*Other titles in the CONTANGO series by Chris Dunn,
all published by Upfront Publishing:*

DEADLINES

DOMUS

CONTANGO

TRICKS

COMMEDIA

Forthcoming titles in the CONTANGO series:

STIR

FOIBLE

TALENTS

QUONDAM

Also by Chris Dunn and published by Upfront Publishing.

The Good Trader – A Year in the Markets

The Good Trader II – The Crash of 2002

The Good Trader III – Greenspan's Game

SPOILS

Chris Dunn

UPFRONT PUBLISHING
LEICESTERSHIRE

SPOILS
Copyright © Chris Dunn 2004

ISBN 1-84426-294-4

First Published 2004 by
UPFRONT PUBLISHING
Leicestershire

26 August '04

for Chris 'Fingers' Moore,

SPOILS

King of the hidden
hand-words!

Chris

PART ONE

SUMMER

It was during the boiling heat of a Berlin summer afternoon that Joe took sudden stock. Abrupt, spine-chilling stock. He made up his mind just after four. At that moment sunlight flamed through the windows of ABC Bank's Berlin headquarters at a slightly changed angle. The shadows altered for a second in the boardroom.

That flicker clinched it for Joe. It was so obvious. He would have to deal with Felix. It was him or Felix. No other solution.

Joe well knew it would not be easy. Felix was no stranger to the killing game. Nor could the move be long delayed. Felix was beginning to run Joe very close indeed.

Noncommittally, but with his mind made up, Joe glanced across the table at Felix sitting opposite him in the boardroom, just to check again on the dimensions of his quarry. A figure from Joe's violent past, Felix gazed back at him blandly, almost innocently.

And was Felix following his train of thought, Joe wondered? Of course he was. Felix was no fool. Felix was a professional. They had trained together in the same hard school of death.

The Quiff, indisputably by his own account CEO of ABC Bank, was holding forth in the cloistered calm of the bank boardroom high above Berlin – the Quiff by nickname throughout the bank and the Screw, or worse, by nature. He had just vituperated against his joint deputies – Joe and Felix – with customary indiscriminate brutality. Both subordinates had nodded almost eagerly in agreement as the tongue lashings continued.

The Quiff was a Spanish practices banker of the old school – graft first; discipline second; and initiative a very poor third. Integrity was unplaced in his book.

You can take a boy out of the Bronx but you can't take the Bronx out of a boy, thought Joe to himself facetiously – and how!

The Quiff paused to light yet another cigarette, coughed heavily as he inhaled, and then returned to the charge, eyes reddened by fury. The spume of exhaled smoke moved steadily like a Zeppelin down the boardroom table, as the Quiff's body language turned muscular. The Quiff was ruthless with his subordinates, hence that afternoon's brickbats. But that was only part of his act. As befitted a man promoted unexpectedly and way beyond competence by invisible and powerful City friends, he also lived in a state of constant anxiety, relative to the continuing fair opinion of his supportive moguls a few hour's journey away in London. As Joe had learned to recognise, the easy smile, the change in accent, the swift glad handing and the practised air of willingness to please and accommodate were never far away. That was the Quiff's alter ego and living ever-present just beneath the skin of his pliant, supple being.

The Quiff was a bought man, purchased on the cheap by talent scouts many years ago.

Outside the Berlin weather continued to swelter. Likewise across all Germany that afternoon.

Both Joe and Felix kept their heads down, avoiding eye-contact with the Quiff. Both knew how to bend with the wind; both had survived far worse in their joint past than anything that might erupt during the Quiff's outbursts now. Just verbal flak from the CEO; nothing life-threatening...Unlike in the past...

In days gone by...Joe's mind was elsewhere as the tirade continued.

He thought about Berlin and the Wall...About the hunting and the shooting and the terrifying chases across the cold windy squares...And he thought about the Felix that he had known in very different circumstances years ago, that same Felix who was now seated opposite him in a fine well tailored suit and sporting more than just a touch of pouchy jowls around his neck and face.

Time come to pay a call...More than likely accompanied by Death...

In those days it had been a starveling Felix who had lived on the other side of the Wall in the mean streets of East Berlin; a Felix who had fixed very nearly everything for Joe in his espionage days; and a Felix who had worked at a senior level for the East German Stasi secret police, along with his father. Felix the Fixer...Always the fixer...The fixer Felix...That was what the Fat Man had called him over the years.

They had depended on him utterly...And Felix had been discreet. It had been Felix who had always smiled quietly and secretly when questioned about just how he had managed to put the papers together for passport control...How he had arranged for such and such to happen... How a lorry would be there punctually at such and such time...And finally now it was that very same Felix who had somehow fixed to turn up as Joe's exact peer in the ABC Bank, tumultuous product of the biggest cross-border banking merger that Europe had ever seen.

And headquartered in Berlin, long time scene of Joe's espionage youth, before the Wall came down...If a knowledge of billiards is a sign of a misspent youth, then what, pray, does a detailed knowledge of all Berlin's mean streets connote...?

The surprise of the ABC banking merger, followed by Joe's appointment had been as nothing compared to the shock of the encounter on Day One when Felix strode into the boardroom with a spring in his step and found himself face to face with Joe. Both had turned to stone; neither had acknowledged the other's prior alternative identity.

They had shaken hands solemnly on the Quiff's introduction. Just like colleagues pledged to work together but in reality more like prize fighters, waiting for the bell. They had both known far, far too much about each other. The Berlin Wall might be down now, but another, no less solid, construction, like dragon's teeth, had sprung up in its place between the two former spies.

How piquant...! How too, too exquisitely threatening...

So far as Joe knew, the Quiff was ignorant of the fact that both of his deputies had played active roles as espionage agents in the Cold War. Not a detail that the vicious, galumphing Quiff might have been expected to take on board. His mind, as ever, was fixed on higher things. Like the remorseless advancement of the afore-mentioned Quiff...

Felix's old nickname clicked into Joe's mind. Bobby – that was what they had called him in the British sector. In those days he had been slimmer, far, far slimmer, almost rake-like, with long blond hair, way down beneath his shoulders, that same hair which now in forlorn memory of his magnificent plumage stuck out in random tufts around his skull. Practically bald but otherwise unchanged. Semper Felix. Still the same knowing smile, the same bland charm, the same ability to ride it all with a shrug of his shoulders.

And no doubt the same deadly intent when it suited him. Joe had no illusions about Felix's ability to bring down his quarry. He had seen Felix in action and under pressure. Very good with a rifle from a high vantage point early in the morning was Felix…

Joe wondered what thoughts were passing through Felix's mind at the moment. He could guess. It was all so obvious. Almost transparently so. Behind those gold spectacles and that smiling easy-going manner, Felix would have worked out Joe's position in his own scheme of things months ago. Ruthlessly. And made his adjustments. Most likely he was plotting the same fate for Joe.

Was ready to go now perhaps? With Joe late to the call? So Joe was lagging Felix by now in his appraisal of the situation…?

But then Joe had always been the baby in the operation, the one they had somehow kidded along through all the truly rough stuff. He had always insisted on an element of leeway – which had always been granted to him, even by the Stasi.

More banking law was being laid down savagely by the Quiff in the heat of a Berlin afternoon as Joe mused still further.

But the leeway that had been granted to Joe had all taken place a long time ago. That had been then. It would not be like that now. It would be mano a mano for the two of them. Joe had no choice on that basis. It was him or Felix. His discoveries of Felix's conduct of his side of the banking business at ABC made it imperative that he took some action. Felix was moving into ABC – and moving on, most likely using the Quiff as leverage.

Joe wondered in a sense of idle speculation whether Moley might be able to help him in some way or other, Moley the old friend from his early City days who had welcomed his appointment at ABC so effusively…Had made a special point of contacting him when the news broke quietly of his appointment…Had rhapsodised over his return to Square Mile business after such a long absence…

Good old Moley…?

Just how could he broach it with Moley, he wondered. Tentatively an idea framed itself in his mind, like a hint of Autumn on a sunny day in August. It was imperative to get to the

Quiff, he speculated. That would be the way to fix it. Could Moley help him on that delicate assignment, he wondered?

He would raise it with Moley as they gossiped about the markets. 'You see, Moley, I have this problem. My opposite number at ABC, Felix, used to work for the Stasi before the Wall came down …I think he's…It ought to be investigated…It's going to create a huge scandal… But he's the joint deputy CEO of the bank, along with me, so it's hard to put a tab on him…Oh and Moley, it's tricky for me because I used to work with him in espionage but on the other side of the Wall, the British end, so we're really blood brothers…'

Savvy, Moley? Problematical, eh? Not bad, eh, as a conversation piece with an old friend…? But all of that too presupposed that the Moley of today was the Moley of yesteryear.

Gazing at Felix across the table in Berlin and mulling the changes that had taken place in his relationship with one old comrade-in-arms, Joe very much doubted if Time had stood still with respect to Moley, another erstwhile colleague.

It just wouldn't work that way. It never did.

Sharing the prospect of an early death with someone and then surviving it all makes for a certain and undeniable bonding sensation, Joe conceded to himself; in the limit, he and Felix were truly blood-brothers. Likewise Moley with whom Joe had shared his early years in the Square Mile? He mused on Moley's likely response to revelations and then returning to earth became aware that the Quiff was still thundering away, this time at him, but that the meeting was drawing to a close. The vituperation was losing its bite and the tone of the criticism had eased from full crescendo.

The Quiff with that gesture that was so characteristic of him, took a final heavy pull on his cigarette, stubbed it out with savage finality in the overflowing ashtray beside him and then rose to go accompanied by his cough as he exhaled with venom. The Rockers quiff at the top of his skull, seemingly fixed rigidly in place from birth and certainly ever since Joe had first met the ABC CEO, went to the door stiff; rigid; and unmoving along with the cough and the Quiff's stumpy bulky presence. The meeting was over. Both Felix and Joe stood up to acknowledge his departure.

The Quiff disappeared out of the door and the cough could be heard all along the corridor outside from the boardroom; his insides seemed to be on the point of expectoration. Not long now before the Grim Reaper pays the Quiff a call, not long at all, thought Joe.

Good old Grim Reaper...

Felix prepared to follow the Quiff out of the room and Joe was gripped by some nameless, inscrutable sense of lunacy, the same that came over him whenever he was faced with danger. Like walking in front of the border guards as if he had been a defector. It was madness but it had never failed him. He walked after Felix to the door and began to hum, quietly under his breath but audibly, the melody from the 'Bobby Shaftoe' sea shanty.

'Bobby Shaftoe's gone to sea
With silver buckles at his knee
When he comes back he'll marry me
Bonny Bobby Shaftoe...'
Berr-berr-boom-boom-boom-berr-berr-boom-boom-boom....

And so on...

Joe, for once, had been able to hum in tune. It wasn't such a bad effort. To an outsider, Joe's gesture would have sounded convincing, almost like a soothing gesture towards a colleague recently mauled in a board room brawl. But that was only the half of it. Sympathy had nothing to do with it. What Joe was about doing was far more significant, and way more provocative. 'Bobby Shaftoe' had been Felix's call sign, the tune he whistled down the phone line from East Berlin to identify himself as he made contact with his British Intelligence control.

With intent, Joe was opening his account with Felix, the new trading account, the one that dealt in death as well as nostalgia.

It was a dangerous move. And provocative. How long was it since Felix had last heard that melody in combative circumstances...?

It was an invitation to hostilities. Unmistakably so.

Felix failed to respond or react in any way as Joe walked behind him to the door still humming just loudly enough to be heard by Felix. Not by a flicker did he announce a response to Joe. But then, as he reached the door he turned and said to Joe quite quietly and without apparent malice:

'Joe, I was not fat but I was fair. Now I'm neither as you can see. Time has not been altogether too kind to me. That makes me a particularly tricky commodity for you to deal with. Don't forget that, will you? Because you too have a past also, don't you, my friend…? And the past has a way of becoming the present, when the unpaid interest falls due…'

He made his comment almost with a smile and the English was perfect. Again an outsider would not have been alarmed. The tone seemed friendly enough. Beside the door, Felix paused for a second. Then very slowly he brought his right hand up to the level of Joe's nose. With an expression of extreme seriousness on his face, he rubbed his thumb and his index finger together in the unmistakeable gesture of the street.

The sign of graft.

Joe was shocked. He had not expected that reaction from Felix.

'You and I have some unfinished business to discuss, have we not, young Joe? Yes, indeed we have, young Joe…As you know well enough, my old friend.'

Then he disappeared in search of the Quiff, leaving Joe in a state of astonishment. What did the gesture mean? Was that an invite for Joe to join in Felix's little game? And what was this unfinished business? Was it a joke?

Hardly – there was menace underlying it all. Joe knew Felix too well to be misled by his tranquil manner. Everyone reacts to danger differently. Under pressure, Felix became ever more eminently reasonable. His calm comments spoke volumes for Joe of the real dangers that lay ahead. Joe had seen Felix in action before.

Very handy with a shooter he had been, even in bars…

Later that afternoon, Joe caught his flight back to London, leaving the Quiff and Felix still in Berlin. He was grateful for the Quiff's absence as he flew back to the UK. The need to hold an audience to his unflagging hypocrisy and self-seeking wearied him. Joe had other matters on his mind. Other business and other matters...His love, Perdita, was now very slowly and quite unconsciously breaking his heart as her troubles multiplied and she fell out of the cradle.

Not that the Quiff was aware of that. The Quiff knew nothing about Joe's home-life. So far as the Quiff was concerned, Joe resided at the Reform Club. That was the address Joe had given when he had been recruited to ABC and it had never subsequently been queried by Personnel. In transit, Joe had alleged...

But even so the counter-jumping Quiff, in flight and perpetual upward social mobility, would have been angling for an invitation to the Reform. It would have offered him the chance to play CEO to all and sundry ...Not that Perdita would have cared a jot about the Quiff, were she to meet him...Joe's heart ached as he thought about her, further away from him almost daily, deep in the Hampshire countryside, with her pathos and her faltering grasp of reality as the visions swept over her...But then that was what hearts were for, wasn't it then, squire, as Stanley, his ex-forex dealer, would say in his villainous way, for getting broken.

That's what they're for, stupid...

Joe decided to worry about Perdita during the descent to Heathrow. She could wait for forty minutes or so.

Meanwhile there was Felix. And the gesture, whatever that meant. And his discoveries about Felix. Perhaps he would broach something of his problems to Moley after all. Perhaps he wouldn't – he didn't know now for sure how it all played, in the modern world of banking, finance and high rolling stockmarkets. And in London...Was it betrayal now in strict tempo or in ragtime, as it had been in the good old, bad old days?

Who knew? Who cared? Only the money mattered – more and more and more of it. Joe felt his stomach twist into knots as he affected a jaunty approach.

But his decision about Felix was true at first light – he had to fix Felix before Felix fixed him. Because if Felix fixed him, he also fixed Joe's very, very hush-hush espionage mission. And that would be a tragedy for everyone all round including the Americans.

Joe rolled his mind towards the darkness and the shadows where another unexpected reality lay concealed.

Felix was just the start of it. Joe had to get his head around other problems, just marginally connected with his job. Like where was the £ going? Up or down? That was the key question, also known as the mighty conundrum. It sounded academic but the direction of the £ on forex would make his espionage stock market deal fly or tank. So was his hunch correct? Was the £ poised to tank, along with the Euro, as the $ soared?

That was what he had surmised, being more or less alone among the senior executives in ABC Bank in taking that view. And with good reason – if the £ fell along with the Euro, not something incidentally that seemed possible to the market, then his cross-frontier takeover was eminently do-able, because of the currency sweetener.

And that deal, once done, meant that Joe could hit the world's highways again, taking Perdita with him and leaving a busted Rivers Pugh, her brother, well behind.

It was tight; and Joe felt cramped and hemmed in by the complications of a multitude of hostile factors; but it seemed to be do-able. Joe was optimistic. But yet again the image that haunted him perennially came to mind – a white anxious traveller's face at the rain-dashed window of a train passing smoothly and silently through field after empty field in the gathering dusk. But in what country? Heading for where? Driven by whom? Nobody knew anymore and nobody cared – only the journey mattered and the oblivion of speed.

And the money…

The maps have long since been burned or discarded, Joe thought. We are pious pilgrims on the road to Nowhere.

* * * * *

The moon was rising as Joe's hired cab approached within a few miles of the gates of Pugh Park. It was full and close to the earth like a friendly but warning presence. Joe was suddenly wide awake. He was alert for the unresolved uncertainties in his situation. They would not be long in arriving, he guessed. He was facing danger now on reserve tanks but with just enough juice to see it all through.

The fighting years were taking their toll.

Joe had been dreaming about Lady Pugh, recapturing in his imagination her bounce and her smile, her charge and her no nonsense earthiness. Such a good honest woman at all times, he thought, even though she was – just maybe – descended from badgers. Such a wonderful presence...The sense of her loss lingered with him from the dream like an invading resentment about the dullness of death.

Coal scuttle up, he recalled, as she tripped off to that wedding of the Stokely's with her extraordinary hat perched on her head. And look at the trouble which that little gesture had caused...Joe recalled her absolute and unflinching resolution to do exactly what she had decided to do at any given moment. She drifted before him in his mind's eye, with a wave and a smile. He recalled the scraps of billet doux from her dead lover of 30 years past flying hither and thither in the wind as her coffin was borne to the grave...The urgency of his love for her and the stillness of the tomb as she was laid to rest...Ancient memories of ancient fires...That was why she had willed Pugh Park to him before her death and not to Rivers, quite irrespective of the mortification which this would cause her son and heir and head of...Or perhaps she had had other reasons for taking the extraordinary action which she had done.

The cab driver took the bend quite wildly and threw Joe about on the back seat. That woke him up some more. Joe knew now that it was time to start managing the various different realities which he inhabited. It was the appointed hour. He had avoided squaring the books until that moment. But it was time. The countdown was starting, especially since he and Felix were going head to head. He needed to be very straight in his mind.

To begin at the beginning, he thought, Rivers was the key to it all. His impact on Perdita was critical, Perdita whose state of health and frame of mind were distinctly unstable now that her mother was dead. Joe shuddered to think of the effect on Perdita of an indiscreet word by Rivers in his direction. It would go down very badly with her. Perdita had her good days and her bad days. They came and went although cumulatively she seemed to be recovering. Hopefully tonight would be one of her better days, when her artful social sallies and wicked dazzling smile flowered at the dinner table. At her best she could be hugely entertaining with her witty and challenging ripostes. On that form she could always set the table in a roar.

Together she and Joe functioned well in public, sharing their jokes around and always working off each other with intuitive understanding, although when Rivers was around it was different...

She was more inhibited then because of her divided loyalties between Joe and her brother and she faltered when Rivers stared at her coldly across the table...

To Joe, who adored the breath of careless, casual beauty she brought into his life, she was like an elegant, mysterious bird, used to soaring high above the seas and the mountains, then drifting motionless on the still summer air above the peaks and crags. And who for some unfathomable reason had mislaid – just for the time being – all her art of flying. She could not soar, just for now. Therefore she was obliged to clump about on the hard earth heavily burdened by her huge wings...

That left Rivers...It all came back to Rivers...He of the beautiful and unyielding nature; he of the understated almost silent contempt for Joe and total ignorance of Joe's rise to power at ABC; he of the chief executive position at Global Aerospace and the many deals he had put through, after reversing his own company, Crecy Systems, into the larger concern; he who had insisted on remaining whenever it suited him at Pugh Park; and finally he, Rivers Pugh, who was about to receive the terminal shock of his life and career when Detroit Fire of the United States of America, largest weapon manufacturers in the world, launched an unsolicited and hostile bid for Global. Rivers' company, no less.

The bid was imminent. It was for this deal that Lucia, Joe's head of Mergers &Acquisitions at ABC, would most likely be obliged to sacrifice the summer and also her summer vacation in Italy.

And who were sponsoring and in effect underwriting the Detroit bid for Global? Why none other than ABC Bank. And who was the prime mover behind the ABC bid on behalf of Detroit Fire? Why none other than ABC's joint deputy chief executive, that grand old man of door stepping espionage, Joe himself who had been ghosted into the job by Pa Lee specifically and by US Intelligence in general in order to put through that one crucial bid.

Tight indeed. And that was before Joe started worrying about the currencies...

The cab was manoeuvred carefully through the Pugh Park gates and began the long haul up the drive as Joe thought how very different possession and ownership always were in Hampshire and in England. Of course he owned Pugh Park – he had legal title to the assets – but as for owning it truly, in a word, possessing it, that was a fatuous idea...The dead Lady Pugh, he reckoned, possessed it more than he did, especially since on occasion Joe, if he looked hard, reckoned he could catch glimpses of her ghost on patrol in the garden or just leaving the kitchen, as she still watched over her darling daughter. Her spirit suffused Pugh Park, like a quiet wind.

His thoughts went back to Pa Lee as they approached the house and he looked out for Perdita coming to the front door and racing down the drive to him. Pa Lee had never spelled out precisely why the bid for Global was important but Joe could guess. Enough hints had been dropped about the US reorganising its global military presence for him to guess that Global contained areas of expertise that the US preferred not to risk leaving behind.

Once the bid was through, Joe could relax. He could sew back together again this problem of the gap between ownership and possession. He was free to go. He could leave ABC if he wanted; he could take Perdita with him to any exotic clime of his choice and ensure her recovery. He could sell Pugh Park. He could do whatever he wanted. He was very nearly a free man again after his years in espionage and the markets. The world was practically his oyster, provided he fixed the deal and avoided any terrifying collateral damage on the way, delivered by the angels of death come to call.

Or Rivers...Rivers was a danger and an enigma. As for his reactions to the loss of Pugh Park through the switch in the inheritance, Joe coped best by closing his eyes to the whole question. What Rivers thought about all of that, nobody, least of all Joe, knew a thing.

The car neared the house...The front door of the house opened quickly and Joe saw Perdita emerge to greet his return. He saw at a glance that she was fine that evening. The eyes looked bright and her blonde hair waved about her head as she gave him her nonchalant windscreen wiper of a special greeting and smiled at him from a distance. Long legs clad in slim jeans, descended the steps with confidence in the early moonlight. Joe found himself whirled into a deep embrace as he stepped from the car in front of the entrance to the house.

'Darling, I'm so glad you're back. I've missed you so much. Everything looks brighter now. Joe, you are a sweetheart to come and see me.'

Joe kissed her back, and then again right on the tip of her nose and she pouted at him with her outrageous moue, play-acting immediately. This cheered Joe.

'I couldn't stay away, could I? It's something in the air down here. It's so hectic. And I get lost so easily...'

'Oh, aren't we the witty one this evening...? So you get lost, do you? Well, what is lost is always found, you should know that by now with me...'

'Sweetheart...'

He blew her a kiss and she laughed at him and held his hand very deliberately. Then he disentangled himself and paid off the cab driver who goggled at, and almost saluted, the vision of carefree loveliness in front of him.

The moon was driving up hard now above the house even as the light of the day faded. The cab drove off down the drive at speed. Joe stood there in front of the house still holding hands with Perdita, perplexed as to which direction to take. It was a quiet exquisite moment of boon for them both.

'It's very large tonight. You're going to have some fun. She's really making up to Rivers.'

Joe raised an eyebrow and then laughed again at Perdita's comment, forgetting his preoccupations for a moment. This all augured very well. She only made that joke when she felt exceptionally fit and limber. It was starting to look like a good evening lay ahead. He began to relax.

True the moon above them was large but her comment referred not to the size of the sphere. It was a reference, and a far more indelicate one, to the shape and size of the posterior of Mrs Gulliver, newcomer to Pugh Park, post Lady Pugh's demise. It was a private joke between the two of them, Joe and Perdita, which only existed when Perdita felt good and fit. Otherwise Perdita cleaved to the conventions of life in Hampshire and respected them. She wouldn't play the game when she felt rocky.

From the front, Mrs Gulliver, the good woman who had stepped into the breach at Pugh Park after Lady Pugh's death, was quite pretty – blue eyes, small delicate nose and a pleasing smile. But turn her around, as Joe had remarked to Perdita when Mrs G had assumed in loco parentis power at Pugh Park, and a very different picture emerged. Her bottom was large. According to Joe, who joked about it almost as a separate persona, it almost hung from her body; he reckoned it would not have disgraced a pantomime horse. 'I know that bottom and I know when it's angry', Joe had stated quite solemnly one evening to Perdita after Mrs Gulliver had swept from the room in high dudgeon. Perdita had promptly collapsed in a fit of giggles.

Problem was that Mrs Gulliver held strong views about life and convention and conformity and Pugh Park and Rivers Pugh. She did not care to conceal her opinions, all of which ran counter to Joe's tentatively expressed suggestions. Joe was new to the business of running the estate as lord of the manor- and it showed.

'Come on Perdita, let's not go in just yet. Let's go and sit on our seat and drink in the view. This is too sweet a night to spend wholly indoors...We could have a little round of quote-speak...'

Nodding her head, Perdita laughed and kissed his hand which she held up to her lips with a meaningful, artful, mock-threatening expression. They walked around the corner from the front door and sat on their bench which commanded a view of the valley sloping away from the house towards the thick clump of trees below, still visible in the gathering dusk. They sat down close together and Joe felt the pains and tremors of the day ease away in the light, moonlit air. He felt more secure for a few seconds. More rooted and protected...

'You're not my patient, Mrs Doodah, you're my meat...'

'That's good one. You've been swotting up, my sweet pea, Perdita. That's cheating, my little cabbage. I didn't think you knew that one. What about 'And keep me a normal healthy girl'? Or 'Welcome back to the old watering hole, Mrs Whatever...'?

'All right take this then – Every day is arbour day to Mr Joe...'

Joe volleyed back without a pause. He knew this game well.

'My wife always has me followed on St Valentine's Day...'

More pouting in disbelief from Perdita.

'As if, Joe, as if....Well then, OK then. OK! You asked for it, mister. 'Do you mind if I get out of these hot clothes?'

'That was quick. No I don't mind at all. In fact, I'm going to take a kiss from you, clothed or otherwise.'

Perdita had been focussing on the game. Joe's threat alarmed her.

'What? That's not in the script. There's no line that says that...You're cheating again, Joe. Have you no code, man?'

Joe kissed her quietly on the lips and she responded, curling her tongue below his with little squirming motions, and moving against him so that she could hold him by the shoulder as she kissed him in reply. It was a moment of sweet calm for them both. They sat together on the bench and they were very close. Perdita enjoyed kissing Joe.

Staring him full in the eyes, Perdita withdrew a fraction from him. But she still held him by the shoulder.

'That's nice, Joe. In fact, that's the nicest thing that's happened all day. I'm glad you're back home here.'

'Me, too. There were some good things that happened today, but nothing to compare with your sweet lips. Honey child...'

'You sound like something out of the Wild West when you say all that. All sweaty and meaningful. You sleep in your vest, of course.'

'I last changed my underclothes when I lunched with Geronimo in '86.'

On his cue, she was launched.

'Ah'm jest a rootin' tootin' kind o' gal, and ah loiks mah men strong and firm, yes, sirree!!!'

'Loiks? Shouldn't it be laikes... Cowgirls are from Dakota, not South Yorkshire. Aren't they?'

'This one strayed, after he done her wrong. In Barnsley, he done her wrong. That was where he did his evil deed. She lit out after that and took a boat travelling steerage. She disembarked in the land of promise and took the first train out of New York, just as soon as she arrived. Jest a rootin' tootin' kind of gal...'

'She knew Butch Cassidy, too, I'll be bound.'

'And Sundance, too. She would have danced fer her Sundance...'

'But he refused to allow it. So she pined away and away... And so, why don't you go out and trace something.'

'Ah, hah!'

Perdita waggled her eyebrows and cavorted about. Joe was playing a treacherous game, trying to take her by surprise. But she bounced back off the ropes.

'Have you seen mah pistol, honey bun?'

'You can't reform me, my good man...'

That was one of Perdita's favourites and she hooted with laughter as Joe pulled his rabbit of a joke out of the hat. Some times the really good lines were hard to remember. That one didn't always come up. Perdita stood up and prepared to do her little jig, the one with the flying feet clapping in mid-air, which she normally failed to execute successfully. She was grinning hugely as she prepared to go for it.

Then Mrs Gulliver wearing her serious face tore round the corner just in time to break up the party. She bustled into view looking responsible. She was apprehensive and clearly in haste to find Perdita. She greeted Joe perfunctorily.

'Good evening, Joe.'

'Good evening Mrs G.'

That was about as much as he was going to get from Mrs G by way of formal salutation. Mrs G was under pressure. The meal was nigh but also under threat.

Perdita's face fell and a frown hurried across her features. She looked deflated. The feet ceased to kick and fly. Joe knew that expression well. She was losing it. It was the sudden switch from one set of obligations to another which jolted her, especially the declension from a state of high bounding excitement to domestic trivia. Tragedy of total tragedies, Mrs Gulliver was not her mother bustling round the corner and insisting on help in the kitchen. That was where the rent in the universe occurred. Perdita missed her mother when she was about to show off outrageously.

Perdita looked constantly for Lady Pugh's reassurance. And presence.

Joe reached out to take her hand which she gave to him, looking suddenly bereft and forlorn. The switch had taken a few seconds. Oblivious to the change, Mrs G hurried on with her messages.

'Look, I'm taking it out of the oven now, Perdita. Would you come and give me a hand, do you think? Rivers is very impatient. He wants his dinner. And Buffet's here. He's just arrived.'

Managing a smile, Perdita tripped after Mrs G, back to the house and the kitchen. Her shoulders were bowed and it looked like a bad attack. Joe tried but failed to avert his gaze from the strongly assertive bounce of the Gulliver rear as Perdita was carried off to perform more sensible duties. He shared her sense of deflation as their play acting ground to a halt – and just when they were getting it together as well...It was a crying shame...

But the joke was over. That was obvious. The ambience had been smashed. Useless now to gag about Mrs G's posterior. It would only make things worse, because Perdita would be careful from now on and withdrawn, at least until she felt better.

It could be a difficult evening to come, he surmised, although he had known her recover in the past quite quickly from her attacks of nostalgia. Halted in mid-stride, though, it would be hard to get her back to balance for most of the evening.

And what about Felix, he wondered as he looked around for his mobile. It only needed an unfortunate intrusion for Perdita to throw one of the biggest wobblies of all time...Joe thought with real fear about the implications for the present of his past life as he located his mobile, stuffed away in the corner of his briefcase, and tapped into it.

Seven calls waiting for him! He flicked through the numbers briefly. Most of them originated from one source which Joe recognised to be Lucia's number. So she'd been chasing him! So was there action on the Global front? That would be a comfort – the sooner that particular box of tricks was parcelled up and dispatched Stateside, the happier Joe would be and the faster he could sort out his domestic situation and spirit Perdita away to Prospero's Cell, somewhere in the tropics...

Joe prepared to take his calls when he heard Buffet's familiar whine on the other side of the hedge. Was it going to be a walking stick night tonight, he wondered? More jokes from the school tuck-shop?

'So, Rivers, and how's the carpet bagger then?'

'Passing fair. Mustn't grumble...Well, I could but there's no point... He keeps his distance and I keep mine. I'm waiting for the day he gets his comeuppance and it won't be long delayed...'

Oh really and oh yeah, thought Joe on the other side of the hedge, as he paused for a second before dialling Lucia. Rivers continued the diatribe.

'Just a couple more deals and then I'll be ready to do the really big one. Then I can move against you know who of Pugh Park, which I will do...'

Joe moved away. He knew what Rivers was about to say about his latest deal. It was common knowledge at ABC among Lucia's team. Lucia had been very thorough in her due diligence. The Rivers deal was worth about £1 billion and it involved a Czech arms manufacturer with impeccable Eastern bloc connections. Rivers was paying too much for the Czech business but that was the direction in which Rivers saw his business progressing. Bottom line, and paradoxically, he was careless about his p & l. He had a very large Russian arms deal lined up for completion in six to nine months time. Massive earnings dilution, or so Lucia estimated. It was no wonder that Pa Lee wanted to take the whole Global operation out of the Rivers' tutelage and into safe US hands. Global was large and ambitious and free-booting, so much so it was almost the ostensible swing factor behind US : Russian relations.

As Rivers undoubtedly knew...Rivers had moved on from germ-warfare...

Lucia had learned all this through sheer hard work. She had located a loose-tongued operative in Rivers' office. Rivers' least movement was known to the camp at ABC. That was Lucia's beautiful talent for industrial espionage. She had boasted quite recently that she had very nearly got her hands on Rivers' agenda diary, so that she would soon know his every movement, hour by hour. Joe had congratulated her on all this, wondering to himself whether he featured or not in the Rivers' agenda. He rather thought he didn't, except maybe as an effigy with a few pins deeply embedded in vital parts...And if Lucia did get her hands on the diary...And if Joe featured...?

Then the deal was dead. Joe was of course wholly; totally; and fundamentally compromised in terms of the bid since he, lead manager of the predator part of the bid, resided under the same roof as the chief executive of the victim company. Should that fact ever emerge, the bid would be declared null and void instantly on the grounds that Joe had acted throughout as an insider. Details, Joe had decided with his heart in his mouth, thanking God that he had given his London club, the Reform, as his main address. Lucia would shoot him, he reckoned, were she to discover Joe's unhealthy proximity to Rivers Pugh.

Joe called Lucia on his mobile, standing beside the summer house, a little way off from Rivers and Buffet who were still talking, he imagined, into the evening air up above behind the hedge in front of the house. Lucia was in the office. She picked up the phone instantly. She was not happy with Joe.

'Where on earth have you been. I've spent ages trying to track you down. You should answer your phone. We have business on the move here.'

No time for niceties. Joe and Lucia knew each other too well.

'Yup, that and other things. I've been talking to people. Also I've been in Berlin, don't forget. What's the story, Lucia?'

'We've had a breakthrough. We did a big pitch, as you know, earlier this evening to, among others, the Pru and Norwich Union and they like the sound of the deal. I have to tell you that because in all honesty I was very surprised by their attitude. They've turned against that blue-eyed sheikh of Araby, Rivers Pugh, which will come to him as a shock. So they listened to us with more than just an attentive ear. They don't like some of the prices that he's been paying for his deals and they also think the world picture for the arms' traders is changing quite fast – more and tighter surveillance by the US. Especially in the light of what's going on in Iraq. So far fewer degrees of latitude from now on for the smaller operators like Global who have had a fantastic run so far. Etc., etc. That's their view anyway. So gently and quietly they think they're going to come in on our side…'

'Well done Lucia. That is indeed good work.'

'Thank you, Joe. That's what I thought, too. So big switch for them. They're heavy sellers of Rivers' futures right now. Young man in a hurry, that kind of thing, as well as youth must be served – they're completely out of all that line of thinking. So they are not impressed. In fact they were quite rude about him for most of the meeting. Bit of a shocker, really, for Rivers. Very much ex-the golden boy from now on. He'll be surprised by all this, bearing in mind that he runs Global with a rod of iron as top-down top dog. But they're not happy with either him or his attitude. They think he's too young and too cocksure and they don't think much of the team he's got around him at Global. Too many fags from Sloane School was how one of them phrased it, with, I reckoned, a goodly smear of working – class malice aforethought. They thought the Global team needed some Northern grit…I gathered from them that they'd watched him with some care over a period of time, and they'd given him his head. They don't like what they see now, so they're prepared to pull the plug on him.'

Joe kept walking as far as he could away from Rivers and his conquistador views as two realities, not twenty feet apart, crashed together. This was very good albeit unexpected news. Good dinner-party chat stuff as well – Oh, incidentally Rivers, don't bother putting in those extra hours on the new deal; you're totally fucked. To be delivered as the cheese arrived...

'This is a surprise, Lucia. We thought they saw the sun shining out from his unmentionable.'

'As you so delicately put it, Joe, from out of his fundament. Well, yes, but that was then. Markets change as you know. Not any more they think he's God's gift. They've done the sums on his growth prospects and they reckon the earnings profile doesn't justify the kind of rating that Global is carrying. They think the p/e is far too high now. They want to cash in their chips. That at least is obvious from tonight's meeting. The old, old story – a deal too far for Rivers Pugh and it all comes crashing down.'

'That's remarkably far-sighted for the Pru. I didn't think they went in for that kind of sagacity.'

'For God's sake, Joe, stop interrupting me and second-guessing me. This is serious. They are suddenly talking to us now. But the clincher for them is something else and I must know more about it. It's this dollar angle you keep banging on about. Now how strong can we go on this?'

Joe's heart skipped a little beat as he prepared to commit himself; his reputation; ABC; and most likely Pa Lee's reputation as well to his own highly idiosyncratic view of the foreign exchange market. It was not a contrarian view. But it was maverick.

'Yes. Very. But be careful. Float it as a possibility, not as set in stone. Don't forget we're still some months away from launching the bid. Just talk about the $ market being capable of reversal. That should do it. For the time being.'

'What on earth do you mean, Yes, Very? Talk English, for God's sake will you, Joe?'

'I mean, yes, you can go strong on that but be careful with the phrasing. It's matter of degree and presentation. You can go strong on hinting about weak sterling. Be affirmative.'

'Christ, Joe, this is really very off the wall. Really off the wall. ABC as a whole is committed to the view that cable will be stable. You've heard the mantra. We don't want to get half way through this deal and find that sterling is starting to rocket up against the dollar or something frightening like that. That will fuck everything, balls and all. So is it just you against your whole bank, taking a view? Do you have anything else backing it up, apart from the undoubted skill and brilliance of your perceptions, Mr Joe?'

'A great deal of hard work on the trend in the currencies but well away from the crowd, Lucia. But believe me, it's going to happen. I can assure you on that.'

'And I can assure you, Joe, that it's crap. I'll run with this on your say-so, but I tell you, I think it's bollocks. The £ is going to be strong and that's a deal- breaker. I feel it in my bones.'

'So be it, Lucia, but the milky bars will be on you.'

The phone went down with a crash as Lucia terminated the discussion. Joe went in for dinner, wondering just how many balls he could keep in the air at once until the bid was announced.

★   ★   ★   ★   ★

'Now Tom, just tell me again what you're going to say to the board?'

Ursula was brushing Tom's jacket at the lapels almost mechanically and staring fixedly at the weave of the cloth as she bullied him into a response. She brushed him down as she might have combed a dog. But there was no malice in her enthusiasm, Tom was sure of that. She was right behind him in her support. She was warm about it all. He couldn't fault her for commitment, just as he couldn't complain about the magnificent breakfast she had served up for him on this, perhaps the most important morning of his career. Ursula was very stalwart, no question at all about that. Tom felt stronger for her presence and her interest.

'So what are you going to say to them?'

He pondered his reply for a second. They had rehearsed this routine many times in the last few weeks, mainly in the kitchen, as his final interview with the Financial Chronicle board came closer; Ursula had played the board, along with the condiments for colleagues.

Doyen of the Chronicle, Tom was up for the Editor's job. But then so too were three other candidates. The board would make its decision sometime soon after the final interviews. The other candidates were very strong but Tom was the in-house choice. Nevertheless, it would be tough fight at the final interviews to impress the Chronicle board and get clear of the field.

'I'm going to be honest with them, Ursula, and tell them I think the paper needs some change to it. The formula is very successful. Has been for years. Never failed. But it needs adapting. Financial journalism is not the game it was, and it's evolving all the time. We have to take on board that we're a huge global operation and that the markets are global as well. I think our style must alter to reflect that. We…'

Ursula coughed; she did not wholly support this line of argument. It jarred with her. As a former financial PR, and chisel-jawed with it, she advocated a more emollient approach to the board, more along the lines of 'We'll cope with change when we see it and we'll deal with it in our own way;' or 'If it ain't broke, why fix it?' Moderato cantabile, in other words. She had also suggested to him that he should treat the Chronicle board with more deference and he had rejected her idea soundly. Nevertheless she remained loyal to the line that Tom favoured and she went on asking the questions, taking the line that he knew his own business best.

And brushing his suit, clicking her tongue occasionally as she flicked a stray hair from the lapel. It was undisputedly Tom's best suit. It glowed with expense. For a moment, Tom had departed from his customary identity – badly dressed and always unimpressed.

'And when they ask how will you change the style, what will you reply…?'

'I'll say that we have to…'

The phone rang and Ursula took the call, perhaps a trifle too hurriedly, but still brushing away manfully.

'Peggy, is that you? Yes, I'm a little tied up just for the moment. No, I'm putting Tom through his paces and doing some grooming at the same time...Yes, yes, it's today and he had his hair cut two days ago so he looks very presentable...He's had a very good bath this morning as well, so he looks clean too. None of that printer's ink on him...Yes, isn't it exciting. We think he'll get it, of course...Of course he'll get it...Well I do, for one...Oh yes, I will do...'

She turned to Tom.

'Peggy sends her best wishes for the interview. Look after the p's and the q's will mind themselves, was her advice. Do you want a quick word with her?'

Tom shook his head, looking well groomed.

'Tell Peggy Thanks but no thanks...I'm too busy concentrating on my pearls of wisdom for the board. But this evening, yes...I'll give her the full blow- by- blow. Ask her...'

But Ursula had returned to her caller.

'He's got stage fright, Peggy, and he's tongue-tied. Really, aren't these men pathetic...But there we are...Now we're meeting this evening, aren't we...? What time are you poling up...? Some time after seven thirty...? Wonderful, we'll see you then...Bye, Peggy...'

She put the phone down.

'She says she's going to keep all her fingers and her toes crossed for you all morning. And so is Graham. She's told him to adopt a rigid posture. Now that's a nice thing for anyone to say isn't it?'

'So uncomfortable for both of them. But Graham...?'

'Can't be bad, kiddo, can't be bad. Graham will always be a dark horse, but better to have him on your side than shooting from the enemy trenches.'

Peggy's Graham was a hidden force in the newspaper industry, of vast inscrutable experience. He was deep friends with Lord Test, chairman of the Financial Chronicle holding company, and almost an eminence grise to him, if the Fleet Street rumour machine was right. But Graham had made no pledging of support whatsoever to anybody's candidacy; he was pleasant enough but he kept his own counsel. Under no circumstances could he be described as one of Tom's backers; both Ursula and Tom knew that Graham's support would be committed to where Graham thought it might most benefit Graham – and to be fair, the Chronicle also. That was axiomatic. His kind words that morning conveyed via Peggy buttered few parsnips so far as the interviewee was concerned; they constituted the small change of commercial diplomacy. But it was good of him to go through the rituals of support. And the small drinks party that evening with Peggy and Graham in attendance should do Tom's candidature no harm, after the interviews but ahead of the decision. Both Tom and Ursula were agreed on that score.

Emboldened by the muted message of support from Peggy and Graham, Tom started to tease Ursula.

'Aren't you mixing your metaphors just a trifle Mrs Woodentop? Dark horses shooting from trenches...?'

Tom called her Mrs Woodentop when he felt daring enough to confront her on her own ground. Obligingly, she rose to the bait.

'Don't call me Mrs Woodentop; don't you dare. You know I detest that term.'

Outside the sun shone fitfully on the Hampshire countryside. The sky was bright but the clouds were always lurking. Rain was a real possibility later that morning.

Ursula brushed the suit down some more like a stalwart. She gave Tom some friendly fire in return for his insult.

'Look, young Stone, if you adopt that hoity toity, superior attitude with me about language there'll be no supper for you tonight, good interview or otherwise...'

Tom kissed her and she yielded with a smile to his embrace. Off and on, they had been together now for a long time. She liked his kisses. There had been another husband for her in between Tom Stone Mark 1 and Mark II, plus children and all the other baggage. But she had always liked his kisses. They had retained their potency over her, despite the years between them.

'You wouldn't deny your hungry little journalist supper, now would you, my darling Ursula, not after his long hard day toiling away at his stories?'

'Your darling Ursula takes a dim view of you monkeying around with her like this so early in the morning. And she's easily distracted, as you know. Now what time is your train?'

'Ten past...'

'Fine. I'll drive you to the station. I want to go to Sainsbury's afterwards. We can go now if you're ready...'

'As ready as I'll ever be.'

'How did the Chron look this morning then? Any comments to make about it to the board?'

Tom frowned, switching from the candidate parading his views to a sceptical interviewing board to the committed journalist who worried constantly about the standing and progress of his newspaper.

'It's OK, as far as it goes, but it needs a remake. We're lagging the Journal in so many ways...Their story focus...'

He was lost to her as soon as he began discussing his precious newspaper. He lived for the Chron and the daily issue was a viaticum for him. He was like a man discussing his collection of rare books. In answer to Ursula's innocent question, he was seized by an impenetrable fit of abstraction. He continued to talk about the paper and his plans all the way to the station as Ursula drove carefully through the Hampshire lanes.

'It wouldn't be for want of a good audience and a strong send-off that he did badly,' she thought as she watched him climb onto the train and then wave her goodbye. And she thought also that he looked eminently suitable for the demanding job of Editor of the Chron. His predecessor, or rather the man she hoped shortly would be categorised as his predecessor, had been a fool. A venal fool at that, which was worse. How he had got the job had been a mystery; likewise how he had managed to hang onto it...

That had defied the imagination. Everybody agreed on that. Meanwhile the newspaper had slipped in a chronic shift of slow declension and morale erosion.

She watched the train pull out of the station and then drove onto Sainsbury's to buy more food for that night's supper. The rain started falling as soon as she started the car but she ignored it. She was still wondering about Tom's interview that morning. It meant a lot to him to land the job, she knew. He had worked hard; he was dedicated. He was a good journalist and he deserved it, even if he was, in the last analysis, a company man. But she also knew that it meant a lot to her as well. Sagely, she was not ignorant of the extra increment of prestige that would come her way in the county if he was appointed Editor of the Financial Chronicle. As a former PR she knew full well the value of prestige; she would never despise it. The two of them, in their separate spheres would rise together. She would be a credit to him but just as important he would be a credit to her. She liked that idea very much.

Then her thoughts turned to Peggy and Graham as the rain hammered at the windscreen. And would Graham be offering his quiet support that morning for Tom via his contacts on the board, she wondered? Impossible to tell. Yet again she concluded that Graham for all his jollity and high spirits was a very dark horse indeed. The thought crossed her mind fleetingly that he might even represent hidden danger for Tom. She didn't even know for example how he made his money. Just what had financed Derby Court, that monstrous pile of bricks and mortar – the shack according to Peggy – that they called their home? Share dealing? Trading? She didn't have a clue, she realised as she turned into the Sainsbury car park.

Graham's money, like his influence and possible support for Tom, were a kind of mental Greenland for her. As they all tinkled the coffee cups in various meetings, she knew neither the mass nor the length nor even the precise location of his power and prestige. But of course she could never say as much to Tom, who was counting on Graham's support deep down.

★　★　★　★　★

At about the same time that morning, but in a very different neck of the woods – just off the King's Road in London's SW3 – Nicholas surveyed the wreckage of breakfast.

In London, which always takes less actual weather than Hampshire, it was still a dull day.

Nicholas looked at seeming miles of breakfast. It appeared to be all over the breakfast room and all over the floor as well by the looks of things. Was the ceiling safe, he wondered as he glanced upwards. How breakfast had expanded itself into such a mess remained a mystery. Had they played baseball with the boiled eggs in some alternative dimension, he wondered? Had particle physics intruded so early in the day? He was intrigued by the effortless way that their breakfast had expanded with such fury.

Grace, in a hurry as usual after her early morning gym, had consumed her fruit and muesli; her boiled egg; and her Earl Grey tea with lemon at the speed of light and had then zoomed off for a post-dawn client meeting in a bustling crescendo of bags; keys; umbrella; snatched bye-bye kisses; and packages. Way to go for the head hunter of the year, bar none…Nicholas had seen her out of the door fairly brightly, trying to mask the dullness of his feelings as, on the face of it, another tedious day as a Chelsea house husband stretched before him. Starting with the washing – up, to be followed by some tactical shopping, a soupcon of dusting and hoovering and the whole culminating in a deep vision of eternity with his head buried in Delia Smith's Cookery Book.

He'd endured nearly three years of house arrest now in Chelsea after his City job had inexplicably come to an end and he'd been shown the door at stockbrokers Fulford Bros. Shown the door, most likely, without a reference. He doubted if brokers Fulford would even acknowledge that he had actually worked there, let alone grant him a reference.

It had all been utterly mysterious. One minute he was flavour of the month with his accurate calls on sterling and the dollar enchanting the traders. But the next instant, he was down the road, there to languish in oblivion and obloquy. It was baffling!

So he and Grace had adjusted painfully and over time to the loss of his six-figure salary. In the meantime, positions and relative rankings within their joint menage had altered, sometimes not so subtly.

The nimble and outspoken Grace, whose career was blossoming, thought that Nicholas failed to concentrate on the job in hand with sufficient seriousness. But she had refrained from hyper-criticism quite successfully. She had a rare skill with people, a kind of diplomatic ease of presence which rarely if ever faltered in 1-1 situations. It was this touch that enabled her to cope with Nicholas' fall from pre-eminence. But the relationship was full of compromises now that Nicholas had ceased to earn. His poor culinary skills represented yet another area where an adjustment to expectations had been forced upon them. Grace had married him on the understanding that it would be she who would retire early.

Fat chance now of that, she told herself bitterly, and daily. She'd be working until Doomsday at the current rate.

Enter, of course, at that point, the alternative agenda involving the office; Simon her partner in the business; and their wager together on Nicholas' future. What had been a light-hearted piece of gambling was now turning into something far more loaded and dangerous; Grace hardly dared contemplate the consequences of the wager if it went wrong for her.

Meanwhile over them both, dogging their footsteps every day, hung the shadow of the mystery – why had he been unable to land another job in the City? Grace herself, whose specialist recruitment field lay away from the Square Mile and closer to Westminster, had been mystified by the lack of interest as Nicholas had received one rejection after another. It was not as if he was unqualified – far from it. He was eminently suited to do the job of global markets' strategist for which he'd been hired originally. But the rantings and the ravings against Fate came to nothing. The one thing constant in Nicholas' life was his inability to land an interview, let alone a job in the City. The bar against re-employment was total, absolute and apparently without remission. Gradually, the two them had reached the conclusion that unwittingly Nicholas had offended somebody, somewhere out there in the Square Mile, somebody very big and powerful indeed who had tipped him the Black Spot, in turn putting him out of lucrative work now and perhaps for ever. It was a chastening thought that such malice lurked unseen throughout those bland and deferential banking parlours, so full of bankers' soft murmurings about credit and deals and profit and darling dinner parties.

Back to the present, sighed Nicholas still contemplating the post-breakfast wreckage. What was it they'd agreed to eat that evening? What had Grace flung over her shoulder as she bounced into her BMW? Nicholas hadn't the foggiest. What they had agreed to eat that evening had gone clean out of his mind as soon as Grace had left the house, partly because of timing. Today was a special day for him. Today was the day that he played ever so gingerly his Ace in the hole.

It was a Friday, that was all he knew. And Friday was a super day for Nicholas. That was the day when he bought the Financial Chronicle, as opposed to reading it at the Chelsea Town Hall library. After buying the Chron, Nicholas scoured through it and worked out some smart calls in the markets. Japanese bonds; Mexican equities; defaulted Croatian bank debt – name the switch and Nicholas clocked it then watched it.

After he'd worked out some clever thoughts, well ahead of the curve, he called Moley on Moley's direct line and talked the ideas over with the City's leading guru. It was a vital call for Nicholas and Moley always seemed pleased to hear from him. This was just as well for Nicholas since Moley was the one person left in the City who was prepared to talk to him. Apart from Moley every single one of his connections with the Square Mile had withered on the vine. Now it was as if he had never worked there. The connection between himself; that fabled zone of money, centred around Threadneedle Street; and big, big salaries grew steadily fainter.

Apart that was from Moley. God alone therefore knew why Moley bothered with him but then Moley was famed throughout the markets as a real snapper-up of trifles; in that respect, he was a true questing beast for special situations. Perhaps that was the reason why he allowed Nicholas to keep in touch with him. Whatever the reason, Moley was a lifeline for Nicholas and Nicholas was deeply grateful for that one slender line of hope that stayed open. It was also a lifeline that sometimes paid its way. Occasionally Moley sent him a cheque for a small amount in gratitude and recompense for his investment advice. That helped to mollify Grace who in truth was beginning to talk now meaningfully to Nicholas about retraining; starting again at the bottom; contemplating a future as a postman; and such-like horrors. Grace didn't like Moley but she had to admit that the odd cheque from him came in useful. The fact of payment could not be gainsaid. It was undeniable. And it was Moley too who advised Nicholas not to give up; kept his hopes alive about landing a job; and who promised to mention his name around in various circles. So when Wednesday came around, and the Chron carried all the job adverts, Nicholas could afford to disregard the tempting offers for Global Portfolio Specialists; or Quants Wanted Urgently. He had faith in Moley. Moley would see him right. Nicholas knew that for a near-certainty.

And thus he looked forward to Friday.

Nicholas contemplated the debris of the breakfast. He knew that as a good and trusty house husband he ought to clear it all away and get the place in good working order, so that it all looked presentable just in case somebody dropped in for a cup of tea. As if...As if..., he thought to himself, as the counter-proposal loomed large in his mind. The struggle was brief but greed and lust won out handsomely over duty. Nicholas left the house – and the washing up – and walked quickly across the street to his newsagent in the King's Road.

Now for some truly scrumptious number-crunching, he thought as he neared the shop. Real mind-boggling stuff...So much better for your teeth than that wretched old muesli... And then afterwards, when he had digested all the data, he would make a quiet call to Moley and enjoy hopefully a long, intelligent chat about the markets; the data; the movers and the shakers; and experience all the fun of the world's topsy-turvy markets...

On an impulse, he called Moley before he bought the Chron, just to check that he was there in his office. That way he could forestall any later disappointment if he called and then found that his man was absent.

Moley's familiar, high-pitched voice answered the phone and the day proper began. Nicholas introduced himself. A slight shock from Moley, a marginal sense of withdrawal, but then the usual fruitiness from the broker in his reply as he inquired courteously after Nicholas' well-being. Nicholas thought he detected real warmth coming down the line from the broker. Nor was there any doubt about his enthusiasm to hear Nicholas' latest investment proposals.

They agreed a time for Nicholas to call later, when he'd done his numbers and worked out his picks in the market. Nicholas had an idea for Moley about Japanese bonds. He had been mulling it during the week and now he wanted to offer the thought to Moley.

Moley for his part sounded more than mildly interested.

'Japanese bonds, eh? It's a long time since I looked at those little fellows – could be interesting. You think the Ministry of Finance is going to switch, eh? Let's talk some more.'

The discussion concluded with lightness and heartiness on both sides. This beats housework hands down, thought Nicholas as he opened the Chron and started checking prices.

*   *   *   *   *

Nicholas was closer to the brink with Grace than he either knew or suspected. Some months previously, Grace and Simon, her business partner, had entered into a bet about his future. Over lunch, and just after they'd done some especially lucrative head-hunting business, Simon had scoffed at Nicholas' chances of ever working again in the City. Grace had rushed to the defence of her man.

'Nothing wrong with him. He can work; he's smart in the markets. All he needs is a break and then he'll be back on track. He's just hitting a bad patch. He'll get through it, you'll see.'

She had played the loyalty card very strongly, grinning at Simon.

Simon had rubbished all of this in a loud voice. He had guffawed as he drank his coffee. Then as if reaching a big decision, he had leaned forward and suggested the wager.

'I don't think Nicholas will get back, but you do. Now, Grace, you know that I fancy you like mad – and you know also that Nicholas is so demoralised that he's not looking after you as he should. I can see that in your face each morning as you come in. So here it is – if Nicholas hasn't found some kind of job in the City in say six months, then I want to spend the night with you.'

She had gaped in shock and awe at Simon's proposal. But she recalled too her excitement at the suggestion. Simon was quite fanciable – it wasn't a wholly repugnant idea. And what he had said about Simon had been true. As her girl friends would have said, in all their raucous vulgarity, she could use a good seeing-to. She listened intently as Simon outlined the deal across the cafe table.

'Yeah, fuck you stupid, that kind of thing. Yeah, the whole bit, no holds barred. The two of us crawling around the bed, shagging like maniacs, as you discover my pecs. I mean it because I'd like to spend the night with you. But also, in all sincerity, and because we're partners in this business and because it's going well and because we're involved financially and because I don't want to see Nicholas drag you down, I would like to offer you a fresh start. What a fresh start, you'll say, quite rightly. But, equally, no point in flogging a dead horse if Nicholas just can't deliver on account of him having been tipped the Black Spot. So if in six months he can't deliver, work wise, you have to move on – and I'll give you the exit card.'

Grace was not in business for nothing. She had a sharp brain and an eye for the main chance. She scented some kind of deal.

'So assuming I agree, which is by no means certain, the lure of your body notwithstanding, what's the other side of the bargain. It's all downside so far, as I see it. You shag me, I may or may not enjoy the experience, and I lose my husband into the bargain. What kind of a deal is that to offer a girl and a business partner to boot?'

Simon had laughed. But he had been serious as well. He said that he wanted to push matters along further and crystallise the position. To her amazement, he said that he would back his words, and while she havered he agreed to place £5000 in escrow. If Nicholas did secure some form of employment in the next six months, that bonded £5K would be forfeit to him, Simon, and would fall due automatically to Grace. No question – he'd sign the piece of paper. Otherwise it was a night of passion at a hotel in Central London or Paris, the venue to be agreed mutually between them like the date – and to be paid by Simon! Unless of course she wanted to buy herself out of the whole trade, in which case it would cost her precisely £5K to avoid the pleasure and the pain of spending the night with him.

Laughingly, she had agreed to the wager. That was two months ago. Nothing much on the horizon since for Nicholas, so far as she could see, apart from Moley and Nicholas' interminable discussions with the broker whom Grace personally thought was too fly by half.

Not be trusted, unlike Simon who clearly was 100% full bore behind his bet.

So she was beginning to concentrate on the imminence of the deal maturing. And likewise Simon. They were both preparing for a denouement, which in truth, given the way the business was flourishing, represented no more than a physical extension of their already close intimacy in matters elsewhere, away from the bed-chamber of the Hilton or the George V. They were both on their marks. Unlike Nicholas, who was rapidly descending in her eyes to the status of tea boy – or worse.

So that was why his position chez Grace was far more precarious than he had ever imagined. But as Simon had pointed out, without insisting on the point, there was no point in flogging a dead horse in the tough and challenging trading environment of London.

★   ★   ★   ★   ★

Emma Bales sat in the main square of Repugia drinking her first cappuccino of the day, and smoking a contemplative Silk Cut cigarette at about the same time that Nicholas was opening his Financial Chronicle with greedy eyes in London's King's Road.

The Italian day was already hot and the shadows stood with aggressive outline among the staircases and gables and doorways which surrounded the square. Passers-by who had ventured out without shades screwed up their eyes against the sun which dazzled in its brightness. Emma took her time. She needed another cappuccino and another Silk Cut before she could put her brain fully into gear in such heat. She had the time to ruminate.

Emma was thinking about her father; wondering when her man in quasi-tow was going to deign to appear from the hotel; and in between those thoughts she eyed the mature but still quite attractive English couple who were sitting at the next table in the square, making heavy weather of Anglo-Italian relationships. Squalls lay ahead in that particular quarter, she surmised.

She took another sip of her cappuccino, holding her cigarette high in the air as she bent forward to the cup. The sun caught her on the nape of her neck and she felt its torrid burn. Just how much longer was Craig going to be, prettying himself up for the day, she wondered.

The deterioration in Anglo-Italian relationships a few feet away was a pity because the couple's waiter, Paolo, was normally quite a happy go lucky Italian. Proud? Yes. Arrogant? Of course, but still for all those quirks of temperament pretty good-natured. Emma had certainly suffered no indignities at his hands during her stay in Repugia which had now lasted for two weeks.

But on this occasion, the couple had rubbed him up the wrong way by being too fastidious in their demands for breakfast tea – yes, English tea – and it has to be made just this way – very hot- and this way alone for Charles, the husband. They had just been too downright snappy and haughty in the way they had delivered the instructions. Ah, the English abroad, thought Emma, how badly they travel...The couple were flustered most likely after their journey, so that the old authoritarian English reflex actions had come out with a vengeance.

Paolo disappeared into the cafe and out of the bright glare of the sun with a backward scowl in the direction of the English couple.

Emma thought about her father a little more as she pulled on her cigarette and then watched the smoke hover in the warm morning air. Him and his tanks! Poor man, how hard he had worked to realise his dream! How he would have relished her success and her independence! How grateful he had been when his inventions brought in just a little bit of money and how delighted he had been when anyone, yes anyone, took him the remotest bit seriously. It was just so unaccountably tragic that he had not lived to see any of her success...The tanks of course had prospered but her father had died before he could see the full fruition of his invention and collect some of the handsome returns which had begun to flow homewards just before he died.

Bad timing, Dad, bad timing, as always, Emma whispered to herself as she felt the sun start to beat on her arms and bare legs. In the heat of the Italian morning she recalled with a shiver of dismay his eyes starting to close as the death rattle started, with a look of surprise and total inexpressible disappointment. He died thinking he'd failed his much adored daughter; his son; and his wife...

The caprice of Fate had cheated him of any satisfaction whatsoever...

There were times now when he seemed to hover quite close to Emma in spirit, to whisper consolingly to her from across the ether which separated the quick from the dead. This morning was one of those occasions. She felt that he was close by, still watching out for her and protecting her, as he always had done during her brief but meteoric legal career. Emma mourned, as she always did, the loss and the absence of her dear beloved father while her mind took in slowly the antics of the couple at the next table.

Charles was now rebuking his wife for some imagined shortcoming in the testy, disappointed way that the over-protected develop as they grow old. His wife defended herself as best she could. She accommodated his complaints and to some extent anticipated them so that the atmosphere of a marvellous day in prospect was not wholly ruined.

Thinking that she too in some ways was living on the same knife-edge as Charles' wife, Emma wondered what her father would have made of her position now, as she prepared to launch herself into publishing. A good marriage, followed shortly afterwards by the death of her Norwich farmer husband unexpectedly, had made all these things possible. And Craig, still invisible within the hotel, was her risky venture into the world of fiction publishing! Her first! Emma reminded herself that Craig was not quite her man – yet. He was her first author, a different matter entirely. They were here in Italy so that Craig could pursue his researches on his novel. Emma, determining to do things with style, had offered to pay for the costs of the holiday. Craig had a good idea for his novel and he had taken the concept just as far as he could in England. A trip to Italy was vital to clinch the detail. So he had accepted.

That, as yet, was as far as it went. They were staying in the hotel in separate rooms. Their relationship was chaste – as yet. Craig was a young classics schoolteacher trying to break out of the rut of his career. He had the earnestness and careful approach of those whose ambition has not yet been mutilated by events. The holiday so far had been a success. Craig had done his writing diligently, and Emma had lounged about the square most of the time, wondering about other areas of her life and the other men in it…

Not a technicolour story in all-around sound but nevertheless she had had her moments…

She was glad also of the break from the ceaseless round of London socialising with its unending triviality and backbiting.

There was also another rationale to the trip which Emma kept concealed from Craig and indeed from anyone. That aspect of things was simply not for public consumption. Just a matter of a meeting and a letter to be handed over. Not more than five minutes in all, she guessed, although it was crucial to stick to her timetable agreed with London. Indeed Emma prohibited herself most of the time from thinking about it at all as she enjoyed her holiday. As well as being her first expedition as a budding publisher, it was also her first trip abroad as a trained agent for British Intelligence. She was determined to make a success of handling the two roles, although in truth the mission itself hardly seemed that demanding. Just a matter of meeting a man in a cafe and leaving an envelope for him in the loo...

Not long now to the meeting... Unconsciously she knew that she was counting the days...Craig was departing that morning for Verona to continue his researches for a fortnight and in that time she would...

Afterwards she could really settle down to enjoying the holiday with Craig. Briefly the image of his sun-tanned body emerging from the shower in mid-afternoon in search of her welcoming body struck her and she quivered a little with the excitement of its potential. That made her nervous. The sex and the espionage seemed to have become entwined together in her mind. She tried to think of other things.

Thrusting such matters from her mind, she pondered the other men in her life. It was not a long story but there again it had its tragic aspects. Gregory, her poet, had been a catastrophe. That could not be denied. He had been a complete disaster, and that coming just at the worst possible time, just when she had thought she had everything under full control...If only he hadn't turned up so unexpectedly in the West Indies. None of what had happened would have happened...

She took another sip at her coffee and another ruminative draw on her Silk Cut as the sun beat down and she felt the sweat trickle down her neck and thighs and across her arms.

Deliberately in order to provoke storms, Paolo brought the wrong kind of tea and placed it carefully in front of the English gentleman and his slightly flustered wife. Emma noticed that Charles, the husband, appeared to suffer from some nervous affliction. At least his hands never stopped shaking. He was upset by the arrival of the wrong tea and his wife knew it. She winced as the hands shook some more. He looked at the label of the tea and then barked some command or other at Paolo. Paolo for his part like all Italians adopted a supremely understanding air. This was wholly bogus; Paolo was quite mutinous. His stance translated quite freely into a desire to create an outburst of total rage on the part of the travellers who were irritated beyond endurance.

As Charles' wife attempted to intervene, Charles turned on her and rebuked her quite savagely.

'Lucy-Miranda, will you please stay out of this. I'll handle it. Can't you see that? I'm used to dealing with Italians.'

Lucy-Miranda shrugged and was silent. Paolo posed in front of them with a look of insufferable pleasure on his face as the English couple bickered away. It was like a silent film at this point, just before the fist-fighting started in slow motion. Emma thought that it was time for her to get involved. Craig would have been helpful at this juncture because he spoke quite good Italian but he was nowhere to be seen.

She leaned across to Charles and Lucy-Miranda, introduced herself as English, and then half beseeching, half cajoling, enjoined Paolo to bring the correct tea.

'Earl Grey, yes, comprende Paolo, Earl Grey?'

She spoke slowly to the waiter as the flames of wrath engulfing the two English began to subside. An early morning Vesuvian eruption was being averted. They both looked at her with gratitude. They were being rescued, as good English people always were in Italy.

'Ah, Early Grey,' said Paolo who knew the jig was up as soon as the Senorita Bales had joined the scrap. Besides he rather liked the look of Emma. For her it would be a pleasure. He was very happy to have become understanding and helpful. He stressed the Grey in the name of the tea as if that had suddenly become a quite new commodity which inexplicably had escaped his vigilant attention. Then he disappeared back into the cafe.

'I think you'll get your tea now. Paolo can be quite difficult, I know, but he's a sweet boy really. Besides, it's far too hot to have disagreements over tea, don't you agree?'

They all agreed in chorus and a shadow fell across the group as Craig materialised from his prinking. He looked fit, chunky, tanned and slightly abstracted, as if he'd spent the past hour writing as the inspiration took him. Other worldly, in a word. Emma suppressed as unfair the thought that he had chosen the right moment to turn up just after she had handled it all, hoped that his writing had gone well and introduced him to Charles and Lucy-Miranda. The image of his naked body emerging from the shower still lingered on the edge of her imagination, not quite wholly suppressed.

'Good morning, all of you. I'm sorry if I've missed something. I've been writing hard this morning and it's gone very well. I'm somewhere in authorial outer space at the moment.'

The schoolmasterly tone, that rasp at the end of the sentence, was quite absent from his voice, thought Emma. The holiday must be doing him good.

Paolo reappeared with the correct tea and placed it without a word in front of them. Craig joshed him on the shoulder and muttered something in his ear, at which Paolo brightened immediately, joshed back and muttered audibly to Craig 'Imbecile' with a smile before departing to cause more trouble at another table.

'This is Craig and I'm Emma Bales. Craig is writing a novel – his first, mark you – and I'm going to publish it for him. It's a new venture for both of us.'

Lucy-Miranda was very excited and turned to Charles in triumph.

'You see, Charles that's what you should be doing. I told you that. You should at the very least be writing your memoirs. But I think you'd be better with novels. You do write well you know...'

She turned to Craig and Emma.

'Charles was in the Diplomatic Service for most of his life. He has some marvellous stories to tell if only he could bring himself to get them down on paper. He was in Moscow during the worst of the Cold War, fancy that. And he knew Philby. What do you think of that? Yes, Philby, the master-spy...'

Charles reacted like a hunting dog hearing his master's 'view halloo' at the mention of the Foreign Office; the Cold War; and the unspeakable Philby. He put out a restraining hand to Lucy-Miranda who pushed it away.

'Charles don't you try and hush me. I will say what you did – I'm proud of it. When are you going to get it into your head that you've retired, that all of that is behind you, and that you can say and write what you like. If it wasn't for me, you'd be a free man. Think of that.'

Rebuked into silence, Charles concentrated on pouring out his Earl Grey tea, while Lucy-Miranda, glad of a change of audience, requested further information about the book. Craig was a willing speaker. The writing had clearly gone well that morning. To Emma, it sounded like 1500 words at least, and all of the very best...

A pang ran through her as she calculated in those terms. It was not fair to anyone to think along those lines. But she had been there before with writers.

Surrogates all for Gregory...?'

Craig had launched forth.

'It centres around this Roman poet called Catullus. He lived about 30 BC, so two millennia ago, give or take, and he had a very passionate affair with a very smart Roman lady called, we think, Clodia who was older than him. She came from the very tip-top senior echelon of Roman society of the day, so it was a sensational affair. But Catullus was smart too. Very much the man in the Ferrari beating up the Italian roads on his way to the next party. It was an accident waiting to happen. To cut a long story short, the affair went badly, he fell apart over it, because she dumped him. She simply moved on. She really was a lady who knew her own mind and she always got what she wanted. Catullus maybe died of a broken heart, we don't know for sure, but in the process he left us with this collection of poems...'

'Lovely,' interrupted Lucy-Miranda quite captivated by the recital and also worried lest Charles started becoming fractious and difficult. She wanted Craig to continue talking. He needed little invitation. Charles continued drinking his tea quite sedately in the morning Italian sun. The shadows moved around the square.

'The poems are magnificent but that is not really the point of my novel. You see, the poetry disappears. It is not seen again for about twelve hundred years. Yes, as long as that. And it is known to us quite by chance. It reappears very briefly in the Middle Ages when the whole collection, arranged we think by Catullus himself, is found either wedging a wine butt in Verona or in the dust of the Verona streets by the town notary. Nobody seems to be quite sure.'

'Just like that, in the streets? How remarkable.'

'Just like that. Totally casual. Like finding the Sistine chapel on the municipal rubbish dump, or a lost play of Shakespeare in a mail order catalogue. But the mystery deepens now. The poems were copied out but no sooner had that happened than the original collection once again vanished. Having lost it, it seems that somebody then stole it back. Perhaps a member of Catullus' family in Verona, or perhaps even a descendant of one of his friends mentioned in the poems. The original collection was never seen again. All we have are imperfect copies of the original poetry, poetry I should add which blisters across time and space with its intensity. This was no ordinary love affair that just petered out after which everybody went their separate ways…It scorches off the page…'

'So what's the novel then?'

Lucy-Miranda was enthralled by Craig's description. Her eyes were shining. For a moment, she looked younger by twenty years. Love had come to call on her just for a second.

'I thought I'd play around with the time sequences, using this funny incident in the Middle Ages as a link. Part of the novel is set in Roman times and describes Catullus' affair, but the other part takes place in modern times. Perhaps set in Italy but more likely London. The man this time is older and his love is just a girl. So the roles are reversed. I can use the poetry to point the way towards what is happening in both time sequences…And then…'

Craig faltered just a fraction as the immensity of the project and the small efforts he had made so far to fill the canvas briefly overwhelmed him. Lucy-Miranda appeared not to notice the lapse of confidence.

'What a perfectly wonderful idea. I'm sold already. And I want to see it and read it obviously when it comes out. So what's the timetable? When's it being published. And what will I look for? What's it called?'

She turned to Emma as she spoke, including her in the discussion. It was a generous gesture. Emma looked rueful.

'We haven't quite fixed on a title yet. We've tried all sorts of ideas but none have quite hit it. We think that there's a perfect title somewhere out there but so far it's eluded us. But it'll come, I know that, it'll come...'

'So how much have you written so far?'

Charles sounded cordial, as he eased his way into the conversation skilfully. Emma noticed how easily he addressed Craig in contrast to his testy treatment of Lucy-Miranda. Craig was pleased by the manly tone of the inquiry. Everybody seemed happy to chat.

'About 40,000 words. Nearly half way there. This morning was exceptional. I've done 1200 and it's only...God, Emma what time is it? I think it may be time I wasn't here. I've just lost a few hours in my head from writing. I've got a train to catch. I've arranged to be in Verona this afternoon. Looking for the notary and checking out the wine-butt....'

Emma looked at her watch.

'Craig I hate to tell you this but we have to break the party up. You have exactly fifteen minutes to make that train. Where's your luggage?'

'In the hotel lobby. That's easily done. But I'd better go and pick it up. Wait here for me. I'll be back. Oh God, this writing, it just takes you over...'

He loped back across the square and they watched him hurry, pursued by his shadow. Emma thought of someone else who used to say similar things a long while ago. Lucy-Miranda broke in on her thoughts. She was insistent, taking control with some emphasis.

'Now that we've found you, I'm not letting you go just like that. Is that your hotel?'

'Yes it is.'

'Well we have a story to tell to you. Not quite as thrilling as yours but a story nevertheless. Isn't this fun, swapping stories like this as complete unknowns, just like real travellers. So what d'you think, Charles? I think we should invite Emma over for drinks early this evening? You're not going with Craig I take it to Verona, judging by the hurly-burly over the luggage? So you'll be free?'

Bullied, Emma nodded, feeling slightly overwhelmed by events but charmed by Lucy-Miranda's initiative nonetheless.

'And we owes you too for helping to sort out the tea just now for Charles. Do come to our little party...'

Emma was hesitant because the invitation threatened distantly to derail her schedule and hence her assignation. But she felt it absurd to be so apprehensive. Besides, she was intrigued by Lucy-Miranda and wished to see more of her. It was a rapport thing. The woman struck a delicate chord with her. She felt comfortable talking to Lucy-Miranda. Emma would not like to be walled up with Charles and she sympathised with his wife.

'No, I'm not going to Verona. Craig wants to do the research on his own. He thinks that if he strikes it lucky he may even run the original manuscript to earth in some Veronese vaults but I think that's wishful thinking and incidental to the main business in hand. Besides I'm just his publisher. I'm not his keeper or his wife. Craig likes to potter round the archives but it would drive me mad, I'm afraid.'

Lucy-Miranda smiled.

'So you two are not married then. Well that settles that. You must come over to see us this afternoon. You'll be missing him whatever you say. This afternoon is when my daughter is arriving from London with her new beau along with a lot of our crowd from the country. From Hampshire, that is. We're staying about 100 yards from here in my eldest daughter's villa. She won't mind a bit, I know, about the villa seeing a new face. She's a Gilston now, so she's used to all this. Besides, she's in the USA just now, so it won't really concern her. So it should be very jolly. You'll be very welcome. You're happy with that aren't you Charles?'

Charles nodded, not really concerned by the hijacking of the stranger who for her part seemed eminently presentable.

'My daughter has given us all the use of her little shack for part of the summer. It's a traditional thing.'

'Yes, very welcome.'

Charles interrupted his reverie to voice his approval again. It seemed to be a settled thing. Emma had mixed feelings. She felt once again that she was being absorbed by that eternal travelling country-house party of the Home Counties' nomenclatura, the same glitterati who had given her such a tough time when she first returned to London, plus a fortune but short of a husband.

44

But perhaps it might be different for her this time, with them all being so far from their natural habitat. She was far more grown-up about it all now.

She began to assent to the invitation in her mind. Who could tell, it might be fun...And she might squeeze in some more chat and gossip with Lucy-Miranda...

Craig arrived back at speed carrying his grip. He panted in the heat. He had lingered too long in the Elysian groves of creative frenzy. Now he risked missing his train. But he was courteous towards his benefactress as he fretted over catching his connection.

'Don't you worry about my cab. I can see there's one over there on the rank. I'll take that. You stay here and chat. There's no point in both of us rushing down to the station.'

Emma smiled at him and then disagreed with his suggestion.

'No, I'll come to the cab with you. Just to make sure that you get into it and start the journey. New young authors are wayward...'

She realised that there was a more pressing matter to complete, and the short walk to the rank would help her do that. It all brought back the old times for her when she had been with Gregory.

They walked the few yards to the rank together in the blazing white of the heat.

As they approached the cab, Emma fished in her bag and pressed a bundle of Euro's into Craig's hand.

'Now take this and don't you think of arguing with me. This is my business venture, and you shouldn't be worrying about money when you do your researches. I'm talking to you as your publisher now. Have some spending money...'

Then she bundled him into the cab before he could protest about her generosity. The cab zoomed off in the direction of the station with Craig waving frantic, grateful farewells from the rear window. Emma returned to her cafe.

Lucy-Miranda and Charles had discreetly vanished but Emma knew that their absence would be brief. She knew how Hampshire behaved under these circumstances. She was to be taken up again and scrutinised. And how would she fare this time around, now that she had added espionage to her round of activities?

She looked forward to the afternoon with a glimmer of relish. And would the dames take her to their bosom a second time around? Emma rather doubted it. Compassion was soldered out ruthlessly from their make-up within the cradle. That was the Hampshire way.

She bade Paolo good-day and he gave her his little boy 'lost and found' look which stated quite categorically that it was there for her alone, on certain terms of course, if she wanted to trade. But it was definitely not there for him. She smiled her rejection as a young and independent female would do and wandered back to the hotel. She found that Lucy-Miranda had moved quickly. There was a message for her at the desk.

The message was handwritten in a tight, educated and controlled fist. The style of the calligraphy came as a surprise to Emma, after Lucy-Miranda's rather passionate and fluttery performance that morning.

'We'd love to see you later this afternoon for our drinks' party. It'll be at the Villa Lampedusa at around five o'clock. My daughter Lucia should be arriving at around four thirty with her party so it should all go with a swing. The Villa Lampedusa is about 200 yards up to the left of the hotel, as you go out by the main entrance and then past the Cathedral again on your left. I do hope you can make it but if there are any dramas in the meantime involving Roman poets; novels; or Verona, here is our telephone number…'

The absence of Craig hit her quite suddenly as she held the note in her hand standing in the lobby. Her surroundings were not cosy, all of a sudden, but rather metallic and quite harsh, she thought, as the loneliness struck her. The sunshine seemed to fade. She would dearly have liked to have attended at the Villa Lampedusa on the arm of her man, exposing herself to the inevitable scrutiny of Chiantishire with someone presentable beside her. But it was not to be for her that afternoon, just as it had not been for her for so long in that contented way, with Geoffrey failing her for the terminal reason of a stroke; and then with Gregory opting out for another…

And then there was Joe of course but she preferred not to think about Joe at all. He was just a great big riddle to her. And the great lovers' tryst in the Caribbean, that had quite simply been a catastrophe for them all. Best not even recalled to mind at this delicate moment in her journey of the spirit through Italy.

She would attend alone. And she would make the best of it. She crunched the note in her hand and threw it into the wastepaper basket in the lobby.

'Bad news, signorina Bales?'

The Desk was worried but she shook her head and took the lift quickly.

She fought with her feelings briefly as she went into her hotel room, telling herself that it was quite unfair to include Geoffrey in her diatribe against the males of the species. It wasn't his fault, poor man, that he had died trying to extract a stubborn root from his garden, so soon after they had married. Geoffrey, she was certain, would much rather still be alive at that moment and travelling with her in Italy…But Gregory…Now that was a different story entirely. Gregory was a shit and a louse. She'd wasted her time with Gregory, time that was now too precious for her even to think about it.

She found herself inveighing about the temporary nature of it all, that massive contingency factor in her life. It was starting to drive her insane. The programme was always the same. If she did this, she might meet So and So, and she might get on well with So and So and it would all lead to a Jolly Good Thing… But if she didn't do what she had planned to do, then either she might not meet So and So, in which case a Jolly Good Thing was off the menu, or more worrying, she might meet him as a result of changing her plans and doing the exact opposite of what she had originally intended. It was just all too fretful, almost as if the only way she could proceed was by continually short-circuiting herself, a performance which would lead ineluctably to the Priory and those strong nurses with their lethal injections. She wanted none of that. She wanted to feel in control, not like some random particle buzzing around the cosmos. She wanted to be settled now, and bedded down and predictable, with a secure round in her days to look forward to, rather than this continual hitchhiking through relationships. She knew that for a certainty.

She felt her stomach contract with tension as she thought about Gregory. She went to the window and flung it open so that the sun off the white square and the blue sky smashed into the room and she could see very clearly the busy people of Repugia crossing and recrossing the square bent on their daily round. Their plodding normalcy comforted her even here in Italy.

Gregory and she had lived together in London for many years trying to make a success of the capital, she as a lawyer and he as a poet. That had been some years ago now. They had been happy in their poverty. The relationship had broken up and she had later discovered that Gregory had fallen in love with a man and was sharing his life with him. She had just about been able to accept this fact without screaming the roof down, even though they were by now living apart and she had married and had then been widowed by Geoffrey. And of course there had been Joe...Yes, Joe had played a full part in all of this grim business...The whole ghastly imbroglio had reached its lurid climax in the Caribbean when Gregory had suddenly turned up on her estate in Antigua at exactly the same time that Gregory's evil genius, her very own wretched, wretched younger brother had happened by appalling coincidence to be there in town at the same time...What ghoulish fun the two of them had enjoyed around her kitchen table at just the moment when she had been preparing to cement her alliance with Joe...

It had been unspeakable...By the time she had sorted all of that out, she had missed her meeting with Joe, who had disappeared to New York, along, so she gathered, with his new career...

She came to herself with a start and made strong efforts to master her feelings. That was then, she told herself firmly and this was now. She was in Italy and she was having a good time. A very good time. The weather was good. Craig was a very nice man and they were getting along splendidly. He would write his book and she would publish it and they would all live happily ever after. Together or apart, it didn't matter – that was the plan. That was her future. If she stuck to the line she had worked out she would be fine, provided she did not deviate one iota from that line. Otherwise, there would be trouble for her...She told herself these home truths very forcibly and refused to weep over her chagrin, not in Italy at any rate and in such beautiful weather...

She continued with the pep talk.

She had met some new people that morning who seemed to be very agreeable. She would have a good time. She was bound to have a good time. She told herself this at least seven or eight times, repressing the obvious thought that Craig was just a pretty boy she had picked up as a replacement for Gregory...

And if not, the doleful thought struck her, why had she known almost to the word just how much Craig had written that morning?

The wherefore to that why was because she had watched Gregory struggle over his poems. On a Friday evening when he had read them over to her, as she relaxed in the bath and turned on the taps with her toes in their rented Earls Court flat, she knew very well just what the wordage count would have been for any given session.

That was why...

But am I to be so shackled by the past, she wondered with a resolute show of mental strength as the birds screamed and wheeled past her window heading for the cathedral. Is everything to be a reprise of what has happened already? Can I not even escape for a moment from the consequences of my past actions, even with all my millions of dollars and the whole world for my playground? This is absurd. I refuse point blank to be shackled by the tyranny of time. I am my own mistress...

The phone rang at that moment. She snatched it up. It was Craig calling from his train. He sounded blissful and bubbly.

'Yes, I caught my train just in the nick of time, literally by seconds. So here I am racing through the Italian countryside and very good it looks too. I was ringing to say Thank you for the cash. That will be a great help. I'll keep in touch of course but I wanted you to know that I thought it was very generous on your part...It'll make a great difference to morale...'

Emma found herself drawn into the role of nurse; sympathiser; and benefactress and she hated her words as she cooed support and sympathy down the line. But she stuck to the role. She thought she had no choice at all but to succour Craig and see it all through. She chattered on to him as his train boomed on down the track. It had been good nevertheless that he had called, she thought. The brief human contact had caught her just in time from sliding into that vast pit of self-recrimination that she knew so well...

She replaced the receiver and decided that desperate situations called for desperate measures. No choice here at all. She opted for the strongest anti-depressant that she knew under the circumstances – sleep. It was time for a nap. When she woke again everything would look and feel different. It always did. Nothing to be done until then but snooze...

And after all she did have a nice party to go to in the afternoon....

She stripped off, and flung her clothes on the chair next to the bed, relishing her nudity as elemental and purifying. She slid swiftly, eagerly between the sheets of the freshly- made bed. She left the windows wide-open to the sun; the breeze and the hooting sounds of daily life meandering up to her bedroom from the streets and the medieval square below. Her spine seemed to merge with the mattress as sleep overtook her in a friendly, rushing wave of complete oblivion that drove her straight down to the ocean floor.

★   ★   ★   ★   ★

'So tell us, Tom, in your own words – of which I know you possess more than just an eloquent few – just why we should make you Editor of the Chronicle, in preference to the other excellent candidates we have just seen today? Tell us why.'

Tom paused and smiled before he commenced his reply. The reference to his column was friendly enough – cue brilliancy in his words now!

Headed by Lord Test in the centre, the board awaited his replies in relaxed fashion, sprawled in reposeful nonchalance around the table. Tom saw that Graham was nodding an unseen, tiny inclination of encouragement to him from the far left, a small hint of complicity that went beyond the protocol of the interview.

This was the big one. Silence fell. Tom cleared his throat.

Tom was the last to meet the board, after he had suffered the coming's and going's of the other candidates throughout the session. It was all or nothing. Either he could make his mark – now – or the decision to take one of the other journalists would not be reversed.

'As I see it, the Chron...'

Tom began speaking along the cautious lines that Ursula had advocated, emphasising the importance of continuity and tradition at the Chron and how he'd been able to fulfil that tradition in small ways because he'd written a column for the paper for many years. He knew the paper well; he was a good safe pair of hands; he could be trusted to rule a bolshie newsroom discreetly; he saw a wider role for the Chron outside of its' traditional parish of the Square Mile and the Home Counties...

It was good worthy stuff...

Maybe Ursula was right, Tom thought, as he saw the domes of varying complexion nod and bob up and down as he spoke. But Graham stared straight ahead of him, refusing apparently, to Tom's way of thinking, to address him directly. Was this endorsement by Graham or was it disappointment? It was unclear to Tom who continued, nevertheless, to toe the Ursula line in his speech, which touched inevitably on revenues; readership and market penetration.

Grip factor? Might be nil, Tom speculated as he rambled down the lanes of talk.

He paused for a second and took a sip of water, still enjoying briefly and vicariously the sensation of being the interviewee, not the perennial newspaperman hounding his victims into indiscreet disclosures. The water refreshed his dry throat as it coursed towards his stomach. Tom felt well in control.

But at that point and in a very public way Graham shook his head in what looked very much like a concerted signal between himself and Lord Test. Thumbs down for the job? Total fuck-up on tactics by Ursula? Negative grip factor? No news, no job?

This semi-public dissent from his statements flummoxed Tom. He felt himself floundering. He stopped himself before he recommenced speaking; sipped more water; and then did the only thing that came naturally to him in such circumstances. It was intuitive. Reverting to newspaper mode, he asked the board a question:

'Any thoughts so far?'

Heavy silence this time. Then as if right on cue after his puppetry performance, Graham shot Tom a query from half-way across the room to Tom's left. Tom wondered if he was shipwrecked at that moment or floating free on the flood tide.

Like a well-aimed Scud, Graham's query hit the magazine.

'How do you propose handling the Bank of England? Some people say we're far too close to the Bank; that we're nothing but the Bank's house journal. That our product is a farrago of nonsense relative to the truth in markets. Is this correct? And if so, how do you propose handling that problem?'

Tom felt the Scud missile brush past him in its flight.

'Wait one,' said Tom. 'I have to think quite carefully about this. About my reply, I mean.'

More silence as the board watched him idly; Tom deliberated for a few seconds more in front of their serried ranks before replying. It was the black question, in Tom's view, and the ball-breaker for all the candidates. How best to answer? And what did the board want? And absent any clues on that score, did Tom follow the appeasement line, as dictated by Ursula, and run with the 'Steady as she goes line'?

Or did he speak the truth as he saw it and look out for the main chance? Leave the safety of the thickets and canter onto the broad plain?

Eventually, Tom decided to tell the truth as he saw it. It felt right. The temporising alternatives bored him and made him feel feeble. His was the exasperated response of a fair-minded professional journalist to the problems of self-censorship which haunted the paper daily. Abruptly, and as he washed out the equivocation from his head, Tom junked Ursula's line and went instead for the jugular.

'I'm glad you asked me that question. I've spent some time on this problem, thinking about it, and it's not easy. I didn't think it would come up, but here we are, and I'm grateful for the chance to make a solid reply. We've spent years in the Bank's pocket, in my view, and it's not healthy for both parties. So let's accept this as fact and move on. Now what I propose is this...'

Tom became aware that the atmosphere in the room had changed. Instead of the idle attention of some moments previously, the board was now all ears to his proposals, in spirit at least crowding around him to hear what he had to say. Their interest had been aroused.

Is this a winning line, and is this what the other candidates suggested, Tom wondered as he threw caution to the winds. Speaking confidently, fluently and from the heart now, he outlined a scheme to put clear blue water between the Chron and the Bank. These plans involved a different, more free-wheeling, approach to currency and bond markets coverage; they were designed to indicate to the Bank that the Chron, although willing to cooperate with the Bank, reserved the right to hold more than just the non-voting loan stock when it came to the business of Square Mile reporting and commentary. It was radical stuff from one of the Chron's die-hard investigative reporters. The board sat in silence either lapping it up or repudiating every syllable.

Tom had no way of knowing. He ploughed onwards.

Either way, after such a speech, it was clear his job was no longer the same. Onward and upward; or onward and out – those were now the only alternatives after his fighting words.

'The Bank may be an Old Lady but the Chron is a young and feisty creature that must be allowed elbow-room. We have to go for it, and hang the Bank. It's a barrier to progress,' he concluded on a quiet but sincere note and looked around him.

'Like getting one of Tom Stone's excellent columns the day before publication,' said Lord Test, glancing around at the other board members, his face wreathed in smiles. Likewise the rest of the board. They grinned at the interviewee. Tom still wondered if he'd hit the jackpot. Were they all just being kind to him before presenting him with a gold-embossed P45 – and fountain pen?

But an atmosphere of glee now pervaded the room. Lord Test coughed slightly before resuming:

'Tom, it is a problem for us, this relationship with the Bank, both now and going forward. So we decided to ask each candidate the same question at some point in the discussion. You got there a little ahead of us, but that's because you're a journalist, I suppose. You seemed to scent the question ahead of time and so congratulations on your pre-empt. Anyway, and to sum up, the short point is that all the other candidates answered the same way – No problem and if so containable – almost word for word. That is what has made today's interviews so astonishing; they all said the same thing, apart from you. We were quite confounded. But this glibness' – here the rest of the board also nodded agreement at Test's words – 'this glibness of the other candidates is to our minds today, and at this point in the paper's evolution, simply not sufficient…Really inadequate…'

It began to dawn on Tom that he might have made a winning selection. Otherwise Test would not have been so friendly. Editor of the Chron, by jingo! He could see it coming up over the horizon now, in just a few moments, like a little golden chariot with Tom Stone marked across it. It was good. He felt himself smiling back at the board.

Wouldn't Ursula be pleased with her Tom, even though her suggested line of attack had been completely wrong! But he would never say that to her in so many words! He paused again.

'…And so, Tom, I think I speak for all the board when I say that we liked your comments on the Bank : Chron relationship. I, for my part, particularly enjoyed the balanced approach you adopted to the Chron. Your opening remarks were well couched and delivered, clearly from the heart. You stressed the need for continuity but also the need for change in this vital area. That was important. So in my view and in that of the board…' – here Test glanced around like a seasoned veteran to ensure that he had gauged the mood correctly – '…Good; no Nays; that is excellent and so we are unanimous.'

More spirited nodding by the domes. Test continued with zest.

'Tom, in our unanimous view, you are the outstanding candidate. Congratulations and well done. I therefore have no hesitation in offering you the Editorship of the Financial Chronicle, effective immediately. What say you, man? Yeah or nay?'

The tone of avuncular familiarity was crafted to encourage. Tom took his cue from Test. He smiled back at the board. It felt very good.

'I think you can take it for certain that I'm not going to turn the offer down. That is set in stone – or should I say Stone? Ursula would never forgive me. But I'm going to take a little bit of a chance and accept the offer even before I've talked it over with her. Want me to sign anything? Apart from my by-line, that is?'

More honest, hearty, grateful laughter from the board as the directors crowded forward to shake the Chron's new editor by the hand. Somewhat to his surprise, Tom saw that Graham had already left the conference. But then, as he recollected, he was due to see Graham later on that evening. How very correct of him to distinguish between his private and professional existences so clearly!

Tom continued to shake the directors' hands.

★   ★   ★   ★   ★

It was close to five o'clock as Emma toiled up the steep street beside the cathedral in search of the Villa Lampedusa. Again she thought about the marked absence of male presence at her side. But her spirits had recovered with her sleep. It was more of a challenge now than a burden – she was looking forward to meeting the Gilston tribe.

A cobbler of some description was hammering away at the sole of a sandal as she passed him seated in the doorway of his workshop.

'Scusi, signor...'

He looked up with a glare and jerked his head upwards interrogatively, still hammering. The black eyes were fixed on her face like limpets.

' Er...Dove Villa Lampedusa, per favore...?'

She felt a fool but she guessed to the cobbler all travellers were idiots; it didn't matter. He jerked his head towards the left and then dropped his gaze back down towards his sandal. Emma felt less of a fool but still stupid and continued on her way.

She was right to feel idiotic. The Villa Lampedusa was unmistakeable. It was the only large building in the street by the time she had passed the cathedral on her left. The main door, set within the high wall of the outer structure, was thrust wide open and she wandered through into a courtyard. Everywhere inside there was bustle, with people disembarking from taxis and flinging luggage about and shouting to each other in that controlled yet exasperated tone of voice so typical of the Home Counties transported abroad. Children were rushing about in high excitement now that the journey from England was over and they could play without restraint. Matrons patrolled here and there, walking in a more stately manner.

The Gilstons had arrived for their summer break.

Beyond the courtyard Emma glimpsed an open expanse of garden, ablaze with colour and flanked by trees, which seemed to give directly onto the sunbaked hills behind Repugia. This intrigued her since she knew that Repugia was built up from the ground on its high walls. But from where she stood there was no sign of that raised elevation in the perspective. She made to advance in order to check her bearings, whereupon a child with long blond hair that desperately required trimming barred her way, like a small sentry.

'Who are you? I don't know you. What are you doing here?'

The child could not have been older than eight, but he had the self-possession and proprietorial assurance of a man of forty. Catch 'em young, thought Emma as she carefully explained that she had come for the party as a guest of Lucy-Miranda and Charles. The young commissar was unimpressed.

'Don't know them either. Not my family. You'd better ask for them at the gate.'

Emma paused wondering if she could call his bluff by marching onwards, when the child abruptly dropped his ferocious bearing and said to her confidingly, as if she had been a life-long friend of the Gilstons,

'I say, it's rough luck on Lucia, don't you think?'

'I suppose so. Tough for her,' said a temporising Emma vaguely, struck by the sudden thought that Lucia, as a name, rang some sort of bell with her somewhere. It was a familiar name, but in what context she failed to recall. She thought she remembered it in some more specific setting but dismissed any connection. Impossible, she thought, that is just too ridiculous as a coincidence.

But it was a good well sounding name.

Dropping all pretence then, she asked the barbarian child what had happened to Lucia. Like a small wizard, the child was only too eager to tell the tale.

'You're not the only stranger here. There's Jake as well. Lucia had to turn back at the airport, at Heathrow that is, I mean. It was very exciting. They made the announcement over the loudspeakers just as we were getting onto the plane. Lucia was absolutely livid, I can tell you. She didn't want to go...Oh, my name's Gavin; what's your's?'

'Emma. Pleased to meet you, Gavin. And Jake? Who's Jake?'

'That's Lucia's boyfriend. They work in the same bank, at least that what Mummy said. I heard her talking about it. She said that Lucia was disgusting. She was only bringing Jake out here for a cheap fuck and even that was possible only because she was his boss and she'd practically ordered him to take time off with her. That's what Mummy said. So what's that, Emma, when it's out and about? What does it mean? What's a cheap fuck?'

'I don't know Gavin. You should ask your mother. She's bound to know.'

'She won't tell me. That's why I keep asking everybody so I can find out.'

The spectacle of this mutinous child marching determinedly from guest to guest in his quest for information was so appalling it was practically comic. But how to escape?

Emma was rescued from his control by a small young girl who flew past them both and told Gavin he'd better hurry into the house because his mother had been searching high and low for him. Gavin made to flee. Lucy-Miranda strolled upon them from around the corner.

Her face lit up at the sight of Emma.

'Emma, how very nice to see you. I'm so glad you could make it. It's so good of you to come. Now let's go onto the terrace and get a good view of those hills in the sunshine. Follow me. There are some drinks laid out as well for us. Charles is there. He's very chatty now that he's got some company. Quite different from the grumpy old man you saw this morning. But we'll have a chance to chat together.'

And indeed Lucy-Miranda spoke true. Like a true diplomat, Charles was working the room, or in this case, the terrace with ease. A smile in his eyes and glass in hand, he was gliding here and there among the guests, smoothing out the rough edges among the welter of personalities. He was the picture of radiant, experienced bonhomie as the Gilston group sorted itself out on its arrival; found its rooms in the villa; and then sped down to the drinks laid out on a long table beside the terrace, now taking the late afternoon sun in all its splendour.

The terrace gave onto the hills from a distance but also closer up, as Emma had surmised, formed an elevation of the city's walls. This created a continuous ledge of rocks, some five feet high above the lawn and the walkway, which ran all the way round the garden, dropping sheer on the other side of the elevated town some 200 feet down to the jungle of undergrowth on the outside of the city's boundaries.

Charles was full of excitement as, starry-eyed, he bobbed around Lucy-Miranda.

'Darling, you heard about Lucia?'

'Yes, I can't believe it. She was practically in the plane. Almost airborne, but they still managed to get her. And all for some silly deal or other. Some stupid takeover.'

Lucy-Miranda turned to Emma.

'My daughter will not be joining us for some time, if at all. She was called back at the airport...'

'Yes, I heard about it on the way in, beside the gate in the courtyard.'

'Such a bore. I practically haven't seen her for years. This was our first chance to get together. Now this has to happen...She doesn't even know Charles very well...Oh, I'm so mortified by it all, I could spit.'

'What kind of a deal?'

'That's the galling thing about it all. We don't even know. It's all very hush-hush. It's like fencing with shadows. My daughter works in Mergers and Acquisitions – at least I think that's what it's called, takeovers, you know, that kind of thing – for that enormous bank that's just been set up, ABC Bank, you know the one I mean, I'm sure you've heard of it. When they start working on a deal they have to drop everything and just get on with it. Live like Trappists – and for months. Can't talk to a soul. So of course even though she was actually at the airport, she had to cancel the idea of the holiday on the spot and go back to the office...Leaving, I have to tell you, one very disgruntled boyfriend in our midst. She insisted apparently that he took the flight and they had a fearful row in the middle of the airport concourse...At least, that's what my spies tell me. Look he's over there. Jake is what he's called. I think he comes from Stepney or somewhere like that. Certainly East London. He's a nice looking boy but rather common I think. I don't think he'll fit in at all. But then all Lucia's boyfriends are like that...Definitely NQOCD, and then a bit more besides.'

A little bell tinkled in Emma's head but still she reserved judgement on the situation. It might be true but then on the other hand it might not. Perhaps it was just as well that Lucia had been detained from arriving. Lucy-Miranda continued to jabber through the Italian evening air about her daughter.

'...She seems to like them rough but this one beats all records. He looks so miserable, I can't bear it. Can you imagine being miserable in a setting like this?'

Emma took in a fairly tall, tough-looking and squarely built individual with a shaven bullet head standing well apart from the group with a glass in his hand and a faraway look in his eye as East London confronted the Home Counties in their droves at play. She didn't think that it was the Italian background that was upsetting him.

But then Charles was off again.

'Look there's old G&T over there with the new baby. Come on Lucy-Miranda, come with me and say Hullo to them. Back in a second, Emma.'

But Lucy-Miranda disentangled herself from Charles.

'No, Charles, you go and talk to them. I'll stay here and look after Emma. G&T will be quite happy for you to keep them company.'

Charles darted off on his mission across the garden towards a young, bright and self confident couple standing with backs to the hills against the terrace wall, facing the throng. He was a burly ginger-haired man with an open shirt; and a broad smiling expression of willing-to-please competence. He was holding the baby in his arms as his wife chatted away to friends in their entourage. But his wife was stunning – a startling red head, tall and slim, with a groomed but rangy, smouldering, volatile look to her. Carrying herself with detached poise, almost translucent in the sunlit air, she was highly presentable, like all of the SW3 goddesses. Yet she looked dissatisfied. They resembled the perfect couple in silhouette, yet subtle electricity flashed between them both.

Emma found the girl quite fearful to observe.

The red hair, tumbling in well coiffed sheen around her chiselled features, gave it all away. She was wild. She looked capable of anything, even extremes. She had resisted all the corralling motions of a highly defined upbringing.

Danger, thought Emma.

The baby squirmed in its' father's arms. It was restless after the long flight and it kicked. But the father held it well without embarrassment and carried on chatting.

'The girl is called Ginnie and the husband is Tommy. So naturally they're called G&T – which just happens to be what they both drink. With names like that, they were destined for each other at birth, which is more or less when they first met. They got married at the first opportunity, straight out of university. I think she's a handful but then that's just my opinion. A fearful temper, really quite volcanic, but he doesn't seem to mind at all. At least, I think he doesn't mind. He's never complained, to my knowledge. He's very placid and he seems to put up with her – and the temper. They get on quite well together as a couple and they're very popular. But I'm surprised to find Tommy here at all. He normally works quite closely with Lucia as her broker or assistant or something like that, I think, on these deals. So if she's in London that's where I would have expected to find him. Strange…'

Lucy-Miranda spoke reflectively as she continued to stare at the couple who were now joined by Charles who gave Ginnie very exaggerated respect in his deferential greeting to her.

'You see Charles is crazy about Ginnie. Older man and younger woman – she touches something uncontrollable in him. He just can't keep away from her. He's like a moth to a flame with that woman. Any minute now and… Yes, I thought so…'

Emma saw Charles start to drag Ginnie away from Tommy towards the house.

'He's found something to show her in the kitchen. To my certain knowledge he hasn't been into the kitchen but that won't stop him finding something to engage her attention. These men really are just the limit. He just seems to idolise her. But then there are times when I just don't care anyway…'

Lucy-Miranda's little speech ended with a quiet sigh and she looked slightly alone and spare in the middle of the bustling group.

Tommy still stood against the parapet still holding the baby as his wife strode along with proud grace behind Charles to the villa. Her head was high. She looked like a Red Indian brave about to throw a tomahawk. Tommy was gazing noncommittally around him, drinking in the atmosphere of the early evening as the crickets started to whir and shadows lengthened on the Repugian hills opposite. The baby for a few seconds was quiet in his arms.

The hubbub of noise around him was gentle and contented as the guests milled about, greeting each other fresh from London, exclaiming about Lucia's absence with some envy and slurping down their Pinot Grigio and Chianti. Ginnie was nowhere to be seen. Emma glimpsed Jake looking vacantly out across the valley conspicuously separate from the other guests, alone and not talking.

The familiar pitch of a mobile phone was heard above the din and Emma saw Tommy pull his phone from out of his pocket still holding the baby and place it to his ear with some difficulty because the baby was abruptly awake now, after the ringing tone. And the baby was fractious.

Emma saw that Tommy was bending forward intent on the call because the reception was poor. Then she saw his head go back sharply and a look of sheer jubilation come into his eyes. He was still holding the baby at this point. But then his brow creased as he listened with difficulty to his caller and she watched him transfer the baby from one arm to another as he manoeuvred the phone from one ear to another.

Up went his hand to his other ear and then – in a fatal lapse of attention which conformed to habit – he placed the baby on the parapet with his hand still restraining its movement as he talked and then listened. Fatally again as he heard some more news he punched the air with his free fist and this had the effect of releasing the baby from his grasp. Tommy was oblivious of this. It was plainly a very important phone call. The baby, delighted to be free, began to crawl along the uneven top of the terrace, unattended and disregarded by her father, who was still all smiles on his mobile phone.

The baby chuckled and gurgled as it set off on a great adventure.

To its left lay a sheer drop to the woods below the walls. One slip and it would be over.

Gradually the guests took all of this on board. Cries of alarm were stifled for fear of prompting the baby into an injudicious move. The talk stilled among the guests as they watched with fascinated horror the baby crawl along the uneven wall. Tommy's words could now be heard more clearly as the noise level dropped among the other guests. A quiet, pregnant silence began to reign.

'Lucia, this sounds like one of your greatest deals. Congratulations. I just want to be in that number. Count me in – you know that. I'll be back just as soon as I can.'

Emma saw Ginnie re-emerge from the villa and then saw her start back with horror as she took in the scene. She moved to scream – and then checked herself. She started forward -and then halted. The baby was now a good ten feet or so away from its father and moving briskly. If he moved to grab it, then he risked sending it over the edge willy-nilly. Anyone coming from a further distance risked an even greater disturbance, with potentially fatal consequences.

There was now dead silence in the garden. Nobody dared breathe. It was going to end in tragedy. That was written in the stars – and the holiday was going to be ruined. Meanwhile the birds sang in the trees and the shadows pranced and cavorted on the hills opposite. The child was bound to tumble down from the parapet on the wrong side and smash itself to pieces on the trees in its fall. There was nothing to stop it taking a terrible, fatal tumble. Women among the guests were now biting their fists in the effort to stifle cries of alarm as the moment of tragedy loomed closer.

Tommy was still rapturously delighted by the deal which Lucia seemed to be offering him. He was shaking his head with joy, head down, tuned into London via the mobile, and oblivious.

The child began to sway from side to side on the parapet as it realised that it had crawled away from something that was no longer there. It started to cry. Ginnie's eyes by now were standing out from her head in her alarm.

They were all paralysed. Nobody moved among the holiday throng.

A maidservant of the villa appeared from away to the right of the party. She emerged from the kitchen and she was still drying her hands on a paper towel as she walked into the open air of the lawn. She was a bright black-eyed strapping Italian girl who took the scene in at a glance – the man on the phone; the terrified wife;

the guests frozen into immobility, glasses undrunk in their hands; and the baby cavorting above the drop.

And, above all, the silence of pure terror.

Without pausing for a second, without even changing expression, as if this kind of thing happened all the time, she walked forward beside the parapet and past Tommy who was oblivious to everything but his phone call. In one swift movement, before the baby saw her, she took a great stride and caught up with it and swept it into her arms with a swing that lifted the baby clean off the parapet. Then kisses and cuddles for the baby held high aloft, whose adventure was now over.

A hiss and a whoosh of relief went through the assembled guests and then everybody started talking at once. Noise, a great babble of the stuff, soared in blocks towards the branches of the trees in the forest. Glasses clinked and waiters bustled. The birds could be heard singing once again. It wasn't a tragedy after all, it was only an incident, just a terrifying might-have-been scenario.

And so the holiday wasn't cancelled. After all. No harm done. The decibel level increased exponentially. The holiday was still safe. After all.

But Ginnie was not satisfied. She was beside herself with rage. Her face was dark beneath the copper mane and almost disfigured with anger, through the pale skin. Emma watched her walk right up to her husband fearlessly and very deliberately; and then snatch the mobile phone from his hand as he looked up in shock. She hurled it over the balcony of rocks. Whimpering in mid-flight as Lucia continued to talk in confidence to Tommy from her London dealing-room, the mobile described an elegant curve through the air, before it crashed into the woods below.

Tommy stood there nonplussed, his hand, empty of the phone, still waving in the air. His voice was strangulated into a croak in mid-phrase. He was thunder-struck.

'What...?'

'That's what,' shrieked Ginnie as she smashed her hand across his face. The baby had started to cry now and the girl was comforting it.

Tommy stood aghast at the unexpected violence, his face puce-white, as his wife stood in front of him still shaking with rage. He was completely shocked. His eyes narrowed immediately in anger. Instinctively, his fists clenched.

Emma saw Jake spin round at the sound of the blow but he had missed the action. It was not wholly clear from where he stood just who had struck whom. He too stood stock still and stared.

Silence tried to fall again among the guests but many of them maintained a nervous chatter. It sounded like a football crowd as the chant died away for lack of support. Feet were being shuffled. There was some coughing.

In a miracle of bad timing, Charles reappeared on the lawn, a tall dapper figure of some apparent consequence. Wearing his polished diplomat's smile he made his way towards Lucy-Miranda via the inevitable detour towards Tommy and Ginny. The two of them stood like statues, still glaring at each other in complete silence as Charles luffed up to them.

'Beautiful evening, I think...' he started. But he got no further. Picking up the appalling vibes, his voice tailed off. He shambled back to where Lucy-Miranda and Emma were standing.

A child was heard exclaiming plaintively in the background, 'Come on, Mummy, what is it then, a cheap fuck? You must tell me. I've asked everyone and they all say the same thing, that you should know?'

The crack of the smack sounded like a rifle shot. More rage, this time from the mother, as her right hand exploded on the child's cheek amid howls and screams. He was dragged off for a very early bed by an outraged mother.

Violence begets violence.

'What on earth is going on, Lucy-Miranda? When I left you all, it looked like a wonderful party. Now it seems as if civil war has broken out. What has happened?'

'You'll find out presently, Charles. But stay quiet will you for just a second?'

Hang-dog, Charles did as he was bidden and Lucy-Miranda concentrated on Ginny and Tommy, muttering in an aside to Emma that the outburst had been in the offing. Wholly predictable, no less.

'He wanted a boy and she produced a girl, would you believe? So no heir as yet, let alone a spare. There's bad blood between them. The cat's well and truly out of the bag now.'

They watched Tommy square up to Ginny as if about to strike her back. His eyes were very narrow. He looked very big and very broad. He wasn't used to taking unexpected violence from anyone, let alone his wife. Two years playing in the First Fifteen for Sloane School had taught him how to use his fists to advantage. Then, very slowly, by an enormous effort of self-control, he managed to simmer down sufficiently to speak.

'Well, I'm off then.'

Ginny was shocked. She started to veer from anger to fear – and then more rage.

'What do mean, off? You've only just come here.'

'I'm off to London tonight. That was what the call was about. Business. You know, that thing I do that...'

Ginny's voice was rising. She sounded shrill.

'You'll do no such thing. You'll stay here and make amends to me. Do you hear that? Do you know what you've nearly just done? You very nearly happen to have killed my baby just now. It was left in your care...'

She was almost in tears with rage now. Her eyes popped hard with anger.

'Our baby, darling, not your baby.'

'You very nearly killed my baby. It was left in your care, you let it alone and do you know what happened...? It was crawling. Yes, crawling, you bloody great oaf...Here, yes, here. Crawling along that fucking parapet and it could have fallen over at any moment. So you fucking nearly killed my baby, as everybody here will bear witness. Yes, killed her. If it hadn't been for Maria here...'

'It was an accident, darling, and accidents happen. Or don't, as in this case. I was just in receipt of the most marvellous news...'

'I don't care if you were taking a direct call from God Almighty above, you still failed to look after the baby. So don't you darling me, you bastard...'

She was about to burst into hysterical tears. Her voice was now cracking at the top pitch and she was suddenly very unhappy.

Tommy, for his part, had clearly taken just about as much as he could stand in public. He had collected himself and he was very angry. He wouldn't put up with these rebukes in public much longer, that was plain. Hard now of feature, he wagged two fingers in Ginny's face.

'Two things, Ginny, two things. Yes, two things, so even you don't have to think too far to remember. Listen to me very carefully. First, I have find my mobile which is somewhere in the undergrowth down there because you interrupted me in the middle of a very important call. I have to find it quickly in order to get back to Lucia. So that's the first point. You'll excuse me, I'm sure, for my absence shortly on that account, my sweet Lady Ginny.'

A look of pure terror now passed across Ginny's face. He was leaving her; it was obvious. Only for a moment but the sensation of separation was already traumatising her. Tommy was inexorable.

'And the second point is this; as soon as I've retrieved the mobile, I'm off back to London. Tonight, yes, tonight. To do some business. So you can stay here and look after your baby and enjoy your holiday – or should I say our holiday? – and I'll go and make some money to keep the two of you, plus me, in house and home. Understood? Yes? Savvy, Lady G? To keep the two of you in fucking house and home. Good. Now, if you'll excuse me...'

Emma watched an open-mouthed Jake absorb the spectacle of the Home Counties' haute bourgeoisie squabbling bitterly. This was by no means clean linen being washed in public at all – far from it.

'Tommy, don't go like this. Please don't leave me like this. I'm sorry I shouted at you, I'm sorry...'

'Excuse me, will you, for Christ's sake, I'm going to find my mobile.'

And with that, like an angry man, he clumped through the group of guests across the lawn and into the gathering dusk, leaving his distraught wife alone with her screaming baby girl and silhouetted in her Huron beauty against the setting sun.

Lucy-Miranda watched him go with some bitterness.

'He didn't need to make such a meal of it, you know. He knows Lucia's number only too well. He could perfectly well have phoned her back from the house. He just wanted to make Ginny suffer in public, and make a drama into a crisis. What a nasty man, what a nasty unforgiving toe-rag of a man. She won't forgive him for this, you'll see. She plays the victim enough as it is, without being given this as an excuse.'

Emma asked Lucy-Miranda whether she should stay or go and received an urbane reply.

'Yes, I think so, but first, let me show you my little square.'

'Little square?'

'Yes, it's just behind the villa on the other side. Let's edge our way through the crowd and if we get lost I'll see you over there to Ginny's right, by the kitchen...'

Lucy-Miranda set off at some pace and with a quiet determination which Emma was beginning to recognise and admire. Lucy-Miranda, alone of most of the women that Emma had met in this neck of the woods, appeared to know her own mind and to act accordingly. Emma followed Lucy-Miranda who spoke to her as they walked across the lawns.

'It's where I go when I want to get away from the Gilstons and all the wrangling when we're on holiday here. From Charles, too, on occasion, although most of the time, he's no trouble. None of them know about my little square, I mean really know about it, because they just don't...Don't...Well, I'm sure you know what I mean without my putting it into words. The English abroad, that kind of thing...When they're all here on holiday in the villa it's just a home from home for them, whereas for me, it's different. I want to feel part of something different. I like to sit down very quietly and absorb the atmosphere of a small Italian town. And if that sounds rather pompous and too touristy, Emma, well then I'm sorry...But I have been coming here for quite a considerable number of years, and you do get to know certain sights – and people.'

They reached the kitchen area unobserved and unhailed. It felt like an escape.

'We just slip around here, Emma, and through that little door and then we're nearly there. Follow me, my girl...'

Which Emma did with little spurts of excitement, feeling privileged to be included in such a clandestine expedition. Lucy-Miranda made the way ahead with assurance. They passed quietly through the small door and into a steep roughly cobbled street lacking a pavement. Then they slowly and deliberately made their way towards the small square which they glimpsed at the bottom of the street. The high walls of the Villa flanked them on one side as they went down the street. Then the street widened into the square, a small dusty nondescript expanse with a couple of trees in the middle; a pathway round the perimeter; some benches to one side; and a few shops or cafes strewn higgledy-piggledy around the expanse of space. It was still warm after the heat of the day, although the light was now fading fast. Light glowed from the cafes as the men sat there looking dapper and relaxed. Noise blared from windows in the high buildings above the cafes and women could be seen moving from room to room, preparing the evening meal.

Lucy-Miranda sounded a trifle anxious.

'I always go and sit down over there very unobtrusively, yes, on that bench there, and see if my calling card is still good. If you don't mind sitting there with me...This is a bit of a treat for me. I've been looking forward to my first little sit-down on the bench but to have a companion as well is really special.'

They both laughed at the outrageousness of the adventure, as Emma sat beside her on the bench. Lucy-Miranda took her hand and squeezed it as she was silent for a few seconds. As they took their places, Emma thought they constituted a simple tableau drawn from life, Seated Women in the Evening, or something along those lines. Something peaceful and contemplative and understated, quite unlike the hurly burly of the Ginny and Tommy show away back at the villa.

And as for the slap...And the mobile phone wheeling in its slow pathetic arc as it fell into the woods...And the drama of the baby... Oh my God, thought Emma as she ran through the rush of events in the last hour...Such turbulence...

Lucy-Miranda was recovering her confidence now that she'd made her escape from the villa.

'You know, Emma, it always takes some time to see if I'm recognised. I don't like to intrude on their lives, I'm really just a stranger in their midst, even though I've been coming here for nearly twenty years. I've been sitting here since Lucia was born, I think, although I'd have to check...I don't know if the people in the square realise anything about me. I mean that I'm a Gilston and that I stay for part of most summers at the Villa...I suppose they must do, because the servants must talk, but they have always been very discreet and polite with me. No one has ever questioned me, they have always just left me alone. So I can sit here and take it all in and if after a few days somebody says Bon Giorno then that's a bonus, I reckon that I've been accepted back into the fold with no fuss. Back on my perch again as if nothing else matters except for this small place in the entire universe that I can call Home. None of that mess about what you are that you have to endure in London and Hampshire as a Gilston. Then once I feel at home again I'll go into the cafe and buy a coffee and...'

Emma felt calmer in the square, seated next to the reassuring maternalism of Lucy-Miranda, than she had done earlier in the day in the hotel room. Lucy-Miranda spoke true. There was something very sedate about the square. It had a well-used feel. Everybody in the neighbourhood at some point in the day would obviously make tracks towards it as a matter of ritual, offering salutation to this small familiar point in time and space. The square was always theirs' by rite of presence, a witness to their lives just as a great cathedral silently absorbs the prayers of the multitude over the centuries. People rambled through the square at their own pace, throwing off greetings, mooching, strolling, reading newspapers or else like the young girls Emma could see at the furthest end of the square behind the trees, creating all kinds of mischief for the young men's hearts at this special moment of the evening as the light went down. The girls were sky-larking around and squealing in their excitement and the boys looked alarmed.

'These things do happen on holidays, I think, Emma. People do run into each other when they're at a loose end and they talk more freely I think than they would do in England...'

'I'm certain you're right Lucy-Miranda. But you've been a great comfort to me already today and I'm very grateful to you. You were right about Craig. I did miss him when he went off to Verona so the trip to the Villa...'

'...Had its moments. I'll bet it did...It was very nearly a tragedy. In just five seconds, too. It just blew up like that. It seems a long way away now but it could all have been very different. They were both very lucky. It was lucky too for him that she didn't have a glass in her hand, she'd have thrown that in his face, I'm sure of it. He got off very lightly did Tommy but it's only a temporary reprieve. She'll pay him out for his moment of negligence, in some way or another...I can see it coming...Now look, look over there, just to my left...I'm so relieved to find she's still here, yes, you can see her clearly, that woman over there walking in front of the garage...'

'I see her.'

'That's Senora Jean. Now she doesn't look anything special, does she, and until I found out about her I never bothered looking out for her. Until I discovered just by chance that she's one of the most important women living on the square.'

'Oh yes, and how might that be? She doesn't, as you say, look that important.'

'It's very simple, Emma, and very Italian. She keeps everybody's keys for them. I found out one morning in the cafe when there was a terrible to-do and she was sent for in a great panic and she turned up with what looked like chains or ropes of keys. It was amazing. If anybody goes away for any reason, they leave their keys with Senora Jean until they come back and then they retrieve them. And anybody of a forgetful nature will also leave keys with her. She's the key-lady for the square. There should be somebody like that for everybody in London. You know how terrified one always is of closing the door of the flat or the house behind you and then discovering that the keys are on the other side of the door...'

'I know that feeling very well. Senora Jean sounds like a modern saint.'

'How well you put it, Emma. But there's somebody else too I want you to see. Very much so. She's very important to me. One of the big reasons why I come and sit here. But so far I can't see her...'

Lucy-Miranda sounded anxious. She was leaning forward on the bench in her apprehension not to miss the glimpse of this special person. But in vain. That special person failed to show, at least for the time being. Lucy-Miranda sat back looking disappointed.

'That's very strange, Emma. She's always around here at this time. This is when she takes a small break. I know all about her time-table. I hope nothing has happened to her. The last I heard was that...'

A small commotion took place to their left about fifty yards away, across the edge of the square. One small dog was baiting another small dog. One dog belonged to an elderly woman carrying a loaf and the other was the property of a young woman who by the cut of her clothes; her self-confident in-your-face carriage; and her sparkling, decolletee glamour was indisputably a whore. High class maybe but still a whore. The whore pulled her dog away with a powerful movement and walked across the square. Eyes, pop-eyed, followed her across the square from the cafes. She had lots and lots of punchy style.

Emma suddenly became aware that Lucy-Miranda beside her was also agog, following the whore's progress step by step with glistening excitement.

'That's her. That's who I wanted you to see. That's Gina. Doesn't she look gorgeous? She is such a beautiful girl. I've watched her grow up from being just a tiny girl and now she's fucking the mayor of Repugia...Hasn't she done well...?'

Gina disappeared into a house opposite and Emma, blinking slightly, wondered if by chance she hadn't stepped into a time warp. There was something surreal about it all. She felt light-headed and nervous about events and her precise location in them. First the near-tragedy of the baby followed by the fisticuffs between Ginny and Tommy; then the escape from the villa, and the philosophical reflexions on the importance of the square in Lucy-Miranda's life; and now that same Lucy-Miranda, who five seconds previously had been the soul of home-spun common-sense, was salivating practically over the local tart... And lapsing from a noticeably precise almost stilted use of language into the argot of the gutter, to boot, with every appearance of familiarity and practised ease of delivery...Truly there was matter here worthy of explanation, Emma reflected.

Just who was this strange woman who called herself Lucy-Miranda?

Lucy-Miranda leaned across and patted Emma's arm. She sounded far happier now that she'd seen Gina.

'Don't worry, there's nothing to be alarmed about. This is all very innocent. It's just a story about a women who had a strange set of experiences in the past and who finds to her surprise that those experiences now mean far more to her than she ever imagined they would, now that the initial pain has faded.'

Lucy-Miranda rose to her feet. She was smiling. The square behind her was filling up as more people returned from work and took their ease under the warm stars, in the bars and cafes.

'We can talk about it tomorrow. Not tonight, I'm afraid – I'm feeling tired and I have to get back and look after Charles, who will be fretting. I've had my little outing and it's time now to sneak back through the looking-glass. But you've been a very good companion, Emma, and I'm very grateful to you for coming along. If you want to listen to an old woman's unusual story, why don't we meet and have some breakfast tomorrow. Charles will be no trouble because he'll be too busy attending to Ginny, assuming that Tommy rushes back to London tonight. So I'll have a little bit of time to myself and I can tell you the tale.'

She paused and grinned at Emma in a devil-may-care way, looking again younger and more carefree.

'Want to hear it all? I've been dying to unburden myself of all of this to somebody, and you might just prove to be the listener that I was after, that is if you don't mind being hi-jacked for an hour or so. I think it's called dumping in some vulgar circles.'

Emma smiled at her in friendship.

'You know that I will hang on every word. I look forward to drinking in every syllable. Name the time.'

Lucy-Miranda waved an inquiring hand.

'Eight thirty? Nine o'clock? What time would suit? When do you plan to surface?'

'Oh, I think 8.30, don't you? I don't want to lose any time over any of this. Where shall we meet? Here on the bench?

'And where else? Once we've done that, and met up, then we can dash to that cafe over there, the one where I heard the story about La Signora Jean, and have our breakfast. I think I'll enjoy this breakfast. Two women in Italy are far less at risk than one. Goodbye for now.'

'Goodbye Lucy-Miranda and thank you for the evening's entertainment, all of it.'

Lucy-Miranda waved a hand behind her in acknowledgement as she sailed off back up the small street to the villa – and to Charles and Ginny and Tommy and the baby and the other guests, plus the non-appearance of her daughter and all the other problems consequent on taking a family holiday.

Family fun, pshaw!

Emma for her part made her way back to her hotel by the side streets in blithe mood. She fell asleep almost immediately, comforted also by the two messages from Craig she collected at the desk. The second sounded considerably more agitated than the first concerning her whereabouts, as if Craig was more than just mildly concerned for the welfare of his patroness.

'How much more satisfying it is for me to be the pursued rather than the huntress,' thought Emma as she fell into a deep sleep. Dear, dear Craig, she mused, as she realised that she had barely thought about him once throughout the entire evening.

* * * * *

At eight fifteen the following morning Emma stepped out of her shower, breathing deeply and feeling slightly dizzy, as she tried to shake off the effect of her long profound slumber. She had lain inert like a log in a stream for over nine or ten hours. The dreams had come but the dreams had stolen away without a murmur. She felt that heavy resilience in the limbs, savouring almost of fatigue, that comes after the sleep of perfect peace. Outside she saw that the sun was already smashing down on the square; and that the shadows had been petrified into submission by the heat. Her eyelids tingled as the warmth rose to meet her. Time to be off; time to be at the square to have her breakfast with Lucy-Miranda.

She towelled and dressed quickly realising as she moved about the hotel room just how much had changed for her in 24 hours. This time yesterday she had been looking forward to a predictable and slightly dreary day, saying Goodbye to Craig and all that jazz...Her mind ran on for a second and then braked abruptly as she remembered something else which had slipped from her mind – her mission!

She had completely forgotten about the meeting she had to make and the letter she had to hand over!

The panic subsided. The meeting was days away. She was fine. She'd let nobody down. London would not be chasing her with an axe...The letter was in her suitcase, tucked away in one of the pockets. In her bare feet and still clutching her towel, she tiptoed over to where she had stowed the case, and ran her finger into the gusset. She encountered the sharp edge of the envelope. Yes, there it was. It was still there. Nobody had stolen it. She didn't know what was in it and she had no desire to find out either, as she contrasted the slightly furtive assignment that she was fulfilling for London with the breezy normalness which life for her in Italy had suddenly assumed. She would do what she had been asked to do and that would be an end to it all, she resolved. No more spying for me – it's a mug's game. Besides, what would Lucy-Miranda think of her if she suddenly discovered that this new friend of hers was a spy. That was hardly something to boast about to the girls, now was it? It was a chastening thought for Emma who had no desire to be kicked out of any circle, let alone one that she had some high hopes of joining. Yes, enough is enough, she thought. Time to call in my markers...But meanwhile no cause for panic. Everything was still on-line.

She left the hotel at 8.20 in high spirits, feeling that a whole day of adventure lay ahead for her and looking forward to her breakfast.

Lucy-Miranda was there before her on the bench and waiting for her. She greeted Emma enthusiastically and with a slight tinge of apprehension.

'I thought you'd come but I couldn't be sure. I'm very pleased to see you again. Very pleased indeed. I had some second thoughts about burdening you with all my revelations but I've managed to conquer all that. It's not a very edifying tale in places, I'm afraid. But I'm determined to make my confession to you. There's nothing actually very sordid about what I'm going to say but it does amount to a change of mind and attitude on my part, and it's this change in my feelings which bothers me. It makes me feel so disloyal. And it's been bothering me for quite some time now. It's high time I talked. I'm not quite the person I appear to be, as you will realise. Not quite the pillar of the establishment that you think you see before you.'

Emma smiled at her as she spoke, still thinking about the envelope tucked away in the pocket of her suitcase.

'I'm sure that everybody has many things in their lives that they would blush to discuss. But the difference is that you're prepared to talk about it all. Now where's that cafe you promised me, and where's that breakfast. I can't function unless I have some caffeine inside me.'

The two women made their way across the square, more or less empty at that hour apart from two old gentlemen seated on chairs in the middle who were reading newspapers; and a crowd of youngsters playing a high spirited game of football. Yelling and shrieking they kicked the ball about as they imitated in their imagination the skills of the stars they knew so well of Italian football. They had all the gestures and mannerisms of the stars and occasionally, just in flashes, some of the skills. The ball bobbed about in the game, out of control for most of the time.

Emma and Lucy-Miranda sat down at one of the tables outside and managed to place their order without incurring either the importunate attentions of the waiter or his hostility. Their presence passed unnoticed. He brought the jug of coffee and the rolls, plus butter and jam, without comment, nodded at them, blinked confidingly at the sun and then wandered off back into the cafe to polish some more glasses and gossip with the bar-flies who were just too busy to contemplate work that morning.

'That's a relief, isn't it, Emma? I don't think I could stand any hassle this morning, not from the waiters anyway. I'm just not in the mood for it. Now where was I? Yes, of course, poised to start boring for England. But meanwhile, I'll be Mother and get on with the serious business of pouring you some coffee. White or black?'

'White, please.'

And Lucy-Miranda began pouring out the coffee. As she did so, Emma saw a slightly familiar figure appear from the entrance to the square which led to the villa. It was Jake, instantly recognisable despite his shades. The bullet shaven head gleamed beneath the sun. He shambled along in jeans, trainers, and open shirt, looking out of place and miserable. He had plainly spent a very uncomfortable night and was looking for succour beyond the confines of the villa. No Lucia; no succour. He wandered vaguely in the direction of the cafe and Emma and Lucy-Miranda, looking quite lost.

'Watch out Lucy-Miranda, your story may be delayed. Here comes trouble.'

Lucy-Miranda looked up and groaned.

'You're so right. He's the last person I want to see. I could do without the sufferings of Young Jake right now. It's all my daughter's fault...She just takes them up and then ditches them. She's always been like that, right from...'

But Lucy-Miranda's recriminations were ill timed. Something exceedingly odd proceeded to take place in the centre of the square. It started when the football bounced out of the game and in Jake's direction. The boys playing the game shouted at him to return their ball. Jake moved towards it with an eel-like sway of his hips, almost in a reflex action. Without pausing in his stride, almost apparently without even thinking about what he was doing, Jake flicked the ball onto his instep very gently and then continued walking across the square, still flicking the ball up in the air but juggling it from foot to foot so that it kept bouncing just a small distance in the air as he walked. It was as if the ball was tied to his feet with elastic.

'I see what you mean, Emma. Yes, my story had better wait a few moments. Jake has certainly got the attention of the locals.'

Lucy-Miranda spoke without irritation as her moment of dramatic revelation was delayed. Meanwhile Jake was still slouching along and not apparently concerned by the object that was attached to the laces of his trainers.

The Italian boys in the game first screamed at him for the ball and then rushed to tackle him. But Jake evaded their rushes by flicking the ball easily onto his shoulder and then onto his head where it continued to bounce in perfect balance. He was still walking across the square as he performed these acrobatics, much to the amazement and then to the enthusiasm of the players who stood back and nudged each other with excitement and started to applaud his skills. In generous measure, too. But Jake gave no hint of acknowledgement, indeed no hint of any attention to anything but waltzed along with the ball still bobbing up and down on his shaven skull and still apparently deep in thought. Heavily preoccupied.

Emma realised that these feats had not passed unnoticed. Attracted by the yelling, the waiter had emerged from the bar to see what was going on and had then dragged out in a rush all his cronies to watch the footballing phenomenon.

Yelling the most was the goalkeeper some twenty yards away from Jake. He made it clear in unmistakeable terms that he wanted Jake to shoot and for him to save Jake's shot. The other boys took up the shout as Jake juggled away. Then he suddenly flicked an arm which indicated to the other players to stand back and for the goalkeeper to ready himself. The goalkeeper crouched between the posts of the small portable goal which also surprisingly contained a net and awaited the shot. Jake barely moved but kept dancing from side to side on the spot, with the ball as always under complete control. Then very slowly it seemed, he allowed it to dribble down the front of his chest until it reached his thigh which he raised in balance, so that the ball sat up apparently in mid air. Almost without looking at it, with cool flowing grace, Jake lashed at the ball. It whistled like a shell at the goal, striking the left post with huge force and velocity. The goal keeper was completely beaten by the shot. But it was worse for him. The ball flew to the other post and then into the back of the net with such force that it brought whole contraption down almost on his head. Ball; goalkeeper; and goal vanished suddenly in a flying confusion of nets and posts and boots.

The square burst out laughing. Both the bar and the players applauded Jake's spectacular piece of football artistry. Unconcerned, shoulders hunched and still rapt in his thoughts and inscrutable, he made his way towards the bar where Emma and Lucy-Miranda were sitting.

'I think our little chat may have to wait even longer. This looks serious,' Lucy-Miranda whispered to Emma as Jake reached their table, to be greeted by back-slaps by the audience. He sat down abruptly.

'Wotcher, ladies, good morning. I thought I recognised you two. You were at the party last night, weren't you?'

Jake was unconcerned by the riots of enthusiasm surrounding him in the bar. He spoke in a matter of fact way. The two women nodded at the celebrity in their midst. Lucy-Miranda bearded him a little with her question.

'Where on earth did you learn to play football like that, Jake? Even I, who know nothing about it, could see that you were doing something quite amazing.'

A steaming cappuccino suddenly appeared on the table, borne by the waiter who made it clear that the coffee was on the house. Unimpressed by the tribute, Jake nodded. His eyes glinted behind the shades. The two women realised together that suddenly their stock was rising in the square because they alone were acquainted with the footballing genius. That counted for massive pull, so far as the Italians were concerned. Suddenly they really were a touch important in the eyes of the locals.

'Youth international. Train wiv the Arsenal. Should be West Ham, but there you go. Arsenal got there first. Offered better terms as well. But Lucky has gone and stuffed me well and truly, I think.'

He poured some three sugars into the coffee. Looking over his shoulder, he raised the cup in salutation to the bar, which grinned back at him in unison as he lounged in his chair, all shades, muscle, tiny waist and the taut limbs of careless youth.

"Ere, tell me, just what is going on in that house where I'm staying, if you don't mind my asking. It's like a mad house. There was an almighty rumpus last night as what's 'is face – Tommy, of course – went back to London. I thought there would be more blows exchanged then as he departed. Then I get a call from Lucky first thing this morning telling me to stay where I am and I am definitely not best pleased by that. I truly feel that I am missing out on something in London over this mystery deal. But she's the boss so that's that. Never argue with the boss I say, especially Lucky, and never trust a man with a Windsor knot. Facts of life. Then Ginny, Tommy's missus – at least I think it's 'is missus – anyway Ginny is walking around on the lawns at some ungodly hour screaming blue murder at somebody. It couldn't have been 'er old man because he was long gone by that time back to London. But who it was, Gawd only knows. And then, to crown it all, I can't find anyone to give me breakfast. I mean, what is all this caper? You come seventeen thousand miles or however far it is, you can't get back and you can't even get breakfast either. It's an absolute and total disgrace. Breakfast, that's what I want. I don't mean this apology for a breakfast they have in this poxy country – you know little rolls and what have you – I mean a real breakfast – bacon, eggs, beans, toast and maybe a couple of sausages as well. And especially toast. I like toast.'

He shrugged his shoulders in such disdainful dismissal of the whole country on account of its failure to provide him with a typical Greasy Spoon breakfast that both woman burst out laughing. Jake bridled behind the shades. They could see that he was offended by their detached response. He was not used to free-thinking, fast acting women who knew their own minds.

'You'll have to get used to a good deal more in Italy than just a change in breakfast, you know, young man. Don't you think so Emma? It's a very big country.'

Emma nodded and Jake continued to look ill at ease in the presence of two women who failed automatically to agree with his every word. He shifted in his chair from one haunch to another. Lucy-Miranda seized her opportunity.

'Tell me, Jake, just who is this Lucky you keep referring to?'

'Oh, beg pardon, that's Lucia. Or rather Lucia Maitland, Number Two in ABC's Mergers and Acquisitions Department and a holy terror to all and sundry in the bank. Known as Lucky throughout the markets on account of the fact that she always pulls off her deals. So she's brilliant. But she's also my girl friend – or was, until we went on this holiday…We've only just started going out together…'

Emma broke in quickly and diplomatically.

'I should tell you Jake that Lucy-Miranda here is Lucia's mother.'

It seemed only fair to him to point that out. This was beginning to be a very small world for them all, even out in the middle of Italy.

Jake was silent and stunned. It was too much for him. He hadn't expected Lucia actually to possess a flesh and blood relative, still less a mother. It did not lie within his calculations. The manifestation of normality and its awesome proximity took him quite by surprise. It rather frightened him too, Emma thought. Suddenly he was running in grooves, and accountable. He seemed caged and at bay.

'I'm sorry, Mrs Maitland…'

Lucy-Miranda interrupted him to prompt. She was hot on protocol, Emma divined. But only on one level perhaps – what about Gina the Trollop of the previous evening?

'Lady…'

'Lady…?'

'Yes, Lady…'

'I'm sorry, Mrs Lady Maitland. I should have realised.'

'No, Lady, not Mrs. And my name's not Maitland either. It's Dawson.'

Jake smiled for the first time. The teeth were white and the grin was dazzling. Emma could see much trouble looming for them all now. Jake could be quite a charmer.

'You've got me well and truly confused here, Mrs…Mrs…No I don't understand and I give up…I have never understood a word of this titles lark to this day.'

Sounding relaxed about it all, he turned to Emma.

'Perhaps you know the answer. This is all too much for a simple East London market trader like me. You don't see that many titles in Manor Park. Except for the cinema, that is.'

It was Emma's turn to confess partial ignorance.

'I think I understand part of it, Jake. Lucy-Miranda is married to Charles, whose correct title is Sir Charles Dawson. So she's not Mrs at all. Never can be, once she gets the title. But where the Maitland part fits in, that I cannot fathom...Who knows? Perhaps Lucy-Miranda, you might enlighten us both?'

'It's simple enough. This is part of the story that I was going to tell you, Emma, so nothing is wasted. My first husband was Edward Maitland. He and his brother, indeed the Maitland family, owned Martins Bank which is now part of the Gilston Empire as you know. But because of unwise market speculations, Martins Bank went bust and my husband...'

She paused and breathed heavily, in some distress. This was all costing her some pain. That was evident. She gazed at the square, witness to multiple breaches of amour propre, and took succour from its windswept sunbaked casualness. Jake stared at her impassively from behind his shades.

'...My husband died. Yes, that's it. He died...Just like that – died. It sounds innocent enough but it isn't really. He didn't pass away peacefully.'

Another pause as she collected herself.

'He shot himself in the dealing room of Martins Bank. Afterwards we discovered that the result of all this speculation was...'

Another pained pause. She collected herself.

'...No, I'll come onto that later, if you don't mind. It's too painful for me to discuss just now. There was a complete history to it all which turned out to be completely unedifying. To cut a long story short, after my first husband died, I then met Charles, whom I married. So instead of being Mrs Maitland I am now Lady Dawson, while my daughter retains the family name of Maitland.'

More bells had started to ring in Emma's head. It was indeed a small world that she was inhabiting. Her mind stole back some years to other scenes, scenes long since buried beneath the jurassic of events… Then her reverie was interrupted. Ginny was in their midst. She had stolen up on them unseen across the square. She stood in front of them, a lithe fiery flame-haired warrior presence, seemingly just a fraction abashed by the events of the previous evening. She wore a nervous ingratiating little smile that ended just above her lips, failing to reach the eyes.

'So that's where you all are hiding. I might have known. There's practically nobody in the house now apart from Charles to eat the breakfast which I've prepared. Is nobody going to eat my breakfast?'

They all knew the answer to that question. Boldly, Emma spoke for the group.

'It depends on what kind of a breakfast you've prepared.'

They all looked at each other conspiratorially and then gazed at her waiting for the reply. She was irritated. She thought they were ganging up on her. Subject to critical appraisal, her firm purpose of amendment was crumbling before their eyes. She became more brittle.

'What do you mean, what kind of breakfast? It's a straightforward breakfast. Eggs; bacon…'

The Aaah in response to the news was collective.

'Beans…?'

This question came from the hopeful Jake whose tongue was very nearly hanging out. He had started forward in his chair.

'Of course, there are beans. What do you think the villa is? Some kind of Little Italy? There's nothing native about us. The beans are practically stockpiled in the kitchen.'

Jake stood up abruptly. Emma noticed that the biceps bulged as his arms emerged from the shirt even though he was rail-thin.

'I'm ready to follow you anywhere, Mrs …?'

'Ginny.'

'Mrs Ginny. No, that's wrong as well…'

There was almost another explosion from Ginny along the lines of the previous evening's detonation but she restrained herself.

'No, my name is Ginny. Just call me Ginny and we'll get along fine. Is that clearly understood?'

'Perfectly, Ginny. Now where's that breakfast you were bragging so hard about?'

The two of them, a bold Jake in his shades and jeans and taut shirt, and a fleetingly deferential Ginny, all shorts and long, slim legs and red hair blowing in the slight morning breeze, faced each other for a second before moving off back to the villa. Emma thought they made a beautiful couple of handsome human beings as they paused very briefly in acknowledgement of each other before setting off. Superb creatures and specimens. But feral too and dangerous both for themselves as well as for everybody else.

Strange things happen on holidays, as guards are relaxed. And these odd events take place more slowly than anyone imagines – but with far more dire consequences.

At that moment, a football bounced into their midst, directed at Jake by the kids in the square still playing away happily at their game. They screamed at him in voluble Italian to join them.

Lucy-Miranda informed Ginny that Jake was an international. Ginny looked jealous of that information for just a second. She frowned possessively.

'Oh so you've really been introducing yourself around have you?'

'Show her for us, Jake, will you? What you can do. Ginny, the Italians loved it. They gave him a free cup of coffee for his tricks. Isn't that so, Emma?'

Jake stood stock still for a second waving at the Italians with the ball behind him at his heels. The boys on the square and the cronies in the cafe all watched in silent anticipation for the maestro showman to perform. Then Jake, with a careful flick of his heels, manoeuvred the ball onto his shoulder from behind, humped it around his head for a few seconds, allowed the ball to travel down his body to his ankles, stopped the ball on his instep so that it bounced up again and then kicked it away with great force so that it rejoined the game -without him. Then he waved Goodbye to the cafe and the boys in the square. It was a perfect piece of showboating diplomacy carried out by an aristocrat of the pitch. The Italians recognised all of this. As he wandered off across the square with Ginny they clapped him again, as if he was disappearing down into the tunnel after being substituted midway through a game; he waved a hand behind him in casual acknowledgement.

'I can see trouble brewing,' said Lucy-Miranda darkly as the two of them ambled away. 'I think she has designs on him. I wouldn't put that past her, not for one moment. Besides, he's very handsome boy, although he thinks far too much of himself; that's painfully obvious from the first moment. But she really shouldn't be doing it, not with that baby to look after. Poor Tom! It will lead to endless squabbling with him. But she won't be told, not even for a second. She's always been that kind of girl. What she sees she wants, and what she wants she schemes until she gets it, no matter what the cost. She's always been the same – I don't think her parents loved her one little bit from the first day she was born and that's when all the trouble started. She trashed somebody's car when she was eighteen, I seem to remember, just because her boyfriend happened to start paying some innocent attention elsewhere. The volcano exploded all over Sloane Avenue on that occasion. I wonder if the same thing isn't going to happen here in Repugia…? And is Repugia big enough to handle this catastrophe on the way…? I wonder.'

Lucy-Miranda smiled at Emma, as if to say that while those two gorgeous love-birds were guzzling their way through their multitude of calories up at the villa, wasn't it time that two women enjoyed their humble breakfast in the far less grand setting of the square and the local cafe?

Following her thoughts, Emma suggested that they get on with their breakfast and Lucy-Miranda, pleased that they could return to the matters in hand, agreed.

'After all, Emma, it's not as if we're going to have any problems in ordering. We do, after all, know the local hero and that must count for something.'

They waved to the bar and service was resumed, with more than just a trifling increment in the respect due to the two women. More rolls and more coffee. The sun baked down now on the square which was deserted, as the boys quit their game. Emma, meanwhile, was thinking about Lucy-Miranda's use of language. It was puzzling. The previous night, when she had glimpsed Gina, she had moved quite easily down to the language of the street. But this morning, when analysing Ginny's predatory attitude towards Jake, her choice of vocabulary had been far more conventional. Two destinies, or two lives, both led in parallel and both of them sealed off from the other? The memsahib and something far more elusive and untouchable, both co-existing within the one frame?

Lucy-Miranda started to talk quite quickly now after the interruptions from Jake and Ginny. What she said did much to clarify what she had been implying so mysteriously during the past 24 hours. But a jumble of thoughts underlaid Emma's responsive attention to Lucy-Miranda's tale. There was something about all of this which she could not quite remember or fit into place, something like a name which refused to present itself on the memory screen. It would come back, yes of course, it would come back to her, Emma was quite confident about that. Her powers of recall were undimmed from her days as a very smart and sharp lawyer. But she must needs be patient, she told herself. No point in forcing it because it was too important. The details lay just a fraction beyond the reach of her memory that morning. She had more than just an inkling of the rods connecting her, wholly unexpectedly across space and time, to Lucy-Miranda and those rods when they finally joined up were going to glow white-hot with energy. So she was content to listen.

Lucy-Miranda choked a little bit on her coffee before she started but the voice, once she got going, remained strong and confident.

'I was just a teeny bit economical with the truth – isn't that what they say these days when they're lying? – when I was talking to Jake. You see, what I should have said, if I'd been really truthful, was that I went completely to pieces after Edward died. Yes, what you see now is not what you would have seen then. I just stayed in the flat and moped and drank and gradually went downhill. I seemed to be falling down an endless, bottomless well from hour to hour and from minute to minute. There didn't seem anything really worthwhile to live for, because all the money had gone and the house had gone and my husband was dead, whom I had loved up to a certain point, even though he turned out to be a really bad lot, and those are all things that you really need to have to get by in Hampshire. Especially the house, although maybe the husband is just as important. At least, having one, although I could never quite gauge any of that either. I just knew that I'd gone from the top of the tree, with all the afternoon tea and friends dropping by with gossip and bridge and dinner parties that comes with the terrain, to a position of absolute nothingness. It had all just vanished overnight. Something else that I really couldn't understand at all became very real instead. So I just lived in town and I didn't see anybody and I didn't answer calls and I became sluttish. Yes, very sluttish. Almost dirty. I just couldn't make the effort in any direction and time and I appeared to have lost all my bones. I couldn't understand it but I seemed to have turned into a jelly or something equally mushy and oozy. I just meandered on from day to day like huge amoeba, getting dirtier and dirtier – at least the flat, so far as I remember, was always filthy – and I just didn't care. Everything was just a haze and always too much trouble. There was nothing I could do about it either, not a blasted thing. I became inert. I have to tell you as well, Emma, that a large daily intake of gin and dry martini had a lot to do with contributing to that haze. The bottle became the first thing that I reached for in the morning and the last thing I touched late at night, before I went to sleep. Me, I ask you, the pride of Hampshire for her clean house and garden and car and what have you, always spick and span. I think I just wanted to die as quickly and as quietly as possible with no fuss or bother for anybody... '

Lucy-Miranda laughed as she reached this point in the story and tossed her head into the sky. She was a brave woman, thought Emma, to tell such a tale against herself, after coming through such an ordeal.

Walkers criss-crossed the square now which had been empty. Over in the distance Emma could see that a man was skipping very deliberately in the sunshine. He looked as if he had some way to go before he lost the tyre round his middle. But he skipped on, nevertheless, with breathless resolution. The trees in the square waved a little in the breeze holding their ground in the cosmos of things.

'Just as I thought that things could get no worse, what with the filth, the bottle and the desolation, they promptly did...'

'No...'

'Oh yes, they did. They truly did. I went out for a walk one day, more like a crawl really, with the absurd idea of finding my other daughter and being looked after. The crawl-walk went haywire. I was abducted, beaten, locked in a room in total darkness and very nearly tossed into the Thames...'

'Oh dear, Lucy-Miranda, I don't like the sound of any of this. This must have been very shocking for you.'

'It was shocking as you say. To cut a long story short, Emma dear – because you are a sweetheart for listening to all of this – I found myself working in a brothel. I didn't know where I was and I could have been anywhere. To make matters worse, I'd been struck dumb by the trauma of it all. I had turned into some kind of terrible mute. I lost my voice. All I needed then was a harelip to make the picture complete. But I survived. How I did that I really don't know, but I did. Early potty training, I suppose, or something like that. Or good school – who knows? But instead of kicking me into the Thames, which they wanted to do at first, the men who ran the brothel decided to keep me on as a skivvy. As the lowest of the low. Can you imagine it? This was a very long way down now from Hampshire. Most of the time I spent cleaning out the lavatories which as you might gather were pretty disgusting. If I wasn't doing that I was taking the drinks into the different rooms where the girls were fucking away with the punters, as a maid. A maid, I ask you. I don't know how long I was there and I don't really know to this day how I actually got out...Well, I do in truth but that's really another story for another day...'

'More coffee, signorina?'

The waiter could not have been more friendly as he appeared in front of them. They nodded at him and off he went, like a lamb, to bring them some more coffee.

'The worst day for me in the brothel proved to be the turning point in everything. It started when one of my husband's old business acquaintances – quite a nice man too, I was godmother to his youngest daughter – turned up there with a crowd of young bucks and there was a shortage of girls for them all. The whole place was fucking like crazy that night. So they wanted to throw me into bed with him. Just like you'd hump a sack of potatoes into a cellar. I was appalled and really frightened. I thought that this was when my entire life would turn out to be one enormous humiliation. Can you imagine it all, as he thrashed around and then finally recognised that the whore he was fucking was the former wife of his esteemed business friend? Oh God, the shame of it all...It still gives me heartburn just to think about it....But again, and this is the unexpected part of it all, that moment was when everything started to go right for me. One of the girls, one of the really tough ones – I forget her name for a moment, but it'll come back to me – took him on instead because she took pity on me. She didn't need to do anything for me and I'd never been particularly nice to her but she saved me out of pure compassion. I couldn't believe it but that's what she did. One fuck here or there meant nothing to her – she could fuck all night if she wanted to. She boasted that no man could exhaust her, that she was insatiable, and that her fanny was steel capped. I believed her too. She was the most popular girl in the brothel. All the men wanted to fuck her. So all of that would have been no more than an aperitif for her... But at that moment in the brothel, when she did that kind thing for me, I decided that there was hope for me; that there was some goodness left in the world; and that I would survive...It was a spiritual moment, I think, so far as I can gather, and I have thought about it a lot in the past few years. I seemed to be invaded by peace in the middle of that terrible place which...No, I mustn't say it, I mustn't talk about any of that... I just can't do that...'

Lucy-Miranda's voice, which had been calm during her narrative, suddenly rose in pitch, testifying to her distress. Emma tried to soothe her with some more coffee. She looked at Lucy-Miranda, who seemed to be shivering and shaking in her anguish.

Silence fell between them for a moment.

'And Charles? Does he know all of this?'

'A little bit, but not all of it. He's not a well man, as you can see, so I keep my troubles to myself as much as I can. Which is why it's such a great pleasure to discuss all of this with you now, Emma, with just the two of us. These things lie dormant and bottled-up for too long. They have to be let out...You see, I met

Charles just an hour or so after I'd managed to extricate myself from that dreadful place. He was in a very bad way as well. We were just a couple of crocks. He'd been knocked on the head by some burglar or other – I never quite got to the bottom of it; I think there was a girl involved but I never probed too far -and he was lying flat out in his flat which, providentially, was next to mine. I saw him lying there and I just cherished him. Here was somebody that I could help, after all these months, somebody that I could look after, so I put my arms around him and I loved him. It was as simple as that. We've been together ever since. I will always cherish him, despite his many failings because he has been my salvation…But somehow there are moments when my sense of duty seems inadequate, as if other stronger ideas keep pushing to the surface…'

She tailed off and sat there in silence again, watching the square for inspiration and support. Emma asked her very gently what it was that she preferred not to discuss.

'After all, you said that you had been invaded by peace at that moment. So what is it that troubles you? You might as well as say it now as not, if you have gone this far in your revelations.'

Emma tried to sound as soothing and as supportive as she could. But it was difficult because she was abruptly seething with excitement. As always, her memory had worked. The name had come leaping into her mind and she could place almost everything in perspective now and fit all – or most – of the jigsaw together. The name she had been seeking had been Prestbury. There it was again after so many years – Prestbury. She remembered two young waifs sheltering together in her old house in Chelsea, fugitives from none other than the self same Lucy-Miranda who was now seated beside her in this square in Repugia, pouring out her heart and soul.

And who said it was a small world? In Emma's experience, it was almost microcosmic on occasion.

Lucy-Miranda was troubled but she could raise enough strength to continue speaking.

'I don't really know how to put any of this together properly now because I'm very confused. The brain went years ago, as you will have gathered by now. But the plain fact of the matter is very clear – I miss the brothel. Is that really very naughty of me? Yes, it's true – I miss it. And I'll say it again. I miss it very much.'

'Oh dear!'

'As you so rightly say, Emma, oh dear. Yes and Oh dear again and as many times as you like. It is bizarre and very puzzling for me and I'm perplexed. Hampshire ladies of a certain age who have had more than their fair share of experiences and who have also been saved quite providentially, do not normally say such things. Best to forget it all. Turn the page, close the book, start afresh – all that kind of thing. The closest most of us come to experiencing such vitality on the whole is by watching it occasionally on the box. Band of Silver, or whatever it was called. We lead very sheltered lives – that is obvious. But I think that I have been altered by my experiences. I saw something else on my travels, something that I never dreamed existed and it continues to fascinate me. That is the only conclusion that I can come to under the circumstances. I tell myself I am the same Lucy-Miranda who was abducted into the brothel, but deep down I know that I am a different woman. You see, what I miss about the brothel is the flesh, yes, just that, just flesh for sale, all around, miles and miles of it. It's elemental…Clothes were irrelevant…Yes, all that plus the excitement of the place, the sheer sense of lust that used to shoot through the place like electricity when the punters were about to hit it. The freedom as well I think. And the girls, of course…Some of them, no, all of them I think, were having fun. They were in their prime. So beautiful…So big, so confident and so gorgeous…So voluptuous… You know what I mean, huge tits, glistening, moist fannies, and tight little bums, and no pretence about anything…They could take on anything, battalions almost, even though they were all being fucked rigid the whole time. I think now that they were also in control, in a way that Ginny, for example, is out of control, because the men came gagging for it…That's the only word to describe how they behaved as they arrived – they were gagging for it. It was a riot in that brothel and I miss it every day.'

Lucy-Miranda tailed off a little. Emma helped her along.

'You use a different language, you know, when you talk about the place. Much more free and easy. Every now and then out comes the old expletive.'

'It's inevitable. That was the commodity – fucking. That's all anybody does in a brothel, apart from smoking and eating. They fuck. That's what brothels are for. But let me explain a little, Emma. I come from a background where money is sex. That's all they talk about, that's all they want, that's all they dream about – making money. His nastiness apart, my husband Edward was a very charming man on occasion but his main interest in life wasn't me – it was cutting deals, worrying about them, getting them right, and collecting a hatful of money at the end. I was an appendage to that. On show permanently, to help the business along. Ultimately just a doll, a possession, something to be taken up and then replaced on the shelf when the time suited. Or, to put it all another way, we didn't make love very often. Edward's interests did not lie in that direction, to put it mildly. Money was sex for him. So I played the role of the dutiful wife and I like to think that I played it very well. My house as I told you was spotless. You could have eaten your evening meal off the floor it was so clean. I know that – I scrubbed it. But I was a housekeeper. And that's exactly what I'm becoming and doing again, even though Charles is not a money-maker but a diplomat. But he has obsessions on a different level and he is not close to me. He would like to be, I can see that, but he just can't fucking hack it, as they would have said in the brothel. Too much upbringing and not enough background – isn't that how somebody put it once? Well it was true for Edward and it's true now for Charles. So now for me it's the same only different, if you follow what I'm trying to say. I'm still the dutiful wife, still handing round the sandwiches and doing all the good social things that I ought to be doing. But my heart is not in it. It might have been once but it certainly isn't now, because I think I just go through the motions of everything. Between Edward my husband-that-was and Charles, my husband-that-is, there was something else that I miss very much, that something else which seems now to have had inexhaustible vitality. Where people were close, too, very, very close – and I miss that as well. I know I shouldn't, but I do. I also know that I'm romanticising the whole thing impossibly – I lost my voice for God's sake there – but I also feel heavily nostalgic about it all. What happened to the girls? That's what I'd like to know. Where are they now? Have they got Aids? Are they rich? Are they happy? Are they dead? Fucked stupid? Or are they all broken-down hags, scrabbling around in the gutter? I really can't believe that – for the most part, they were all very smart and very street-wise…They were taking a view on all of what they were doing…For some of them, it was a business decision.'

Lucy-Miranda looked at Emma defiantly. Then she laughed.

'And what's worse, I don't know what to do about it. How could I get in touch with them all again? Impossible – they will have scattered to the four winds now. So what do I do? I have one set of values in public and another quite different set of the same when I'm alone with myself and being truthful. That's why I like to come and see Gina. She keeps me in touch with this dark side of my life which now seems, perversely, to have been so bright. I like to see how Gina is, see how she's bearing up as she fucks her way through half Italy, and just…Well, I like to watch…You know, watch to see how well she's dressing, that kind of thing and whether she's taking care of herself…Almost as if I'm playing the game of being her maid, if that idea doesn't disgust you too much. I know that I find it a very frightening idea to return to the brothel in any shape or form, but there again, what can I do, if I'm being truly honest. I miss it, not desperately, but the sense of loss is there. We may be born to a social position but that doesn't automatically cater for what we really want, now does it, Emma? Or cater for what we discover that we want, which is perhaps worse. So I do the best that I can. I just take an interest in Gina although very much from afar, because I'm really a lonely old woman now with all my values turned upside down. I'm fixed in one groove but my thoughts lie in another. I'm doing what everybody else does – living life at one remove. But once upon a time, it was the other way around – Sex was Money and that was far more exciting. I just can't seem to get it out of my mind and adjust to being a boring old Hampshire housewife again.'

Lucy-Miranda paused for a second and then shaking her head, went off at a tangent, signifying that the discussion was over at least for the time being.

'I do think that you'll have to get that Craig of yours back here for a little while. Otherwise God knows what Ginny will get up to with poor Jake. He's a babe in arms compared to her. I think perhaps Jake is going to need moral support, if he stays out here with us for any length of time. Ginny is going to take advantage, I'm sure of that. He'll need some help.'

*   *   *   *   *

Tom prepared to leave the Chron after putting the morrow's first edition well and truly to bed. It had been a good day. With the Chron's powerful, supportive splash on the rising Euro, written under Tom's exclusive promptings, it felt like a good edition of the paper. At long last, the Chron was taking an independent line with respect to matters financial within its Square Mile parish. Tom felt in full control. The solemn, pulsing vibes of the paper were running through him starting with the soles of his feet and then moving upwards. It was a solid sensation. Power ultimately is personal electricity, Tom reflected.

But that was just how an editor in charge of a newspaper now barrelling forward at 20 knots under full sail, after a period of calm under its ex-helmsman, Old Venality, ought to feel, Tom reckoned.

Thus he, Tom, erstwhile inky-fingered journalist and columnist on the Chron, marked his transition to newspaper executive by nodding a cordial Goodnight to the backbench subs as he exited. Suit-clad and, unusually for him, wearing a collar and tie, he left the newsroom in search of his driver.

'Goodnight gents, one and all. And good sailing. Be sure to call me if you need me.'

That renvoi had speedily become his call sign to the subs, who formerly and over many years had chased and harassed him with curses in search of late – or early – copy.

But not now – times had changed. The dog-eared notebook had been briefly put away out of sight, to be replaced by a large gold-topped fountain pen, a present from the highly supportive Ursula to mark his ascension to the editorial purple. Showing the editorial presence by using the pen, he edited on occasion some of the front-page copy with his feet up on the Chief Sub's desk.

Within the discreet, highly secretive cloisters of the Chron, the crucial role reversal had proved acceptable; Tom seemed to have made the transition from hack to editor smoothly and successfully. The subs, in particular, had responded positively to his elevation. They liked the fresh edge to the news coverage that Tom, professional newshound above all else, had insisted form the coping stone to his regime. The memory of Old Venality's long meandering reign was to be fading fast as the old gave way to the new. The subs seemed to be awakening from a centuries' old torpor. Even the headlines within the paper were being written more carefully these days, with extra bite added where necessary to juice up the story underneath the head.

The paper seemed to be renewing itself. The subs wished him Godspeed.

'Night, Tom, well done…Good paper tonight.'

Not exactly a Hallelujah chorus but better in fact. Just a quiet murmur of support.

Tom smiled a final Goodnight to the newsroom. It seemed happy enough. And so home now to Hampshire and to a contented Ursula, increasingly spreading her wings in both town and the country as consort to that new arrival in society's first-class carriages, the fast-rising and well-liked Editor of the Chron. The texture of his social life was altering for Tom, both in the warp and in the woof. The Chron's Editor wondered what social delights Ursula had arranged for him that evening.

Lap dancing…? Get away, he laughed to himself.

The high spot of the day had been his fact-finding lunch with Graham. Just checking on progress….

This had gone well, with no obvious friction arising between them; Graham had gone out of his way to make Tom feel relaxed and comfortable in his presence. Indeed, Tom, by now adjusting rapidly to the complex and formerly misleading vocabulary of power, reckoned he had received a good deal of encouragement from his friendly mole on the Chronicle board. In Tom's book, this amounted almost to an endorsement that his fresh initiatives regarding the paper were being well received where it counted – on the tenth floor of Chronicle House. Even though Tom continued to step warily in the new job, a successful lunch with Graham counted as a plus in that continuing popular saga of Tom Stone, Journalist.

Before that had come an epic news conference when in principle he had confronted and faced down what looked like a small revolt ('not many dead') from the news writers, led by Captain Legless. After running through the news schedule at conference, and finding little if anything of interest on offer that day, Tom had proposed splashing on currencies for the next day's edition; the Euro was moving up at the expense of the $ and the role of the £ was highly ambivalent. Tom had also suggested running a crash feature on Stobart's extraordinary career at the Bank of England which had taken him, a rank outsider in the hierarchy, right to the top as Governor in just a handful of years.

Amazingly, the Chron had never written an analysis of Stobart in any shape or form, merely recording by frequently-reported anecdote just what a warm and friendly, life-enhancing Governor the afore-mentioned Stobart had proved to be. This, in Tom's view, was not wholly an accurate picture of the Governor, well known throughout the City as somebody quite different. Tom wanted to set the record straight. That way the Chron could draw a line in the sand, vis a vis its previous highly dependent relationship with the Bank, and start afresh.

Tom had offered his ideas fairly casually to conference, although they were carefully thought out; undiscussed with Ursula; and formed part of his long-range plans for the paper.

Legless was on his feet in a flash to protest. This was hardly surprising and Tom had expected him to react badly. Legless had spent some time on secondment from the Chron to the Bank –

learning their methods as the Head Cashier had put it grimly. Thus in a typical switch of loyalties within the Square Mile, Legless had been transformed from fearless journalist looking into the Bank into apologist reporting outwards from behind Threadneedle Street's windowless walls. He had become a fervent, intuitive supporter of the Bank's view on everything, from the weather to the shape of the UK yield curve.

He was also rumoured, scandalously throughout the paper, to be a major beneficiary of the Bank's secret largesse, notably via a large mortgage at highly preferential terms, like nil per cent interest. In other words, in Tom's view, Legless was now a bought and kept man.

So they faced each other in conference. The tall, rangy Legless stared angrily at Tom from the well of the news meeting, twisting his neck as he spoke as if to escape from beneath an invisible yoke. The huge hussar moustache, draped across his upper lip, quivered with passion. Legless' totally bald head glowed angrily beneath the lighting.

'Knock it off, Tom. That idea just won't fly. We never cover those aspects of the market. They are far too technical. We leave that to the Bank. That's how it's always been. Don't you start innovating in this direction, Stone. You're only an editor but this is a newspaper; we're not here today and gone tomorrow as you may be. We need the Bank's help and its goodwill to operate on a daily basis. So don't even think about it. As for Stobart, leave him alone. We have good relations with Stobart. He's very useful to us. Let sleeping dogs lie, can't you?'

Then like a grotesque, Legless stood there in the middle of conference, gyrating in silence at the new Editor as his head twisted here and there in vain attempt to escape the invisible shackling yoke. It was quite a performance. Some Legless stooges mumbled support in a quiet background roar. Tom thought of that zero rate on Legless' mortgage as he faced the angry, frightened journalist from behind his desk. He was tempted to inquire there and then about the mortgage and the rate but he desisted – bad timing, he reckoned.

Instead he played it cool. Rather than shriek the usual nostrums about a free press at Legless, Tom worked a different ticket and decided to throw it out to conference to discuss.

'Well, what say you, the rest of us? Let's debate it for a brief while. It's important and we've heard what Legless had to say. So...? What's it to be? Do we run with Legless and go for the custom and practice approach? Or do we try to break fresh ground by doing something that's good for the paper? I can't order you guys to cover stories if you don't want to. But I do think we should try to set the record straight on Stobart at the very least... You may think differently. So let's chat awhile...'

The result of the ensuing debate was an eye-opener for Tom. He very nearly rubbed his eyes in disbelief. The bulk of the journalists present practically salivated at the prospect of getting their teeth into such a succulent target as the Bank; at least five of them volunteered to write the definitive piece of knocking copy on Stobart. On the face of it, and purely in terms of numbers, there was no contest – the paper wanted a free rein to go after the Bank.

The Ayes had it by a street. Tom's enthusiasm for reform was catching fire within the paper.

But where Tom started blinking was over the Nays. They numbered about six; all were of a type, old, grey, even grizzled; and all were slightly hazy in outline and allegiance, the kind of subfusc editorial men who always passed muster without question within a crowd. But remarkably all six occupied key production and editorial positions within the Chron; they controlled all the main bridges within the paper. If necessary, therefore, in the case of armed insurrection or – and Tom was forced to admit this to himself – the initiatives taken by a reforming editor, they could in combination block the editor's suggestions and run the paper themselves. It seemed unlikely to Tom but there it was. Quite inadvertently, and very possibly before they had been able to concert a filibustering agenda, such had been the speed with which he had moved, he had isolated, in full view of those with eyes to see, a potential fifth column within the paper.

And were all six in receipt of the Bank's secret largesse in the shape of soft coupon mortgages or better still, kept well supplied on personal a/c via the Bank's ample credit lines? So that, in other words, way ahead of the outbreak of any hostilities, their support was guaranteed because the Bank had established an impregnable fall-back position? And a position that ensured that Chron coverage of the markets would go the Bank's way, irrespective of the Editor's stripe?

It was a sobering thought, Tom had reckoned, as the Ayes shouted their enthusiasm for the new editorial line and the Threadneedle Street Six stood their ground. Toughing it out, with no apparent thought for future careers or advancement, they petitioned for calm; reflection; and a return to the old ways of Old Venality. Tom had been fascinated.

And even more beguiled when that afternoon, after his lunch with Graham – to whom he had not breathed a syllable of his findings – he had found the entire newspaper in quiescent mode. There had been no opposition at all to his suggestion that the Chron lead on the Euro. The Threadneedle Six had nodded it all through without a whimper, even though it was something of a disappointment to Tom that Legless had not after all managed to complete the crash feature on Stobart.

But there it was – first blood to Tom; his story lived. Witness the splash story currently adorning the Chron's front page which covered the rise in the past few days of the Euro; the fall in the $; the concurrent geo-politicals; and the ambivalent role played by the £ in these movement on foreign exchange.

Not a bad paper, he thought. Not a bad, bloody paper at all...Ursula should be proud of him.

And so Tom left the Chron that night in buoyant breezy mood, looking forward to receiving the first editions by special delivery sometime after ten that evening at home.

Oh day of success, he thought as he greeted his driver outside Chronicle House and prepared to be ferried back to Hampshire; home; fun; and Ursula.

★   ★   ★   ★   ★

The following day, Tom's remodelled version of the Chron delighted at least one reader, Nicholas, and certainly dismayed one other, Joe. The Chron's new line on the Euro very nearly reduced Joe to despair.

Nicholas, now buying the Chron daily – and early – noted the paper's shift in emphasis immediately. He was on the phone early to Moley before traders could say 'War Loan' three times backwards.

'The Chron is plugging the Euro, Moley. That must mean a shift in tack by the Bank. The Chron wouldn't dare take such an independent line without the Bank's say-so. Time to buy, I guess. Blair has made his pitch and we're going in,' he exclaimed happily to Moley, certain that he was assured a privileged hearing by the Great Man.

But Moley failed to sound at all happy at the news; at the Chron; at Nicholas; indeed at the entire world. In fact, he sounded grumpy, as if he was planning to renounce the market; its pomps; and certainly its currencies within the space of a mood swing. Moley did not exactly put Nicholas down but he made it clear that for the time being his correspondent should consider limiting his calls to the minimum. This disconcerted Nicholas who by now had grown used to the idea of an early comeback to the City.

'That currency, the Euro, is accursed and it always trips me up,' he thought as the brief conversation with Moley drew to a defined conclusion. Moley had gone to some lengths to ensure the line was kept open with Nicholas. But he had also made it clear that he wanted no more talk about the Euro, especially one that was strengthening. The chat was very short; Moley was preoccupied by the markets.

'I'll know better next time than to talk about that wretched thing called the Euro; it can trade where it fucking well likes,' Nicholas told himself as, chastened with his ears well boxed, he returned to his house-work. 'I don't think the deal with Moley is in jeopardy but I'll have to walk and talk straighter in future. Certain topics are obviously off-limits.'

Meanwhile Joe was glimpsing Armageddon ahead. The bid for Global only made good sense with a currency kicker; without that even Joe, as a seasoned investment banker, could see that it was doomed. Too many bells and not enough whistles. And even less chance of pulling off the deal if the $ started falling. So he calculated his chances of pulling off the takeover if the currency was wrong; enduring Felix's murderous assaults; and surviving the Rivers Pugh show at Pugh Park – and found they were pretty slim.

He was grateful to Tom Stone, whose appointment as new Editor to the Chron he had noted, for clarifying the fragility of his position. But it didn't make it any easier....

$$\star \quad \star \quad \star \quad \star \quad \star$$

Lucy-Miranda had discovered that Emma played bridge. That piece of information had emerged into the discussion quite easily one morning as the two of them sat on their bench in the square in the sunshine, surveying the world and gossiping about this and that. It made for an even smoother absorption of Emma into the Gilston circle. Indeed she had been making headway in that direction ever since the evening of the Great Fiasco with Tommy and his mobile phone. Her face seemed to fit. Ginny seemed to accept her. She spent an increasing amount of time at the villa. Hence an invitation to play bridge that afternoon came as no shock but rather as a pleasing prospect.

Prior to the hour stipulated for play, she had met Lucy-Miranda at their cafe, mentioned that Craig was returning to Repugia in a day or so and received the appropriate bulletin of news from the war-front from Lucy-Miranda as they wandered back to the villa.

'They'll just be the four of us playing, that's Ginny, you, me and Stella, but Jake will be there minding the baby. Charles, who does play, is taking a nap.'

'Jake minding the baby? That's a bit trusting of Ginny isn't it? After everything that happened...?'

'Ginny, the cunning snake, has moved fast since we last discussed her grand plan. Jake is now very much in charge of baby walks and baby talks, along with Ginny but under her supervision. Apart from telephoning my daughter at the ABC Bank, he does nothing else and loves the baby-minding which is only to be expected since he's more or less a child himself beneath that macho image. What do you expect – he's a footballer and a market trader. Barely out of the trees. So they all play together in total innocence. Meanwhile I see very clearly what she is about now. She aims to enslave Jake and turn him into her domestic, so that when she does take him – which she will do when it suits her – he will have no come-back on her because she had already placed him in an inferior position. Which he has accepted. He does not and will not hold the voting stock, as Edward would say, in this relationship. I think that is the way her mind works. Very intuitive by Ginny. She will revenge herself on her husband, enjoy Jake's body for a little while in the hayricks of an Italian summer but with no comebacks on her – nice work if you can get it. Isn't she the lucky girl! But see for yourself. See what you think. I think she's getting him nicely trained up so far for the job in hand – and poor Jake! I'm sure that he'll emerge the loser from all this in some way or another. But what can anyone do. He's like a lamb to the slaughter. None of any of this is a great deal removed from that other place I was telling you about just a few days ago…The decor is more attractive but that's about all…It does all seem horribly familiar…'

They turned the bend at the top of the street and made for the small entrance which allowed them access to the villa.

'You'll be partnering me, Emma, and don't expect too much from my bridge. It went the way of my brains years ago. Stayman and a Weak No Trump and that's about my limit. I'm sure from the modest way that you dismiss your bridge that you're brilliant at it but be assured that anything imaginative will be resolutely ignored by me – or misunderstood. Ginny will play with Stella. I'm sure you'll like Stella. She looks delicate but she has a will of steel. Great table presence too although not the most cunning of players. She's Colombian, although you'd never guess that from her accent. I happen to know that after some revolution or other in Colombia she, along with all her family and her father, were given twenty-four hours to get out of the country and over the border into Venezuela. They made it apparently with minutes to spare with just the clothes they stood up in. Again you'd never guess that from her appearance...She's a very elegant woman. She admitted to me once that she took with her... Well, you try and guess what she did take with her. No time to dawdle if you've been told to leave, remember.'

'A tin opener?'

'Not bad for a sighting shot. And how practical! No, she took three pairs of Gucci shoes and One Hundred Years of Solitude by Marquez. How about that?'

'Such presence of mind. The selection conjures up quite a picture of assumptions about the future. And her bridge?'

'Wonderful, of course, but still on the border-line...'

'Very witty of you, Lucy-Miranda. You are on top form this morning.'

'Her bridge is substantially more complex under pressure, although you never heard me say that. But it has its moments.'

'Quite so. As indeed does all our bridge.'

'That is certainly true. And so here we are...'

They passed through the small door and onto the lawns to find a scene of idyllic splendour awaiting them – Ginny's baby crawling happily around on the lawn in the shade and gurgling with pleasure, followed closely by Jake who was teasing it with a blade of grass as he leaped around with a great fat child's smile all across his face. The whole ensemble was watched in supervision by Ginny, sitting beside the pram in shorts and t-shirt. Emma thought she looked like a goddess in the sun and the breeze and the quiet of an Italian afternoon as she tossed her head back into the sun and her hair blazed in its rays.

A table sat some way apart from the small group towards which a slight woman was making her way with delicacy as she picked her way across the lawn. Next to the pram, Emma noticed as she crossed the lawn to the table, there was a football, some weights, a bench and various other implements of sporting prowess.

'Jake will train, as we play. He trains every day so far as I can gather, for about three hours. That way he gets to keep his hand in with West Ham or whoever it was that he plays for. He also keeps an eye on the baby and maintains his magnificent physique. One way or another I have to tell you, I've seen quite a lot of the Jake torso in the past few days and it never palls. ...And this way Ginny plays her bridge, looks after her baby and savours some of the pleasures yet to come in the shape of her willing suitor as she steals the odd glance in his direction. Don't be surprised to find...Ah, I thought so, yes how foolish of me. Ginny got there before me. She's already booked her spot at the table. How very advantageous for her...She keeps on eye on everything from that angle.'

Stella was polite and controlled and slender. Her fingers were very slender. Emma detected no malice in her, just a sort of yearning for goodwill and a quest for sanctuary, almost as if she had made a pact with the Almighty so that every now and then he'd give her an even break. Like prison, sneaking across the Venezuelan border changes a woman, Emma thought as the play progressed.

But Stella played a solid thoughtful game, watching the dummy like a trapper expecting some kind of animal to surface from beneath the cards, her eyes flickering back and forth from her hand to the dummy and then back to the cards in the middle. Ginny, by contrast, was a mess. Obviously her mind was on other things, like the footballing maestro balancing the ball on his head some fifteen yards away as he went through his paces. She could see him directly since he was exercising behind the table. He lay directly in her line of vision. Ginny played almost as if an alternative presence was lurking around the table ready to check and condemn her performance at any moment. She was a hunted soul and the bridge brought forth, as it always does for those in such torment, a vision of seething anxieties and apprehensions. For her part, Lucy-Miranda buried her cards in her fist and hunched over them like a fortune telling lady about to try and pull a fast one.

As ever with bridge, during the play the truth in character beamed through the trappings of concealment.

Before long the frictions began to surface. Ginny sounded aggressive. Stella was in Four Diamonds, just making. Ginny was unappeased.

'I rather thought that you were going to bid Three No Trumps with that hand. It does make, you know.'

Stella was adamant. Her voice rose a trifle and the accent tottered as she replied. Meanwhile the sunshine lay heavy across the garden and played in the wind with the trees across the valley beyond the terrace.

'No, no I don't think so, Ginny. If they lead a Spade it goes off because I am doubleton and the King is not...I mean if I get the King wrong then I am down...'

Mumbling to herself Ginny pulled the cards towards her and prepared to deal. Her mobile phone rang in her bag beside the pram. Rather than interrupt dealing the cards, she called across to Jake who was now doing heroic things on the bench with his weights to look in her bag and bring the phone across to her. She asked him politely but there was no doubting the underlying note of instruction. Nor the sense of intimacy broached or barriers breached as Jake inexpertly rummaged around inside Ginny's holdall. Penetration took place on some basis not far from the real thing. Then Jake hopped across the lawn obediently with the ringing phone. Emma and Lucy-Miranda exchanged a quiet glance of complicity as they took in the black-haired torso now running with sweat in the bright sunshine, and the willingness to please.

'Hullo,' said Ginny urgently, wiping the sweat from the phone. Then she spoke less swiftly as she realised that it was her husband Tommy calling her from London. Her face tightened into an unforgiving moue. Tommy spoke at some length. At the voluble sounds emerging from the machine, Ginny began to shake her head and roll her eyes, intimating that this was just more typical jaw-jaw from the wretched Tommy. She motioned to Lucy-Miranda to carry on dealing the cards, since she was briefly otherwise engaged.

Ginny focused on the caller. She seemed to have the upper hand.

'Yes I know that, Tommy. You made all of that abundantly clear at our last meeting. Which was here in these very gardens, if I remember correctly. You won't be back for some time. That was what you said. You have a deal to do. That was the arrangement wasn't it? You in London doing your deals and me in Italy with the baby. Or did I get that wrong? Am I being stupid? Tell me, Tommy.'

This sounded like a peace overture from Tommy being soundly crushed at birth. Of course Ginny could afford to talk tough in this way. She had her little Jake around to keep her warm, or so she thought. And she also had the baby, who poor creature was not yet old enough to realise what she really represented – a trophy of war to be captured or surrendered in the permanent armed siege between husband and wife. But her name was already down for Gabby's, Britain's leading girls' public school.

So she might get something out of the family Trojan War at the last.

Lucy-Miranda dealt the cards in silence. Jake was back playing with the baby. Emma and Stella watched the cards fly onto the table in small neat heaps as Ginny and Tommy conversed bitterly across No Man's Land between Italy and London. Ginny was about to land a real pile driver as she touched on the question of the christening ceremony. Tommy was angry too as control of the situation ebbed away from him across the eternity of space between him and his wife.

Too few jokes along the way in that household, Emma thought as her mind turned yet again to the odd relationship which she had unearthed between Lucy-Miranda and herself, a relationship which was about to take another twist after she had read the note handed in for her that morning at the hotel. Lucy-Miranda would be pleased when Emma told her about the missive.

Ginny droned on, grinding out a triumph.

'Yes, Tommy, I hope the deal goes as well as you think. Just don't worry about me. Now about those names we were discussing...'

The note had been from Paolo, strutting bantam cock at the cafe where Emma had first encountered Lucy-Miranda and Charles. It requested some further information regarding the 'admirable magnifico futboller seen with her some mourning last in the piazza. Please to communicate pronto.' The note had been written with care by many contributors, all convinced about the fluency of their English. In that rambling, obsequious yet insistent and deadly Italian way, the waiters and indeed all the observers, had pieced together their side of the story. They had connected Emma with Lucy-Miranda, who lived at the Big House and who was therefore unapproachable. But an approach could be made to Emma who was more charming and less grand than the Signora Lucy-Miranda – and better looking too, with better legs. Hence the note, not intended to give offence, scusi!

And why the approach? Emma guessed very well.

For the small matter of the introduction of such a wonderfully talented footballer like Jake to an Italian club, there would of course be a handling fee, perhaps quite a large fee, which would be shared out in unequal proportions to all the wretched mafiosi involved in the introduction…Emma could see that all very clearly and likewise see all their knuckle-headed Italian skulls clustered together as they worked out the returns.

'…Yes, I'm definitely starting to change my mind about Samantha. Maybe it's the air in Repugia. But Samantha sounds too English and provincial. Perhaps we ought to go for something more Italian, like Claudia or Sophia…Or perhaps even Maria…?'

It was deliberate provocation on Ginny's part, as all the players around the bridge table recognised. She was taunting her husband. Tommy was a true-blue Englishman who regretted missing Agincourt. He thought that Hampshire should introduce passport control and declare UDI from the rest of the UK. He wanted his daughter to sound English. The very idea that she should have a Wop name…Predictably enough, he exploded down the phone. Ginny with her eyes turned Heavenwards, removed the phone a few inches from her ear as the sounds of wrath rolled across the airways and blinked poutingly at the girls. They disregarded her. But she was winning her point. Tommy was being outmanoeuvred. His unreasonable behaviour allowed her in that weird mental universe she inhabited to derive sanction for what she was planning to do with Jake. And that was what she was scheming for, as she wound up her husband mercilessly.

She had to remain victim, because that gave her licence to behave as badly as she wanted, child or no child. And if it didn't look as if she was being badly treated, well she would jolly well arrange things in such a way that he would go for her, preferably in public and in front of a large audience.

Ginny did victim, and that very artfully.

Emma could well understand why some poor chap's car got trashed one fine morning by this human cyclone – and most likely to his utter amazement, as he discovered that Ginny played by different rules.

Ginny gestured to the girls to start playing and they picked up their cards at last. Emma's hand was nothing special and so she thought some more about Lucy-Miranda as the din of Ginny's battle with Tommy raged about their ears. It seemed very simple. Lucy-Miranda had kicked her daughter Lucia out of the family house – this was some years ago – after she'd escaped up to London for a good time with someone she'd picked up in a chat room called Prestbury. Prestbury was exquisitely formed and very black. She and Prestbury had had a diverting time in London from what Emma had been able to glean later about the row. Emma at that precise moment had been busting up in a wholly tearful, gut wrenching but, as it happened, conclusive way with her long term lover and confidant, Gregory. To square the circle of all these stateless people drifting around she had then sold her recently acquired house in Chelsea for a massive profit to the Maitland family. That way the Maitland's reckoned they could park the errant Lucia there while her other, far more respectable, sister completed her solemn and full fig nuptials, unmolested by the druggy presence of Lucia with her socially unacceptable boyfriend. Nuptials, as Emma had gathered later from Joe, had been organised around a terrific stockmarket deal which fell apart at the last moment and resulted in the death of Edward Maitland by his own hand in the Martins Bank dealing room.

Not nice for Edward or Lucy-Miranda… But then neither was life…

So it was *that* Lucy-Miranda, who had booted out her daughter, doubtless with good reason, and whom she had known about at arms' length many years ago who turned out to be the self-same Lucy-Miranda who had been sobbing into her beer in Repugia about her time in the brothel and who was now playing her cards with the greatest of care as she plonked them down stolidly on the table, seated with her back to the hills of Repugia in the summer sunlight just a foot or so away from Emma opposite!

Incredible, unbelievable and wholly disturbing coincidence!

Emma could piece most of it together now...And Joe...The thought of Joe struck her abruptly. Like a nemesis. Where was he? Where was Joe? What was he doing now? Did he ever think about her? Joe the Elusive broke in on her thoughts like an assassin stealing through the door. Joe was important to the story because it had been Joe, the ghostly Joe, who had brokered the whole of the deal over the house in Chelsea just as it had been Joe who in Norwich...Yes, Joe...And in Norwich...

Norwich had a lot to answer for one way and another... And Joe too, for his sins...

It was the first time she had thought about Joe for many months. She knew it was a mistake, sunshine and fair weather above her head notwithstanding.

She thought some more about Joe for a little while and then decided to forget about thinking about him for the time being. She was being stupid and reckless to dwell for more than a few seconds on Joe. She had far too much on her mind to allow it to become cluttered up with useless and painful reminiscences. There would be time to think about Joe later, she told herself.

Emma played a card and found to her astonishment that she had managed to follow suit. That was clever of me, she thought, in my abstraction – I'm not even sure that I'm aware I'm playing bridge. It could even be snap for all that I'm aware of anything.

Ginny terminated her discussion with Tommy on the worst possible note by pointing out to him that she had to end the conversation because she was in the middle of a hand of bridge with the girls – and she had to bid her hand! It was a race between them both as to who beat the other in snapping off the connection. Ginny won by a short head as Tommy's voice rose to an extinguishing shriek across the airwaves.

'Revolting man. I just don't know what I ever saw in him,' she remarked desultorily as she closed up her mobile and consigned her entire marital status to the dustbin. She placed the mobile carefully beside her on the table, ready for the return ding-dong. Peace reigned for a few moments on the airwaves between London and Italy. The girls got on with their play.

Emma could see that Ginny from her position at the table was eyeing Jake with a kind of lustful relish. There was an anticipatory gleam in her eye as she stared straight ahead of her in such a way that she could not fail to take into her field of vision Jake's aggressive work-out. Judging by the grunts and the groans, Emma guessed that he was hammering the weights to death, much to Ginny's gleeful and suppressed anticipation. Emma could guess only too well what was running through her head. 'Don't take too much out of yourself, you gorgeous hunk of unexpected pleasure, because I'll be there very shortly to relieve you of whatever spunk you have left – and more besides. You have absolutely no idea, you thrilling little guttersnipe, just what I have in store for you as I strip you right down to skin and bone and then attack every single little porous cell of your being...And then discard you forthwith – like that, pouf ! – after you have done for me what I wanted you to do...Revenge for me is a dish best eaten hot.'

The phone rang again and Ginny snatched up her mobile and flung it to her ear, her mouth tightening yet again into a familiar expression. Sadly it was the wrong phone. She looked puzzled for a second, silhouetted in a blaze of red and gold against the sun. Then she realised that it had been Lucy-Miranda's phone which had rung. Looking only slightly deflated, Ginny replaced the phone on the table as Lucy-Miranda fumbled in her bag in a growing panic before pulling out the shrilling instrument in a cascade of make-up; chequebooks; and junk.

'Yes, yes, it's me here. I'm sorry...I'm sorry...Who is that?...Oh yes, Lucia, how nice to hear from you. How are you? I expect you want to speak to Jake, do you? Yes, yes, he's just a few feet away, playing with the baby and doing his work-out...Yes, he does look very fit indeed, I agree, we've all been very impressed…Yes, just one second…'

She called out for Jake and at that moment Stella's phone rang as well. Stella picked up her mobile as if it had been a ciborium. Ginny pursed her lip in vexation. She wanted her kiss and make-up call from Tommy to be well witnessed by the girls.

'This place is becoming a madhouse. I'm going to tend my darling little child…My little gorgeous sweet bunch of lovely kisses…'

Her expression softened as she approached the child and Emma glimpsed a different Ginny hidden deep beneath the armour and the war paint. The Ginny who rushed to the surface was a tender, kind, loving and sentimental girl, full of beauty and shape and élan, who needed support, a vulnerable Ginny who was barely a woman, who had been run hard by a harsh loveless system which had moulded her gullible simplicity into something hard edged, demanding and quite inhuman. It was a chilling sight of complete emotional deprivation. Emma understood a little, just a fraction, regarding her compulsion to attack and conquer and destroy. She didn't know what she wanted, so once she had it, she didn't know what to do with it. So onwards, ever onwards, to the next conquest…And meanwhile her good looks would always be working for her, so that men would always come running at her beck and call. The many swain would always be there, clambering the gates across the fields to get to her as she crooked her finger…Jake was only the first of many males doomed to do her bidding, succeed, and then find themselves rejected utterly as she moved onto the next victim…

Jake meanwhile was finding discussion with Lucia quite difficult in the presence of her mother. Fortunately she seemed to be doing most of the talking.

'Yeah, Lucky, this is a bit difficult for me to talk…Well, I'm embarrassed, what with your mother being right beside me here. No, I don't think she realised that her daughter was called anything else but Lucia. But I have been singing your praises here. Yeah, natch…'

Here Jake turned to Lucy-Miranda and shot a frightful leer of conspiracy and complicity at her. But Lucy-Miranda remained expressionless and very memsahib. Whom her daughter chose to associate with was very strictly her business and nobody else's. She was of an age to know her own mind now and that was that.

'...Yeah OK, Lucky, you're the boss, so the message is just stay here until you can come out...Yeah, that's what I guessed, I'm conflicted...So you can't talk about the deal, yeah, I realise that...But I hope it's going well. It sounds an absolute cracker and I'm sure that you'll handle it brilliantly...Yeah, total cracker...OK, now look, is the Tank anywhere to be seen? He is? Terrific, can you put him through, I want to ask him a favour... No, Lucky, no problems, apart from the fact that I'm missing you...And the food is good, especially the breakfasts...A flying visit? Yeah, that would be great...Just great, Lucky...It would be brill to see you out here...'

Ginny heard that sweet sound of affection and she didn't like what she heard, although the compliment about the breakfasts was just about acceptable. But her disapproval of Jake talking sweet nothings to Lucia was obvious. To be added to the volcanic temper were the multitudinous seas incarnadine of her jealousy...Oh dear, thought Emma, oh dear. Poor Jake... He really is going to get it in the neck at some point. I feel it in my bones.

'Look Tank...Yeah and up yours too, you wanker...Now that's enough of that rough market talk from you, I'm in company here...Polite company too, like what you, my son, are never ever likely to encounter. Yeah, yeah, yeah and the same to you... And how is Superbum...She's good? Moving well? Great. Just give her one for me, will you?...Hah, hah, hah, Tank, you do know how to make a girl feel good, don't you, Tank...Now look, will you look in the second drawer from the top in my desk...Yeah, you're there? OK, now fumble around, will you, and somewhere in that heap of rubbish you'll find a training schedule...Black, spiral bound? You've got it? Great. Now fax it to me will you. I've got so much time here I want to hack the really tough schedule and get into great shape for the opening game...Wait one, I'll check the address here.'

Jake was back in market mode and speak. He turned to the women still seated in silence at the table in front of their cards.

'You guys got any idea what the fax number is here?'

Lucy-Miranda said that the villa didn't possess any such thing and Jake's face fell. He wanted his training schedule immediately. But Emma leaped into the breach. Her mind had moved quickly. Establishing a little bit of independent contact with Jake would be no bad thing.

'Jake, there is a fax at the hotel. I've got the number here.'

She read the details out to him from the back of her hotel booking slip and he repeated them faithfully down the line to the Tank in London. So problem solved. The schedule would be over immediately and Jake could get on post haste with the serious business of burnishing his body into a perfectly moulded wand of a projectile. Ginny approved of that course of action, up to a point.

In a quiet way Emma had established a small line directly to Jake. That counted for nothing she knew in the overall scheme of things but one never knew...As Annie always said, seize every little bit of information that you find comes your way...

As the mobile phones were extinguished and play was about to recommence, Stella made her contribution to the total sum of universal elements. She spoke in her clipped precise tones, waving slender hands just a little as she made her point with a Colombian smile.

'That was a call from Patti who very surprisingly is in Petana with all the rest of the group on a bridge holiday. Julia and Barbara and Trish – they are all there, all the group, and we are invited, once they've settled down, to go over there in a few days and play with them... Isn't that exciting...The group is alive and well but in Italy...'

Emma saw a hard gleam come into Ginny's eye as she digested the news. Yes, very, very, very exciting for some of us, she thought. This will be Ginny's first opportunity to launch her strike, which she will do...Of that, I am quite sure.

And so the play at the bridge table continued in all the sunshine which an effervescent Italy could muster.

Afterwards, in the square, whither Emma and Lucy-Miranda had mooched quite naturally after the bridge had finished, Lucy-Miranda asked Emma what she made of Ginny's performance.

Mindful of just how much and how fast her relationship with Lucy-Miranda was changing, Emma spoke cautiously.

'She's a study. I think she suffers from panic attacks in the brain. Once they set in she doesn't know what she's doing at all. She's a completely unguided missile. Completely out of control, baby and all.'

Lucy-Miranda digested what on the face of it was quite a constructive comment.

'And Jake?'

Emma had told Lucy-Miranda about Paolo's note.

'Well, obviously, we have to talk to Paolo, I suppose. Find out what he really wants and then talk to Jake about it. I must say this is all very thrilling, doing this negotiating. I like negotiating. That was another discovery I made when I was in...'

Emma had decided not to reveal to Lucy-Miranda that in a past life she had been the kind of lawyer who ate those deals hours before breakfast, four or five at a time. The time for intimate revelations had come and gone. It might return but Emma wasn't betting on it. She wanted to preserve some room for manoeuvre, ahead of Lucia's arrival in Repugia, an event which might on its own oblige them all to rethink their relative positions.

Because Lucia would of course recognise her...End of the holiday fun?

Emma was beginning to steel herself over relations with Lucy-Miranda. She could feel the iron entering her soul.

'Emma, is it my imagination, or do the natives seem friendlier? You see that woman over there, yes, the one with the little black dog in tow. You see her?'

'I do indeed.'

'Her name is Giovanna. In all the time that I've been sitting here over the years, she has never so much as glanced in my direction. But now she seems to be smiling all the time at me.'

'The next thing you know she'll be offering you a sweet. I'm not as sensitive to the atmosphere as you are, Lucy-Miranda, but if the air has turned warmer for us, it's because they're softening us up for the negotiations.'

'Such a pity. You're probably right, in fact I'm sure you're right, but how disappointing. I thought they were starting to accept me at last...'

'If there's a deal there for them with Jake they'll offer you the freedom of Repugia, Lucy-Miranda. What would you say to that?'

Lucy-Miranda thought for a moment and guffawed – a good nasal honking snort. It was startling in its frank vulgarity.

'Cor, what a treat!'

'What's that in Italian?'

'Corra, whatta treata! Give-a me some pizza!'

And they both laughed out loud. Such a pleasant day it had been, just wandering around in the town in the sun and playing pasta bridge of the worst, most stupid kind. Stella had been quite offended by their nonchalance at the bridge table. Even Ginny with all her rapacity and insecurity fell into place in this scenario. Now they were just two women sitting together on the bench in an Italian square gossiping away and having a good relaxed time. Emma thought it was wonderful.

The sun licked at her toes as she placed her sense of reserve about Lucy-Miranda to one side, almost in cold storage.

'Emma, when did you say that Craig was coming back? It's about time he showed up, in order to frustrate Ginny's evil designs on Jake. A little bit of the old male bonding ought to give him some protection against her predatory designs.'

'Next week, just for the day. He'll be here in the morning and early afternoon. Then he has to go back. It all sounds highly mysterious. He's wildly excited about his discoveries. He can't wait to tell us all some more about Catullus. He thinks he's definitely stumbled on something. He was in the library in Verona, grubbing about in the archives, as only Craig can do...'

'Are you sure he's a novelist and not just a researcher?'

'Who knows? He seems to be doing the work and that is all that counts for the time being. He hasn't mentioned the writing much but then I don't really care, between you and me, what happens provided I see the project through to the end. It's only a trial run for both of us and there are other things that are beginning to come between us...'

'Like what, for example...?'

The cold hand of reason and self-preservation clutched at Emma's heart. She must not tell Lucy-Miranda any more than she needed absolutely to know. It was a pity, but that was her stony road...

'I'll tell you more when I've sorted myself out more. But publishing may be only just a part of it. I'm starting to miss someone else very much indeed. I've only just realised this. In fact I only started coming to terms with it when I was playing that Three No Trumps contract, you know the one that I should have made if only I hadn't buggered up the Spades. I felt a pang, a really deep one, and it quite put me off my stroke. Ginny was over the moon about getting me down.'

'Yes, she did rather gloat, didn't she...? I wondered about that contract... It all started off so well too but then came the moment of abstraction...I could see the little grey cells beginning to lose their sheen as the Clubs failed to do their thing...But it's understandable. That's what Italy does for you. It brings all those little hidden particles to the surface. It's the sun – it brings it all out. I know just how you feel. I'll tell you a thing or two about that in due course. I loved someone else very deeply a long time ago. But...'

'Scusi, signorina. Please to talk with you...?'

The voice was respectful, quiet but insistent. They turned round. It was Paolo, a rather beseeching Paolo, who stood there awkwardly, almost on one leg, hoping that his overtures to them would be acceptable. Not quite the proud strutting waiter of the main square but also not quite the full Italian shilling either.

'Paolo...!'

'Signorina...!'

'Paolo, I got your note. Now what did you want us to do about it. You wanted us to put you in touch with Jake...?'

A flurry of beseeching hands, as he sat down between them; there had been a modification to the original plan. That was what he had come to inform them. Emma was conscious that most of the cafe behind them was watching this performance by their nuncio. It was serious stuff. Now the two of them were down in the market place with a vengeance.

'Jake...I do not know...I hear that 'e do the most marvellous things with the futbol...'

'We saw it too, didn't we Emma? He was like a god. Really Paolo, just like a god.'

Lucy-Miranda rather screamed the word at Paolo in the hope that he would understand.

'Lucy-Miranda, don't oversell it. In any case, Paolo wouldn't understand any of that, would you Paolo?'

Paolo ignored her.

'We 'ave some plans for 'im, if 'e eez that guud, but...'

Paolo gestured at the square impotently and made kicking footballing gestures as his English failed him. Emma saw what was afoot. She grinned and nudged him kindly in the elbow then turned to Lucy-Miranda.

'I think I know what's going on, Lucy-Miranda. They think he may be wonderful but they need to see whether he can actually play football. He may be just a juggler and being Italians, they're naturally suspicious, deep in their peasant souls. So I think they want us to lure him down here and get him to play with the boys in the square, something like that so that they can gauge his form. Yes, I think that's it. And of course when he does that, they'll have their man here as well so that he can report back to the vigilantes just how good he really is...'

Paolo was nodding away in half comprehension as she gabbled all of this at Lucy-Miranda.

'So what do we do, Emma?'

A mischievous thought struck Emma, one of those blinding flashes of intuition she had enjoyed when she was last a lawyer, the moment when the whole of the contract and all the attendant Gordian knots of problems lay in crystalline clarity before her and she knew exactly how to solve it all, as the rest of the team stood around wringing their hands at three o' clock in the morning.

'We tell Jake that we have been offered an English breakfast by the Italians, on the house free gratis and for nothing, provided he comes down here and does his stuff by playing a little football with the locals. We'll really bully him into it by saying that it's important for your standing with the locals, so that way he can't refuse. We'll get Ginny down here with the baby too. And just to put on a good show of it all, we'll lay it all on for the locals the day that Craig arrives so that we all have a fabulous time here in Repugia. How about all that?'

'What a marvellous idea. I say, Emma, aren't we starting to have fun? Now how are you going to convey all of that to young Shylock here?'

'Very easily. Just watch me…Now Paolo, we bring Jake here for futbol Tuesday next week, comprendi, Tuesday?'

'Si si. For futbol, si si.'

Paolo looked happier already.

'But he like breakfast, English breakfast, so mangiare English breakfast at café' – and she gestured towards the cafe as she spoke, the while making an eating motion with her hands, – 'after futbol…'

Paolo nodded in full comprehension now. He smiled. He could see the dollars coming over the horizon.

'Tuesday, futbol, English breakfast…'

'Si, si,si…Momento…'

Paolo stood up and loped off back to the cafe to report the news and receive further instructions. He disappeared into the bar and then reappeared after a few seconds, clutching what was obviously a menu. He waved it under their noses. Grubbily, with more than just the odd olive oil stain obscuring its gothic print, there was advertised an Englishes Breakfest. Emma pointed to it and gave Paolo the thumbs up.

They all shook hands in high excitement at the selling of Jake.

'Tuesday, si! At ten o'clock, here.'

Emma pointed magisterially to the square.

'Futbol, si si…and…'

'English breakfast.'

They all laughed and shook hands again. It was a trade. Neither side would break the covenant. So much was obvious. Paolo saluted them with the dancing smile now back on his lips as the mission was accomplished, and then he headed off back to the cafe to confer some more with the other brokers of the square, in on the deal.

The two women resumed their vigil on the bench, feeling like native-born Italians. More sunshine warmed them on the bench.

'Any more of this, Emma, and we'll be going to church each morning with our rosary beads and our scarves round our heads...You were magnificent. Congratulations.'

'We'll meet Gina on the way out, wearing a perfume called 'Odour of Sanctity'...'

'Now that's a come hither for you...'

Again the two women laughed in full merriment at the crazy situation that was evolving almost day by day before their eyes. Craig; Ginny; and Jake had been situation rich enough. But now there was Paolo and the great football game, not to mention some bridge with the Sloane Square dames who had suddenly turned up in nearby Petana!

What larks!

'What was that you were saying, Emma, about Craig and Catullus before we were sidetracked?'

'Ah, yes, before we were sidetracked, as you said. Well, Craig was in the library researching away and checking out what he hoped to find out about the family and the friends of Catullus. Apparently they have some full dossiers on these very points, so he was plodding through the catalogues, when suddenly one of the Italians started to take a great interest in what he was doing and struck up a conversation with him. Very knowledgeable too about Catullus and his background apparently. The upshot of all this is that he's been invited to Sirmio which as you know – or maybe you don't, I forget how much of this has been pumped into me by Craig in his tete a tetes – anyway Sirmio was where the Catullus family home was located. There's even a poem he wrote about being rowed across the lake to the family home with all the retainers out there waiting for him, which is very sweet and evocative. So Craig clearly thinks that he's onto something. I doubt it very much, but then in Italy, as we are discovering, anything can happen...'

'Maybe we'll discover that Catullus was a great footballer.'

'No, a futboller, correction.'

The two women laughed together. The presentiment of impending disaster was just for once briefly absent.

Lucy-Miranda assented very happily to that judgement, which suited Emma very well. The day before the great football trial she was due to make her little clandestine trip a few hundred kilometres away to the west of Repugia. Nothing would happen; it would be uneventful; just a little touch of local espionage. It happened all the time – Emma had the distinct impression that she was not the first young woman of independent means who had been asked ever so discreetly by London to take an envelope or a package from A to B and then report back. After she'd done the drop she could get on with the business of holidaymaking. But the logistics needed careful organisation as well as some concentration because she needed to call London afterwards to confirm that she'd made the drop. She needed to step into another identity, albeit briefly, but that could hardly be done with full focus, if she was also spending all her time sky-larking around with Lucy-Miranda et al...

As it was she was having difficulty in recalling the passage of the week from one day to another as she relaxed into the country house party that went on 24 hours a day in the Gilston villa. But this way it should all work out fine and her absence would not be queried...

★ ★ ★ ★ ★

Joe paused in front of the entrance door to one of the tower blocks in the Barbican. The wind howled down the passage ways and across the piazzas, tearing at his coat and ruffling his hair. All around him lay blank brown brick squares, empty of meaning and filled with architecture. The Barbican, a huge soulless housing and arts complex located just inside the Square Mile, is much inhabited by stockbrokers and bankers who like to live close to the City action.

Joe was visiting Moley, his comrade in arms from the old City days. Moley very much wanted to live as close to the action as possible.

Joe was calling on £100 million and then upwards, all made within living memory, from small beginnings, trading on the old Stock Exchange floor.

For Moley, money was the action. There was nothing else for Moley. His presence in the City was all pervasive. And all powerful too, most likely. Moley was a new boy but he had a finger in nearly every pie. Joe thought, but could never prove it of course, that it had been Moley who had supplied the Gilstons with the vital scratch on credit lines to run a position on sterling the night the bank very nearly went bust some years ago. George Gilston knew but he would never tell ever – George was dead now. Moley did business on that kind of scale. Unknown to the world at large, Moley was everywhere and everybody in the City. He could make a money call to anyone at any time of the day or night. That was real, backstairs, power

Joe was miserable about his deal at ABC; it was treacherous and going sour. He was obsessing about Felix as well. He was worried about both Felix and his deal. The currencies were wrong and it was stalling. Nothing was moving, apart from Lucia's angry eye-brows, the raging circumflexes.

Time to take some time out and visit an old friend, Joe thought. Who knew what he might learn?

Joe stared at the control panel beside the door. Again he reflected on the importance of the numbers. A few digits, random but correctly aligned and punched into the panel, would open that door for him and secure access to Moley. But one digit out of place and the system would refuse to function. Confuse a 9 with an 8, not a huge error all told, and everything was barred – such was the margin between success and failure. Huge endeavours could fail as they lay stranded between integers and the door stayed closed...

It's not the boulders that trip you up, thought Joe, but the small stones that lie in your path. Avoid the small stones and everything will be fine. Or should be fine, super snafu permitting...

Joe played around with the numbers on his fingers, exploring the pattern of Moley's code before finally pressing the numbers home. He stepped back a touch almost as his fingers explored with seeming familiarity the pattern of the arrangement. He found to his surprise that there was knowledge there. The spread of the hand was known to his memory. Recollection seeped through the touch of his fingers. They slotted together quite naturally in an old configuration. He tried again, and watched the inverted triangle of the first three numbers sit atop the natural triangle of the second three to be followed, using the final numbers, by the composition of a...

Amazing, he thought. Both numbers are very nearly the same. As I tap into Moley's control panel in the Barbican, I am in fact calling Control. That pattern is my old telephone call sign. The numbers are so very nearly the same. Only the 5 has been transposed into a 4. Otherwise the pattern is identical...Who would have thought it...? Did he but know it, Moley's door panel could take someone almost into the heart of British Intelligence.

And, of course, were the computer panel on the door wired up to BT...

Joe smiled at the connection as the wind screamed in its frenzy down the blank passageways and then out into the empty squares.

Undeterred by the similarity and refusing to acknowledge the existence of coincidence, Joe finally punched in the data, and pushed on the entrance door which opened softly to his pressure; he was still thinking about Felix. He slammed the door behind him and the wind ceased. He smoothed his hair down and caught the waiting lift. Then he sailed up the twenty or so storeys to Moley's apartment, rising higher and higher into the sky as the lift chugged boldly on its way.

How typical of Moley to live so high up in the Barbican! How very typical...!

He and Moley were very old friends. They went back more than twenty years. They had met when Joe had just emerged from university after his recruitment by British Intelligence and before his epic and perilous time of spying in Berlin with the Fat Man, for the most part in squares very like the Barbican. He had been parked by British Intelligence for a small while in the City with L'Houblyn, a quiet blue-blooded little stockbroking firm located somewhere in Finsbury Circus, to learn a few numbers. That was what the Gents had told him.

'You'll need numbers Joe,' they had added ominously. 'They're always handy for someone like you. They'll provide you with a bolthole.'

There in the old City, as a blue button on the old Stock Exchange trading floor and as an oik indistinguishable from everyone else, he had been friends with Moley, likewise a blue button and learning his trade in the old gilt-edged market. Moley of the rigorous approach and unspoken, undisclosed views, he of the Puritan voice and the fluttering eyebrows and the excruciatingly bad Oxford experiences...Moley of the threadbare suits which he wore as a protest against the porcine City philistinism...That had been Moley in the old days, a refusenik like them all. He had not exactly advocated the nationalisation of the stock exchange but the then senior partner at Fulford's would not have been pleased to hear his star analyst's true and heartfelt views on various investment situations.

And now twenty years or so later on, on that windy evening, in a place that so very closely resembled Cold War Berlin, the two of them were meeting, in order to play chess together and relive some old times in the halcyon days of their youth in the City...

Who would have thought it, who seriously would have ever dreamed that such different paths might meet again, if only for a brief encounter? And by the same token, who seriously dreamed that it was possible to go backwards in time?

Joe watched the numbers of the floors succeed each other and wondered what had become of Moley. They were fairly benign thoughts. He had fond memories of Moley. He wished that he could think the same even-tempered thoughts about Felix. No such luck – Felix the Assassin advanced just a further step in his direction every day and he, Joe, was powerless to stop him.

It would be Death by a Thousand Cuts and Joe was braced for it. Felix had penetrated Joe's investment meetings now, a very big breakthrough for him. His influence at ABC grew daily, almost by the hour.

Ready when you are, Death babe, Joe thought, as the lift climbed into the skies.

In the old days in the myriad of small bars and drinking clubs which ringed the old Stock Exchange, Moley and Joe had played chess in the early evening, as Moley had fulminated about the markets and Joe had listened intently.

In those far away days, when the City was a busy bustling prosperous village, almost a medieval manor in some respects, Joe had flitted from job to job between Berlin assignments, his path crossing that of Moley from time to time as he, Moley, marched on solidly to his first fortune and then to his second and then onwards again…The millions were never enough for Moley who had obsessed at every turn about his pile of gold and its height. But they had always found the time for some chess somewhere in a dark City bar. They had stayed remotely in touch, if such a phrase had ever had any meaning.

More thoughts by Joe about the altitude as the lift grunted to a halt somewhere in the clouds, clearly at risk from low-flying choppers.

What kind of person was Moley now, Joe wondered, as he stepped out of the lift and touched the bell to Moley's flat, dismissing Felix with difficulty from his imagination. Moley and he met that evening as old friends, that was understood, but each was a stranger to the other beyond that friendship. That too would perhaps be understood. Twenty years is a long time in a relationship, just as five minutes is a long time in the markets. People change. Without a chance meeting in Throgmorton Avenue a week ago, after Moley's earlier congratulatory phone calls, there would have been no meeting now. Moley and Joe were not exactly close now.

Serendipitous chance lay behind this meeting, thought Joe. But who was Moley now, beyond his colossal fortune?

The door opened and there he was, like Time reformed, tall, smiling, slightly askew, eyebrows fluttering as ever, hair in a haystack, and looking shabby in his pullover. Yes, shabby as ever, Joe had forgotten that detail. Moley kept an entire wardrobe of rumpled suits to suit all occasions. That was comforting. So nothing had changed because the dress code was still the same?

Same old Moley?

Fat chance, thought Joe as he buttoned into the situation. But maybe his chess has improved…?

Moley's hand was outstretched in welcome and the smile was on the eyes and the lips. Clearly the intelligence was still there.

They shook hands as old friends and Moley motioned Joe into the sitting room. Outside the flat lay a magnificent, stunning backdrop taking in the City with its spires; the curve of the river Thames; and then further out behind the dark straggling hinterland of South London, the Surrey hills. It could all be seen quite clearly in the setting sun.

A chess set, fully crewed with its pieces, sat patiently in the sitting room between two chairs. Ready for action! Without further ado! Ready to resume the chess movements and the friendship of twenty years by a tiny and insignificant, almost mechanical, movement of the chess pieces like Pawn to King Four, Knight to King Bishop Three, etc. etc.

And so time flowed ever onward for them both…Turn it on and turn it off….But was it that easy, Joe wondered, as he adjusted to the view.

'Just like old times, eh Moley? I see that you're ready for the off.'

Moley laughed and pointed towards the bottle that stood beside the table.

'Drink? Red wine? Or white?'

Joe nodded and full of camaraderie made a slurping gesture with his cupped hand. That had been traditional with them in the old days.

'And why not, Moley. I'll have some white.'

Smiling, Moley the Millions stepped with great deliberation towards the wine bottles and poured out a glass of white wine for Joe. Joe saw that it was a Chablis. Some things never seemed to change…

Still talking, Joe accepted the glass and true to the spirit of the occasion, took a quick swig before Moley had poured out his own wine. That was how they always drunk in the past – there had just been no time for niceties. Too much duty drinking to get through in the session for protocol to matter, for God's sake.

Yes, for God's sake draught it down and let's have another – Joe could hear the roaring of the bloods of his youth in the City bars as he quaffed his wine with gusto.

Joe placed his glass carefully on the table beside the chess sets and hovered beside one of the chairs.

'I'll need some more of this to play some chess with you, Moley. I don't play that often these days.'

Moley smiled again.

'Me neither. I think it must be over five years since I last picked up a chess-piece. And so cheers... Here's to our game. And of course to our serendipitous meeting...'

Something clicked in Joe's head. That didn't sound quite right for some reason. Not wholly Moley? Would he have deferred like that in the old days? Putting his moniker on the situation so obviously? Had the meeting been quite so accidental?

Joe's attention flickered for a second. No, he wouldn't have deferred like that – that was the correct answer. Senses began to stir at the back of Joe's head as he kept the smile pinned to his face.

Moley raised a glass to Joe, who hastily picked up his own glass from the table and then raised it in equal salutation, matching the gesture to the occasion. Both were smiling at each other. Then Moley sat down at the board without further ado, clutched a white and a black pawn into his two fists and ran them behind his back. Ancient ritual. Joe pointed and guessed wrong. More ritual – Moley always picked right. The white pieces fell to Moley, who crouched over the pieces in frowning concentration. A finger and thumb plucked away his right eyebrow – Moley's gesture, borne unchanged to that precise moment in time over all the years when they had not been in correspondence!

Then out came the move, as might have been predicted – Pawn to King Four. Moley's favourite opening, the one he used to semi-deadly effect, until it got to 8 in the evening and the Finsbury Circus drinking pole-axed him.

'Thank God for that, Moley. I thought you were going to make me sweat for a moment there, Moley. A Queen side opening, perchance, or something even more exotic?'

'No chance. I wouldn't know a Queen side opening from a hole in the ground these days.'

'Me neither!'

Joe felt reassured. So they were truly just a couple of City hoofers on the lam from the markets. He made the conventional chess response to Moley's opening and then off they both went, straining and struggling to recall the openings and play at least the semblance of presentable chess. Silence between them for a brief time.

Pawns advanced; knights gambolled; and bishops slithered. Action chess, to say the least. In the old days they had played with a portable chess set between them in the corner of a bar, sheltered from the jostling of the open-necked, roaring pinstripes by the angle of the door frame, as they struggled to concentrate; a bottle at least of Chablis stood between them. And now they were playing the same game but in very changed surroundings...

After very different careers, too. Joe doubted whether Moley had ever conceived of even the idea of Joe's Berlin days. Too busy making money to think about that little divertissement. So Joe too came with baggage to their quiet moment of nostalgia.

As ever, too, there were pauses between chess moves and the pace of the game slowed. There came the quaffing again of the wine as the level of the bottle sank rapidly; and then by unspoken agreement the inevitable chat about the markets commenced and claimed their attention. The pieces now were a medley of disconnected power spaces in suspended menace as both Joe and Moley slowed the play down and talked about the bonds. The pieces could wait for a brief time.

In the discussion, Joe played to Moley, who responded or not as he felt inclined. That was the way they had always conversed. Joe served and Moley returned serve. With accuracy and venom.

'Greenspan has problems.'

'No question. But he doesn't have refinancing problems ...'

'Yet...!'

'Good point, Joe. But those yields...'

'There's a paradox here. The bond yields are too high so junk doesn't stand a chance. But if he can't reopen junk, then Greenspan's New Age economy goes straight up the pictures.'

'Correct. Because the New Corporates can't refinance through bank credit. And they don't have any cash flows to speak of. So...'

'And the dollar...?'

It was a deft, careful piece of work by Joe, that question about the $.

'Good point again, Joe. We'll talk about that later. I have some thoughts about all of that. Now are you going to move that Bishop or do I have to take it with my Knight?'

'You take that Bishop whenever you like Moley. It's all part of a carefully laid plot, as you will find out.'

Kitchen chess a la Barbican. No move was sacred and second thoughts about strategy were allowed, albeit only just.

'Joe, you always were a chancer. If you think that I'm going to allow that pawn of yours to make the back line, then you must think that I was born yesterday.'

More tugging by Moley at his eyebrows. Joe made the obvious replies.

'Day before, Moley, day before. Meticulous inaccuracy as ever, Moley. But I don't want to flatter your vanity by giving the game away... Anyway I'm not moving the Bishop. So you take it and see what happens. It's a sacrifice, know what I mean?'

'I know exactly what you mean. OK, I take....'

Moley reached across a confident arm to take Joe's Bishop. Then quite late in the day he saw Joe's nasty little stratagem. Circumspectly, the arm withdrew, like a crane slowly regaining its position. Joe registered perhaps by reflex that Moley was very keen to win their chess game. That was new. In the past neither of them had cared. But now, years further on, winning at chess might just have become a matter of prestige for Moley.

'...Or rather I don't take. All is revealed, Joe. So I push my pawn instead...Like so.'

The pawn edged across the board in all innocence and Joe realised that Moley had missed it completely. He thought some more about the game with difficulty, as Felix and Joe's special deal against Rivers Pugh flitted through his mind. Soon it would be time to confront that deal. Time enow but not time enough...

Joe stared at Moley's pawn. Tragic thoughts concerning Perdita oozed through Joe's mind and he suppressed them with savagery. He fingered a rook and then changed his mind.

'That was a very nasty idea you cooked up there, Joe.'

'It came naturally enough, Moley. Just thinking about it all paved the way. But now that you've seen through my little game, I'm going to do this. I'm going to shift my Bishop. Like so.'

And Joe moved his Bishop and Moley fell to a hideous frowning as he contemplated the impact of the move. Through the window, from where he was seated high aloft, Joe could just glimpse the peaks of the skyline, the spires of the City churches, the topmost points of the skyscraper blocks, and the edges of the hills bathed in the setting sun. A glorious peaceful scene.

And so who was Moley now, this creature seated opposite him, who was so desperately keen to win out during their little, mutual, but insignificant Proustian moment ?

Fingers tugged at an errant eyebrow as Moley stared at the board. A hand strayed towards his glass, and he slurped down some more Chablis as he continued to focus on the pieces.

Joe reckoned that it was easy enough for Moley to work out as they both stared at the board. Joe had made a mistake around move three and that had thrown his whole game out of kilter. His position now was hopeless. He was at Moley's mercy. But whether Moley realised that and shifted his pieces accordingly was quite a different matter. Moley had the choice. Or the option, as Joe's lawyers always said in cold deliberation.

In chess as in life, Joe remained remarkably still and waited for the imminent coup de grace. The game should be over very quickly, according to Joe's calculations.

Or not, as the case might be…

It was up to Moley now. Moley puffed and pondered and eventually reached his decision, as Joe waited for him to deliver the killing blow, very prepared to concede at once and start a fresh game. Not long to go now.

Moley reached out a hand and moved his King!

The King, the King, the King! Not the pawn! But the King! Wrong move! Quiet drama in a high room. Joe felt his eyeballs bulge. He breathed again… He paused a few moments, drinking in the sense of respite and wondering whether or not to enlighten Moley concerning his missed opportunity in order to force a swift mate there and then.

After a few moments Joe decided on balance to remain silent. He had dismissed the click in his head. But friendship, nevertheless, might have its limits. Best to play safe. It was a long time since he'd seen Moley, after all. Who knew where he'd been?

Joe sipped some more Chablis, and then made his move. He blocked his highly vulnerable centre with a Knight in order to protect the King and take him out of danger. He had been swiftly conveyed to a place of greater safety by the move. But who would have thought it? The game would now stretch on until midnight if not beyond, a chess match of classic, bitter attrition.

Oblivious to the opportunity which had gone begging, Moley nodded away in approval of Joe's move and then raised his head, gazing directly at him across the board.

'You're at ABC now I gather. How is that suiting you? A fine return to the City, I would have thought. It's a very big bank.'

Joe thought it was a very direct question for Moley to have asked. But he failed to bridle, indeed to react at all. The question still lay comfortably within the traditional parameters of friendship. Joe replied lightly about the huge burden of business and responsibility under his stewardship, much as all old friends can chat whose careers have prospered in tandem.

'Too early to say with any certainty. We have problems of course, but then doesn't everybody. Running three banks into a cross frontier merger takes a massive amount of administration. No holes in the accounts so far, at least not so far as I know, thank God and touch wood, but rearranging the personnel takes time and then some. Building the teams is a nightmare. And then there's the US election on the way as well…We just cannot work out which way the currencies will jump. Strong dollar and weak Euro or what? Strong pound? Who knows? It's a nightmare. Banks based in one country only have to worry about the domestic parities. But we're across frontiers. We see it all the time. It can be quite hair-raising. But what do you think, Moley? How do you see it?'

They were talking as they had always talked. That was one right back against Time, straight off the wall. Moley shrugged.

'Snowden wants a strong pound and what Snowden wants, he generally gets even if he loses something else as part of the bargain. Like his industrial base, for example. But you know what the UK is like – it can only do one thing at a time and that with difficulty. So I think I'd be betting on a 'No Comment' strong pound... I think the UK does 'no comment' strong pound rather well.'

Moley looked smug as he made his pronouncement. But it was pure bollocks. That was new for Moley, Joe thought. He had never for a moment appeared to be complacent in the past. But his comment suggested Moley Mark II had a PhD in smugness, or market, talking bollard, rubbish. Joe adjusted. He was tempted to disagree with the sage but in his idleness he refrained from comment. If I want strong pound arguments I can get all I want at the office, he thought. This is no place for fine tuning the discussion. Right now, I want some more Chablis.

'Quiff treating you OK?'

Again Moley was insistent in a way that puzzled and slightly irked Joe. More clickings in his head which Joe dismissed as paranoia. This was City talk on a higher level, Joe concluded. Even so, he found it mildly intrusive. The preamble had been too brief ahead of the interrogation. Joe lied easily, quickly and evasively in reply to Moley's question.

'Wonderful boss, Quiff, and extremely capable. I like him very much indeed. I think we're lucky to have someone of that calibre running the show. After Malcolm's death, it's a wonder we didn't finish up with some retread. But not so, it didn't happen like that, and we were lucky. The right man I think got the job in this case. He's been very supportive to me the past few months.'

Well versed in City speak, Joe sounded glib to the point of mendacity but his comments appeared to satisfy Moley who turned his attention back to the chess board. By instinct and forcing the point perhaps unwisely, Joe added a few more gobbets of flattery in order to test the market reaction.

'It's his grasp of a situation on a daily basis which I find so impressive. He's always there and he's always right on the ball. Such a fine ability to finesse a situation. Yes, we're lucky to have him.'

Joe needn't have bothered with the overdrive. Moley nodded absently. His attention was elsewhere. He was scrutinising the board, apparently satisfied by Joe's replies. The brow was well plucked by the fingers like tweezers as the Chablis smashed down. That is significant, thought Joe. Moley wouldn't have been so blase about my flattery some twenty years ago. At comments such as Joe had just uttered, Moley would have been hooting with laughter, stuffing his napkin into his mouth or biting the cuffs of his shirt, eyes streaming with tears of laughter and derision at the Pigs as he called the partners in his stockbroking firm.

But not so now. Joe had answered correctly and that was all that mattered to Moley apparently. The quality of the dialogue had deteriorated, in Joe's view.

Moley stared at the chess board, plainly trying to work out how to win the game. The pace slowed as he pondered. The pieces lay inert on their squares as the sun went down in the sky outside.

Joe thought again about the combination that he had punched into the door downstairs. Better not to mention its alternative meaning, he decided as he morphed by instinct and by degrees from frank sincerity into presentational mode, right there in front of Moley.

No, he told himself, I don't think that discussion about Cold War Berlin in the Eighties would serve any purpose just at this juncture. No purpose at all. For the time being I'm just a lucky banker sprung from nowhere who's made it in the City. That's what he wants and that's what he'll get. It's pro forma time all round. I'm a dummy. And a pliant one at that. Just watch me bend with the wind and the client.

Still more eyebrow tugging from Moley.

'You've certainly given me a problem here Joe with that move of yours. I'm going to have to think about all of this.'

'It's no big deal, Moley. You just lose a couple more pawns here and there and then you concede and we start a new game. Easy.'

Moley wrinkled his brow. He was not conceding. A fortune of £100 million plus does not give up like that.

'Just a minute, just a minute, Joe, let me think about that. I've been thinking about something else for the past few minutes…I've been distracted.'

Silence between them for a little while. What was on Moley's mind? Then Moley shot his question out at Joe quite abruptly, staring at him again across the board in a way that gave Joe much subsequent food for thought. Not much trace of erstwhile friendship in Moley's expression, that was for sure.

'You were at Martins before ABC weren't you, Joe? CEO for a while, I seem to remember? Very briefly. Yes?'

'That's right, Moley. Very briefly. Some one else wanted the job. Very urgently. So I resigned and the bank went bust. Amazing coincidence.'

'I remember. It was much talked about at the time. You got out at the right time. No question about that. With a very large cheque, as I recall?'

So had Moley arranged the funding for the Gilstons that evening? If he had done, Moley wasn't telling. Most certainly he would have been mixed up in it, like guaranteeing some escrow account in New York for George Gilston. He was now a true City Father; he had been 'made' in that respect. But Moley wasn't telling. Besides, that wasn't the purpose of the discussion, as Joe realised. Moley was trying to make a separate point. Very carefully as well.

Very, very carefully.

Joe was all ears. This was turning into an interview. It wasn't a meeting at all. Joe felt his insides starting to turn green, partly through excitement.

'And then you simply disappeared, Joe. You went to ground. No one knew where you'd gone. You became the invisible man. We didn't think we knew you anymore.'

The unspoken question hovered between them like an unresolved chess move. So what were you up to during your period of absence, eh? Answer the question, boy! Not part of the City gang – unthinkable! Not playing the game! We couldn't keep tabs on you…

Moley persisted. He was not the slightest bit friendly now. The Quiff's right-hand man at ABC was being put through the mill, just ever so slightly and far more than somewhat.

'One or two people in the City asked me about you and where you might be. I tried to be as helpful as possible but I couldn't tell them of course because I didn't know. That was during the period when we weren't in communication, if you remember. They asked me, these people that is, most of whom you will most likely know by now, they asked me how well I knew you and what your background was and where you'd come from. That kind of thing...They wanted to know more about you...'

Brief pause by Moley as he recharged his glass, emptying the bottle in the process. Joe thought about the entrance ticket to Moley's exclusive City club, which plainly came cheap these days at £100 million. A snip at that price. Moley draughted down a little more Chablis and resumed his speech.

' ... And I of course spoke out on your behalf. Quite eloquently, Joe, on your behalf. I don't think it cost me to be so supportive, but you never know these days in the City. It's not the place it used to be, I can vouch for that. But I didn't count the cost. Who cares, for an old friend one must make these sacrifices. I was resigned to that. But it did emerge in the course of discussion just how elusive you had been during your career in the City. Those periods in the Eighties, I recall, when you seemed to go from job to job....I didn't realise that you'd had quite so many jobs during that period. You never told me that. Your career was more like the Scarlet Pimpernel's than that of a City broker.'

'Experience, Moley, experience. That was what was driving it. But it was all a long time ago. Nearly every firm that I worked for has disappeared now. And it hasn't worked out too badly.'

Joe had not spoken defiantly, although he felt shocked by Moley's questioning mode. He tried to keep his tone of voice as light as possible. But Moley was putting him on the spot. That was obvious. What he had said about Joe not being truly known was ominous. The City hates an outsider. It squeezes them out.

But what Joe had just said about his jobs had been true, up to a point. Every job that Joe had done in the City had been organised for him by British Intelligence. They were careful about spoors and they left no traces. The pathway had vanished and no tracking was possible. And likewise the Gents had seen to his disappearance after the Martins' debacle, although his isolation then had involved pain of a different order. But for some reason and strange as it might seem, Joe felt reluctant to blurt out all of that to Moley, especially when Moley constituted such a sceptical audience. Joe was not disposed to reveal or discuss his alternative existence with anybody these days. A forest of alternative identities beckoned at that moment. He was a banker who had perfected the Indian rope trick – that was the story line and good enough for anybody, Moley included. Perhaps he was even quite a good banker, although he had to agree, it was the Indian rope trick that drew the crowds.

Moley changed the subject.

'This bottle's empty. I'm so sorry Joe, I hadn't realised we'd got through the Chablis so fast. Let's have another one. I want to talk about the Chron as well. I think it's going off the rails. Stone is taking a very independent line these days on the Euro. Not the City view at all. That's bad for him. He'll catch it sooner or later. Friend of your's, Joe, this Stone man?'

Joe made to reply, but Moley was too quick for him. He stood up and flicked his fingers, making a dry cracking sound with the bones. Imperiously. On his own manor.

To Joe's astonishment, a boy's sallow face appeared around the far distant door at the end of the sitting room, followed by a body that advanced into the room and moved towards them reverentially. So they had not been alone! Moley had not seen fit to reveal the presence of his eavesdropper! This was a very different Moley that Joe was encountering. Moley would not have withheld like that in the past. Some people might even say that concealing a third party on such an occasion, billed as a tete a tete, constituted sharp practice in the extreme although Moley would be bound to disagree with that comment. But Joe was shocked to find that they had not been alone. Moley had definitely not mentioned this small and trifling piece of information to him.

The young boy stood before them in penitent and regimented pose. He was perhaps a shade over twenty. He had the dull eye and scrawny head of a young seminarist committed for life to the highly structured love of God. He looked neither fearful or resentful, merely resigned. He stood in silence awaiting his instructions. His eyes were deep pools of obedient, total blankness.

Moley spoke to him briefly in what Joe thought he recognised as Italian. The instructions were clear – take away this bottle and bring me another one. Moley spoke with authority in his voice and without a trace of affection. The boy nodded understanding of the instructions and then went away. He returned almost immediately with a second full bottle of Chablis which he placed in front of the chess players. He then departed for a second time and disappeared. During the time he had carried out Moley's commissions, he had not spoken a single word.

Moley refilled their glasses with gusto.

'I can see that you're worried that something you might have said will have been overheard. Impossible. He – Petro that is – doesn't speak a word of English. That's why I bought him, so that I could have someone utterly discreet in the house, whether I was here or not.'

This is not a moment to display a fragile liberal conscience, Joe thought, old friend as Moley might be or no. This is a time to accept the status quo.

'Where did you buy him?'

'In Italy. On holiday. Just below Salerno. Nice chap isn't he? I must say we get along very well together. Famously. He really fits into my household. I found him in a village. I was staying with some friends in a villa down there; he was doing the serving; and we became aware that his mother was impossibly over-burdened financially. So we came to an arrangement, whereby I send the family some money and in return I get the use of Petro as my houseboy. I've had him for over a year now and it's proved to be a most satisfactory arrangement. He can be sulky but it passes as soon as it's pointed out to him.'

Moley paused expectantly but Joe made no reply. He concentrated on the chessboard.

'And the Chron? You don't like Stone's line?'

But Moley wanted to show off his house-boy some more. Briefly the Chron had faded from his mind.

'I don't think his English has improved very much since he's been in London but his knowledge of fine wines has come along by leaps and bounds. That's something worth acquiring, I would have thought. I take full responsibility for that aspect of his education.'

Poor little bugger, thought Joe. That's exactly what he needs to know for his pasta shop. His chances of survival must be zero. His papers will be out of order so he will have no hope of getting back to Italy or wherever, his mother won't want to see him because she wants the money, and meanwhile he's stuck here up in the clouds in the Barbican with Moley of all people. What a nightmare for anybody!

Joe reckoned he was beginning to see what Moley's game might be. But he said nothing; he wasn't sure of the drift in his thinking. Moley interrupted his reflections.

'This game will go on for ever and I don't think either you or I have the time for that kind of thing these days. I, for one, have some business to put through in New York. What say you to putting the board to one side, keeping the pieces just as they are, and resuming another time? That gives us an excuse to meet and have another chat, which I would like, I have to tell you, Joe. Yes, I would like that very much.'

'Excellent idea, Moley. I hadn't thought about it in that way but now that you mention it, it seems optimal. Just like the old days. Yes, definitely another meeting. With some Chablis, of course.'

'Of course, the chess and the Chablis come up with the rations. It's rare to be able to meet and chat with such old friends, so all of this is wonderful. Now whose move was it when we resume? We must keep a check on that point at least.'

'Yours,' said Joe without hesitation as he thought he saw Moley's game even more clearly, wondering about the sacred ties of friendship. Was Moley somehow in breach, and at risk from the Gods because he was in breach? Did trashing a friendship constitute some kind of awesome crime in the eyes of the Furies?

'What ever happened to Ratty, Moley? What became of him in the end?'

In the good old, bad old days of the old gilt-edged market, when order or Mr Peter reigned supreme and all gilts business stopped for the Government Broker, the Lord Cromwell, to finish his morning cuppa char in his office, Moley had been close, close friends on the gilts pitches with another oik, highly prone to being ragged by the jobbers on the trading floor and then losing his temper. Hence, naturally, Ratty. And thus by swift extension, Moley had emerged as himself and as Moley , such was the eye and predilection of the old market for nicknames, pet names and sobriquets.

'A bad business, Joe. He got his money as we all did at the end of the Eighties, when the brokers were taken over, but he decided to spend it. Aggressively. To cut a long story short, he spent it very well and very quickly. I lost touch with him because he seemed to live for most of his time in New York playing blackjack. A couple of months ago, he was found dead in a field somewhere in Blackheath clutching a bottle and quite, quite penniless. Hadn't eaten for days, apparently, they discovered. Such a shocking end for such an old friend. I was distraught for a time.'

'We all have to go, Moley.'

'Yes, but hopefully, not quite as badly as that. Imagine, in a field with the bottle. That bottle was half full, too. And cheap wine.'

'Ratty wouldn't have liked that.'

'I dare say. But he was such a sharply dressed broker all his life. Such a stickler for…Ah well, you know what I mean. I mustn't dwell on any of that. It's long gone like Ratty, I must confess, all of that little world which we inhabited for so long. It is still a mystery to me just why the English trashed their financial empire the way they did at the end of the Eighties. But that's what they did. And who am I to complain…?'

'Quite so, Moley, we mustn't grumble.'

'Now when shall we try to meet up again?'

'To be decided by telephone? I can make this time of the day quite easily. All my meetings are over by early afternoon for the time being on this particular day.'

'Perfect. I'll keep the chess set safe here and we can resume just as soon as you turn up…And maybe chat some more about currencies?'

And you can resume your questioning about relations with the Quiff, thought Joe. Just to keep tabs on me, so that any untoward comments can be reported straight back to the Quiff and the rest of the neighing feudal hordes in the Square Mile. Such a neat little set-up. I can of course duck out from the chess games but much good that will do me. I'll be tagged in some other way, mark my words. And marked down for hue and cry. Moley is just taking time out, amidst all this passage of arms, to tell me that I'm not trusted; that I'm on red alert for good behaviour; and that I'm guilty until proved innocent.

And the slave? The slave has been produced, I guess, to warn me what my true status should – and will – be if I step out of line. As a piece of stage management this has been superb. Not a line out of place...Pure pantomime, but beautifully done...The Margrave couldn't have done it better.

'Tell me, Moley, is it possible to step out onto the terrace? I just want to feel the wind up at this altitude.'

Joe felt the need for some air.

'Of course you can. I keep it locked for obvious reasons but by all means step out. Be careful, though. The wind is very strong up here.'

Moley tugged at his pocket and produced a bunch of keys. He selected one out of the bunch and walked across to the windows and fiddled with the key in the lock. Then he stepped back and pressed a button in the wall. The patio door slid back a fraction and the wind howled like a beast in pain through the exposed crack, driving the curtains every which way.

Mayhem and disorder in the room instantly. Joe quailed from the implications.

'On second thoughts, I think I'll pass on the panoramic views, Moley. You're right. It's too windy.'

Moley smiled and closed the patio door. Then he saw Joe carefully to the lift. No sign of the boy as Joe left. The flat seemed empty of life to Joe as he left it. But where was the boy hiding? And how would Moley treat him on his return, when the two of them were alone?

'Until next week then, Joe, or sometime soon. This has been a real treat and I look forward to the next meeting – and the chess of course.'

'Me too, Moley. This has been a truly epic encounter. Keep those chess pieces in order. Guard them well, especially that knight of your's on that exposed square. Or was it mine? I can't quite remember now.'

The lift rumbled down its many storeys as reluctantly as it had ascended them. Joe reached the ground and went in search of his driver. He was in a hurry. Next stop was not quite Hampshire but somewhere on the way. He still had time for a small rendezvous with his man Stanley in a small pub somewhere en route to Perdita; Pugh Park; Rivers Pugh; and of course, Mrs Gulliver, self appointed presiding genius in residence of Pugh Park now that Lady Pugh, keeper of the household, was dead and buried.

The very thought of Mrs Gulliver was enough to make Joe shudder. He needed to talk with Stanley even to be able to contemplate dealing for two minutes with Mrs Gulliver. Mrs Gulliver truly gave him the pip.

★　★　★　★　★

Annie sat in the car with Pa Lee as they drove from the US embassy in Grosvenor Square to Pa Lee's home in Notting Hill. It was not a long trip but throughout it Pa Lee stayed in radio contact with the embassy, holding the microphone in front of his mouth and just mumbling away to it, so that his voice was heard constantly back at base. It was routine. No one expected a rocket attack on the car that day just beside Hyde Park in London; on one level the UK was very well surveilled. But this was the US abroad. It took no chances. Annie sat beside Pa Lee and said nothing, listening to the mumbling. She waited for the journey to finish before launching into the real points under discussion.

The points were serious. Very serious. The UK was under pressure. Big pressure. It was all going to take a lot of explaining. It was not going to be easy.

The car reached Pa Lee's house and stopped in front of the gates. The gates eventually opened to the car, which drove into the complex very carefully and then down a ramp into the underground parking space. Only then when the engine had been switched off and the car was completely protected within the parking space did Pa Lee turn his radio off and cease to communicate with the embassy. From the parking space he could step straight into the house, one brightly-illuminated stride away. Impossible for an assassin to be lurking there because of the surveillance cameras which would have picked him out instantly.

Annie followed Pa Lee into the house at just about the same time as Joe was waiting in vain for Moley's coup de grace on the chess board.

Pa Lee escorted her upstairs and into a pleasant sitting room that gave onto a garden in yellow summer bloom, now taking the early evening sun. He left her there in order to change out of his suit and into jeans. He liked to do the real business dressed comfortably. Some minutes later he reappeared, looking like a cowboy, with a tray of drinks on his arm.

He checked the phone in the room very briefly. The last time he and Annie had spoken in this room, the discussion had been broken off temporarily as Pa Lee took a call direct from the President. Pa Lee preferred to be wearing jeans when he spoke to his boss.

The drinks were fixed and Annie chose sparkling water. Pa Lee sat down opposite her and then started talking at once.

'You know exactly what our game plan is so I won't detain you long over it. Since Vietnam, America has located its investments in Asia to build a ring of thriving economies around China and it has placed its military hardware in Europe as a counter to the old Soviet empire. Now we are switching these two because we see China as the main military threat. So we're pulling investments out of Asia and putting them into Europe and relocating the hardware in Asia. As we sell in Asia and pull out investment from that area, the dollar is going to go through some very odd movements as you might expect but we've allowed for that. Simple. Now where does that leave you, Annie?'

Pa Lee might have been discussing his geraniums, he spoke in such matter of fact tones. Annie twiddled her glass and then replied:

'The old Soviet empire has regrouped and is starting to pursue an expansionist policy. That is obvious. Oil prices are high; the IMF has been milked dry; and the Soviets – let's call them that for want of any other term and in recognition of the reality of things – are flush with cash. They think they're back in the game, which they might well be. They are out to cause trouble and they are reactivating their old core units abroad, where they can. Ahead of the US election, and they expect Kerry to win so that the Clinton open-handed policies will continue, they see many opportunities...'

Annie could see the difficult part of the analysis coming up fast. Best to get it over with as quickly and as smoothly as possible, she thought. She braced herself. It would not be pleasant but there was no other way. Pa Lee would not be pleased, but the words had to be said. Those sounds constituting words and adding up in total to communicable intelligence had to be emitted across a short distance to Pa Lee in this pleasant room bathed by the setting sun and they had to carry their full quota of meaning.

Better out than in... Words are very important in the intelligence world.

The words in turn, once emitted, would make their short journey in space and time and would then register with Pa Lee in his brain and make their appropriate impact. And he would react accordingly. That was all that could be said about this future event, impending very shortly and impacting on arrival. But again she braced herself. It was not going to be pleasant. But there again name anyone who was delighted by the disastrous turn of events in the UK.

Another confession of the UK's appalling inadequacy? Or just a fuck-up and as such unavoidable?

Meanwhile Pa Lee nodded. All of Annie's statements were known. Nothing new there.

Annie took a deep breath. This was how and where she had come into game years ago. But the confession was not going to be easy.

'The biggest and most prestigious of the Soviet satraps abroad obviously was the Bank of England. Inheriting this jewel from the old Russian Secret Service, the Soviets controlled the Bank almost throughout the twentieth century, which accounts for the frequent oddity of its decisions. As a prize it outranks everything outside of Russia in terms of its sheer importance. So…'

Her voice tailed off and she glanced around her briefly.

'We thought that we had nailed the Bank and cleaned it out when we got rid of Gloster…'

Pa Lee sat impassively, listening to her dreary tale.

'But we were wrong. We glitched. There is no other word for it. We glitched enormously. All our work went for nothing. The Soviets regrouped.'

A quizzical look came into Pa Lee's eye as his features tightened a fraction but otherwise he made no response.

'We timed the coup against Gloster to coincide with the Election which was fair enough. Many years of preparation all worked perfectly. Gloster went and we had the Bank where we wanted it. We were all ready to pull it into structure and clean it out immediately after the Election. But what we didn't know, couldn't have known in fact, was that Snowden, the incoming Chancellor, had his own plans for the Bank which had been formulated for him, in Opposition, by a Soviet plant on Snowden. The old Soviets had seen Snowden coming and they were afraid that the Bank would come under even closer surveillance under a Labour administration than it had done under Clarke and the Tories. They had made their own plans for the Bank which they duly fed to a gullible Snowden. Came the Election and came the revelations which for us were shocking. They amounted to full-scale independence for the Bank. It was out of the cage again! The Bank had wriggled free of us. The Bank was back in Russian hands.'

Pa Lee nodded. It was neither a nod of sympathy nor one of acquiescence. It was simply a nod. He was following the story. That was all Annie had to go on.

'The Soviets had a replacement for Gloster waiting in the wings at the Bank called Stobart, a career official at the Bank who duly got the job as Governor as a stop-gap after direct representation to the Prime Minister to keep out any outsiders and the most God-awful departmental in-fighting in Whitehall I have ever seen. I have to admit that we bungled almost the whole of this. We were not prepared for the coup, nor the way that the Soviets had been able to position. The Bank was able to exploit this, as well as its' new-found freedom. The Bank always falls between the cracks in the UK – none of the security services has direct responsibility for monitoring the Bank. It sits at the crossroads of the Foreign Office influence; the Home Office; the City; the Government in Whitehall; and Westminster. And it is always deferred to because of the massive power of its patronage in the City. Not every civil servant wants to be a hero and many of them would like to have a portfolio of company directorships at the end of their careers. So the Bank is the civil servants' Shangri-La. It is never monitored and when it is subjected to some surveillance, well, it is very light – all you can see up my sleeve is my elbow, that kind of thing… But it is just as much a physical reality and identity as Saddam Hussein's Iraq. And just as much as a force for Soviet influence, too, under Stobart's new management.'

Pa Lee spoke dryly.

'I can see that. This all leaves the IMF pretty high and dry in its attempts to discipline the Russian economy, I guess.'

Annie continued after sipping her water.

'This tale gets worse before it gets better, I can assure you. That is only part of it.'

More water. Annie needed it.

'To continue… Stobart, the present Governor, gets the job and sets about immediately reorganising the Bank so that our coup against him and the Bank will not be repeatable. Never, ever. He plans to make the Bank truly independent, liker a self-contained city state in the Middle Ages, so that henceforth it is invulnerable to any attempts at control. Quite literally. Of course the fact that the Bank is now de facto independent means that he can proceed with absolute impunity. Snowden indeed encourages him to act with resolution. Knowing this, Stobart moves very fast indeed. First, he arranges for the Deputy Governor to be recruited from one of the Soviets' old and highly reliable stamping grounds and source of trouble, Balliol College, Oxford. He puts in Dr Q, as he is known. Dr Q is a long term plant by the Stasi – as Professor of Economic Strategy at Balliol, he has been waiting some fifteen years for this moment. Now Dr Q is no banker and perhaps not very good as an economist but he is a professional. Top flight. Fully trained by Stasi and Moscow. He knows exactly how to go about consolidating control at the Bank. After Angola, the Bank was easy meat for him. And everything surrounding the Bank. He is a very brutal man indeed is Q and he is not squeamish about his methods. He butchers the place, all under the guise of modernisation. He is feared and hated within the institution within a very short space of time. So, for example, the Monetary Policy Committee, half composed of academics drawn from outside the Bank which Snowden installed at the time of the Bank's independence, is bounced around from pillar to post. It is hustled and frightened and intimidated by all manner of violent threats, all orchestrated by Q. In theory this Committee takes its decisions about rates on the evidence before it. In practice, the Committee does what the Bank tells it to do. And that means Stobart and Q. Nobody else counts. All the decisions about rates which they take are then rubber stamped by the Committee, so that in effect Moscow is now running the UK's interest rate policy, and hence the currency. First blood to the intriguers and then some.'

A little more water for Annie before she resumed speaking. God, but this is hard going, she thought, admitting to all of this! We might as well become plumbers, for all the good we do as an espionage operation.

'Having cowed the Bank, Stobart and Dr Q go about the second stage of their programme; this amounts to an ethnic cleansing in the City. The Soviets are not going to lose control of the jewel in their crown a second time. They are very thorough. Very nearly all the fund managers and analysts known to hold views at variance with those of the Bank on anything are fired over quite a short period of time. Dissent becomes dissidence in a very short space of time. The ethnic cleansing is not so difficult for Stobart and Q to accomplish since the Bank can establish from the trades going through the markets; investment returns; and the economic reports just where fund managers are invested and what the analysts' views might be. And they see all the reports anyway as a matter of protocol. Hence the Bank's patronage is massive; not a single senior appointment can be made within the City unless it has been approved at the level of the Governor's office. A mere phone call from Stobart's office indicating disapproval of what Such and Such has written or purchased is all that is needed for the said So and So to be given his cards. The refuseniks are thrown out en masse. So they all come to heel with great rapidity. Dr Q also revives the idea with great vigour of the Bank's black lists, a feature of the Bank's traditional methods of control within the Square Mile. These are circulated to all headhunters on a weekly basis. It is very systematic. Q is thorough. Eventually, as I said, no appointment can be made in the City without the Bank signifying approval. The ethnic cleansing takes place very rapidly with great efficiency and, irony of all ironies, with the outspoken approval of the Labour administration since the Bank appears on the surface to be doing such a good job. Snowden congratulates himself in public that he's in control and that he's tamed the Bank. It is all very surrealistic. But the bottom line is that the bad boys are thrown out of the City and no good boys can get into it because of the blacklisting. To sum up so far, Stobart and Q behave like old-style Soviet party bosses, running their little piece of empire with ruthless precision, the only difference being that their power base just happens to be located in London. We were wrong fundamentally. We thought the Soviets were seeking a warm water port – which they were but it just happened to be a friendly centre of capital, not warships! And just to be sure that the Stobart : Q duo hangs onto its power this time, they have reactivated an old but very rich ex-stockbroker Soviet sympathiser called Moley. His job is to inspect the borders between the City and the Press and play vigilante. He roots out what he; Q; and Stobart would describe as intruders. Moley is really the master card in all of this, almost the master-stroke of the whole coup indeed. Whomsoever the Bank thinks will prove supple is offered some form of bribe; corruption, anyway, is encouraged among the journalists. No comebacks that way. But Moley adds an extra dimension. He acts as a kind of game-keeper for the City demesne. No question but it is a very successful policy – Moley is rich and can therefore act with impunity because he is protected by his wealth as well as by the Bank. He is well known within the City and also to the Press so that he has an instant calling card. He can patrol the border at leisure. Meanwhile, the bulk of journalists pose no problem since the bulk of them, as I said, have been bribed into silence or submission long ago by the Bank. The institutions are the main threat to the Bank's total control. But Moley is active on this front too, holding and hosting a series of impromptu meetings which just coincidentally help him – and the Bank – to identify the diehard refuseniks. Over lunch...To be followed by a call from the Bank...A call from the Bank to any institution which has hired someone not instantly acceptable to the Bank will result in the loss of business by that institution if the unacceptable individual in question is not fired by lunchtime the same day. So you can guess what happens – it works every time. This is a totalitarian system in full working order, using cruelty as its maximum weapon. Now...'

Annie paused again. This was really going to be excruciating. She would almost prefer to have cut her tongue out than say these few short words. But she ploughed on. They had to be said. It was a mess, a total mess. Pa Lee looked at her steadily without comment.

'Yes, to continue... Because of the Bank's complicated relationships with the Home Office and the Foreign Office, it will be immediately clear to anyone like Dr Q taking this kind of interest just where the British agents are located, not so much abroad but certainly in the City, because that was where we could always hide them until we needed them. Because the Bank has always been trusted, you understand, although that in itself begs so many questions I will have to come back to it later...Anyway we had shown our hand in the coup against Gloster, the coup which failed through bad timing, Murphy's Law and God knows what else combination of cock-ups... So of course Dr Q weeds out the agents immediately. They are winkled out and they are all fired. More or less at once as soon as Q takes over. A complete clear-out.'

Pa Lee looked at the ceiling. Then he spoke. He was shocked too.

'My God, this is awesome. You've got no one there.'

'No one at all. We've been stripped bare.'

'So London, the second financial centre of the world, or maybe even the first, is now under the total control of the old Soviets.'

'That's about the size of it. Yes, just about…But it is worse even than that…'

'I don't believe that's possible.'

'Wait until I tell you. Still here? There's not much more left to tell.'

Annie could see Pa Lee eyeing his phone. There was going to be a call put through to the US very shortly and she could guess exactly who would receive that call.

'We know that there's another mighty coup planned, one that will drag the UK into the ambit of the old Soviets permanently. It is a coup involving the markets in some way. We think it may be a currency coup but we have no real way of knowing. We have gauged this from other sources but essentially we are flying blind. So what the coup involves; and where or when it may happen, we have absolutely no way of knowing. We are blindfolded. We know absolutely nothing. And why? Simple – in the past we would have relied on the Bank to provide us with this information, which we now realise might have been bogus or otherwise. But now there is no information at all coming out of the Bank, unless it suits Q and Stobart. And that means, as of now, no information. Those two have declared UDI, fully supported by Snowden, our elected Chancellor. So we know nothing about any coup impending. The Bank can just about bring itself to show us the weekly returns – and there's absolutely damn all that we can do about it. It's a coup; game set and match; and we're out of the game.'

That was it. She'd said it all. Nothing left to add. She sat back in the chair. Pa Lee looked at her again.

'What you're telling me, Annie, if I understand it all correctly, amounts to this – your intelligence effort is completely paralysed. There is no further input from you guys that can be trusted.

You've been wiped out. MI6, MI5 and the rest of it, forget it. It's over. Correct?'

'Correct. Our intelligence effort still functions on paper so to speak, and functions very effectively but it cannot actually do anything. To all intents its brain has gone. The whole thing is non-functional. The links from the Bank run everywhere throughout Whitehall in a way that even we did not quite understand at the time because of course we trusted the Bank. We took it for granted, not realising that was exactly where the precise centre of the UK was located. So when we tried to get rid of Gloster we treated the whole thing as a one-off. We thought that just getting rid of the spider was enough. But we overlooked the web. We are as much a part of that web as the Bank itself. So with Stobart and Dr Q in charge we're paralysed. Relations between the Bank and MI6 were always very close. But now that we know that the Bank is a hostile force, we cannot be certain that MI6 itself, for example, isn't either fully penetrated or its plans known well beforehand. It would be entirely likely that MI6 is wholly penetrated at the senior level because Spanish practices are not unknown to that organisation. The Bank has always been on feed to them by way of jobs etc on retirement. So why not? So we're paralysed. We can't make a move. We know, for example, that the Soviets are planning a political advance from where they are located in the City, but when it happens and what it amounts to...Well, that's anybody's guess. Certainly not ours. We can't trust our own information and even if we do that we can't act on it because we're not clear that it isn't already known. We can't be sure about anything. We're out of the game.'

Pa Lee looked at the ceiling.

'My God...'

Long pause. There comes a moment in the career of any official when the template fails, when the signposts point the wrong way and when the road maps are plain wrong. Pa Lee had reached this moment. He was in a black hole and at a dead end after five minutes of discussion. Black uncharted infinity loomed. He could have been anywhere. Every supposition he might have made about the immediate future was now invalid. Pa Lee did what all officials do under these circumstances, short of holding a meeting. He reached for reassurance. He asked about his deal. He borrowed some time.

'And Joe? How safe is he, doing our deal?'

'Safe for the time being but that won't last. Dr Q is closing in on him. Not life-threatening yet but in a month or so…He's on the list, that's for sure. Just as soon as Q can find a way of dislodging him from ABC, he will do so – and then very quickly. Very likely by using Moley himself. Moley and Joe used to be friends in the City years ago. Very good friends, but that was before Moley took the many Moscow shillings on offer to him – the bribe can never be to excess for Moley. Q, via Moley, will know how to exploit that. Very likely Moley will have been in touch already with Joe with the idea of applying his usual squeeze. They're bound to start meeting.'

'That takeover deal has to go through…'

Pa Lee started to run through in his own mind the implications of what Annie had just told him. He was still impassive; he could still receive information, like any other human being. But he was agitated as well. His brain was in a turmoil. He stared at the ceiling and very slowly ran a finger round the inside of his collar. It was the nearest Pa Lee ever came to admitting that he might be racked by tension. But it was a telling gesture. Round and round the collar went the finger as he slowly digested the implications of the words which Annie had just fired across the room at him. He raised his eyebrows too as he evaluated her briefing. Very slowly and with great caution, he enunciated a sentence.

'You know, Annie, this might be a winning line for those Moscow boys. They might just have got us licked with this one. Yeah, just might have got us licked. I see no way of dislodging those two guys, Stobart and Q. Do you?'

Not a bad comment from a man who has just seen his country's first line of defence ripped away in a flash. Pa Lee was still functioning as a sentient being- but only just.

Some news is just too hard to bear.

Annie hesitated before speaking. She had to take it all very slowly. The meeting was evolving as well as could be expected, but it was still very tough going. Trust is an elusive concept, especially when you've just admitted to letting a super power down in a very big way.

'We think we may have a plan...Just the glimmerings of something, but it may act as a holding operation.'

Silence from Pa Lee. This might have been an occasion which called for a wry smile from him, plus a kind of joshing 'Yeah, you and your plans' reaction and a sceptical shake of the head. But not this time. Pa Lee snapped his head up and down a couple of times but otherwise he kept his face very straight.

'Uh huh.'

'It is a very simple scheme. And it looks as if it might work, in terms of destabilising Stobart and Q in their positions which for the time being have to be viewed as permanent at the Bank. But it is very much a plan conceived au naturel, if you like.'

'Explain all that, if you will. I don't follow you, Annie.'

'It works using the country's legal functions in a very straightforward way. That plus a few other tricks which I will tell you about. All very ingenious and plausible but as such it takes time. Our scheme has to meander along in its own sweet way for the time being although I have to tell you that appearances will be deceptive. It has all been conceived very much with the US election as a background element in respect of our timing. And that is not so far away now. So the ploy won't continue indefinitely. During this present dead time, there is nothing we can say or do with respect to any of our people, like for example Joe, which might be viewed in the slightest way as indicating our help for him. We must withdraw all support for him. Everything must proceed as normal. There must be no sign at all that we are in the game. Otherwise, Stobart and Q will surely get wind of our plan and react accordingly. They can still – just – protect themselves. If they see what we plan, what we're on about, then they can manoeuvre their way free by simply not taking the bait, bait which in the context of their fears about the next US President they are bound to gobble up. That is our scheme and the path is well baited – and that is all we have to offer by way of solution in this impossibly troubled situation. So Joe and the others must fend for themselves, I'm afraid. That is the bottom line of all of this. They are on their own.'

Pa Lee whistled quietly for a second then leaned forward to ask his question.

'And his, or rather my, deal? The only reason we're doing this deal, the only reason that we put Joe into ABC, is for him to do that deal. That is all he must accomplish. Can he do it? Is it feasible? I shudder to think what might be the reaction in Washington, if they think that the Soviets can get their hands on some of that hardware. That bid must go through. As we shift our military capability from West to East, we cannot take the risk of leaving anything behind here in Europe which the Soviets might be able to pick up. That company that he's trading contains enough bio-warfare breakthroughs anyway...'

Pa Lee paused.

'I won't continue. You know what I'm talking about and you know how important all of this is. So can he be protected?'

He looked at Annie for a moment in vain hope and then answered his own question.

'No, of course he can't be protected. How stupid of me even to ask the question. So our deal is also in jeopardy?'

Annie nodded.

'Everything is in play. It all depends on the Bank of England. They control the whole of the City. Always have done and always will do. As of now, and for our purposes, that means Stobart and Q. And you now know what they amount to. So if they get wind of what lies truly behind the facade of Global, then they will intervene and try to swing the deal in the direction of more friendly companies. That means Russian-based companies. They can do that quite easily. You see, once you control the City, you control all the big institutional shareholders as well, especially since you've cleaned out all the refuseniks. The institutions will respond to the promptings of the Bank. By tradition, by deference and by idleness. That is how the City functions. But now on top of all that obedience coming up from the banks and the rest of them there sits a hostile direction. It is as if you were trying to do a deal in Moscow, not London. Think of it along those lines...And all of this is before we've thought about including the Russian oligarchs in our calculations.'

It was Pa Lee's turn to nod.

'I begin to get the picture. Yes, I think I see what you mean. Of course…'

He smiled at Annie, who was shocked by his sense of humour breaking through.

'Yeah, Annie, I guess this kind of redraws the lines a little…Food for a little thought, I guess…And this coup which you mentioned? I mean your coup…?'

Annie managed a wan little smile in reply. She felt that the clouds were lifting just a fraction and that the worst of the interview might be over. It had been hard going and an enormous amount of briefing with Pa Lee lay ahead of her. But the emphasis in their discussion was shifting from the confrontational to the constructive. That was something to treasure. And she had liked Pa Lee's smile at the very bottom of his despairs as she was unfolding all the bad news just now. She thought Pa Lee must be a very brave and resilient man and she felt just a little more at ease and reassured.

'Could I have some more water before I launch onto that and what we know of the Soviet intentions…?'

'Of course, Annie, let me fill your glass. And then let's talk.'

Pa Lee stood up and walked across to her with the bottle of water and refilled her glass. Outside the sun had just finally set and the garden was full of summer shadows. A beautiful setting for a tragic discussion, Annie thought. Wasn't Nature wonderful?

★　★　★　★　★

Joe's driver had problems with traffic all the way through London but Joe did not fuss. He sat in the back and brooded at first about Moley and the sadness of the ambivalence of his old friend. He didn't like the idea of the slave one little bit. Joe had survived too much exposure to people who had been stripped of their rights to accept those pale dead eyes of Moley's presumed catamite with equanimity. Outside the car the solid mass of stationary metal snarled and jerked in line all the way round Hyde Park. Moley was not going to be easy, that was for sure. Good friends did not threaten like that. And did Moley have ideas for some kind of set-up? Who knew – Moley & Co were now all tinged with grey and shot through with violent lights in a way that Joe had not anticipated. Moley would take some careful reflection before Joe reached his decision about his old friend.

Joe's driver was reassuring in an insistent way that they'd be out of London shortly and fair flying along but Joe paid him little heed. The driver made his point strongly and eventually Joe mumbled away in his replies before he gave up on placating him. No point in arguing and none really in chatting. Joe didn't trust his driver one little bit. He didn't trust anybody at ABC. Not after Moley's pep talk that evening.

Eventually Joe got bored with thinking about Moley and his attention veered round to Felix.

Worlds collided as he did so.

There was Felix Mark ABC which he knew all about as Felix with a smile went to work on slicing his way into Joe's empire and cutting Joe out of his job. Joe was watching the process of insertion by Felix with fascination. There might be a two-way street fairly shortly on that business if Joe's researches on Felix matured although Joe couldn't be certain that the disclosures would register much anyway with the Quiff. The Quiff struck him more and more as a bought man; the body language said it all. The Quiff was a man on the take as well as the make, most likely cheaply purchased by Felix, and a negligible force for good in Joe's universe. Enough then of Felix ABC – that was all a known commodity and events would take their course. Joe reckoned that it would still take Felix a further year or so of departmental intrigue before he could really start to embarrass Joe to the point of absorbing his empire, by which stage Joe would have done his deal and be out of ABC for ever. Unless of course Felix had some other coup planned which would unhorse Joe rather sooner...

But there was more to it all than that. Joe continued to reflect on Felix, registering unconsciously that his car suddenly appeared to be moving. Cars thinned out on either side of him as they gathered speed. But Joe was buried deep in memories of people he'd known years ago. He was oblivious to the traffic. He was thinking now about Felix Version Master Spy, of whom Joe knew a great deal. Joe tried to recall, but couldn't do so with total accuracy, whether or not Felix had been mixed up with the Hitler Diaries fraud of years ago in Germany. He remembered Felix dancing into their hotel in Berlin and claiming that he'd made a great deal of money out of...? Out of whom? Now what had been the name of that German fraudster? The Fat Man had known him well – that was for sure. Indeed, as Joe now suspected and as indeed the pattern of events coming back to him over the years strongly indicated, the Fat Man might well have arranged the whole thing. That kind of scam would have been right up his street... But what was the name of the forger? Yes, just what had he been called?

'We're here Joe. We've arrived. How long will you be on your little drink?'

The driver broke in on Joe's thoughts and Joe looked up more than a little surprised to find himself well clear of London, deep in the dark countryside. They were parked in the usual spot, beside the tiny complex of pubs in the village which lay on his route three quarters of the way back to Pugh Park. Time for a swift glass of country beer with Stanley, before he encountered the delights of Mrs Gulliver across the dinner table...

There was always a great deal of behind in what that woman said.

There were two pubs in the complex, which lay cheek by jowl together on the outskirts of the village, adjacent and almost but not quite contiguous. Stanley, Joe assumed, would be sitting waiting for him in the further establishment, connected to the first pub by a common Gents lavatory. As Joe had discovered, they do things differently in Hampshire.

As a precaution in order to wrong foot his driver, should his driver, a company man to the manner born, ever get so curious as to check up on him, Joe always went into Pub No 1, nipped out through the back bar and then into the Gents. From which glorious point of locational neutrality he then entered Pub No 2, to encounter Stanley seated beside the hearth in the saloon bar, reading quietly beneath the orange lamp and just nearing the end of his first pint.

Stanley was important to Joe. He had become his honest and impartial eyes and ears in the markets. Joe didn't want anything brutal to happen to Stanley that could be averted. Hence out of habit he took precautions.

Joe bought the drinks and Stanley gave him the benefit of his views on the markets, especially the currencies. That was the deal. Joe trusted Stanley because Stanley was an honest man and his views were worth a hearing for a busy chief executive like Joe. Stanley, one of Joe's old dealers from a few jobs back, had retired without the golden nest egg which the partners had taken home on their retirement; so far as Joe could gather Stanley was very nearly broke. But Stanley was a traveller, possessed of a ferocious sense of independence as well as an encyclopaedic knowledge of currencies. He had taken to the road, the better to traverse the forex highways. He would accept none of Joe's money, apart from taking a small loan to help pay for his annual season ticket. Joe asked no questions and made the £3000 advance – not as a gift but as a loan – which bought Stanley his ticket, enabling him to roam the rail network of London and the South East. So far as Joe could gather Stanley was also practically homeless. There were allusions every now and then in their discussions to a portfolio of wives. Joe presumed that Stanley's domestic affairs were very likely a chaotic and catastrophic mess. That meant he was on the run most likely from the sisterhood. Joe thought he rode the trains these days, travelling here there and everywhere on his ticket, perhaps sleeping in various waiting rooms up and down the Home Counties wherever was convenient, the while devouring the financial pages of any paper he could get his hands on in order to follow the markets. Effectively, Stanley was a high thinking and intelligent toff vagrant.

But Stanley had traded currencies for Joe back in the old City days, times which now seemed so far distant as to be almost prehistoric. But days also when Joe and Stanley had talked seriously about Pesos and Rupees and Yuans etc etc. up and down the dealing rooms. Not everybody shared the fascination with markets. Mostly the dealers had jeered at their long-drawn out analyses of whither the Canadian dollar or how the Swiss franc was pricing, with the derision reaching a crescendo when Stanley, Joe's subordinate by a multitude of tiers in the broking house but his equal in an intellectual context, had lent him in all sincerity his favourite book – the French Franc Between the Wars – and sternly advised him to read it for his personal benefit. This in front of the entire dealing room! Stanley's gesture had gone down a storm among the yahoo traders and helped form a mutual bond between them.

Moley and Stanley had never met, to some extent by Joe's design. But just as Joe had bumped into Moley by accident in the City, so too he had run into Stanley at Waterloo, opposite Platform Seventeen to be precise, and the relationship with his ex-dealer had re-blossomed from there. The old sense of mutual dialogue had survived the passage of time without alteration. They had picked up the discussion immediately.

So they met now in this obscure pub for further dosages of the drug – whither the markets? And what was cheap or dear?

In part they were like a couple of moral theologians trapped in a concentration camp and talking about sin. But only in part – Joe wanted Stanley to offer him some light at the end of the tunnel. He wanted to hear about the $ lifting off for the high blue yonder like a supersonic fighter-bomber.

Fat chance?

Joe emerged from the car; told the driver he'd be gone the usual 30 minutes or so; and strode across the lot to the pubs. In at the first as usual, round the back as per custom, and then into the saloon of the second, where Stanley like a wizened gnome, with his white Clemenceau moustache blackened and yellowed by the smoke from his roll-ups, was seated as he should have been, beside the empty hearth under the orange lamp and reading his Wall Street Journal!

On schedule! A docking! Connection made!

He looked up as Joe appeared.

'Usual, Stanley?'

'Don't mind if I do, Joe.'

Stanley's glass contained the residue of some beer, but no more than that. That was timing from the King of the Road…

Stanley was in a hurry to talk.

'Now look, while you're ordering, Joe, let's talk about the dollar, shall we?'

Noncommittally, but with a pounding in his brain commencing, Joe agreed to discuss the dollar; he pushed over to the bar to place the order. But he was far less nonchalant than he appeared. He felt a tiny pang of fear at what Stanley might say. Ahead of his deal and in order to help it along, ABC was running a huge dollar exposure, on Joe's say – so, at a time when only the earnest exhortations of senior US officials appeared to be keeping the currency aloft. It was perilous stuff.

So what did Stanley bring to the party that Joe's army of economist and statisticians at ABC had missed? Was the dollar about to tank? Was it time to sell? ABC was certainly terrified of the dollar exposure which Joe had orchestrated very quietly. Down in the dealing room it was known as Joe's Folly. Would Stanley's quiet words in some country pub in early summer indicate a misreading by Joe of the variables?

Over a humble pint of beer, Joe would soon find out.

Markets are very democratic. Anyone can play the currency game and anyone can be right – or wrong. By no means do the professionals have a monopoly of wisdom in this sphere of human activities. So billions of dollars, like ice floes in the Antarctic might start to roll on Stanley's words. Because Stanley might have found the line. He might be proved to be right…

Joe rather hoped that Stanley's words would be supportive as he picked up the drinks. A fiasco for him over the dollar would give Felix rather more than a sporting opportunity to strike at him. Joe would be dead meat at ABC, even more so than he was anyway at that moment in time. And his deal would be dead in the water. Just like that.

Joe brought the drinks back to the table where Stanley was seated, his newspaper thrown now to one side.

'Cheers, Stanley.'

'Cheers.'

Stanley drank deep into the pint and then raised his muzzle from the glass and brushed the froth from his moustache. He looked at the now half empty glass of beer with a distant look of great affection.

'The dollar, Stanley? Whither the greenback?'

'Yes, Joe. I agree. The $...! I've been doing some work for you on it. Just checking it, you understand. Taking the temperature, nothing stronger, and plotting the coordinates – simple stuff. There's something odd going on. I can't give you a definite fix, but I think it's going to...'

Stanley took another swig at the beer and Joe's heart skipped a beat as he waited for the great sage to opine.

'...behave in a very unexpected way.'

'Collapse?'

'No way. At least no way that I can see...'

Something like a great weight rolled away from Joe's heart. That felt better already. Oh my God, did that not feel better – a rhetorical question by Joe to himself and one clearly inviting the answer 'Yes'. Joe hit his own beer running.

'Like another drink Stanley?'

'In a moment but you might tweak the barman's eye for us... I don't know what your exposure to the dollar is right now – and it's no business of mine to find out or to know...'

'Very small, Stanley. We're not position-takers as you know. This is an academic conversation.'

The bank was very nearly under water in dollars but Joe was saying nothing strategic at that point.

'Glad to hear it. But there's a big moment coming for the dollar. It's starting to look very odd. It's showing symptoms again...'

That was the Stanley phrase of phrases – showing symptoms. Any moment now and the dollar would out in a rash, according to Stanley. Just itching to go...

'When you say 'behave in an unexpected way', Stanley, what exactly do you mean by that? All my boys at ABC have been telling me it's going to fall at worst and do nothing at best. Is that what you mean?'

Stanley was crisply dismissive. No, that was not what he had meant.

'Not at all. You can see all this on the cross-rates, especially in Asia. It's like a wave out on the ocean starting to gather strength. Those Asian economies are tied to the dollar and they're all starting to fall back. Where they run a forward market for the local currency against the dollar, there's real carnage starting to happen. The central banks are doing the best they can but mostly they are helpless. It's like watching a balloon starting to take off. In a small way – and only so far, like tiny – it's happening all across Asia. There's a ripple effect as well. It'll hit Australia and New Zealand soon. And then of course…But it's small as yet, as I say. It could all peter out as the enthusiasm wanes. I myself don't believe that will happen from the pattern of the market, but I can't positively swear to it all. Because I don't know why it's happening in the first place. And of course, all of this may put the Euro into play in a way that I can't fathom either. Or at least I can fathom it, and the conclusions are too crazy even for me to try and understand.'

'We'll see some of Stanley's theories tested against experience, won't we?'

It was one of Stanley's maxims that the old Commonwealth countries still lay on the cusp of the dollar area and London. So a run on the Australian dollar would impact sooner or later on London, after India, South Africa and Pakistan had taken their pounding. London was where the routes on the currency maps all converged.

'We will indeed. Indeed we will. And do you know, I don't have a clue as to why all of this currency movement should be taking place. It's very mysterious. And that in itself is quite disturbing.'

'You know, Stanley, for an uneducated man and a trader at that, you can be quite lucid and eloquent in your reasoning. You're a natural intellectual aristocrat.'

Stanley sniffed and drank some more beer, delighted by the chaffing. Suddenly for a few seconds he was back in Nirvana, checking prices in the dealing room and positioning for a daring contrarian trade. The beer swept from the glass down his scrawny ill-shaven throat in a continuous flow.

Joe watched him drink. He was starting to feel very good indeed by now. Witness the benefit, he told himself, of the impartial observer. Stanley speaks truth. He has not been paid to lie, unlike the army of droogs that I have on the ABC payroll masquerading as honest analysts, who would sell their mothers without a blush for just one day's mention in the Financial Chronicle.

Time to buy some more dollars, perchance? That really would put the frighteners on Felix if I can get a position like that wholly correct? Time to load up some more? Joe could feel his fingers starting to itch at the prospect of the dollar ballooning ahead in forex. What Stanley had said lay within the range of Joe's hopes and fears. A surging dollar, eh? And against the market's expectations? That would wipe the smirk off Felix's face. Just as a collapsing $ would have the opposite effect...

'Stanley, are you back on solids?'

Stanley looked a trifle discountenanced by the abrupt question. 'I...er...'

'Stanley, for a railroader, I've suddenly noticed, you're looking quite plump. Those bony hands have got some flesh on them. The nose is not so bulbous; nor does it stand out like a prow any more. What is going on? You are longer the human skeleton. Almost human looking, I would say.'

Stanley looked embarrassed. The moustache quivered distaste. He stared around the room.

'I will tell you but fetch me more beer, Joe. It's the same old problem. I can't help myself.'

The barman had anticipated the request. He approved of his odd couple disputing with vigour in the corner of the saloon. He was already approaching with his laden tray. Stanley eyed the new pints with relish and lashed into one of them with speed and enthusiasm. More brushing of the moustache after he had smashed down extra inches of ale.

The roll-up flamed at the end like a torch as Stanley relit it for the umpteenth time, inhaled heavily and then breathed out a spume of foul-smelling tobacco smoke. He leaned back in his chair. Stanley was hitting mid-season form.

'Did I ever tell you, Joe, that I had trouble with women?'

'I believe you touched on the matter briefly on the odd occasion. Kingsley Amis wrote his little novel with you in mind, I think you once said. Stanley and the Women? Was that the title?'

'Correct. A bedside book. Kingsley didn't know it was biographical at the time but then how was he to know? Anyway, I've been married four times. Well, three actually, I was never actually married to the second because we never got around to it. She was on the game, you see, and didn't want to be married because she was afraid it would interfere with the business. So call it 3 1/2 wives...'

Joe sipped at his beer, thinking about the dollar, wondering if Stanley was right about the currency, listening to his odd guru enumerate his connubial problems and estimating that this was indeed a golden fleeting moment. How truly wonderful it would be for him if the dollar soared...On this basis, he could even face Mrs Gulliver that evening.

'Well, if I'm not careful I'm about to do it again.'

'Making 4 1/2 now.'

'It won't come to that yet but I can see it in her eyes. Station mistress just a few stops down the line from here. Husband's dead and she...'

Joe laughed.

'Has designs on poor helpless young Stanley here?'

'It's actually a bit more complicated than that. Someone I was travelling with one morning down Kent way told me about Maisie – that's the station mistress -and bequeathed me his interest in her for some Old Holborn and a packet of papers. He was going away. Australia, I think. Told me Maisie went through the card, which she does. Very satisfying indeed. Very nice card.'

'And she's feeding you up now?'

'Like a fighting cock. She cooks one of the meanest breakfasts I've ever tasted. Bacon, eggs, tomatoes, even black pudding if I ask for it. Trouble is that she knows the railway timetables as well as I do. Most of the ...er... ladies I encounter on my travels require a maidservant to look up the times of the trains for them, not being able to do such things for themselves. So I can always escape via the platform and the next train. But Maisie...She's crafty. And she's in the rail business. She's even bought shares in the railways.

So she knows where I'm thinking of going before I've thought of it myself and she knows what time I'll be there and she also knows – and this tragic – when I'll be coming back. So she's there, waiting for me…'

'The little woman, with the evening meal to boot. What a horrid way for you to go, Stanley. Come to think of it, you do have a hunted look. A plump look but also a hunted one. So when are the nuptials?'

A pleading look of horror came into Stanley's face.

'She's making preparations, even as we speak. She's invited me to meet some of her friends. That's just the start of it.'

'You'd like that. The friends, just think of it. It's a big step, Stanley. Think about it…'

'I know. Perhaps I'd like it, perhaps. And then perhaps I wouldn't. That's all I'm saying. There are friends and friends.'

'Australia beckons, Stanley? That's where the first chap went to.'

Stanley looked hunted.

'I may need sanctuary somewhere one of these days. I can see it coming. She's a big woman, all woman in fact, and she won't be denied.'

'Well, you should know all about that, Stanley. Flee to the hills time?'

'And beyond, and then beyond those too.'

It was nearly time for Joe to depart. Maisie sounded more like Mrs Gulliver by the minute. He checked some details with Stanley.

'You've got all my numbers haven't you? Any time you really run foul of anything, just call me and we'll fix it.'

'And Maisie?'

'That might take longer. I think you may be in the bear pit alone on that one.'

'And here am I devilling for you all the hours…I can well believe the bear pit touch, though. It's her enthusiasm I find so unsettling. She's like a charging rhino. She shouldn't feel so enthusiastic about someone like me at her age. Should she?'

'A loveable sex kitten like you Stanley will kindle lust wherever it walks. Pure charisma. You ooze it Stanley and you know it. That's all it is and nothing else.'

'It's been said before, I must admit. There's something goes on between me and women, even though – and this is a funny thing – I actually prefer the company of blokes. Even yours, on occasion, Joe, despite those steely eyes of yours.'

Joe produced his wallet.

'Money, Stanley?'

'Not for me. I don't need it and anyway I believe Maisie goes through my pockets when I'm asleep. She would literally go crazy if she found some money on me. Imagine it, can you? Where did you get it? Who gave it to you? What did you have to do to get your hands on this money? No, just don't bother; it's not worth it, apart from a tenner...'

Joe handed over £20. Stanley took it without comment and the note vanished somehow into his clothes, drawn inwards by an invisible wind.

'The sight of some folding stuff would bring out the beast in her. She's a jealous woman as well. She'd take it the wrong way. But I can get rid of this quite easily.'

'Sounds like a good woman and then more besides. But the money is there if you need it...'

Stanley nodded. Carefully, Joe returned to his theme.

'And the dollar? How convinced are you about this? How right does it feel to you.'

They were back in the dealing room now with the shouting and the dealers leaping up and down and the flashing lights and the information channels running pell mell round the walls. So how does it *feel* to you, amidst this chaos...?

'It maybe has to be right, Joe. Maybe it just has to be right, I don't know. But there's something going on that I can't absolutely nail to my satisfaction. It's the silence at work in the process that is so fascinating; it's the creeping forward in the market and the kind of freezing over of the exuberance in the daily quotes. I will work on it for you so that when we next meet...'

'Care to make a forecast?'

'Index or rates?'

'Whichever.'

'No, no forecast, it will sound crazy. I don't want to make one. But what's cable?'

'$1.65 or thereabouts. Been there for years. Trades in the range. Very stable.'

'You might see $1.35. That's how it looks to me. It's a big call. But I'm just thinking the unthinkable.'

Joe gaped a little at the prediction and then whistled.

'That big a fall, eh? That is a very strong dollar, my son, and no mistake. That'll make the analysts chew on their pencils and no mistake.'

Stanley shrugged and absorbed some more beer. The rate of change in his consumption was increasing.

'Stanley, you said there was something else that was odd.'

More wiping of the moustache before Stanley replied. Joe had half risen to go. Mrs Gulliver now beckoned.

'I can't put my finger wholly on it, Joe, but it's something to do with the press coverage of all of this. The press isn't firing on it, or if it is firing, it's shooting blanks. It's muted. Maybe they just haven't woken up to what's going on.'

'And the Chron?'

'You can't blame the Chron. They're reorganising. That's what Stone is trying to do there. I can see all that. It's a fascinating paper to read day by day as he rings the changes. Stone was straight with the readers in that editorial of his. He said the paper was going through changes and he admitted that the quality of coverage might vary. Which it has, no question. No, it's the US press which doesn't quite seem to be awake at the post. That's the part I don't understand.'

'Point taken. And as a matter of interest, Stanley, purely in the interests of science, where do you find your Wall Street Journals of a morning?'

Stanley shot him a look as if to say 'Stay off my patch'.

'Clapham Junction around 8.15 in the morning can provide some rich pickings, if you're ever down that way at that time.'

Joe was half way to the door now and he blew Stanley a cavalier's mock-heroic kiss.

'Same time? Next week?'

'I'll try. Thursday could be good. I'll be here even if you miss. Meanwhile think of me with the station mistress. And pity me.'

'I'm thinking about the friends, Stanley. That's where you'll come a cropper. That's your Waterloo. They'll eat you alive.'

'Pray God you're right. This close attention is killing me.'

'Don't take your eyes off those newspapers.'

'I won't Joe. You can rely on me.'

And Joe was out of the door, into the loo, through the other saloon and then back in his car before his slumbering chauffeur had time to register that he was back, leaving Stanley alone in the saloon with time and money to brood some more on the dollar.

Very abruptly, Joe went through the usual calculations as he slumped in the back of his car. It was a small detail but vital. His deal was priced eventually in dollars. A rising greenback changed all the variables. It made the deal just that much more attractive in terms of the cash element...

Joe hoped that the station mistress wouldn't work Stanley over so much that he lost interest in his currency predictions, at least for the next month or so; or conversely that he left the country in flight and fright at her zeal for his bony little carcass.

★   ★   ★   ★   ★

A few days later, Emma and Lucy-Miranda were back in the square on their bench, watching the evening shadows lengthen across the hard ground. Time stopped in defined space. Like all the rest of the inhabitants, they both felt obscurely that they possessed the square. Part of it was theirs, just as part of it belonged to everyone who took a stroll through it every day. Again obscurely they felt that if they held on tight to the experience of the square, then somehow they got the better of time and everything that could happen by way of time. By choice they were locked into that slow certain wheel of the day which involved spending some moments in the square. It was the certainty of their presence there, at some point in the day, which gave them protection against whatever else might happen; the wheel of the day rode shotgun for them against all hazards.

Meanwhile they thrilled in a dark primitive way to the nightly spectacle of the comings and goings in the square, all accomplished either with frenzy or at a slow measured pace. There was room for everyone's personal cadence. They watched the young girls pace purposefully in one direction, arms linked and all moving together while the boys gazed at them in wonderment. Then under the sheer pressure of the excitement of it all, plus the shouts and jeers of the boys, the girls' attempt at solidarity disintegrated. Their closely disciplined lines broke up. Then it was mayhem and screaming as the boys chased them mercilessly, hunting them down in one's and two's.

More cooking scenes could be seen in the houses around the square, as dinner time drew near, and there were more faces at the window, shouting comments at the antics in the square or just gossiping very loudly with the neighbours. Up above, the swifts wheeled and turned in great arabesques over the gables, dark twisting figures in an azure sky moving this way and that as they looked for the gusts of hot air rising from the chimneys to help them glide across the sky. Giovanna waved at them both as she walked her dog in the company of her two friends. The plodding little caravan of gossip and earnest discussion walked slowly around the perimeter of the square in the opposite direction to that of the young girls. Youth and age going their ways, clockwise for the teenagers and appropriately enough anticlockwise for veterans like Giovanna. The men returning from the day's work lounged now in the cafes, reading the newspaper, drinking a little or just staring silently into space. Tea was brought for Emma and Lucy-Miranda as a matter of course from the cafe by a small waiter, almost a boy, who tottered across to them with his loaded tray and treated Emma with absurd deference. Lucy-Miranda marvelled outspokenly at the change in their status.

'It really makes me want to spit. I've been sitting on this bench for God's knows how many years, hoping and praying that someone would throw me the bone of a kind word, like some kind of wretched Vestal Virgin. Now, total change. Overnight.

Through what is obviously just a pure accident of blind fate, I'm practically part of the family of Italy, with my every whim anticipated. But why couldn't this have happened before? It's so pleasant now and it was so horrible before, in retrospect. It's all just so galling.'

'We owe Jake a lot although he doesn't know this, Lucy-Miranda.'

'Yes, indeed, I'd be the first to admit it. And talking of whom, have you noticed just what is going on between Ginny and Jake now that they're getting into their holiday modes? It makes rather a change, I must say. I don't think we've heard a single explosion from Ginny for about four days now, not so much as a whimper of discontent.'

'How could I miss it? It's so blatant. But I don't find it the slightest bit offensive. How could I? They both seem so happy together.'

What Lucy-Miranda had mentioned and what Emma had described was the almost animalistic moving towards each other and cleaving together, day by day and hour by hour, of Jake and Ginny. It had started, so far as Emma could establish, with the morning ritual of Jake's workout, which naturally he did before breakfast, because breakfast, as all the world by now knew, was a serious matter for Jake. So early in the morning, around 7.30 according to Lucy-Miranda, Jake was out on the lawn with his weights and his football and all his paraphernalia of top-grade athlete. It being hot even at that early hour, Jake naturally worked out in just shorts and trainers. Practically nothing about the dimensions of his buffed burnished and browning body was left to the imagination. Gradually Ginny had taken to appearing on the lawn at around the same time, flaming red hair left unbrushed and very definitely not smart, partly to give her a little time to play with the baby and partly of course to take the early morning air after some difficult nights with the child. In truth the child slept like a log in a hurricane but that was the excuse, or the pretext as Lucy-Miranda called it quite ponderously, and it was accepted. So far as the villa was concerned, with its complement of 15 or so guests, maids, servants and what have you, nothing untoward was taking place. No protocols were breached and no etiquette infringed. What would have been unthinkable in England was no more than commonplace out in Italy. Barriers were falling and new fresh and quick links were being forged in the Repugian heat. So every day the two of them together were alone just after the dawn on the green lawns in the hot sharp crisp air of a fine Italian morning, he in his wholly appropriate semi-nakedness and slim taut muscularity and she in the tasteful flowing deshabille of a young mother on holiday relaxing with her child. Whites and browns and greens and golds and heavy reds all intermingled in a frieze of slowly evolving passion and trust and contentment. As Jake skipped on the terrace to the monitored regularity of his stopwatch with concentrated focus, eyes glazing with effort as he listened to his breathing, Ginny crawled about on the lawn with her baby, giggling with the child, kissing it, talking to it and just occasionally throwing Jake a word as he moved from one stage of the work-out to the next. But it was a friendly word with more than just a hint of encouragement, support, complicity and shared enthusiasm for the moments they were enjoying together. More the commonplace word which a contented woman would offer to a strong spouse close by, certain of it being understood at a deeper level than a casual comment thrown to a chance acquaintance.

And he, just as often, moving in natural harmony but taking great care, would roll the football in her direction so that she could take a punt at it with laughter or offer her some weights to brandish in the air and give to the baby with its surprisingly strong grip. When he took a break from the workout, she would wander across to him on the terrace and standing close up but without taking her eyes away from the baby she would chat to him. Behind the two of them, the shadows of the early morning sun flashed across the hills and deep down into the valleys and raced through the trees as he steamed beside her with his sweat coursing down his body. He answered less curtly than before and with more understanding and tolerance. Just as he found it surprising that she knew so little about the life he had led with its toughness, its street cred obsessions, its sharp angles and its East End based mobsterism, so she delighted from time to time in explaining aspects of her life, like how she had met Tommy at a party so many years ago; how little she had enjoyed school, being so much away from home; how university had been a surprising bore for her, because she hadn't been the slightest interested in the History of Art and because she had missed her friends from school; how defined and in a sense satisfied she now felt with her early marriage to one of the most successful young merchant bankers in the City. No, she found that she couldn't summon up all that much enthusiasm for Tommy's wonderful deal, but there it was, that was his life and she'd better learn to stick it. After all, she had the baby didn't she, even if Tommy had seemed remarkably unimpressed by her reproductive powers so far. No hint of having to stuff it passed her lips as their new house in Hampshire and the friends and Tommy's job loomed large in her discussions; if anything she exuded a sense of stoic endurance rather than any sense of rebellion.

But little by little in the intimacy of the sunshine and the early morning romps, the obvious differences in background between them began to give way to a sense of shared experience – they were both stranded in another country; they both had agendas; and they were both in some senses adrift. They were young and felt they still had choices to make. Time and opportunity were on their side. By way of exploring that sense of choice at an oblique angle, Ginny admitted that she shouldn't have snatched Tommy's mobile and flung it over the terrace walls. But the provocation had been considerable, she stressed; he might have killed her baby by his stupid negligence. Jake, by the same token, averred that Lucia should not have left him here on his own, pleading slightly lamely that she was always her own boss but with the obvious slightly fearful inference to be drawn that most certainly was not for repetition – because she was after all his boss – that Lucia was a damned selfish bitch who most of the time thought only of her own success and self-glorification. By this stage, normally it was around 8.45, the phones had not started to ring from opposite sides of the lawns- both emerged each morning with their mobiles tactfully located in the gardens – and so it was truly time for breakfast. On a particularly good day, when they'd been well and truly in a state of blissful communion, Jake would hoist the baby onto his shoulders and march her into the house with Ginny following close behind while the baby shouted its enthusiasm for its newly acquired daddy to the rooftops.

The baby was going to be called Sam after all. Ginny had executed a strategic withdrawal on that point, knowing like all great generals when to cede a small amount of ground to the enemy when she could glimpse a huge terrain over yonder that was there for the taking. In this case it was practically a country called, coincidentally, just Jake.

On the grounds that she too had been taking wholesome exercise, Ginny slightly fussily and certainly clumsily would supervise breakfast- up to a point – by going down into the villa's kitchen and checking on progress for the fried bread and the bacon and the eggs, much to the disgust of the Italians in the kitchen with whom Ginny was not popular. Lucy-Miranda said she had heard them with great amusement imitating Ginny's clipped Sloane Ranger tones of instruction between themselves on the stairs as they did the cleaning, laughing to each other.

In the morning room, which gave onto the hills at the back of the town, Jake in jeans and tight-fitting top and with all-devouring eyes in his hunger would consume whatever was placed before him, wolfing it down more or less with both hands, as Ginny took the first call of the day from Tommy, just after he emerged from his morning meeting in London. Tommy in the natural course of things was anxious. He was missing his wife and his child and his attractive domestic set-up which normally ran on well defined grooves. But it was too bad for Tommy. His commitment to the job and the deal came first. That was the sacrosanct arrangement. So he had to live with the pangs of separation although he was clearly discontented. This showed up in the hectoring tone of his questioning which was noted critically at the other end in Italy by Ginny; it did not add to Tommy's shining hour. What detracted also from the brio of his repartee of course was that he needed to be fairly muted in the discussion. There wasn't a great deal he could add from his end. The deal was obviously a big one and he was obliged under the rules of the Takeover Panel, to be wholly discreet. That did not leave him a large amount of scope to redefine the world according to Tommy in Ginny's eyes and ears. So the levels of exchange were strictly procedural. How was Sam?

What was the weather like? How were the other guests? What were they planning to do that day? The line of questioning was flat to the point of bathos. To all of the questions Ginny returned adequate enough, but nowhere close to sparkling, reply. As she spoke, according to Lucy-Miranda, her eyes never left Jake or the baby. Like a Nordic warrior in the heat of battle, she had simply and swiftly redefined her emotional locus so that its centre was now somewhat removed from London and most likely camouflaged in hiding somewhere amid the Italian hills.

Climaxing her sense of alternative existence and identity was the emergence of her joke syndrome. As Lucy-Miranda suggested to Emma on their bench, and as Emma had already surmised, there was little outlet in Ginny's life for humour. People in her circle simply did not tell jokes, with all their unexpected rib-tickling capacity to dissolve authority into nothing. Too much dignity was at stake for that. From her first waking moment, Ginny had been taught to walk the line, in line, as gracefully as possible and also to make bloody sure that she walked that line correctly even if she did nothing else by the book – in line and according to the precedence laid down at birth, so that everybody could see her walking like so. That was the mantra which Ginny had followed from birth – stay in place, stay in line, stick with all the others. For Jake that was all quite incomprehensible. The line did not exist. The rules were that there were no rules. Bred in the streets of Manor Park and a fortunate fugitive from its unlicensed boxing and career criminals because of his God-given talent to play high grade football, Jake's response to the slings and arrows of fortune was a shrug of the shoulders; a loud laugh; an uncomplaining attitude towards Dame Fortune; and an ''Ere, you heard this one...' This threw Ginny. She couldn't cope. She couldn't even begin to understand. She simply couldn't deal with the freedom to react which Jake's shrugging implied, the sense that whatever the universe happened to throw at him, well it would do that wouldn't it, tough shit, now have you heard this one? There was no line. Without that of course, without some guaranteed standard of conduct or behaviour, Jake left her with no point of reference, no beacon. It showed in their discussions according to Lucy-Miranda who was enjoying herself working out what was going on between them both. Once according to Lucy-Miranda when he thought he'd badly ricked his ankle one morning, Jake said blithely, 'Well, that's me crocked up for the next fortnight' to which bland comment Ginny asked him with some asperity whether or not he cared about being crocked up. Because if he didn't, he jolly well should. 'Well, what happens happens, don't it, there ain't nothing I can do about it' was Jake's off-guard reply at which point Ginny tore into him for an absence of personal responsibility. Jake retaliated – and defused her rage to boot – by reciting a limerick to her at point blank range. Ginny had not expected humour at that point. Nor had she expected to find the limerick funny – which she had done. She had hooted with laughter; tried to remember it; failed; tried to write it down; failed; and finally had asked Jake to repeat the limerick at the breakfast table. This he had done successfully. She had listened to the performance with all her eyes. Later that day, Lucy-Miranda had come upon her in the garden, in a quiet sunny corner with the baby, duly reciting the same limerick to herself and trying to catch the nuances of Jake's delivery which had so amused the breakfast table. It was a form of deference on her part to him which was the more striking for it being so unexpected – Lucy-Miranda had expected, as she informed Emma, for the opposite to be taking place. But Jake in the limit was unquenchable. He could always call upon that quicksilver sense of survival which is bred in the gutter and which she for her part had never needed to employ. But now that she saw it in operation at close quarters, saw indeed how Jake could work the room on his own terms and in his own time if he needed to, she was impressed. Like a market trader, which he was, Jake always left something for the others when he cracked his jokes. He had a natural politeness. He also operated intuitively, just as he did in the markets, and he rarely forced. He didn't try to nail down everybody's reactions as part of a programme of self- assertion, he just let the room go with the flow – and then giggled. This too was something foreign to Ginny's experience. Leaving in the shortage for the other guy was entirely outside her realms of behaviour. I's in her life had been dotted and T's crossed from birth. It was part of life, like the overwhelming importance of the verb 'to seize'. But out in Italy life had switched to a different tempo. Thus Ginny began to experiment with alternative forms of self-expression. She didn't exactly start to simper over Jake. Far from it – she was too smart for that. She simply went away and tried to work at her own act. Hence Lucy-Miranda's discovery of her that afternoon trying to tell herself a joke and letting it reach her on the summer breezes so that she laughed. Which of course she didn't – only a very special form of egotist laughs at her own jokes. Nevertheless she persevered and that quite cunningly. She obviously prodded Tommy into telling her some jokes when they chatted together alone in the evening – an inquiry from his severe and strait-laced wife which must have shocked him rigid – and these she proceeded to try and retell in the morning, every now and then, at breakfast. She started off well enough, Lucy-Miranda confided to Emma, but she couldn't manage the punch line and the attention of the room both together. Either she forgot the punch line or she faltered as the intensity of her audience's attention struck her dumb. 'Why is the hot dog the noblest of all the dogs?', she inquired of the guests challengingly and in a loud voice as they spooned their muesli into expectant mouths. Heads shook as all confessed ignorance. Smiles flitted through morning eyes as they waited for the killer line. Jake sat back with a fat smile on his face as he partook from afar of the atmosphere in the dealing room. He didn't care who told the jokes provided the ambiance was there. Ginny bellowed forth. 'You don't know? Well, I'll tell you – because it....' Pause then silence, then total confusion. 'You know, I haven't the foggiest how that joke goes on', she confessed disarmingly to the assembled guests, 'I've completely forgotten the punch line. Maybe telling jokes is just not my forte. It's gone clean out of my head.'

Much sympathetic banging of tables with spoons and hoots of laughter and guffaws at her brief amnesiacal seizure. But the guests clapped nevertheless at her brave effort and she cut an entertaining figure anyway as she craved the audience's indulgence quite charmingly. Inevitably she leaned across to Jake and tried to tell him the joke, which she succeeded in doing in the greater intimacy of their duologue. He, the hero of a thousand tough exchanges of repartee in and around the Square Mile, nodded at her and wagged a finger at her and seemed to gargle a reply at her, squinting at the ceiling. Finally she got it straight in her mind, and tried again, an initiative which all agreed was brave on her part and added to the holiday larks and general sense of repose. 'Ladies and gentlemen, why is the hot dog the noblest of all the dogs?' A sudden long wail from Sam interrupted the proceedings briefly but Ginny ignored her and Jake quieted her by rocking her back and forth. Staring at the ceiling, with hands very nearly twisted behind her back, Ginny persevered – and got it right. 'Because it feeds the hand that bites it,' she almost snapped out in an agony of paralysed staccato. But nobody cared about her quality of delivery. From everybody, it was well done, Ginny, for being so plucky and such a good sport. Much laughter at her witty gag, more stamping and much more banging on the tables with spoons, to the delight of the Italians clearing the tables who thought that the English when they came to the villa were a stuffy Northern Protestant lot who had no sense of fun whatsoever. But this year it had been different. Even Ginny was almost approachable. But then of course, as the Italians had correctly surmised, she had a reason to be more simpatico, and that not only because she had the bambino with her. There was this handsome young man, built like a rapier, whom she talked to each morning as he did his gym and whom...

Much laughter in Italian at this point. There are no secrets from domestics, still less in Italy. They all gossiped away about what Ginny and Jake had got planned for each other when Signor Tommy was still in London... And then what about the football and Signor Jake, they whispered amongst themselves as they cleared away his plates...That was going to be really something, they told themselves, something which Signora Ginny was not expecting...Because we Italians know how to arrange something when we really want to, and we can produce a surprise, the like of which...And then according to Lucy-Miranda who had heard most of this later that morning as the stairs were being cleaned, the two cleaners went off into one of the bedrooms to change the sheets still chuckling to themselves. Lucy-Miranda could not eavesdrop any further.

But something was going on. The fair folk of Repugia were plotting a coup.

Emma interrupted her at this point as they took still more of their ease in the early evening air.

'This football game is going to be really something, you know, Lucy-Miranda. I think the whole town is going to turn up in one way or another. I can feel it all stirring out there. There's definitely something brewing. My instincts are never wrong on this. Each time I meet Paolo, either in the street or in his cafe, he winks at me and rubs his hands as if to say ' Isn't there something truly amazing on its way? Aren't we going to have fun?' He's so viciously conspiratorial, it's unbearable.'

'I agree with you Emma, but I think it's just these greedy Italians who think they're going to get their hands on Jake; his football boots; and some extra money. Now, Emma, what do you think? The sun must be over the yard arm by now. Do you think we can risk ordering some nice Italian wine without losing our reputations?'

'Certainly I think we can. A couple of glasses of vino bianco before dinner? That won't harm our reputations.'

'Good idea. If you like to wave, because you're better at attracting their attention than I am…Oh look now isn't that a cheering sight. There's Gina. We haven't seen her for a few days. Doesn't she look smart? Isn't she doing well? She wouldn't look as good as that if the punters were treating her badly. It tells on a girl if it isn't working out, as I told you.'

And in truth, Lucy-Miranda was right. Gina looked sensational. She was dressed in an impossibly tight, figure hugging outfit which showed off her long legs and shy almost discreet but still wanton bosom. Watched in awed silence by the two women, she slinked gracefully across the square and into a large limousine which awaited her on the other side just beside the church steps. The chauffeur stood there for her respectfully holding the door. He tucked her in with care as she slid through the rear door and perched on the back seat. She folded her legs in beneath her but not before some six inches of thigh had been revealed fetchingly to the world, like the promise of an experience inevitably about to take place.

Absently, and almost as a dreamy aside, Lucy-Miranda said she hoped that Gina would fuck the brains right out of the Mayor of Repugia's skull that evening because he deserved it. Emma once again remarked on the two-tier language system which she employed, wondering in turn whether she had ever lapsed into the patois of the brothel at an inappropriate time.

Emma must have raised her eyebrows instinctively at the foul language. Reading her thoughts, Lucy-Miranda laughed and said that Yes, there had been one time when she'd lapsed. Charles had invited some of his ex-colleagues round from the Foreign Office and they'd been discussing some posting or another where the ambassador had lurched right off the rails and gone native with one of the local girls, finishing up, as might have been expected, spending most of his time in a house of ill fame. Such had been his lust for experience. Charles had wondered aloud rather naively just what the ambassador, whom they had all known for many years, had got out of the experience, whereupon Lucy-Miranda in brothel mode had snorted in reply 'A jolly good thrashing most likely.' At this all the mandarins had coughed together most discreetly, like ecclesiastics hearing a minor heresy. When Charles had gently alluded to her comment after the drinks' party, Lucy-Miranda had insisted that she had said 'A jolly good ear bashing' and asserted that a car backfiring outside had distorted her words. 'Oh,' Charles had said quite innocently, 'so that was it, was it? I thought you had said something completely different. It just goes to show you, doesn't it? Information is inevitably garbled in transmission.' He promptly went off at a tangent, leaping onto one of his favourite hobby horses.

'Which reminds me, Emma, are you still missing that chap you mentioned a few days ago?'

Emma nodded in such a way as to discourage analysis of her precise frame of mind. She wasn't in the mood for it and tomorrow looked like being a long and trying day. It was time for them to separate anyway for the evening, Lucy-Miranda back to the villa and she, Emma, back to her hotel. The time for her to discuss the state of her heart had come and gone so far as she was concerned for that day.

The two of them prepared to leave their bench and to quit their gentle meandering gossiping. As Emma had taken the greatest of pains to inform Lucy-Miranda during that day, she was obliged to leave Repugia the following day in order to motor across the Italian countryside and visit a distant relative of her mother's. Hence she wanted an early night in order to prepare for the journey and make an early start the following morning.

But she answered the question.

'Yes, I am missing him. Perhaps and I don't know this for certain, but I think, perhaps a great deal. He certainly occupies my thoughts a lot of the time. I've been doing this thing, which I'm sure is fatal, of imagining that he's just going to walk around the corner at any moment when of course he's nowhere within five thousand miles of Repugia. It's so stupid of me and I must stop it. I'm going to think about him tomorrow on the journey and see whether or not I'm just fooling myself. I haven't spoken to him for some time and I'm not entirely sure that I know how to contact him. But I may try. It all depends. I'll see how I feel about it tomorrow. I can't see that it would do any harm to get in touch with him, provided I can find some pretext for contacting him. But I may be fooling myself. I may not feel so strongly about him after all. We'll see, Lucy-Miranda, we'll see. I'll keep you posted about all the mood shifts. And I'll be back in town tomorrow evening. I'll see you then and I can give you a full report.'

'I will miss you tomorrow, Emma. Repugia won't be the same without you. I'm not sure that I want to sit on our sweet little bench without you. Maybe they won't serve me with the same willingness. Now that would be a tragedy wouldn't it? Just when I thought I'd secured squatters' rights in the square. I couldn't bear it if that happened.'

'I'll be back. And you'll be fine. I won't be away for long. You won't be left alone with the young lovers for too long. Nor with the capricious Italians in the square. So fear not.'

'Heaven forbid! Anyway so far as Ginny and Jake are concerned, I would interfere and ruin their billing and cooing by giving them too much advice, advice of the most practical kind, no less. But that reminds me, Emma, I wanted to tell you sometime all about the love of my life. Yes, I wanted to wallow in it all, while we're in this confessional mode. That way we could exchange tales of horror and imagination.'

'On the bench!'

'Exactly. On the bench. How suitable. I met him, my lost beau, at university you know, so it was a long time ago but I...Well, never mind, another time. You don't look in the mood for it tonight.'

'I'm sorry Lucy-Miranda but I've got a long day ahead of me tomorrow.'

'Yes, how foolish of me. I should have realised. Well, I suppose I must be getting back now to Charles and what have you...'

Suddenly Lucy-Miranda looked older and more discouraged. Joyful holiday-making, the equivalent of building sandcastles on the beach, was over for the day so far as she was concerned. The past with all its promise and hopes of fulfilment was catching up with the present. A little heavily, she toiled from the bench, looking grimmer and far less attuned to the presence of another quiet person close to her. The jokes with Gina and Ginny and Jake had suddenly gone flat as her own experience weighed hard on her. The tally did not seem to be in her favour that evening – one husband dying by his own hand, another who seemed to be fading into a nothingness of obliging stupidity, and all the time she was carrying this tiny little torch for someone else who in all likelihood she would never ever see again.

On the soft warm air of an Italian evening she could plainly hear the quiet whisper of mortality across the square. Just a prompt from those dear little wings but it was sufficient to alter her mood.

It was time to say Goodnight, before the mood of the meeting changed irrevocably. Lucy-Miranda plainly did not relish returning in that frame of mind to the villa but nevertheless she was prepared to put up with it. But she would find the going heavy. So much was clear.

We are deceived, thought Emma as she accompanied Lucy-Miranda back up the steep street to the side entrance of the villa. We are dupes. We think that the people we have known are just a phone call away, as they were in the past, and that they will always be there for us. We think that it is all settled because that is the way that it features for us in our imaginations. But it isn't true. It simply isn't true, whatever we might think. The friends we have known move away on their own paths and do not tell us where they have gone. Nor what they have become. They stay frozen in our memories. But our memories cheat and lie to us and are not to be trusted. The friends go or they have gone and they leave us behind with just our memories of what they were. We have no way of knowing whether that conforms at all to what they have become. And so what is the use of memory if it deceives us like this...? It is just too big and too tragic for me to comprehend all this fully but that is what Lucy-Miranda is suffering at this moment...

They said Goodnight with a great display of affection at the entrance to the villa. On her return to the hotel, Emma was sufficiently struck by Lucy-Miranda's quiet chastened look of dull resignation that she called her, after an interval of an hour, to check on her morale. Not to be found was the reply; perhaps she'd gone out for a walk.

Emma knew where she was and where she'd gone – back to the bench and to the usual contemplation of the solitary... That was where she'd be the following day, keeping the vigil, and the day after that, if Emma did not return from her journey, a figure rapt in the long weary process of squaring the books after the hard business of living, making certain that the balance sheet balanced...Fat chance for her of making the sums add up and fat chance for me, thought Emma as she turned out the light and prepared for her little journey the following day...

*   *   *   *   *

Delivering the envelope was the easy part of the day.

Emma rose early and descended to the lobby of the hotel, there to find the car which she had hired for the day parked outside. It was large and it looked serviceable. Emma was unconcerned by its provenance. She thought it was a Fiat but she couldn't be certain. It was something Italian, she knew that much. She had breakfast and then she departed. As she flew along the Italian roads, making for the small country town of her destination, it all seemed so straightforward. All she had to do was to find the cafe in the street which had been marked out for her in her London briefing with Annie, a street rejoicing in the improbable name of the Happy Pilgrim; presumably in the Middle Ages, the town lay on the pilgrim's route to Rome, and not too far away either. She had to saunter into the designated cafe carrying a copy of an English newspaper – any English newspaper would do, it had been stressed – and then drink a cup of Earl Grey tea somewhere in the area close to the bar. Early in the morning would be best, if she could manage that, because the cafe would be less crowded at that hour. And then...

Emma drove on with everything well prepared. She had her English newspaper safely stowed on the back seat. She had come well prepared for the trip. The letter was in her handbag. She had prepared for her little piece of espionage as she might have done for a board meeting.

Finding the cafe proved to be slightly more difficult than she had imagined. Her instructions had been less than precise on this point. It turned out that in the Street of the Happy Pilgrim there were in fact three bars, all of which might have answered to Annie's description back in London. By dint of careful observation, Emma decided that only one of them could fit precisely the rather vague description which Annie had given her and she sauntered into the cafe. Nobody reacted to her presence as she pushed through the door. It was exactly 10.15.

A woman behind the bar greeted her brightly in Italian and Emma, still keeping a weather eye open for the person for whom she was about to deposit the letter – whoever he might be – asked in a flustered kind of way, in her dreadful Italian, for some tea. The cafe around her buzzed with a sort of early morning energy. Outside she could see the scooters whizzing up and down the street in the sunlight. The kids in the street were having lots of fun. No one paid any attention to her inside the cafe. She wondered if she'd selected the wrong place.

'Earl Grey, please, if you've got it.'

'Si, si signorina,' came the unhurried comfortable reply as the serving woman bustled about behind the counter. Emma suddenly wondered what on earth she was doing in the cafe, playing the role of some kind of cheap imitation Mata Hari. The idea hit her like a streak of lightning. She almost stood outside herself as two sides of reality – the humdrum day to day programme of her ordinary life and the more charged version which came with the espionage – confronted each other. But the mood passed with the arrival of the tea. She stirred the teabag deep into the boiling water and watched the water darken – and then thought of Joe.

More lightning.

According to instructions, she paid for the tea immediately. And then nearly panicked, she felt so low about it all. Joe was still in her thoughts.

It was inevitable. The mood had been coming up behind her for days. She had staved it off quite successfully by gossiping with Lucy-Miranda but now it hit her right amidships like a broadside from an angry hostile fleet of personal demons. The old questions hit her with more than usual force. Where was he? What was he doing? Was he thinking about her? What was she doing? And how much thinking about him had she been doing? And was it all worth it? Yes, that was the question – did it add up to anything more than just a row of beans? All the usual queries overwhelmed her with the intensity of their interrogation. But one in particular screamed at her from the lower depths. Was he thinking about her at all? That was the question which went right to the bottom of her stomach and took away all her insides with one great scalping cut, leaving her gasping – had he forgotten about her?

She thought about Joe because this was the kind of situation – sitting in a strange cafe waiting to do a dead letter drop – which she was quite certain he had been doing all his life with extraordinary aplomb. Joe was like one of those card sharps she had occasionally encountered in Oxford Street, doing the three card trick. First, the card sharp showed it all to you so that it looked dead easy; then he invited you to have a go yourself – and just when you were about to recoup your losses, the Ace would in the wrong place, you'd lost your fifty pounds or whatever, he'd place his hand over the whole caboodle and gather it up, wafting away into invisibility down a side street like a Demon King – and with your money. It was uncanny the way Joe managed to be both wholesomely corporeal like a very solid presence the while and yet simultaneously he resembled some kind of Ariel, light as thistledown and capable of turning up somewhere like in Ethiopia in a twinkling. She'd always suspected that he was really a spy, but she'd never quite succeeded in pinning him down to an admission about it. All that stuff about Berlin had never really added up to much in her mind, except as a series of good stories. He had always been very vague about what he'd actually done in Berlin. So maybe it was all true…How could she tell – she had no way of knowing. Emma was glad she was wearing her shades because she could feel her eyes starting to water at the sense of loss of him, right at that special moment when she needed to be so calm and so collected. She was enraged at her weakness. And then she thought about him because it was long overdue for her to brood about him anyway and because the action in the cafe – or rather the lack of action because there was nothing going on at all, outside of her imagination, either on one side of the bar or the other – provoked the onset of these terrible throat-grasping blues. It was very simple. She could see that. And she felt sick. She knew that too. She hadn't realised just how shielded from reality she had become by life at the villa and by her gossiping with Lucy-Miranda. It had all been very easy for the past few weeks. She'd forgotten just how vulnerable she could feel in this world. Now the demons were letting her know that they'd been sitting there in wait for her all the time.

Time to suffer.

Meanwhile she continued to stir her tea as the clouds burst inside her head and she felt very close to tears. Joe was a million miles away from her and he should have been very close to her. But she struggled with her feelings and she succeeded in turning the pages of the newspaper with something approaching calm. There was a news story about some peer losing his acreage in Norfolk and she noted that. She also managed to take a sip of tea. Then she looked at her watch. Yes, it was time now. She'd been sitting there long enough. Time to act, and time to get on with it. Now that the time was due she felt more resolute. But her knees felt wobbly nevertheless.

She stood up and walked to the bar and asked the woman behind it, who had served her the tea, where the Ladies was located. Upstairs to the right came the reply, conveyed mainly by signs with a smattering of English. Feeling more resolute now, Emma walked through the swing doors and up the stairs to the Ladies. The plan was very simple and she followed it to the letter. She took the envelope out of her bag and placed it behind the cistern above the loo itself and secured it with a small piece of sticking tape. Then she left the loo, carefully flushing it behind her, and just as carefully left her handbag, which contained nothing at all of value, in front of the mirrors by the wash basins. She exited from the ladies and went downstairs and sat down again – and waited. The woman behind the bar was nowhere to be seen. After pausing for about 30 seconds, and sipping her tea perhaps once, she then stood up and exclaimed about her handbag and made to go out again through the swing doors and upstairs to the Ladies. She was forestalled by the Italian serving lady, who charmingly had found her handbag in the Ladies and brought it down for her. Emma mustered all her self-control and took the handbag, thanking her for finding it for her and returning it.

'Niente, niente,' came the reply with a smile.

Following instructions, Emma did not linger in the cafe but left it almost at once, thanking the woman again for returning her handbag. She did not pause or look back until she had paced the 200 yards or so which took her to where she had parked the car. She got into the car and drove off carefully, heeding Annie's warning that she should take it easy because the adrenalin high caused by her espionage could quite easily lead to her stamping on the accelerator. She moved into the traffic and negotiated her way out of the town. Only then did she stop the car. She pulled over into a small lay-by, stopped, braked, and turned off the engine. Then she opened her bag.

It should have been empty, but it wasn't.

Somebody, somehow, in the tiny interval which had elapsed between her leaving the bag and retrieving it, had managed to insert into her bag a small very delicate white rose. It sat very snugly at the bottom of her empty bag and its perfume was strong and exotic.

As Annie said to her some fifteen minutes later, when she phoned London to inform them that the mission had been completed, 'Well done. They must have liked you. Normally, they just return the bag. You must have made an impression on them. It's rare for them to make any reaction at all.'

Emma, too full of emotions for words to help, listened dumbly as Annie thanked her. Then as the adrenalin began to ebb she realised that the demons which had been circling around her for the past two hours would now launch a full scale attack... It was useless to drive. She might well go off the road. Her hands on the wheel were trembling. So she climbed out of the car and stood against the bonnet and took in the glories of the Italian hills directly in front of her and the long stretch of water between them which led on towards the sea. The wind was whipping off the hills in a mad, gadabout frenzy in the sunshine.

It all felt quiet and clean and cool.

It was a small lay-by located just before the road curved round in a bend. Only one other vehicle had parked there, a dormobile of some description, from which a small party of boys had debouched led by what transpired on closer examination, and judging by the exuberant cries of the boys, to be an English priest. Plainly they were on their way to Rome and had been obliged to make a stop because one of the boys was suffering from car sickness. Emma could see his frail form stretched out on a huge rock overlooking the drop down to the deep waters below; he was ashen and appeared to be trembling as he drank in the fresh air. Very gently the priest was feeding him some water. But the other boys, capably marshalled by the priest nonetheless as he tended one of his charges, were strolling about in the early morning sunshine at their ease, young fearless and self-confident protected from doubt by their faith and by the presence of their Holy Man, the priest. They seemed to dance around the edge of the cliff in their high spirits.

The wind blew hard up the gulch from the water and Emma felt its heavy tug at her hair as the sun flamed down from the blue empty sky.

She had more thoughts about Joe, none of which helped to please her. She felt stupid to be so assailed by his memory. She was a mature woman and she ought to know about these things and how to handle them. Either the relationship was over and done with, or it was still alive – she agreed with herself on that. But how did she know what was the status of the relationship when it must have been well over a year since she had spoken to him? It had been just before that disastrous tryst in the West Indies, when he'd been waiting for her on the seashore, perhaps a year ago, carefully parked there via her manoeuvrings, all present and correct, because she'd spoken to him the evening before after he'd completed his journey of love and affection which had taken him, following her business proposition, from the Coffee Room on the top floor of Peter Jones in Sloane Square all the way to Antigua...And then to lose him, at that moment...at that moment of all moments...Was she always doomed to lose her men in dramatic unforeseen circumstances...? Her brother, wretched bane of her life, had turned up out of the blue ...And with Gregory, of all people! Twin evil geniuses for each other, no question of that! And both drunk, both keen to see her for a spot of sponging, and Gregory in particular desperate to make some sort of explanation of his past conduct, a Gregory who looked seedy and slightly plumper and somehow tarnished, like goods damaged in transit and then some ... But time had passed while she sorted them out, valuable time, hours of it, lorry loads of precious minutes, before she had been able to rid herself of the two of them, by which time Gregory was completely smashed, likewise her brother, and she'd left both out cold on the floor of her villa. She had sent an emissary and then she herself had rushed to keep the appointment. But Joe, by the time she'd actually managed to make it round to Galley Bay, had disappeared. Gone, vamooshed, disappeared into thin air, typical Joe. She gathered from her investigations that there had been quite a party. First, he'd received a telephone call from New York; then a young girl had turned up along the beach and he had danced with her.

Emma knew nothing at all about the young girl. That was new for her. She wondered who the girl might have been. Next, according to reports, there had been more telephone calls and after that he'd taken a car to the airport, after putting the young girl into a separate vehicle, and simply vanished into thin air. She'd left messages for him on his answer phone in London but to no avail – he had not replied. Perhaps he had never received them. How could she tell? How was she to know?

And so here she was, immaculately dressed in her pure Versace numbers and rich, very rich, sitting against the bonnet of her hired car in the sunshine of a beautiful Italian day, absorbing a spectacular view of the hills, and actually moping after somebody whom she hadn't seen for over a year and who very probably had forgotten that she even existed... Oh yes of course, as she reminded herself while she tried to locate herself in some form of recognisable reality, don't forget that all this heart to heart scenario she was enjoying that morning was taking place after she'd completed her first piece of serious espionage in another country delivering God knew what to God knew whom in some seedy backstreet cafe at the behest of somebody whom she just happened to know very slightly in London but who was undoubtedly one of the top intelligence chiefs in the UK. Nice work if you can get it, she whispered to herself, feeling far from home and a long way from familiars like the memory of her dead father, her mother and a few odd snatches of similar brushwood reminiscences.

She sighed again and felt the tears beginning to well behind her eyes as the wind whipped along the grasses at her feet, curving them over in hoops. It was all so unfair and peculiar, she thought, and it just didn't work out as planned at all. It had all seemed so easy and straightforward years ago. But no, it just didn't work out as planned. Years ago, she had envisaged no difficulties at all. You worked hard, you had a guy in tow, you wore good clothes, you had some good fun in London and everything else just seemed to slot into place. Virtue had its own reward and there was no need to worry about approval-seeking or power relationships; the future could take care of itself. But now, as she had discovered, it just wasn't that simple. The guys weren't reliable and they saw things from a different perspective. And they would not, repeat not, commit. No way would they commit. Either you shared their point of view or…No, it was true, they weren't ever in line in the way that she'd been in line. They were always shooting off in some new unexpected direction. So why did Gregory have to discover that he was gay for God's sake? And why did all those chinless wonders that she'd dated in London after she became rich have to be such Mummy's boys? And Geoffrey, her dead husband – why had he felt just so obliged to wrestle with that root and give himself a coronary? And why hadn't Joe simply waited for her on the beach in Antigua, instead of haring off wherever he'd gone? Why did they all have to have a separate agenda? Why couldn't they just wait to be told like everybody else? What was it about these men, that they always had to be doing what they wanted to do? Could they never stop to listen for once and just try to share things a little? Couldn't they even try to negotiate just for once?

As if, she found herself saying to herself ironically.

Guys…Negotiate…As if…

She moaned away to herself as she watched the young boy on the rock gradually recover his colour and sense of movement, thanks to the ministrations of the priest bending over him with the water bottle. Now he was stirring some more and trying to stand up, while friends in the group came rushing over to him to check on his progress in convalescence. Another pang struck her, this time smack amidships, as she watched the small scene evolve before her eyes – where are my babies then? What had happened to them? What have I done with my time in that respect then?

The pang seemed to gather all her stomach up into a ball and then twist it about with razor blades, the sense of pain was so acute.

Just as Emma prepared to grapple with this fresh threat to her sang froid, a voice broke in upon her thoughts, a voice that was familiar but which nevertheless she failed to place at once. The voice was English, quite high pitched and very confident, with a form of deft insistent fluting at the end of the phrase. It was the voice of a woman who knew her own mind even from minute to minute and let consistency be damned. And likewise anyone who ventured to disagree with whatever the line might be from minute to minute. The voice knew its own worth, in England, in Italy, or in any damned place in the universe... Emma listened some more, the while sliding discreetly round the bonnet of the car so as to remain unseen. A confused rather lower pitched mumble from another female, perhaps not English, responded to the voice. So there were two of them, thought Emma as she carried on slipping around the car, adjusting her shades at the same time. But that was all she knew. So far she had failed to put a face to the voice. But she felt some danger. She knew she had no wish to meet the voice. All she could report at that stage was that the voice had not always boded well for her, as confused memories of England and London surged about in her head. Who could it be? But without a face, she still couldn't tell.

The voice then inveighed against her tennis partner that morning and Emma thought of Norwich where she had played a good deal of tennis when she'd been married to Geoffrey. No luck with that part of the memory bank. The accent was wrong for a start. The voice had no Norfolk in it, but rather a fine plummy tone, which could only come from Surrey or Hampshire or......

Or...

The voice completed the sentence and Emma's memory bank kicked in hard with the data, sending her back to an epic moment at the Liz Playfair Bridge School just off the King's Road, in Lower Sloane Street, SW3, London to be precise. The voice belonged to Babs, who had been one of the group of women who had played at Liz Playfair's before the famous incident...And Babs was with Gay...And Gay and Babs...Emma recognised the voice now, just as she recognised the situation too, as she very quietly unlocked the car and slid into the driving seat. She'd forgotten about that little detail of her life, now about to impact on her. But now she had started to remember. And my, wasn't it a small world even in Italy? Wouldn't there be some fun, wouldn't there be just, enormous great heaps of it at least?

Some devil in Emma prompted her to leave the window wound down so that she could continue to listen to them unseen. Babs and Gay were standing not one foot away from her, but gossiping away to each other and they were oblivious to the presence in the car beside them, beshaded, ostentatiously looking the other way – and eavesdropping.

'Yes, it may be a bore playing bridge with them, but then I haven't seen Stella for a month or so now, so it ought to be a pleasure to play with her. What fun all of us just meeting up like this in Italy. I wouldn't have believed it possible not in my wildest dreams. It just shows you the power of the Sloane Square mafia. We are everywhere, feared throughout the land. Just when you think you've got rid of us, up we pop with savage force…Mind you I don't know about the others who are coming over. I don't know Ginny at all and I've never heard of Lucy-Miranda and I certainly don't know what kind of bridge they play. But then, Gay, there are still one or two odd people in Hampshire that I haven't met. Not many I grant you but there are some. And as for our bridge well it's nothing to write home about at the moment is it? If only you'd sent me a Spade back last night, everything would have been so different. I certainly gave you a McKinney, when I dropped the seven of hearts, at least I thought I was giving you a McKinney…Why you decided to return a Club I really can't make out at all, but then all of our bridge last night was a bit like that…The locals couldn't make sense of it but then neither could we, which was a pity, although I'm sure that we enhanced our reputation for deviousness. But at least it put me in the mood to play some really ferocious tennis this morning, I felt so cheated by last night's dismal performance. The Italian girl really didn't know what had hit her and I felt quite sorry for her on occasion. She spent most of the game just trudging from one part of the baseline to the other or picking her returns out of the net which was depressing for her… Emma, the other girl in their group, I can't place her at all. There was an Emma knocking about somewhere in our bridge circle who I think was mixed up in some kind of incident but that was some time ago now. I seem to remember that she was excessively rich and slightly vulgar but I may be mixing her up with somebody else. I wasn't there at the time anyway, so I couldn't tell. It may even have been boyfriend trouble but I can't be certain at this distance. If it is the same Emma, then she was very friendly with Nancy, but I don't suppose it is. There are so many Emma's nowadays, I really can't keep track of them all…I say, Gay, just look at that view will you…Isn't it just quite stunning. It makes you want to tear your clothes off and plunge in doesn't it, like that advert from M&S, advertising the normal woman…You know the one I mean, the one where the Size 16 or whatever struggles to the top of the hill, starkers, and waves it all about to the clouds in the sky…'

Sloane Square arriba, thought Emma as she quietly started the car, grateful that they had nothing more on her than a confused recollection of her newly enhanced status, which would of course be quite completely soldered out from even their memories by the time they all came to meet up for the bridge. Meanwhile, as Emma reversed, she saw that the two women had wandered closer to the edge of the rock shelf, the better to gaze at the sky and the hills and the water. Emma had forgotten to adjust for that little festival encounter that was coming up shortly, courtesy of Stella, and in truth she was forgetting about it now. The women would vaguely recognise her from the past but only faintly. She could very easily fade into the background as she played her bridge with them. That was easy; that's what she had been trained to do by the capable Nancy. But meanwhile she had found another tie with Joe. The comments of the two women brought back all her memories of that odd time, when she'd returned to London as a rich widow in search of Gregory. Joe had been very helpful to her on that occasion, even though Joe had been broke at the time – and looked it. But Joe had been devious too. It was Joe who had tried to set her up in that situation, she was more or less sure of that, and it was Joe who had weasled himself out of it just as rapidly when she tried to catch up with him.

Emma spun the wheel as she rounded the corner with the hills still on her left and still brooding about the dangerous wraith which had come to touch her life in so many different ways and yet which still eluded her.

'Joe, Joe always that wretched man hovering around me, like a spectre. And I put up with it every time,' she told herself half in anger but also half with regret because she could tell from the way her mind was working that some kind of cross roads was approaching. She was going to have to take a decision. It was time she came to terms with him and sorted it out one way or another,

191

she thought as she passed a signpost indicating just another 40 kilometres to Repugia. How about that for negotiations then, she wondered to herself, how about getting into the lists with Joe for a quick spot of duelling? She did not relish the prospect but she felt determined to persevere with her train of thought, now that the memory of the cool excitement and concentration of the letter drop was starting to ebb away.

'This has gone too long for it not to be resolved now one way or another. Craig is all very well but I think that he's just a substitute Gregory. I have to accept it – Gregory has gone for ever and I must beware of the surrogates. The past is what happened a long time ago. Craig's a nice boy and I'm certain that he'll write a very good novel about Catullus and I'm sure that I'll make a great deal of money out of it. But that's not where the action is for me, not any more, sadly. Sadly, because Craig is nice and straightforward and he might have done for me very well about ten years ago. But as of right now I think I'm going to have to reopen the Joe file once again. Because Joe is charming and elusive – and dangerous. That's one of the things I like about him – he lives with danger all the time. It sounds romantic and it sounds stupid but it must be right. I live surrounded by people who do what's right because they don't know any better and they've never done anything else. But Joe…I doubt if he's ever behaved himself once in his entire life. And look where it got him…'

She drove on and into the late morning sunshine.

Emma spent the next thirty-five or so kilometres wracking his brains about the appropriate approach to make to Joe in order to re-establish communications. It had to look right and it had to be dignified too, so that if he definitely wasn't interested she could retreat in good order – and start all over again. That was the point of the whole exercise, she told herself. She felt that she was drawing a line in the sand now and beginning to take charge of events once again. She was putting ticks or crosses against the list once and for all. That cheered her immensely. But even as she approached Repugia, driving at a slightly more relaxed pace because she really did want to find a way of contacting Joe, she was mortified to admit that her famous intelligence had for once let down. She couldn't think of a single ruse whereby she might contact him without losing face. She was greatly chagrined by this breakdown in her keenest faculties, so much so that she very nearly ran down a shepherd nonchalantly driving his flock across the road without so much as a backward glance.

She wound down the window to scream some rebuke at the shepherd, realised that she only knew how to order a glass of wine in Italian – not the most appropriate phrase in the language to express her true feelings at that moment – and then started to laugh, much to the amazement of the shepherd who had been expecting a tirade and who wandered on with some astonishment painted on his features as the laughter followed him up the path.

Emma had found the key; she had stumbled on her bit of Morse code for Joe; it was OK now; she knew exactly how to contact him. It was so simple. Joe, she knew, spoke German and Joe belonged to the Reform Club. She knew that only too well from her first delicious encounter with him at his club, when she'd gone to great pains to have her hair cut becomingly. That had been some time ago. Coiffeurs died at her feet daily now. But very well – she would write to him at his club and she would say that she was planning to learn German and did he have any old tapes she could borrow to make a start on the business of learning the language? Or could he advise a good way into the language? Some such cunning ruse. That would be her starting gambit and anything could happen from then on in. That was up to him. He could take up the gauntlet or he could leave it lying there in the dust. But she could make her approach to him quite fearlessly now...Even better too if she wrote to him from Italy, so that her craving for German would look all the more authentic. But first she would make a call to his club...

Relieved that she'd found her way out of the dilemma, largely because she had been unable to produce a volley of abuse in Italian at an errant shepherd, Emma drove on her way. She was anxious now to get back to the square and to Lucy-Miranda and to the gossip – and she even started to feel quite tenderly disposed towards Craig.

Which just goes to show, she thought as she pulled up at the hotel, just what crazies we women can be on occasion....All it takes is just a teeny-weeny bit of affection and we fall over backwards with our legs apart, gagging for it...Her mellow mood was enhanced still more by the two messages from Craig which awaited her on her return at the lobby, both of which expressed regret that she had not been around when he had called to confirm that he would be arriving at around lunchtime the following day.

Perfect, thought Emma. He'll arrive just as the great football match is finishing, so that we can all have a great lunch up at the villa and talk about Jake's footballing skills and I can introduce him to the circle, and he can ramble on about Catullus and we can all have a fairly jolly time. Which reminds me...Where's Lucy-Miranda? I must make contact with her. She'll be brooding if she's left alone for too long.

Further inspiration about Joe struck her as she emerged dripping from her shower. She was having a good day, she decided, in terms of cutting through the mental undergrowth.

'I will ring Joe at the Reform Club and check that he's still a member and whether he's been seen in the club recently. It's the obvious thing to do. I know that he belongs to the club; I've known that for years. I've had dinner there with him and it was there that Gregory made such a frightful exhibition of himself by getting pissed; falling backwards in his chair at the dinner table; and then trying to rape Pascal – oh happy, happy days. After that everything between me and Gregory went downhill. So that evening was really the start of everything. The Reform Club has a lot to answer for in terms of my love life, so it can jolly well tolerate a small inquiry from a lonely seeker after truth plus TLC in Italy. And anyway isn't that what clubs are for – so that members can be contacted easily? It's marvellous idea to ring him there and it won't cost me more than a quick telephone call.'

Still dripping and clutching the towel around her, but feeling decisive and briefly empowered, she reached for the phone and almost immediately got through to the Reform Club in London's Pall Mall via the international directorate and a couple of misdials. Communication after such a long silence should never be that swift, she thought, feeling that one foot was launching forth into the dark of empty space.

'Reform Club, good afternoon. Can I help you?'

The voice was low and confident and seemed to hark back to a previous century of deference and adventure. It sounded so normal.

'Good afternoon. My name is Emma Bales and I'm calling from Italy. I was hoping to speak to one of your members. You probably know him by sight. Joe…?'

'You've just missed him, Ms Bales. He left the Club about ten minutes ago. I believe he was heading back to his office. If you know the number, you could always reach him there. But I can take a message for him, if you wanted to leave one, and put it on the board for when he's next in the club.'

Nothing could have been more straightforward. Oh fantastic day, thought Emma. Such a good strike! She wanted to pummel the air with her fist. I'm on my way.

'Can I really? How wonderful of you. That's exactly what I do want you to do. Tell him that I called – that's Emma Bales, if you missed the name – and say that I'm writing to him today from Repugia. So he should watch out for my letter arriving in the next few days. Does that make sense? Have you got it all?'

'Yes, indeed, Ms Bales. Anything else we can do?'

'Yes, just one second, let me think…One second…Yes, I've got it, will you just put in a postscript that it's about Germany and German. Can you do that? He'll understand more when he gets the letter.'

'Of course, Ms Bales. Consider it done. Can we help in any another way'

'Not for the time being, but thank you all the same. I'd better get on with writing the letter now. Thank you so much for your help. Goodbye.'

'Goodbye, Ms Bales. I'll see that he gets the message.'

'Thank you again for that.'

Still wrapped in her towel, which she thought highly appropriate to her status as femme fatale brackets failed, Emma sat down at her dressing room table and scribbled out a note to Joe to the effect that she needed to learn German in a hurry and could he perhaps help with tapes etc. Many apologies for the imposition etc. She was sorry that she hadn't been in touch but she was tied up with a new publishing venture which had absorbed all her time etc. Hence the German. She'd be in touch again as soon as she returned to England – in the meantime, her London number was the same as it had been – and here she quoted it – so would he be kind enough to acknowledge receipt of the letter by leaving her a message etc? She hoped he was well etc. Such a pity about the meeting in Antigua but he'd never guess what had happened…And so on and so forth…

She read it through and was pleased by the tone – it was cool, businesslike and matter of fact, indeed almost dull. She particularly liked the careful untruth linking publishing with her desire to learn German. Beneath the flat prose there was a neat charge of explosive which might, just might, produce the desired response in that most uncharted of territories – Joe's heart.

Before she had time to reflect on her course of action, or entertain any pusillanimous second thoughts, she placed the single page of correspondence in an envelope; sealed it; and rang for Room Service which, upon its prompt appearance, she commanded to take charge of the letter and ensure its safe arrival in London by first class posting.

Or words to that effect.

Room Service smiled, took the letter and scurried off and Emma threw herself back in the chair, wondering in a mood of sudden fatigue whether her move had been wise or simply long overdue.

Eventually she tired of the question. So much so that by now half dry she crawled into bed and fell deeply asleep, thereby neatly avoiding both the heat of the day and her own beating questions. So what the hell, she thought before sleep overtook her, it's only a bloody letter. No one could object to that. And it's not as if we're complete strangers. Anyway, the Reform Club didn't sound too snotty about it, so that's one good thing…

And then off she dozed on a magnificent journey into sleep. Maybe espionage did stimulate the brain after all, she mused, sinking swiftly to the lower depths…

After a further hour or so, by now well after lunch, the reawakened and refreshed Emma made her way up to the square in search of Lucy-Miranda, feeling bright and confident and thinking just a little occasionally about her letter questing on its journey to London.

But there was no sign of Lucy-Miranda.

The bench in the square was empty. The square went on with its business – the wind in the square raised little puffs of dust; the women were still strolling anti-clockwise; the cafe was full of men lounging about; and the man on the other side of the square was doing his skipping, looking as round in the stomach as ever. Time stood still for them all, as it always did. But there was no sign of Lucy-Miranda. The bench looked forlorn in its emptiness, almost like an empty house.

The boy waiter could not help.

'She no been seen today here at all,' he said, practising his English on her with a flourish.

Emma was disappointed not to find her companion waiting for her. She had a whole series of lies packaged up to tell her about the trip, all of which conveyed the flavour of the excursion without ever alighting on precise detail. It seemed a pity to waste such an elaborate exercise in deception. So Emma with little better to do, but with no sense of life's emptiness, remained seated on her bench for most of the next few hours, recovering her tranquillity after the violent emotions of the morning; drinking in the ambiance of the square; and allowing time in this tiny finite piece of space to roll along quite undisturbed. It struck her after an hour or so of pleasant daydreaming that she'd become almost Italian in her outlook, as she looked forward to meeting Lucy-Miranda in the public gathering of the square, in the middle of the hurly-burly, rather than in the fast privacy of their various abodes, as they almost certainly would have done in the harsher Northern clime of London.

But still no Lucy-Miranda.

After some time, even the cafe started to register its concern. It was used to the sight of the two women roasting away together in the sun, or of Lucy-Miranda brooding there on her own. But for Emma to spend all afternoon quietly seated on her bench alone was an event out of the ordinary that called for some comment. The boy waiter was sent out as an emissary to glean fresh information. But Emma could not help him. She had no information to impart. The boy waiter staggered back to the cafe almost bent double beneath his heavy tray, after he'd collected in all the glasses, and unable to throw any fresh light on this unaccountable departure from the norm, so far as the square was concerned.

Eventually Lucy-Miranda turned up in the square round about six in the evening. Emma saw her walk rather heavily into the square from the street that led up to the back entrance to the villa. She rose to greet her from afar waving her scarf at her to attract her attention. Lucy-Miranda clumped across to see her, looking relieved. Her expression brightened at the sight of her friend.

'I can't tell you, Emma, how nice it is to see you here. I've missed you so much today. I really could have done with your help, but it's all been sorted out now, so I can sit down and have a small chin wag with you instead.'

'So what has happened? The square was worried. They all missed you. They wanted to know where the Signora Lucy-Miranda was 'iding 'erself away. Pronto.'

'Did they really, the little Italian darlings? Well, isn't that nice of them all. I was coping, that's what I was doing. Charles had one of his little turns.'

'Oh, I'm so sorry…'

'Nothing serious. He has them all the time. You can see from the nervous state of his hands that he's seriously hyper – it's the result of all those years on foreign assignment, which is how he chooses to describe the weeks and years he spent hanging around in the basements of embassies. Well, if you live on your nerves for thirty odd years, it catches up with you in the end, which is what has happened to him today. I think his whole system just goes into reverse, or at least that's what it looks like. So I spent most of the day putting him to bed, encouraging him to take some rest, reading to him – he adores Evelyn Waugh these days, so I read him some of the Sword of Honour – and then as soon as I was free, I scooted down here to the square, hoping to catch you on the bench.'

'Exactly my thoughts. I was hoping to find you on the bench. So here I waited – on the bench.'

They both laughed at the pure serendipity of their reunion.

'Of course. And such a dear little bench it's become for us all…And isn't it odd, dear Emma, just how continental we've become all of a sudden. In London, we wouldn't dream of meeting like this, out in the open.'

'We've gone native, Lucy-Miranda, that's what it is. We're wops now…'

'Sssh, some of them know that word from the milords they have to serve in the main square. Now what are you going to have. It's time one of us was sensible this afternoon, at least until Charles wakes up. So what will you have?'

'I thought…'

'Exactly, our thoughts are identical. Indeed, the same. A couple of glasses of vino bianco would not go amiss at all.'

Emma nodded with a smile. Lucy-Miranda waved away imperiously at the relieved boy waiter who came running over promptly at her signal.

'I do believe I've cracked it, Emma. The way to survive in Italy is to treat 'em rough. Nobody makes pasta like Momma makes pasta – that's the deal. That's how these tough guys are brought up. They have an inner weakness from birth. I intend to profit from my knowledge.'

And Lucy-Miranda placed her order with all the confidence and swagger of a woman whose loyalty had been sorely tried throughout the day, who had come through that testing ordeal without protest and who was now proposing to have a little R&R in the company of a friend with a cheering glass of Italian white wine in her hand.

The boy waiter took the order without a whimper.

The glasses arrived and they clinked. As they raised their glasses, Lucy-Miranda remarked with deadly intent that there had been developments between Ginny and Jake that day.

'Developments? What kind of developments?'

'Let me tell you…'

'I heard you make that promise once before. But you never did.'

'I forgot and I forget. But this time it's different. Let me tell you, Emma. First they had a terrific row at the breakfast table. I think Tommy was to blame, but they really went for each other.

Like lovers, we all thought. She was very nearly in plate-throwing mode. She was hissing at him, as the anger machine went into top gear. But then they made it up. I know this, because I accidentally ran into them – when they had their backs turned to me – at the very end of the gardens, by the statues. They were holding hands, and she was looking very obedient indeed. She almost had her head on his shoulder, as she balanced the baby on her left arm. It was a very touching little scene involving our village Romeo and Juliet.'

'I don't think I'd ever describe Ginny as a village Juliet. Goneril , yes, or Lucretia Borgia but never Juliet. No, never Juliet.'

'Maybe you're right. Do you know, to this day I think Jake assumes that it was Tommy who thumped Ginny rather than the other way round. Jake is the old fashioned sort, a chivalrous being at bottom…'

Lucy-Miranda was enjoying her gossip, as she gulped down another heavy lungful of vino bianco.

'So they've reached the physical stage?'

'Looks like it, Emma. You can't hold hands and not reach the physical stage. Or can you? On the Internet perhaps?'

'Not in my experience,' said Emma, joining in the banter but thinking with yet another pang about Joe. What if she were to discover that she truly loved him? Had always loved him? Couldn't live without him? Now wouldn't she look just the prize idiot, if he slipped through her fingers after all? And what if he didn't reply to her note? The consequences were too tragic to contemplate.

'You can judge it all for yourself tomorrow morning. We're all coming down to the square to witness Jake's soccer prowess – Charles, if he's sufficiently recovered; Ginny plus baby; Jake, of course; and yourself, as co – founder member of the Jake Soccer fan club.'

'And the Italian presence?'

'I think they'll have the cameras there for sure. Italian national news, no less.'

'How droll, Lucy-Miranda, how very droll.'

'Now Emma, you have to be sensible on this occasion. Do you think I can risk another glass before I have to return to my abandoned charge?'

'I think so and I sanction it.'

'So be it. I agree. Now you try to call him over....See if you can master the Italian boy male...The best approach is to hold your head up – so – and you do the matron look; like so; then you swivel imperiously – like so...'

'This looks like synchronised swimming. But it's working. Besides, he's been watching you like a hawk. He's on his way...'

'You see, it works, and nobody makes pasta...'

'...Like Momma makes pasta...'

'Exactly.'

And so they enjoyed another glass of white wine before departing up to the villa together. Emma had the invite to the villa party if Lucy-Miranda was around, but otherwise, not so. She was sensible enough to realise this and she refused to chance her arm alone. Ginny had that kind of fixed look when she was crossed, Emma had decided, which meant she would deal with intruders very brutally. Emma walked warily. She had no desire to be on the receiving end of Ginny's basilisk glare.

★   ★   ★   ★   ★

The following morning, Emma sat on the bench, after a fine night's sleep, and waited for the contingent from the villa to arrive. Much excitement in the square – the word about Jake's football trial had gone all around the town.

The working definition of the conceptually impossible is an Italian Trappist monastery.

The square was far fuller than usual with many of the people Emma recognised from the main square in the town just happening that morning to find an excuse to walk through its dusty expanse at that precise time on that exact day. The cafe was in a state of high excitement. The boy waiter had approached Emma more than once to check on the menu. Giovanna and her dogs, plus her friends with their dogs, had found multiple excuses to linger on the perimeter of the square, mainly by encouraging the dogs for once to amble more slowly, the while airing their own grievances even more volubly than usual.

The boy waiter could not resist pestering Emma with his requests for information.

'Is Eengleesh breakfet – yes?'

'Correct.'

'Backon, hegg, tomato – yes?'

'Yes. But what about fried bread?'

That flummoxed the boy waiter good and proper.

'Fry bread? What is, please, fry bread?'

Emma regretted introducing the whole idea of 'fry bread'. It would lead to a whole heap of multiple troubles.

'It doesn't matter. Forget fry bread. Just concentrate on backon.'

'And hegg?'

'And hegg of course.'

'Si, si…'

And off he hopped, like a small bird. Emma was relieved not to have mentioned black pudding. God alone knew what he might have made of that particular English provincial delicacy.

Emma gazed around the square and took in the presence in front of the cafe of a very determined looking group of Italians, all with a kind of rapt concentration in their look. They were swarming, she thought, but with an impression of hidden power. She concluded that these must be the town bosses, come to run their eyes over the latest potential starlet. Then she saw that there was another group quite close to them, which was quietly deferential to the first and composed almost wholly of strong, tough looking young men all wearing tracksuits and trainers…She looked more closely and discovered that they weren't trainers at all but football boots. The young men looked more like a football team than anything else…

Not many schoolchildren about either, kicking the ball at random around in the square, she suddenly realised.

And so Emma discovered the first stage in the Italians' elaborate game of subterfuge. Jake thought he was just performing in some kind of exhibition game. Perhaps that was so but it was not wholly so – the Italians were laying on a full scale opposition to test him to the utmost. They were serious about it all. If he was a genuine football star, they wanted to know for certain. Just playing in a kick-about with school kids was no kind of test for him. Emma found herself wondering vaguely about Jake's contractual commitments with Arsenal and his injury insurance, should anything go wrong – those young men looked pretty tough to her eyes.

But then if he was indeed as good as he looked, then none of it should pose any problems for him. And then as she looked again, she picked out more changes. She could see that the fairly ramshackle goals which the boys used had been replaced by a far smarter but miniature set-up, carefully placed in the square a good distance apart so that there was good play for the football. But goal scoring had become so much more tricky. Clearly some deep Italian thought had gone into all this arrangement. It was subtle, it was discreet but it was also the real thing.

Little had been left to chance.

Out of the corner of her eye, Emma saw the contingent from the villa emerge gradually into the square – Ginny looking dazzling in white jeans and blouse, with her copper-red hair glinting in the morning sunlight; she was carrying a small bag. Lucy-Miranda and Charles were walking in between slowly, with Charles looking quite determined; and on the other side, riding nonchalant shotgun, came Jake, carrying the baby, and simply dressed again in white jeans and a blue top; he was wearing his shades. As they came closer, Ginny reached across and took the baby from Jake. He gave a little skip of anticipation as he in turn took what was obviously the kit bag from Ginny. He was getting the feel of the football surface. Unbeknownst to the party and following at a discreet distance came most of the staff of the villa; they had found occasion, again at that unusual moment of the day, to attend to urgent extra-mural business in the square, all at the same time.

How very surprising!

It was going to be quite a party.

There was room on the bench for Ginny and the baby; and Emma; and Lucy-Miranda. The baby was quiet, very nearly asleep, and she was no trouble. She slumbered away with resolution, deep in contented dreams like a small animal in hibernation. Ginny sat in the middle of the group, and Charles hunted round for a chair to drag up beside them, which he eventually found. The English contingent was in place, as Jake prepared to play.

He casually peeled off his pants revealing the shorts underneath, and then doffed his top to reveal the hard muscles of his abdomen and the tight bunched pec's of an athlete on top of his form. The women gazed at the body with undisguised interest, Ginny most of all. She had a hard and hungry predatory look as she studied his torso.

The original idea, of being revenged on Tommy, was still in place. But it had been overlaid by a more basic impulse, to the fulfilment of which the row with Tommy had now provided fundamental causality. Emma thought that nothing short of a nuclear explosion would come between her now and the bedding of Jake.

'Doesn't he look marvellous? He works out all the time,' she said idly, as if she was normally in charge of the training schedule and his muscles were part of the programme. Jake was looking to change into a football shirt and glancing around at the square, and slowly removing his shades in slight abstraction as Ginny spoke and he nodded as if at his personal trainer. To an outside like Emma, there were now extra degrees of intimacy between Ginny and Jake which had evolved quite naturally during the time they had been together. No one could measure these because they existed between them as a kind of barrier against the casual stranger's interest. They seemed to move together rather than separately as if unspoken but nonetheless deeply formed, unstated pacts had been agreed between them which others might observe but could hardly understand, still less condemn. What lay between them was something that had grown up quite spontaneously in the heat of an Italian summer – no more nor less than that. It was invisible but somehow palpable in the dust and the quiet breezes –

and it was almost self-sanctioning because of its spontaneous formation.

It was then that the Italians sprang their second trap. It was neatly done and with hindsight inevitable. This was sport, Italian style. The Italians know all about handsome young men – and what they need.

Bait!

The baiting of Jake took place quite naturally. He realised that the game he was about to play was slightly more formal than he had been led to believe. So he wandered across to the other players to find out some more about the team selection etc. still in his shorts but otherwise almost naked. It was the natural uniform at that stage in the proceedings for Jake who had been playing quality grade football most likely since he was five or six.

As he moved in the direction of the other players, a young girl, perhaps eighteen or nineteen years old, detached herself from the group in front of the cafe and approached Jake, now walking across the square. She was carrying a football top which she proffered to him as she walked up to him with the unhurried sway and self-confidence of the young and the totally beautiful.

Blond, unlike Ginny, and slightly ill-kempt like all teenagers, but with a fine slim body and a caprice in her eyes which to a young man like Jake would be irresistible, she drew near to him. He stopped with a smile as she approached him. She gestured with the shirt and he assented, ducking his head. She then actually clothed him in the top in the middle of the square. She did this with the tender care and concern for detail which she might have brought to the dressing of an altar, particularly the smoothing down gestures as the top went over Jake's head; these seemed to Emma to resemble an act of homage and obeisance.

Then quite naturally, with a delighted laugh, she took him by the hand and led him into the group of Italians. She had been told what to do, most likely by her father, one of the town bosses, and she had agreed to do it, albeit grudgingly. But she had had no idea at the time just how pleasurable it would all be for her, especially the progression into the group, hand in hand with Jake.

Beside her, Emma felt Ginny gasp as she drew her breath in very suddenly.

'That's a bit overpowering isn't it?'

Emma could sense the jealousy beginning to spume from her as she dandled the baby with savagery in front of her.

'That's what you might expect from the Italians. They're always up to this kind of thing. She's just bait for him. If he's any good, then they'll do all they can to sign him up – and what better way than with one of the local beauties, if not the local beauty. And perhaps even more besides… That must be her father who is standing next to Jake now. He looks more like the local town boss than anyone I've ever seen. Jake could do very well for himself this morning…'

Emma added the last comment just to test the market for Ginny's reactions. She wasn't disappointed.

'Well let's hope Jake plays well – but not too well. We don't want to lose him to the opposition. Think what Lucia would say if she turned up and found that her beau was living down in the square with the local Jezebel…'

Emma very much doubted that Jake would be shacked up down in the square if events came to pass in that way. More likely in a monstrous hacienda somewhere up in the hills. Nor was that gorgeous young Italian girl, by now laughing with ease in the middle of the footballing group, even remotely connected to the oldest profession. But she understood what Ginny's over-statement implied. Claim jumping! All of her speech intimated, freely translated, that if that damned blond strumpet attempted to lay just one finger on her Jake then she, Ginny, personally would rip her throat out with her own nails and throw it to the dogs…Because she had found him, she had brought him on at her own pace, and he belonged to her and her pleasure and not to anybody else – at least, that was, until she'd finished with him, after which he was anybody's for the taking.

The baby rocked up and down on Ginny's knee like a metronome.

Ginny plainly did not like to feel there was any competition around to queer the pitch for her with Jake.

Bait indeed!

Comprende, wopette and hands off, was the exact meaning of Ginny's sniff which immediately followed her words.

The game started, with all the players lounging around in positions before the kick-off. Jake was playing in mid-field. The ball was passed back to him and he sprayed a fine pass across the square almost without looking at the ball. His first touch was sure and Emma could tell by watching the subfusc gaggle on the touchline that the bosses were impressed. Instead of following the game with detachment, they were scrutinising Jake's every move and chattering among themselves in commentary as he moved around in the play. He seemed to lope from position to position, a slim almost ghostly presence on the pitch. But his sense of timing was always seemingly just right and he emerged inevitably from the loose play with the ball at his feet. To be followed by the simple push of the ball or the defence-splitting pass which changed the direction of the play, creating oblique angles of possibility as the two teams massed and charged and then massed again.

Jake made it all look so easy.

The essence of his game was speed and simplicity allied to spellbinding technique. Emma could see very clearly that he had benefited from the daily hard workouts. He was normally just a shade faster than the opposition and he out – thought them on much of the play. His colleagues in the pick-up team lacked just that extra centimetre of speed to match his speed of conception and execution. Jake saw and read the game very fast. Once he executed a superb back heel which left the goal wide open to the player following behind him. But the shot was hasty and flew wide. Another time he exchanged a string of passes with a fast black haired gorilla of a footballer, but the last carefully weighted pass could only be caught by the gorilla anticipating the final open space – which he failed to do. Emma meanwhile was fascinated by the chivalry of the encounter. The Italian players looked beautiful but they played hard with commitment so that there was the occasional hard bump of one player into another. But there was no animosity in the encounter. Handshakes were given and accepted. Players were hauled with generosity from the ground. The speed of the game was such there was no time for rancour. When Jake, suddenly bursting through for a shot, went skidding away at an angle as he was neatly dispossessed, the acknowledgement of the skill on the burst and the exquisite timing of the tackle was immediate. Both players smiled at each other and then shrugged at Fortune. Emma thought that was important. Jake seemed to fit into their game and understand the underlying metaphor. They for their turn respected his twists and turns quite obviously. They rarely tried to crowd him, which was a good sign.

The men on the touchline were more silent now as they weighed his skills, nudging each other occasionally. Emma saw too that the blond teenager was simply staring quite openly with fascination at Jake as he glided around on the pitch like a slim, tanned ghost. She exuded both the gaiety and insouciance of youth. But as she stared at him there was a longing in her eyes for closer proximity. This seemed to confer an extra fiercer maturity on her. Youth was calling to youth but there was another message there as well, as the girl drank heavily to Jake with her full, liquid eyes.

She wanted him – that was obvious.

It had to happen – both ways as it turned out – but it should not have happened both at once. Jake picked up the ball in the middle of the square, feinted to go right and then changed direction very fast, taking the ball on his left foot. The opposition were tiring slightly now and they wheeled just that fraction too slowly. A gap opened up in front of goal which Jake took in at once, smacking the ball with a tremendous strike of his left foot through the thinning ruck of players in front of him.

An 'oomph' went round the square at the audacity of the shot.

As the ball flew towards the goal like a shell, Ginny's mobile phone in her bag rang with a clang. Inevitably it was Tommy calling from his London counting house. 'Yes,' she barked into the mobile as Jake's shot crashed off the low crossbar of the miniature goal and cannoned away across the square, to the handclaps of the spectators and the players alike. It was a magnificent effort, even though Jake had failed to score. He turned away, raising an arm like a gladiator in acknowledgement of the applause.

But he looked disappointed not to have scored.

Tommy wanted to explain something but Ginny wasn't having any of it. She was curt.

'Yes, yes. I got that the first time.'

Mumble, mumble, squeak from the mobile.

'All right, all right, I've got the message. Now what do you want me to do?'

She's starting to blow, thought Emma beside her. It's thundering Aetna time...She's under pressure from both Tommy and the blond beauty over by the café. Somebody's going to catch it...This could be a Jake too far for her...

Yet again Emma wondered at the capacity of the English shirearchy, even when abroad, to conduct the whole of their most intimate business as if calling to each other across three fields, oblivious of the audience. Everything was out there in the open to be discussed – except the true agenda, of course, which was never discussed at all.

'So you'll be arriving when? Next week, you say. Oh, I see, business permitting next week, but certainly in a fortnight. Well that's something to look forward to isn't it, and I'm sure that we'll all be here to greet you... No, of course not, of course I'm not being sarcastic, don't be so bloody pompous, Tom...Well, I am your wife, or have you forgotten that already... What am I doing at this moment?... Well, I'm minding my own business for a start, and I'm in the square and I'm watching a football game...Yes, it's very exciting, I think we're just about to score...'

The crowd in the square roared with anticipation and even Charles stood up to watch in the excitement of the moment. But no goal was scored. Jake's final, treacherous ball, threaded through the defence to the gorilla, bounced awkwardly on the uneven surface of the square and then ran out of play. The gorilla was mortified.

So a draw it was, after all the hard running.

The final whistle went. The play stopped. The exhibition game had been a great success. One by one all the home players went over to Jake to shake his hand or clap him round the shoulder. Emma could see that he was smiling, well pleased by his performance. Some of his play has been spectacular. He was right to feel delighted with himself.

All of his supporters were delighted for him, and one in particular, a highly nubile blond. Meanwhile the Hundred Years

War was continuing to go bosh-bosh-bosh in her ear from Ginny beside her.

'Don't be brutal with me, please. I can't stand it. I'm just sitting here in the square, being no fuss to anyone, watching the football with Charles and Lucy-Miranda and you have to come on the phone and start beating me up. Don't do it, please.'

First fall back position, thought Emma, the victim pose. Prone.

'Tommy, if you're having a tough time on your wretched deal, well then it's your tough shit. You haven't asked once about your daughter. Aren't you concerned about her. Don't you even care about her one little bit. I know you don't rate me very highly, but your daughter...Well...But of course, we all know what you very nearly did to her, so really I'm not surprised in a way...'

As Ginny's knives went in across the airwaves, each one well aimed and well thrown, Emma watched the blond saunter studiously away from her father's group and towards Jake as he approached the touchline. After a moment of hesitation she made her decision and started forward. She went up to him and kissed him proprietorially but also delicately and almost submissively on the cheek. Jake smiled at her and Ginny's eyes nearly started out of her head at the effrontery of the Italian girl.

She looked very much the Huron brave by now.

More screeching down the line at Tommy who must have been having more than just second thoughts about the wisdom of the match. Ginny was gradually working herself up into a fury. Emma recalled just what the Italian maids had been giggling about as they did the cleaning in the villa and how they would all, from a distance, have been relishing Ginny's intemperate reactions to the on-going, attempted seduction of Jake by the local beauty.

Tommy was getting very short shrift indeed. Ginny's voice began to rise in anger. Her fury was overwhelming her brain, it seemed to Emma.

'Yes, yes, we'll be here...Of course, we will. Now look, Tommy, this a bad moment...A very bad moment... The game's just finished and I can barely hear you...... We'll speak later on today. Good-bye.'

So saying, she snapped the mobile into fold position so that she could conclude the conversation; cut her husband off; and also pop the machine back in her bag all in one simple movement. The intercourse between husband and wife was over for the time being. Tommy presumably went back to his deal in London with his head ringing.

The boy waiter approached them to take the drinks order. All around them in the mid-morning sunshine, the chattering crowd in the square was dispersing in high good humour, after watching a session of football which had lived up superbly and surprisingly to the advance billing. In the boy waiter's enthusiasm, just as Ginny concluded her conversation with Tommy, he motioned in the direction of the baby in her lap with a friendly leap as if looking for someone to join in some football with him and as though the baby too constituted part of the crowd and might have been a playmate. It was a friendly lunge. But he could not have been more mistaken. Ginny's baby was never a playmate in that setting; it was an English baby and such it would remain, heavily sequestrated from the mob. Ginny glared at the boy waiter so fiercely for his effrontery and breach of protocol that he stepped back with a kind of horror in his eyes as he glimpsed her rage. He cowered before her mighty anger. Ginny's fist was clenched tight and she might very nearly have raised it against the waiter and struck him, had there not been an unexpected intervention.

'Hullo, everybody. It looks as if I got here just in time to miss all the fun. A game of football – I'd love to have seen that...'

Emma spun on her seat. She knew that voice. It was Craig, back from Verona on an earlier train than planned and looking relaxed, tanned and really quite chunky and attractive. Emma briefly was glad that they'd stayed in touch during his absence. The schoolmasterly tone was banished from his voice. The voice no longer requested attention, or threatened unspeakable punishments if that attention was withheld.

'Ginny, I don't think you met Craig to any great extent before he went off to Verona on his researches. Craig, this is Ginny who, as you can see,...'

Emma gestured towards the baby, now stirring in Ginny's lap and looking keen to play a starring part in any melodrama available or around in the next few minutes. Ginny shook hands with Craig with a slightly 'damsel in distress', faltering look in her eyes, as if she was inviting him too to ride to her rescue from the abominable Tommy.

Emma realised that Ginny had a formula. Taken to the limit, this involved a capacity for generating quite extraordinary destruction all around her, and then for her walking away from all the rubble, saying she'd been misunderstood and she hadn't meant that at all. Power without responsibility...Worlds might crash into smithereens but as the eternal victim, swaddled in fantasies of her own creation, Ginny would always disclaim all or any responsibility.

Such a dangerous woman...! And so highly protected by the high barricades of the wealth that flanked her around...!

Lucy-Miranda sprang to her feet and gave Craig a deep hug as if to say that he was welcome back from wherever he'd been. Craig smiled a deep smile at her enthusiasm for him. He hugged her back and they looked at home together in their clinch in the Italian sunshine.

Lucy-Miranda wanted to hear the whole story as she welcomed him back to Repugia.

'Now how's the writing going, Craig. I hope you haven't been neglecting your novel for the sake of your...er... researches...'

'The researches were so-so...'

'I was always a bit suspicious of those researches, as you called them. More an opportunity for doing nothing, I thought...So how much have you written so far? I thought it all sounded most promising.'

'No, the researches served their purpose – and I had a couple of adventures too while I was away which are worth the retelling. But the writing is going very well. I've finished – more or less – Part One of the novel, at least I've written the gut of it, and I've now launched into Part Two, which is writing a lot more easily than Part One, I must say. Modern times are easier than B.C. Republican Rome, although I guess it all converges to the same moment of ecstasy and despair in the end.'

'Strong words, Craig.'

'I've been writing dialogue all morning, Lucy-Miranda, and I'm still reflecting my characters' facility for shallow glib talk...'

'Well said, young man, well said.'

Words were clearly emerging from Craig and onto paper at top speed. To Emma, as his backer and editor, this looked like a definitely good thing. Lucy-Miranda nodded away at his comments, as one who is accustomed to sit and read on a hard chair, considering writing and writers as serious phenomena in the landscape and worth the comfort sacrifice. Ginny glinted at him as another potential victim of her outraged amour propre, just as a sweat-stained and quietly exultant Jake joined them. He slipped back into the group discreetly. His nipples stuck out proudly beneath the t-shirt and the sweat streamed on his skull. It had been a tough workout even for him. Mentally he was still juggling the ball at his feet, and feinting from left to right, looking for the break. He was just a touch breathless.

'Those Italian boys really know how to play a bit. Know that, doncher. They read me right all the way through the game. Very impressive of them. The one-two's never work in England, but here it was working every time…They never lost their bottle either – amazing…The heads never went down… Brilliant…'

Then he stopped, aware dimly that he was stepping out of role and voicing serious views on a sacred topic in front of people who wouldn't know a wall-pass from a yellow card. Nonplussed and out of synch, he looked around.

Ginny stared at him, or rather at his nipples. Craig intervened.

'You must be Jake and you must be from Stoke Newington.'

Jake looked startled by the accusation, like a comic figure from Dickens, a sort of circus Bill Sykes. Craig stepped forward to introduce himself. Jake spoke to him,

'Not me, I'm from Manor Park but my Mum, she was from Stoke Newington. Always talked like that, even though they laughed at her in the street. But how d'you know all of this? I'm just an ordinary guy, honest I am, Guv…Know what I mean?'

East London was suddenly very present in this group of expatriate patricians. A relaxed Craig laughed in the sun. The two men were hitting it off, menaced as they were by compatriot women in a foreign land.

'It's way you said bottle, Jake. You pronounced it bottol, which is a characteristic way for Stoke Newingtonians to use their 't' sounds. Elsewhere in East London, they simply drop the 't' altogether and say 'bo'ull, swallowing the 't' at the back of the throat.'

'Froat'.

'Stoke Newington is a little speech island all on its own.'

'Bleedin' 'Ell, Craig, you sound like a teacher.'

'I am a teacher, Jake but I'm taking time off to write a novel.'

Jake nodded unafraid and the group stirred. The baby was getting restless and so too was Ginny at the evident bonding process. The boy waiter approached them on tiptoe, as the two men grinned at each other in the sun.

'Eengleesh breakfest, please, now, pronto...'

Emma broke in on the discussion.

'I forgot to tell you about any of this, Craig, but there were two things happening this morning – first a little game of football involving Jake, as you can see; and then an English breakfast involving us all, including yourself if you haven't already stuffed yourself with coffee and buns on the train.'

'What a glorious idea, Emma. Yes, I'd love to join you, although I did have the odd croissant en route, it must be said. But Jake here, doesn't he need to shower first?'

'I can do that in the cafe. They've given me the bathroom to change in, so I can join you in a few moments.'

'Don't be long, Jake. Otherwise we'll have scoffed the lot. Then where would you be?'

'Not happy, that's for sure. A man needs his breakfast after a game like that. Some of those tackles... Wait one – I'll be back very quickly.'

Jake moved off at some speed towards the cafe, with the boy waiter tagging along beside him. Emma saw the blond detach herself, a trifle hesitantly, from her group, and move towards him. They spoke briefly together at the entrance to the cafe and Emma thought she detected a snort and a frisson of rage from the Fury beside her. But she might have been mistaken.

Jake disappeared into the cafe and the blond swayed back towards her father, one haunch delicately following another in a faun-like movement, head held high in evident great delight. Her father now ranked as a very great man, in her eyes, for introducing her to Jake.

Emma could just see the storms ahead, despite the brilliance of the day all around them.

They all arrived at the cafe, and sat down at the table prepared and set aside for them. Great chattering all around them at the brilliance of Jake's play. The waiters and the owner were out in force in order to serve up the feast and the air was filled with the clatter of plates, the poop of water bottles fizzing, the scrape of chairs, and the odd whoop of enthusiasm from one or other of the waiters as they relived memories of the footballing display, waltzing in and out from the kitchen, an imaginary football at their feet. The pungent smell of the bacon sizzling away in the kitchen ranged through the cafe – breakfast, English style, was hitting Repugia.

Attention focussed on Craig in Jake's absence. He talked about his experiences in Sirmio, in pursuit of the real Catullus.

'Sirmio was Catullus' family home, up in the North of Italy, just on the shores of Lake Garda. He has a poem in the collection which describes the sight of the servants coming out to greet the young master as he is rowed across the lake on his homecoming. He's dog-tired, and says more or less in the poem that there's no place like home and your own bed…Not very original, but there again, he says it all very sweetly…So anyway, when I met this guy in Verona in the library who took an interest in what I was researching, he said to me that I ought to go and visit Sirmio and that he would come with me. Well, I thought that the contact might lead somewhere, you know, manuscripts suddenly appearing out of walls and that kind of thing, but no such luck. It didn't, I'm sorry to say, but I did get to Sirmio and something very odd did happen to me there, which was, and is, quite inexplicable. If you look at it all from a certain angle, I mean…'

A showered Jake rejoined them very quietly and took his place unobtrusively at the table, carefully avoiding interrupting Craig in his discourse. He looked pale but composed now that he was recovering from the game.

'I travelled up there with my guide, who turned out to have relatives in a place called Desenzano, most likely the village where Catullus hired his boat two thousand years ago. Anyway we parted company after a fun journey, and I hired a boat and read the actual poem aloud as I was being rowed across the water to the family home. Nothing so odd about that, apart from it being a very romantic tribute. I landed at Sirmio, and I wandered about. I then made my first discovery...'

Plates loaded with sausages; beans; eggs; and bacon, with – miracle of miracles for Jake – fried bread to boot, arrived at the table. Somebody from the villa, who knew about Jake and his breakfasts, had been talking to someone else in the square, passing on information. Coffee in steaming jugs was plonked here and there, and bread arrived by the basket. The cafe owner then arrived in person and shook hands with Jake and embraced him on both cheeks. Jake took it all in his stride as a matter of course. From where Emma was seated she could see the blond and her father in a huddle outside still discussing the game. This problem, she thought, is not going to go away. In fact, it's going to get closer. I can see that. You don't need to have gone through a crash course in espionage to deduce that little verity. The minute that blond takes it into her head to make her move...

They all plunged into the food, as Craig continued talking:

'I found there were sparrows all over the place, especially on the beach. As you know, Catullus' greatest poem is to Lesbia's little sparrow. But I'd never seen sparrows in such profusion anywhere else in Italy, so all of that maybe suggests that Catullus took Lesbia to the family home...'

Politely, Jake inquired of Lucy-Miranda what in all the world Craig was on about. Lucy-Miranda obliged in her best 'bringing the tablets down from the mountain' manner. But it was well done with no hint of condescension, just a concern for accuracy.

'Craig's novel, in Part One, deals with a Latin poet called Catullus who has a real hot and heavy bone-shaking affair with a rich Roman lady called...Called what, Craig?'

'Clodia was her real name, although Catullus calls her Lesbia in the poetry.'

'Yes, and Jake, she was an older woman, like me, so you'd better watch out...'

Lucy-Miranda muscled up against Jake suggestively and they all laughed, Ginny included, although Emma saw that she was glittering and glinting away at Jake like a Christmas tree.

It can't be long now, thought Emma, especially since her husband is now threatening to come out to Italy shortly and round her up. And then there's the blond outside, hovering like a hawk...No, she's going to move in very shortly...It's a matter of personal honour with her, especially after this morning's little love murmurings with Tommy...

Emma saw that Charles was well snuggled up to Ginny, seated as he was on her right. He was helping Ginny with the baby; crooning to her; feeding her whatever she wanted on the table; and in general behaving towards Ginny and her baby like a large but obedient courtier lapdog. Outside the cafe, the town bosses, big men in their jackets and suits were mooching about together in the square, talking, gesticulating, and clearly arguing one or two points quite vehemently. The blond hung about hesitantly, not certain whether she should feature or not in this particular scene.

Eventually, Charles tore himself away from his preoccupation with Ginny and standing up in front of them all, said that he wanted to congratulate Jake on his great performance that morning. The English breakfast was going down well, and disappearing with speed from the bowls and dishes on the table.

'It was really excellent. I don't know how anyone can play like that. You were a pleasure to watch, Jake. Whenever I've tried to play football at all seriously, something happens to my legs and they don't do what they're supposed to do.'

Laugher at this point. Emma wondered just how much of Jake's performance Charles was planning to hi-jack for himself by attributing it all to patriotism, thereby milking the credit in his own direction. The answer came quickly enough – about 90% or more of it. Raising his mug of tea to the assembled group, Charles made the inevitable comments:

'You were a credit to us today, Jake, and we have to thank you for it. You kept up the standards. As a nation, we fall short in many things and we acknowledge this. But today was different. I'd like to think that today you helped to instil just a trifling amount of respect for the British way of life among these...'

And Charles crouched low, Archie Rice style, and whispered behind his hand with a grimace,

'...Wops...'

Laughter, for the most part genuine enough and unforced. Emma was upset to see just how grimly Charles went about the business of putting the correct imprimatur on the morning's doings. She was even more disturbed to note that Craig by his applause seemed to endorse what Charles had said. This startled her. Craig's eyes were shining with enthusiasm. He had liked the allusion to the British way of life and he was gazing at Charles with something more than just approval. Emma was shocked. Could she have been nurturing by any chance a full blown fascist snob? Someone who actually believed all this nonsense? Was there a social climbing viper in her bosom in the shape of Craig? Yet another Englishman yearning for Agincourt and a toast to the Queen?

Perish the thought, she decided but it was hard to shake the idea from her mind. Jake then stood up and replied in a few well chosen words. For a boy from East London he was remarkably pithy and poised. Jake did public speaking quite naturally.

'I never thought that Hackney Marshes would equip me to play a game of football in the middle of Italy. But there you go…That's football for you…All those kickabouts were worth it. As we say back at the old ABC, we count 'em in and we trade 'em out. That's showbiz for you. Many thanks to one and all for all turning up on this very important day for me when I do declare I have eaten just about the best English breakfast it's possible to eat – that is until Ginny gets to work and does the same for me up in the kitchens at the villa. Now you must excuse me. I'm starting to feel just a tad fatigued and I also have to go and talk to Lucky fairly shortly and inform her of the gruesome outcome to my encounters with the…'

Stage pause. It was well done.

'…Wops…Was that the word? Or did I mishear that one?'

More applause. Some banging on tables in good English rowdy fashion. Jake's timing was good.

'Perhaps we could all put our hands together and give Mr ….'

'Signor Rossini,' said Ginny in a very loud whisper.

'Yeah, all right, I think I just about got that.'

Jake scratched his earlobe, holding the audience's attention effortlessly.

'Do you think I'm deaf or something, Ginny? Mind you, I wouldn't be at all surprised if my eardrums had gone all to pot, after dealing with that baby of yours. She sounds like something in pain on the Thames some days. '

Ginny was not pleased at all by this display of familiarity, as her frown of disapproval showed. Jake continued:

'Anyway, that's by the by. She's a wonderful child, most of the time and you can see exactly what she'll be like when she grows up by looking just about half a foot North of her sweet little cherubic face…'

More laughter.

'…So isn't she the lucky girl? Anyway, without further ado, can we all give Mr Rossini a big hand of applause for his breakfast this morning. Ladies and gentlemen, I give you breakfast a la Rossini.'

Lots of applause, stamping of feet, cries of Rossini, Rossini, Rossini, whereupon Sr Rossini in person appeared in front of them all. He was an archetypal stage Italian. Plump; short toothbrush moustache; fussy manner; and hands waving for silence.

'Pliss,be quiet, pliss. Congratulations on brakefest. But quiet pliss again. Shortly we maybe 'ave some news of something else. Just one little moment for us all to wait…Be quiet, pliss…'

The blond suddenly materialised through the door which led to the square and swayed into their sight. Ginny controlled herself sufficiently not to hiss at her – just. The sunlight followed her through the door. The long blond hair fell about her face in unruly, uncontrollable fronds, testimony to her shyness. She had been charged with a mission from her father. She looked important, because of the mission and because it involved Jake. But she was also deeply apprehensive because she was not used to commanding the podium so decisively. She feared that her mother would turn up at any moment, overwhelm her with reproaches, bully her and then chase her off into the kitchen to complete her chores.

Ginny stared at her blankly as one would discountenance an intruder.

'Jake, Jake, my father, he want to talk with you about your football…'

She subsided into silence, cowed into muteness by the attention of the British and her own lack of stage confidence. But she still stood there, like eternal youth, tall, graceful and swaying like a ripe peach on a bough, slightly buffeted by the wind. She held her ground because of Jake.

Jake for his part looked slightly weary as if he had been expecting such an overture.

'Sure. I'll come with you, Angelina. Where is your father? Still outside? Lead me to him. He may be in for a shock when he discovers that I'm tied up with the Arsenal. But who knows…I might be able to sell him a few US Treasuries at cheap prices in the meantime, though…'

Lightning had flashed through Ginny's eyes at the rapid intimacy implied by the mutual use of Christian names. Things were going far too fast for her now and she would have to intervene. Lucy-Miranda interrupted Jake.

'Charles, you've got Italian haven't you? I do think you should go with Jake and help him if he needs anything translating from Italian. It could be worth quite a few millions to him, if you were there. Don't you think so?'

With a veneer of politeness which barely covered his reluctance to be separated from Ginny at the breakfast table, Charles scrambled to his feet and took charge immediately and inappropriately.

'Come along with me, young man, I'll handle these negotiations for you. We'll see if we can't diddle these Eyeties on their own back doorstep.'

The three of them – the blond; Jake; and Charles – exited into the sunshine. Emma saw the three of them reach the group outside, and registered how warmly Jake was greeted by a man who was obviously the blond's father. Patronage, Italian style. More gesticulations; more pacing about; this time with the arm around Jake's shoulder.

Ginny seemed quite calm inside the cafe as she fed her baby and waited upon events. Some silence at the table. This was Craig's moment, come yet again. To some degree importunately, he resumed the tale interrupted by the rapid furnishing forth of the breakfast.

'Anyway, there I was in Sirmio, looking at these sparrows and ruminating away about the novel, when all of a sudden I realised that it was late. There seemed to be no way that I could get back to the railway line at Desenzano. If I couldn't catch a bus from Sirmio then I was stranded. And I did in fact turn out to be stranded – no bus at all. So I started to walk back, which was hardly a pretty prospect because it was about thirty kilometres or so, and the romance of the journey had started to wear off...'

Craig had their attention back now. Teaching must be worth something, thought Emma, if you can grab and hold an audience like that. She listened with half an ear, still taking in what was happening outside. Charles standing almost to attention in the sun was doing his translation bit valiantly.

' So, as I said, I started to walk, hoping to thumb a lift, or something like that. Nothing doing. There was just no way that the Italian drivers were going to stop for me. They whizzed past at top speed gazing at me in the half dark as they went by, as if I had been a vagrant. So I decided that I was in for a long walk, tried to make the best of it, and off I started. Now the point about Catullus is that he spent a lot of time travelling here and there on trips, mainly in Asia. So did his friends, with the fervent hope which they all had as they shot off and away that they would meet up again, at Sirmio or some similar place, even Rome, and swap travellers' tales. So, I thought, if I read Catullus aloud in the boat on the way over Lake Garda to Sirmio, as a mark of veneration, I'll read him again just before I set off again on a far tougher trip. Which is what I did, and in quite a humble frame of mind. Catullus will understand, I said to myself, as one does. You know the prayer, I'm sure – hey, if you're out there somewhere, Catullus babe, send me a cart or an ox or just anything to take the burden out of the journey. I picked out what I thought was the most appropriate poem to read under the circumstances – one about one of his pals getting home safely and how they all rejoice when he arrives back – and I solemnly read through the whole poem aloud in the night and in the hedgerow, a poem, mark you, written almost exactly two thousand years ago, as the cars crashed by on the road. And what happened…?'

Silence from his audience. They gazed at him like the Pied Piper.

'A car stopped within two minutes of my finishing the recital, two jolly Italians picked me up, and I was back in Desenzano within a half hour. They bought me some drinks too, and gave me a very hospitable trip. Cultivated guys – they chattered on and on about Latin poetry. Now what do you make of all that – sparrows and then some magic on the journey? Isn't it remarkable? It's all going into the novel, I can tell you, Emma.'

Silence from his audience as he finished his tale which had been well told. Then a little round of applause from Emma and Lucy-Miranda, praising the artful raconteur. Lucy-Miranda took Craig's hand and told him how well he was looking.

'I think Emma will be very pleased to hear that her author is on course for writing his best-seller. How are you going to work the story into the novel?'

'Possibly it will fit best in Part Two, the modern bit. But if you all read it there, you'll know where it came from.'

Ginny showed sufficient interest in Craig's project to ask when publication date was scheduled. Craig replied to her. Again Emma was struck by the tone of respect, almost deference, that he adopted towards the haute bourgeoisie. It was something in the craning of the body, she decided, like an involuntary genuflection in mid-air outside a church. He seemed to grant her extra attention beyond the required measure.

'Some time after I've finished writing, I'm afraid, which won't be before Xmas at the earliest. So add on a year to that, roughly, and you get the approximate date of publication. There'll be a launch party, of course, Emma permitting, so obviously I'm hoping…'

His slightly hamstrung gesture at that point seemed to indicate a willingness to invite all around the table but only provided that his backer, Lady Emma Bales, showed willing. The body language was unfortunate. Emma thought that Craig was slightly pre-empting her role in the matter of his novel and its publication but no matter. She was too fascinated by what she took to be the hierarchical by-play between Ginny and Craig to take any offence. So she nodded vaguely at the whole idea.

'Of course. The launch party will be the talk of the town...'

The discussions outside were still going on. In the sunshine of the square, Jake was going through his repertoire, closely watched by the Italians. He was balancing a football on his instep and flicking it with continued accuracy onto his shoulder and then his head, where he nodded it up and down with total control. This was serious stuff. The Italians were very definitely interested. They were going to make him an offer of some sort. Charles was scratching the back of his neck, presumably flapping slightly as terms like 'libero' and maybe even 'catenaccio' flowed back and forth. Ginny was also craning her neck to take in the scene outside with an expression of feigned detachment.

The blond was very close to Jake, almost playing a supportive role. Her foot was pawing the ground and scraping out patterns as she moved from foot to foot. Craig was still talking about the novel and Catullus, mercifully. The suspense regarding the negotiations outside was mounting.

'There's just one little passage in the poems which brings the whole affair with Lesbia to life for me. He's talking about the friend who lent Catullus his house where he and Lesbia could meet...'

Emma noted that Ginny seemed to wake up at this point or at least register her attention afresh. She seemed more relaxed all of a sudden and her ears certainly seemed to prick up.

'Catullus says that this friend opened up a wide path for them through a closed field, which looks like an obvious allusion to the exact location of the house. Well, that's no use to man nor beast now, because we don't know where the house is – or was. But then Catullus says about the house, in something of an aside, that his white-skinned goddess, visiting him there and on tiptoe, smiling, would put her bright sole on the smooth-worn threshold, foot poised on a creaking sandal...Doesn't that just tell the whole story...? Isn't that a moment from the past come to life? Lesbia has been dead now for two thousand years. She returned to primeval dust many years ago. Yet reading that line, she is still so very much alive, just hovering on the threshold of the house, in the sunshine with her faintly tanned skin and waiting to see her Catullus in their secret hiding place where the two of them can't wait…'

Lucy-Miranda congratulated him on his literary detective work and Ginny sat there in silence at the breakfast table, nursing her baby with a far-away look in her eye.

Another covert, approval-seeking glance at Ginny from Craig, Emma noted.

'Catullus must have died in a total agony of remorse. But no, that may not have been the case. Just wandering around the streets brings you in full frontal contact with the Italian mentality, which is to live and let live. They are such a casual people with their beauty and their countryside and their sun – they've seen it all before so many times. So perhaps he got over it all, although he was supposed to have died of a broken heart at the age of thirty something.'

Ginny was listening to all of this, which was being delivered for her benefit, with half an ear. She had turned off long ago, as soon as she heard that the novel would not be available immediately. No need to warn her friends yet about something sensational on the way from an unknown writer she happened to run into in the villa in Italy. But Craig was not to know that. He, the skilful teacher, failed to read the signs of inattention in part of his audience. The grip factor was fading. Or perhaps he didn't dare acknowledge to himself that he'd lost the plot, as he tried to cope with his first morale-shattering exposure to Hampshire society and its highly restrained attention span.

'There is a very small poem right at the end of his collection which talks about a moment of reconciliation between himself and Lesbia, when she's come back to him, as he thinks, and they're together again and still in love and enjoying each other. The pain in the gratitude which he offers up to the gods just tears away at your guts as you read it…'

Ginny had lost interest. She ignored Craig and his tedious twitterings. She was looking at the square outside.

Jake returned back into the cafe from outside, looking preoccupied. His re-entry mercifully killed Craig's monologue and Emma felt relieved. He had rambled on just that little bit too long, with the teacher in him overwhelming the audience-sensitive raconteur. Ginny sparkled somewhat as Jake sat down at the breakfast table, now a sad little desert of half-full coffee cups, empty bowls scattered here and there, dirty plates and the debris of bread, butter and jam. Here was new sport for her, and just in time before the holiday tedium set in.

Jake spoke to all and sundry at large, with a smile but with an expression as well of concern. Charles regained his place at the table beside Ginny who made room for him. The blond had disappeared, presumably with her father.

'Well, this is all going to put the kybosh on lots of things for me...I didn't realise that I was being set up here, although it doesn't matter. It had to happen sooner or later and an English breakfast is maybe a small price to pay for it all. You see, the Italians out there want to make me an offer. They want me to go and play in a serious trial for them, at Roma. Now any of you know what kind of a football club Roma is...?'

He spread his hands on the table, very much the trader back in the market, asking his people to follow him on a reasonable point.

'Well, I'll tell you, it's a very big and important Italian football club. So in theory this is a very big break for me. They're offering me a way into top flight Italian football. I have to tell you that Italians don't pay peanuts either, if you make the grade. The noughts on the contract go off the paper.'

Ginny was paying very close interest indeed to Jake's words, but still with visible detachment. She was fondling Sam in a sweet motherly way but she was keeping quite quiet, away in the corner of the restaurant. Socially, she had decided that Jake was a non-starter, baked, boiled or fried, Emma had guessed. The fact that he might suddenly be worth an enormous amount of money cut precisely no ice at all with her. His position in the world according to her hierarchy remained unchanged. Jake lacked tone. She could not introduce him to her friends, not in a month of Sundays. So that was that. But the social fatwa was not necessarily fatal to his chances with her personally. Lots of other nice things were by no means ruled out of court, far from it...In fact they might even become more accessible because of his total social impossibility...

Like a tigress on the bough, Ginny would bide her time.

'Now my problem is, and always has been, that I have this deal with the Arsenal. You know, we football stars – that kind of thing. It's not much of a deal, but it was negotiated by my agent, who is now very much my ex-agent. He turned out to be a complete tosser. He's done this with lots of people on his books. It was a mistake my ever getting tied up with him, I know, but there you are, what's done is done and there's an end to it. I blame my mother, which is about all she's good for these days.'

Emma saw Lucy-Miranda wincing at the roughness of Jake's street-wise comments. It was understandable. But Jake was nothing compared to the impact that little Lucia would have on her, the little Lucia whom Emma had last seen as a shy very late teenager and who now presumably had matured into a markets' toughie of the first water. Lucia might very likely shock her mother rigid with her foul language and her instinctive claim for first-round control in almost everything.

'So I have to go back to the Arsenal and tell them what's going on. Now, they don't like dealing with the players direct for obvious reasons; they prefer to trade with the agents. But I don't have one, so they're going to have to talk to me, at least temporarily. It's all a matter of presentation, I can tell you, and they will talk to me but how they're going to take it, God alone knows. I was supposed to be up for the first team squad next season which is why I've been training so hard but now...Well, Roma's a big club and you can't just walk away from them, can you? I wish Lucky was here to advise me. She's good on that kind of thing...'

Jake looked out of his depth and a long way from home. Lucy-Miranda made the obvious comment as he smoothed his hand over his skull in a gesture of embarrassment.

'Can't you just ring my daughter up and discuss this with her? It seems to be the obvious thing to do. I'm sure she'd love to talk to you.'

'First of all, you don't know your daughter very well or the position she's in right now if you think that, Mrs...'

'Lady...'

'Lady Mrs Dawson ...'

'Oh for heavens' sake...'

'Well, whatever. I really can't handle these titles at all. They set my teeth on edge. But you see, with Lucky, I'm a trader, and I trade the market mainly for her on her deals. Now she's involved in a massive takeover deal, which means that she can't talk to anyone outside a small circle. She's got to be careful how she talks to the cat in these conditions, because the cat may not have signed a confidentiality agreement. Some of them refuse. It's been known to happen in the past. So if I call her up and say 'Wotcher Lucky, how's it going and know what's happened out here etc etc,' and then something goes wrong and the share price of whoever they are trying to take out goes haywire well then we're all in deep trouble then aren't we? The finger of suspicion is never very subtle in the way it points. If anything went wrong, Lucky would be out on her ear hole, like me and all the rest of them...I know she's my girlfriend but one has to temper desire with discretion here.'

'I wondered why Tommy wouldn't tell me a thing about this deal. So that's the reason is it? How fascinating...'

'No, I'm going to have to handle all of this myself. I think I'd better have a good think about it all. Now what's happened to that coffee. Is there any more of it? The Arsenal people are not the easiest of folk to chat with, and I'll need the caffeine, after all this running about this morning.'

On cue, Sr. Rossini bustled in with more coffee, and evident hopes in his eyes that the commission paid to the men and boys at his cafe who had spotted Jake's potential would be very large indeed. He clapped Jake on the back with a big smile on his face with his other hand waving towards the middle distance, towards Rome.

'Roma, eh, Roma.'

He blew a large kiss with his fingers towards the Eternal City.

'Big, big football club, Roma...You will be so 'appy with them...'

Jake did not look as if he was in the mood to sign autographs. As the breakfast party started to break up, he buried his face in the coffee cup, lost to them all in a mood of abstraction. Emma wondered whether or not to step out of role and reveal herself as a fairy god-mother who knew about the law. On second thoughts she decided that to take such an initiative would be unwise... So she would remain in role and wait until she could discuss it all with Lucy-Miranda on their bench at the earliest opportunity. She was missing their duet on the bench. What with the breakfast and the blond and Ginny, her world seemed to have become very crowded all of a sudden. Emma also realised that she would need to park Craig somewhere at some stage for whatever time it took while she enjoyed a council of war with Lucy-Miranda. She rather resented his presence on that account. He niggled. She'd forgotten about him by and large. Provided he did lots and lots of writing, everything would be fine but the plain fact of the matter was clear – life had moved on somewhat for her, leaving Craig still stuck in mode as the aspirant writer. While he had been thumbing lifts on the road from Sirmio, she had actually been doing her bit of espionage...And lots more...And these things counted as a force for change in the long run.

Emma caught up with Lucy-Miranda as she was leaving the cafe and intimated that a small tete a tete would be most welcome. Lucy-Miranda looked surprised but gratified by the invitation and they agreed to meet the next morning, early but not too early, by which stage dear Craig ought to be at his writing desk and scribbling hard. And if he wasn't, then she, Emma, would like to know the reason why...

And that was how they left it, with Jake walking slowly back to the villa with Ginny, deep in thought like a younger Achilles and carrying her baby.

The blond was nowhere to be seen – for the time being.

$$\star \quad \star \quad \star \quad \star \quad \star$$

Joe was spending a lot of his time watching the screens and waiting for a sail. Not a lot else to do – the proposed bid had reached that stage familiar in all hostiles when the assumed shock of the future event, when the bid would have been announced, was equally matched within the ebb and flow of Time by the slow on-going of the present, when nothing untoward happened.

So, and against the expectations of the predators, Rivers Pugh's operation sailed on unconcerned...

And Joe watched the screens where equally nothing happened. The $ refused to boom and the Euro trod water and the £ bobbed and ducked within its range. Stasis on forex.

No story... Joe watched away, waiting for his sail, sensing at the same time that his stock was falling daily within ABC; his audiences with the Quiff had become less than perfunctory. A man who claims to make the weather will necessarily find few buyers of his personal stock in the personality futures markets when his predictions of storm and stress ahead are found wanting. A supremely self-confident Felix now openly queried many of Joe's views of the market at conference, always prefacing his jeering remarks by a little seemingly innocent squiggle of thumb and forefinger together. Those at the meetings reckoned that Felix was questioning the value of Joe's market views. Quick to jump on the bandwagon, the gesture spread to the traders in the dealing rooms where Joe's sparse appearances were greeted by a forest of graft signs.

Good natured, of course, but increasingly with a slight edge to the mass gesture as the traders sensed that Joe's formerly high flying rating was experiencing a trip to the credit rating agencies. It's worse than being told to fuck off, Joe thought. I'm actually being hacked off physically.

Isn't Felix a good operator?

And so no deal either...At least not for the time being, although the ABC dealing room was not to know any of that, such was the secrecy that attended the diligent preparations for the hostile... Lucia and Tommy worked hard and pumped the institutions dry with suggestions about Rivers and his operations. But in the limit and as happens in hostiles their calumnies were almost counter-productive; the reservations expressed by the dynamic duo about Rivers' performance paradoxically raised the exit price. The buying or selling bias had fallen in the institutions' favour and they could afford to ante up without fear. Absent the currency kicker the deal was going to be hard…The odd buyer of Rivers Pugh futures could be seen here and there.

Tom Stone isn't helping either, Joe reflected for the nth time as he gazed at the dealing screens, tracking the cursor and simultaneously perusing the Chron. Sure, it was increasingly a new look, new broom Chron and very pretty to look at with its fresh lay-out. Joe liked Tom and respected him as a journalist; indeed he had managed to use him many times in the past on his own behalf, very likely contributing to the advancement of Tom's career. But Tom's freshly found independent editorial line was a pain. It blocked Joe's project since it consisted for the most part in preaching the virtues of the Euro; the attractions of Europe; and the fading charms of the $. This, in turn, had actually helped boost the European currency on forex as the market, with some bemusement, adjusted slightly to the Chron's line. It assumed as usual that the Chron, traditionally the house-journal to the Bank of England, was in full, heavily motivated signalling mode, as Whitehall debated endlessly the pro's and cons of the £'s entry into the Euro. And for the time being, the pro's had it…

So no play for the $, not at any price…And no deal for Joe…

Joe continued scanning the screens as his mind, idly, ranged across Time. From mulling Moley and his much-altered persona – only to be expected, Joe told himself, and there are many unanswered questions there – he fell to brooding on the very different Lucia he had encountered in the past, as indeed she bustled in and out of his office still intent on sewing up the deal but increasingly sceptical about Joe's capacity, indeed ability, to deliver on same.

Joe knew that both she and Tommy had been given a very hard time from their loved ones, abandoned perforce in Italy, as they slogged it out seemingly fruitlessly during the summer in London's Square Mile. Tommy, in particular, had been on the receiving end of any number of brickbats from his dearly beloved, ever-loving Ginny, now swanning it in the Repugian sun. Tommy's reaction had been stalwart . He had closed his mouth up – so! – in repressed rage and buckled to with a will, hoping to drive down deep into the depths of Lethe the shrewish comments of his spoiled, misunderstanding wife.

But Lucia was less involved. She was cooler. Across the continent by heavily-monitored phone, just like Tommy, she spoke on occasion to Jake, whom Joe in fact admired as a clever trader, in a fairly off-hand way. But she talked to him flatly with no sign of Tommy's inner torment – business was always just business for Lucia; Jake faraway had reverted in identity to the trader she knew in the dealing room rather than the stud she had hand-picked to service her when she required. She was like her father in that respect, rather than her mother; she was a true Maitland; and as such born to trade. It was in her blood, in her skin and in her pores. Thus it was almost like a force of nature that she just continued trying to do the business.

And stroking her nose in a meditative kind of way...Just like her father, Spongo Maitland, had done before her...And reflecting on the business in hand, with that quick eye for the main chance...Just as her father would have done... Her father, Spongo, who had been Joe's old boss at Martins, would have approached the dilemma of Joe's bid with caution, sniffing the air just as his daughter was doing now...

Thus does Nature, pleased with its initial handiwork, repeat itself rather than deviate from the first winning line...

As the forex trades flickered up and down on the screen, watching them with more than half an eye, Joe allowed himself, briefly, to follow such a meditative line about Nature, because he well knew in which direction his thoughts were latterly tending...

And they would get there soon enough...

Towards a full reprise of Lucia's erstwhile bad girl behaviour before she discovered her true vocation in the City. This was never, ever discussed between them...But not only towards Lucia but also beyond her, as his thoughts began to circle round her mother, Lucy-Miranda, also just as well known to Joe in a previous life. Well known to Joe in a way that daughter Lucia, now thrusting some files under Joe's nose, would have found wholly shocking...

Because at university, Lucy-Miranda, older than Joe by some considerable margin, had been his girl-friend...And because they had travelled frequently together in Italy, riding the railway systems in carefree, blithe, go anywhere in summer mode...Because also they had stopped more than once in the Repugian region, not at the town itself but somewhere close by – a Roman fort, Joe seemed to recall – in order to do what had to be done urgently at the time...And very nice and cosy it had been too, that Roman fort, he remembered, although that was then...Almost as long ago in History as the Romans themselves...

One thing is sure in all of this, Joe told himself, I will not be going back to Italy and I will not be seeing Lucy-Miranda again; the first re-encounter was bad enough at that dinner-table, with Spongo dancing attendance and the mad brother prowling around... Having her daughter running this bid for me is tricky and dangerous, but not quite impossible; besides, the bid hasn't flown, which puts a different gloss on everything. But as for meeting Lucy-Miranda again – No, that is just too much; coincidence can go so far and no further; I wholly reject the possibility. Anyway she's married to Charles and I know that for a fact, so I'm safe as houses from her.

Good old Charles...Let the Grim Reaper keep his distance for a while.

And Joe thanked God for the very, very, very low profile he had opted to keep at ABC. His true role in M&A was known only to a few and principally to those within the most senior echelon of the bank, Moley always excepted. Here today and gone tomorrow as soon as the market turned with Lucia taking all the credit, he told himself. Meantime they won't lay a glove on me.

To the outside world, it was Lucia who was running the deal, as Joe had arranged; she was the super-star in charge, not a role she visibly eschewed in any respect. Content with the front he had found in Lucia, which he could manipulate, Joe was, if anything, just a walk-on part.

Graft signs apart, that is.

And that's the way it's going to stay, Joe thought with finality, letting his reflections return to Felix and the far more dangerous imbroglio he faced from that quarter. Difficult for him to retain the same level of invisibility with regard to that gentleman, Joe conceded as he found himself twisting finger and thumb together in the gesture of the moment.

But what could Felix mean by it all?

The quotes on the screen remained as flat as Joe's expectations, as he wondered just when Felix would move to strike at him. Judging by the friendly, avuncular way that the Quiff discussed market matters openly now with Felix on the top floor corridor, matters that normally fell within Joe's domain, it wouldn't be long; both of them were edging Joe out together, such was their desire to make sweet music together in the boardroom – and Felix was an expert in such ingratiating manoeuvres as Joe knew from old.

Once Felix had the Quiff in his pocket, Joe guessed that he would make his move and that could not be long delayed. The Quiff had spent so much of his life in one pocket or another, he practically passed for marsupial at a distance...His favourite business position was on all fours.

Good old Quiff...Good old Quiff's cough...

And good old Grim Reaper, when he chose to make his timely entrance and claim the Quiff, at last, for his own...

★   ★   ★   ★   ★

'So where is it? Is it still there?'

Simon was being even more nauseating then usual, Grace decided as he burst into her office interrupting her reflections in the late afternoon. Such a squalid little man in so many ways...But quite loveable in others...Almost a little boy really...

And very good at his business.

It had been a good day for her and for the partnership. They had just placed a very senior man within the Whitehall village, plucked complainingly from industry at astronomical cost, and at a huge placing fee into the bargain.

Placing fee to accrue to her and to Simon and to their business naturally.

And who cared now that Chancellor Snowden was free-spending so heavily, as part of the inevitable gear shift from

Labour austerity to tax and spend. Except that there were no taxes…But that was another story…Meanwhile the headhunting business was booming. So there were plenty more cheques on their way, much like today's or even larger.

'What do you mean, where is it? Oh, yes, I know what you mean. It's here…'

And Grace reached into the lowest drawer of her desk and pulled out a savings book. This was the famous escrow account – a Chelsea building society account in both their names and signatures, which contained just £5000.That was the cost of the fuck, or the night of passion, depending on how it was sliced, which Simon had negotiated with her, catching her at a weak moment all those months ago.

She regretted signing up on the deal. But then again Nicholas was turning out to be such a wet blanket that it might in the end be not such a bad thing. It would help crystallise matters between her and her husband. And so what was a fuck anyway…? It mightn't turn out so badly, her night of passion with Simon, especially if the hotel was good. And it was bound to be. Even in Paris, the £5000, which Simon planned to spend on their night together, would go some way towards partial compensation for her loss.

Her regime shift…!

Grace was philosophical about the trade with Simon. Idly she wondered just what kind of nightwear she should buy for the occasion. Kit to turn him on, something dark and sensuous? Or something to turn him off, like a chaste shift?

She didn't know and she didn't truly care too much either. She had an open mind. She was prepared to let events take their course, especially after the deal they had successfully completed that day.

She felt so good-tempered after placing her industrialist and seeing the massive windfall of the finders' fee heading in her direction that she could quite cheerfully have taken Simon on that afternoon across the desk, dealing forward on their wager.

Now that would shock him, she thought to herself, if, ahead of schedule, she suddenly stood up, tugged off her blouse; released her bra before his gawping eyes; groped his flies; pulled off her knickers, and called his bluff...

'Come on, big boy, what are we waiting for? Let's do it...Take me now, now, now,' she bawled in her imagination as she opened her legs wide and glutinously to him on the desk...

'Not long now, eh Grace? Now let's see...'

And Simon began counting the months that remained before their bet fell due.

'Yes, just two months. It's down to weeks. Any news about Nicholas? Nothing, I suppose.'

And Simon licked his lips. Not gloatingly but nervously, she observed with interest. This was a new Simon that was emerging under pressure. Perversely he now wanted to hear good news about Nicholas' prospects as his story altered. Simon was changing course.

Grace realised that he was most likely quite terrified now about the entire venture. Girl friend problems, new or old? Wife difficulties? Grace seemed to recall that Simon had married young, like her, and then divorced. But it didn't matter; he was definitely backing off from the whole idea. That was why he wanted to look at the account and was so doing now with his Mad Professor look all across his face. Perhaps he wanted the money and regretted his expansive gesture – £5K was still £5K of anybody's money when all was said and done, even though they were heading for the record year of all record years...

Simon stood reading the Chelsea account book in a state of some tension. That encouraged her to feel more aggressive about it all, not least because she did not want Simon to feel less than positive about her. She had found herself glowing inside after he had said so categorically that he fancied her like crazy. That had been nice, more like the rampant Nicholas in the old days...

'I've got a brochure here. For a hotel in Paris. What do you think? Do you think we need to book?'

Looking again slightly demented, Simon plonked a gaudy brochure down on her desk advertising what looked like a two star hotel in Paris. She stared at it in disbelief. Haughtiness flew to her aid. This was off the wall.

'Not quite what I had in mind, dear Simon.'

He looked relieved.

'You mean…Somewhere else…?'

He's thinking about the money, poor lamb, thought Grace. Well, if that's the case, he's got another think coming.

'I was thinking more of the George V actually, or somewhere similar. I'm not having a cheap fuck in Paris with just anybody, still less my business partner. The surroundings have to be right.'

'Are you sure, Grace, I mean…'

'Simon, I mean exactly what I say. If we're going to spend a night of passion together, then you'd better be man enough to make it worth my while. And if that means digging into that tight little pocket of yours…'

And she tapped him familiarly on the chest as he backed away from her, looking alarmed. She wondered whether or not to cause a commotion by unbuttoning her blouse there and then in front of him, and letting her bra point menacingly at him from beneath the folds. A dress rehearsal? With regret, she decided he wouldn't be able to stand the strain – and that maybe he'd run. She couldn't have that. She needed Simon around as the business boomed. Any disruption to the flow would be fatal, just as they bobbed off on the Snowden flood tide to fortune.

So she smiled and tried to look less predatory. More sweetly, she urged him to get a more comprehensive brochure for Paris.

'Michelin are very good; they have the very best hotels in their guide,' she added as she closed the door on a flustered Simon; replaced the account book in her desk; and resumed her reveries about the flow of new business. Bra or no bra, definitely with Simon, but maybe minus Nicholas – business was looking good. And it required reflection…

★   ★   ★   ★   ★

Joe's attention was caught by a small paragraph deep down in the Chron's Appointments column. It stated, almost as an aside, that

Lord Test would shortly be replaced by Graham Dune-Jones as Chairman of the Financial Chronicle. This surprised Joe. He had lunched not a fortnight previously with Test, a bluff, good old boy, who had assured him with great excitement that he intended to remain on the board for as long as it took for Tom Stone to play himself in as Editor and make a success of reconstructing the Chron and restoring its editorial independence.

'I spy mischief here, just a little bit of naughtiness,' Joe added, turning the Chron this way and that to see if he could shake some more disclosure out of it. The early departure of Test would be a shock to Stone, that was certain. That would cramp the style of the new editor, if he failed to see eye to eye with the new Chairman.

Joe fell to wondering about Dune-Jones. Nobody was born with a name like that; it must have come straight out of a TV quiz show. Joe reckoned it was a made-up name, one of those nabob verbal constructs that the City's nouveaux created for themselves after they bought big houses close to the Hampshire littoral with their bloated City doubloons – and sought more street cred with the local squirearchy, even though joined-up writing was still a problem for them on Mondays.

With half an eye on the screens, and watching the market frolic, Joe wondered what manner of man Dune-Jones was, that he had been able to ease himself, albeit unknown, into this key position on the Chron's board, to such an extent that he could boot Test into the great unknown. He must have pull, Joe concluded, massive pull.

The only Jones that he had really known in the City was way back, when he played chess with Moley up and down the City bars after the markets had closed. His name was Graham Jones but he was known universally as Gazza. He was a burly young man, with a bullet head, who specialised in analysing engineering stocks, because he had studied engineering at Cambridge. Moley and he were quite close because their parents knew each other in some obscure way that was never quite spelled out clearly; Joe had been given to understand that they had shared political affiliations of long Thirties' standing. So Gazza on occasion turned up to chat with them as they played through their chess game.

'Move this pawn,' he would say to Moley impatiently, pointing at the board. 'Move it here at once. Can't you see the angle, you idiot?'

Moley would bridle at this, because Gazza saw the board very fast,and that was something that Moley aspired to achieving. Prod, prod, prod went the finger over the portable chess set as he sluiced the beer down his throat, one pint after another.

Very, very outspoken he had been, and very left wing; the braces were always red and the talk non-stop, always about the shortcomings of the partnership. Joe seemed to recall some scandal involving Gazza singing the Red Flag when pissed on the firm's annual outing; he had been ejected from the coach for screaming socialist abuse at the Senior Partner. Then shortly afterwards he had married a young Russian woman to everyone's great surprise whom he had met on a flying trip to Moscow. It had all been very odd at the time, but overshadowed by the Senior Partner's fall down the stairs at the Xmas Party. Sad to relate, he had been carrying a full bottle of whisky in his trouser- pocket. His life and his leg had hung literally by a thread for weeks...

But Joe also recalled a moment of inspired, splendid street-theatre from Gazza. The quarterly bonuses had just been paid; Joe and Moley were drinking and playing chess together in the Watling just by St Paul's; and Gazza heaved into sight, well tanked. First, he had made an unfortunate reference to a woman standing beside the two of them, describing her as a 'dwarf with tits', not a cool thing to have done since the woman in question was the wife of a colleague of Gazza's.

Next, he had unzipped his flies, placed the bonus cheque in his pants so that it hung out tantalisingly like a prick; and then he had limbo-danced his way across the pub saloon floor, singing loudly as he went 'Fuck 'em all; fuck 'em all; the long and the short and the tall' as the scandalised pub witnessed with dismay such louche behaviour from one of London's young stockbroking finest. Only Moley's intercession with the landlord had prevented Gazza being flung out into Watling Street on his ear, the size of the bonus notwithstanding.

And so could this Dune-Jones have any connection with the wild Gazza. Highly unlikely, thought Joe. Gazza will have been long dead and buried. But I can find out if I want, it being a slow day in the markets.

He called a cuttings agency in High Holborn and asked for a profile of Dune -Jones, yes, the Graham Dune-Jones featured in the Chron that morning.

'Any urgency ?' he was asked. Not the slightest, Joe reassured the researcher and promptly forgot about the commission, even though he was in truth vestigially interested to find out more about the Dune-Jones who had supplanted Test so easily and so discreetly

★　★　★　★　★

Lucy-Miranda was almost beside herself with excitement the following day when the two women met up together on their bench, coming to the point of rendezvous from different angles of approach but at almost exactly the same time. It was nearly nine in the morning. The sun was high in the Italian heavens, and throwing sharp shadows all across the scrubby stony expanse of the square. Giovanna and her cronies, who had watched the football with great enthusiasm the previous day while restraining their animals with difficulty from joining in, were walking the dogs as usual, in deep discussion about the usual personal grievances. The man was doing his skipping as usual on the other side of the square and to Emma's untrained eye, he seemed to be slightly larger than before. A quiet breeze blew from East to West across the square. All had resumed its semblance of normality again. It was Emma and Lucy-Miranda's square again, and they were both grateful for the sensation of painless repossession. In that square, the wind blew for just the two of them and likewise the sun shone. Sitting on their bench in the square was a way of trapping reality, of cornering it and of getting it under control. It was just wonderful when it seemed to happen. The boy waiter kicked stones all the way up to their bench; grinned at them as family as he took the order; and then kicked stones again all the way back to the cafe. Jake's legacy lingered on.

'You'll never guess, Emma, what has just happened. I was very nearly witness to a murder. It was really quite frightening. And so early in the day, too.'

'Lucy-Miranda, this is a very strong way to start a conversation. Are you sure about this?'

'Let me tell you and you can judge for yourself. I woke up early because Charles was huffing and puffing a little – I'll tell you about that in a moment, if I may – and I decided to wander down into the garden because it was such a fine morning. I'd quite forgotten about the Ginny and Jake show at that early hour and I thought I'd have the garden to myself. So I slid into my jeans and off I trotted, to find the two love-birds at their customary billing and cooing positions – he's doing all those amazing things with a football and dancing along and she's drooling over Sam on the lawn, and they seem to be in perfect harmony. I have to tell you that the two of them looked so utterly beautiful I could barely take my eyes off them. Talk about young love in young bodies -my God you could have cut it with a knife, and I'm no prude, as you well know. I've seen a lot of young women's bodies, as you might imagine. But there was a sort of electricity flowing between them which said to anyone who got in between just 'Get Out' – I'm sure you know what I mean. So I excused myself as the obligatory old trout in attendance, and I wandered over to the other side of the garden, beside the dining room. And who do you think I should have seen sauntering through the hallway, and looking as if she owned the place, but Angelina. Yes, Angelina, looking as pleased as punch and as if she owned the place. The servants must have put her up to it. There can be no way otherwise that she would have known that the early morning was almost the very best time for her to be around and catch him. Oh the malice of those servants – it takes some beating doesn't it? I tell you too that Angelina had not just fallen out of bed five minutes before and decided to pay Jake a call on the off chance. No sir, no way sir, not her, sir. She had been up since five this morning, if not earlier, working out just how best to present herself. Well groomed? You bet she was well groomed – she looked as if she'd just dropped in from the catwalk at Milan. Everything beautifully simple – just a cotton blouse, a pair of white jeans, and a pair of gold sandals – but in the sunshine she looked more like Aphrodite than a human being. Teenagers at that age when they put their minds to it can be very sexy indeed – and get away with it, too, just by being themselves. She looked sensational – and she knew it. She was coming to pay a visit to her man, to her uomo, the one her father had so very kindly picked out for her, much to her initial disgust, I bet.'

'My God, Lucy-Miranda, I can see what you mean about murder on the premises. Because just around the corner, and playing with her baby was the Goddess in residence who...'

'...Did not take it well at all. She didn't exactly bare her teeth at Angelina and hiss at her but she went about as close as she dared. She saw Angelina before Jake did, so she had plenty of time to warn her off the sacred turf of her and Jake by glaring at her...But it didn't work. Angelina stood her ground, flaming away in the morning sunshine like...Well, not like one of my old girlfriends from you know where, but just simply radiating sex and love and youth all over the gardens like some force of nature, I think. She had no reason to do anything else. To her Ginny is just a ridiculous English woman with a baby who has public rows with her husband in England over the telephone and who likes to get her own way. That's what the servants will have told her and Angelina has no reason to disbelieve them. They wouldn't dare lie to her anyway because of her father...'

'Agreed...Agreed. So? What happened?'

'Jake had his back to her so he didn't see her at first. He was still juggling his balls, which sounds appalling, but that's exactly what he was doing. He was engrossed. Eventually, Ginny ground it out to him, in a voice that sounded like pressed steel, that he had a visitor, a very early morning visitor, from the square. She made Angelina sound like a local alley cat of some ill famed description, the way she announced her. So Jake turns round and sees her and still thinking about his discussions with her father about Roma most likely puts on a little exhibition for her of his ball control, which again sounds appalling but I can't think of any other term to use. Anyway, he's bouncing his balls together – ha, ha, ha – and going through his tricks in the early morning sunshine, with Angelina watching and applauding and looking like something out of a fashion show, very much at home in the ambiance thank you very much, on one side; and Ginny is there on the other side, feeling distinctly spare and under-dressed in some smock or other she had on. And so it goes on, this frozen moment of horror, until her phone rings and it's... Well, you guess, it had to happen of course...It was Fate...'

'Who was it? This story terrifies me. Who was it?'

'Tommy, of course, ringing slightly earlier than usual in order to try and catch his wife at a good moment. Well, as if poor Tommy had a chance. Every day is a bad hair day for Ginny. He got the cold steel in the voice treatment, just like Angelina, but in the interval that she was talking to Tommy, before she could cut him off, Angelina sees her chance and wades in with what I think was an invitation to dinner with her father. Nothing Ginny could do about it. It's a perfectly legitimate overture for her father to make, and he'd be a fool, which I don't think he is for a moment, if he operated in any other way. His daughter is tasty bait for Jake. That's why he sent his daughter with the invitation. So there we had it. Invitation offered and accepted; the blond smirking all over her face at the success of it; and Ginny seething away at being out-manoeuvred on her own territory and looking sick as a dog because Tommy confirmed that he – and my darling daughter Lucia, from whom I have heard precisely nothing, not a cheep – were coming over to Italy sooner rather than later. The deal has not gone as well as they thought and may even be on ice briefly. So they are getting close to being a little more free and easy about town as well. Their holiday apparently can be taken out of cold storage for a brief while. The Panel has assented, it seems, whatever that might mean.'

'That doesn't give Ginny much time at all now.'

'If at all. Jake is like a little boat which is about to sail out of harbour all on its own and there's very little that Ginny or anybody else can do about it.'

'What about Lucia? He belongs ultimately to Lucia, doesn't he? She was the one who brought him into all this in the first place.'

'I wouldn't trust my daughter with men as far as I could throw her. She's always had an itchy fanny when it came to the male of the species and so far as I can see she always will have. If she gets a whiff of what is going on, well...She's a very quick-tempered girl, I can tell you that as well...'

'She throws a good punch and Jake had better watch his step?'

'He is treading through a mine-field of female psyches. Knowing his sensitivity, know what I mean, I would be very surprised if he managed to avoid blowing all or at least some of us to smithereens. Know what I mean...?'

Lucy-Miranda gave a fairly accurate rendering of Jake's slack-mouthed mode of delivery, at which point Emma very nearly fell off the bench with laughter.

'Know what I mean?'

'Know what I mean?'

'Ha ha ha ha...'

'That's good, innit, know what I mean...Now dahn Hackney Way, which is where I come from...And all of my fourteen bruvvers an' sisters...And that's not forgetting Auntie Lill in Gants Hill...'

'Lucy-Miranda stop it, or I will do myself a mischief, as my grandmother used to say...And I wanted to ask your advice on something else. I know the odd lawyer in London. Do you think I should get in touch with them and warn them that Jake's business might be in the offing?'

'Know what I mean?'

More laughter. Lucy-Miranda took control of her self. She sobered up with a smile.

'Yes, Emma I think I would do that. It can't hurt anyone to do that. Can it? I don't think so. No, just go ahead and make some contacts for him. I'm sure he'd be delighted. And it most certainly should come in handy. Know...'

'Don't...! I mean it, Lucy-Miranda.'

'What I mean?'

'Ha ha ha ha...'

'I will do it this morning, Lucy-Miranda. And when is it exactly that we go to meet the girls in Petana?'

' Ginny doesn't have a moment to lose.'

* * * * *

The morning of the departure for Petana and the encounter with the bridge-playing girls from Sloane Square was marred by some tension – or 'stwess', as Lucy-Miranda called it...

They had decided to go en masse to Petana, taking Charles with them as well because he was now feeling very much more perky; he had bagged travelling space with Ginny, whose party also included Stella and Craig. Jake, Emma, and Lucy-Miranda would be in the other car. The plan was to get half-way by noon, take in a Roman ruin on the way for lunch, and then arrive at Petana around 1.30, in time for the Bridge – what fun to have an excursion planned in the middle of a holiday!

It all felt like high jinks to Emma, who in truth had started to feel just a trifle hemmed in by the proximity of the group. The sun didn't help either – it was ever-present and always hot. She lived in its harsh light in the open squares or as a fugitive from its beams in the angles of the shadows. She was finding the sun discomforting...

Plus, they had all been living in each other's pockets for weeks now, without moving around within space as they might have down back home in London or Hampshire. So the prospect of a little break from routine and a little expedition into the unknown was cheering. Emma dearly loved her tetes a tete with Lucy-Miranda on their bench in the square and she was pleased by the progress that Craig was making with his novel as he beavered away. But it was all too static and too well defined for her liking. She could not as yet accept the rectangular definition to her life which these events described, not least because she still nurtured unfulfilled expectations about Joe. Joe was the time-out for her. In her house in London, having arrived at some unknown time, there would be a letter from him lying forlornly on her mat. That he had responded to her letter she knew without doubting. He would not have spurned her overtures, although he might be circumspect about the follow-through. She knew all that without thinking about it. So she wanted to take a look at that missive and digest its contents before she finally caved in and embraced whatever kind of limits to life she was going to be forced to accept. Was Joe her last chance before she made the Great Compromise? She shuddered to think that might be the case and fled the conclusions of her ruminations. So for that reason also she welcomed the trip out and away from Repugia. That way she could escape from her darker thoughts.

But then came the tension. It started with Ginny at the breakfast table, who could not prevent herself from hurling a series of barbed remarks at Jake, who in turn looked bewildered. The previous night had been a triumph for him. He had wandered off down into the town, in his shambolic way, to dine with Angelina and her father, after surviving a rigorous kit inspection by both Emma and Lucy-Miranda. Some articles of clothing he had been forced to change in order to alter his appearance from footballer/market trader to respectable Englishman abroad. After the usual caterwauling of complaints from the two women ('You can't possibly wear that, Jake; just what do you think you're doing; it's just too naff for words. Don't even think about it') he had given in to the pressure of their disapproval and worn whatever they had recommended. They had watched him depart with pride in his appearance, feeling slightly satisfied that something closely approximating to presentable was on its' way to an important meeting, courtesy of their handiwork. Then they watched him return some hours later, still immaculately turned out and looking cool and dapper, and heard the good tale he had to tell. Yes, there was a possible deal on the table; Angelina's father was very definitely interested in taking it all a stage further. He had talked to Roma, told the football club about the genius who had been spotted in the backstreets of Repugia. Naturally, Roma wanted to hear -and see- some more. That was being arranged. Then Angelina's father had questioned Jake very closely about his background and Jake, being Jake, had been able to give good report of himself. Jake described him as an easy man to talk to, under the circumstances. Yes, Jake thought he might need a lawyer in London. And yes, Angelina had fussed over him the entire evening in a very grown-up matronly kind of way, aping her mother, and very nice it had been too, although he was looking forward to seeing Lucky again when she finally made it to Repugia from London with Tommy. Jake had said that carefully for the benefit of her mother, Lucy-Miranda, who was very present at the post-mortem to the dinner, out in the gardens of the villa under a clear dark Italian sky where a fat yellow Italian moon beamed down so closely that Emma felt she could reach out and touch it. Lucy-Miranda had accepted his comments as being possibly, indeed most likely, sincere but also almost certainly motivated by a desire not to upset her. Jake was emerging as a very straight forward, attractive young man whose mind was intuitively half made-up on most things. As Lucy-Miranda confessed almost tearfully afterwards to Emma, the mere fact that he had thought about her feelings at all made her go quite weak at the knees at the peculiarity of it all. Her family life up to that point had not accustomed her to such generosity of spirit.

All of which made Ginny's bitchiness the morning afterwards at the breakfast table, just as they were preparing to depart on their expedition to Petana, the harder to bear with equanimity.

'So how was your girl-friend last night, then, Jake? Still looking like a fashion model? Or were you too tired to notice?'

Jake who thought he was doing the right thing but found himself caught in the wrong in a way that he failed to fathom, struggled to reply. He wallowed in the quicksands of her mercurialism. Scenting a lesion of weakness, Ginny pressed home her advantage, dandling the infant Sam on her smooth bosom.

' I suppose it'll only be a matter of a few weeks before you'll be away from here, now that you've found a better billet. I can't say I blame you although you have to admit that the hospitality has been splendid.'

More consternation from Jake. Some murmurings from the rest of the guests, on whom Jake had grown little by little – but only up to a point – during the holiday, warned Ginny to still her venomous remarks. This indeed she was obliged to do because her phone rang with the usual morning call from Tommy. More role reversal spinning on a sixpence. Tommy, of course, got a Ginny full of sweetness and light, not the customary harridan who let him have it square between the eyes with both barrels, because she had already loosed off her thunderbolts against the hapless

Jake. Tommy was treated to a rhapsodic description of the infant Sam that morning, instead of the usual curt formulaic replies. Ginny's kindness to him left Tommy feeling ecstatic, so far as could be gathered from the squeaks coming down the line.

But Jake was confused. He simply was not used to this form of quick-draw double-dealing and he fell silent, looking awkward and short-changed.

So the expedition began on a sour note. Ginny was still scowling as she climbed into her car with the other designated occupants. Craig, instead of Jake, who was in the other car, had been deputed to hold the baby, something which looked like a meticulous snub to the watchful chorus of Lucy-Miranda and Emma.

But the rage and the bitchiness could not be sustained. Moods started to alter as they sped out of Repugia and into the surrounding countryside. The force of the elements in the Italian countryside soon put paid to any possible sense of rancour. The two cars following each other at a comfortable speed, went some distance towards Petana on the autostrada. Then they turned off onto a small side road which led across country to the Roman ruin and then afterwards onwards towards Petana.

Langour replaced rancour as the kilometres ticked away on the clock. There were trees overhanging the bumpy road; sudden switches from sun to shadow and then back to sunshine; there was speed on the road; ripening corn in the fields, swaying to its own special rhythm of growth; slow joy of abundance; wide, wide expanse of fields sweeping across the land towards the hills, rippling in the wind; and the crazy spectacle of the car in front bouncing along the road between the fields which raced past on either side.

Arms began to wave from car to car through the roof in a simple expression of well being. Eventually, the cars drew level with each other, with no danger from oncoming traffic because the sight lines ahead were so clear; and they drove more slowly. Emma was at one wheel and Ginny at the other, both smiling away in the sunshine, one hand on the wheel, both splayed out in their shorts in the heat across the driving seat, and taking the breeze. Sam was hoisted up by Craig through the roof to take in the fields and Sam, a small baby but larger now than she had been a few weeks previously, squealed in pleasure at the sights and waved at Nature. Jake just smiled back in the other car, as well he might have done with what looked like a lucrative footballing contract very nearly in his pocket. Ginny nodded to him absently between the cars.

Sun now rising high in the sky, as Emma drove along thinking quite hard about what lay at the end of the journey for her, taking the breeze on her face as much as she could to tone down the heat. It might all become quite complicated. She was bound to know most of the girls they were due to meet in Petana; she had after all seen most of them play at Savages many months ago, hundreds of miles away in London, just before her infamous debut at Liz Playfair's which had gone both spectacularly wrong – because she had falsely presumed upon an invitation which proved to be phantom – but which had also gone very right for her, in an odd kind of way.

Thanks to her friend Nancy, eventually she had secured some right of entry to the most exclusive of bridge salons, the Liz Playfair Thursday morning group, most of whom were now awaiting her a few kilometres down the road in Petana. The pity of it was that almost immediately afterwards the Liz Playfair school had ceased to exist because poor Liz…Well, it could happen to anyone, and thank God it hadn't happened to her, but poor Liz…She had seemed to be such a nice good kind of person as well…And where was she now, poor Liz Playfair…? How could somebody just disappear as she had done? The group had moved on, leaving her marooned somewhere in unknown time and space.

So the girls were bound to recognise her, up to a point, and perhaps even make much of her as another fugitive from the rigours of Sloane Square life and times. But, and this was the real point she was turning over in her mind, she had not so far mentioned to Lucy-Miranda that she knew these people. Would L-M be upset by this reluctance to reveal and treat it as a betrayal? Emma sincerely hoped that she wouldn't and anyway doubted that she would; she was hoping for the best. She was going to take the risk. She felt pretty thick with L-M, what with their daily, almost hourly meetings sometimes, on the bench in the square, the walking around the town and the confidences exchanged about Jake; Ginny; and whoever else had come within their sights. She felt confident that their friendship could withstand any buffeting from the crowd in Petana, given her own conscious reticence. Besides, if the worst came to the worst, she could always blame Stella; that was what Stella was for. She could say that she, Emma, had had no desire to steal her, Stella's, thunder by laying claim to prior knowledge of these people without being certain they were actually the same folk that she had known in Sloane Square and the environs. And that she still enjoyed landing rights with them. A little lie if need be; a tiny economy with the truth; and a small evasion of reality – that should suffice, she thought, as the Roman ruins came up clear across the plain of waving corn, the two cars still bumping together along the road. They prepared to stop for lunch, exactly as planned.

But perhaps I should just mention, in passing to L-M over lunch, that I might know some of these people, Emma reflected. That should help to smooth over any unpleasantnesses and ruffled ego's…Just a quiet mention to prepare the way for subsequent revelations involving a small world?…Yes, that's what I'll do. That looks to be by far the best policy.

And so thinking she brought the car to a halt in the car park in front of the Roman ruins and prepared to pull out the lunch hampers.

It was easy to see why the Romans had built their fort and town where they did. Situated on a huge slab of rock outcrop, the complex commanded a view for miles all around across the waving cornfields. As such it was practically impregnable. The Romans had added an amphitheatre to the complex at the back, so secure had they felt in providing the legions with R&R. The Romans had been right. Nobody could have approached within a few miles of the complex without being spotted, as Craig, whose idea it had been to visit the ruins, pointed out. Meanwhile the cloths were being spread out among the rocks and the food lugged over from the two boots of the cars.

'Most likely it was built around the second century B.C., as the Romans started their push outwards from Rome in order to pacify the whole of Italy. They built where they needed to protect territory, as here. Eventually they took control of the whole peninsula. And they built for keeps as you can see...'

It was Craig the teacher and guide who flung out a demonstrative arm which embraced the lowering walls; the narrow gateway entrance; and the mass of streets within the complex which led towards the amphitheatre at the rear. Emma, listening carefully, swore to herself she could hear the tramp of the legions up and down the streets from many centuries ago. Echoes resonated over the millennia.

Then Craig was silent, as a long Italian loaf, crammed with cheese was handed to him, along with a glass of Italian red wine. He crunched hard into the bread sending a shower of crumbs into the air and they all giggled at his eating performance. Jake looked long and hard at him and ruminated to himself, as Stella, waving her thin arms around the food, prepared to take some salami on board with an exquisite refinement of personal delicacy. Sam, meanwhile much to the amusement of the locals and the guides who gathered around the picnic, wandered on tottering uncertain legs from one to another in the circle squealing with pleasure and closely watched by a more relaxed Ginny from one side of the circle. The locals loved Sam immediately.

'How far you got in your book, then?' Jake finally asked Craig, who very nearly choked on his roll trying to reply.

'Stilll steaming. It's got some critical mass behind it, as Emma will be pleased to hear. It's going well. All the characters have done exactly what I wanted them to do, which is a bonus. I found that Catullus himself worked well for me. He's an excitable, warm man and full of friendship, whereas Lesbia is a cold fish who just gets what she wants more or less all of the time. Rather a sad figure I thought. Now in the modern version...'

Craig took another bite and glanced across at Emma who nodded back at him with a smile which she hoped looked less than proprietorial. It was, after all, his book, because he was writing it. She was just supplying the financial backing, which in turn reminded her about some calls she needed to make to London about registration. Meanwhile she had been daydreaming about Joe and that dangerous look which came into his blue rocks of eyes, if you looked carefully enough, when he was crossed over anything. Such a sinister man in some ways, she thought, and with such potential for violence. She thought more and more that she wanted to see him, as a matter of urgency in order to discuss matters arising with respect to personal parameters.

Emma then looked around for Lucy-Miranda. When she failed to spot her within the group – and she'd been there just a few minutes past – she pulled herself to her feet and went in search of her. After a few yards, she could see her wandering close to the walls away to her right, so she walked more quickly in order to overtake her.

She was shocked when she caught up with Lucy-Miranda. L-M was sobbing her heart out in a silent paroxysm of grief, with tears streaming down her cheeks, as she stumbled amid the rocks at the base of the town complex.

'No, no, you must leave me alone. I'll get over it, I know I will but just now it's all caught up with me, so please, please, leave me alone.'

'I most certainly will not leave you alone. This is awful. What has happened? Has somebody said something to upset you? What is it, Lucy-Miranda, come on, do tell, just a tiny bit. It's heartbreaking for you to be so unhappy. Do let me comfort you, please. Please, L-M…'

They had turned the corner of the complex away from the picnic so that they were unseen now by the others.

Lucy-Miranda stopped to confront Emma with red-rimmed eyes and tears still streaming down her cheeks. She looked totally miserable. Almost deflated in a way, so that she seemed suddenly smaller. Emma took her hand and clenched it and Lucy-Miranda, slightly comforted, glanced at her and then looked at the ground, still weeping and drawing long large breaths.

Almost in tears herself now, Emma took both hands of Lucy-Miranda's in hers and squeezed them tight, saying at the same time, as forcefully as she could:

'Now come on, Lucy-Miranda, what would our bench say to all of this? Think about that. And our growing army of swain back at Repugia. What would they say? You know as well as I do that tough girls don't cry.'

Lucy-Miranda whimpered some more, adding between sobs that tough women cried all the time. Emma, trying desperately to bring her some cheer, hugged her hard. Then, and after looking over her shoulder she said meaningfully:

'Know what I mean...?'

Lucy-Miranda did not exactly corpse with laughter at the sally but she managed a small brave grin through the tears cutting furrows down her cheeks. Taking a huge breath, she sat down heavily on one of the rocks. Emma sat down beside her, taking in the vast expanse of corn in front of them, waving and hissing away to them both and to the world in general beneath the wind.

Impervious Nature at her most munificent.

Lucy-Miranda sobbed away some more, still trying to catch her breath and banish the evil ideas from her mind. Every now and then she succeeded and the breathing became more regular. Gulping in air, she prepared to speak. Then, just on the point of recovery, the ideas impinged again and she halted. Emma held her very tight, and rocked her just a little, murmuring quiet words of encouragement to her.

Little by little Lucy-Miranda was able to string her breathing together so that it no longer came in spurts. Finally, and very red in the face, she managed a whole sentence.

'Emma, I'll be OK, honestly. And you've been very kind, tracking me down like this, and I'm very grateful to you. It's just that...'

She heaved down a great sigh and her eyes bulged with the effort of containing the grief. She got the words out one by one, with great difficulty. She strained after each syllable.

'I've...been...here...before. Not... once... but... twice. It was awful for me then, and...I thought I could handle it today...but, well,... You can see... how well I've handled it now...Oh God, oh God, why do these things have to happen to me. My life is just one long walking disaster area...'

She got that last sentence out easily enough but then she relapsed into more sobs. There was another pause and then silence between them. Emma broke the silence.

'Do you want me to go away now just for a moment and let you get over it?'

Lucy-Miranda looked at her with hopeless eyes.

'You know that I don't want you to do that but yes, I think you should. I have to get over this myself I think…'

She started and looked at her watch.

'…And quite quickly too…'

More heavy breathing. More staring at the ground. Emma spoke to her sternly, but with great affection.

'I'll go for a little wander around the amphitheatre and other parts of the town for about five minutes and leave you alone. Then I'll come back here. Either you'll still be bawling your head off, in which case I'll give you a quick rabbit-punch to finish off the job, or we can walk back in good order to the picnic…Is that understood? Know what I mean…?'

Lucy-Miranda nodded. Then she sniffed and ran a handkerchief around her eyes and gawped at the muck that appeared on the material and groaned again.

'You sound like something from Cell Block H, Emma. I didn't think you could be so tough. It's so impressive.'

'You'd be amazed what I get up to in my spare time. Martial arts, kung fu, the lot. You name it and I punch it…'

Lucy-Miranda smiled a little at Emma's wisecrack and shook her head.

'Oh God, what a fucking torment all this has turned out to be…I thought it was bad, but today…Oh God, it's terrible, just awful.'

'Why don't we talk about just a little, when you're feeling more like it?'

Dully Lucy-Miranda said that she be delighted to spill every bean she could.

'On the way back, L-M? I think Stella will be staying with the girls, so we can easily dump Jake with Craig and Ginny.'

'We can try, I suppose. It will look a bit odd, because that makes four in their car and just two in ours, but we can certainly try. Otherwise, I will tell all on our bench as soon as I can…This has been a bad attack. They're not normally as virulent as that but when they come…'

Lucy-Miranda was recovering.

'I'll be back in about five minutes. Until then, look after yourself....'

Lucy-Miranda laughed with slightly more vibrant gusto and Emma, casting the odd backwards look at her, wandered away to give her time to recover from her little spasm.

She walked along beside the city walls for about two hundred yards and then driven by curiosity regarding the amphitheatre, stuck in this isolated outpost of Roman power, she struck inwards through the walls, still thinking about Lucy-Miranda and wondering what terrible moment in her past had caused her to break down so abruptly in such magnificent surroundings. Musing that it must have been a man, because only men provoked such titanic responses, she clambered among the boulders and came out at the very topmost rim of the mighty construction, all pillars and seats converging on a stage some fifty yards away.

For a moment she was silhouetted against the sky. Then she dropped down out of sight on the outermost side of the rim. What she had seen she should not have witnessed.

Down on the stage, but secreted almost to one side of it, so that only somebody coming upon them as Emma had done, from the top of the amphitheatre could see them, were Ginny and Jake. They were standing very close together. Very slowly and with concentrated attention, Ginny was undoing her blouse, to reveal a very white bra underneath on dark tanned skin; and a swelling bosom towards which she very deliberately guided Jake's hand, so that he caressed the outside of the cup as he stood straight and firm beside her. No sound could be heard; Emma was merely witnessing the action from afar.

Ginny grimaced with pleasure as she felt Jake's fingers ease around her breast over her nipple and she reached up to him with her eyes closed so that she could kiss him full on the mouth with her lips and tongue. She moved against him the whole time, easing her body against him and raising her leg against his in an agony of frustrated desire... Then very slowly, still driven by the lust for Jake's body and the desire for revenge which had been pounding away at her throughout the Italian holiday, not wanting to miss any moment of opportunity, she eased her face down the length of his chest and beyond, past his navel...Fumbling a little with his shorts, she managed to unhook the fly. Emma saw her plunge her face and mouth into his groin and watched her head rise and fall slowly and rhythmically for a few seconds as Jake stood to ramrod attention, taking the careful, painstaking and skilled fellatio she was giving him, like a soldier on parade.

'She's doing it at just about the speed that I like to do it,' thought Emma. 'I wonder if she's got her eyes closed. I bet she has. I always do it with my eyes closed. It feels so much bigger that way. And I feel so much fuller in my mouth.'

Emma could see Jake's straight legs and his firm tight back and the buttocks tensing beneath the shorts, as Ginny's head continued to move up and down, up and down, slowly up and down. She certainly knows what she's about, thought Emma. After a brief time, Jake must have come because Ginny with her eyes shining with pleasure, raised her head out of his groin and stood up very slowly, and then kissed him again on the mouth, the while fastening his flies, leaning a little clumsily against him so that one of her boobs slewed heavily as it went lopsided against his chest.

Then in a matter of fact way, like one saying that business had been concluded but only for the time being, Ginny restored normality on the sex act that never took place by buttoning up her blouse. Primness returned by magic. The boobs and the bra disappeared. Modesty was restored. She kissed him again and touched him on the cheek, as if to say that there was far more where that came from, if only he could wait just a little while. Then she took his hand firmly and ran it over her chest, still staring at him. The two of them moved away from the stage and back in the direction of the picnic like a couple of sightseers who had stopped for a quick cuddle in the ruins in order to assert their continuing vitality among the dead; the monumental; and the stones.

Emma stood there breathless and realised that Ginny had made her move. Pretty decisively too, so far as she could gather. Angelina could take what she wanted now. Ginny had got there first and snatched what she needed, as well as what she wanted.

After the small sexual intermezzo she had witnessed, there wasn't a great deal more for Emma to do except retrace her steps.

Feeling slightly spare, she wandered back the way she had come. Not finding Lucy-Miranda seated weeping on her rock, she continued on her way towards the picnic where she found them all lolling about and looking totally serene. They were clearing up the debris of the picnic and pacing about on the grass, impatient to be gone. It was uncanny – nothing seemed to have happened. The wonder of it all was that Lucy-Miranda looked bright-eyed and bushy-tailed, as if nothing untoward had happened to her in the past two hundred years. The tears had gone and likewise the red-rimmed eyes. How she had effected such a transformation remained a mystery. Likewise with Ginny. She went about the usual business of looking after her baby, fussing over it with all eyes as it crawled about on the grass, wholly unconcerned. Meanwhile Jake was talking casually to Craig, asking him whether he had ever taught in East London. Jake looked and sounded like a Londoner out on the spree, standing there with his hands thrust into his pockets and legs splayed wide apart, rather than a man who had just been given the expert blow-job of the century, not ten minutes since, among the ruins.

The breeze still hissed off the cornfield and the sun beat down from high in the heavens. Bliss in Italy. But the weather had to remain unchronicled. They were behind schedule now. It was time to go if they were all to make the date in Petana with the girls. Time was marching on.

Craig denied all knowledge of East London Latin, whereupon Jake, abstracted and all innocence except in Emma's eyes, said that there had been a very famous young teacher of Latin in a school in West Ham, just by the football ground, who had been first derided by the boys for his interest in Latin – tough nuts every one of them – but who had then secured acceptance throughout the area on account of everybody's spelling and grammar getting better.

'There aren't many Latin teachers in East London, as you might well imagine, and I thought it might be you, because this geezer taught my cousin, who was not the fastest, I grant you, but who learned so well that he could actually fill in a job application form. He got a job out of his Latin and he was very grateful. Even in our street we thought he was an idiot and Strone Road was famous for its stupidity. So I was going to say thank you for the help you gave him.'

'Not guilty, Jake. When I did teach in the state system, I taught over in South London, down Peckham way.'

'That must have been tough. They're animals, south of the river.'

'They say exactly the same, south of the river, about East London. But the spelling did improve, I have to tell you.'

'It would have needed to. Knives and forks are a challenge for them in Peckham.'

'Not knives, Jake. Definitely not knives. They well know how to use those.'

'Yeah, I can imagine that.'

It was a flat knowing matter of fact reply that spoke volumes about the casual violence offered and accepted around the streets of South London; East London; and indeed any part of London, if you went looking for it. Even standing almost knee-deep in the bucolic setting of a ripening Italian corn field in the late Summer, it was impossible to mistake the sense of mean streets abounding in Jake's 'Yeah, I can imagine that.'

Emma's sense of strangeness over the unseen events that she had witnessed began to pall as the hampers were loaded back into the respective boots; cars occupied; and doors slammed. Schedules were under pressure; agendas reigned. It was time for the off. Emma was in the lead this time, and she reversed carefully away from the car park in front of the fort, and then swung powerfully onto the dusty road. There wasn't a great deal of time to spare now before they were due in Petana. It was the moment to make tracks.

They sped onwards into the sun. Jake seated in the rear of the car promptly fell asleep. Emma saw this through her rear mirror and thought 'Yes, you lucky bugger, just you sleep it off like that – I'd like to have had some of what you've just been up to. Fat chance though for a while…But it's nice work if you can get it…'

Then she kept her eyes riveted on the road, as L-M fussed a little bit over the dormant Jake, sprawled out across the back seat with eyes tight shut and fists slightly clenched and legs curled under the seat, saying how sweet and young and innocent he looked when he was asleep.

'He looks exactly like a child in that pose. Look, Emma, look at him. You wouldn't dream that he was a famous footballer to be, would you, with him looking like that, now would you? I'd put him at about eight years old with that expression.'

Emma rather demurred about this to herself but mumbled a vague kind of assent to L-M in public, still keeping her eyes on the road, as the countryside swept past on both sides in a riot of fields and birds and sunshine.

There would time for her to question L-M shortly as well as for other forms of revelation to be made perhaps later. But her time would come, she had no doubt about that. She drove onwards.

After some fifty or so kilometres, with Jake still sound asleep and snuffling gently in his dreams, Lucy-Miranda broached the point first. She sounded cautious.

'I suppose we can talk with Jake out cold like this.'

'He will hear nothing. Assume we are seated on our bench. That's the best approach. Consider yourself back in Repugia.'

'I suppose you're wondering what all those tears were about back there at the fort.'

'It had crossed my mind, but before we get into that, I have to congratulate you on the recovery programme. I've never seen anyone put away grief at such speed. How did you do it...?'

'Early training, Emma. We were brought up to feel it but not to show it. At least that's the theory. All complete bollocks of course. In reality, the loos at Gabby's were – and are – full of messed-up damsels screaming their heads off but that's another story...No, it all took me unawares, and I just couldn't handle it at all. But recovery time is what counts in this game...'

'Are you going to tell me what it was all about?'

'I suppose so. I'll tell you by degrees. I don't want to start bawling my head off again, so I'll try to remain calm and composed. But just to recap, imagine that I've just been married; that everything's wonderful; and that my mighty all-powerful and all-conquering husband, whom I subsequently discover to have been a crook, takes me on my honeymoon.'

'And you come here?'

'Not immediately. We stay in Venice; we stay in Rome; we stay in Pisa; we stay here and we stay there; and we have a good time. Lots of fun. Really a very good time. Spongo seems pleased with me, and I discover, if you want, that he's not such a bad bloke after all, as the girls would say back home in You Know Where – a sweet little fucker was their highest form of praise. On such trivial foundations are mighty dynasties formed. Of course, all the subsequent revelations about how he swindled Martins Bank were years away, and likewise Gerald...'

'Gerald? He's new on the scene.'

'My lover, while I was married. Spongo found about about him and had him killed, as I later discovered. He had a yacht and he used to come and see me when we lived down on the coast. He would boat in from the Atlantic. He was a very expert sailor, but Spongo did him in, somehow and some where.'

'Not bad, the ancient mariner sailing in from the sea with lust in his heart, I grant you. But golly, you have lived a bit, haven't you, L-M? One husband committing suicide; one lover killed; one bank collapsing; and then any amount of time spent chained up in a brothel...'

'Which was, of course, the best time of all, because I went dumb. I couldn't have got up to any mischief, had I tried. I know, I know. Spare me the actuarial bit, Emma, there's a dear, because I know it tots up. I know it all sounds terrible. That's what I meant when I said my life was a walking disaster area. I seem to be one of those people who just attracts bad luck...And also one of those unfortunate people who tears other people's lives apart.'

'But you still haven't explained why you burst into tears back at the fort, oh life wrecker...'

Lucy-Miranda was silent, and stared through the windscreen at the road ahead and the sun above and the fields still racing past on either side of her.

'It seems so obvious and trite when I say it and explain it but then that's what it all boils down to in the end, isn't it....'

She seemed to shake herself to find comfort in the simple reality of existence.

'No, the reason why I burst into tears is that Spongo did bring me here, to the fort on our honeymoon, and we had a very good time walking around it and admiring it and even having a good cuddle among the ruins…My husband was fascinated by the past, including the genealogy of his own family which dated back well into the Middle Ages, so he was very pleased to be strolling about among the ruins.'

I don't believe this, thought Emma, I just don't believe it. This must be a well known trysting point for the shirearchy. God alone knows how many heirs and spares have been conceived on those old stones; it's a key spot on the tourist route. But I'm not going to say anything. I'm just going to keep my eyes on the road and I'm going to keep driving.

Lucy-Miranda continued inexorably.

'But what my husband did not know was that years before I had been to visit that fort with somebody else, where I'd had an equally good time, indeed a better time…So you can see why I felt so emotional about it all…'

'And this other person?'

'Oh, I'm not going to talk about him. These things happen, and I've done enough blubbing for today. Me and my guy met at university and we spent a lot of time together in the vacations just travelling about on the continent, but mainly in Italy. We used to take trains all across the country from town to town and if we didn't like a town we'd get on another train and move on…'

'How fantastic. It doesn't sound like my time at college at all. I had to work. My father had died nearly bankrupt and left us all in penury. My idea of a good time was taking an early night off from the bar where I worked in the evening. But enough of that…We all make our own luck…And the money came in the end. But the fort. There's no railway close by.'

'There is a bus service. Or there used to be one. We'd had enough of travelling by train so we decided – or at least I decided – that we'd take a break. So we took the bus out here. Or rather there. I was determined to say nothing about it today at all but it hit me as we sat down and picnicked and I watched little Sam wander about and I thought about…Well, times past and what happened and what might have happened and all that kind of thing. So I broke down and here I am, sounding like a complete tit going on about it all. It was all over and done with long ago.'

Lucy-Miranda spoke with an air of finality which rang completely false. Emma, intrigued, pressed her a little.

'So why did you marry Spongo when you were in love with the other guy?'

'My father. He's to blame. He thought he knew best. He knew that Spongo was a good match, so he bludgeoned me into it. He locked me up in the house over the weekend and said that he refused to allow me out until I consented to marry Spongo. Which of course I did in the end. He held the whip hand.'

'And the other guy? What happened to him? And what was his name, by the way?'

Here Lucy-Miranda looked shy, confused and evasive.

'Don't let's talk any more about it, Emma. I'll burst into even more tears if I do…And there, just right on cue, I think that dear Jake is starting to wake up…Saved by the bell, as usual…Isn't he just a darling…?'

Which was true. The tousled head of Jake emerged over the seats. The world's greatest footballer was very sleepy.

'Where am I? Who did it? You can't hold me…'

'The coffee was drugged, Jake, and we've abducted you. That's the good news. The bad news is that you have to fulfil our every demand now, and I warn you, we're women of passion and molten desires. Both of us. You up for that? We refuse to take No for an answer. So brace yourself to accommodate our every whim. Not that you have any choice in the matter, since we're in charge of your destiny now. Prepare to submit gracefully to us.'

'Wotyewonabart……?'

This polysyllabic single word was from Jake who plainly had been brought up in a household chockfull of adoring females all poised to anticipate his every desire, and that all in his own good time. It was back to the breakfast syndrome.

Sounding more restored by the chaffing of Jake than she looked, Lucy-Miranda changed the subject with brutal emphasis and proceeded for the rest of the journey to talk to Jake about his football prospects, something which the normally quite taciturn Jake was happy to discuss. The car bowled along the remaining kilometres to Petana. As the town heaved into sight, Lucy-Miranda whispered to Emma conspiratorially that she would fill in all the gaps as soon as they were back on their bench in Repugia.

'Honest?'

'Honest, know what I mean.'

Emma giggled, still driving at some speed. Jake caught something in the repartee.

''Ere, you're taking the mickey out of my accent.'

'Impossible, Jake.'

'Know what I mean, Jake?'

'How should I know what you mean, you couple of clowns......Know what I mean? Cor blimey.'

He joined in the banter quite easily after thawing out. He had an infectious, uncomplicated, 'come hither' smile.

'No, I don't know at all what you mean, Jake, know what I mean?'

''Ere, lay off...'

And he waggled his eyebrows at them both.

That was the signal for practically mass hysterics. They all fell about laughing as they rolled into Petana, and waited for Ginny to catch the car up. Then they set about looking for the bridge club and the girls and the next instalment of the adventure of the expedition.

Eventually, they found the designated address, thanks to Charles' stage Italian. He looked quite flustered and red in the face with effort but he managed in the end to make himself understood. The cars pulled up in front of a low building close to the river. Out they all tumbled, and the door of the building opened – and there they all were.

Quelle surprise!

It was Liz Playfair's establishment in Lower Sloane Street come back to life again. They might all have been having coffee in Oriel in Sloane Square for all difference the change in surroundings had made. There was Trish and Mandy and Barbara and the rest of the gang, all looking slightly tanned and more relaxed and somehow more outward going as they found themselves free of the great burdens of office, not least the principal element – their husbands who were not in attendance on the trip. The girls were less memsahib and more themselves, just as they used to be thirty years or so previously, as they cascaded out to greet the travellers.

'Stella, Stella, how nice to see you…So pleased you could get here…Isn't this just a lovely surprise. And Ginny good to meet you at last…And you too Lucy-Miranda…And what have we here? Girls, look here, just see what we've found. Girls, who do you think it is…? It's Emma, a founder member…Oh, what larks all of this is…Come on, Emma, what are you doing here of all people…Where did you spring from, we'd never have guessed that you'd be smooching around here in Italy…You're supposed to be in London…Or was it the West Indies? I forget but I know it's one of the two. So how's your bridge these days…? Played any at all?'

Explanations were given at top speed, received at the same velocity and the conversation ricocheted around the building into which they had all more or less converged, a happy, suntanned, brawling band of English women suddenly reunited in a foreign land…Happily for Emma, the fact that she knew some of the women from old, in London, was obscured by the general bonhomie of the welcome, so there was little opportunity for Lucy-Miranda to derive even more chagrin from the day's events by discovering that her close bosom buddy was an intimate of these fabulous creatures from back home. The Italians were also on good form. They were fielding a team to play against the English women that afternoon, and they contributed to the general mayhem which reigned briefly in the bridge salon.

It was a happy moment of relaxed kicking and shoving and gouging in the run-up to the bridge itself. Lots of smiles and embracing as the travellers were made welcome.

Eventually the situation settled down and the teams prepared to compete. Emma was playing with Lucy-Miranda and by chance, because of the imbalance of forces, they were paired with the Italian team in opposition. The two of them took their place at the tables and prepared to face Trish and Stella, both late of Liz Playfair's, who as usual looked ferociously competitive.

They glared at Emma and Lucy-Miranda, now part of the enemy, and asked them what conventions they were playing. Suddenly they looked like a couple of mercenaries from the Hundred Years War.

Hard core!

'As few as possible,' said Lucy-Miranda stoutly, not to be overawed by outrageous Hampshire behaviour.

'A weak No Trump; Stayman; and Optional Double over your Threes,' said Emma. It couldn't be simpler. We've been playing in the sunshine. It addles the brain. We're completely stupid with the heat. We'll be easy meat for you.'

Which was probably quite true. Trish and Stella played frequently together and were greatly feared at the Friday afternoon duplicate at Savage's. Lucy-Miranda laughed and the snort of battle came from Trish and Stella as they reeled off a host of bidding conventions that would not have disgraced the Magna Carta.

It was formidable.

They all reached for the cards and prepared to do battle.

Looking round at the familiar faces bent over their cards as they sorted them, Emma could for all the world have imagined herself back in Sloane Square on a Tuesday afternoon at one of the many bridge clubs in SW3. Only the dress code was different. Even so, despite all the spontaneous expatriate gaiety of the occasion the code was still fairly subdued and biased towards the sensible. Hampshire ladies are reluctant to dress down even on holiday.

Emma had played a tiny amount at Liz Playfair's before her club had broken up. She looked in vain now for the sight of Liz, striding between the tables, eyes swivelling from hand to hand; she missed not seeing her six foot blond majesty, ever present in the past as a permanent feature of the territory like the worn statue of Sir Hans Sloane himself in the middle of his eponymous square in London beneath the trees. Liz Playfair remained a deeply sympathetic figure.

Instead of catching sight of Liz in her sweep round the room, she took in Jake and Craig – neither of whom had an inkling about bridge – kibitzing together at one of the tables. Predictably enough they were at Mandy's table. Mandy was one of the most majestic of all the Hampshire dames in the group, a real Mme de Pompadour of the genus who would prefer to die rather than allow a human reaction to disturb protocol. It was wholly within trend that Craig should have made a beeline for her. Emma was beginning to get to know her Craig's little predilections quite well and reverence for the Great and Good was one of them. He just could not prevent himself from genuflecting to rank – he was programmed to defer.

Charles, as per usual, was seated just behind Ginny's elbow at her table, looking intent and devoted both at the same time. He was also holding the baby on his lap.

Trish and Stella were into the bidding too quickly for Emma's liking, haring like rabbits for the slam which they fondly and not unreasonably imagined was there for the taking. Lucy-Miranda sat there opposite Emma impassively. Eventually Trish and Stella reached their Six No Trumps and L-M just as rashly, it seemed to Emma, doubled their contract.

Yes, it was true. There was no doubting L-M's bid. The red card sat on the green baize like an assassin's dagger. L-M herself sat there looking composed and unrepentant.

A gasp from Stella and a snort and glare from Trish and off they went on the play. It was all fairly hairy and it made Emma think of Joe again, a person whom she did not wish to bring to mind at that precise moment. Emma knew that Joe was a great gambler, a lifetime player of the odds and the probabilities. She knew also that he would have relished the defence at that particular moment with the two women going for it with all their might. He would have played it very cool indeed with his blue rocks glinting at dummy and his face screwed up in that special look of concentration which he adopted in quite tough contracts, his cards as ever lying face down on the table as he focused on the breaks. But she preferred not to think about Joe at that particular moment because it was too painful and evocative. So she tried to clear her mind of extraneous detail like her ex-lover and concentrate on the play.

Which in fact turned out to be quite easy. Childishly so – Trish was mortified. Lucy-Miranda led a Heart, which didn't seem to get anybody very far. But when Trish played for the drop in Spades, it was not only quite unnecessary, because the Clubs were coming home. She also failed to take into account that Emma had three Spades to the King over Dummy. So she won with her King and dutifully returned a Heart which predictably won because L-M had Ace, Jack over Trish's King, with Queen on the table. A good though very risky double, and a nice fat top for Emma and L-M. Both Trish and Stella were livid with each other during the post-mortem, while Emma and L-M chortled away in silence, rejoicing just through eye-contact. The slam should have made quite easily but, as Trish complained, she'd been put off by the double and that made all the difference. Stella insisted on going through the bidding again. By the time that little exercise in cruelty had been completed, the smoke was practically billowing from Trish's nostrils.

So far from home and yet so close to familiar territory, thought Emma.

All in all, Italian bridge didn't seem so very different from the SW3 version, except that the temperature was higher. Outside, that was. The centigrade count within the building was the same as anywhere that an English social duplicate was being played.

The next two boards were fairly run of the mill with no great excitements to tantalise the players. Since there were three board rounds it was then time to move – even in Italy. The conventions were the same the whole world over. Emma and L-M bade good luck to Trish and Stella, who were still investigating the fault-lines in their bidding, almost too preoccupied to acknowledge their departure. Just a wave and a glare.

Pure SW3. The no 137 bus might have been rumbling past the window.

Onto the next table – and another greeting from an erstwhile member of the Liz Playfair group with Emma doing the introductions yet again. More surprises. L-M discovered that she had a common acquaintance with one of the girls who should have been at the bridge table, Betty, who might also have been on holiday with the gang, as a last-minute replacement. But her departure had been prevented by the marriage of her son, Marcello. Betty was certainly not part of the gang. She lived in the wrong part of the world. There was a great deal of chattering away about her, with Betty being described as practically running around in skins because she lived in Hertfordshire. Then there was talk about her son, Marcello; there had been some early trouble with him apparently after he left home abruptly but now all was well since he'd eventually come rolling back home of his own free will – reportedly. Emma distrusted those reports from the front from past experience but there seemed to be some credibility in this one. With the marriage, plus the work he was doing for his father in the family business, Marcello sounded as if he was well integrated into the main stream. Emma mused about what it might have been that made him drop out in the first place; Marcello sounded like quite an independent character.

As the cards were picked up for the play, Lucy-Miranda whispered to Emma that Betty was the friend who had found her running down the street and looking like a tart with her boobs flying around all over the place when she made her escape from You Know Where. Emma gawped for a second as two worlds that normally lay far apart came very close in her imagination.

No surprises at all in the hands. They trundled through a few part score contracts and then resumed the gossip. Emma swore to herself that if she listened carefully enough she could hear the roar of London traffic beneath the window outside. Lucy-Miranda insisted to the go-between that Betty be made aware of her existence and the go-between promised faithfully to convey the message. Links, thin trails of invisible gossamer nourished by chat, were being established between Repugia; Petana; and wherever it was in Upper Sloane Street that Lucy-Miranda lived with Charles.

Lucy-Miranda was very insistent with the go-between about Betty.

'Tell Betty, will you, that I'm sorry that I haven't been in touch with her as much as I should have done but I have had a few problems. There's my new husband, over there…And oh, he's actually playing. Well, I wonder. On his own head be it. I don't know if that's good for him this afternoon…'

Emma looked with Lucy-Miranda and saw that indeed Charles was playing at the table, in Ginny's place. He was looking calmer and less flustered; that augured well. And of course, he was playing in Ginny's place. But of course... He was predestined on that occasion to play in her place. Of course he was. Emma saw everything in that moment and wondered at her stupidity at not unlocking the elegant little subterfuge beforehand. So carefully arranged and so simple...It was all part of the cunning little plot hatched by that oh so glamorous and oh so lustful and oh so manipulative young opportunistic Sloane, Ginny, the red-haired charmer. Ginny with her eager, hot little fanny. That was why the compliant Charles had been brought along – to take Ginny's place while she flitted from the room, with Jake in tow. It was all so deadly and so effective in its invisibility. That way Ginny could take advantage of her one opportunity to hit on Jake, while no one noticed her absence or could remark on it. Part One among the ruins – the blowjob -had been just the aperitif – literally. But Part Two, while the bridge was taking place, was the real raw red meat of the entree, in every sense.

Lady C, an old acquaintance from Liz Playfair's, was playing at the next table and she welcomed Emma very cordially. Emma doubted however whether Lady C actually recognised her or remembered her. Not that it mattered – life just went on in its unchanging way for Lady C. She was a little plumper than before so that her spoiled darling 'mistress to the King' look was even more pronounced than before. The Carolingian curls were in place, as well as the pout, and so too was her sashaying 'watch but don't touch' walk as she rose to her feet to fetch herself a glass of water. But she seemed just a trifle distraite. She fingered the cards absently as if they were refusing to speak to her of their limitless possibilities. She seemed barely involved in the proceedings. Emma wondered what the news was about her daughter, the very capable Ateh who had mysteriously turned up out of the blue, the product of a mesalliance by Lady C in her hot careless youth. Ateh had been kept very much under wraps throughout Lady C's very public life; such seemed to be the case now. She certainly didn't seem to be accompanying Lady C that afternoon. Some time back, the revelation of Ateh's existence had been the talk of SW3 for a brief period at the very height of the storm surrounding poor Liz Playfair. The bush telegraph had practically pumped itself dry with excitement. The gang had closed around Lady C in support, while at the same time booting Liz Playfair out into the snows for her misdemeanour.

As might have been expected – an education shared is a bond for life. But, mysteriously, no mention of Ateh that afternoon, and Emma did not see fit to venture further questions. Lady C seemed discouraged in some vague way. The old hair-trigger brittleness of her temperament had given way to a sort of specious melancholy, a kind of sallow brooding. Emma was pleased in some ways to note this change in Lady C. The last time they had encountered each other, at Liz Playfair's, Lady C had given her a series of blistering rebukes such as might have quelled for ever any inclinations Emma might have nurtured about socialising in the upper reaches of SW3. But that seemed to be all long gone. Not now would she have been so fiery. The flames looked to have died down and she seemed charred rather than lively, almost frumpish in some ways. The viperish tongue was less in evidence.

Lady C greeted Lucy-Miranda very civilly nonetheless and they started the play by picking up their cards. The bidding began but it had no sparkle to it. Again both sides trundled through their contracts; the play came to an end; and it was time to move on, this time to an empty table because L-M and Emma had to sit out the next round. Lady C bade them farewell without much more than a glance and the two of them repaired to a secluded part of the room.

They were joined almost immediately by Lady C's partner at the bridge table, scurrying over to them conspiratorially. Lady C's partner was someone whom Emma did not immediately recognise although in manner she was visibly and massively part of the Dames genus. She spoke quietly but insistently to them both as if she was imparting world shattering news.

'Don't worry about Lady C, Emma. She's having a very bad time all round just now. She's not getting on at all well with her daughter, and I believe they had a stand-up shouting match over the phone this morning. Ateh and Lady C may be mother and daughter but they've had very little time to iron out their differences and there are temperaments between them. Differences…She'll be OK but she needs time to cope with it all. The death of her husband didn't help, so…'

'How did he die then?' asked Lucy-Miranda, always keen to hear whether her own tragic tale could be topped by anyone else's.

'Oh, he just died...Yes, he just died...He found that...Well, he wasn't well...So he -er...Yes, it was a great shock to us all but he threw himself out of the window of his house during a party...A bridge party actually...And killed himself, of course...Anyway, that's neither here nor there, is it now, because it's water under the bridge so to speak if you'll pardon the expression, but that's what's going on between Lady C and Ateh, just so that you know. I must be getting back to the bridge, but I just thought you'd like to know about Lady C. She needs a lot of cheering up these days...'

'So do we all, dear,' was L – M's tough-minded comment as the acolyte rushed back to fulfil her devotions.

'Emma, I like the sound of this Lady C. I want to know more. She sounds like a woman after my own heart. A founder member of the League of Distressed Gentlefolk, brackets Women, I think. Might hold the world record for crying into her beer, late at night. I see possibilities here. I want to get to know her better. We could become friends.'

'With Lady C? Impossible.'

But Emma laughed as L-M began to sparkle again and feel at home. Then as Emma looked around the room, she noticed Charles, as he was playing a hand. She wondered just how long lived L-M's moment of blissful caprice might be. Charles' face was redder than ever and he seemed to be breathing heavily as he scanned his hand and then looked across at the dummy. His eyes looked globular in their intensity.

But her attention was distracted by the arrival of another of the English contingent at their sit-out table, this time the Betty go-between.

'I'm dummy and the hand plays itself so I thought I'd just nip across and mention something else I should have remembered to tell you about Betty. Did you know that she's set up a kind of a bridge school where she lives?'

'No but it wouldn't surprise me. Betty's that kind of girl. But I've been out of touch, so I wouldn't have heard. I didn't think that she was that keen on bridge, though. This is a new one for her.'

Lucy-Miranda spoke easily about her absence from the scene. The go-between persisted.

'Yes, but I thought you might have known the woman who's doing the coaching at her school. She's called Liz Playfair...Do you know Liz Playfair?'

It was like the sound of champagne corks popping in a restaurant. From one table to another, the bridge players with their alert ears picked up the name and repeated it, so that it went all the way round the room.

'Liz Playfair?'

'Liz Playfair?'

'What's that about Liz Playfair?'

'Did I hear you say Liz Playfair?'

'Who said anything about Liz Playfair?'

Cards were breasted from table to table as attention was distracted. Heads bobbed up and down. The Italians were nonplussed as the English contingent almost downed tools at reference to the hitherto unmentionable name.

'Scusi!'

'Scusi!'

Heads swivelled in the direction of the little group comprising Emma; Lucy-Miranda; and the go-between at their side table. But etiquette prevented them all from quitting each and every table and bounding across en masse to hear the news about Liz.

'Who is this Liz Playfair, Emma? Do you know?'

L-M posed the question as this time the go-between returned to her table, after detonating her bombshell. Emma replied to L-M very quietly.

'Yes, I do as it happens. She ran a bridge academy just off the King's Road – there are lots of them there – and something happened to her. A very brief affair and with a woman...'

'They all chucked her out.'

'Lady C included. She was the leader of the rat pack. Or the witch hunt, in this case.'

'I can well believe it. That's exactly what they'd do. Exactly what I'd have done in my old days as a leader in Hampshire society. Before I knew better. So they all told her to fuck off just for that tiny thing. Quite, quite predictable. I can tell you that in You Know Where...'

Emma noticed yet again how the vocabulary changed gear as L-M's mind neared the brothel. It was uncanny.

'In You Know Where, it wasn't rife, but it existed and where it did exist sometimes it made the girls happy and sometimes it didn't. It didn't alter the human condition one tiny jot. Sex is always a la carte. That much I have learned. So...'

That was about all the philosophising that Lucy-Miranda had time for. The hands had finished, and the girls bounded across. Emma and Lucy-Miranda were surrounded by a sea of expectant faces, all bursting to hear the news.

'What's this about Liz Playfair? How is she? What's she doing? Where is she these days? How's her bridge?'

Emma spoke with calmness.

'Apparently she's running a bridge school somewhere in Hertfordshire, I think. The cross-connections are a bit hazy, but it belongs to someone called Betty.'

The chatter of the responses was immediate, excited and confused.

'Betty? Do we know Betty? I don't think we know Betty, do we?'

'Yes we do. You know Betty, of course you do.'

'I don't think so. She doesn't ring a bell with me.'

'Wasn't Betty supposed to fill in if Mags couldn't make it?'

'Oh that Betty – I remember now. So is it true that she's given Liz a berth? That's bold of her. Very bold, I say.'

'I don't know. Ask Emma over there. She seems to know.'

Emma prepared to fend off the questions, wondering just what the heightened level of interest in Liz Playfair could actually mean. Were they suddenly in favour of her now , just as they had been hostile towards her at the time of the Great Crisis? Were they poised to take her back into the collective SW3 bosom, after kicking her out so brutally? Who could tell – it was inexplicable, this abrupt change of mood and sudden reawakening of interest. Emma, not herself the best advert for inclusive group behaviour, prepared to cope with the sea of faces, as if about to give a press conference.

Just then a small brown-skinned man with a heavily receded hairline and a serious, tired and responsible professional expression pushed his way through the group and asked for silence in Italian and then English. Voices could still be heard at the back of the crush twittering on like song birds about Liz Playfair. Gradually a reluctant silence fell in anticipation of the man's words.

'The Englishman who was playing at the table is very sick. His heart is not well. Please we can have no more bridge for a little while until he is carried to the hospital. And please, can we all go outside. He is very sick indeed. We do not know if he will live.'

Charles had had a stroke in the middle of playing a hand. He had collapsed but nobody had noticed – the tension had caught up with him at last as the world turned its back to find out more about Liz Playfair. At the news, the crowd let out a terrible gasp of anguish and disappointment.

No more bridge…!

As the crowd parted in front of Emma Charles could be seen lying on the floor, quite quietly but breathing very heavily, looking absent-minded and almost lifeless, surrounded by the crouching paramedics who must have arrived there in a flash.

A whole sequence of events had taken place quite unbeknownst to the group whose attention at those critical moments had, quite understandably and forgivably, been focussed elsewhere.

The beautiful Ginny chose that moment to saunter back into the bridge room looking relaxed and limber and without a care in the world, having concluded very evidently her business with Jake to her own manifest satisfaction. She seemed very relaxed. Very deliberately she took her baby from Craig who had been entrusted with its care, after Charles started to play; placed it on her knee; and began to croon to the child, quite unaware of the drama taking place at the other end of the room.

Tommy was due back in Repugia very shortly. Mission completed by Ginny and just in time! Revenge, as Ginny would have agreed at that moment, is a kind of wild justice, and nothing else...

'Nice work if you can get it and hang the cost. It's a victimless crime, if that,' thought Emma to herself as the group trailed out into the sunshine, to be followed eventually by Charles looking helpless, with the oxygen mask over his face, on the stretcher, and headed for the hospital and the life-support machine. And a very new life, provided he managed to get through the night...

*　*　*　*　*

'It was that snake Ginny wasn't it, Emma? I should have guessed.'

The two women sat on their bench in the square in Repugia. Three days had passed. They had made the journey back to Repugia alone. The other members of the group had gone on ahead. Charles was still in hospital in Petana, undergoing tests. The medical reports spoke favourably of him making a speedy recovery. But given his age the Italian doctors were taking no chances. The paralysis was said to be mild and ought to wear off in due course. Charles could also speak, albeit with a slight impediment. L-M had endured a tough few days but she sounded philosophical about it all.

'She arranged it all, didn't she, Emma?'

'I imagine so. I couldn't say for certain either way but it certainly looks that way. She took Charles along to act as a stand-in for her while she met Jake outside...'

'And then fucked his brains out in some dugout. I know, I should have seen it coming. But there again, what could I do? It was inevitable that something like this would happen at some point. Charles just couldn't resist Ginny. I feel very sorry for him lying in his hospital bed, and I watched over him the last few days with a great deal of compassion because in many ways he has been a very good second husband to me. But Ginny was always going to be fatal for him. He just couldn't say 'No' to her. He could always deny me but never her, and that was a fact of life I realised very early on. He would always do whatever she told him to do. The fact that he's still alive is a bonus. She was always going to use him in one way or another, so I have to assume that I've got off rather lightly. At least they got him into hospital in a trice, so I've got that to be grateful for. That doctor really was truly magnificent. It was just so fortunate that he happened to be playing bridge there on that afternoon...'

L-M paused as the life of the square in the early evening went on around them. Emma did not intrude on her reverie.

Lucy-Miranda did not seem to be in the mood to discuss the love of her life, amid rhapsodies of previous trips to Italy down memory lane. Emma steered well clear of those topics because she too was not disposed to the intimacy of such revelations whose moment had come and gone at the Roman fort. But she had love and affection on her mind nevertheless and it was beginning to ache inside her. Joe was weighing heavily on her mind. It seemed like weeks now since she'd written to him. Had he responded to her letter or not? Was there a letter from him lying on her front-door mat? A letter which contained some intimation of remembrance and recollection on his part for her? That was the vital point which she now wished to clarify and she yearned to know. She listened to Lucy-Miranda spouting onwards with some outward show of support but her mind wandered. She could feel the Italian holiday drawing steadily to a close. It was nearly time now to be off and doing other things. Craig's novel for example was very nearly finished. It had been a very successful few weeks for him and he looked pleased with himself. With his novel on the brink of the last few chapters, and a new teaching term poised to begin in a few weeks, which required him to return to London, the justification for Emma remaining in Repugia was beginning to wane.

Life was moving on for them all. Soon Ginny would be back in London, just ahead of the autumn. She would be reunited with her circle and with her husband who at that very moment was presumably sewing up the last details of his deal ahead of flying out to Repugia. The bankers and the traders in the party were due back the following day and a large lunch party had been arranged to celebrate their return. So it was all nearly over. Ginny had taken her revenge on Tommy for his outrageous behaviour over the phone call and the baby – with no comebacks for her. Charles was collateral damage but she couldn't be held responsible for his cardiac malfunction. So no comebacks. Emma sighed once more over the nonchalance and the mobility and the invulnerability of the English rich, so well-embedded and so comfortable within society.

The boy waiter toiled towards them with their drinks. It was the early evening and the night life of the square was just starting to sparkle, with lights going on in the windows of the flats round the square; women calling to each other across the square from the open windows here and there; and the usual gaggle of familiar beings walking here and there at their own favourite pace from point A to point B in the square. Hands were waved frequently in their direction as people passed. They were both very well known now to all and sundry as the English ladies who sat on the bench. Occasionally they were consulted on tricky matters involving Anglo-Italian understanding, on which subject they were considered to be authorities. Meanwhile the boy waiter was growing his first moustache. It looked terrible, like a piece of vegetation spreading across his soft little face. But diplomatically the two women had said nothing untoward about the vegetation, merely uttering encouraging but non-committal sounds when he tried to discuss the problems of puberty in Italy. The boy waiter was very proud of his moustache. Lucy-Miranda had told him it made him look like a man. He was very pleased by her compliment; he kicked the stones all the way back from the bench to the cafe.

The soft evening light fell gently from the Italian sky.

'You know, Emma, my life is just continuing to be some God-awful fuck-up all round, just as before. I've given you the tally of disasters so far. Charles fits into the pattern very neatly. Well, I've had an idea about all of this. I'm fighting back. It came to me while I was watching poor Charles battling for his life in the oxygen tent. I've decided to change things. I've decided to take charge. Rightly or wrongly, I feel empowered.'

276

'I thought you were in charge, L-M. You always gave me that impression.'

'Superficially yes, but in reality no. It always escapes me at the critical moment. But this time, it's going to be different. I'm taking charge.'

'I've heard that before from women and I've always believed it and they always finish up grovelling away as before with nothing changed. So what are you going to do that's going to make such a difference?'

'I'm thinking about it...'

'Hah. There you are, you're thinking about it. I told you so, didn't I? That's as far as it'll get, thinking about it.'

'Not necessarily, young Emma. Just wait a little and allow me to explain. Now while I sip my wine, tell me some more about Lady C.'

'What you'd expect, given her background – selfish; tongue like a viper; the absolute centre of the entire universe, bar none; and basically I would say disappointed in life. Would probably benefit from a short spell in prison to straighten her out. That, or a succession of regular beatings.'

Lucy-Miranda looked jubilant.

'That's exactly what I wanted to hear. You put it so well, Emma. I'm going to offer you a place on the bus as well.'

'Bus?'

'Never you mind. You'll be told all, and all in good time. Now tell me about Liz Playfair.'

'Have you called Betty yet?'

'I was waiting to hear your report before I did so. Liz is vital to my plan. I have to know more.'

'Plan? What plan?'

'I told you just now that I had a plan and you disbelieved me. Now you think I might have a plan. You will just have to wait before I tell you anymore.'

Emma told Lucy-Miranda what she knew about Liz Playfair – the career as an up and coming bridge player just on the fringe of the England team; the little bridge salon which she'd founded in the heart of SW3; the problems with her husband and the short affair with someone who turned out to be a freedom fighter from somewhere in Asia; and her sudden social eclipse as SW3 dumped her. Emma wondered whether to mention Joe in the context of Liz, because Joe was more or less the fount of all knowledge on the subject – and he'd liked Liz very much – but she decided not to risk a mention of Joe to Lucy-Miranda. It was a conscious decision to keep Joe's name out of it. It might bring on the whole series of threatened reminiscences about the love of L-M's life – whoever he was – and Emma preferred that evening to hear more about The Great Plan.

L-M duly disappointed her. After digesting what she'd been told about Liz, she cut the discussion short.

'She sounds perfect. Thank you.'

'How absolutely infuriating of you, L-M. So you won't tell me any more?'

'Not tonight, Josephine, but tomorrow I will speak, after they all turn up again from London to collect their loved ones. My daughter in particular will be very surprised. She thinks her mother is an old fool. Well she may well be that, but just before she goes into her dotage, she has decided to do something which will either confirm her idiot status, in which case public opinion will be entirely satisfied, or...'

'Or?'

'She'll be the talk of the town. Yup, top hat and tails and flying down to Rio. That's all, Emma. It's one way or another now for Lucy-Miranda and her rather odd life.'

'Again how every infuriating of you, L-M, but then again, how brave of you even to be considering taking any kind of initiative at this point. Charles is after all at death's door.'

'Thank you Emma. You said that very sweetly and it is a great encouragement to me. Now I propose to finish my wine; keep a lookout for Gina, who has not crossed our sightlines so far this evening on her way to bring heartache to the mayor of Repugia; and relax. No more revelations until tomorrow. Understood, girl?'

They both laughed.

'Know what I mean?'

'Know what I mean?'

''Ere...'

'Didn't he look sweet as he woke up to find himself with 2 crazy women…?'

More laughter as the two women drank their wine together. But L-M was true to her word. After her enigmatic statement, she refused to say anything further of enlightenment and insisted on talking about the weather and the lunch party the following day, much to Emma's chagrin.

★   ★   ★   ★   ★

Emma woke up in the middle of the night in a cold sweat of fear. In her panic, she threw off all the bedclothes. Outside, the night was a very still and silent watchful confidant to her thoughts.

Emma had forgotten all about Lucia and her arrival later that morning.

'This could make L-M very angry indeed. Not telling her about the SW3 girls in Petana – well, I just about got away with that in the excitement. I don't think L-M ever put two and two together. But this is different. I actually sold a house to Lucia and her boyfriend via Joe. That must have been when she was still married to – what was his name? Spongo? Yes, that was what she called him, although I seem to remember the name was Maitland. Yes, of course, it was Maitland, because there was all that horseplay about names when Jake arrived. And if I recall correctly the house was actually in Lucia's own name, for some reason, so that she got to keep it even after Spongo's whole estate went belly-up. I remember it all now perfectly and so will L-M when there is a connection made between Lucia and myself. If any of this comes out – and I don't see any way that it can't as soon as Lucia arrives – there's bound to be trouble. Lucia is bound to recognise me. She can't fail to…It's inevitable. I haven't changed that much in the last few years. There's going to be trouble. Yes, big trouble. I can smell it on the way. L-M's no fool. She's bound to smell a rat and she'll think that I've been holding out on her. Oh bugger, bugger,

bugger…I really don't want to lose her as a friend, but it looks as if I'm going to do just that in a few hours time. I just can't stand it…'

And Emma, deeply alarmed, sat up in her bed, and then got out of bed and began to pace about the hotel room in her agitation as she envisaged the sad and catastrophic consequences of her meeting later on that morning with Lucia after her arrival in Repugia from London. And what about Lucia's reactions if she so much as got a whiff of what Jake had been up to while she'd been away…?

'Oh my God, it just doesn't bear thinking about. Lucia is a successful banker in a man's world, the kind of girl who is used to taking snap decisions, based on hunches. She's going to make a fuss. I can feel it on its' way.'

Emma knew the type. From all L-M's comments about her, and from Emma's own experience of her, she was certainly a girl who could live with the consequences of those decisions. Just like her father, as L-M always said. She was quite likely to make merry hell, on her own terms, if details of Jake's rather casual and probably quite unthinking philandering started to emerge.

And then what about Angelina? Emma had forgotten about her. Had she been invited to the lunch party? Did she know about it? Had Jake signed up with Roma, or whatever his football club was called? Was she going to turn up and cause a scene as well? As well she might…She looked well capable of that, like one of Nature's born foot-stampers…

The perspiration began to run down her back as the deadly clairvoyance of the morning's small hours revealed just what a powder keg they had all been casually tossing about in Repugia for the past few months. And now it was about to explode in their faces…The lunch party which had been arranged for them all was going to be a disaster… That was abundantly clear…

Feeling more than somewhat distraught, Emma tried to compose herself for the morning which lay ahead and grab some more sleep. Without a great deal of success. She tossed and turned until at 4.30 in the morning by the clock. The hands moved very slowly round the dial.

It was all going to end in tears. It was inevitable.

But she need not have worried so much about Lucy-Miranda and her daughter Lucia flying in from London. Events conspired to protect Emma. Round about five in the morning she got a call from L-M. It was a rather shaky voice that crept down the line. No bounce at all. L-M sounded old and tired and discouraged.

'You'll have to hold the fort for me at the lunch party and say Hullo to everyone for me, Emma. I'm off to Petana immediately.'

'I'm sorry, Lucy-Miranda...'

'Yes, bad news. Charles has had a relapse. A bad one and it's come at just the wrong moment, when he was starting to get better. They say that he's very ill now and may not last the day. It's simply touch and go. If I'm there, they say, he may rally, but who knows. If I'm there it might prove fatal, what with my track record. Anyway, I'd better be there, so I'm off now on my mercy mission – I've got a car waiting downstairs – and with luck I'll be there by eight or so. I'll ring you as soon as I've got some news...Enjoy yourself at the party and say Hullo to my daughter for me, will you?'

'Of course Lucy-Miranda. I'm so sorry...'

'Just as well I have my plan, isn't it?'

'I could sympathise a little more, L-M, if I knew what the plan was about...'

But no guffaw from Lucy-Miranda. She didn't sound at all jaunty as she put the phone down. Emma returned to a horizontal position, torn between remorse at the worsening health of Charles and sheer jubilation that she would now avoid the confrontation with Lucia under the gaze of her mother.

But it was all very sad...

*　*　*　*　*

The events at the villa got under way smoothly and quietly enough at the beginning. To welcome the prodigals' return from the City, albeit temporarily, a huge table had been set up in the gardens, right in the middle of the lawns and taking the shade of two of the trees from the hot late Summer sun. It was a feast of feasts. The kitchen had been labouring since early morning with the pasta and the chicken, the lamb and the rice. Meanwhile the fruit; the bread; the wines; the plates; the cutlery; and the glasses had all been loaded upon the table. Chairs were placed fairly casually all around so that no fixed order would be seen to prevail. Emma wandered about, missing Lucy-Miranda and thinking about Joe in the late-morning sun. She wondered if Jake and Ginny had enjoyed some form of meeting early that morning on the lawns – perhaps their last – just before Lucia and Tommy arrived and reassigned each of them to their respective partners – another sign that the holidays were over. But in Lucy-Miranda's absence, she had no way of knowing; from Lucy-Miranda, tragically, there had been no word. Emma hoped fervently that she had arrived safely in Petana after her journey. But she feared for her friend L-M and also for Charles.No news was definitely bad news at that point.

Lucia did not at first admit to recognising Emma when she at last set foot in the villa. Emma saw her arrive and she was very much as Emma recalled her from some years ago only emphatically more so. Work in the City had emphasised into prominence what was latent anyway. Sharply dressed in crop top; shades; designer jeans; and loafers, every inch the busy preoccupied can-do banker working on a deal but not too busy that she couldn't dress the part for a feast, she swept into the villa without very much of a sideways look to all and sundry awaiting her arrival in the hall, tucking her mobile away in her handbag as she did so and passing Emma by without anything more than the flicker of a glance. Lucia was self-possessed and immediately at home in her surroundings, as anyone might have been who had been brought up in a dozen different houses and locations throughout her youth. She had style and presence and money by the yard but she was not flash. That was immediately apparent. Instead, she had pedigree. But she also possessed a lean and hungry look. The call to London still reverberated in the air as she hunted the deal. She was looking for Jake too and she was in a hurry to run him to earth. She soon found him in the garden, leaning against the parapet from which Samantha had so very nearly hurled herself some months ago. Jake was looking very slim; young; tanned and casual after his holiday, almost detached in a way from it all like a slender creature, while Lucia by contrast brought some of the bustle and cares of the big city with her as she whirled in haste across the lawn towards him, despite the careful camouflage of her fashionable clothes. They embraced each other cautiously and not passionately, just around the waist, almost carefully and with reservations as if they were trading each other's stock, still uncertain whether what they were holding so close was a Buy or Sell or merely a tepid Hold.

And did it carry a bonus? That was another large question which required negotiation. And how big was the bonus – questions, questions…There seemed to be a hierarchy in their relationship which made Jake immediately deferential. This was not surprising since he was holding his boss in his arms. Jake reverted immediately to the dealing room parlance, upon which culture presumably his relationship with Lucia was founded. But Lucia did the talking after Jake greeted her.

'Wotcher, Lucky. Long time, no see. How's the deal?'

Lucia pulled her nose in that gesture that was characteristic of her as she held her ground and commanded her space. She took careful stock before answering his question. Precautionary finger to lips…

'I think it flies but it's difficult. Very tricky in some ways. We've had a lot of problems one way or another. The market hasn't helped one little bit, it's been so volatile. But maybe we're nearly there…It's hard to tell… You know, I had to get special permission from the Takeover Panel to come out here this weekend…It's that tricky these days with Compliance and confidentiality agreements…That tells you how much I feel about you…'

Jake nodded his understanding as she put down her marker. They chattered on, gossiping away about the markets.

Emma wandered over to the two of them and introduced herself. Jake smiled as she spoke her name, because she and Jake had got on well during the summer. Jake for his own part had hit it off with Craig once he had mastered his consternation that

Craig was actually writing a book out of his own head and without help.

But Lucia frowned at Emma's name and muttered something about meeting once before but couldn't remember where or when and turned back to Jake. Emma realised at once why she seemed so amnesiac and she could have laughed at her own stupidity at not taking the point immediately. When she had sold the house in Chelsea to Lucia, Lucia had had a different boy-friend named Prestbury. In the tangle of subsequent alliances and Lucia's ruthless development of her own career, backed by her father's ever-resonant name in the City, Prestbury had of course been jettisoned. The existence of a former beau was not something which Lucia, power dressed as she was, wished to recall at that precise moment. And if she didn't wish to recall it, well then it wouldn't be recalled. Lucia had Nelson's blind eye off to perfection. Hence her combination of aggression towards Emma and her temporary absence of memory recall as the sun blasted down on the gardens in the villa.

But she managed both of these feats with instinctive aplomb. Emma decided that Lucia all in all was a very formidable little piece of machinery indeed. A tough cookie. Not to be crossed.

Jake, ever the eager and deferential one where Lucia was concerned, told her about Craig who was writing a book. Lucia showed an immediate interest, if only to change the subject away from her prior acquaintance with Emma.

'Let me find him for you, Lucia. I'm sure you'll like him. He must be here somewhere…'

Lucia nodded in a 'Go fetch' kind of way and Jake sloped off in search of Craig. Lucia's mobile then rang shrilly from her handbag. Before answering it, very much with Jake's back view in sight, she fixed Emma with a chilly eye, which betokened no nonsense. In a simple statement of fact, addressing the point between Emma's eyebrows, Lucia said very directly:

'I really can't think it helps anyone for the world to know that we once did a property trade together, does it? Particularly one where I paid so much above the market. That galls too. I wouldn't pay that now for that house. So we say nothing? Understood?'

'I couldn't agree more, Lucia. Who the hell cares anyway…'

'Exactly. Wait one, Dickie...On the button...Yes, on the button. Dickie, now I'm with you.'

Lucia turned dismissively to her phone call just as Jake heaved into sight escorting Craig towards Lucia. Lucia was brisk down the line.

'Well, if that's what he thinks, let him think it. I couldn't care a flying fuck what Joe thinks. It's what I think that counts here.'

She snapped the call to an end.

'Joe?'

Emma's question was mildly interrogative.

'Friend of yours? Of course, stupid of me, I'd forgotten. Didn't Joe broker the deal over the house? It's all very hazy now in my mind.'

I'll bet it is, thought Emma. It was her turn to be evasive.

'It's maybe not the same guy. There are millions of them around and about. Who's this Joe?'

'Number two at ABC and my boss. But not for much longer. He's on the way out. Ring any bells? If so, I'd forget him. He's fucked huge. Dead meat. It's only a matter of weeks now before he gets the chop. Felix and the Quiff have got him by the throat – and they're squeezing. They are just lining him up for a turkey-shoot. It's all over for him. Arsehole. History.'

A terrible pang gripped Emma as she heard the bad news about Joe but she managed to keep a straight face and respond quite nonchalantly.

'None. My Joe was a librarian.'

'Can't say I know many of those. Not my line of country...But this must be Craig. Craig, good morning. My name's Lucia. How's the book?'

Lucia had a way of spinning light and attention around her like a lighthouse beam. Those who were in the line of the light etc. felt flattered and cherished. Everything else lay fast bound in darkness and could rot. It was a very effective technique, automatically placing Lucia in pole position in any conversation. Emma needless to say had been cast into darkness as Lucia focussed on Craig. Craig for his part was flattered by her attention and shuffled his feet a little. Then he began to talk very quickly about his book; about Catullus and his love affair; about how he was nearly finished; how wonderful Italy had been that summer; and then, almost as an after-thought, about his publisher, Emma, who was standing right there behind Lucia.

Lucia cleared her throat at the news that Emma had some role to play in the scenario and paused. Then reaching out an invisible crooked talon, which tore where it touched, she swiftly acquired a tiny sliver of equity in Craig's book:

'Yes, I'm familiar with Catullus. He's a superb writer, I agree. We did lots of Latin at school, and I always thought there might be a book in that situation with Lesbia. No time to do it myself of course, unfortunately. Too busy in the markets, I'm afraid. But congratulations on spotting the angle. It should sell well. Film rights sewn up?'

By the way she was standing in the gardens, at the angle between the lawns and the terrace, Lucia was holding both of the young men enthralled in her triangle of radial influence while shutting Emma out completely from the flow of the discussion. It was brutally and neatly done. Suddenly the beautiful and benign Italian garden, so full of flowers and sweet thoughts, had become a power cockpit of jostling ambition.

Thinking that this was how life should always be organised, plus similar dull thoughts, Emma wandered away to another part of the garden. Lucia was for the time being just too much; too retro; and too overpowering for her to tolerate.

Ginny and Tommy were standing together with the baby close by the spot where Tommy had nearly had his fatal accident. Tommy was talking to Ginny very fast about the deal and waving his arms about as, in his own mind, he brought home the bacon. Ginny was holding the baby and looking angelic, submissive and maternal in cream pants and a t-shirt. The red-copper hair was scraped back off her face with its very pale skin, making her look oddly youthful and vulnerable. But there was something odd about the way the two of them stood together. It was only after a small pass about the couple which took her to the parapet and then back that Emma realised the problem. She noticed that Ginny was listening to Tommy but only with half an ear.

In reality, she was looking away from him, almost through him in fact and Emma guessed that she was focussing on Jake over in the corner with Lucia and Craig. Emma felt a twinge of alarm. Ginny should not have been behaving in this way. It was too obvious. She was standing with her legs apart, holding the baby it was true, but she looked aggressive and proprietorial almost as if she was about to dump the baby on Tommy; walk over to the group; and yank Jake away by his ear, after punching Lucia a classic one in the chops.

Emma stood with her back to the parapet unobtrusively. Glancing about as if taking the air on such a marvellous day in Italy in late summer she drank in the bellicose ambiance, from where she stood, arms outstretched along the parapet and head raised to the sun. She could just overhear what Tommy was saying – and what Ginny replied. Ginny sounded brusque and truculent, with her mind on other things as she spoke to Tommy. She refused to let go of Jake. That was obvious. She could not surrender title to him. And unless she did so, there was bound to be trouble.

Claims and counter-claims, all pressing, and such like matters...

Emma mused away. Perhaps Ginny had done wrong in scheming to fuck Jake rigid through all the weeks she'd been in Italy with him. But no one had seen anything; no one had held her conduct up to critical reproach; she had ruffled no feathers; it had been personal between her and Jake, a private moment of pleasure between two consenting adults. Society had not been affronted with the sole exception of Charles who had all too obviously allowed himself to be used as a gofer. Silly old Charles! It might all -just – pass without sanction. But for that to happen, Ginny had to back off – now – and just forget about the whole thing, leaving Jake to go whither he might wander. Ginny had to return to her baby and her husband and her close circle of friends in SW3. That was where she belonged. Meanwhile Jake had enough problems of his own, right now. A super-dominant Lucia, to whom the word 'Maybe' had never been uttered, had reappeared on the scene. Angelina, unknown to Lucia as yet, hovered somewhere in the background with a strong interest in Jake, backed up by football contracts and large amounts of Euro's at her disposal. Jake had problems enow without Ginny adding her own slab of gelignite to the conflagration. She had to accept that it was all over, like the fast fading summer.

Jake was free to go. She had to release her grasp.

Emma wondered exactly how Lucia, let alone Ginny, would react to the presence of Angelina, if the flower of Italy managed to find an entry onto the crowded stage of the villa's gardens. Fists? Guns? Knives? Bombs? Anything might happen...

Emma could see Ginny's shoulders begin to straighten even as she held the child. The bum was beginning to poke out; it was angry. It was steaming with rage in fact. Even from where Emma was positioned, Ginny seemed enraged. Up front she must have looked like a Valkyrie with both eyes blazing as the hapless Tommy bored on and on about his deal. The mental circuits were starting to glow white hot as they gradually infused with rage. Emma tentatively could piece together what might be happening in Ginny's brain at that moment before desire and lust gradually blew out all the entire mechanism.

It was jealousy, the pure and unadulterated flying visit by the green eyed god. The sequence of causality was almost traceable. Tommy seemed to put her down when he talked about the deal, so he obviously reckoned she was nothing more than a flame-haired bimbo. Good for child bearing but otherwise not serious. So she felt inferior on that account. When she was with Jake however, amid the seduction of same, there was no way that she could feel inferior, not with somebody quite so amiable and good-natured and easy-going as Jake with his jokes and nonchalance and intuitive, beautiful, tanned sleek, athleticism. Like an Ancient Greek athlete, Jake was a cup-bearer to eternal youth. He offered nothing more nor less than delight. In other words, he had been good for her that summer. But of course Ginny could never admit this to herself. She could never say that she had entered into relationship with Jake, because that would entail her making choices and perhaps surrendering some of her much cherished social status as an idolised, iconic Chelsea Mother. Which she couldn't possibly even contemplate doing, not in a month of Sundays. So on one level, Jake was just a fuck for her. He was a villein who lived in the village beside the chateau and he existed for her much as firing or kindling might have done in the Middle

Ages – something to be taken at will and consumed and then thrown away. That was what having it all meant for Ginny. But of course the fucking of Jake was not the whole story. It all went far deeper than that. Jake of course wasn't just anything so simple as that for her. Ginny was fooling herself to think she could rationalise it all away by an act of self-denial – no more rough trade sex. She and Jake had shared some confidences and intimacy and trust, even in her rush to get him into bed, as he worked out in the morning and she tended her baby. They had enjoyed some genuine Garden of Eden sensations together which were all the more real for having been so unexpected – and unobserved. They had simply grown together during the summer, like any boy and girl meeting together during the summer and little by little falling in love. Now Ginny was regretting the loss of all of that as Tommy turned up. So Ginny, far from being the happy predator, was herself fucked stupid by her own feelings...

For her this was worse than the remorse of the cheque book stubs.

Emma realised with regret as she framed her thoughts in this way that L-M's louche choice of vocabulary was gradually influencing her own verbalised stream of consciousness. But no matter. The situation was too tense for her to worry about a few obscenities. The fucking of Jake would shortly be followed by the fucking of Ginny.

Yes, Ginny was fucked not two, but three ways. She had the husband back with whom she did not enjoy a specially close rapport. Privacy but not intimacy – that would be about the measure of it. The sex was a backup to the job, a necessary adjunct. That was bad in itself. At the same time she was having to suffer the agonies of separation from Jake who was happily chatting away to Lucia; that was bad number two. No more lovely wonderful unconstrained sex with Jake. Not good at all. Poor show, in fact. But he was chatting away as if she'd never existed. That was the point – as if she'd never existed! Far from her dumping him, tra la, tra la, it was Jake who was dumping her...!

He was casually walking away from her, as if he had accepted her decision to dump him with gratitude. So she was nothing to him, and the life in the village was somehow superior to the life in the chateau...! Impossible. But that's what he thinks, then is it? He just doesn't have the right...

Emma could almost see the thoughts form within her skull, as the mental overload started to burn and the shoulders squared another notch and the feet scuffed the ground in anger as the baby bounced around on her arm and normality reasserted itself and Tommy explained again and again what he had been up to, without of course being specific because the Takeover Panel had forbidden him to be anything more than just vague...And Ginny boiled just a little bit more with rage, anger, chagrin and self-imposed mortification as the summer started to end and the London autumn beckoned.

The last time she was put in this position, thought Emma, she tossed Tommy's mobile into the forest and slapped his face good and hard. God knows what might happen this time. She's about ten times more angry...And of course, she's bound to cast herself in the role of victim. That means her behaviour will be all the more outrageous because she'll go all the way without constraint.

Oh my God, there could be a total incident here in about five minutes time...

Emma slid away from the scene of the explosion and wandered about some more as the villa servants began bringing out the lunch and calling the party to the table. Poor Joe, she was thinking, poor, poor Joe. What had happened to him? Why had the career gone belly up as Lucia had suggested. Why was Joe, the arch-magician when it came to finessing a situation, now in the scuppers? It was just unthinkable that he could go down...She gazed at the hills and mused about him some more. She thought that perhaps – if the occasion warranted it and if he had responded to her overtures – she might try to bring him out to Italy and give him some TLC.

Might even take him to those ruins which had caused Lucy-Miranda so much distress and Ginny so much pleasure...She persisted in her thoughts as she day-dreamed about Joe, refusing to believe in her hearts of hearts that Lucia could be right and that Joe, the conjuror of opportunities, could be going down...

Such things just did not happen...

Right!

One of the maids came up to her and told her that she was wanted on the telephone. It was Lucy-Miranda, she was told, calling her from Petana. Emma hastened into the house and clattered down the polished wood floors in the hall in her haste to reach the phone. The receiver lay on its side looking bereft on a small occasional table, the flex trailing down from the cradle. The maids watched her bustle up to the phone. They were silent and grouped together. They knew that Sr. Charles was sick and they suspected that he was now dead. But they did not speak to her as she picked up the receiver. They simply clustered.

'Lucy-Miranda? It's Emma here. What's the news? Good or bad?'

L-M was not jaunty. But she was not tragic either. More like undefeated.

'He's at death's door but he may have acquired another life. That's what the doctors have just told me. They are amazed. He seems to have found some strength from somewhere and he's rallied in the last fifteen minutes. Before that, they thought he was heading for the bins. Now they're not so sure. So he may be at death's door, but he may not actually be knocking on it. That's the news, Emma. Now what about things at your end? Has my daughter arrived?'

'She's just got here and she's in the garden with Jake. They are reconciling.'

'I won't disturb her. Tell her I rang, but don't tell her much about Charles. As you might imagine, she thinks he's a silly old fart – and that's when she's feeling charitable. Say he's got flu, or something stupid like that. She won't believe it, but who cares. It'll do for the time being.'

'Know what I mean?'

A small giggle at the end of the line proved that L-M was still alive and kicking.

'I know perfectly well what you mean. And how is the old 'Know what I mean'?'

'Holding his own, Auntie Lill. 'Ere, you're a wicked woman, nuffink' less…'

L-M giggled again and then rang off, leaving Emma to face the crowd of assembled Gilstons with a small smile on her face which said that the news was bad but not tragic.

Emma returned to the gardens and found them almost deserted. Tommy and Lucia had departed upstairs to change; Jake and Craig were chatting away together by the parapet; and Ginny, ostentatiously separate from the boys, was playing with her baby on the grass way over on the other side of the lawns, making the point that she was utterly detached from them. Detached my foot; she's infatuated by the whole thing, thought Emma as she saw the small quick covert glances that Ginny continued to direct towards Jake as she played up her role as doting mother on the grass.

But then there was no more time for play-acting. Lucia and Tommy descended from the bedrooms looking like every one else on holiday in jeans and t-shirt and the food began to be served at the table.

Lucia suddenly looked very tired and Emma knew that feeling. She after all was a veteran of the legal all-night sittings. She knew exactly how Lucia felt as the adrenalin of battle suddenly started to ebb, to be replaced by a sense of sheer burned-out fatigue which seemed to gather in the ashen pit of the stomach and pull every muscle inwards. Her face was abruptly drawn and she raised a slim long arm in utter fatigue towards the water bottle, glancing around the while as if to convince herself that she truly was seated in a blooming Italian garden and that the roars and screams of City institutions in the committee rooms were now just a ghastly, ghostly memory of 24 hours ago.

Again she pulled at her nose in an expression of some confusion, and again Emma knew how she felt. Eventually, all deals were the same, differing only by degree. Did the numbers still add up? Would that mezzanine fly? And the currencies? Would that fly too? Were the institutional shareholders about to rat on them and back the other side? Clearly a cascade of thoughts were racing through Lucia's head, who was afraid to give up on the concentration but who was near extinction. Because of fatigue she was running the whole thing through her head just one more final time before she was overtaken by oblivion.

And still the deal was on the runway. It hadn't even started to fly...It wasn't even airborne yet.

Dressed in her jeans and huddled at the table surrounded by the maids who were pitchforking food at her, she seemed suddenly vulnerable and terribly over-burdened by responsibility. Hoping to lead the conversation into quieter channels, Emma asked Tommy, who was playing with the baby as if with a stranger, how he felt about the deal. Was nearly finished?

'Of course I know nothing of such things, I've never been involved in that side of business but it must be very exciting...'

Lucia glanced at her sharply but Tommy responded well enough to the lead.

'I'm glad it's nearly over because it's been very hard going. I can't really be more specific than that until the deal is announced and that may be some time away. But what I can say...'

Lucia was gazing now fixedly at Tommy willing him not to be indiscreet. Ginny's attention had veered round again to Lucia as she picked up on the control vibes emanating from her. So her husband actually took his orders from this creature....

Not for long, he didn't...

'Don't say no more, Tommy, there's a good man. Can't you see that Lucia will have your guts for garters if you so much as breathe a word out of line.'

Jake added by way of explanation that Lucia was very hot on compliance, well known in fact for that aspect of corporate vigilance throughout the City. Lucia nodded, smiled a shallow smile from the jawbone and then attacked her melon as her mind went elsewhere. She was procedural if nothing else. Tommy did not take kindly to Jake's hectoring interference. In front of his wife, to be cheeked by this barrow-boy, who just happened to be having some kind of relationship with Lucia – it was not to be borne. Ginny stared at him in a belittling kind of way, and she reached across to take the baby, as if to infer that he was no way man enough to be left in charge of something so important to her after being told to hold his tongue by the barrow-boy. Tommy blushed scarlet for a second and then buried his face in the salad. Emma thought that that would be the end of it.

She was mistaken. Much thinking went on, along with the chomping. When Tommy's face arose from its inclined position near the plate, he wore a different more aggressive expression. Tommy had evidently decided to tell it as it was because that was the way his wife wanted it and his wife's opinion was the one that counted. His natural caution had been cast to the winds, perhaps because he too was tired and oppressed by the constraints imposed by the deal and its pressures. He was muzzy and fuzzy and he had started to lose it.

'No, I think you're wrong there, Jake, we can talk a little about it all, I think. We are after all on holiday now so that gives us some leeway. On a sunny day like this we can be more relaxed.'

Slowly Lucia began to focus on Tommy and his words. She interrupted him quite gently.

'Not now Tommy. I just can't stand it. Let's talk about something else. Craig, tell us some more about your novel. I'm fascinated by it. That'll take our minds off it all. Come on Craig, talk to us. Tommy, let me tell you that this is by no means a done deal. Far from it. And you know that. You're giving the wrong impression. So can we chill on that, please? And if you want a second opinion, that is not a suggestion that I have just made, it is an instruction. OK?'

For Lucia, that wasn't too bruising a passage of arms.

She might have been exhausted but she was still the centre of attention, a remarkable feat. Craig for his part began talking with great excitement, again with that mixture of assertiveness and deference which Emma found so irritating. Lucia stared at him attentively as Ginny waggled her baby at her across the table in an ostentatious gesture which seemed to indicate contempt for Lucia's non performance so far as a female reproductive agent. The baby gurgled and kicked and wriggled and did what babies do under such circumstances – she played to the gallery. It was a wholly unpleasant and unnecessary gesture on Ginny's part but one that a woman whose pedestal was rocking might be tempted to make. Lucia stared at Ginny in stupefaction as Craig rambled on about how many pages he had written; how he'd been disappointed in Sirmio; how the last 50 pages had been a joy to write; how he hoped to finish the novel shortly; and how upset he was about having to return to teaching in a fortnight's time. Lucia looked at him briefly as he said that, as if teaching was somehow an occupation for chimps, but she added nothing.

She reached out a hand and laid it across Jake's thigh and turning to him gave him a quick kiss. Jake responded to her and they embraced each other gently. Lucia looked like a very young girl as she kissed Jake. She was still very slim and she seemed quite vulnerable as she buried her face in Jake's. Emma watched Ginny's eyes burn at the sight. Her brain circuits by now must be on fire, thought Emma.

Not two feet away her lover of a few days ago was now shamelessly moving onto a new conquest...Another scalp on his belt...That was not how Ginny was accustomed to trade her experiences...No way, Jose...She had not, repeat not, given herself to this guttersnipe to be spurned like this...Emma looked around her to see whether or not Angelina could be seen burning away on the lower edge of the distant horizon. But mercifully she was not be glimpsed. The presence of Miss Italy of the Millennium was all that was required now for the holocaust to begin.

Ginny asked Tommy to say something – just a little bit – about his sodding deal. She sounded very hard as she spoke. Tommy was not the man to deny that tone of control.

'After all, we've been sitting it out here all summer just moping around with very little hard news, you understand, Lucia, hard news, to go on. But Jake here has been very attentive, especially when he's been doing his workouts in the morning so he's helped a little. I've been very grateful to him. Very grateful. But we need something harder to go on. So come on, Tommy, spill some of the beans at least.'

Jake looked very alarmed at Ginny's words. He knew about situations getting out of control. Tommy, nonplussed, was caught between his boss and his wife, exactly as Ginny intended. Emma in an attempt to alter the molten channel down which the conversation was coursing, asked Craig whether or not he'd mind fetching some of his manuscript from the hotel and perhaps giving them a reading. Craig sprang to his feet at speed and darted off, eager to oblige both Emma and Lucia.

Lucia watched him go, looking envious. Emma caught a glimpse of a young girl yearning to be out of it.

Some seconds passed, and they all ate assorted morsels of food.

Ginny asked Tommy again if he'd kindly be more specific about what he'd been up to in London and waved the baby at him, as if to say that he'd better make a choice between his wife and his boss – and he'd better make it good and fast. Ginny was going to needle somebody until they cracked. She was out of control. So much was clear from her behaviour. Preferably it would be Lucia, whom she clearly hated, who finally went bananas.

But in the end she didn't really care who she upset. She just wanted more vengeance. Jake; Tommy; anybody would do at that stage. She was enraged beyond endurance by the sight of Lucia snogging her man and by the feeling that Lucia and her husband had somehow been enjoying their own secret rapport throughout the summer in London working on the deal. She felt inadequate.

The overload in the circuits was now dancing its way to the Heavens.

Emma realised at that moment that Ginny was actually crazy. It should have struck her a long time ago but there were impediments to understanding, like her beauty and her youth and the protection to candid observation which her social situation procured for her, like a hedge around a beautiful but poisonous bower. But she was mad, nevertheless, like any other local crazy.

Problem was that her insanity had lain for so long undetected.

Tommy cleared his throat and prepared to speak. Lucia interrupted him. She spoke very clearly. What she said could not possibly be misinterpreted.

'If you utter one word now about that deal, Tommy, you'll be off the case and I personally will ensure that you never work again at ABC. Is that clear? This is not the moment to start doing indiscretion.'

Jake looked very startled and afraid at such a naked demonstration of power. Tommy began to whine. Ginny clicked her tongue in disapproval at Tommy and at Lucia, as if they were both small children requiring chiding. Lucia's expression hardened. Reaching a decision, she stood up from the table. When she spoke, she sounded quite composed. She might have been addressing an investment meeting.

'I'm fed up with this whole thing. What on earth is going on and who is this crazy woman. I come here to get away from things and to find my man and what do I find – bitching, bickering, tension all around; everything moving out of line and worse all manner of innuendo coming from that woman over there across the table. What she's telling me, Jake, just what is her take on all of this? Is she just making trouble because she's a crazy or is it something closer to home. Come on Jake tell me. Has she been fucking you this summer. Now tell me – is it true or not?'

She looked very small and slim and determined as she spoke to Jake, and also full of disappointment.

Jake was no dissembler. He hadn't been brought up to play such games and deny even the most blatant and flagrant example of the truth with a straight face. He did not have the requisite PhD in Mendacity; not enough early training. His face flamed red as Lucia shouted at him. His guilt looked signposted all over his face. Lucia hissed at him with black eyes as she went dead puce with rage.

Lucia then stared at Ginny who glared back. There was a moment's pause again amid complete silence. Then very deliberately almost as if in a dream and looking detached from it all, almost in fact as if turning to go because it was all over, Ginny picked up a full goblet of red wine which shimmered on the table; held it balanced for a second in her hand, a mite contemplatively, almost academically, as if still considering a course of action, so that the sun flashed on the wine in the glass as well as on her red, red hair.

The garden stilled for a second.

Then, decision taken, Ginny hurled the wine with force in Lucia's face. It flew like a bomb from the glass in a solid flux of liquid. In the bright sunshine of the garden, the wine struck Lucia right in the mouth and then exploded across the table. The red wine spumed all across her face in a great wave and she looked quite dumbfounded as, in an instant, the wine dripped from her nose and mouth and eyes. The t-shirt was soaked blood red in a flash. It was the work of a second and yet it changed everything.

Outraged amour propre now fully placated, Ginny seemed to giggle at Lucia's shock and discomfort from the other side of the table.

As mayhem broke out all around her, she looked down at her plate and began to play with her food moodily.

Subsidence of the circuits as the storms abated in Ginny's mind.

Tommy and Jake seemed to spring to their feet with open mouths and arms outstretched in horror at Ginny's action. There was frozen silence in the second or two which elapsed after her act of war. Emma who had witnessed similar outbreaks elsewhere of mad behaviour found herself totting up the list of Ginny's misdeeds so far, as she watched Lucia shake herself free of the shock of the impact of the wine, salving Ginny's contempt for her.

Emma continued with the reckoning.

'First there was Charles, who's at death's door; then there was Jake, who's obviously now lost his job and his girl friend; there's Lucia, who is going to throw the biggest wobbly of all time; and there's still Tommy to come. The damage which she's done to his career cannot even start to be measured...I don't quite know where Angelina fits into all this but she's there somewhere. And all, all for her glory...'

It seemed like a moment of crystallisation. Three sets of people and three destinies soldered into structure by Fate and Ginny's act for the next thirty or so years...

Lucia handled it all well. She kept her dignity, inciting Emma's admiration at the same time. Shaking her head so that the wine sprayed off her hair like in a shower, and wringing her wet hands, she said throatily but very simply:

'We'll see about all this in a moment, shall we? Right now, I think I need a clean top. And a dry napkin.'

Impressively, she was still mistress of the occasion.

Then the action speeded up. Nodding madly at Lucia and almost laughing in his hysterical attempt to find a bottom of normality, Tommy tried to hustle Ginny away. Eyes flashing like fire, she protested and thrashed about with her arms. A bustling Craig rushed out of the house waving sheets of manuscript, and escorting Angelina, who came most eagerly upon her hour, walking along beside Craig with a kind of strutting, fashionista voluptuousness.

Bingo! Full house!

Emma watched in fascination.

Angelina wanted everybody to know she was on her way to see her man by permission of her father who wanted to talk to him about a big contract with Roma …And for tea with Momma…And all the good things which followed from that including a very quiet wedding in the cathedral at Repugia, with no more than 500 guests including just a few of her school-friends, so far unmarried, to be followed by almost as many bambini…Repugia was opening its arms to Jake. Angelina still hadn't completely made up her mind on the guest list, but it could wait. Meanwhile wasn't life just so wonderful and simple?

All of that was implied by her pawing, swaying walk towards them in the bright sunshine, and her bright, steely smile.

Craig rushed up to Lucia and mercifully misunderstood what had happened. He took charge, fussily and over-protectively. His presence and his reactions were exactly what the situation required. He saved the situation from even worse disaster by behaving like a booby. Everyone else was stupefied by shock. He was Heaven-sent to cope with the outrage.

'Oh I'm so sorry, Lucia, what a terrible accident to happen to you here on your first few moments of holiday. But it's always the same with jet lag, so I'm told. Don't worry, you'll dry out.'

He began sponging her down with a napkin. Then, finding that she was completely soaked and still talking at the top of his voice in a schoolmasterly over-control kind of way, he led her out of the garden, still mopping, and into the house, as if Lucia had been doused in ink because of some classroom incident. An unprotesting Lucia suffered herself to be taken away to be washed clean.

If Craig had not existed at that special moment, he would have needed to be re-invented…

Meanwhile Angelina took Jake by the hand; kissed him again but this time with more confidence, reaching up to his mouth with hers; and walked out of the garden with him through the little door at the end.

The two of them disappeared quite literally into a new life. Football; Italy; and much else beckoned for Jake.

Tommy and Ginny by this time had moved together with the baby back to the parapet where the original incident with the mobile phone had taken place. They stood together in the sun as a stiffer breeze began to blow. This lifted the skirts of the table clothes and ruffled the heads of the flowers in the beds across the lawns.

Autumn was on its way as Tommy and Ginny looked forward to a different future, standing together in the sunshine. Much irrevocable destiny had crystallised for both of them during the lunch. Under pressure, these decisions were taken very quickly in the immediate aftermath of the crisis. More breeding for her, so that she could be cloistered for anything up to the next twenty years in child rearing.

After the wine incident, Tommy simply needed a larger family.

For her now there loomed the school run; the worries about a choice of schools as she tended her growing brood; the chilled presence, standing on the touchline and yelling encouragement at her many sons and daughters during the soccer or hockey matches on a cold Saturday afternoon; and the local admiration in Hampshire as she managed her husband's career by staying well in the background, far away from anywhere and anything where she could cause trouble by a scene.

The incident would never ever be referred to again. Officially it had never taken place. There had been no witnesses, that is to say nobody had seen what had happened who could speak up and make a difference. Omerta would reign. It would never be discussed.

Strictly speaking, it had never happened. Something like the incident had taken place but the reports would be confused and the witnesses unreliable. They would be disregarded.

Tommy would speak to his father about it all, adding that Lucia had seemed to be a little stressed; women were always women whichever way you sliced 'em. Perhaps the deal had got to her, he would hint, carefully misrepresenting the facts as he pleaded Ginny's case. His father in turn would speak to the

Gilstons. Amid quiet confabulation, most likely in an aside over lunch at the City Club, it would be decided whether or not Tommy could remain at ABC. Most likely he would – the deal was far too advanced; tricky; and potentially lucrative for any change in the team to be contemplated realistically. That way the commission might be in jeopardy. Rome wasn't built in a day and nor was it built on sand.

In other words the British financial empire was not going to be rocked by a single incident in an Italian rose garden. It was far too solidly based for that. So Yes, it would charge on; and No, nothing had ever happened. That would be the line and in years to come they would all laugh about it, Ginny and Lucia included.

Such little local difficulties arose all the time, most of the time accruing from misunderstandings. Both the women had been under pressure.

Emma sat in the garden at the table and realised that she was almost alone there. She felt comforted by her solitude as if something artificial and almost distasteful had suddenly and mercifully been resolved. She was free to go, she suddenly realised unexpectedly, and the summer was over. Whatever happened to Craig's book would be via the good offices or otherwise of Lucia. He had thrown himself at Lucia's feet; he would not immediately be allowed to remove himself from that position of prostration. He was far too useful to be cast aside, at least for the time being.

Henceforth, Emma realised she was out of it. Craig had deserted her as Lucia had switched in taste away from jumped-up proles, albeit with foot balling feet of genius, to litterati. In the twinkling of an eye, Lucia had moved on, just as in his own way Jake had.

The summer was dead.

For a brief moment she understood just how Pontius Pilate had felt as he washed his hands in the clear cold waters of the bowl placed before him. The wind still blew across the garden, ruffling her hair and the napkins on the table, and she was grateful for nature's small soothing gifts. But yes, it was over for her too. She felt calm because she also had had an inkling of sudden destiny. It all seemed so simple now – she was going back to London to find Joe. She had no other move to make. It was Joe or nothing. In her view, that was how the equation factored. The sooner she found out about her destiny the better. That was how it would run now. For the time being, there was nothing else left to do.

Her reverie was disturbed by one of the maids who said that Sra Lucy-Miranda wanted her on the telephone again. Very slowly Emma walked into the hall and took whatever news L-M had to impart in that small but elegant hallway, as the maids yet again clustered around at a distance.

L-M sounded very tired.

'Yes, he's out of danger but I don't think there's much left of him.'

'A vegetable?'

'Just about. I can authorise them to turn off the taps now but I can't quite bring myself to do that. So it's life with a mummy...'

'We should talk about this, Lucy-Miranda. On the bench.'

'On our bench?'

'Exactly. On our bench, Auntie Lill, know what I mean?'

'Emma, you are a great comfort to me. I can be there by tea time.'

'Five o'clock?'

'How English and how civilised. It seems almost too long to wait. We can chaff the Young Moustache. And drink our wine...'

'Be careful. There is an ill wind about today. Wait until I tell you what has happened today. There has been a drama. Involving Lucia...'

'Plate-throwing stuff?'

'You're warm. Very warm.'

'I knew it. I felt it in my bones. I'm on my way and I can't wait. This hospital gives me the pip as I wait for Death to show up. I'm on my way, darling Emma. And thank you very much.'

★ ★ ★ ★ ★

Lucy-Miranda, deeply experienced materfamilias, shrugged at the end of Emma's tale.

'At least, Lucia didn't throw something back. Like a knife. That's a comfort. There's only injured pride at the bottom of this. Nothing mortal has happened. It can all be put right again. I will speak to Lucia and tell her on no account to try and engineer Tommy out of ABC. I will talk to her like her mother. That way she has no choice but to listen – and to obey.'

Emma listened to the soothing tones of reason from L-M, as the Establishment voice got to work. It was like clockwork. L-M added that she dimly recalled some kind of spat over ponies between Lucia and Ginny at a gymkhana when they were both very small, years ago.

Old scores...

'If that is the case, and my memory is slightly faulty here, then it was bound to happen...Better that it should come out here, miles away in Italy, than at some dinner-party in Sloane Square where there might have been real damage to reputations...Didn't I tell you Ginny was a complete bitch? Wasn't I right? An eruption waiting to happen?'

Lucy-Miranda then changed the subject and told Emma about her great idea. The collapse of Charles had made it more, not less, attractive. She was going to set up a house for Women who had Fallen. In Repugia itself, and in the beginning, using the villa.

'It's empty for most of the year so this will be putting it to far better use. It won't be for fallen women, you understand. I've done that one and I've decided that I'm not going back into that. The girls will have to pine without me, I'm afraid. No, this place will be for women who have made a mistake of some description or other and who need some time and space to get themselves right. Like Liz Playfair for example. She's perfectly OK; anddeeply remorseful for what happened. But completely confused. Something happened, as it does, which she still doesn't understand and she just needs a lucky break. So I'm going to get her out here in due course and use her to set up a little bridge salon whither the dames can repair from SW3 whenever they feel like some bridge in the sunshine. That way Liz can work her way back in, if she decides that she wants to, and the dames can decide just how good they want their bridge to become. As if they had a choice in that...And it will do Liz no harm to build up her bridge reputation here in Repugia. Likewise Lady C and her tough daughter, two more casualties of SW3's richly decorous pattern of crucifixions.'

'It's like Candide cultivating his garden.'

'I don't know about any of that, dear Emma. I'm not in the end a book-learned woman, although I dimly remember something like that at university. All I know is that if I carry out my little plan, I don't have to go back to England. Now that Charles is more or less kaput, England has no charms for me. It's been the scene of non-stop humiliation for me for the past thirty to forty years. With my little Shangri-La here in Repugia, I can still sit here on my bench in the square and...'

'Merge'.

'That's it.'

'And you can also watch Gina going off to screw the Mayor of Repugia!'

'How crude of you, Emma, to put it that way. You're not normally so foul-mouthed. You must have picked it up from me. But yes, as you say, the thought had crossed my mind....Gina...And the mayor...Inseparables... Ah, how enlivening and how spiritual. And I can also keep an eye on Jake. I've rather fallen to liking that feckless young man so I'll mother him a little as he makes his fences with young Angelina...Everyone in that situation needs someone to make the running, and I'll be more than happy to do that for him.'

They paused as the boy waiter with the hedge of a moustache made his way towards them with the drinks.

'And you, Emma, are you going to stay here and help me with the project?'

Emma paused. Lucy-Miranda looked expectant but not hopeful.

'I will be here but not immediately...'.

'Ah...'

'Lucy-Miranda, there is something that I must do in London, amidst trips to Antigua. But I will be with you in spirit and it won't be long before I'm back out here, sitting on our bench again...I promise you that quite fervently. Like you, I'm reaching some decisions. It'll take some time for it all to work itself out, but it'll happen.'

L-M looked more relieved now.

'There's a man at the bottom of this, I can tell. And it's not Craig either. It's another, isn't it?'

But the drinks arrived at that moment, borne by the Moustache and they spared Emma the embarrassment of an explanation. She nodded vaguely in answer to L-M's question. By the time the drinks were served, L-M was off on another tangent, this time about Lady C for whom she had high hopes. Emma asked her a pointed question.

'In your house of correction, would you allow to stay, for example...'

'Yeees...'

'Ginny, perchance?'

L-M paused.

'I'd like to be given the option on that one. You know Ginny would start a fight in an empty house, she's so crazy. So what would happen if I let her loose in a house full of women all in spiritual mode and grieving away? No, I'm afraid Ginny wouldn't qualify. She needs a shrink and deep sedation, not some kind of female R&R, which is what I'm proposing. The minute Ginny made it across the threshold, I'd be out by the backdoor. We could dedicate the place to Ginny but we dare not let her in.'

'We could hang her coat of arms across the threshold.'

'Know what I mean?'

'Exactly. That's what we'll call it, but in Latin of course. Whatever it is in Latin, and God alone knows what that is. But that'll impress them no end. The Italians revere Latin.'

Both of them fell about laughing again, because it was a good joke. Meanwhile the square rambled through the day with its customary somnolence and assurance. Giovanna was walking her dog as usual, and again as usual discussing her customary grievances and laments. Everything was as it should be.

Emma eventually wandered back to the hotel. She thought about Joe, about London and about her fortunes as she prepared to make her run, out of the safety of the thickets and across the open ground. She knew as she went through the entrance to the hotel that upstairs there would be no Craig waiting for her and no book either on Catullus for her inspection. That bird had flown and the situation was now defunct...

Putting his instinctive deference to good use, Craig would be comforting Lucia and Lucia would be lapping up the attention from an unexpected but diligent presence. Craig would pass muster for the time being, before she moved on again. He was someone who had a reasonable story to tell but who most important came from beyond her social circle and who was thus out of her particular loop. No comebacks at all – he held no equity in the situation and never could. Lucia had traded well and taken out a completely new market position, which she was now poised to explore. Emma hoped her Latin, at least, would improve, courtesy of Craig's endeavours.

As for Ginny and Tommy, well the wires would be red-hot between Repugia and London as Tommy launched a full-scale damage limitation operation and Ginny just sat there complaining yet again about someone who had come between her and the light. Lucy-Miranda, meanwhile, was probably just sitting on her bench in the square, drinking up the ambiance, looking for Gina, rejoicing in her heavily qualified freedom, and feeling her way towards a sense of direction.

As for herself, it was obviously going to be either Emma Arriba or something infinitely more painful for her as soon as she returned to London...

But she too wanted to see something resolved. She wanted to experience definition, however harsh, and she wanted to commit to something even if it meant embracing permanent detachment. It was time to get sorted, Joe or no Joe.

She asked for her bill from Reception. It was time to go back to London.

★   ★   ★   ★   ★

With great satisfaction, Joe noted that events had marched on, judging by the Chron's appointments page. As forecast, Lord Test had indeed been replaced by Graham Dune-Jones as Chairman of the Financial Chronicle board, with immediate effect.

'I spy mischief here, although what it amounts to, Heaven only knows. I can't see that it will benefit me – or my deal – in any way. Too bad.'

Joe was still watching his screen, waiting for the currencies to move. Fat chance, he told himself as they traded sideways day after day. Forex was about as flat as his deal.

But then the cuttings duly arrived on Dune-Jones and the plot thickened. It was all laid out for Joe to scrutinise, and that process took him all of some 50 seconds to complete. His excavations into the deeper vaults of the personal Joe memory bank had yielded pure gold. All was correct. Yes, Dune – Jones had reinvented himself and that very successfully; yes, he was one and the same with the drunken Gazza Jones who had married the Russian girl overnight in Moscow; and yes, he would now be very rich indeed. Very, very rich. Formerly an equity partner in Montgomery, Mills, he would have collected some £5 million when the broking firm was taken over in the late Eighties, during the mass dissolution of the Old City. That capital sum appeared to have been augmented throughout the Nineties, according to the cuttings, by a judicious series of job hops, taking him gradually higher and higher within the City hierarchy, but clearly by the back, dark and winding stair. Dune-Jones had advanced cautiously. Most likely, in Joe's view, he would have been guided carefully along and across those treacherous cobbles from job to job – it all looked highly implausible because of its very plausibility. There had also been a couple of divorces along the way, so the Russian wife was long gone by now, most likely back to the dacha. The names of the new wives grew longer and more elaborate, Joe noted. Finally in 1998, Jones had taken the supreme step and changed his name by adding the hyphen to what most likely had started off as a middle family name.

It was almost like a change of sex for the Midlands roughneck. But nevertheless the transformation was complete – he had the double-barrelled moniker and the county entry. He had made it into nabob land, he had become a figure of respect. He had become a toff as well as a City paper shuffler within his own lifetime.

But none of it rang true for Joe. The memory of Jones limbo-dancing in those pink braces across the floor of the Watling saloon bar while shouting out 'Dwarf with tits; dwarf with tits' at the top of his voice, the bonus cheque hanging down the while in derision from his undone flies, with the colleague's wife standing no more than five feet away, came back to Joe with a force that made him almost laugh.

But equally it had to be admitted that Jones was now a power in the land. To hold the chair at the Financial Chronicle was to occupy a position of considerable potential influence. There could be no doubt that Graham, after his long journey through the foothills of power, would stand for no nonsense as he reached the summit of the mountain range, still less from something as flimsy as an Editor, now that he, Graham Dune-Jones, ran the Board of the Chron.

'If young Stone gets on the wrong side of Dune-Jones, then truly I don't fancy his chances one little bit on the Chron, new broom or not. Graham has simply too much money riding shotgun with him to take any crap from the likes of Stone. And Gazza is a professional, I'll give him that; he knows just how to plunge the knife in. Stone has no chance. So we shall see...'

The faint stirrings of an idea about forex flickered through his mind and Joe was enchanted by its possibilities – could Stanley have been right? Joe thought about it some more and dismissed the idea as far too fanciful. Too many wings to fly as a good notion, he reckoned.

But nevertheless, the idea had structure. It existed within potential symmetry; that was undeniable. So it might prove to be correct...Might just...

Joe put all the bits together of the cuttings and his interpretation of possible events and was struck by a single salient factor. Moley and Graham were still most likely in close contact. There must be some cultural consanguinity between them. What had slipped out on that memorable night in the Watling had been unforgettable – Gazza's parents sang the Red Flag every night before they repaired to bed, while Moley's folks were what he himself had described as 'rigid atheists'.

In other words, both sets of parents were Thirties Moscow fellow-travellers, along with the rest of their generation...

Trick or treat, wondered Joe as he continued glaring at the screen. So was it time to play some more chess with Moley and test the market again?

★   ★   ★   ★   ★

PART TWO

LATER, DARKER

Tom Stone, editor of the Financial Chronicle, was on the lookout for the lights of Ursula's house to appear distantly through the trees in deepest Hampshire. He reflected on a day's work well done as his chauffeur swung round the tricky chicane in the lane just a few miles away from the house.

The events of the day were not over yet, not by any means. He had Ursula's dinner-party to get through and the paper had not wholly been put to bed. He didn't actually have the first edition in his grubby little hands and he wouldn't rest easy until he physically felt the ink on his fingers from the first pull of the Chron that night. Yet for the most part the day was over. The big things had happened and they had been hugely satisfying, apart that is from the deep melancholy of Bill Bell's leaving drinks party an hour or so ago. Tom had looked in for a moment on his way home from the Chron to offer his sympathies and commiserations.

Seeing Bill on the way out, standing there in the middle of the Harrow's back bar with a glass of champagne in his hand, very much an ex-financial editor and a standing victim of someone else's more powerful but invisible hatreds and caprice, had been devastating. It had been like losing another tooth.

. He and Bill had been rivals, colleagues and near-friends in the financial journalism game for over twenty years. And now Bill had gone, sacked beyond any possible hope of recall...He had bounced back again in the past, had Bill. But this time...? Age would play a part here... Tom thrust the thoughts of remorse and the spectacle of Bill's abjectness in the Harrow from his mind and focussed on the other good things to have happened between sunrise and sunset on that glittering day. Bill's leaving- do had been only a small part of the story. The rest of the day had been pure gold. He had found a good story all on his own at lunchtime. He had passed it onto the news boys who had chased it well, so well in fact that it qualified as the splash on its own merits.

In the course of all this, he, Tom Stone, had put together what he considered to be the best front page of his career.

Today is the day that I really earned my money as editor, he told himself. This is what I got hired for to do. Tomorrow's front page of the Chron, in his view, marked a turning point for the paper. Tom was marking out territory here, not always with the support of his ever-willing staff of journalists, who had not wholly seen the light as yet. They were not entirely with him as one as yet, that bastard Legless in particular. Nevertheless the mix of stories which he had pushed onto the front page marked a radical change for the paper, in particular the detailed analysis of the UK trade numbers. Tom had insisted that these come in above the fold.

Plus the sparkling fact of his leader on page 400 or something...

Tom was reaching into those innards of British policy formation and making plenty of inroads as well as waves. Test had gone, but Graham was now Board Chairman and counted as a friend. Tom had high hopes that Graham would be even more supportive than Test had been.

Too bad he wouldn't be at the bash tonight...

Tom's mind went back to the Chron that night. The Chron didn't normally try to fish in those particular waters, or at least, traditionally, hadn't tried. But today was different. Yes, today really was different. Cheek by jowl with Tom's story on the Nest and above the fold was a story on UK trade, plus – and here Tom could see himself making this point to Ursula in the kitchen with stabbing forefinger extended by way of emphasis – plus, mark me, a really good tale on the US Presidential Election which tipped Kerry to win handsomely against the odds and Bush.

That's a strong page, a good page and an honest page, he told himself as the driver negotiated the last stretch of the journey. None of your close encounters of the curd kind or similar nonsense here. This is journalism. Good, direct frontline journalism. And I liked the trade numbers story; young Giles did well there. The boy wrote well, especially the way he linked the numbers up with the £'s reaction on forex. Bound to tweak the Bank of England's tail, that kind of thing. Stealing into their territory, step by step, as the Chron's domain expanded.

Now that is journalistic class, he told himself. Giles had simply used his imagination, as he'd been trained to do...And he'd used it well...

As for the Nest story...Well, that took him back in time just thinking about it. Tom stretched out in simple ecstasy at the recollection of it all. Hoofing, that was what journalism was all about in the end, simple hoofing. Knocking on doors. It was that simple.

And Tom waved a fist in the air in the back of the car in most un-editorial enthusiasm.

He had attended one of Mark Lomax's parties at lunchtime. A simple gathering of head media honchos in a small backroom at the Ritz – nothing serious. That was the kind of gathering that ex-peer Lomax, a suave and dapper boulevardier of the most polished variety, was accustomed to organising. All over town, similar discreet and influential lunch parties were taking place as Tom well knew – it was most important, as a successful editor, to get onto this particular lunchtime circuit and Tom now seemed to have mastered the art of acquiring the crucial invitations. Inside track, inside track, that was all that counted, as Tom told himself on countless occasions. It seemed to be working. Lomax, he flattered himself, knew him rather better than slightly by now. And for his part, he now ranked higher with Lomax than just a telephone connection.

At the gathering, there had been seated around the table the head of BBC TV; a relative of Lomax's who was trying to buy the Express Group; he, Tom Stone, editor of the Chron; and a rather quiet and silent individual who turned out to be the world's greatest expert on the old 'cash for questions' sleaze saga in the House of Commons, as well as on the man himself.

Lunch had followed its inevitable trail, course by course, with Mark, an excellent whip, orchestrating the conversation with ease. Tom had spoken for the most part with BBC TV who it turned out had similar problems to Tom in motivating journalists to cover business stories with gusto and accuracy.

But not much of a story there in that chat.

But then it had happened. Tom leaned back in the car and savoured the moment when hard news had started to fly.

Mark, sipping his coke as per usual and looking very fit, had dropped the name of Guy Lambourne into the conversation. Tom had reacted sharply to the allusion while the rest of the table continued chatting away about other things. His alert response was appropriate, since Lambourne, one of London's movers and shakers, was at that very moment negotiating to pay +£100 million for the ill-fated Nest down in Dulwich, one of the gems in the extensive portfolio of Snowden Follies. It had transpired that Lomax and Lambourne did business together. Lomax had the inside track. Lomax was the man. Tom was suddenly very pleased to be taking lunch with Lomax.

'Oh,' Lomax had remarked, leaning forward to Tom, 'you didn't know that Guy was planning to walk away from the deal?'

Almost consumed with excitement in a flash at the suggestion, Tom had shaken his head silently. His pulse rate was up in the 200's by now.

'Watch the old ticker,' he told himself. 'It's pooped out once. A second time might be fatal. They'd be sorry, then, wouldn't they...'

The Lomax briefing had continued as Tom tried to contain his breathing.

'We took a look at the accounts, such as we were shown. They were bad enough. But then we discovered that they only covered half the business. Most of it is off-balance sheet and completely out of control. They don't know what they've bought and what they've sold. There are no financial controls at the Nest whatsoever. Down at dear old Dulwich, it could be worth £100 million, or it could be worth threepence. Nobody knows.'

'Hard to close on a deal with accounts in such disarray.'

Tom had made his reply crisply, restraining himself – but only just – from reaching into his jacket pocket and pulling out a notebook to get it all down on the record and then phoning it through to Copy.

This felt like a good fat chunky story that would write itself, after no more than one phone call. One phone call – that was how the very best stories came.

Lomax persisted.

'That's why Guy is walking away from it. As he said last night, winning the rights to pitch for the Nest was the hardest thing he'd done this year, until he saw the accounts. So the next hardest thing will come today or tomorrow when he chucks. He's on the brink now after the duffing-up we gave him last night.'

Tom thought he had been cool in his response to Mark, as the chat ebbed and flowed around the small table.

'Is this to us?'

'If you want it, and if you're quick enough, it's to you. But why not call Guy himself. I'll give you his mobile number in a second.'

Mark had then changed the subject, asking his son in law David Hyde across the table just how much he was really prepared to pay for the Express Group, a subject on which Tom himself had strong views. The number that came back across the table was startling in its exactness and provoked further questions. The direction of the flows in the conversation had altered for the remaining half hour of the lunch. Misty-eyed, Mark had talked at length about the pain of no longer enjoying entry to the Lords, now that he had been dispossessed of his peerage in a stitch-up by White's. Lomax spoke impressively. Tom thought he had been brave about the whole business and wondered if he would ever care to visit them in Hampshire at some future date.

But nonetheless the steer from Mark to Tom remained unchanged. At the end of the lunch a crisp piece of embossed pasteboard was pressed discreetly into Tom's hand by Mark. On further inspection Mark's card carried Lambourne's mobile number on the reverse. That was all Tom needed.

The rest, as they say, was showbiz. Tom went into top gear on his return to the Chron, gathering his hacks around him. Lambourne the Great Asset Trader coughed beautifully – and quotably – and they had the story wrapped up within an hour. At the late editorial meeting, there was no question about the lead – they splashed on the Nest. It was just like old times. Tom got a clap on the back from the news editor and was told there would be no problem that week with his expenses. There's facetious for you, he thought. Smiles all round from the gnarled veterans who made up the Chron's back bench. They were all happy with the story, which scooped obviously. None of the others had even so much as smelled the pending Lambourne pull-out from the Nest. So for that reason the back bench were prepared to go just a little bit of the way down the road with Tom on his innovations. For once he had had no problem with the subs in getting his UK trade story onto the front page.

It has been a happy day apart from poor old Bill, thought Tom, as the car pulled up in front of Ursula's front door, after racing up her short drive. Tom's driver bade him a temporary Goodnight, and looked forward to seeing him a few hours later with the first edition.

The car drove off and Tom turned towards the house with its brightly lit windows, right in the middle of what was left of the Hampshire countryside, telling himself again that he was a lucky guy that day. Tough tit for Bill, though, as he stumbles out of the Harrow later tonight and into the street with a swimming head and no future. But that's Fleet Street for you...

Now for the Ursula beanfeast...

Light and tight, right and bright – that's how newspapers should be written. Don't get it right, get it written.

Feeling bright and right but not tight, Tom entered his house by the front door

The hall and the morning room were thronged with people, all slightly hard faced and focussed, especially the women, who looked as if they were in a meeting. Tom made his way through the milling throng to find Ursula. She was in fine form talking to a woman whom Tom did not know about her bridge. Ursula's audience listened respectfully to the exposition. He kissed her and she paused briefly in the narrative to acknowledge his return.

'Tom, thank you for dropping by. Only 30 minutes behind schedule. For you that's a miracle.'

Tom opened his mouth to talk about his great scoop but she forestalled him.

'Later, Tom, later. The Great Scoop can wait until the later editions, like pudding. Just now there's someone I particularly want you to meet before dinner. It's Bella Harper and she's sitting over there talking to Gloria. You see...?'

Tom saw. He was used to these assignments. He raised an interrogative eyebrow.

'We don't have too much time before dinner, Tom, so talk to her now if you'd be a sweetie about it.'

Tom trooped over to talk to Bella as Ursula resumed her bridge anecdote. On cue, as Tom approached, Gloria stood up and departed, leaving Bella alone on the sofa.

'Hullo, I'm Tom Stone.'

She looked up with an expression of some muted anguish. Tom knew what was coming.

'Oh Tom, I'm so pleased to have the chance of a quick chat with you. Won't you sit down here for a second, so that you're comfortable. Was it a very hard day for you at the...I mean, on the newspaper.'

'So, so. A story here, a story there. Routine. After a while, only the headlines change.'

'It must be such an exciting world, the newspaper world. I know nothing about it. Lloyds' yes; Fleet Street, definitely not.'

There was a residue of suppressed emphasis to that sentence as Tom moved to sit down. She made exaggerated room for him to be seated next to her. The wrinkles around the Harper eyes told the whole story – acres and acres of them around bright blue, bitter eyes, where the tension of gratin existence had taken its toll. Tom sat down beside her, and the crowd milled round above them. She twisted her fingers in and out of the palm of her hand.

'I'm very worried about Andrew, that's my youngest. He just doesn't seem to be able to settle to anything. But he does like writing, and he's done lots of it, so we thought perhaps that journalism might suit him. He's even had some things published, although that was just in the school magazine, before he left, but still...'

Tom was being asked to fit Andrew Harper into the Chron. Tom temporised, as he always did.

'Has he thought of taking a course in journalism?'

'Yes, we talked to him about that and told him to make enquiries but he's such an impatient boy, he doesn't want to go through that kind of rigmarole. He wants to make his mark at once, which on the face of it seems improbable. So we thought if we sent him along to you, you might be able to talk to him and give him some advice and guidance...'

Like how to fiddle his expenses from Day 1, ha ha ha!

Tom thought of the lonely hacks out there in the provinces filling miles and miles of newsprint with their stories, driven by blind and hopeless ambition to make it into and onto the Street. But he said nothing and listened to Bella Harper talk about how he could cut her son in and onto the fast track.

And toll free!

Well scripted by Ursula and well versed by now in these desperate encounters with apprehensive mothers, he knew the drill. He fished in his pocket and pulled out his card. Ursula always stressed that it was important not to offend anybody by his response because that interfered with her networking.

'Just tell him to give me a call and we can talk over the phone. If he's got any copy that I can look at, that would be helpful. Some writing of his own that he's done, that kind of thing. But do tell him to ring me and I'll look out for him. Tell him to make it early in the day. After about eleven, things start to move on newspapers and there's no time to talk to anybody. We're too busy fire fighting after 11.'

She nodded understanding of the concept of schedule, took the editor's card as if it had been Holy Viaticum and filed it very carefully in her handbag. Tom was left in no doubt of the gravity of her response. The call would come the following day at 10.30 on the dot. Tom knew that for a fact. That was when they always rang, the mother standing behind the hapless child almost with a bayonet poked into his back. That was when the first words of halting introduction were followed by a mixture of bluster and bombast as the said difficult son tried to make his mark over the phone, coached and scripted in his own mind by movie idols.

Bella Harper snapped her bag shut and stood up abruptly, smoothing her dress as she did so. Her mission was finished now and it was time to socialise. She looked younger already, appreciably so. Contact had been made; that was all that counted. There was nothing further to discuss; the old feudalism was working well especially with a nouveau like Tom in a position of job-hiring authority. She nodded at him in a business-like way, assured him that Andrew would be in touch, and melted away into the crowd, leaving Tom alone in the throng.

'You're Tom Stone aren't you?'

A petite and shapely blond person stood unbidden at his side. White teethed and attractive, Tom noticed.

'Indeed I am.'

'I'm Jilly Smart, the novelist.'

Tom smiled at her.

'Never read them, I'm afraid. I do apologise. I should have done. Every else round here has read them. They swear by them.'

'Thank God for that – a virgin audience. Someone I can talk to for a time. I know they've read every blasted word of them, and I'm sick to death of the attention. I know that they're my readership and my bread and butter, but there are limits to the amount one has to give. Everyone I've spoken to tonight wants to know what happened to her favourite character. Perhaps I can just roost here in sanctuary for a while, close to this madding crowd, and we can talk about nothing in particular.'

'Delighted to offer you a perch. What shall we chat about?'

'Style. Words. English, the usual rubbish. I'm obsessed by the whole thing of language. The pity of it is that I never worked on a newspaper, so I never had the chance to develop a straightforward way of writing things, you know where the language just becomes second nature…I missed out on that…I miss it.'

This was manna from Heaven for Tom, who loved to chat about newspaper style. He blessed the timely presence of La Smart at the party. Tom had not exactly edited the Chron book on house style but he had taken a very close, some said sanctimonious or obsessive, interest in the contents.

'Yes, you see…'

Suddenly Ursula's voice could be heard above the throng. The voice was high. She was panicking.

'Tom, Tom where are you? There's a phone call for you. Can you take it somewhere but not here? Tom, Tom can you hear me?'

Tom apologised to the novelist for his disappearing act.

'That'll be the paper. We have a strong front page tomorrow. I'll be back. Sorry about this.'

Tom struggled away from Jilly and pushed past Ursula who nodded at him, and handed him the phone. Holding the receiver, he made his way into the hall and then half way up the stairs where it was abruptly quieter.

'Stone here. Can I help?'

'Q here. Bank of England.'

It was not a friendly voice. But it had a powerful sound. Dr Q spoke abruptly and very quickly with great assurance. Tom felt his stomach sink to his knees.

'We've never met except at Bank press conferences but we will be in closer touch. I can promise you that. I want to see you tomorrow at the Bank for a little chat. Say 10? Is that OK?'

Tom bridled at the speed of encounter.

'I'll have to check my diary.'

'Your diary will be fine. We've already checked. You'll be there and don't be late. Oh and another thing, we've changed your front page for tomorrow.'

'You've what?'

Tom felt the blood rush to his forehead.

'You heard me. We've remade your front page. We've improved it for you.'

So what had happened to his Nest story? The universe seemed to go up in flames and smoke. Tom now felt blind rage cascade through his veins.

'I don't believe this. You can't mess around with my paper like that.'

'We not only can mess around with it, we have done. So you'd better believe it. We changed the front page because we didn't like it. It was unhelpful.'

'What do you mean, you didn't like it. It's none of your business...I'm the editor of the paper not you. You don't have the right...'

Dr Q barely paused for breath. Down below Tom, the pre-dinner conversation continued at a loud pitch. The Chron editor felt as if he'd stumbled into a nightmare. Q did not leave him alone.

'You don't seem to understand but it's everything of our business. We're still the Bank of England. We have a responsibility for markets. So you don't go running stories that might affect the markets without our say so. If you don't like any of this, talk to your chairman, Dune-Jones. We already have done so tonight and we've set him right on one or two things. I think you'll be seeing him tomorrow as well. I don't think the interview will be a pleasant one for you. I'll discuss this with you more clearly tomorrow so that you know exactly what you're supposed to be doing in future. That is to say, for us. We're the Bank, don't forget. Until tomorrow then and don't be late. 10 o' clock sharp. Is that understood? We're busy men. Goodnight.'

Tom was left standing halfway up the stairs holding the phone in one hand and feeling utterly bereft. Waves of rage seeped through him at Q's action. He wanted to hurl the phone down the stairs irrespective of his guests and give vent to his anger. It was his front page, he was the editor, and what went into the paper was on his say-so, not this blasted Q idiot from the Bank...

Wasn't all that true? Of course it was true...That was why he had got the job in the first place.

But behind the rage, and this happened almost immediately, there was just a tiny amount of fear which seemed to tick insistently in Tom's head. It warned him to be careful – if Q had simply called up his proprietor as simply as that of an evening and secured audience on the nonce and given him chapter and verse about Tom's front page, then Tom's job as Editor was by no means as secure as he had thought...Watch out, said the still small voice, Q must be a very powerful individual indeed. Staring at the crowd down below, phone still in hand, Tom fell back on folklore as his guide. It was an operating maxim in financial journalism that tycoons had short fuses and were liable to explode at any moment. They tolerated journalists – just about – so when the wind blew, as it always would, there should always be a shelter to climb into...

This could be that defining moment when the maxim was tested to destruction...

Tom held the phone in his hand and wondered about calling the news desk and asking them what on earth had happened to his page. But again, as the seconds passed, one by one after the call, he temporised as he grew more cunning at understanding his predicament.

To call the news desk would be to intimate that he knew something had happened to his stories that day. But in truth he didn't actually know what had happened to his page. He didn't know what the Bank of England had changed. They might have done literally anything to his front page, as he now realised. He was in their grip quite firmly. So he would look foolish, more like an office boy than an editor, if he rang requesting information about something which had already taken place, if he himself did not know what that something was...

Far better to wait until he'd actually seen the edition before reacting...He did not want to make himself look foolish with the Night Editor, that was for sure.

Then he saw Ursula in the hallway downstairs marshalling the guests for dinner and he thought just a little bit more deeply about his situation. The guests thronged impatiently as dinner was called and was about to be served – Ursula was a good cook and her dinner was bound to be far better than just edible. Still just a few moments into the revelation of the Bank's coup and still staring at the throng of guests, Tom realised that he was not alone. Far from alone. There was Ursula to take into consideration and she was a mighty handful. It behoved him to step warily. He felt still more alert as these thoughts ran through his mind. Ursula liked Tom being editor of the Chron. It pleased her in many subtle ways. She feasted off his position, and he sanctioned this, because of the simple pleasure she took in exploiting his success. That gratified him. Moreover she played her part in consequence of that feasting by converting his Fleet Street success into the hard currency of social intercourse. That was the deal – the Tom Stone, viewed purely as a currency, was strengthening. Tonight was a perfect example of that and of their teamwork. No way would such a glittering cavalcade of guests have been assembled here in Hampshire without her hard work across the bridge tables etc. of the county. Tonight's beanfeast in Hampshire was the flipside of his endeavours on the Street. So could he just go, boots and all, for the Bank and neglect that factor...? Could he afford the luxury of petulance?

Unlikely. Highly, highly improbable.

Step warily, young Tom he told himself as he descended the stairs, you have a lot to lose here including…Tom could barely bring himself to utter the thought, but he knew what lay at the back of his mind. Editorship of the Chron carried a knighthood and Ursula wanted to be Lady Stone. And did he have the right to jeopardise that ambition merely by querying the composition of his front page on that specific night, one out of 350 or so nights of publication in any given year?

Perhaps there had been something wrong with his stories that day? Too much exuberance? An excess of zeal?

Tom positioned to rejoin the guests feeling more comfortable with his decision to wait and see on the small matter of his front page's recomposition when another stinging tragic thought struck him. It very nearly knocked him off balance as he went down the stairs – if he surrendered over his front page that night, then he gave away everything about being editor of the Chron. If he couldn't run his splash and select what stories went into the paper, then he couldn't run anything. It wasn't his paper any more. It belonged to the Bank of England – again – and he was just the office boy. Tonight was the thin, thin end of a long, fat wedge. Tom had his first inkling in that moment of the perils of closet servitude; of the uncertain life led by those who tack in the face of power; and of the comically implausible nature of partial integrity ('I'm honest up until 11 at night on a Friday. Then I let rip').

Not that Ursula would understand any of that line of thinking. Ursula had grown up in PR. The very concept of editorial integrity was foreign to her. Newspaper stories were just stories to her. She was interested in promotion. So she would never understand if he took a hard line over all of this, saying that certain modes of behaviour were ultimately unacceptable…

Many, many acts of journalism, many bitter disputes with Ursula concerning the unsullied concept of a story, and many interviews, notebooks, discussions with Copy, extra phone calls, rewritings for later editions and anguished discussions with editors, subs and sources had led Tom to that precise moment in space and time when, standing on the stairs above his hallway, he was offered a choice of direction.

The phone call said it all; it summed up his career in thirty seconds flat. It was all so clear. He could go this way, and shrug and say: 'Well, they were bound to catch up with me one of these days. Just a bit of fun really and everybody's doing it. So be it.' Then he took the money. In other words, went for the gong, irrespective of the issues. That was the sensible route. Ursula would like all that. Or he could refuse to go thattaway, striking out elsewhere. He could say most unfashionably to the Bank and others, in a way that would pain Ursula mortally when she got to hear about it: 'I guess there are limits. I can bend and stretch just so much but in the end and most regrettably I cannot accommodate you, Sir, beyond this point. You cannot hope to bribe or twist, Thank God, this British journalist...Most reluctantly, Sir, I have found there are boundaries to my latitude and no one is more surprised by this discovery than myself. My stretch factor has reached its absolute maximum. Thank you but no thank you'.

Very, very boring that route. Tom could see that immediately. Not a popular choice.

Away in the distance of his mind's eye, quite proximate over time and almost in faraway sunshine, Tom could see these two paths forming quickly, consequence of his phone call from the Bank of England. For a few seconds, inconsequentially, he thought of Bill Bells, still in the Harrow as the leaving party drew to a close. Tom sympathised with his fuzzy head as he took anguished cognisance of the possibility that he too might be stumbling into the street, and alone, like Billy, before too long. Tom knew that street and he knew how the wind howled with joy down its long dank expanse. He'd been there before in his dreams and nightmares after it all went smash.

Soon be there with you, Billy boy, soon be there with you, he found himself whispering to himself as he rejoined the guests. Ursula stood at the entrance to the dining room marshalling the guests through the door. She barely had time to give him a second glance. The food was ready to be served any minute and people just had to find their allotted places before that happy moment!

Tom was nudged in the ribs by a large confident man with a florid almost perspiring complexion.

'You're Tom Stone aren't you? You're the Editor of the Chron, I believe.'

'Correct.'

'I want you to know, Tom, that I think you're doing a very good job there at the Chron. It needed shaking up. It's been doing the same thing mindlessly for years and now it's started at long last to explore some new avenues. I don't suppose you're getting a lot of thanks for what you're trying to do but it has my vote – and the vote of a lot of other people in the City. It seems to have a voice all of a sudden...We all liked your editorial when you said the paper had to change. That was much discussed. It was well received in the City...'

'Thank you, sir, thank you. That is very kind.'

Tom had no opportunity for further discussion. The two of them were swept apart by the tide of guests as they both approached the dining table. Before they parted, Florid Man reached into his pocket and pulled out his card and handed it to Tom.

'Call me if you want to chat some more about the paper. I have the odd idea. We all care about the Chron.'

Tom thanked him again, said that he would be in touch and smiled, realising the futility of his comment. Half an hour previously, and he would have been delighted to arrange a discussion on Whither the Chron? But that had been then. As of now it would be an empty moment. The axe had fallen and Tom's card had been well and truly marked. The Bank was a powerful player.

Tom found himself dividing into two as they all sat down. Ursula, he noticed, looked very serene at the end of the long table. He sat at the other end – Tom the Editor, who looked and played the part. To his right sat Jilly, with whom he had enjoyed the start of a convivial moment before his phone call. As he sat down, she resumed talking to him immediately about the subjunctive and Tom the Editor, who had strong views on moods, responded at once. This made a good impression on his section of the table. He and Jilly played some clever real tennis back and forth among the condiments, on the knotty topic of English grammar. Jilly knew what she meant when it came to grammar and so did Tom; it was virtuoso stuff. He was heeded as the manifest embodiment of what an editor of the Chron should resemble. Tom played the part well, since he knew from experience what he was doing. The table was pleased by all this easy knockabout. Conversation at dinner tables is always a hazardous business so that anyone who takes the strain brings a smile to anxious faces.

But that was not the whole story. Within Tom the Editor, there was another, alternative Tom peeping around the corner, just out of sight, who was saying quietly 'I may not be Tom the Editor much longer. This is all coming to an end. Don't be fooled folks. I mean this quite sincerely.'

His sense of impossible duality climaxed when there was a knock at the door. It was around 9.30 and late for any one to call. Everybody started at the sound. Ursula reassured them all.

'Don't worry. It's only Tom's gofer with the first edition. He has to look at it to check that everything's all right and that he's done his job right as Editor. This man turns up every night and it's a real bore. Isn't that right, Tom?'

Tom the Editor nodded and laughed and scrambled to his feet to answer the door watched with admiring and appreciative eyes by the Lady Smart. Meanwhile the inner Tom, Tom the Realist, very nearly gulped with rage and tears and mortification at the artificiality of it all. What on earth had they done to his page and what on earth was the mayhem that had been created back in the news room by the Bank's intervention?

He found out very shortly. He took the first edition from the man from the Chron at the door and bade him Goodnight. Then he went back into the dining room for a second. Waving the paper unopened above his head he said to the attentive guests that they should continue their meal without him; that he must attend to his newspaper; and that they should talk and eat quietly among themselves, preferably in active voice. That crack raised a chuckle from Tom's end of the table, as Ursula frowned at his levity.

In another room, he dared to open the fold of the paper and look at the front page. He was right to be careful. The page was a shock. The Bank had gone about its work thoroughly. The lead story on the Nest had disappeared completely, to be replaced by something anodyne on world copper negotiations. Such a heavy splash story and so worthy! The second lead concerned something life-threatening about sprockets. Big deal! Tom's UK trade figures story, which he had sweated blood with the back bench to see included above the fold, had also disappeared, to be replaced by something anecdotal and whimsical about a revered Parliamentary figure. The Chron front page was its usual boring and amateurish mess. It was about as stimulating as a drink with an ex-girl friend, now married with three children and trailing a husband with money worries.

In other words, business as usual for the tedious old Chron!

Tom began to learn a thing or two. He could now glimpse the hidden wiring between the Bank of England and the Chron, wiring that he had not dreamed existed until that evening. Somehow they were in cahoots. Along with matching personnel, there was present the indispensable muscle to back up the deal. He flicked through the pages of the edition, and failed totally to find his Nest story. God alone knew what had happened to it. Dropped most likely, like the dead donkey before it...And his trade story...? Where was that? When he finally ran that to earth, on page 32 and a long way down the page, it had been entirely recast to take in a fresh angle. This happened, by chance, to be statistically incorrect but it was one which favoured the government. The story had also been written by a different journalist on the paper, one Morton, who had only recently joined the Chron and who Tom barely knew. Certainly not one of his toughies, part of the crack elite! Tom found himself looking at a Chron as it ought to look and as it had always looked, a study in mental inertia, edited by the usual fustian bodies, and conforming to some ancient set of worn out journalistic precepts.

The page as laid out before his eyes was a warning to him – don't get smart, Stone, and stray off the beaten track... Your job is to keep the Chron on the road, travelling sedately.

As such, it was another journey into alternative realities. Of course, he was still the editor of the paper, but now only in name. The paper had been taken over in a stunning and efficient long meditated coup. That was obvious. The insult to him was calculated, as indeed would be his interview the following day with Q.

Tom pondered it all briefly, still with the edition in his hand, standing alone in the middle of the room and listening to the clatter of plates next door. Ursula's Beef Wellington was going down well...The guests sounded happy. Tom realised that his career had now entered a fresh phase. There were decisions to be taken now or later.

Did he resign on the spot? Did he march into the room next door looking like Henry Irving, fling the paper down onto the table in front of the guests, cry to his astonished audience that this was not good enough for him, m'lords, and e-mail his resignation on the spot? Hardly. With a wry expression Tom thought to himself that Ursula would not be best pleased by any of that behaviour. Tantrums were out, at least for the time being.

It occurred to him, as he pondered on his position and as these things strike the insulted and the injured at such moments, that there was a pattern to it all. He recalled an incident of some months ago, when Griffo of the Bugle, another stalwart from the good old, bad old days of financial journalism, had been summarily dismissed from his job as Financial Editor for running some perfectly innocuous story about the pound. So Griffo, then Billy and now him – was there a structure to all of this...?

The phrase appropriate to his course of action drifted through his mind at that moment.

When in Rome, thought Tom as he decided against calling the news desk and asking just what had happened to his front page that evening. Tomorrow would suffice for the row or the whimpering. He thought he would box clever for the time being. He was on the run and this was no time for heroics. That was how his instincts as an old investigative reporter counselled him. Tonight he had a part to play, that of Tom the Editor, for his guests. Sufficient unto the moment...That would be his watchword because the story sounded too good to miss...

Shriven of doubts for the time being, Tom rejoined the dinner party, looking blithe, and without the first edition which he had left elsewhere, carefully stuffed into a waste paper basket.

'No problems at all. That's such a relief,' he said blithely to his deeply impressed audience. He then recommenced his discussion about grammar and the evening continued on its gay, carefree way...

The evening in fact was a great success. The party didn't break up until after midnight. Ursula was very pleased with Tom as they chatted about the event, after the guests had gone.

'You know, Tom, I was really very pleased with you this evening. I don't think you put a foot wrong all evening. Not like in the old days in Hampstead, when you were still learning to be a human being and use a knife and fork correctly...'

'But that was before we had taken each other in hand...'

They eyed each other with cool surmise. And one thing then led to another as it normally did when they found each other in chatty, giving mood. After so many years together and then apart, miraculously they could still kindle that electricity between them that leaped across space and time...

Tom said nothing about the fiasco of his edition and concentrated for the time being on matters arising from Ursula's familiar gulps of pleasure...

Tom's driver, cheerful as ever, picked him up at 9 the next morning. Tom felt suspended between unrealities as they motored up to town and he queried whether or not he had misunderstood what had actually happened. But no – that was impossible. He had the front page spread out on his knees. No mistake was possible. That set of stories on page 1 was not the arrangement of news that he had sanctioned the previous evening before departing.

He paid a brief visit to the Chron newsdesk before departing for his meeting with Q at the Bank. Complete routine all round. Nobody there apart from a junior manhandling the tapes.

Newspaper offices are clean and quiet and cool in the early morning; that day was no exception.

The scandal of the previous night had melted away with the early hours and the late editions. There was nothing left there to record what must have been the consternation and sheer blind panic of the news desk when the Bank pronounced its fatwa against Tom and deemed the planned first edition of the Chron last night as unacceptable. Tom could picture the scene, like an early black and white film with journalists and editors running every which way, all yelling. The Bank had planned its coup with care. He didn't always leave the office so early.

All that recalled the typhoon of the previous evening was a note from his secretary to call Dune-Jones, to set up an urgent meeting.

That is real enough, thought Tom as he hurried from the building towards the Bank. Dune-Jones will not be pleased to get a complaint from the Bank about my editing. Black mark, whichever way you look at it and very much first blood to the Bank.

The Old Lady's perfidies take place behind the camouflage of the commonplace, thought Tom poetically, realising that it was a phrase worthy of Jilly Smart. Should he note it down and call her later, as a renvoi of an entertaining evening?

He thrust the thought from his mind as belonging to a previous era and concentrated on the here and how as he walked through the grim dark entry to the Bank and asked for Dr Q. He was expected. A pink-jacketed flunkey walked him at once through the barrier behind the entrance hall and then to the right of the Bank's elegant garden in the centre of the complex. Tom noted the right turn with some interest. Normally he turned to the left, which passageway led to the Governor's office, the way he normally went towards the smiles and the handshakes when he had been in favour.

But to the right...? This must be where they took the special prisoners, those destined for the first circle of the Bank's Hell, Tom speculated as he wandered with the flunkey through a maze of dark winding corridors, up some stairs, round some corners, across a lift area and then in by a small oak door to a broad study where a small plump man with a fluted head; stubby fingers; and round thick spectacles was seated writing at a desk.

He looked up as Tom came into his study and rushed from around his side of the desk, hand extended. They shook hands somewhat incongruously, smiles on both faces. Dr Q motioned Tom to a seat.

He sat down opposite Tom, arranging himself delicately. His words came with a rush.

'I'm so sorry about last night, and I'm sure you'll understand when I say that we just had to do it. I'm sorry your page was butchered but it was imperative that we took that story about the trade figures off the front page. Very bad for the markets. Won't you have some tea?'

'I'll have some tea, thank you.'

Dr Q rang a bell and another flunkey appeared. Q made plain his requirements and the flunkey disappeared.

'You do understand, don't you, that we had to do what we did. We are responsible for running these markets. That story, especially the way it was written, would have sent the wrong signal to the markets. So that was why we did it. And that's why we're having our little chat this morning. Extra briefing for you. So that you understand.'

Like managed democracy, it all sounded so reasonable, Tom thought. But then all invitations to connive at the truth would be framed likewise. The basic facts remained the same. It was his paper, not the Bank's.

Or used to be.

'And the Nest story?'

'A different matter entirely. Not my responsibility at all. That was Stobart's decision. He deals with that aspect of the press. No, my responsibility is purely financial... You must ask Stobart about the Nest story, if you're still upset. I know he's around this morning until his meeting with the PM. That's at noon, so you may catch him. If you want to, that is.'

Tom found the switch from last night's deadly aggression over the phone to this morning's gushing friendship and affability hard indeed to bear. This was the Bank's alternative face. This man is an actor and a charlatan, he told himself, with an agenda all of his own. I want to get some of this into the notebook for future reference. The minute I get out of here, out comes the notebook...

The notebook was lodged, as ever, in his left hand jacket breast pocket.

Q continued blinking at Tom in a mild Pickwickian way but he said nothing. He was expecting Tom to speak. Tom said nothing but stared back at him mutinously. No words between them. A little time passed. Q wanted Tom to play to him and Tom was refusing.

Finally Tom spoke, to break the silence which had fallen between them. Bound to his routine, Tom realised that, after all, he had a paper to edit and that it was getting later in the morning.

'You asked me here. I think it's up to you to do the talking. You fucked up my paper last night and ruined what would have been a first class edition. We had good stories on that front page that we had worked hard to put together. That hard work went for nothing. I think you owe me an explanation for all of that extraordinary behaviour. So over to you, now, Dr Q.'

The door opened and the flunkey bustled in with a tea tray held high through the door and approached the table. The atmosphere was chilly but that would have lain within Q's calculations. Q glanced at Tom. The tea tray approached, borne aloft. As the flunkey prepared to place the tray on the table Q motioned to him to remove it from the room.

'Mr Stone has changed his mind. He won't be taking tea this morning with me. Take it all away at once.'

'Your words, not mine, Q.'

Tom glared at Q and then shrugged as the flunkey with evident ill humour crashed back out through the door. Q's eyes flashed rage and power behind the lenses.

'That is extraordinarily rude of you, Q. Is there any point in my staying here and talking to you at all? What do you think this is, a Nazi interrogation centre?'

Q was not displeased by the idea. He was plainly playing by different rules. He made that clear at once.

'If it was, you would not be sitting there with a mutinous look on your face and maintaining your uncooperative attitude. A man breaks quite easily after …But no, enough of that. That is just play-acting and you know it. More likely there are other solutions in this day and age. More than likely, you'll be packing the shelves at Tesco any day now at this rate. The market for ex-editors is extremely thin, I can assure you of that…And you should know that Dune – Jones was shocked when we spoke to him last night about our reaction to your stories. And your responses this morning…'

Pause, as Tom mulled what Q was saying. Threats, just brutal threats. Conventional stuff. As someone had once muttered prophetically to him, just after he took the job at the Chron: 'You must watch out for the Bank. It can be pretty nasty when it wants to be.' Like now. His informant had been right. Q was a thug, just a heavy, as perhaps one might have expected. But Tom's job? Forget it, Tom thought. That job was now hanging by a thread after the Bank had dealt direct with the crucial element of power in the equation – Graham Dune – Jones – who until now had been pretty friendly towards Tom and his reformist measures.

'I think, my friend, there are one or two things you must know about the relationship between the Chron and the Bank. I didn't want to have to spell them out but I will, now that you're making it all so very difficult. Let me put it you very simply -we run the news in the Square Mile. Does that make sense to you? Because we make the weather here, we also make the news. We, the Bank that is, not you, editor of the Chron, decide just what is news and what is not news in this part of town. And when I say 'Not', that's exactly what I mean. Your job is to take down accurately what we say and not to change established custom and practice. Understood? You run your newspaper in conformity with what we decide is correct. Understood?'

Tom said nothing.

'I said, understood?'

Tom shrugged and again said nothing. Q was unlike anything he had encountered before at the Bank. This was all quite bizarre. Q's act was a hard one to top.

'You had a fair run at first as Editor because we wanted to see just how you'd shape up. But as soon as you started to change things, we decided to step in. Does that make sense?'

'In so far as what you say is understandable as English, yes. Otherwise, it's remarkable. This is a country which likes its newspapers. The Chron may have been the house journal of the Bank for centuries but it must all start to change now.'

'That's as may be. It may be remarkable to you, Mr Stone, but it matters a great deal to us here at the Bank. The reporting by the Chron must be fair and unbiased – and mustn't rock our boat. That's the important thing. So you'll find that what you may call drivel we treat as a very hard commodity indeed. In order to ensure that, now that you're here and we can discuss it, we are going to insist on a few changes in the reporting lines on your paper. They are very straightforward, they won't take long to outline and we're sure you'll agree. We want Morton to cover all foreign exchange stories. That is very important. We can rely on Morton because he's a first cousin of our Chief Cashier. Family, you understand. Not much risk of him going native. We want Alexander on the news desk because he did a good job for us last night, and we want a more reliable presence there. We also want a lot more input to your leaders, especially over the next few months, because the Bank is going to have a hard time of representing itself to the Chancellor. We don't want any irresponsible and ill-informed gung ho journalists queering our pitch by thinking – and then writing – things out of turn. That is just far too dangerous for us to contemplate. So we want Gunter as Senior Leader Writer.'

'Gunter?'

Q sneered at Tom.

'You probably know him better as Captain Legless. What is unmistakeable is that he is one of ours. And wholly reliable.'

Tom shrugged.

'This is the theft of a newspaper. You realise that, don't you?'

Q smiled. He had a winning line and he knew it.

'You're exaggerating again, Stone. This is no more than the restoration of the status quo. We are putting things back to how they were. It has worked well in the past and it will work well again. You are the oddity in all of this, not us. We are tradition here.'

'And editor?'

'Oh you can stay as long as you like as editor provided you're happy with all of the changes. We're not so worried about you as editor provided we have all the rest, all the essentials. You play the part very well and everyone's impressed, including some of your dinner party last night. They reported back on you and your showing very favourably. On that point, incidentally, beware of guests who proffer their business cards too readily. Yes…? Make sense?'

336

Tom gaped at the power and reach of the Bank's intelligence. Q continued.

'You can even have a cup of tea with me now if you like, although I am busy. I'll call the waiter back. Our main business is now completed and I'm certain you're going to see the justice of our requirements. It'll take a lot of the strain of editing off your back after you fall in with us, for one. Your salary will continue to be paid, of course. But I have to tell you, that if you don't agree to all of this, well, that phone there on my desk' – and here Q indicated his phone across the room – 'will be connected to Dune-Jones' number just as soon as you leave the room. I don't think your job will be worth much after we've finished our discussion with him.'

'Call him now if you like. The job's worthless anyway now.'

'No, after you've gone is better. We don't want a scene. And you make a mistake, Stone, when you say the job is worthless. That is quite wrong and very shocking of you to say so. The job has simply been redefined and you have failed as yet to adjust to that modification. That is all. Think it over and don't be hasty. A job is always a job and worth having, especially one that carries the prestige with it of Chron Editor. That knighthood is still waiting in the wings, you know. Don't be hasty. A K is always a K.'

Dr Q was cunning and Tom could see that. There was an alternative approach to the crisis and Q fed his suggestions into the discussion with great skill. Tom could see that knighthood hovering above his head, rather as the Desert Fathers had apparently glimpsed the Paraclete. It couldn't be ignored, especially when Ursula was also in the frame.

'Any redress from any of this.'

'Unlikely. Dune-Jones has been in the City for years. He knows our little ways. He is also ambitious. So he's not going to stand out against us, not in a million years. It's our forcefully expressed opinions to him against your…Well, there's no contest, is there? So call it whatever you like, takeover or anything, but we're in a hurry. Our plans… Well, they don't concern you…But they are well laid, I can assure you.'

Tom felt some more questions form themselves as he grew conscious of the notebook tucked away comfortably in his jacket pocket. There would be some writing down to be done, the minute he emerged from this crazy discussion with Q. Much might have been lost so far that morning but the basic gumshoes instincts of the reporter still remained. Perhaps were all that remained? He felt his fingers itching to be writing.

'Why did you allow me to become editor in the first place?'

'We had someone else in mind but it was just too difficult and disruptive to steer him into the job. He'll get the job in due course. So we decided to play it long. We let you ease your way in, we watched carefully, obstructing when we felt it necessary, and then we picked our moment. You have been very useful to us. The Chron wanted a more liberal voice, so it got what it wanted for the time being. But by putting you into the job, that way we were able to identify all the potential rebels on the paper, which we have now done. Needless to say, all that category of journalist will now be quietly eliminated from the Chron, so that it will revert very quickly to what it has always been for us – a pliant mouthpiece. And if that process of cleansing can be effected from behind the facade of the liberal voice, that is to say with Tom Stone still as Editor, so much the better for us, ahead of the appointment of our genuine, long-term selection. Last night was important and we needed to reclaim territory fast...But afterwards...'

Q shrugged.

'Anything further? No? I can see that you're beginning to adjust to my suggestions. A K is always a K, Stone, don't forget that, especially if you do nothing to earn it beyond keeping a seat warm.'

Tom shrugged in turn. It seemed a futile gesture but he made it. Q was so far ahead now that he was almost out of sight. It had been quite a coup.

'One more thing, Tom. I'm assuming that, dazed as you are, you're going to agree to what we want. Otherwise you would have left the discussion a long time since. Of course, of course. So on that assumption, don't go back to the Chron office immediately after our discussion finishes, which it will do in about thirty seconds. Allow about an hour, which gives us time to make certain that all the main changes are in place by the time you get

338

back. You can announce the changes later today if you like, but you'll find that your editors are fully apprised of the moves. We want everything functioning as normal by this afternoon. There's a big leader we want written up for tomorrow's edition which will set the Chancellor right before too late. That is a first priority. Snowden is itching to make a move on taxes but he'll think again after the Chron has taken a swing at him. The leader is written already but it needs guaranteed insertion before it goes live, if you understand me. We have one or two others in the pipeline, of an international forex nature, but they can wait.'

Tom felt like the bull, motionless in the ring after the matador has tormented it to such an extent that the head starts to drop. It was time to go before he keeled over completely. The notebook was weighing in his pocket as he contemplated a new and unexpected existence. It was time to start writing now that he was no longer the Chron editor. Or, more accurately, that he was still editor but strictly non-executive.

Tom stood up, controlling himself carefully. He forebore to hospitalise Dr Q by smashing him in the face, breaking his jaw in fourteen places. Convention still forbade such displays of excess spleen, even by journalists. He left Q's office without a further word or even a glance towards him and happily without taking any of Q's tea.

Game, set – but perhaps not yet match – to the Bank of England and Dr Q! Tom acknowledged that freely as he was escorted from the building.

He was bowed obsequiously round all the corridors by the pink-clad flunkeys attendant on him at every corner as he retraversed his route back to the Bank's main doorway. The Versailles of Louis XIV must have been a similar mix of frustrated intelligence, cruelty and orchestrated fawning, he thought as he exited from the Bank's headquarters and into the bright morning sunshine of Threadneedle Street. Tom was adjusting rapidly to a new-old life as a journalist. He was back with a pen in his hand and with ideas on writing.

The idea had come to him quite suddenly in the middle of his tete a tete with Q. Writing all this down would not be enough. The notebook alone would not suffice. A tough road lay ahead of him which, quite conceivably, he might not survive. Just regressing to gumshoe journalism would not be enough. The situation was too complex and too important for him to exhibit a stock reaction. So he had decided to keep a diary of events subsequent to his effective dethronement as editor. A permanent record, no less. Pepys had done it, he recalled, at crisis moments of his career, and he would do the same. It was his only solution.

Useless for him to discuss any of this morning's events with Ursula. He would remain silent with her about the interview with Q. There was simply no way that she would understand what was at stake and what was in play. Admirable though she was in many ways, when it came to the integrity of the press she was pretty much an airhead, as he had frequently told her. She had no idea whatsoever that newspapers were important or that the Bank's coup, for example, reached deep into the intellectual formation of the country. As Q had said, the Chancellor was planning a move on taxes and the Bank was going to short circuit all of that by its control of the Chron, in general, and by its leader the following day in particular. The Chron would be used as an instrument of control to keep the Chancellor in line. Nothing outwardly would have happened at all; Tom, for example, was still editor; and the big, menacing changes that the Bank had proposed would be quite hidden from the public or even Whitehall's gaze.

But everything had changed in reality. The Chron was no longer what it had been until 24 hours ago when Tom had taken his call from Q. It was now back in long-term role as the house journal of the Bank. Every word that appeared in it henceforth would be after sanctioning by the Bank. That was what could be read quite easily into Q's words. Like the Vatican, the Bank now had its own daily instrument of propaganda, recaptured and intact.

That was as far as Tom could see but he had no doubt that it all reached a great deal further than his vision allowed. The Bank was out to capture the Chancellor and who knew what else besides. What had happened to him that morning was a clear act of expansionism, a powerful and long-meditated gambit in a specific direction. The Bank was moving onto the offensive in a way that seemed to betoken some crucial event. It was all very sinister, very important, and it had to be recorded. So he would keep that record. He would not resign as editor. Instead he would accept the humiliation of the downgrade and watch out for what happened in upcoming months, exploiting in turn his privileged position as editor of the Chron. And he would talk to no one. He had accepted, as the interview raged with Q, that he was alone now, a man caught in the limbo of conscience with all the craziness of those uncharted longitudes and latitudes. Decision time had come to him when he had least expected it, on the very cusp of his moment of triumph. Now he must adjust. In default of Ursula, bless her outbursts and her chagrins, he would confide in his diary. He would reinvent himself as an investigative journalist, going back to his roots. That way, in some slight fashion, he could palliate the shame he felt at his capitulation to the Bank over his editorial integrity; it was like meeting himself, but a different oh-so-changed self, warts and all, in a parallel universe. He would never have believed that what had happened to him could have taken place, had he not experienced it for himself. Such had been – and was – the mighty shock to his morale.

He had lost the Chron. That was the realisation that lay on the seabed of his anguish. He had lost his paper, his pride and joy. It had slipped from his grasp. It belonged to others now.

Small tragedy, not many dead…!

Then in some months time, when he had made his decision, which he could see looming more and more on the horizon; when some of the wounds had ceased to bleed; and when he had had enough of the Fleet Street farce, Ursula could read his diary and understand at least why he had done what he had done.

By then he might be long gone. Or long departed. Or whatever. It was anybody's guess.

Anything could happen now that he was caught in a wilderness of mirrors between two states of being. But in the meantime he would keep his diary.

To his surprise, his plans seemed ready formulated as he left the Bank; they needed no further referral back to judgement and control. Like an automaton, he tripped down the steps of the Bank and marched across the street to the Royal Exchange where a small but exclusive stationers traded in the shadow of the Old

Lady. There he bought a ring-bound notebook with plain unruled pages. And another bottle of black ink, just to be on the safe side.

He would start by handwriting the diary.

After all, he had the pen, Ursula's present to him after he became Editor. So it was back to basics for him. He would start by scrawling in his diary in odd quiet moments. Then as he grew more emboldened he would transfer it all, warts and all like his vision of himself, to his computer. It would all go into the journal. If he couldn't run somebody else's newspaper, well, then, he would write his own.

To Hell with the lot of them! The Bank had tried to strip him bare. But, inadvertently, it had left him with something fundamental, his writing skills, that he could now use to hoist himself out of the pit into which he had been hurled.

Tom found a coffee bar in Queen Victoria Street. He well recalled walking in haste up and down this street in the old days when he was new to City journalism and chasing stories. It had been the scene of triumphs and disasters as he filed good, bad and indifferent copy.

'That's all in the past,' he said to himself as he sat down on a high stool in the window of the bar which commanded a panoramic view of the outer ring of the City. He stirred his coffee and then filled the pen. He took a sip of the coffee and then opened the notebook.

Quite carefully at first but then more fluently as the habit of handwriting returned and the words flowed, he began to write.

'This diary is addressed to my darling Ursula, whom I have loved, lost and then loved again throughout my life. I fear, darling Ursula, I may be about to lose you again after the grave setback to my position as editor of the Financial Chronicle which I have suffered at the hands of Dr Q of the Bank of England between 10 a.m. and 11 a.m. this morning. I foresee many months of strife ahead during which I may be wholly discredited. My life is not what it was before the meeting with Dr Q. These facts are not for your ears now. But I may lose you and my ship may not come safely home. If that happens then I will bequeath to you this testament of mine, written in all good faith over difficult months, so that you may understand why I have done what I felt I had to do. But darling, darling Ursula you must never forget that I loved you first, best and always. And always will.'

Tom read through what he had written and was pleased with the prose. It struck the note he wanted. Then he looked at his finger and saw the familiar bump appear on his forefinger, testimony to hours of scribbling as a journalist in a pre-computer age. He smiled at the link established with the past. He felt calmer and less devastated. Very briefly, he then wrote a factual account of his meeting with Dr Q. He kept it tight. There would be many such entries to come over the next few months. Death to prolixity. He wanted to to establish at once the style of the diary, so that Ursula would have no difficulty in reading the saga. He knew just how limited her attention span could be. In effect he wrote the passage as a straight news story. After he finished writing up his diary entry, he read it through again and liked it. The prose was flat but it had good rhythm and it flowed quite easily from point to point. He was pleased that he could still put a simple pen onto plain old paper and make sense. That stirred something inside him. Then he drank up his coffee and prepared to leave the bar. It would be time for midday conference shortly which he must host, erstwhile editor though he might be.

As he left the bar, packing the diary into his overcoat, he felt better than he had done for some 24 hours. The air was fresh and there was sunlight all around. He saw his shadow looking limber on the ground. He felt solid enough. There seemed to be a release taking place inside him and a freedom in the air which he did not wholly associate with the act of writing.

'Strange,' he thought, 'I should be on my knees after Dr Q this morning, but not so. Not so at all. I feel good, I feel strong, I feel ready to cope. I thought I would feel ashamed to take conference this morning. Quite the contrary. I want to see how they look at me, knowing about the disgrace of last night. I almost want to feel their scorn because it is renewing in some odd kind of way. They are staying where they are but I am moving on. That is for sure.'

He patted the pocket where the diary was stored.

'And I have the diary to write. I am ready to confide as well. Now that can't be bad and might even be fun. Who knows? And

Sam Pepys, this is for you – I now know why you needed your diary as confidant in moments of crisis.'

He caught a cab back to the Chron offices and arrived just in time to take conference.

★　★　★　★　★

Joe told his driver to hang a left on the outskirts of London as they came into town from the country and this his driver did, practised as he was in obedience. The car swung left. But Joe caught a glimpse of the chauffeur's face in the mirror and it was a picture of dissatisfaction. So had the news got to him as well? Was he also ready to play fast and loose with Joe?

Joe rather fancied not, at least for the time being. In an organisation as vast as ABC Bank, it would take time for the news of someone's imminent demotion to filter down that far into the jurassic of structure. But it would only be matter of time now before Joe's driver starting giving him the Look. The Look that betokened Shock and Dismay. And Departure. Joe knew all about the Look – he'd seen it before. Felix was deadly. He was starting to accelerate the process of Joe's discrediting. He was spreading rumours about Joe, most likely via the secretaries. The secretaries should have known better but then what secretariat could refuse to gossip and reject the bait. Gossip was part of the job. Felix knew his market and Joe knew his methods; a gullible secretariat that lived off face values was meat and drink to a cold-hearted operator like Felix straight from the Eastern bloc. Felix was an actor as well. A hint here and a suggestion there with eyes rolling and then his stage gesture of silence with the finger over the lips – yes, Felix had always been good at that. The secretariat would believe the mime, the more so since it came from such a normally straight laced and highly elevated source. Joe had seen him operate at first hand years ago in Berlin. It worked a treat then and it would work again now, against Joe. Felix never failed to edge his intended victim off the stage. He had a kind of knack for setting people apart and then subjecting them to hostile group disapproval. It must have been a technique he had learned from the Stasi or anywhere east of Berlin. It felt like Eastern bloc and it never failed.

Felix was a professional. He had now inveigled two of his men onto Joe's investment committees, so that he occupied key vantage points on Joe's territory; he had the ear of the Quiff in a way that Joe would never enjoy because Felix and the Quiff were both bankers and Joe was a trader. And now he had started the rumour machine full blast. Joe felt like a man on the outside of a skyscraper block hanging there by his finger tips 100 storeys up. So far so good but he was just starting to slide...

As Joe's car roared into London from a different angle of approach, Joe wondered what foul story it was that Felix had spread around concerning him. He could see it in his staff's eyes daily. 'We thought he was such a good guy, but now that we know better. Ugh!'

That kind of thing.

Felix's rumours were like a noxious low level cloud that he released into the atmosphere at careful discrete intervals, just keeping the rumour alive by giving it careful oxygen. Sooner or later Joe would find out the substance of the rumour but most likely by then the damage would be done and it would be too late. Already his power base was corroding, little by little. Joe reckoned power was about reach and grasp – would a man do what he thought you wanted him to do even when you were not around to check up on him? Like when he was working at home for example? That was power, when the reach equalled the grasp, irrespective of your presence.

Joe knew about power and he could feel it slipping from him at ABC...

Joe's Financial Chronicle lay opened but scarcely read on the seat beside him. Joe had skimmed through it, noting that Tom Stone seemed to have played and lost. The paper had a familiar dull feel. Long windy and chary of conclusions, the Chron had reverted to its old ways abruptly, positioning daily to be a reliable second with the news, although Joe did admit that something vaguely out of place in the markets section had caught his eye briefly...Something that seemed oddly well informed for the Chron as it reverted to traditional know-nothing mode...

More structure...?

Joe wondered how long Donnelly, his number two, would hold out before changing sides and transferring his loyalties to Felix. That would be the defining moment in Felix's campaign against him. That would be when Joe knew that he was on his way out of the bank and his job. A month? Or two? Three? Not longer. Impossible. Donnelly couldn't afford to back a loser at this point in his career and he was gradually reaching the conclusion that Joe would not go the distance. Joe could see that in his eyes. Donnelly was a brisk, no nonsense, well put together, thickset banker with some imagination and flair and more than just a touch of the cattle-rustling Celt about him. He had made an unexpectedly successful switch from conventional mainstream banking into investment banking years ago -and it had paid off! He had prospered after discovering a talent for conservatism that held the wilder investment ideas for deals in check. He could dialogue with extremism and retain his street cred; this in turn had saved his employers millions. His talent had brought him through the ranks to the exalted position of number two to Joe at ABC. Donnelly could see preferment beckoning and he would not allow, in Joe's view, trifling considerations like individual loyalty to interfere with his broader horizons. That, too, was the evasive Celt in him. He would seek ways of escape from his allegiances. Joe could see it all daily in the way that Donnelly averted his eyes from Joe's gaze at the start of the discussions. His investment ideas, once so crisp and well formulated, had grown vaguer of late as Donnelly considered his position and turned deeply risk-averse; even cash was tricky for him in the investment meetings. Joe couldn't say that he blamed Donnelly; they had both come to their jobs from very, very different experiences. Not everyone's CV in banking included a long spell in Cold War Berlin as part of the Gents' crack hit squads...While Donnelly had nothing backing him apart from his ever-loving wife. He had to get this one right, now that the children were all at private schools...No, it would be an epic moment when Donnelly switched sides, Joe was sure of that. He could envision quite easily the way that Felix's eyes would gleam momentarily in triumph behind his spectacles as the moment of betrayal approached...

And then took place, as Donnelly most likely moved clumsily around the boardroom table and closer towards Felix in symbolic act of vassalage...

And meanwhile Joe was going in search of Felix. That was why he had taken a different route that morning into London. He was en route to seek out Felix's perfidy. A chance to even up the score, if only briefly, as Felix forged ahead round after round.

Joe had made his discovery weeks ago. Flicking through the lists of ABC's major advances and loans outstanding, which just happened to have been left in his room, Joe had made little of the strings of names that followed each other in orderly fashion on the print-out. So, as one does, he had tried finding names that might fit his own interests and preoccupations. He had a few minutes to kill before his next meeting. No need to bother with the Pugh's – Joe knew all about that already. He skipped the 'P' columns. Rivers Pugh would come later in the day, at 11.30 in the morning to be quite precise. Noting the sums advanced and the coded references in the margin, he tried this and that permutation of names, running his eye idly up and down the columns until under 'F' he had looked again idly for the name of Fat Man, thinking that it was one name which would never appear in the august lists of the ABC loan portfolio.

The name had leaped out at him from the cold black print – Fat Man Enterprises – £25 million – SI, or Special Instructions. No repayment details were listed and nor were the interest rates on the loan. SI covered the whole loan schedule.

Joe had recoiled from the printout. He was suddenly full of quiet rage. It was impossible, he told himself, that the dreaded name should appear yet again in his professional life, tracking him down as before across time and space from their experiences together long ago in Berlin – and with Felix. But there was no mistake – the Fat Man's name sat in the column like a spider eating its prey, black squat and self-assured.

Then it had been time for Joe's next meeting. No time to make further investigations. Noting the account number and the various codes of Fat Man Enterprises, Joe had laid the print-out carefully on his secretary's desk as he left his office, and prepared to do some research when the time permitted.

Gradually over the next few weeks, by dint of careful and discreet investigations, he had established that the Special Instructions referred to Felix's number two no less, another glib-tongued smiling German who held special responsibility for the account devolved from Felix himself and the Quiff. No other manager was in the command chain. Just Felix and Felix's number two had charge of the account, and the Quiff of course, although it was unlikely that Felix would involve him in monitoring such triflingly small sums. Fat Man Enterprises was Felix's baby and the bank was in for £25 million and upwards. The head office was in London, just on the outskirts. It was an import-export operation of some description with mainly European interests. Joe had even found out the address, using his secretary in a roundabout way.

And so now, early in the morning, Joe was paying Fat Man Enterprises a surprise visit, just to check out the terrain and see whether the ghost of the Fat Man still lurked in the machine. Yes, the Fat Man had always been enterprising, that was for sure. The name had been well chosen. He had always been remarkably coy, for example, about that currency problem he'd once encountered at Sydney Airport. No way that Joe had ever been able to worm the whole of that story out of him...

They were heading towards Putney now at some speed given the constraints of the morning rush hour traffic...Unbidden the name of the German forger who had hoodwinked the world over Hitler's Diaries, and whose name had eluded Joe for weeks came into Joe's head. His name had been Kujau. And why had Felix been so thick with him? Easy – Joe recalled that detail also. It was a morning for nostalgia. Because Felix and he had come from the same town in East Germany. They had most likely grown up together. That was why Felix and Kujau had been so close....

They were crawling down Putney High Street now in a traffic jam that was quietly gathering strength and critical mass. Joe had the A-Z out in front of him.

'I want you to go left at the next set of lights and then full speed ahead about 400 yards and then stop. I have to deliver a letter to a friend of mine. I won't be more than five minutes. Then we're on our way again. Understood?'

'Yes, Joe, perfectly.'

That seemed courteous enough. Perhaps the bad news about Joe really hadn't travelled as far as the chauffeur yet…They swung left at the lights, covered the next quarter of a mile quite rapidly, and then stopped. Still clutching his A-Z, Joe got out of the car, nodded at the chauffeur, and then traversed a fresh 50 well rehearsed and well imagined yards towards a turning on his right.

Something stirred in him, something told him that none of this was quite right.

The early morning breeze plucked at his hair as he walked along the road and his black shiny shoes clicked on the pavement. It was a warm summer morning, but it still wasn't right. Foreboding gripped him. He continued to walk nevertheless, still methodically checking the terrain against the map in the A-Z. No question of it. The A-Z was correct and so too was the address, assuming the secretary had done her job correctly – which she always did. Her information would be bang up to date. She was that perfect kind of secretary. Joe even called her the Perfect.

So…So….

None of this is right now, Joe told himself. He was opening up a fresh dimension in his relationship with Felix. He had a sick feeling in his stomach.

Joe had found the turning and he had found the street. So far, so correct. But no way had he found Fat Man Enterprises, and that for one very simple reason which leaped immediately to the eye.

The whole street had been demolished. Not a single house or office was standing in the region of the turning. Instead, it was a construction site. Cranes wheeling about overhead; hard hats; and men walking about on the site with that purposeful look of construction workers bent on a day of hard physical endeavour.

Clump, clump, clump, and cigarettes hanging from lower lips.

Where Fat Man Enterprises might conceivably have been located was now just a thirty foot deep hole in the ground. No way that even the Fat Man could trade from that setting.

Stuck for a response, Joe turned and waved to the car, holding up his fingers to indicate a fresh delay of some five minutes, and then plunged down the road and onto the site.

The loan figure of £25 million kept leaping into his mind. Would he now be acquiring some leverage relative to Felix, by chance, with his discoveries that morning? Not even ABC, he reckoned, would be so foolish as to lend £25 million, or perhaps even more, to a hole in the ground. So was he, Joe, on the brink of a small break though in the war of attrition against Felix? If true, it would be a pleasing thought.

It is good to bring chips to the table, thought Joe.

Without too much trouble, Joe found the site foreman and asked him the inevitable question.

'I was trying to deliver a letter here to a friend. But now I find...'

Joe indicated with an incline of his head the devastation of the site.

'...Any way of catching up with him?'

The foreman shoved the hard hat to the back of his head and laughed for a moment.

'If it's money your friend is owing you, well then he's no friend of yours. He's given you a bum steer, mister. This site had been derelict, by orders of the council, for about five years before we started work on it a month ago. He hasn't gone away because there was no one here living to go away, apart that is from the winos, and nowhere to go away from. How much did he owe you?'

'What makes you think it was a debt?' said Joe, wondering if after all there was a God above who protected him.

'Men always say they have a letter to deliver when they're chasing someone for money. It's a standard formula...Hey, Pete, watch where you're going with that digger. You're supposed to be over here, you fucking eejit...That road you'll be down that fucking hole, you clod-hopping Scouse moron...'

Touching his hat to Joe, he bade him good morning and continued with his day's work of demolition and then reconstruction, leaving Joe to stumble off the site and back to the waiting car full of thoughts.

The chauffeur was eager to please.

'Find him did you, Joe?'

'Oh, I found him all right. Yes, thanks, I found him.'

'Pleased to see you, was he?'

'He was surprised, let's just say that.'

'You've been around haven't you, Joe. You know some odd people.'

'A lot of people say that. But it's not quite true. All bankers know funny folk. It's part of their profession.'

And some funnier than others and some very close to home, thought Joe, as he mulled his discovery and wondered just how to put it to greatest use. So Felix, by any criterion, was milking ABC for millions, using his relationship with the Quiff to talk the approvals through, the while undermining Joe as cover for his activities.

Quite a sexy little trade by Felix.

So that was it? Or was it? Just the tip of the iceberg thought Joe. Felix was more subtle and would be playing for higher stakes. He might be bent, but he wasn't cheap. No sir, Felix had never been cheap. The hole in the ground only told half the story.

The chauffeur was disposed to be chatty as they set off for the City and Joe's office.

'I see what you mean. I've always thought of bankers as very pukka people.'

'Used to be the case but not any more. They can be as common as any other criminals. They just have more opportunity.'

The chauffeur shut up like a clam the moment he heard Joe's philosophical words lifting the discussion onto a quite different moral plane. He didn't want to talk about anything located too far from East Enders. So now he concentrated on his driving. Joe sat back in the seat still thinking about Felix and picked up the Chron. He was now about twenty minutes from the office and slightly ahead of schedule if the traffic was kind. Time to catch up on the markets...

Joe's phone rang in front of him. It was Mattie Mat his head forex dealer, a sharp featured man who looked and thought and traded like a man doing bird with a shaven head to boot. As a result, he took home about £1 million a year in basic salary. He and Joe enjoyed good rapport. Mattie Mat was good on fringe currencies, but not so assured with the big hitters, like the dollar; he didn't croon with the greenback and therefore slightly lost it with the big boys. But Joe had a good feel for the dollar, via US Treasuries, and that helped. They tended to work together and off each other.

'Seen anything, Joe?'

'Just looking, Mattie Mat. I'm a touch behind the curve. I've been thinking...'

'Never a good thing for you to indulge in...Too early for you, Joe, to be thinking.'

'To be discussed and to be continued...How are they looking this bonny a.m.?'

'Fairly stable for once. Not much movement. Can't see many heads above the parapet. Could be a dull day. Taiwan dollar's a plonker again but then that's nothing new. Any day now China invades but then that's nothing new either. They've invaded Taiwan many times in my lifetime already. The market's waiting for the US non-farms, and maybe won't budge before them.'

'The market's a fool. There's plenty going on, but the problem is that neither you nor I can see it. We're on the dark side of the screen. I'll call you shortly if I see anything in the Chron. I'm just delving now, but I have the Trib and the Journal to read as well, so I may be a moment or so...I'm still obsessing about the dollar, Mattie Mat. Any thoughts?'

'None printable or repeatable.'

Joe had fed Stanley's views into the forex team but they refused to believe it. They were dollar bears to a man just itching to sell the breeches out of it. So Joe had not insisted. He had just whispered the thoughts around his departments, planting ideas without commitment – the big decisions would come later and he could maybe wait. Not for very long but maybe time was on his side just. His deal was maturing but only slowly and he still had all the time. He didn't think for one moment that even he and Stanley together would get the timing of the dollar so totally right that they would be way ahead of the curve. Just slightly ahead of the flow and the turn in the dollar – that would be good enough for him, Joe reckoned. He didn't want Felix gloating over some terrifying forex fuck-up when they were long billions and the thing was careering down and out of control – the ABC politics of it all just would not tolerate that degree of exposure.

Joe had another reason to be cautious. Most of the time he could read the world's financial press like Braille. It was his special talent, his gift to the ABC team and a dubious but highly profitable legacy of his Berlin code-breaking of years ago. It wasn't always the case but on occasion some things just leaped out at him from the day's newspapers.

So far he had seen nothing in the press ever since Stanley's epic statements in the pub halfway to Pugh Park; no hints and no steers. Stanley might well be right in his call, but so far Joe had remarked on no stirring in the long grass about the dollar from the world's press. That was crucial in his assessment of how the dollar might move and in his judgement of Stanley's perception. The central banks would signal via the world's hacks. They would breathe their view of the market to select friends in the press if they saw a change in markets looming. They always played the game that way and there was no reason why this time it should be different.

So he could wait for a sign…

He went through the Journal and the Trib. He saw no stories as yet on $ strength. The Trib and the Journal tended to concert their market stories, leaving the Chron lagging some way in the rear. The US empire is a vast one. There has to exist some form of noticeboard function for its legates scattered here and there across the globe. The US press tended to perform that function where necessary and when danger threatened the US, leaving spoors of information for the hungry eyes of Joe and his ilk to absorb.

But that day, seated in his car and en route for ABC Bank, Joe saw nothing. The market stories were conventional – fears about a fresh fall in the dollar; Greenspan's dilemma about tightening; and the inevitable upward march of the US trade deficits. Joe returned to the Chron just to cross check the various lines on the market adopted by the UK press organ. Yet again, no story…Mattie Mat would be disappointed. He had nothing to trade as things stood for the rest of the week...

Then Joe saw the detail that had taken his attention; it had been the name of the new journalist writing the Chron's forex column, Morton. Morton who, thought Joe? And who Morton? For years, Chris Leadon had done the job faithfully and on occasion adequately, given the Chron's rigid self-censorship. For a few months, in the Prague springtime of Tom Stone's editorship, he had blossomed miraculously, writing clever well researched stories on faraway exotica like the Canadian $ and the Indian Rupee. Traders had commented on the wealth of information in the Chron until, inevitably, the axe had fallen and the Chron had returned to its old leaden self. As a piece of tragic ritual, Leadon had disappeared for a day or so, and likewise his column. Now, as Joe had noticed, the column had returned but not written by Leadon who most likely had now become the Chron's Siberia correspondent. He had been replaced by Morton, presumably a typical Chron apparatchik, long on obedience and short on talent.

Many drinks consumed with the City's forex boys, but not many paid for by Morton

Joe scanned his column and threw it to one side beside him. Nothing there whatsoever, he thought, absolutely nothing. All straight off agency...Same old dull Chron fare...

Poor old Tom Stone!

And so it was into the City with Joe gazing out of the window of his chauffeur-driven car and thinking about Perdita. Tall blonde slender and terrified Perdita... Perdita for whom the system had failed and who was afraid now to pass beyond the friendly and familiar confines of Pugh Park...Her sense of territory was now so circumscribed...The business day was closing on Joe and he wished he was still in bed with Perdita back at Pugh Park, cuddling her and comforting her and encouraging her just to take a few steps of adventure that day, as she clung to him in hope and love and he coaxed her into optimism. Her mother's death had brought such dire dreams to her. Such wreckage of young hopes...

They would walk together now on daring expeditions, in the early morning alone and together across the territory of Pugh

Park, she clinging to his shoulder and he with his arm around her so that, locked very close together, they explored just how far she could adventure from the house before the demons took control.

Small steps for Joe, giant strides for Perdita. She had not been well since her mother's death.

Thinking about similar bucolic trips that he had made in Pugh Park with Lady Pugh before she died, Joe gave her all his gentleness, coaxing her like a trainer into her stride. Perdita had not been bred up to face the ordinary stresses of life. It was not very far, perhaps forty yards or even slightly less from the house for her when fears of the unknown took over and she was forced to turn back and return. Up to the limits she was her old self again, pushing forward with vim and contemptuous of the slackers; she was Perdita the Bold, very blond and beautiful and tall and slim. But at the limits of the territory, she faltered and grew quiet and shivered, as if the ghost of her dead mother, Lady Pugh, had materialised from the trees all around like a dryad and warned her to go no further, shaking an admonitory finger at her. Lady Pugh, whom Joe had loved and who had succoured him, was all around them in the atmosphere of the house. She was a kindly invading presence but not apparently a sufficiently powerful spirit to lay the ghouls as her daughter trembled on the threshold of maturity and then regressed, fractured in spirit.

But more or less every day Perdita tried to make headway in gaining territory, trudging with resolution to the outer limits of her tolerance, hand in hand with Joe. But failing in the attempt?

Now as the day crept up on Joe, he lacked her. Day by day she seemed to drift away from him, like a spirit straying across the marshes as he watched from the safety of the dry turf. So he relished his vision of her that morning, sleeping soundly and deeply with abandon for once with her hair splayed across the pillow as he tiptoed around the cold bedroom. Then she had started into wakefulness as she heard him fumble with his shoes...'Joe,' she had said plaintively, 'Joe, is that you? Are you there, darling?' 'Yes, darling,' he had replied, 'Yes, I'm here right here, I haven't gone away.' He had moved towards her in the deep warm bed. Her arms had come straight out of the bed to hold him in their embrace and she had smiled her old carefree smile at him and nestled at his shoulder as she swam upwards from her deep slumber…

Now in the car, chugging towards the City past Ludgate Circus and daydreaming, Joe warmed to his visions and thought of the seas pounding the long beaches in the early sunshine somewhere far away when they had escaped…When they had escaped and they woke from their sleep and once again Perdita looked around with her old carefree confidence, not in this fright and apprehension which gripped her now wickedly and so unexpectedly.

To help her get over her mother's death, he thought that he should give it all up, banking, trading and everything and devote all his time to her, take her somewhere far away, somewhere simple and primitive where he could start to help her rebuild, where he could try to remould that shattered psyche so that it could cope with ordinary life…

But then there was Pugh Park, to which she belonged and also Rivers, her brother, disinherited from the family acres in a final act of dying revenge by Lady Pugh which had made Joe the master of the Pugh acres. Pugh Park could not just be sold on like any old house. In that respect it was a millstone round Joe's neck, impeding his freedom of movement, his freedom to take some decisions and to breathe. Gradually the county was pressing in on him, obliging him to behave in a certain kind of way, which he resented. But that was only to be expected. Pugh Park was a fixture in the life of Hampshire, just like Mansfield Park for Jane Austen in the Napoleonic era. Ownership and possession mattered…

And then there was Rivers…No reason to do anything with Rivers still in the offing. Joe's stomach turned somersaults at the thought of Rivers as his mind turned away from the potential in the situation. It was just too ghastly to contemplate how Rivers might react when he found out the truth of the bid for his company. And Christ alone knew how Perdita would take it, although he doubted whether she would genuinely take in the full implications of the story as it unfolded. He had done his best to camouflage his role in the whole thing, hoping to God that the

Americans would protect him in some way when the deal finally surfaced.

He could always resign from ABC when the deal was done. Resignation might be strong. Resignation and then flight, precipitously....But Felix might well get there before him on that.

The day yawned ahead of him and he braced for the inevitable conflicts as ABC's London headquarters loomed on the horizon at the end of Queen Victoria Street. It was a big bank with an edifice to match. The minute he arrived it would be into the morning meeting, ahead of his investment meeting. Markets all over the world, perspectives across the globe, trading, risks, losses, shouting, and positioning as the paper shuffled from buyer to seller and then back again – that would be his day from the moment he stepped out of the car.

The early part of his day at ABC was highly structured. After the investment meeting, he had his meeting with the Quiff alone to discuss investment exposure, and then came his special secret meeting with Lucia Maitland at 11.30, in order to go through just what had been achieved so far with Trojan, code name for ABC's most elaborate and dangerous bid so far, and one which might quite easily torpedo Joe's entire domestic set-up, Perdita included.

Trojan was aptly named as a bid situation. It did not have a lucky feel. Trouble was that no one quite knew who the horse was; who were the Greeks; or where Troy featured. It was a very mysterious bid indeed and a very big bid too, worth billions. The CIA were behind the deal, as Joe well knew, but it took some selling in and around the Square Mile, even if the Shades were helping things along, as they put it so felicitously.

Lucia was handling it all very capably as she always did. Like a true professional, she had barely griped at being summoned back from the airport weeks ago on the very point of departure for her holiday. That had been part of Joe's plan. It enabled him to force her to work in semi-isolation, a long way away from M&A. But Trojan was complex and delicate – and that was just on the surface of it all.

Lucia had only received half the story from Joe who indeed had brought the deal to ABC, courtesy of Pa Lee. But even the half she had seen made it a real swine of a bid – a hostile offer by a

US company for one of Britain's largest exporters. And Joe was at such risk from the various City surveillance authorities, like the Takeover Panel etc…He was conflicted in a dozen different ways on this bid. Not, of course, that Lucia knew any of this. Just as well he had been so evasive on personal details when he had joined ABC.

But then Pa Lee when he had broached the idea of the job at ABC had been very insistent. 'Joe,' he had said, 'you are the only person in the City who can get this bid through for us and we want you to do it for us. This is one of the reasons why we put you into the job…We'll look after you. You'll be safe with us…'

Fat chance, thought Joe. No way that anybody in this game could guarantee protection. If they tried to underwrite the protection, as Pa Lee was trying to do, then it was a sure sign they were lying. The intelligence game was always about lies. That was part of the territory. Deals of this size just didn't come with a safety net. But Joe couldn't turn ABC down. The job was too big for a start. It took in the entire world in its spectrum of responsibilities. That in turn meant wholesale and very discreet rehabilitation for him in the eyes of the City, a not inconsiderable attraction for an ex-gofer for British Intelligence struggling to re-establish his credentials within normality. Joe felt as if he had been on the road just a few years too long now for comfort or credibility. Nor could he reject £5 million a year before bonuses, plus all the stock options in the world he would garner from ABC. If the deal went through, he would be very nearly a very rich man indeed…

The palm trees beckoned for him and Perdita, provided he could collect on his deal…

So all he needed now was time and a following wind, in his estimation.

And so it all went on. It was a tangled tale. He lived in a messy complex world. But now to add some spice to what seemed to be an impossibly over seasoned dish anyway, he had discovered that his former colleague in espionage, Felix, was taking something like £25 million out of the bank on his own authority and the security of a hole in the ground…That's power lending and how, he thought to himself. The account had been aptly named Fat

Man Enterprises; the Fat Man himself would have been proud of Felix had he known. Nice money if you can get it, Joe thought as he exited from the car, thanked the chauffeur for his cooperation and took the fast arrival lift to his office in the skies, thinking that sooner or later he would have to lunch with Felix.

As a prelude to Felix taking him out, of course. Or of him taking Felix out, which seemed far less likely as the weeks went by. But he still wanted to lunch with him. Felix and his expensive hole in the ground intrigued him more and more. And was it a possible bargaining tool between the two of them? Did Joe suddenly have some leverage on Felix as a result of his discoveries that morning?

Unlikely in the short term, he decided. Felix was too smart and too deeply stitched into the Quiff for an act of denunciation to carry much destructive firepower at that stage in the hostilities. That was Joe's view that morning.

He was full of thoughts about such possibilities as he said Good Morning to the Perfect Secretary, took the reluctant smile of reply on the wing, dumped his newspapers and exited sharply again from his office in search of his morning meeting. It occurred to him that Felix would not be involved in such an obvious open scam like the hole in the ground in Putney unless something threatened quite shortly.

Sooner or later he would have to talk with Felix, not least because as Felix stepped up his campaign against him there was just a possibility that he would play the domestic card; trail Joe back to where he truly resided; find out about Pugh Park; and go for Joe at home. That really would be fatal then...That really would crack Perdita wide open, if shades of Joe's old life came to call. She had trouble enough coping with the day to day phenomena. Men in raincoats and snap brim hats would rip her apart in five seconds...

Time to think about that one...

But the moment of meeting with Felix face to face came sooner than Joe had expected. It took place at the end of that busy morning.

Joe coasted through most of the morning and the markets were kind to him as he went from meeting to meeting. Nothing jagged emerged in the bank's exposure anywhere. Awkward questions which might have been asked slumbered, uncalled, in dulling, uncaring minds. Nobody for the time being cared about anything but profits; they were all just too greedy to become masters of the universe as prices zoomed away and ever upwards on the Dow; S&P; and Nasdaq.

It was relax and get rich time.

At the morning meeting, the bank's chief economist, a naturally gloomy man with Joe suspected a serious problem of self-assertion as well as an irritating attention to detail, was heeded with barely scant respect as he went through the 7 million reasons why the markets looked expensive. The traders lounged around indulgently and paid no attention to him at all. It was a slow day for prices and gains but it felt rich and full for the bulls. Dr Gloom could go and do something unmentionable to himself and good riddance – that was the traders' view. When the markets were slow, so too was everybody in the markets, paying no attention to the catastrophes of the morrow. It didn't mean it was all coming to an end instanter; it was just the pause that refreshed.

Donnelly was especially obsequious in the morning meeting which Felix had also attended; Felix was taking stock and counting heads. In silence, Felix glinted around the meeting proprietorially, his thick lenses and bald head well to the fore. He might not have liked the way Donnelly had played to Joe but if that had been the case he failed to display ill-temper at his future vassal's acknowledgement of Joe's presence. Donnelly should have been less attentive to him, Joe reckoned, and more responsive to whatever rumour Felix was putting around about him. Donnelly would smart for that later, following the great denouement when Felix became King, Joe estimated. But Felix could afford to wait. That was what the body language screamed to the room at high volume.

Lucia too was making progress on the deal. The institutions were coming round to the idea of a US hostile but as always they were greedy. But their greed was natural. If a huge UK exporter was going to go to the US, then they all wanted their palms greased extra heavily for the privilege of selling a good old UK name down the river to the Yanks across the pond. That was about the strength of their reaction, which seemed par for the course to Joe. Indeed as he discussed the deal with her, Lucia and her team seemed to be slightly further advanced than he had thought. Almost ready to go but not quite for the obvious reason... For the umpteenth time, Joe asked her what difference a change in the dollar would make to the terms on offer and she glinted at him in typical Lucia style.

Already up with the pack as he spoke.

Joe thought she looked more refreshed after her flying visit to Repugia. Younger and perhaps more feminine. Jake doing his business? Or had she found somebody else to keep her happy?

'Huge, Joe, just huge, if the dollar was rising. They could all sell out with a clear conscience, especially if it was a knock-out cash deal in dollars. They could arbitrage it all over town and they'd make millions on the side. That way they could salve their consciences for the policy holders and still go out to dinner...'

Joe laughed at her vehemence and trundled out his line.

'Nobody believes me about the dollar but we'll see. I have a man who looks at these things and he swears that the dollar is about to take off...'

'Who is this guy, Joe? He sounds a fruit cake.'

'Chap called Moley, old style City chap. Lots of nose for situations. Not many of his ilk left now. A dying breed. He swore to me that the dollar would boom...'

Lucia was too young to understand about street arabs like Stanley. Moley sounded better. Truth was a variable where she was concerned. She might have heard of him and if she was familiar with the name then it would have a refreshingly reassuring sound to it for her.

'Tell me something, Joe, while we speak... Rivers Pugh, Global's CEO, now how well do you know him? Did you ever run across him in your travels?'

'Never once Lucia. He's a mystery to me as much as to you. I've met him from afar on the circuit but no more than that. He's young isn't he?'

'Very young. But capable. Very capable. Impressive. Until recently, that is. When he started off, he seemed to know how to cut a deal. Very few of them went wrong for him, from what I've been able to establish with some certainty. But then the successful deal flow just dried up. His touch seems to have deserted him. That's why the institutions are not so friendly or supportive now.'

'Of course. But he's one of Sloane School's finest products,' Joe reassured her.

He refrained from adding that in his view, and with plenty of evidence to back him up, Rivers Pugh was a natural born killer. Not helpful at all to add that small detail, he judged.

And then of course Lucia didn't know Rivers as Joe knew him, residing as he did cheek by jowl with Global's charismatic enigmatic and maniacally driven Chief Executive at Pugh Park. Lady Pugh's death had not affected him like his sister Perdita. He seemed barely to have registered her demise, so keen was he on closing his next deal – or the one after that. He worked all the hours and he never let up for a second.

'I'm surprised you don't know him Joe. I would have thought he was just your type…'

'Don't forget Lucia that I was out of things for a while. And that was when he was making his mark at Crecy, before he reversed into Global… If you miss part of a generation, you miss the whole shebang in my experience… He took over from…Now what was his name…?'

Lucia quoted the name.

'That's right. That's the fellow. I didn't know him either.'

That was Lie Number Two in the space of two minutes. Joe recalled a grisly death of Sir David, Global's chief, by his own hand to be followed by a charismatic and tasteless exhibition of public mourning by his widow Lady C. But that was not part of the Rivers story. He declined to make reference of it to Lucia. She was too young to know about such things. No point in burdening her with premature disclosures of information.

'If Rivers went on the board of Detroit Fire, then it actually might almost look like a reverse. It could be promoted in that way. The Chron would certainly buy that line and once you've got the Chron you've more or less got the rest of the London press. So it all looks good, as of now. Over to you Joe. How good is this guy of yours, Moley? What's the strength of his strong dollar story? It is almost certainly a deal making factor for us.'

As she spoke thus so appraisingly, Lucia tugged at her nose in an act of vintage Maitland mannerism which took Joe scudding back to his good times at Martins Bank; Spongo Maitland her father; and then by an odd quirk of memory presentation, to Emma Bales herself. She crept into his mind with her twirl and her broad smile and her optimism. He wondered briefly just where she was now and what she was doing...With that money and her reconstituted shape, she ought to be doing well for herself, especially since Emma hunted on a global scale. The Caribbean seemed like a long way away in both miles and time.

Then it was back to matters in hand. Lucia had some extra news for him.

'Oh and Joe while we're about it, Jake's off the deal but Tommy's still on it. So if you hear any rumours about Tommy, you've just had the truth of the matter.'

'The very idea of a reshuffle amazes me. I didn't think it was scheduled.'

Lucia ground out the news from Repugia with aplomb.

'Jake has decided to stay in Italy. You remember he was conflicted in a small way, so he stayed in Italy while I worked here during the summer. Seems that he was spotted playing football in the park and now he's been signed up by Roma.'

Joe looked at her quizzically.

'Does that make a difference to the team'.

'Not really. He was always better at football than trading. That's where his true vocation lies.'

End of subject; end of Jake; let's move on...Typical Lucia.

She turned back to the papers piled on her desk. That was Joe's cue to depart. He was dismissed. Lucia had lost interest in the discussion. She was back in the deal. She couldn't help it, despite the undertones of extra femininity which had blown into the room alongside her; her new guy was obviously pleasing her. She was a well brought up girl with impeccable manners away from the markets – but then something happened when she was involved in a deal. She had an abruptness and almost a harshness to her then that formed the hallmark of her operating style. She was feared for her intelligence and her directness. Away from the deals, she was like a lily, she was so reticent. But when trading, she was like a tigress. She functioned in manic bursts of energy and perception where good manners came a long way second, and her hands were on the deal's throat.

Curiously, that was all accepted quite easily by the markets.

Joe left her office and wandered through the dealing rooms, gauging the excitement of the market by the depth and pitch of the shouting. Not much to be heard ahead of New York in an hour or so; London and Europe were waiting for the traders out of the US. One of the girls was slowly waggling her bottom in teasing derision at a trader away to Joe's left on the Italian bonds pitch. He watched her closely as he gorged on a sandwich. That was about the strength of the activity at that hour. The rest of the traders were reading; eating; drinking coffee; or staring quietly at the ceiling. Noise levels were low.

Slow day, he reckoned, slow day...

He fetched up at the director's dining room for lunch as an afterthought and there as luck might have it he found himself face to face with Felix. That shocked him briefly. He would have preferred more time to mull Felix and his game-plan. Also Felix's hole in the ground. But there was nobody else in the room apart from the waitress. They had both arrived simultaneously. Just the two of them in the dining room. There was nowhere to go to hide.

Nothing for it but to lunch together, especially since the waitress, seeing them both come in together, naturally assumed that they were together.

'Mr Joe and Mr Felix, my two favourite directors. How nice,' she said as she positioned them together at her best table right next to the window which gave onto the City; the Thames and the rest of London. So she hadn't heard the rumours either, thought Joe as he took his place opposite Felix. She at least is still smiling in my direction.

'Morning Felix.'

'Good morning Joe. And how are we today? I must say, Donnelly thinks a great deal of your expertise. I was very struck this morning by his deference towards you at the meeting.'

This meant that Donnelly would have it pointed out to him quite forcibly at a future date just where his best interests lay.

Nothing in that statement was lost in translation. Felix was fast onto the attack in a commanding way. Joe let him come at him. It was an intriguing moment for him, which he planned to savour.

Just think of it – £25 million advanced on nothing, a hole in the ground deep down there in Putney. By the open-handed Bank of Quiff, no less. Amazing…!

So here they were seated together as serious and respected players at the ABC bank, former comrades in arms in a dark and dirty trade of yesteryear which had no purchase or respect in the commercial currency of today. Now they were so deeply divided to the point that both were contemplating the extinction of the other. Such was the strength of society's conventions that this could never be admitted by either of them. So they would sit there and eat their food together, each with his hand trembling over his dagger – and they would talk…

'Tell me Felix, just what was the name of that forger you made so much money with, you know the man who forged the Hitler Diaries and swindled Stern? You were so pleased with that deal I remember you nearly got shot by the Wall guards.'

Joe also was fast to the punch. Felix had not expected the sally. He was taken unawares. He wanted to concentrate on the here and now as he ground Joe into the earth. The reference to his past flummoxed him. He paused, failed to prevent himself from looking around the dining room conspiratorially, and then smiled at Joe as a last resort. It was like a release. He showed his teeth as he grinned. He looked younger fresher and more like the Felix of old but very fleetingly. He shed his responsibility very quickly.

The waitress hovered over them with a smile as she took the order. She did so delight to see those two directors together at lunch! They were in her view the best of the ABC bunch! Her approval added to the ambiance of the occasion. The waitress bobbed off and Felix prepared to speak.

'For one moment, Joe, and just one moment, I am prepared to speak about the past. Do not think for one moment that you can escape from me but I am prepared to enjoy a truce with you for just this lunch…'

Like the Felix of old, he then looked at the ceiling and laughed.

'His name was Kujau, Konrad Kujau. We came from the same town, you know, Loebau, which is quite close to Dresden. About forty miles distant...He was fifteen years older than me...'

Felix looked as if he was enjoying himself as he strolled through memory lane.

'Again Joe do not think that I am letting up on you because that would not be true. I have old scores to settle with you and the Fat Man, serious scores which we must talk about and very shortly, before you leave the ABC Bank, which you will also do very shortly. I am arranging for you to leave shortly, as you know.'

Joe raised an eyebrow at this assertion as Felix ploughed on like a man in a hurry released unexpectedly into a secret garden.

'...But meanwhile Kujau...You know we took Stern for over £2 million...All for diaries which he aged by pouring tea over them to make the pages look old. You wouldn't believe it! And the diary entries! They were so puerile. We were astonished. Konrad used to fall asleep writing them, they were so boring, and I had to take over. The world marvelled at our prose I can tell you when I revealed a Fuehrer obsessed by his farting and his bad breath!...Must not forget tickets for the Olympic Games for Eva, that was the kind of thing I put in the Diaries. And this from Hitler who took on the whole world in war. There were no limits to the gullibility of the West. That was the first thing I learned from the Diaries...'

He paused, looked round again to see if anyone had observed the old Felix saunter from his lair and then reassured, continued.

'Poor Konrad, it all drove him mad. He couldn't take it. He was making £50 a word – a word, mark you – from the diaries, so he started to go insane with the excitement of it. He would go to nightclubs and insist on being addressed as General Kujau, and then spend £3000 a night on drink and drugs. That kind of thing gets a man noticed in a small town... It was hardly surprising that the police caught up with him and that he went to jail...But do you know, they never got the money back, so even when Konrad came out of jail, he still had enough left to start a gallery of forgeries in Stuttgart...Genuine forgeries of Hitler's paintings were what he exhibited. That was what he called them. It was preposterous...And the reason why he could do that was because I took charge of his money and kept it for him while he was in jail. When he came out everything had changed because the Wall was down by then, so our little game of milking the West had to take on a different aspect…'

'You don't mean that Stasi were behind the Diaries?'

Felix looked evasive, as he always had done when asked a direct question about the East German secret police, even in the rain beside the Wall years ago.

'Of course they were Joe. You are not the complete idiot, I trust. It was just a scam which worked. OK so Konrad went to jail for a time but that was a small price to pay for the privileged position he came to occupy in the West. He was trusted by you – I mean the West – and that was a great help to us.'

Joe stared at Felix and thought about the Fat Man. The Fat Man had been very, very interested in Konrad at the time, Joe recalled. So had Felix and the Fat Man been doing a little private line together?

'But that's all over now, isn't it, Felix?'

Felix's tone of voice began to change. It was tighter. The humour had gone out of it now and the communing was over. It was back to global warfare again. Such a pity, thought Joe. Gossip can be fun, especially about old times beside the Wall.

'Of course, Joe of course. Everybody knows that we are all friends now. The Wall is down. It is ridiculous to imagine that the Cold War continues.'

'Well, that's good to know Felix. Now what's this about my leaving ABC shortly. I have no plans to go. You surprised me there.'

Felix tried to contain himself but failed. In the limit all self control breaks down under stress. It was happening now with Felix before Joe's eyes. Felix was like a man wrestling with a boa constrictor within him.

'No, Joe, you know that you have to go – and quite shortly. It is important that you understand that. I don't think for a moment that anyone actually believes that you are a Communist agent….'

'Ah…'

So that's it, thought Joe, that's the rumour you've been spreading, you squalid little fucker. You've been saying that I'm some kind of fucking Stasi agent, while all along it was you who did that particular turn. What a neat little trick – and how typical of you, you rat-faced louse. No wonder the secretaries have been turning their noses up at me when they've been fed that particular anti-patriotic line, you sneaky bastard.

No, nobody truly believes it…

'Felix…'

'Don't worry Joe it won't last much longer…It will all be over shortly. But you see, you have to go because otherwise I will really have to kill you. You have no idea just how angry I am with you…That is why you have to go. I have been bottling this rage up for years and now it's starting to become quite uncontrollable…'

Joe was feeling the heat on the breeze. He also noted that Felix's English was breaking up under stress.

'OK, Felix, we're old hands at this and we know what we're talking about – Berlin, all points East, the Fat Man and all the rest. We've both been there. I don't need to talk about a thing. So you just tell me why, quite coolly, you plan to take me out. Just tell me why, OK? This is a civilised place, so we can talk about it calmly before you blow my head off. So why…?'

'Mind if I join you?'

They both looked up at the same time, realising that their heads had been almost knocking together as the temperature in the discussion mounted. It was the Quiff, cigarette between his dark brown finger tips, who had stolen upon them unobserved. They sprang apart. The Quiff had addressed his question in the main to Felix. His head was tilted in that direction. Joe noted the focus of the Quiff's attention. That was ominous, too.

The Quiff took a long drag on his gasper, and then exhaled smoke all over the table as a mark of his authority. Coughing as he took in some of the smoke, Joe hoped it was the Quiff's 50th of the day already. He glanced quickly across the river in the distance hoping to spot the Reaper on his way.

In vain.

'We were talking about the dollar.'

Joe got his hit in first as Felix appeared to reconstruct his face from eye-popping, tack-spitting anger and back into its normal mould of caring, almost bovine, Teutonic stupidity. The Wurtemberg courtier's smile etched itself across his features like the pattern of machine-gun fire in the sand.

'Good thing to talk about the dollar. You were very impressive about it this morning, Joe, but I believe Felix here has some views on it as well, don't you Felix. Let's give Felix a chance to give his views an airing over lunch shall we, Joe? It can't harm anyone to hear the alternative view on currencies and...Just one moment, Andrew, yes, I'll be with you in a second.'

The Quiff had spotted a well-connected acolyte in the other corner of the dining room. It was his clear duty to help such people in their brief moments of distress, using his patronage to maximum extent. That was the Quiff's management style. He saw his job as an integral part of his assault on the shirearchy.

Kamikaze attack, Joe hoped and trusted.

'...Be back in a second, boys. I'll have my usual, Felix.'

Pausing to light yet another cigarette, the Quiff moved off heavily in Andrew's direction, leaving Joe almost leaping out of his skin with rage at Felix's implied promotion above him. Joe felt himself glow white with anger. The mental circuits burned away.

Felix seized his moment. He sounded almost sympathetic as he gave Joe the deadly information.

'Listen carefully Joe while I explain it to you. We won't get a second chance so I will tell you very quickly. No e-mails for us, my friend. The Fat Man was running his squad in Berlin, of which you were one. Correct?'

'Correct.'

'And me too?'

'Correct again.'

They might have been talking about the weather.

'Towards the end of his time there – and your time, too – the Fat Man got bored with espionage. He could see it was all coming to an end, that the Cold War was over, and that the Wall was bound to come down sooner or later. So he would be out of a job. End of his toy time. So being the Fat Man he turned to other things in search of the angle...As you well know.'

Felix held up his hand in front of Joe and rubbed his thumb and second finger together in Joe's face for the second time in living memory. The Quiff was at his most attentive far away across the room.

'Not enough money in espionage,' he said to my father. 'I know this because my father told me, after the Fat Man had involved him in his racket.'

'Racket, Felix? This is news to me.'

Felix sniffed in disbelief and then nodded curtly.

'My father was part of Stasi too. Like the whole family. The Fat Man had the bright idea that he could start an import-export business in Berlin but this time in people. There was confusion all around in Berlin as you know at the time because everybody higher up in Stasi knew what was going to happen as the regime came to an end. But the guards on the ground weren't told until the last moment. So there were lots of people who wanted to get from one side of the Wall to the other in a hurry to stake their claims – both ways – but they were impeded by the controls. So that is what the Fat Man cooked up with my father. It was highly profitable as you might have imagined and my father....'

Felix' eyes grew moist as he spoke. The emotion locked within him was at seething point. Joe saw both his hands clench into fists at the effort of self-control. The eyes were still moist. He spoke more slowly, but the words still came out, little by little.

The waitress appeared at their table looking less sunny now that she knew where the Quiff was lunching and with whom. Joe intervened. Speaking casually, and with a wave of his hand, he indicated Felix, now dabbing his eyes with a handkerchief and told her that Felix had hiccups; he was holding his breath.

'The Quiff will have his usual.'

The waitress took the order without comment and showed concern for Felix who intimated in turn that the problem was passing. In a frenzy of clucks, the waitress bobbed off again.

With one fist still clenched, Felix continued. The agony of confession had eased slightly but not much.

'...I loved my father, I loved him very much...The Fat Man's idea meant a lot to us all because suddenly we could see some form of freedom...We talked a lot about how much better life was going to be after the Wall came down, and we were very close. The Fat Man of course kept charge of the money because there was no way that my father could entrust it to the East German banking system. You understand that, don't you Joe?'

'Perfectly, Felix.'

'When you want to look innocent, Joe, you know that you can always assume the pose. It fools everybody. You were always able to play the part to perfection in Berlin of the little boy lost which is why I suspect you so much now...I have watched you manipulate the Quiff round your little finger with admiration...And you mean to tell me that you don't know what happened then?'

'I haven't a clue Felix. This is the first time I ever heard tell of anything like this racket of the Fat Man's. I swear that to you, so help me God, whoever She is.'

But Felix was not amused.

'You are so rich now Joe. It's well known at ABC. How did you come to get so rich?'

'Trading the market Felix. It's all my own money. I made it myself.'

And that was where the problem lay. Impossible for Felix to believe that Joe the fresh- and open – faced lad who had done his bird in Berlin, obedient to the Fat Man's wiles as he dodged the bullets, could have matured into Joe, the artful and knowing stock market operator.

So now Felix gave him a look of blank and unconstrained hostility, as if to say 'Just don't come the old soldier with me, my friend. This is far too important to play games. Be serious for once'.

Joe met his gaze levelly and defiantly.

'It's true, Felix. Why should I lie to you?'

But Felix had been through the same espionage training schedule as Joe – if in doubt, lie. Lie blankly, openly and lie big. Lie huge, if necessary. That made for a serious collision of perceptions as the past collapsed into the present. For both of them. And most likely fatal for one of them at least.

Felix ploughed on with his tale of tragedy and catastrophe. The eyes wobbled in their sockets.

'You can imagine what happened, indeed you will know what happened. Some body informed on my father and he was taken away one morning. The Stasi called for him, for one of their own, and bundled him into a van. We never saw him again. Well, that is not quite true…We did see a little more of him…'

Joe was silent as Felix stared at the ceiling, fighting for control so that he could ejaculate the words. Joe could see that the Quiff was concluding his discussion with Andrew to their mutual satisfaction and preparing to take his leave. Much handshaking amid those special office smiles which display mutual support. The Quiff was setting the world to rights, to his assumed advantage.

'About three months after my father disappeared, we were sent his fingers in a box. One morning they arrived at the door. All ten of them , with his ring on one of the fingers for the purposes of identification. Nothing more. We never saw or heard from him again. We presumed that he died in one of the Stasi torture dungeons, quite alone and screaming in his pain. We have no way of knowing this. We never buried him. There was no service, no ceremony of farewell…No ceremony at all…'

Damp eyes popping with pain, Felix had managed to make his statement and now stared straight ahead of him looking bereft as the Quiff lingered briefly by another lunch table to deal more crisply with another, less socially advantaged, suppliant.

'The Fat Man disappeared, and so did you. That was years ago. Five, ten years, who cares? It all happened around the same time. My father disappeared, so did you and so did the Fat Man. Pure coincidence, of course, as you will tell me, oh Joe with those bright and oh so innocent eyes.'

But, Felix, the Fat Man is dead…

Joe realised at that moment that he was most likely doomed, caught in a trap of truly terrifying dimensions. In a fit of murderous rage, it had been Joe who had killed the Fat Man. Years ago. But that would cut no ice with Felix who would automatically assume that it was Joe now who had collected on the transit deals. Because Joe was rich. And no Fat Man around to say 'Nay; not true' to all of this because he was six feet under now, courtesy of Joe's shot that caught the Fat Man between the eyes and tore his brains out.

In Fleet Street.

Murder most foul…

So if anything it was Joe now who had all the loot. All the more reason therefore for Felix to blow Joe's head right off his shoulders. He definitely had that option.

'It was suggested to me, in passing, that it had been a Westerner who had informed against my father and that was why drastic action had needed to be taken. So you can see the scenario quite easily can't you Joe? My father does all the hard work of getting the people ferried from A to B across the Wall, or vice versa, and the Fat Man takes the money. Then when he judges the moment is correct, he informs against my father so that he can impress his superiors back in London that he is doing such a good job busting into Stasi, at the same time as he gets rid of his Stasi business partner. An elegant double-cross, yes, Joe? The Fat Man collects both ways. I can tell you, Joe, that I have waited a long time to explain this all to you… Because as you know, as you alone know, the Fat Man was certainly capable of doing that. He had that kind of mind, as you alone know again, because you are the only living testimony apart from me, to his existence, let alone his duplicity. As for the money, well of course there was no trace of that anywhere after my father died. The Fat Man had never actually told my father what he had done with the money so how were we to know where to look? As if it mattered anyway when he was dead and all that remained was…'

Small, very sad, pause.

Felix had a touch more self-control now. His moment of madness was passing. Sanity was slowly returning. He had told his story about Berlin's mean streets.

'The first, Joe, that I see of you again is when we meet here at ABC Bank and I find that you are very rich, Joe. As for the Fat Man, I presume that he has escaped to some exotic island where he is now enjoying his ill-gotten gains, eh Joe? You would know that, Joe. You were always very close to the Fat Man. So where is he now Joe? Where is the Fat Man?'

Improbably, in the midst of such anguished Berlin memories and in the plush surroundings of the ABC Bank, Joe was rescued from a reply by the Quiff, who just then sat down heavily at their table, red faced, and took a deep draw on his cigarette before extinguishing it reluctantly in the ashtray beside him on the table.

The mercurial Quiff was close to cursing mode. Joe welcomed that as a diversion.

'Ordered for me have you, boys? Good. It's about time we all had some lunch together…Good banking is about long talking, that's what I've always said and always will do. We don't communicate enough. It's an old-fashioned business despite the hype. And I want us to start sharing our contacts, you especially Joe. You're far too close about who you know and don't know in the City. You should spread these contacts around. Don't you agree Felix?'

His platitudinous bonhomie was almost clammy in its impact. Neither Joe nor Felix blanched. They both attended to his words with rapt attention. They were used to the Quiff's treacherous ramblings. He always without exception spoke with forked tongue. In that respect he was a small perfectly formed replica of the Bank of England itself. Joe saw Felix with perfect composure take a sip of water. The hand holding the glass shook a little but otherwise his calm was absolute. The features were rigid and the eyes were dry. Suddenly, he was the very model of a very modern banker.

Bravo Felix but oh Christ what a fuck-up this all is, thought Joe, left to his own thoughts as the Quiff talked to Felix about the training courses he wanted to see him take. The restaurant hummed genteelly with the busy, bristling lunchtime chat of senior bank executives keen to stay in line with the team while showing enough initiative to advance personal career prospects.

Eventually the conversation between the Quiff and Felix became so intense that Joe was able to exit from the table without breaching protocol. No sense in staying as gooseberry. He wandered down the corridors to his office in a mental whirl, stunned by Felix's revelations.

What to do, what to do?

Give Felix money to get him off his back? Confront him with the truth and admit that he killed the Fat Man? Warn Felix that he knew about the loans to Fat Man Enterprises? Maybe get close to the Quiff and shop Felix? That would be difficult if it backfired bearing in mind how Felix viewed Joe's integrity. That would invite an immediate bullet from Felix's hit men, treasure or not.

So what to do, what to do? Yes, what to do? It was not a rhetorical question. Very likely Perdita was now in play assuming Felix eventually trailed Joe to Pugh Park.

And blew his cover and the Rivers Pugh deal all at once.

It was quite a little cocktail Joe was holding in his hand.

Running through all Joe's thoughts was the doleful realisation, in itself quite devastating, that the Fat Man had been a crook and a thief, a blackmailer and a blackguard. All his life most likely, yes all his life. The Service lent itself to such deceptions, relying as it did on trust in men skilled in deception among far flung fields. Feet of clay, Joe told himself. He had been a fool and the Fat Man's patsy. Putty in his hands. All of this was very shocking. The Fat Man had been an icon in Joe's landscape. He had guided Joe in his career and his development. His maxims peppered Joe's thinking. His counsel was Joe's counsel. Joe had grown up via the Fat Man and reached maturity with the old man, dead or alive, dinning wisdom into his ear along the route.

And now...?

Such wisdom...

Now the Fat Man was indisputably worse than sheep droppings in the fold. Worse, far worse...This was treachery and betrayal and everything else. There could be no doubt whatsoever that Felix was telling the truth when he spoke in the restaurant.

People do not lie when they weep in public, and certainly not somebody with the blazing sincerity and grief of a Stasi-reared Felix. The eyes had it in spades. He had not been faking it.

For others, this would be comparable to the tragic discovery that a very beautiful drop-dead gorgeous woman, adored and pitied by all on account of her husband's brutalities and infidelities, was no better than a worthless hypocrite, faithful only to her vanities. But – and this is the difficult part – even after her lovers' discoveries, life and her beauty would continue to impose their sway, so strong was habit, the lure and the addiction.

Such cowardly repentances...

Likewise for Joe and the Fat Man. As he well knew, extirpating the Fat Man from the depths of his being would be impossible. The syntax of allegiance was second nature.

But adjustments had to be made...Felix's words could not be ignored. Nor the clear and present danger which they implied.

Joe rambled down the corridors in shock. He found his office, closed the door and tried to think, alone in the room high above the bustling City.

Such a shock as the one administered by Felix required wholesale rearrangement of the mental furniture. British Intelligence faced a similar problem when it tried to acknowledge that Philby, former head of MI5, had always worked for the Russians. Always, always, always...Had in other words been a complete mountebank, assumed stammer or no assumed stammer.

In Joe's case, the purgation needed to be done quickly if he was to survive. Unerring was the word. He felt that immediately. He knew he was at risk. It had to be right. He had to be accurate in the process of expunging. It behoved Joe well to make a swift and sure adjustment because Felix was after him with a knife and a gun and God knew what else – and Felix appeared to enjoy a winning line at ABC Bank, despite milking the bank for untold millions.

So Joe was a cipher and Felix was a powerful force in town with the Quiff safely suborned and eating from his hand... Felix was the governor sound in all of this and Joe had better get used to that.

'Oh my God,' thought Joe, 'oh my God. This is impossible. I see no way out of this at all. I'm totally doomed. It is literally impossible for me to tell Felix what really happened to the Fat Man – that I blew his brains out in Fleet Street one fine sunny morning. Felix will treat it as an excuse to do the same to me. And just wait until Felix gets a sniff of Pugh Park and goes to town on that little box of tricks...'

Joe told himself that Felix must not get to that little port of call. That would surely rip him apart to see Perdita torn to pieces by Felix's machinations. Fingers, he thought to himself, yes, fingers delivered to the office with a Hampshire postmark. One finger would carry a pretty ring for purposes of identification…

Oh Christ, oh God…The cruelty of it was unthinkable.

Joe shivered in the warmth of his office.

Distraught and wondering what his meetings schedule for the afternoon might be, as if he cared, Joe phoned his rented telephone number for messages. Pure subterfuge on his part. At the time Joe had thought it a clever, precautionary idea. His number was tagged with a Sloane Square exchange. That way he appeared to live close to London's SW3, whereas in fact he resided deep in Hampshire. More camouflage and more concealment.

He thanked God for his instinctive camouflage.

It was the same with his Hampshire address. Pugh Park was equi-distant between two railway stations in the county, both of which had taxi ranks. Joe always made his driver drop him at one of the stations, making much of the temporary nature of his stay and inferring that he was a paying guest on the lookout to purchase a property. At no other time than now had Joe been so grateful for his intuitive sense of concealment and evasion. It might not have been pretty, but it had served him well – as now. He left few traces. His driver was so bamboozled by it all that he collected estate agents' notices on houses for sale while he waited for Joe at either station.

There were two messages for him, one from Treadwell shouting 'How about some Bridge you elusive swine' and then one from the Reform Club saying that there was a letter awaiting him at the club from Italy. Apparently, the letter had arrived some time previously. Joe could not have seen it; he had been avoiding the club recently. Then there had been a follow-up telephone call for him at the club from somewhere in Italy requesting confirmation that the letter had arrived. The caller had asked whether or not Joe could be contacted soonest to pick up the said letter. The letter was not urgent but important, as the messenger from the club stressed at the end of the call.

Joe was intrigued. He knew nobody in Italy. His interest in the country had ceased as soon as his relationship with Lucy-Miranda had broken up, now many years since. So who was writing to him so urgently that it provoked a check call from the club itself?

Pascal? Impossible. He had seen neither hide nor hair of her since the great gift-fair entanglement. Lucy-Miranda…? That was always a possibility. That would be rich, he thought. But a Lucy-Miranda with or without Charles, her new husband – that was the key point. Emma? Joe ruled her out of the frame automatically. He was off her list. Ever since her failure to keep their appointment in the West Indies and plight their troth on the beach to the pounding of the midnight waves he had written that particular young lady out of his life. Besides, Italy was not her beat…Never had been…But who knew what these days…?

Meanwhile there was a letter. That was fact.

The thought of a mystery letter caught his fancy, especially one which had been flagged so heavily via a follow-up phone call from Italy…He noted that his agenda might just allow him to call at the Reform Club en route that evening for Pugh Park.

So who had sent him a letter and then made the phone call?

More from the habit of routine and still immersed in his conjectures, Joe ventured forth from his office to check with the Perfect what his agenda amounted to that afternoon. The Perfect barely bothered to check the diary. She knew the agenda backwards – or the adjusted one.

She flashed her teeth at him in reply. Her expression of detached and moveable loyalty spoke volumes. After all, she had it on good authority that Joe was a Communist spy. So how could she continue to serve him with all the commitment at her command? All her body language spoke of withdrawal.

'You've had a few cancellations, Joe, so you're basically free to roam this afternoon after three o' clock.'

Joe sensed power start to pass from him with a crash as the Perfect knelled his involuntary removal from power at ABC. Nobody but nobody had meetings cancelled in that bank. It just didn't happen. This was the Quiff at work extinguishing the awkward squad.

'You surprise me with those cancellations…'

The Perfect tolled another clang. She said it all with near-aplomb like an understudy suddenly called upon to play a much-rehearsed part.

'You know that Hans is taking over from Felix as Head of Banking for the time being?'

'Hans?'

Who Hans?

'Yes, Hans, Felix's deputy.'

'I didn't know this. When did this happen? Has it been announced?'

'It's been on the cards for weeks. The rumour machine has been full of it. I'm surprised you hadn't heard, Joe. It's not like you to be out of the loop.'

She sparkled brightly as she informed Joe, her now- reviled Communist boss, of his vital information deficit. She had played this part a thousand times in front of her dressing-table mirror at home. She adored her lines.

'You see, Felix is off on his course.'

'Course?'

'Yes, the Quiff has decided that Felix has to learn more about the markets…'

She paused for effect, half opening her mouth to flash her crowns, just as the girls did on the soaps when they delivered an ultimatum. She felt empowered.

'…Your area…'

Joe nodded as he saw the pattern unfold before him. He was getting the bad news all at once and it fitted together neatly. Felix's attack at lunchtime; the Quiff's insistence on a tete a tete with Felix; and then the bombshell of Hans' promotion. And what about that £25 million, he found himself saying under his breath as the Perfect completed her pattern-bombing raid.

'He'll be away for some time and then there are some more changes expected…'

Joe completed her sentence for her.

'When he comes back…Big changes.'

She closed her mouth and raised both eyebrows like a tollgate. She looked miffed at the interruption. This was not in the script.

'How did you know that?'

'Intuition. It comes with age. You'll get there. Quite quickly, I would think.'

Joe went back into his office and stared at the prices screen as the currencies went bob-bob-bob up and down across the world. Yes, the Quiff was in a hurry. Doubtless worked on by Felix, he wanted one deputy now, not two, and to fill in Felix's ignorance in vital areas, like the whole of world markets, he was sending him on a course. Ahead of Felix's big promotion, just to get him acquainted with the big picture. During the time of Felix's absence, or most likely just before his return, he, Joe, would be fired. That way Hans, Felix and the Quiff could all enjoy their little scam together. Let peculation thrive, thought Joe. They're welcome to it all. They're skunks.

Joe calculated some more. It wouldn't take long to achieve all these changes, Joe was certain of that. The Quiff would be ruthless, once unchained and unafraid of the consequences. The Perfect considered it a done deal already.

Dolefully, Joe thought about his probabilities. He found a tiny piece of cheer.

'I might just have been able to complete my Global deal by the time the Quiff boots me out...It will be a close run thing but the bid may be more than just launched by the time he moves against me. The timing of that small part of my Pandora's box may be just on my side...Once the bid is up and running, Lucia can take charge. She'll do it standing on her head. Provided it all sticks to the rules, she'll be fine...If it runs on grooves and everything hangs together, it'll be fine.'

'And pray God she never finds out where I live either. I'm already conflicted in about 500 different ways on this bid. If she finds out that I'm actually living at Pugh Park with Rivers, Christ knows what she'll do...'

Once a Maitland, always a Maitland. Spongo would have taken a whip to me...Good old Spongo. '

Idly, his mind elsewhere, from sheer habit, Joe continued to stare at the screen, letting the ideas flow through him. He was thinking about Felix and the Quiff and Hans and the Perfect, trying to get a line on them all. It was all very tough but it might just be make-able. Now that he scrutinised the scenario more closely, he could see that time and opportunity might just, and very briefly, be on his side. He might be able to slip his deal between the cracks in the groove as the shooting started. But not if his life collapsed into one single compartment, that was for sure.

He stared some more at the screen. He was puzzled within his abstraction. The changes in the currencies registered with him but left him baffled. There was something going on amidst all this chaos that he failed to understand. There was a lesion in structure where no lesion should have featured. It didn't hang together in the matrix. Something was happening out there, small, indistinct but definitely an aberrant movement, like a radio signal from the distant stars.

His phone rang. It was Felix. More death threats most likely. Joe talked to him while looking at his screen. He switched to the matrix of the forwards as Felix barked at him. But that was no more helpful. If anything more pronounced. More lesion but this time even clearer. Rents now in forex.

So just what was going on? Where was Stanley? When could he talk to him?

'You got the message, Joe?'

'Which one Felix? There have been so many...'

'Don't get so smart with me, Joe. That's another of your failings. This is very serious. For you. I told your secretary to mention to you that I was going away for a time...'

Felix's English was back under control.

'Oh that message. Yes, I got that. It was kind of you to let me know – and her of course. You'll enjoy learning about the markets. Quaint little things they are...'

Meanwhile an unknowable bing – bing – bing from the currencies on the screen in front of him.

'She was very happy to take the message. As you will have realised, she will be working for me very shortly. So she is just getting acquainted with my management style. We'll get along very well together after the Quiff has ratified it all.'

'That was certainly the impression she gave me. I think she'll give you all the loyalty she has given me. More, possibly.'

Felix failed to spot the irony but carried on hectoring. Joe continued staring at his screen in fascination as they spoke. The price movements were really starting to look compulsive. The forex matrix was busting up all over the globe. And the $, like some Moby Dick of a currency, was beginning to blow. Salvation is only ever a state of mind, thought Joe.

'Of course, that is as it should be. Your secretary knows her place. Which is just as well for her. Now, Joe listen to me. I will be thinking about you while I'm away on my course...'

'Learning to take over my job...'

'Learning my new job. You heard what I had to say at lunchtime. I meant every word of it – and every word is true. When I come back, you and I will have another little chat but that time it will be backed up by just a little more – how shall I say...'

'Bite?'

'That will do as a word. But you know what I mean, of course. Berlin Rules. That kind of thing.'

Joe did indeed know what Felix meant by Berlin Rules. Explosions and not many left to tell the tale – that was Berlin Rules. Shoot first, and very quickly, before your man was even awake. That was Berlin Rules. It wouldn't take much to bring out the hit man in Felix anyway. Joe knew that as well.

'Any obvious way out for me, Felix? You know that all of this is a mystery to me, Felix, as I said to you at lunchtime. I know that you don't believe me, although it's the truth. So there we are. Do I have any chance of a recount?'

'I want to know where the Fat Man is; where the money is; and what happened to my father. I want answers to all three questions. You're the only man left who can tell me. So that's what I want to know. Come up with those answers and you'll be fine. Just dandy.'

'Can I phone a friend? Or just ask the audience? Maybe we can go 50 : 50?'

That floored Felix. His command of idiomatic English failed him. He was silent. Felix didn't like jokes very much. Who could blame him?

'Felix, what if I don't know what happened to the Fat Man; to your father; and to the money? What do I do then? What if I'm completely innocent in all of this.'

'I have been on the road on this for too long, Joe, to be...'

'...Fobbed off?'

Felix's English normally cracked under strain. But he was an obstinate man.

'…Put off by you now. But I will give you a tiny benefit of the doubt. During the time I'm away, I will be making some inquiries about you…'

'Good. That's better.'

Joe's heart sank. That was the worst thing he could have heard. That meant Felix and his heavies would be combing through his background. Would they get to Pugh Park? As soon as they did that and discovered his stately way of life, there would be no holding Felix's paranoid suspicions. An English gentleman, to boot…Living in grandeur and seclusion and both unsuspected by all and sundry at the Bank. Joe could almost hear Felix's brain grunt into gear as he meshed Pugh Park in with his suppositions about Joe, money and the Fat Man.

An idea occurred to Joe, an inspirational suggestion that winged its way towards him via Hermes, God of Shadows and Spies, while Felix was reaching for the jugular. It stemmed from Felix's faint suggestion that the position might be negotiable. And it brought in its wake the distant tinkle of another far more reaching thought.

All Joe needed was time. And he might be able to buy that, although the idea of trading Felix's dead broken and tortured father for cash revolted him.

'Felix, you think I'm lying and I say I'm not. Agreed?'

'There is no compromise possible here. But on the face of it, yes, I agree.'

'But we were colleagues of a sort, years ago, which must amount to something residual in terms of trust, and I do have money which you know about. Know all about, perhaps? You're a thorough man, Felix, and you've done the checking up. Agreed?'

Joe was thinking about that £25 million loan account in the Fat Man's name. That had to count for something. Felix was not wholly the gentil parfait knight he claimed, not on his previous form which included larking about on the town with Konrad the great forger.

Joe edged towards the crack in the puzzle as Felix grunted again down the line.

'Agreed.'

'This is my proposal. In good faith, pending our further discussions – and clarifications – I will set up an escrow account, not at ABC but somewhere else, and I will pay £1 million into it. Tomorrow. That's not a down payment on the Fat Man but an earnest of my intentions to reach agreement with you on Berlin and its rules…And I say again, I'm not guilty of anything, although you think I am, so let's talk.'

Long, heavy, suspicious and very familiar German brooding pause from Felix.

Joe said nothing and let the television in front of him waft him off to distant climes of speculation. Like his suggestion to Felix, the screen was odd. It looked too much like an attack on a currency not to be an assault of some sorts. It was certainly along the lines of Stanley's suggestion but it was different.

Very different. The wind was blowing hard now on Joe's deal. All he needed was some extra time.

But now Felix had to bite. £1 million is a sizeable sum. Joe sent a prayer back to Hermes. Felix replied. He was puzzled in his convictions. Joe's gambit worked but only up to a point. Hermes was in deaf mode. Or asleep at his post in the clouds next to Jupiter.

'There was far, far more money involved than that. You are talking about a drop in the ocean here. It was £1 million just to get over the Wall. Either way. The traffic at its height was constant. These were very senior officials who were being transported in flight towards the West. Towards the East, there were people trying desperately to repossess their properties taken from them before the War by the Nazis. You must know this, Joe. You were so close to the Fat Man. So you know they were happy to pay big money to stake their claims…Or so they thought. Check with the Fat Man wherever he is. There might be as much as £100 million to £250 million involved. That was how much my father calculated that the Fat Man had made. It might even be more…But the Fat Man will tell you. He will confirm all of this for you. And for me…Just give him a call.'

It was Joe's turn to be astonished. This was a vast sum. His suggestion sounded pitiful.

'I'm astonished by all this, Felix. And I mean that.'

More silence. Then Felix appeared to make up his mind.

'No, Joe, I don't want to enter into negotiations with you. We'll stick to the original arrangements...As discussed over lunch.'

Felix's turn to be formal. Joe felt very sick. He shuddered.

'So you'll come back from your training course, take my job, blow my head off, and stick the £1 million offered in good faith right up your fundament without answering any questions about your father's death?'

'Fundament, what is fundament? But no matter – tell me where the Fat Man is hiding and we might start to talk. But not before...Meanwhile, I'll be watching you.'

Then Felix rang off, leaving Joe without a reply, assuming presumably that he would stew in suspense for however long Felix would be away from the office. Typical Stasi tactics, thought Joe. Always the heavy hand. They can't help it. They can never change their terror approach, democracy or no democracy.

But thank God Felix was departing for a brief while. He would take no action against Joe for a brief period. That was certain – Felix had been brought up in the Eastern bloc and they were trained to proceed by degrees. That plodding approach might just give Joe the chance to wrap up the deal. It only had to be announced and Lucia could do the rest...

Then he was free to roam, as the Perfect had intimated. And roam he would, like crazy...

Joe looked at his TV screen again, took in the aberrant movement of the currencies and was pleased to think that he had a brief rendezvous arranged shortly with Stanley. More matter for mooting over the pints. This would all bear tough, intense discussion over the beer in the back bar of their little pub with Stanley wiping the bubbles from his moustache as he pontificated about his findings.

Joe was starting to recover a little from the shocks over lunchtime. He felt more resilient. He was ready to deliver a little deft rebuke to the Perfect. While there's hope, there's life, he thought as he padded out from his office towards her lair.

'Yes, I've had a brief word with Felix and it's all arranged...'

She looked a touch distraite at Joe's blithe words and pouted away at him with unforgiving eyes across her board, hoping for enlightenment.

'You can get an e-mail to him while he's away on his course can't you?'

'Certainly.'

Her willingness contained a touch of panic. This was no way the script she had written for herself should be evolving. She had Joe biting the carpet in tears at this point.

'Felix and I go way back, as you know. Way, way back. We used to work together, as you know. He never told you that…?'

The Perfect shook her head, looking frightened. Joe was remorseless.

'That surprises me. He must be cooking up something for you if he didn't tell you that. Everybody else knows that we used to be colleagues. Anyway, be that as it may, that's your business. You'll find out more about Felix in time to come. But as a surprise for him on his course I want you to send him this very simple message. Tomorrow. Not today but tomorrow without fail, first thing. Just say this: The Fat Man's very dead. Got that? The Fat Man's very dead. He'll be amused. Tickled pink, in fact. It's a private joke between us of years ago. I know Felix and his sense of humour. He'll roar…'

The Perfect's startled eyebrows moved in perfect symmetry like windscreen wipers as she went through the motions of jotting down the e-mail. So how many Communists were there then working for ABC? And if Joe was supposed to be a Communist but he worked with Felix, then was Felix…Wait until she told the girls all about this…

Like many a Mr and Mrs Blockhead all the world over, she gave up. It just didn't add up very clearly for her. She bent over her machine.

'Where's my driver got to, please?'

'Waiting downstairs as usual for you.'

'Good. Tell him to be ready in five minutes please. I have an urgent appointment in the City.'

The Perfect brightened at that. So Joe had another job in the offing? That was good news. She could tell the girls about that too – and Felix as well. So it would all be fine for Joe in the end.

Joe padded back to his office to gaze at the screens again and to call Moley and confirm their meeting. He was off to see him shortly for a discreet game of kitchen chess. If he could bring the meeting forward, then he could make a gap in his day for the Reform Club and his mystery mail before attending dinner at Pugh Park. Joe was sure that Moley would oblige.

Whether his driver would be so accommodating was another matter. Would he still be willing to ferry him from A to B? The car facility might be the first to go or the last, depending on how the Quiff executed the Last Rites over his dismissed executives. Knowing the Quiff and his eagerness to cause offence to the vulnerable, Joe didn't reckon on holding onto his driver for very long...

★　★　★　★　★

Annie was nervous. She sat at her desk in her office high above the Thames and bit her lip, with the heel of her hand supporting her chin and her fingers clenched like a bunch of bananas in front of her mouth. She was deep in thought. What was to be done? There had to be something which could be done, even for an Intelligence Service so outsmarted, like her own, that it was out of the game completely.

She had received a panic-stricken call that morning from one of her agents. Leadon had been fired from the Chron. The loss of Leadon from the Chron was a big blow. It followed hard on the heels of other gaps suddenly opening up in her line of agents in and around the City as they were mysteriously, and very swiftly, picked up and thrown out of the Square Mile or systematically marginalised. At first the process had been gradual; now it was accelerating. Stobart and Q were wasting no time.

Leadon had been key for her. For years, he had sat there patiently filing his copy and writing to order what he had been told to write either by the Bank of England or by the Chron editor – which amounted to the same thing. Perfect cover. He had been highly intelligent eyes and ears for Annie while viewed as an idiot and a fool by all and sundry in Fleet Street and the City. Again perfect cover. His flow of information had been constant and high grade. Then in the Prague Spring of Stone's new regime, he had stepped out of line in a fit of wilful enthusiasm and shown himself to be a far better informed journalist than anyone had imagined. Result? Wholly predictable. He had now been chopped down by the Bank and replaced by one of its own apparatchiks. Q refused to allow the grass to grow beneath his feet, or anyone else's.

More blindness and more fog for Annie as the Bank of England gradually disappeared from view in a mist of its own making. It was like watching a liner steam into darkness on the high seas.

Leadon had taken it badly. That was clear from the call. He had accepted being a hack but he wasn't taking being an ex-hack at all well. He was out of a job now, after he'd been kicked out of the Chron. He was highly distraught because he had lost the cachet of working for the Chron and because he was despised by former colleagues for having been stupid enough to buy into the new editor's vision; take an independent line; and get himself sacked. Freedom of the press, eat your heart out, thought Annie – the hacks had had their mouths stuffed with gold and stock options by compliant proprietors and loved the whole idea!

Abruptly, the oxygen of approval by his peers had been cut off and Leadon was reacting badly to all of that. He wanted money too, in recompense for all his years as a faithful agent. This was a fair enough request on one level because he had been highly reliable, but it didn't wash otherwise. Agents didn't command a premium rating for all their years of spying once their covers were blown because in actual fact they received their stipends during the years they were on the job – it came up with the rations, not afterwards.

Not a lot of agents understood that small but pertinent distinction. The only one's who did, in Annie's experience, were the ones forced to learn the hard way – like Leadon. Equity was a moveable feast and dividends could be passed – one of the main axioms in intelligence work.

Meanwhile could Annie find a use for Leadon? Could she find something for him to do which would provide him with funds to tide him over? Annie pondered the point. Reinstatement should not be a problem for Leadon – eventually. But meanwhile he should not be left alone for too long, so that Battersea Bridge and the Thames tempted him into a injudicious gesture…Dead agents were no use at all to her…Maybe he should just carry on writing as if nothing had happened.

Maybe…

Now there was a thought, she mused. There might be something in all of that. What happened if he just carried on writing as if nothing had happened? Now, there was a thought, she mused.

And meanwhile what about Joe? Annie was worried about Joe, her longest serving, most reliable and bravest agent. He was out there on his own and taking the hits. He was out of range of her and she was not in communication with him. That was serious. Annie disliked that separation. Agents should not roam. She fully respected Pa Lee's observation and instruction that the encirclement process of the Bank of England was so delicate that no hint of complicity could be allowed. The merest puff of wind on the surface of normality might be enough to alter expectations at the Bank so that Stobart and Q then shifted ground. The plans, as conceived in outline, did not provide for any movement at all by the Bank. It was all too delicately constructed. Otherwise the two parts of the bridge as projected might not meet in the middle. There was no leeway at all in any of this. But nevertheless she wanted to find a way of signalling to Joe that he was watched, and to some extent protected.

Agents should not roam…

She carried on biting her lip and watching the Thames waves flow past her window, lost in thought and speculation.

Again, agents must not be allowed to roam. That was her strongest operating maxim. Annie left her office and went walkabout in the direction of the Tate. She always had her best ideas looking at simple things like pictures. Over time she had found that Picasso was the most stimulating of them all, in terms of bringing forth the ideas.

Dali ran him a close second...

*   *   *   *   *

Joe was stirred into observation on a number of occasions that afternoon. But whatever pattern emerged was too complicated for him to unravel that day. He opted to think about it all another time.

First his driver seemed to know where he was going even before Joe had issued his directions. Almost as if he had been told where to go beforehand. The Barbican and Moley's flat were not so very distant from ABC Bank but it was a complicated journey through the backstreets, requiring precise instructions. But Joe's driver found his way there unerringly. Joe had barely expressed a desire to visit the Barbican to see an old friend before the car had roared off towards Moorgate and London Wall. Joe sat in the back and marvelled at his driver's virtuoso skills in tracking down the precise way into Moley's part of the complex. Normally his driver was a goof when it came to navigation; the first time they had gone to visit Moley, he'd taken the wrong turning 3 times. But this time he could have driven his way there blindfold. That was clear from the way he handled the car. Perhaps he too knew somebody who lived in the Barbican...? Was he used to the in's and out's of the terrain?

Joe let the matter ride in his mind. He didn't have a monopoly of Barbican dwelling acquaintances, that was for sure. Maybe the driver had a secret relationship.

His second observation was more serious and more thought-provoking. It came as he sat looking at the chess board that was placed before him after Moley handed him some chilled Chablis and then sat down opposite him. The game looked the same as he had left it when he last saw Moley. But there was a subtle difference. Moley had switched the pieces on the chess board. Not by very much admittedly – he had pushed one of his pawns ahead by just one space. It looked insignificant. But it was enough to convert the dynamics on one side of the board from passive to highly active. It gave Moley a small but very crucial edge. Joe was now threatened on both wings. He would have to play like crazy now in order to hold Moley to a draw.

So had Moley cheated? Joe was certain of it. It could never be proved, of course, because they hadn't written the positions down after they paused in their friendly play the last time. But Joe did not forget chess positions. Like old bridge hands, they were branded into his memory. Moley had definitely paltered with the truth. That was conclusive.

That told against the continuation of the friendship.

Joe said nothing but sat at the board in Moley's flat and stared at the new positions of the pieces high above the Barbican and London. Moley was at his smoothest and most accommodating as he fussed about with the bottle of Chablis and broke all the sacred ties of friendship.

This changes a lot, thought Joe as he stared at the pawn that had outgrown itself.

Do I throw it, now that I know that Moley wants to win so passionately? Throwing it would be so simple. I only have to move my bishop fractionally, like so, as if to say 'OK, let's tango' and that gives him an indisputable winning line. So maybe I submit to Moley's signal and we play another game...? It's a possible play.It's an option. Maybe but who knows – it's quite a different game of chess now. To concede might be to concede on another more subtle plane. This is too complex for me to grasp all at once. Perhaps I should play for time.

Maybe I don't throw it? That enables us to prolong the agony and to talk, especially since if I don't throw it, then Moley will think that I've bought into his little game of covert chess adjustments and that I'm even more stupid than I really am. That would be good to convey...And so he'll talk, because he won't be able to contain himself at the idea, strange as it may seem, of legging over one of his oldest friends and acquaintances...Who cheats wins…That could be the new mantra. That could be Moley's new game. So chess-wise I may lose this game by playing on in this faked position but otherwise I may gain…I may learn something…

Joe fingered the bishop and Moley's eyes gleamed. Joe replaced the bishop on the board and thought about the game some more. The gleam died. Moley subsided as the bishop's move came and then went as a possibility. In imperfectly suppressed mortification, he sipped more Chablis and stared out of the window as Joe continued to ponder his next move. Morley had been hoping for a rapid mate, early spoils of victory.

Joe pondered his move. The board lay before him. All the mistakes were there, waiting to be made.

But why should Moley have cheated? Had he become so impossibly corrupt? City life, like prison, changes a man, but not to that extent. So was Moley always bent and I just did not have the eyes to see it at the time? This is not good behaviour from a supposed old friend.

Ah, thought Joe, this is all quite another story and requires a quite separate set of explanations. But it does mean, I guess, that my friendship with Moley is at an end. I must view him in a different light. This heralds the passing of an era. We're going to be awfully jolly together. We're going to go through all the motions of friendship and we're going to recall all sorts of special times together as we grew up in the old City. Yes, all that and more. But the switch in the chess pieces is a betrayal. It is not acceptable behaviour. It looks like a small thing, but it isn't that at all. It's the opposite of dictum meum pactum; now it's something like dictum meum fuctum. It tells me that Moley wants to win above all else and that therefore he's no friend of mine. Not any more. Used to be but not no more…Like the weather, he's changed.

Perhaps he never was a friend at all – now there's a thought. Joe felt a sensation similar to his experience when Felix described the Fat Man's racket. Not so much betrayal as ejection and severance. A place like a cottage had been kept warm in the memory, a hearth that contained quiet breathings and girth slackening and recollections of mirth and jollity and shared responses. But a long time ago. Now no longer. Now it was just blasted sticks and bricks in the wilderness of the moor, a roosting place for the crows. No place there for a weary traveller seeking succour and sanctuary.

Joe thought about Moley's slave, purchased in Italy and presumably hiding somewhere in the flat. That was the clincher. Nobody kept a slave and protested his integrity with conviction. It was laughable. Joe thought about the silence of the slave, only able to come out when it suited Moley, a being kept in complete servitude. That did it for Joe. He'd forgotten about the slave until he saw the chess board. Now he recalled that mute unhappy young face. He hardened his heart and made his move. He pushed a slow but puissant pawn. It was wholly inadequate in response to Moley's rejigging of the board but it held the line until Moley's next move. It was safe and wouldn't cost a piece or a tempo. Joe was going to wait and see.

Joe made no reference whatsoever to Moley's retouching of the chess positions. He was on the alert now. He was watching and waiting for Moley's next move as a friendship that linked youth to maturity died between them over a long afternoon and a bottle of Chablis.

He didn't have to wait for long. Moley had assumed that Joe would move his bishop and had positioned accordingly. In his mind's eye, he saw immediate victory. But the pawn move...Ah, that was different. It would all take a little longer now. Moley decided to take his time. He sat back in the deep leather armchair sipped his wine and stared at the board.

Silence between them for about five minutes. Not wholly a harmonious absence of sound either. Moley failed to make his move after some thought. But then he broke the silence and broached a few points.

'Quiff still treating you well, Joe?'

'Mustn't grumble. He's a busy man. It's big bank. He has a lot to survey. Great banking man, though. We're lucky to have him.'

This is very irregular, thought Joe. Moley is not treating this meeting as off-limits. But he will show his hand quite shortly. Gesture and stance provide the clues. I sense this, he thought, and I will wait. He has a reason for all this elaborate preamble. Like all dishonest operators his great efforts to play straight in appearance whilst dealing from the bottom of the pack just help to show up his crookedness. Revelation takes place despite concealment. I've seen all of this before. He's not a friend, he's a spiv. 'Ware Moley, you guys…

More silence. Then Moley with a great show of reluctance to take any initiative, shifted a knight to the back line. In Joe's view that cost Moley a tempo. He should have pushed his pawn.

'Ah, the knight move. Very cunning, Moley. I approve of that. Very well thought out. You really have been working at it.'

The pressure was off Joe in the game just a little. He settled down to think again about his move but Moley interrupted him. He had business to transact. Moley sounded now like a man in a hurry. So there was an agenda.

'While you're thinking about your move, Joe, let me fill you in with an idea of mine. Well, to be honest, not so much an idea, more of a favour I'm requesting for old times' sake. It involves a young man of my acquaintance who is full of bright ideas on the markets and who does some consultancy work for me from time to time. Good track record, in fact very good. He has been known to have some very unusual ideas on the markets which can go wrong, I admit, but recently he's been very right. He's on a roll. You know the type, I'm sure – very willing, very bright, just a little bit raw and lacking that extra bit of perception that comes with experience. But with good ideas and in some cases quite exceptional market vision. We've all been there, ourselves included, Joe. I need hardly mention the name of Mr Garraways for it to come flooding back to you, including the hang-over.'

'Especially the hangover, Moley. It was that cheap red infuriator did all the damage. He was always just a stout victualler out to make a buck.'

'Exactly. He should have been a chemist not a purveyor of fine wines. Now back to my young man as you work out your move. He needs a little exposure in the City so that he can find a place with a good house. Not with you, of course, you're far too big for him. He'd be swamped by a house the size of ABC and then eaten alive – which is something which I don't want to happen to him. So I've been thinking about a compromise. I wondered if you could find it in you to give him a little bit of podium time at your morning meetings. Not a lot but just enough so that he got himself noticed a tiny bit. He could be introduced as a freelance thinker on the markets...You'll find he has some very striking ideas.'

What Moley asked for, Moley duly received in this neck of the woods. Backs would be scratched just as youth would be served.

'Of course, Moley, I'd be delighted. Just get him to give me a call.'

Joe sounded just a little too eager in his willingness to take the idea and the young man on board. Joe was faking it. But Moley did not appear to notice. He was in a hurry.

'No it shouldn't be a problem, Moley. Tell him to get in touch with me. What does he want to talk about?'

It was a simple question, calmly posed. Joe slid it into his reply apparently as an afterthought. But it was far more treacherous than that, a mere sliver of a dagger but a weapon nonetheless. And it hit home.

'I...'

Moley paused the key fraction before recovering.

'You must ask him when he calls you. His name is Nicholas. I'll get him to ring you.'

Joe kept his eyes trained on the board. Moley's momentary stutter was enough. It was a set-up. Moley had been too excited by the theatre of it all to contain himself. Not detached enough. What Moley had nearly said before he checked himself was something like 'I haven't told him yet what to say but when I do, then he'll know what to say. And that's how you'll know.'

So much was obvious. It was a set-up. For a bust.

Unfortunately for Moley, Joe had been around in stranger places than Moley could have imagined. He was used to betting on nuance; frequently his life had depended on drawing a certain inference. Such gambles might not make for attractive social encounters but they helped preserve the carcass in life-threatening situations. And not everybody turned out to be such a nice guy in the end. Joe had seen that before as well. The substance of the encounters with Moley was turning grainy.

Tranquilly, Joe sipped his wine and pushed another idle pawn. Moley thought he was a patsy. Well, then, let Moley carry on thinking along those lines. It had never harmed anyone in the past.

'I'll look out for his call, Moley.'

Moley looked at the board but without enthusiasm. He was losing interest in the chess. His main business of the afternoon was done. He had effected an introduction for Nicholas. He stared at the pieces without rapport.

Oh,' he cried with his schoolboy enthusiasm, 'I think it's time to do this.'

And he castled with aplomb. So did Joe, instantly, and then stared at the board again. Discouraged, Moley drank some more wine and looked flushed; the grog blossom bloomed across his features. With a sad expression, he pronounced an end to the encounter for the time being.

'We can put the board away, keeping the pieces as they are and meet again shortly. I don't have too much time left now for fun and games. You can tell me how young Nicholas fares at the hands of the ABC traders...I'd like to be kept in touch. He's something of a protégé of mine.'

Joe wondered where the slave was at that point. Lurking in the kitchen? And what about Nicholas? What was his status in the Moley entourage? Chess counsellor? It sounded as if Moley kept a harem of young men in and around town. Would this young man be too outrageous at the morning meeting? Unlikely – Moley was not the flamboyant type.

'Delighted to tell you the outcome, Moley. I'll certainly do that. Let's be in touch very shortly and thanks meanwhile for the wine and the chess. That's a mean position you've got me into. It'll take some evasive action on my part to avoid a crushing defeat.'

Which was as much as to say to Moley that he had full licence to rejig the board yet again. This Moley would undoubtedly do. On the next encounter, Joe would be surprised to find he still had so much as a king left among his pieces.

Moley walked swiftly to the door and opened it quite brusquely. He then bowed Joe out of the flat graciously with his courteous broker's smile, which by implication of its concealed insult placed Joe on a par with Moley's other clients. To be mulcted as such – and as much as possible at high speed.

It was not the smile of a friend. Too many teeth on display. Moley had been a broker for a very long time.

Deep in thought and trying to put the pieces of the puzzle together in his mind, Joe took the lift to the ground, found his driver, and headed off for the Reform Club. Not a lot of it made sense, Joe decided as they sped through the light traffic to Pall Mall. He didn't want to push or impose on the situation to try and gain some purchase, he just wanted to lean into its mass, Moley and all. He wanted to feel his way around the dimensions of it all. A pre-empt would be premature. It was time to reflect but not time to form a judgement he concluded. He resolved to await the telephone call from Nicholas with his wild views before he proceeded any further in his analysis.

But Moley was bent. That was totally obvious. Bent in every direction bar one. Like them all. He had the mark of Cain on his forehead as surely as if it had been etched there by the village smithy. The friendship was dead, dead, dead, much to his dismay. But it was a fact. The carefully phrased contours of Moley's behaviour towards him were most distressing. Moley was playing him for an idiot and trading on their previous assumed friendship as he did so. It was all too complicitous, like a friendly beating in a headmaster's study.

Dishonesty takes a man in the features, as the Fat Man always said. Joe caught himself echoing one of his mentor's saying and was forced into a wry smile. So if that was so true, how come he never clocked the Fat Man as a thief and a rogue, eh?

Eh?

Big questions to which Joe had as yet no reply.

At the Reform lobby, he thanked the desk for its help over the letter which he collected from his pigeon hole. It had been there for some time, judging by the Repugia postmark. Joe wandered back to the car, tearing open the envelope as he went down the club's steps.

Emma had written to him, to his surprise. It was a letter from her, yes, from Emma. From Emma Bales and who would have thought it? Emma who had stood him up so brutally in the Caribbean all those months ago. And an Emma Bales who had decided to learn German!

She should concentrate on English first, thought Joe uncharitably. She's got a long way to go before she masters that satisfactorily. Legal gobbledegook is one thing but the English language was quite a different matter. And foreign to her.

But it was a sweet letter which she had written him, he conceded, and in the midst of his problems Joe felt sentimental about her. They had after all had some fine times together. He couldn't deny it. So he would help her master German, of course he would. He would do what he could. Moley and the Fat Man between them hadn't quite slammed the gates shut on his capacity to respond with compassion. He could unbend to the extent of wanting to help another human being. He determined to find some tapes to send back to her. That was how he had got started in a manner of speaking. He thought about it some more – tapes, tapes and then tapes again. Now there was a question – where were they? Where were his tapes? He had been given tapes of commercial German when he had first gone to Berlin by the Fat Man. Those, plus his university German and his German of the streets, were supposed to equip him totally for the job in hand at the time.

But now...?

Commercial German should do for Emma. Of course it would, Joe reckoned. Perhaps the tapes would also do for Emma – but where were they? There was a book too which came with the tapes and which contained lessons and vocabulary – Joe recalled that all the Germans in the lessons went sick immediately from overwork, something which had amused him no end at the time. Frau Braun had been the name of his German coach who had lashed into him during the tutorials before his posting to Berlin. The books and the tapes would help Emma master the language.

But where were they?

Joe could picture them quite easily but he could not quite fix them in his mind's eye in a precise location. They were not at Pugh Park. He knew that for certain. He had nothing there which related in any way to his old life. The London flat? Impossible –

that was rented out. In storage at the Reform Club? Impossible – there was nothing there....

The car bowled down the motorway, freshly directed by Joe in the direction of Stanley and then Pugh Park. Belatedly, Joe had recalled that it was a Thursday and time for his meeting with Stanley; the previous week he'd stood him up, such had been his preoccupation with the bid. Stanley had called him up in some distress at the office and reminded him of Joe's No Show. Joe didn't want to take another tongue-lashing.

Meanwhile Joe was failing to establish, successfully, just where on earth he had left the wretched commercial German tapes. He could always buy some new recordings. But Joe felt that it was more correct somehow, and more personal, for him to send the older versions which still had some sentimental value for him.

Then just as the car was turning off the motorway towards Stanley and the pub, his memory bank obligingly opened up and provided him with a snapshot. Suddenly he knew where the entire language course was located. It was all stowed in the bottom drawer of his desk in the office. He had placed it there on purpose, just after he had started at ABC, not because he had been afraid of forgetting his German – that was impossible – but so that he might have recourse to a more refined and correct commercial German should the need arise. Joe spoke the language of the Berlin streets. It was not, on occasion, a pretty sound. He had been afraid that his commercial German might be out of date.

He rummaged in his pockets for Emma's letter. He could fix this straight away. The Perfect would still be at her post, Joe trusted. Even she could not have found cause to depart so early, despite her switch in loyalties.

He checked the letter. Yes, there it was – Emma, like a good, sweet lawyer, had given him all instructions, like her London address and telephone number. Yes, he could arrange all of that tonight. Joe rang the Perfect from the car and evidently caught her on the way out. Judging from the tone of voice, she had her hat and coat on and was hot-footing it away. An early Pilates class? She looked the type.

After the usual heavy breathing indicating dissent, she clumped off to check his desk and returned to the phone just as the driver was parking the car in front of Stanley's pub. Yes, she had the package in her hands. Joe asked her to take the package down to the ABC reception and leave it all there for the driver. The Perfect agreed to do this with a sort of limp tone of resignation to her voice and Joe rang off. Stage One completed successfully.

Joe issued his instructions to the driver.

'Don't bother waiting for me. I'm going to have quite a session here. I'll be a few hours. What I want you to do now is return to ABC Bank and pick up a package from reception. Then deliver it to this address.'

He gave the driver Emma's Pelham Crescent address which, he noted, had not changed from the last time he had become aware of where she lived, when Joe was practically a hobo. Still living in a fine part of town Emma my girl, he told himself. He added Emma's telephone number, to be used only if the driver got into difficulties with his commission.

'You will be able to get home, won't you, Joe?'

'Good question. I'm being picked up later on for a dinner party in the King's Road, so that's not a problem. Then it's back to the Reform Club. So you deliver that package and then take the rest of the evening off. It's a fine night. Enjoy yourself. I'm going back to town shortly, but I'll be driven there. The boys will do that. No need for you to wait.'

The driver barely bothered to reply before driving off. He was in a hurry to go. Joe concluded that the demotion news had got to him as indeed it had to sooner or later. Taking the usual precautions, and checking that the cab rank beside the pub was still operating – which it was – he wandered into pub number one, looking for Stanley in pub number two after passing through the common urinal. As he did so, the revelations of the foreign exchange screens that afternoon returned to him.

Joe could see that if he put 2 and 2 together successfully, in the correct order, he could make 78. But somehow that seemed improbable. He decided to wait upon Stanley's commentary.

★   ★   ★   ★   ★

Annie wandered about the Tate but it offered her little inspiration on this occasion. Even Picasso had failed her. She had worked out something quite neat for Leadon – that he should continue to write about markets but this time via a newsletter which he could set up – but that was easy. Not a lot of brain power involved in that solution; it was small beer. He could send it out on the net and she was certain she could arrange for some discreet funding for the venture. Her main slush fund was full to overflowing at that moment and no 2 fund was not exactly short of cash. Funding should be easy, and Leadon could be protected in other ways as well – perhaps he needed a young pliant assistant? The girlie factor could be arranged...

So they would have a voice. And that would keep Leadon happy for the time being.

But her mind was elsewhere as she sat in apparent rapt admiration in front of a Chagall. Mentally she had passed on from Leadon. She was thinking with some bafflement about the whole business itself. Gradually she was forced to admit that she found it brilliant. It was not so much that the bits failed to add up – on the contrary, they did so with great plausibility. She accepted what she had told Pa Lee, namely that the Russians had been smarter to the punch and that they had consolidated their position brilliantly via a well dug-in and well-entrenched occupation of the Bank of England. It was a fact. Just a few miles down the river, almost within hailing distance there they were, strongly positioned behind the Bank's thick and well nigh impregnable walls, especially since they possessed and controlled the Chron as well as an outer bulwark. And how best to deal with all of that...?

There were little inklings in her mind of just how that position might be exploited. She wanted to explore the green shoots of an offensive strategy in a cool casual way with no preconceptions about the whys and wherefores. The office was not the best place for relaxed lateral thinking, despite the waves. She found that her best ideas came from simply playing with things, trying to act them out in a charade and clearing her head completely of the cares of the moment.

Espionage was necessarily about pattern; by definition, in the last extremity therefore it was about linkages, however improbable, between variables. And those linkages formed the pattern. Once the pattern had been glimpsed then the counter-offensive could be plotted. And as she frequently reminded herself, on the other side careers rose and fell, waxed and waned on the outcome to those configurations which had been fed so carefully into the seemingly impersonal flux of events. False moves, because of excitement or whatever, could be made and denouements reached prematurely. That was her job – spotting the gap and building on that observation.

Paintings helped on occasion but not that afternoon. They failed to spark anything. They were mute as she sat before them and let her mind roll on. The wild patterns of the Impressionists did not connect with the feral suppositions that surged through her imagination. The vital connect was a blank and didn't happen.

Time for tea she thought after a while.

She made her way to the Tate restaurant and stood in line with the other art-lovers as she pondered the intricacies of the mission. Such inadequates as Picasso and Chagall and Dali, she thought as she neared the check-out. Slumbering at their post, as usual. Don't these guys know how to make – and keep – a girl happy?

From the point of the checkout, if she craned her neck, she could very nearly see her office. She duly craned, she glimpsed the office and she paid for her cup of tea. She wandered back to a table where with a little effort she could even glimpse her office window. It was her favourite seat in the restaurant.

She found it a comforting thought that her office could be so close…She could play mind games with all of that idea with hugely satisfying results. So, for example, from where she sat in the Tate, she could see where she should have been sitting, if she was still in her office, instead of taking time off and lounging around looking at pictures and drinking tea like any other solitary young woman in London with time to kill. She could always pick out her own window in the complex if she stared and counted correctly…Annie liked that idea of peeking inwards towards an office which ought to contain her – and would contain her shortly – but which did not contain her at just that moment...

Inside and outside – that was the name of the game. What was seen from the outside was not always what could be seen from the inside...The congruence was not exact...

She sipped her tea, rearranged the position of the cup and saucer along with the milk and the small teapot on the table and attracted by the bottles and cruet in front of her she began to play with the condiments. The ketchup was Europe – obviously. Japan looked like the mustard. Now for the big boys. The USA was the salt cellar and Russia was the pepper pot. That was obvious. So she juggled the bottles of condiment together so they achieved crudely the rough outlines of grouping that existed in world geopolitics.

Now back in the Eighties, Russia had become obsessed with global overstretch and had retreated from its European empire – like so: and she moved the pepper pot back. So the USA was impelled into the gap which the Russian withdrawal had created by the sheer momentum of change; it was forced to occupy that space for fear that the Russians would try to reoccupy it – like so. Annie moved the salt cellar forward. All very symmetrical and satisfying. But then the Russians very cleverly had moved back into a space which was very unexpectedly left vacant for them – the Bank of England – and so now they were right up against the Americans in a way that the Americans really could not tolerate. Offshore to Europe, the UK via the Bank played the same role in the vision of the Russian strategists that Cuba had played in the early Sixties. Annie moved the salt cellar and the pepper pot together, so that the pepper pot was right hard up against the salt, in fact positioned behind it...Like so...

Exactly that – like so. She stared at the patterns on the table. Small ideas stirred but nothing of any consequence or pattern. Maybe she should finish her tea and return to Picasso.

She played around some more with the objects on the table...

Her thoughts rolled onwards...

So just at a time when they had all thought that the Russians wanted a warm water port, what Moscow had in fact been seeking was a soft credit area, like London, so that it could wave two fingers at the IMF and indeed anybody else who tried to discipline them – and continue to collect the money...And utilise the credit...and run its secret empire. It was all so simple and so clever and it had all been worked out so neatly. Like a chess game. Very much like a chess game. The Russian strategists had pondered all of this for years – that was obvious and now they had a clear and unassailable lead. There was really no point at all now in doing any work at all in London. The essential brain cell of the UK had been paralysed by the Russian coup. No way that intelligence work actually meant anything any more. No way either that the Cold War was over on this basis, especially since the US relocation of its military forces in the direction of China left the Russians with a giant pincer movement across all Europe, gripping it from both the East via Moscow and the West, via London...Very soon Moscow would start to consolidate its position by closing the borders of the old Soviet bloc to the West, after consolidating its access to Western credit systems via its controlling position in London.

Annie left the condiments where they were and drank some more of her tea. Then after she had finished the tea, wearying of the proto-chess game, she picked up the two receptacles and swung them together locked in her fingers like castanets, reflecting the while that the US and Russian positions were pretty much like the positions relatively speaking of the Chron and the Bank. The Chron was the outerworks to the Bank's well fortified citadel with lines of communication which went directly from one to another, like a medieval passage...Yes, that was it, they were connected, of course they were connected, that was the way the Russians had set it up, so that one piece reinforced another, like two queens on a chess board...So that to communicate with one you had to communicate with the other...Knock on one door and you knocked on the other...Yes, that was it.

Knock, knock, who's there...? Yes, who's there?

She knocked the salt cellar and the pepper pot together in rhythm as she mused.

Suiting the action to her thoughts, she then placed the two receptacles back on the table the one juxtaposed against the other and fantasised about their positions on a chess board, the while realising that she ought now to be heading back to the office. She looked up and saw that the sun was flashing a blinding reflection on one of the windows of the complex and thought for one moment that it was her office and that if it was, then it was just as well that she had played hooky for an hour or so. The light would have been blinding and it would have been torture to draw the blinds on such a beautiful summer day…

And so her mind rolled on as she stared at the salt cellar and the pepper pot and prepared to leave now that she had finished her cup of tea…

…And then it came to her. Just a small flash of lightning that exploded in her mind soundlessly.

And it came there so soft to where her mother lay…As dew in April that falleth on the spray…

She had it, yes, it was true, she had it. It was like a silent clap of thunder or again an invisible flash of lightening, so decisive and stunning was the impact of the perception, there in that quiet little restaurant beside the Thames with the waves outside grinding and flowing towards eternity and the slow trade of people in the restaurant, up from the country and queuing for the exhibition of that particular afternoon…Yes, she had the idea and it was incredible. The perception stole upon her like walls falling down in the theatre, or a fold opening in the universal cosmos to disclose a wholly unexpected pattern.

Yes, she had the idea.

It was viable too. Hugely viable. No question of that. No more than a containment operation, no more than that, but it would act to slow the Russian juggernaut. And it would work – she had no doubts on that score. And beyond? Again she had no doubts. She had found the flaw in the Russian position. It was indisputable. They were vulnerable, hugely, enormously vulnerable. It was true. Annie was certain of that. She had found the gap in their system. She had found the flaw. There was a tunnel into the whole edifice and she had found it. The Russians were totally exposed, provided they assumed that their little game had not been rumbled. And there was no reason at all why they should make that assumption, That was the key point. Everything followed from that. It was all so simple. Because they had been rumbled. That was the key piece of vision.

She had looked at it all from the angle of incorrect perception. Annie very nearly laughed out loud at her folly. She had done this because of what she knew about the Bank of England and the Chron. Because she had been afraid of the consequences of the Russian position. But that was wrong. Completely wrong. Moscow was not aware of her perceptions. All Moscow knew was what Moscow knew. And working off that assumption blew Moscow and the whole of its precautionary position apart...Because she knew more than Moscow knew provided Moscow never knew that she had edge on the information score.

Annie rose to her feet, feeling delirious. She was a happy woman. She had a winning line. In her bones, with all her experience of espionage, she knew that to be true. She had cracked it. And she could proceed now, within the shadow of the US game plan, and she could bring it all safely back home. She clacked the salt cellar and the pepper pot together again like castanets. Was this the end of the Hot War? Could it be that big? Unlikely, she told herself. She cautioned herself against exuberance with all the heavy, cold zeal of the professional spy master.

But no, she told herself, let's not get too excited. That might be the measure of it over time but certainly not now. The possibilities are massive, but so are the risks. This Bank of England: Chron salient is the final throw of the Russian old guard, the guard which has refused to come into the tent with the rush of the new and which prefers the old certainties of the arms race; the Soviet tyranny; the traditional enclaves; and the old balance of terror arguments. So if they lose – and I think I know how they can lose now over time – then they've lost everything. It's all over for them. They must be finished, if I've understood it all correctly. And so, roll the change...And the dice...

There was only one danger, so far as she could see. Stone must stay at the Chron. That was crucial. He had to stay. No way that he could move, at least for a month or so. Unwittingly, he had become the agent in place.

Annie made to return to her office, and then checked herself. Time for sending up a small prayer of thanks to Picasso wherever he might be for his reconstruction of her universe, she thought. She padded back to contemplation of one of the great man's lesser works. She sat in front of it and focussed on the daubings.

Yes, Stone had to stay where he was at the Chron. That was crucial. I'll get a man onto him right away and I know how to do that, she thought. In fact, I know exactly how to do that. Stone will not be a problem.

Her mind rolled on some more. By caprice, Picasso appeared to acknowledge her musings and to respond to them, just like the Blessed Virgin Mary. He sent her another idea. A very good idea which was a supplementary to her first dazzling perception.

These things happen all the time in pagan lands, she thought in her jubilation.

If I assume that the Chron and the Bank and the Russian Old Guard form a solid bloc, then I can tweak all of this by putting some pressure on the Bank and reinforcing its sense of the defensive – because it is after all functioning as if it was located in foreign territory. The Bank is not what it should be and therefore will be susceptible to pressure, any form of pressure. It will act to preserve its camouflage and it will try to soak up the pressure. But it will react internally. Stobart and Q will feel it; they will be at action stations. So that pressure will extend automatically within the Chron: Bank: Soviet bloc both backwards and forwards, backwards into Russia and forward into the Chron. Because it all functions as a bloc. That must be true axiomatically.

So I can tweak it. I can do it by using Leadon and by encouraging him to write the truth, so far as the markets are concerned, about what is happening. And that will rattle Stobart and Q. And they will transmit their concerns back to Moscow, causing concern again at base camp. Which in turn will know no better because it is feeding for the truth in the situation off the Bank and the Chron in London. But these elements, by definition, must relay flawed information because that is their function relative to the outside world of the West. So they misinform the old guard back in Moscow, lusting for the kill. They have no defence against the plague virus of the truth.

Correctly handled the whole structure blows up...It's so beautiful...

Now, she thought as a weeping Madonna with four set of eyes and two heads scrutinised her from the wall, the means of putting pressure on the Bank lie all around because of the Bank's record of intransigent behaviour in the past – towards the creditors of BCCI, for example, over whom it rode roughshod when BCCI when bust in the early Nineties and the creditors were left without a penny. The Bank was utterly rigid in its responses. Thus, the instruments of persuasion are to hand. Merely by using them and turning the heat up on the Bank via these old grudges and grievances, I reinforce their defensive posture. This means that when the time comes for me to spring my trap and deliver my coup – which I can now see even more clearly is a winning line, provided certain assumptions hold – then it will have the impact of a detonation, such will be by that stage the high state of tension within the Bank.

Weeping Madonna and British intelligence chief went eyeball to multiple eyeball at this point.

I am sure, thought Annie, that when I start doing my detailed analysis, I will find that every single fact that I uncover goes with the grain of what I'm planning. It just has that certain feel to it. Not a single factor will be wasted. The Don will flow home to the sea, even though a hero of the Soviet Union stole and then claimed the original manuscript for himself. That's just the way that it's going to be. I know it in my bones. Truth is the winning line – amazing.

Annie nodded to the poly-headed virgin as she rose from her seat and left the Tate, feeling blithe, cool and back in control. Poor Stobart and Q, she thought. This will all come to them as a great surprise. They won't be expecting any of it.

★   ★   ★   ★   ★

Stanley might be right in his forecasts but for the wrong reasons, thought Joe as he went into pub no 2. Now to task the brains of that middle-aged time traveller with some fine searching questions!

He found Stanley looking older, plumper and more desolate, as he sat in front of his well-timed empty glass. The barman brightened as Joe appeared and bustled into action. He had plainly wearied of the phlegmatic Stanley, seated in solitary gloom and hugging his half inch of beer at the bottom of the glass.

'Usual, Stanley? Sorry about last week. And the last few weeks, in fact. I glitched. Sorry again. I missed our discussion very much.'

Stanley looked at him with a mournful eye.

'That's enough apology. Let's talk about the beer. If you twist my arm, I suppose I must have another one. But only if you must…'

That added some exponential spring and zest to the encounter. But Stanley still looked desolate. Joe took in his mournful countenance some more. Stanley stared stolidly at the centimetre of beer in his glass.

'You look exactly as I always imagined Don Quixote to be, sad gloomy, transmit and not receive. Stanley, it can't be that bad.'

No reply from the pillar of gloom.

'You are not happy, Stanley. I can see that, the bar can see that, and I guess the whole world sees it. What's happened? Has Maisie proposed?'.

Stanley sighed.

'Worse…'

The barman arrived with Joe's drink, plus the Stanley refills and took away the empty glass. Stanley grabbed the glass and raised it to his lips. He almost bit into the beer as he tilted the glass into his moustache. The angle of elevation of the beer altered rapidly as Stanley took a deep draught. Then it sloshed back to the horizontal as he replaced the glass on the small table. Around a half pint was now travelling down to Stanley's innards after his gulp. He brushed the drops of beer from his moustache delicately and gazed mournfully at Joe.

'It's all over. It's hail and farewell and goodbye to my freewheeling existence. I've been a fool. It's all because I've still got a cute little butt. Maisie fancies my butt. She's told me that. But so do her friends. That's my whole problem.'

'Some weeks ago, Stanley, when we met here in this place, and you had nothing, we talked about the dollar with animation. You had views and ideas. We frisked about in forex. This time I find you down in the mouth and unwilling to chat while I in the meantime have made some discoveries...Truly startling discoveries...About the $, no less. And I want to check them out with you.'

Stanley heaved a sigh.

'Don't take it the wrong way, Joe. You know very well that I've come with ideas for you too. But Maisie has stumped me and I'm just getting to grips with the problems she has caused. She's made me infinitely depressed. We're taking a holiday and we're off shortly...Such a total waste of time.'

'A holiday? You can't be serious. This is very bad news. Where are you going? For how long? I forbid it. I can't lose my eyes and ears like this. Let me give you a mobile. Without you, I'll be exposed to the rogues in the bank and they're paid to lie...'

'Italy. That's where we're going – Italy. All over it. On a joint rail ticket. She's found some way of wangling it, what with her being in the rail business. I'll be gone a month. She's decided that it's the best thing for us to do, so that we can try some painless cohabitation. She's never been to Rome. She wants to go. She wants to see the Pope. Can you imagine it – the Pope?'

'Ouch, Stanley.'

'Exactly. The Pope sounds bad but the cohabitation is positively evil. She's a large lady. She's built along robust lines.'

'More Brunel than anything else. But built for comfort?'

'For endurance and nothing less. But there's lots to hang onto, I'll give her that.'

'Sounds like wedding number five, Stanley, on the way.'

'I think that as well. It has that feel to it. I feel as if I'm being slowly absorbed.'

'The bells, the bells...?'

Stanley nodded his head in agreement and remained silent.

'And Stanley you're a connoisseur of marriage, as you've pointed out. But if you do marry Maisie, you must be sure to stay on the wedding night in Pisa in the Hilton.'

Joe said this as innocently as he could. But Stanley still eyed him with suspicion.

'And why would that be, master Joe?'

'It's been renamed the Tilton. Very apt for you and Maisie I would have thought.'

'Very droll, Joe, very droll. I'll drink to that. The helping hand you seek is at the end of your arm.'

Stanley drained his glass abruptly and called for more beer with some irritation. Joe wondered if he'd gone too far and changed the subject. Stanley was not amused.

'What about the currencies, Stanley?'

'Exactly again. The very nub of the thing. Just when they were getting interesting, I have to abandon my studies and traipse around St Peter's, sightseeing. Such a waste of time. I was on the verge of a break-through on the currencies but now I'm on the way to a breakdown. I wish I'd never met the blasted woman. I should never have slept in her railway station. I'll be so out of touch by the time I get back…It'll take weeks to catch up. I'll be useless for you, Joe.'

'Did this happen after you met the friends?'

'Immediately. Of course I got on well with the friends who all clucked around me, so that was fine. But Maisie flew into a series of jealous rages and accused me of flirting with her friends and her friends of flirting with me. Result? I'm to be removed from the scene and given a good pounding of 24 hours a day exposure to Maisie alone, so that the friends…'

'…Will encounter a remodelled and reconstituted Stanley whose first and only thought will be in Maisie's direction.'

'Something like that. It just doesn't bear any further thought. I'm devastated. Now Joe…'

Joe realised that Stanley's glass was empty again. Joe nodded at the barman. More beer appeared. Stanley quaffed again, but this time with less speed and aggression. He seemed a touch sated.

'A pleasure, Stanley.'

Stanley drank about three times faster than Joe, but then of course he had less time to put it away.

'Thank you Joe for hearing me out. It's a tragedy for a man to cry...Far better to drink beer. Now to the forex. Just what is it that you wanted to discuss.'

'Last time we talked about the dollar. You thought it was going to rocket, agreed.'

'Agreed. And it's not doing too badly, is it. Look at the pounding it's given the Asian regionals. That's what we discussed last time...But this is small stuff. We're just at the beginning of a shift, so the market hasn't really seen it yet. It's still just a wave out there on the ocean, minding its own business. It hasn't turned yet into the sixty-foot high colossus of a breaker that it's about to become.'

'That's not the point, Stanley. Something else is happening to reinforce that forecast. Within that dollar strength, there's something else afoot. There's an attack on the Euro taking place. A really ferocious one at that.'

'How very interesting, Joe. How very, very interesting. Tell me some more...How clever of you to spot that. Well done, young man, you're coming along famously. You see I'm out of touch already and I haven't even got on the train to Italy. So tell me some more. What's going on?'

'Unmistakeable. It's the way it traded today. I sat watching it on the screens for half the afternoon. I was completely fascinated. And when I say attack, I mean just that. This is Panzer tank stuff. Somebody is trying to destroy the Euro.'

'That's imaginative. The Germans attacking their own currency. They've done that before...'

'Pay attention, Stanley, and listen to me. Don't be diverted by trivia. Now you know how strong the Euro's been.'

'Awesome, yes, I know but what are you calling it now? I've been spending too much time with Maisie. I'm really out of touch.'

'Just around a dollar and a quarter. $1.20, $1.22, somewhere around there. But looking rocky and then some...Really weak, you know, as the £ used to look before Wall Street opened. Where the ECB is these days, God alone knows, but it certainly hasn't been biting the market's legs as usual the last few months. Like the Bundesbank used to do. But anyway as I said I'm watching the Euro this morning at $1.25, or thereabouts. And it gaps down...Gaps down hard. And nobody's there, minding the store. That's what I think. What do you think?'

Stanley was very attentive. He stared hard at Joe. The beer was neglected for a time. Then he started nodding in time to the recitation from Joe.

'No lurch followed by a bounce, you understand, but a lurch followed by another lurch, and then a very sickly partial recovery, and then another bang...And down it went like a stone. And this after a long fall from $1.30 or thereabouts...That's an attack. It was down for a count of eight in the fifth. That's how it looked today.'

'Could be. Sounds like it. Could well be an attack, come to think about. It might be wide open. And as you say, is anybody out there minding the store?'

'Who knows. You know what Europe's like and just how long it takes to get a decision through. The ECB is like a Tower of Babel.'

'How did it finish? Through support levels or just holding? And on which side of the support level?'

'When I left the office, it was focussing on $1.20, with no intimation of any support at all. Two, three, four cents down on the day, but the loss of those cents looks crucial given the threat of that move through $1.20. And it still has to get through New York tonight. The boys will be looking out for it and as soon as they smell weakness... There could be quite a party tonight in New York for the Euro. A bonfire, no less.'

Stanley drank some beer with careful and considered sips. His eyes were fixed on Joe. Joe persisted.

'Now how would all of that look on your charts, Stanley, always assuming that you might still be keeping a chart on the Euro?'

'Pretty terrible, I would guess. Dropping through all the support levels, that's bad. Free fall, that sort of thing...I don't like the sound of that gapping down...That means there's no texture at all to the forex trading...No friction as it falls, nothing even after such a swift fall from $1.25...By the sound of it, you have two weakness factors. You have the weakness against the dollar, because the dollar is strengthening although we don't quite know why. That is to say, nobody knows for certain although I now have a theory about it all. If I can firm that theory up, Joe, then I'll call you from wherever in Italy – I promise you that much. Then you have the secondary weakness of the European currency itself, which amounts to a double whammy on the Euro. So it's very, very vulnerable. And that can only mean one thing, Joe...'

'What are we talking about Stanley?'

Stanley straightened up. He was back in stockbroker mode, poised, polished, responsible and operating at his very professional best. He looked younger and less dishevelled all of a sudden. He stroked his moustache reflectively. He might have been addressing a meeting of important clients instead of Joe in the back bar of some country pub. The eyes were shinier and the hands were itching to make their rhetorical points.

Too many wives thought Joe. That's Stanley's trouble. His Achilles heel was in his groin -or was it his butt? No matter – he couldn't resist. They dragged him down by sheer weight of numbers. Monogamous, he'd have ruled the world. He looks superb now, just like a mid-19th century German banker. The wives distracted him. They were a diversion. Stanley prepared to speak.

'Let me quote just two things to you, Joe, by way of explanation. I see something else which I will come back to in a second but that must wait. Now first, I think the dollar is going to continue moving ahead. It's got a life of its own which in turn is fuelled by some very odd fundamentals. These I now think I understand.'

'Alone among your kind, Stanley? Notwithstanding Maisie?'

'As you say, alone among my kind. ...And forget Maisie if you'd be so kind, that's a cross I will bear later... So I think the dollar's going to the moon. It's going to take off like a Saturn V rocket over the next few weeks. That's one thing we can take as given. Maybe, maybe not, but pro forma so far in the argument it's boom-boom for the $. Agreed?'

'Agreed, Stanley. You look magnificent.'

'Thank you and don't interrupt me. Now the second factor meshes in with all of this insofar as Europe, and we mean Germany here in real terms, tends to lose its currency roughly every thirty or so years. After the first world war, the D-mark was worthless; after the second world war, the D-mark was worthless, and now give or take a decade...'

'It's going to get smashed to bits again?'

'That's the risk. Europe is wide open to such an attack. And that's the trend. It's time for it. You must be right, Joe. The Euro collapses and the $ soars.'

'So what happens to Europe?'

'That's what I was going to say...Maybe it falls apart. Cigarettes and nylons as currencies and the nobility prostituting themselves with the servants...That kind of thing...The important thing is that we've been here before. This is nothing new and there is a precedent. Complete social break-down. It's happened before, as I say...The markets know this.'

'But Stanley, is this feasible?'

'It sounds absurd but countries do go off the map if they make a serious mistake and show weakness. The markets rule. And countries go off the map very fast. That is the lesson of the twentieth century. After the first world war, the Austro-Hungarian Empire was wiped out... They didn't think it would happen, but it did.'

'OK, so how do we quantify all of this?'

'Easy. There's been an attack, you say, which you witnessed today in the forex markets. That's nothing so far, apart from the risk that the currency might part company with everything else in the market because of the rise in the dollar and because nobody appears to be minding the store so far as the Euro is concerned. So if it recovers tomorrow or the next day you've just been alarmist. Big deal and no story. But if it doesn't bounce back, and weakens again, then we're into something quite new...'

'How far does it fall?'

'How far do you think it will fall, Joe?'

'Perhaps to 95 cents against the $?'

'Rubbish, Joe, think big. You're a big boy now with a big job. Think big. Think massive.'

'I dare not, Stanley. I'm also a banker; that fact alone inhibits intelligence. You think it. And then you say it...'

'All right I'll do it for you. I may be the older man but you're a moral coward, Joe. And you know it, banker or no. I'll give you 50 cents to the dollar. Got that – 50 cents! Total collapse with the currency ending up as worthless. How about that? It could even go lower...Think about it – raging inflation; political collapse; all the rest of it. The pity of it all is that I'm inventing nothing. We've been here with Europe before...'

Joe whistled a long sound with no tune.

'You drive a hard bargain, Stanley over the forecasts. You take no prisoners, ever. Ever, ever. But 50 cents sounds extreme.'

' Rubbish. Think big, Joe. I'm just doing a job, sir, just doing a job...Thinking the unthinkable... Extrapolating from trend. Playing with the Doomsday scenario. I can tell you with Maisie in tow, that is almost second nature.'

'So to sum up, Stanley, Maisie or no Maisie, we're talking strong dollar?'

'Unavoidable. The strongest you've ever seen. That's the way it looks and that's how all my thinking falls into line. That's the trend and that's the signal coming out from the Fed as well. Just why they're pursing that line, who knows but I will be able to tell you fairly shortly.'

Joe was starting to feel happier already.

'And a weak Euro into the bargain, Stanley?'

'Not a weak Euro, Joe, but a collapsing Euro. Imagine a Europe with no currency at all, where you can't buy or sell anything without using dollars – or pounds for that matter.'

'Wheelbarrow money?'

'Exactly. That's what we're headed for, in Europe at least, if your tale about the attack is true and if the currency really starts to smash down.'

'Stanley, the thought occurs to me – and it may be crap, I freely admit, maestro – but has someone here been very smart? Has someone seen that the dollar would be strong, spotted that the Euro might come under pressure and launched an attack on that basis? Could this be orchestrated to any extent?'

Stanley stared hard at him and began to drain his glass. He made no reply but continued to drink. Stanley was a forecaster but not a conspiracy theorist. His mind refused to stray towards those tantalising pastures of reflection. But Joe had been in the business itself. He'd seen conspiracy at work – and play. He could see the timing of it all, fusing with the opportunity. And he was involved in this market because he had a deal to complete. That focussed his attention in a different way.

A hard silence fell between them as Joe toyed with the fantastic possibilities of it all...

But it was nearly time for him to depart. Joe was looking at the clock, then at the barman for another drink and a hail to a cab outside. The barman hustled over towards them to take a fresh order.

Joe was also thinking about the impending dinner with Rivers and Perdita and Mrs G and the gang. At that moment Joe would have given much of his fortune to have been able to enjoy a quiet night at Pugh Park lounging and larking about in the sitting room with a Perdita scantily clad in that very, very short black nightie she liked to wear for him. Alone with her. Chatty, the two of them, beside the fire, deep in thoughts of a varied nature, that sort of thing... But sadly there were social obligations to fulfil...

For the most part rowdy obligations...Was it a Buffet night, he wondered?

There was Rivers to deal with. His mind shrank away from confrontation with the ambiguities of it all. He was in it up to his neck with Rivers and his gang. The meeting in particular with Rivers he was not anticipating with relish that evening. He could live without a staring match in silence across the table with the saturnine Rivers Pugh.

Stanley spoke again, fortified by more ale.

'Now you come to mention it, Joe, the symmetry of it all is impressive. Undeniably so. I can see that. There are moments in the development of great enterprises when they are still weak and therefore at their most vulnerable. This could be one of those moments in the history of Europe. And outside the loop there is someone who can see everything that's going on and who is positioning to strike at Europe's vulnerability because there is enough fire power at his elbow to do so…And to make it happen. Yes, I can see that. That makes sense. Yes, Joe, well thought out. That's perfectly feasible. This looks like bye-bye to the Euro on that basis. So don't be caught long will you, Joe…? And won't the Germans be upset? I ask you, won't they just be niggled…?'

Stanley attacked the new pint of beer as Joe prepared to take his leave of him. The barman was waving to the effect that Joe's cab was awaiting him outside; Joe was impatient to be gone. But it was a doleful sense of departure. Joe did not want to leave the pub. He felt rooted to the spot by the discussion as the beer chortled within him and the sense of mutual conviviality with Stanley grew stronger with the imbibing. It all seemed ripe for a session of uninhibited drinking, especially since Stanley would be off shortly to foreign climes, along with Maisie, leaving Joe knee-deep and alone in the whole ghastly mess of it all.

No friendships at the top, Joe told himself as he fondled Stanley's shoulder briefly on his way out. Take it like a man…

'I'll think of you in Italy, Stanley, as the Euro parts company with reality. You may not even be able to get back to Blighty. Call me if you get stranded, OK? I'm good for your train fare at least, ha ha ha, even if you may not have the scratch by then.'

Stanley sprang to attention as he departed.

'As soon as I've worked out what is actually going on with the dollar, Joe, I'll call you.'

'Bye, Stanley, and you do that. Thanks for the chat.'

'Thanks for the beer, Joe, A pleasure to be of assistance. We've had some good discussions…'

'Indeed we have. Take care of yourself. Don't forget – call me if anything goes wrong and if you need some help.'

'I will, faithfully. And Joe, I won't be gone long. I'm not spending the rest of my life in Italy. This is just a flying visit. With Maisie. On the wing.'

Joe gaped at him in shock and awe then waved an arm with a smile as he exited from the pub. It was still a bitter farewell for him. Suddenly and abruptly he felt that there had been too many partings of this nature. It was like a distant view of a setting sun, an intimation of impending mortality, a brush with polar cold.

But Joe was strong enough to dismiss the sensation. There was still business on hand, still Pa Lee's bid to finesse with all the ramifications which that might cause. Undeniably he had had a flash of the muleteer in the setting sun waving his whip as change – huge change – threatened to bubble up from the sea and ground. But the deal was afoot! That was the excitement of it all. The moment was not to be missed. The forex switches were being thrown; they were like an Open Sesame to his deal.

Joe settled back into the cab and wondered exactly what his driver was doing at that precise moment. Had he found the tapes and delivered them to Emma in Pelham Crescent? Or had he simply ignored the instruction and gone home? That outcome would not have surprised Joe. Power is about reach and Joe's was shortening all the time.

Then quite quickly Joe was struck by a whole raft of fresh ideas, so much so that he leaned forward, tapped on the window and instructed the cab driver to go more slowly. He didn't want to arrive at Pugh Park with the ideas, as yet unconsummated by reflection, still coursing through his head.

The taxi-driver began traversing half Hampshire in the direction of Pugh Park at a snail's pace.

★　★　★　★　★

To begin at the beginning, thought Joe in his slow-moving taxi, I can take some of Stanley's thinking with a pinch of salt. These currency heads always rave and rant in front of a captive audience and they always overstate their case – they're too used to wowing the morning investment meetings with blood-curdling stuff. They get carried away.

Wheelbarrow money? 6 billion Euros to buy an egg? Yeah, maybe, but not overnight, Stanley, so spare us a thought. Get real.

But on one point, Joe reasoned, Stanley is to be respected – the $ is going up and the Euro is going down. That looks to be set in stone. So that in turn leaves one currency unaccounted for – the £. We didn't talk about that little maverick darling. So let's address the problem now – whither sterling? It's a fascinating conundrum because it most likely holds the key to my deal; to Pugh Park; and almost to the rest of my future existence. I'm well and truly in the frame with the £ now.

And the £ is going to fluctuate violently. That I know for a fact…

If the £ follows the $ upwards, then that's a catastrophe for me. Plain and simple. There's no deal afoot; Perdita most likely gets murdered by Felix; and Pugh Park is blown up. Oh, and Rivers escapes my clutches and gets to become the biggest arms' dealer in the world. Not good, indeed very bad. That's what is most likely to happen. So, let's fold our arms and give in and surrender – it's all over.

Oh, and Perdita, forget about that marriage we were planning. There will be another ceremony but it will called something else…Something darker…We are in the grip of the Vulcan Gods on this one…

But there's a twist to all this that cannot be ignored. If the market goes the other way and if the £ follows the Euro downwards – and it well might just do that, because PM Blair still wants to take the UK into the Euro and so the £ is bracketed with the Euro – then the sun comes out and all sorts of wonderful things start happening to the deal. It flies as the £ crashes; I'm quickly away from ABC, taking Perdita with me, and Rivers is wholly and totally stuffed, as the Yanks pour in to grab his company. The spooks are happy because I've done the deal and everything is hunky-dory.

Tickety-boo time…?

Possibly and perhaps, Joe told himself, feeling the dead weight of high pressure responsibility lift from him for just a fraction. But then the thoughts returned, increasing a hundred-fold. Not so fast, my friend, he told himself. Nothing is ever that easy. This is a far more delicate play than you can imagine.

Because there's also another twist to all of this, he told himself, which is partially but not wholly covered by my interpretation. Where do those good old soldiers, Moley and Gazza, fit into all of this. They are both crooks and swindlers, as has been established, and they are both obviously playing some kind of different game to different rules. For example, I've just agreed, for Christ's sake, to let Moley's catamite or whatever address the morning meeting at ABC, so that's real enough. Meanwhile, young Stone has clearly been mugged into oblivion as Editor of the Chron and is crying into his beer somewhere as his Chron which tried to climb out of the intellectual slime has now been firmly thrust back into it. So this is a high stakes game, with big professional operators seated at the table. Moley has always been very careful about his money. I remember very well his reluctance to pay for a round of drinks years ago. He would wait outside the pub for the rest to turn up, so that he could avoid paying for the first round. Moley is tight. So it has to be a big deal for Moley to get his toe-nails wet. Pretty well copper-bottomed, in fact.

Moley doesn't like losing out.

So, what's going on? Yeah, Fat Man, what's doing…?

The habits of obedience to the Fat Man's calls died very hard.

Outside, the countryside crawled past the window as the cabdriver, with reluctance, maintained a steady 30 mph from village to village; normally he would be flashing along at 60 and terrifying all the schoolchildren of the area into the hedgerows. But Joe gradually felt a bigger idea stealing into view across the membranes; he could glimpse a more massive structure, although he was not completely sure that he trusted his sense of vision here.

He asked the driver to stop the cab.

He noted the time – it was 5.15 in the afternoon.

The cab slammed to a halt. The cabdriver didn't like stopping.

Joe could hear the Fat Man barking out something, away in the distant halls of memory. It was a rarely recalled axiom of the Fat Man's. It went to the effect that most strategic thinking was wrong by definition; it placed the thinker at the centre of the action, rather than on the fringes of something bigger. It was an enchanting concept because it enabled the analyst to locate himself in the antechamber to bigger conventicles. Joe had always loved that idea of the Fat Man's, because of its whiff of cheating geometry; of somehow faking it along the Milky Way.

'So, if in doubt, young Joe, and if the solution fails to materialise, think again. Roll it through the mind a second time. But this time imagine that you're watching an alternative scenario take place, to which you are no more than a witness, for better or for worse...Just a walk – on part...Your causality is not central to the action you are watching, it is tangential. Then see where happens then to the interpretation. It's amazing, Joe, just how many times it yields the correct line of interpretation as you take it on the bias...Trust me, I know about these things.'

So had said the Fat Man in his prime. Just prior maybe to his betrayal of Felix's father?

The Fat Man had been a dynamic force for something. On that point at least, Felix and Joe were in agreement.

And now...?And now...? Oh, Fat Man, Fat Man, where art thou, as you saunter in Hades' shades?

Joe could see that relocating the vantage point of the analysis wasn't a bad approach. That helped locate Moley and his machinations on a different plane to his stratagems, with very likely a completely separate agenda in play. Joe liked the idea very much, that somehow he was participating in deployment of an agenda that had nothing whatsoever to do with his main frame scheme...He was like an accidental tourist, an onlooker being caught up, so to speak, in the back draught of something massive and yet completely unknown to him, like a pilgrim arrested during a hi-jacking.

And Moley was certainly up to something. Nobody cheated at chess like that, unless there was an underlying agenda.

And most likely Gazza too at the Chron could be bracketed in with Moley.For the purposes of the argument he was very likely again acting in concert with the broker. They had been colleagues in the past; Moley was plotting something; that meant Gazza was involved in skullduggery too at the Chron.

So far so good but what were they up to...?

Joe went back over the trail again, noting that it was now 5.22 in the afternoon. His driver sat sulking and smoking a busy cigarette in front of him.

Bemused, Joe picked up the Chron, to refresh his memory about a story from Tokyo which the Chron had clearly pulled,

422

failing to mention even the most basic facts. At the same time, Joe decided to push the cab door open to get some fresh air. He tugged at the notches on his belt. Recently he had lost some weight, consequence of Perdita's chidings, and the belt was looser around his waist...

He pushed the cab door open...

The idea hit him hard. It was true at first light. It sliced through the rubbish in his thinking like a vorpal blade. He had it! He'd cracked it! He was there! Universes collided in the outer cosmos.

But he had it! He was sure of that!

And the deal flew, as high as the sky, just like a bird!

Instantly, and to the consternation of the cab driver, he was out of the cab, pulling the belt away from around his waist and buckling it together – so! – in the later afternoon sunshine. He was also telephoning the Bank of England on his mobile. He wanted Stobart's CV from the Public Information Office at the Bank and he wanted it fast. He might just catch them before it closed at 5.30...

The idea had gelled in his head. The two ideas had come gliding through the ether like Vergil's serpents – and they fitted. Joe reckoned he had the whole thing now. He'd found the missing link – it was Stobart. And it all made so much sense. Stobart, the Unknown Governor who never spoke, who never gave interviews or appeared in public. He was the missing link in the chain which brought both Moley and Gazza into play. To give Stobart a role, correctly following the Fat Man's precepts, was also to locate the Bank of England equally correctly in the elaborate piece of global espionage, orchestrated by the Russians which was designed to strike at the US at its most vulnerable chink – the $.

Hence the belt! So mundane and yet so astounding!

And he reckoned that the £ would fall like a stone with the Euro. So the deal suddenly was moving ready for take-off, assuming Joe was right. Joe thought he was very right at that moment.

The algebra was irrefutable.

It was 5.23 in the afternoon. Joe knew the Bank's number well
– 7601 – 4444. Everybody in the City knew the number of the
Bank of England.

'Hullo, Bank of England here.'

The usual fruity tones of the Old Lady's switch, nice and
Limehouse – tuned.

'Your Public Information line, if I may.'

'Certainly. One moment, sir'

Public Information answered the call quickly in such a way as
to suggest that the call had better be important because the coat
was on and 5.30 loomed.

'I'm sorry to call you so late...'

An enraged voice from Public Information like a grizzly bear
intimated that he should get on with it. Yeah, as Joe told himself,
the Bank sure knows how to do rude. Years of practice, indeed
centuries, on that one.

Such a petulant Old Lady at all times of the day and night.

Joe assumed his sweetest telephone manner.

'I wonder if you'd be kind enough to fax across to me tonight
Governor Stobart's CV.'

That was not a popular idea at 5.29 p.m., witness the virtual
gnashing of teeth in a growl that greeted Joe's proposal. Public
Information really does want to go home early, thought Joe. He
doesn't want to provide any Information at all.

'Who are you?'

Joe ignored the obvious non sequitur in Public Information's
query. He identified himself, quoting his rank at ABC.
Immediately the atmosphere altered. It became warmer but also
semi-accusatory. Joe ought to have made himself known earlier in
the discussion. Delighted to be able to help...No trouble at
all...But you really should have said, sir...

Typical Bank, thought Joe, either at your knees or at your
throat...Or both at the same time in the Old Lady's quantum
universe.

As the official fawned away, Joe seized his chance and popped
the key question. It had to work within the symmetry of structure.
Joe had to receive an affirmative answer to his careful question;
everything hinged on the reply, because that was how the stupid

Soviets would have set up their scam in the first place. That was what the belt was all about...Or to quote Moley, the good Moley of yore that he used to know, one man's surplus was another man's deficit.

Everything fitted if Joe received the answer that he was expecting to his question. So here goes, he thought. Let the die fly high.

'I'm pretty certain that Governor Stobart is married to a Japanese but I wonder if you'd be kind enough to confirm that. And also where she comes from in Japan...?'

The grizzly at the Bank pondered that one for a few seconds as the thaw continued to wax hot down the line. Joe waited with baited breath as the official either confirmed the query or made a quick call to ABC Bank requesting that Joe be sectioned forthwith. It was all very bold, hard core conceptual stuff.

The information was grunted out.

'I can't be certain but I think she's from Tokyo. I can check if you would like. It'll be no trouble...'

With his heart beating in overtime and with his voice resisting the temptation to say 'Yoh' loudly, one hundred times in succession, Joe was quick to reassure him that there no need. It was information merely supplementary to an occasion in the near future when he would be meeting Governor Stobart socially; he had wanted to confirm early that his facts were right in order to be able to greet the Governor's wife with the correct small talk.

And in the meantime here was his fax number.

Please to fax, sir?

By definition of Joe's cooing tones, if the Bank official with whom he was at that very moment in contact could see his way to placing the Governor's CV on the fax machine in the next 30 seconds and then dialling up the requisite number of digits in the afore-mentioned order, then, he, Joe, would be in that official's debt for as long as it took him, Joe, to extricate himself from this embarrassing position of obligation by purchasing sufficient alcohol on the said official's behalf to ensure his maximum satisfaction.

Something like that, at least.

But over and out now. The theory lived.

'Of course, sir.'

The conversation concluded with the Bank, Joe told his taxi-driver to drive like Hell now to Pugh Park.

'Make it snappy. I'm in a hurry now. Just go for it.'

The cab driver grinned. This was more like it. Off he raced. Joe sat in the back of the cab chortling as he was bounced about. And staring at his belt. He was pretty certain now that his deal would fly but he wanted to retrace the steps in the logic. That way when he got to see the Stobart CV, which again needed to contain just one piece of data vital to his argument, he could reposition very rapidly.

Step One in the argument was the obvious one – relocate and reassess what was already known, notably that Moley and Gazza were a couple of crooks, most likely old Soviet sleepers being reactivated, as the time drew near for the coup, whatever it was, to be launched. Step Two took place in the forex market. The dollar was being pushed ahead and the Euro trashed very possibly in a concerted piece of action by agents hostile to the US. That also seemed pretty clear; that was what Stanley had been discussing.

But the old Soviets couldn't do this on their own. That was the key to it. It was a coup too far for them. They lacked the firepower to force the $ ahead and the Euro down in the market-place. They didn't have the financial muscle to do it. But the plan was to smash the Euro apart…Because the old Soviets had their forward position located in London's Square Mile. They refused, therefore, to contemplate the construction of a rival currency in Europe because that then entailed the need to construct a wholly new forward salient in Frankfurt…Which the Russians couldn't achieve; it had taken them 50 years or so to get the Bank and the City under control and the loss of Gloster had been almost terminal to that espionage strategy. But they couldn't leverage the $ to rocket and smash the Euro alone. Only the Japanese could achieve something similar; the Japanese had reserves coming out of their ears. But it was quite unlikely that Tokyo would come in on the side of the Russians, after the bitter war between Russia and Japan at the turn of the 20th century; the Japanese had defeated the Russians, which meant in turn that the Russians detested the Japanese.

So impasse...So no deal...So forget it...That's what the forward planners in Moscow had said to the whipper-snappers with the bright ideas...

But what if – and here Joe gazed at his belt again, pulling one end through the buckle – there was a linking agent between these two powers, Russia and Japan, something like the Bank of England, which could act as a hidden intermediary between them and unite them in pursuit of the common enemy, the United States?

The buckle on the belt which linked the two ends?

And for that idea to work, the key player was not Q, although he was the talk of the markets with his very peculiar approach to Square Mile administration, but Stobart, the invisible Governor and the man who always hugged the shadows to the point of being unrecognisable within popular City parlance. Stobart was vital, if Joe was right. He was the necessary connect between the two global powers while Q did the administration on the ground.

And for that idea to work, Stobart had to have proven connections with both the Japanese and the Russians. Via Joe's lightning perception of possibilities and drawing on his Cold War experiences, that would have been how the stupid Soviets would have set the scheme up; they were always fixated by self-balancing elements within structure. Because they didn't trust their structures abroad. That was why they made them self-balancing.

So far it all made sense, with Q in the foreground as the operator and Governor Stobart in the background with the vital connections that extended symmetrically in both directions, one towards Japan and one towards the old Eastern bloc. That was why Joe had posed his 'wives and sweethearts' question to the Bank, half facetiously and fully expecting the answer 'No, get away, you young impertinent, he's married to Betty Bloggs from Whitechapel. Childhood sweetheart etc.'

Or whatever...

But he had struck gold, purely by pursuing Ariadne's thread down the twists and turns of the labyrinth of this most ingenious piece of global espionage. The invisible Stobart had married a Japanese woman. So he was tied in on that side of the puzzle. Bound hand and foot, more like. Were Joe to investigate further, he would most likely find that Mrs Stobart was descended from families of senior officials in the Japanese Ministry of Finance. Stobart would be niched into Tokyo structure very solidly. That was certain. If he was tied in on the other side, in an obvious way which the CV would identify, then Joe could go to work on a fresh set of assumptions. It would all fit then. He would know what he was contemplating in the markets and he could proceed accordingly.

And then, because Joe knew how the big picture worked, he could craft his deal, which was tiny by comparison, to splice in with these great movements.

And that way he could pull it off...The $ was obviously about to rocket.

This really is like riding the tiger, he told himself, staggered by the majestic simplicity of the scheme he reckoned to have uncovered. The Riddle of the Sands, with the German fleet riding at anchor in the mists, had nothing on it...

So where's that Stobart CV?

Faster, he told the cab driver with a smile. Get a move on, I'm in a hurry.

The cab flew along the Hampshire lanes.

* * * * *

Mrs G minced towards him as he entered Pugh Park by the kitchen door. She was waving a piece of paper as she greeted him with something approaching enthusiasm. No, there was nobody at home yet and yes, Perdita was away doing her CAB work. But for him there was a message from the Bank of England.

'Very impressive I must say, to get something from the Bank of England,' she added. Mrs G was in just 1 loop – her own – as Joe had frequently acknowledged to Perdita. She bustled away and back to her cooking. Joe watched the bottom – her G spot – ease around the corner.

He stared at the blank side of the sheet of fax paper.

This, my friend, is where all your smart ideas meet their Waterloo, he told himself. And he turned the sheet over and began to read.

Shocks and alarums. He was astounded.

It was all there in the first few lines. Immediately after leaving Balliol and joining the Bank of England, Stobart had been seconded first to the National Bank of Hungary; next to the Moscow State Bank; and finally to the National Bank of Rumania. Stobart had spent his first ten years at the Bank working behind the Iron Curtain, at the height of the Cold War. Impossible to find a better match between data and theory.

Bingo, thought Joe and reached for a glass of wine. And knowing Stobart, I bet his Russian's still useless.

But this was going to take some fathoming. If anything now, he was way ahead of the curve – and motoring. How best to exploit that winning line?

Time to gee up Lucia? Or better still, perhaps keep her in the dark?

But it was time to launch the bid. Only a matter of days, in theory.

★   ★   ★   ★   ★

Darling Ursula, all hail from Tom, your sad, sad consort. So that you may understand exactly what I have experienced day by day on the Chron after my epic meeting with Q at the Bank of England and just before I departed from you for ever – perhaps? – let me describe just how the newsroom is working now that I have lost complete control of my newspaper.

Sad, sad to say such things. Who would have thought it could all finish up like this…

I am writing this in the light of your delighted, sparky attendance at the Woman of the Year award this morning, when you were so pleased to be there and in such exalted company. I could have wept – and I of course was overjoyed to be squiring you to the gathering as the all-powerful Editor of the Financial Chronicle.

Smiles all around across the acres of faces of the women as you enjoyed being out with the Editor of the Chron, making your contacts, spreading the net and looking, if I may add, wholly beautiful and brilliant. I am as much in love with you as ever and always will be – you must always bank on that. You should also know that when you come to read this diary, after I've gone.

But this morning was a sham. It was a piece of make-believe. I am no longer the all-powerful Editor on the paper. I am editor only in name. My writ runs nowhere, apart from possibly with regard to this pc into which I am typing my doleful diary. You don't know this and I haven't told you but that's the truth. Even the pc may be looted in due course. The work – the gorgeous work which I loved so much -of running a newspaper and putting it to bed of an evening goes on all around me but it does not require me. In fact, it has as much to do with me as the National Lottery. I am no longer involved at all. I wander through the newsroom like a ghost, wholly ignored by the goons and clones whom Q at the Bank of England has insisted should be eased into their various jobs. Occasionally one of the old guard on the Chron, with whom I shared a passion for Fleet Street ink, has the temerity to smile at me in acknowledgement and recognition, but that is about as far as it goes; his smile fades quickly as he looks around fearing retribution for his wink at me.

My detachment from the paper is almost total. All the ink and dirt and stories and the shouting and the hustling and the excitement of edition time and the first edition dropping with a good strong lead story – well, that's ancient history now for me. It's as if I never was a newspaper man in any way at all. It's just gone. It's not so much as if I've been put out to grass, more that I've been stuffed with the bloody stuff. I have no control over news selection; features; editorial line; in a word, nothing. My career has gone up in smoke. It started well with a big story and it is finishing on a quiet sombre note – that is the best that can be said for it.

From gumshoe to bum shoe…

Captain Legless grins at me as we pass in the corridor, more in sorrow than in anger, and then emits his short barking humourless laugh. He twists his bald head beneath the invisible yoke, bristles his moustache at me and then wafts off to write yet another leader praising the Bank – macabre.

I'm just a front man now, which makes our appearance at the Woman of the Year award so much more piquant. I've become a public relations man not a journalist which is something that ought to make you very happy, Ursula; I know that that's what you always had planned for me from the start in an ideal world. The takeover by the Bank's boys is complete and they run the show. And they know this and they make it plain in editorial conference and throughout the paper, every hour of every day. They are in control. We don't dare breathe when they're around. We are just the house journal of the Bank. The stories which the Bank wants shoved into the paper go in pronto and the rest is suppressed. I feel completely bitter and idiotic about the whole thing. I think the correct word to describe the behaviour of the Bank's agents in place is 'swagger.' I'm beginning to understand just what happened in Europe when the Nazis rode to power. Whatever they say just goes and there is no redress. The sound of their jackboots is everywhere, clumping up and down the corridors. I am a simple prisoner here. The paper is a joke, a sickening fraud. Everything that I tried to achieve on the Chron – yes, everything – has just been kicked into touch. I feel a complete fool, like a total waste of space.

And I'm carrying the can as Editor, for all the bad stories that we're running. That's what makes it all so much worse. In tomorrow's paper, we are leading on the Euro and saying just what a crappy currency it must be. I disapprove because the balance is wrong but so what – my input is precisely nil. We have the wretched Morton on his currency page saying exactly the same thing about the Euro – so that's two stories hammering the same dreary line – and I think we also have a personality piece on Dowberg of the European Central Bank; this says that he should be known as Dim, not Lim. This is astonishing stuff. Leadon would never have written such inflammatory copy. I'm amazed the Bank itself allows such lack of balance. But under the attack, the currency is weakening too. So the plan, whatever it is, looks as if it is succeeding. The Euro is toppling, which must be what the Bank wants. Everybody knows that we stand on the edge of a first class financial crisis if the Euro continues to fall. But on we go at the Chron, disregarding all this, and hammering away at our line. Any more of this and it will really start to fall apart- and of course we will stand ready to give it some more kicks on the way down.

I wonder just what exactly the Bank is planning.

Just watching the self-confident way that the Bank's boys set about their daily tasks fills me with great foreboding. I can't help thinking that there's a deeper agenda behind all of this which I've failed to grasp. I cannot for the life of me think what the Bank of England has in mind when it manufactures all this destruction. It is so sinister, especially since these things are cumulative and self-fulfilling. If a paper of the standing of the Chron hits a currency like the Euro, day after day, then it stands to reason that eventually it will start to react and go on the slide, purely because of the herd mentality as the traders latch onto what is a safe bet – selling the hell out of this bum piece of Euro crap. Even I can see that and I am in some ways the least aware of markets now of any one on the Chron staff.

So just what is going on? I'm buggered if I can work it out, just as I'm buggered if I can understand why I've been dumped like this. Maybe that's just showbiz…

But Ursula, there's something else that I wanted to mention to you in my sad little chronicles…And this is by no means sad. No, that last paragraph was the end of the dreary stuff. I feel as if I'm on the brink of something new. Yes, truly, and here's how, darling. By dint of sitting around and watching the paper go about its ways and just observing it all, I'm coming to the conclusion that I may be finished in newspapers anyway. Strange but true and yes, you read it right – finished. Kaput and end of story. These things happen all the time, so I've been told.

Now you've grown used to a life shared with the editor of the Chron, whatever your reservations about journalism, and that revelation will shock you. But I think it's correct. It may be time to look around and do something quite new… The fun has gone out of it for me; it's a young man's game; maybe it's time to move on. The stories are the same even though the headlines are different – it's just like what the backbench always said when I first started in newspapers. It palls. News is no longer news, and reporting events has become just too passive for me, now that I've been forced into an even more backseat mode than usual after my dethronement. Now I didn't start this diary with that idea in mind but it has kept returning to me gradually as I've written it. There has been a process of exploration and gradual self-discovery which I'm amazed to say that I have recorded, step by step, looking back. I've kept the diary fairly diligently every day and turned various thoughts over in my head and I've come to the conclusion, little by little, that it may be time to move on and do something completely different.

Surprise, surprise…? Well, that's showbiz too.

And now we come to the really big question – you, darling. Whether you want to come with me on this mad venture, darling Ursula, that is something only you can work out. This may all be very painful for you. In a very convoluted way we may be saying goodbye. It's a nasty decision and I don't feel the slightest bit heroic about it. I saw this morning just how delighted you were with my prestige as Chron Editor at the Women's awards and I wouldn't like to injure you, not in the slightest way. But you should be aware just how I've been thinking. I may have to start travelling by a separate route. You should know this. This may be the only way I have of telling you the truth.

Because I think we should be truthful with each other now, if at no other time.

You see the other thing that I've discovered via my diary is just how much I still enjoy writing. This may not show through in my diary, which I suspect is appallingly badly written, but it's true – I look forward to each and every moment that I can put pen to paper. My capacity for writing remains undimmed, despite the years of strain at the Chron. The Style has been preserved intact. So I have to go for it, I think. I have an idea for a novel which I fully intend to explore and who knows I may be successful in carving out a fresh career. Or not, who knows – but I intend to try at least…

Now how I broach all of this to you, and get over the nasties without a first class row, that I do not know. But the moment of revelation is fast approaching. I sense that. We will talk soon. Perhaps the best thing that I can do is to resign fairly shortly from the Chron and place my diary in front of you so that you can read it through and make up your mind exactly what you intend to do... Darling, the choice will be yours. I have no very great hopes that you will come with me on this foolhardy venture, darling Ursula, but at least if we do have to part, after such a long time spent apart and then after finding each other again and being happy with each other, at least you will understand why I have had to do all these things...

I must close now. I have to go into late conference and go through the motions of talking about tomorrow's paper. A bore, I know, but at least it takes my mind off the thought of leaving you. That, I confess to you darling Ursula, will be very nearly unbearable...

★   ★   ★   ★   ★

'Nicholas, I don't believe you. Just say all that to me again.'

Grace had received a wholly unexpected telephone call from Nicholas at her office. She sat stunned by the news at her desk. She felt happier than she had done for months. So he could bring home some bacon at last!

Scrummy, wonderful bacon!

Nicholas obliged with an amplification.

'Grace it's true. Moley has come up trumps. I've just been on the phone to him. Not three minutes ago. He's arranged for me to talk at morning meetings with about three or four City institutions. So it's back on the podium, starting immediately. Mind you, he's given me a fair idea of what to say on the currencies, but I don't think that matters so much as the fact that

I'm going to get some exposure and I'm going to get paid for doing it.'

'Darling, you clever darling, I take it all back about Moley. Immediately and without reservation. Isn't this just wonderful news?'

'I feel as if I could jump over the moon. I'm thrilled to bits.'

'I'm not surprised. How long is it since you last worked? Three years? Or longer? That's a long time not to be in work, I know. We see them all the time here. We call them the Hopeless Cases. And when does he want you to start?'

'Immediately, at the double. Moley sounded as if the whole thing needs to be done straightaway. I have to telephone various people to confirm the arrangements but it sounded to me from what Moley said as if that was just a formality.'

'How much is he paying you for each appearance?'

'I'm not going to tell you over the phone but it's good money. I'm too superstitious to be too precise. But it will be a fee fully consistent with my previous status. That's what Moley said and that's what I can tell you with a clear conscience. Extra noughts, at the very least. We should celebrate – and that means tonight, sweetheart.'

'I absolutely agree, darling. Now just let me think…'

Mischievous thoughts flowed through Grace's mind as she waggled the phone and concurred with the idea of a feast with Nicholas back in Chelsea that evening. She looked out from her room to see whether she could spot Simon. Flood Street would be happy that night. But somebody else would be quite miserable. And serve him jolly well right. Just wait until she got off the phone from Nicholas and gave Simon the good news…That would wipe the gloating grin right off his face, wouldn't it just…

Executing a 180 degree swing in loyalties, she felt saved from the precipice, just in the nick of time…Time to put the frillies away, hiding them beneath the sensible nighties? How very passe Paris suddenly seemed.

Or time to keep the frillies out, but available for someone else, someone closer to home?

That sounded more like it. She liked that thought.

Grace returned to the topic under discussion.

'Now, Nicholas, let's be practical for once. Have you got any money at all on you as of right now.'

'Not a bean. No credit card either. Moley has turned up in the nick of time.'

'Fine, fine, that's not a problem. But just tell me what would you like to eat tonight? Just tell me and I'll fix it for us.'

'How about some of that steak from Kurnicks? We haven't had any of that for some time. That would make a good celebraggers…'

'Yes, yes, I think that's an excellent idea, now why don't you…'

Simon suddenly materialised at her side, like Mephistopheles. He scented danger whenever she spoke to Nicholas. He sounded for a moment uncertain about his prey. Grace improvised.

'…Just look up the number will you, while I wait…'

'I'll be back with you in a second.'

The phone went down with a clump as Nicholas scrambled to find the telephone number of Kurnicks in the Fulham Road. A feast, a feast, what ho! What ho indeed!

Grace seized her moment. She felt in charge of the universe. For an odd reason that she couldn't place, she also felt richer.

'Simon, can I come back to you in a second? This is quite delicate. Nicholas…'

Simon looked more cheerful.

'The boy wonder's glitched again has he? That doesn't surprise me. Born to fuck up and then some. We're still on for our drink tonight aren't we?'

The drink had been arranged so that they could both firm things up in terms of dates etc in Paris. The identity of the hotel remained very much an open question for debate.

Simon was 100% confident that he and Grace would be sliding between the sheets together as the bet expired and he collected. He also seemed more than 100% confident about his commitment to the event. His walk certainly suggested as such. He wandered towards the door of Grace's office like some conquistador about to annexe Peru.

'See you in a second, Grace babe. Don't forget…'

Grace smiled at him still holding the phone and thinking with gleeful anticipation of the shock she was about to administer to him in just a few seconds. But not too much of a shock – business was still good and she needed a second pair of hands at least. Simon was still key in terms of her work-plans. So she mustn't overdo the moment of triumph, to the extent that he exited from the office and the business in a towering rage.

Nicholas returned post-haste to the phone. He sounded very much more cheerful.

'Grace, here's the number…'

She took it down.

'Now Nicholas here's what we'll do. I'll ring Kurnicks now, and pay for the meat over the phone with my Visa card. A couple of pounds of contrefilet should do it, don't you think? If you can pick it up afterwards that'll be fine. I'll call Oddbins in the King's Road as well – don't worry I've got that number in my diary – and I'll order some wine from them. If you can pick that up as well, we're all set. We've got some vegetables so we can have a wonderful feast, just the two of us…This is fantastic news, Nicholas, and well done and congratulations. Now I must fly, I've got a client arriving in two minutes, but don't…'

It was their mantra through thick and thin.

'…Worry about a thing. Yes, indeed. Perhaps you're right, Grace. Perhaps this has all been a bad dream…'

She rang off thinking that he sounded more dominating and in control than she'd known him for months. That was good too. A man had to be a man, not a doormat…It would be good to have a man about the house again…

She marched in to see Simon who greeted her with an expectant face and a half smile as he looked forward to the early evening tryst.

She came straight to the point, with rare pleasure.

'Bad news, I'm afraid, but also good news. I have to cancel this evening. I have to be at Flood Street.'

Simon's face fell more than a mile. It seemed to implode with chagrin. Long vistas of charming and provocatively posed set pieces suddenly collapsed into nothing.

'What?'

Grace came swiftly to the point, eschewing triumphalism.

'Nicholas appears to have a job. We're celebrating. That was him on the phone now. Isn't that good news. Want to hear all about it?'

The exquisite image of a carefully planned and long term adulterous relationship turned to dust also before Simon's eyes. The hot sheets of lust vanished, whisked away by a chortling Pan. He looked as disappointed as a boy of three whose toy train had broken down.

Grace turned on her heel and left his office. Then she remembered something.

'Sorry to be a bore about this but didn't we have a bet about this. Is it time to settle our account? I've got the book in my drawer. Ready when you are. It needs two signatures, you know.'

She flung that over her shoulder with the greatest of pleasure as she waltzed back into her office. Time to think of cooking her man a good solid meal and time to say Goodbye to Simon. The bet was over and she'd collected.

So fuck you, Simon, with interest, all 5000 smackeroos of it!

    ★   ★   ★   ★   ★

Darling Ursula, the strangest thing has happened and I am beside myself with excitement. I know that as a hack I'm supposed to be schooled in sublime indifference to anything external to my own expenses claim. Nevertheless what has happened has intrigued me totally. I have to write this down for your subsequent inspection. I'm thrilled by the sheer mystery of it all. Also this event may have a bearing on my plans. So when you read all this rubbish, these outpourings, you'll understand everything better, I hope.

And in the event you may not get to read it at all…Things may be changing fast…

To tell you everything from the beginning, darling Ursula, I had arranged to meet Barry in El Vino's. You remember Barry of course – a really good journalist. We clashed years ago over some deal he was covering, and there was one helluvva stink, but since then we've been really quite friendly. He's always been quite open towards me at least. So he had come into my office at the Chron and very softly suggested that we go for a drink. I, of course, said that I'd be delighted to meet him off the premises and so we made our arrangements. I think he'd taken pity on me as the Ghost Editor. I got to El Vino's early and hung around for him a little at the bar before settling down at one of the tables.

Very few of the old soaks were there and I expect most of them are dead now, so I waited more or less alone for Barry to show – and for some time too, because he was late. Too late I remembered that he was always late. Eventually I fell into conversation with one of the haunt's habitues – nothing special about him – but he said the most unexpected things to me. It went as follows: 'You know the situation, I'm sure, sir. You were at school with one of those prize idiots, whom everybody knew to be a classic thicko, and then years later, lo! you find that this buffoon has risen high in his chosen profession, so much so that he is representing his country somewhere. You ask yourself – how can this be? The man's a dolt and yet here he is, starring at X, or Y, or Z profession. So is it me? Or is it him? Have I missed something?'

My El Vino's man asked me the question and stared at me fiercely. I stared back and asked him who he had in mind and he replied instantly, without hesitation, 'Stobart, of course, the man's a blithering fool and yet here he is running the Bank of England with that odd sounding man, X or Y or Z or whatever. You can depend on it, Stobart, sooner or later, will make a hash of things. I know this man. So I can make that forecast without contradiction – I was at school with him. His mind is all thumbs, let alone his hands...So mark my words...He'll make a terrible hash of it one of these fine days. And if you don't believe me, well here's my card, and you tell me. Think about it.'

And then after saying all this, he left me, quite abruptly, with his card in my hand. Ralston was his name. I don't even need to remember that since I have his card in front of me. I've even put the number into my mobile.

So I wondered – what was all that about? Is the editor of the Chron the kind of man to get himself picked up in bars? Far from it, you would have thought. But there again, there are some editors…You see there may be more to this than meets the eye, Ursula. I think I might have mentioned in a vague kind of way that I did have a very mild connection with the spooks years ago. Everyone in Fleet Street has had a brush with them. I did a little bit of fetching and carrying for them, but no more than that. Nothing cloak and dagger. But I know enough about it to realise that these chance encounters in bars are how things start. So the big question for me is this – was this a one-off? Or is this the start of something? Is somebody trying to tell me something? It's quite a big question. If there is something behind all this then it will alter my timetable. My plan is to resign soonest and then take the next plane to Thailand, which is where I plan to start researching and writing my Fleet Street novel. But the trip to the mysterious East may have to be delayed…

★   ★   ★   ★   ★

Annie took the call and was delighted by the news. The caller was jubilant. Annie felt better for that as well.

'Yes, Stone swallowed the whole story, hook line and sinker. I caught him in the bar, trashed Stobart about 120%, and then left him my card. So he knows where he can reach me, and I know that I can always contact him at the Chron. So we have a line open there.'

'Well done, Jamie.'

'He's not the brightest, is he? His eyes were out on stalks as I chuntered on about Stobart. You could actually see the thoughts passing through his brain. They were pretty obvious – is this a pick-up? Am I being fingered by British Intelligence? What do I do now? Call the wife? Or go to the loo? He is utterly transparent.

No, Stone is decidedly not one of nature's geniuses. Open book, basically.'

'That's enough, Jamie. You know perfectly well that the job of Chron editor does not call for an intelligence of the highest order. That's why Stone got the job in the first place. He'll do very well in this position, working it all out for himself...'

'...With a little help...?'

'...From his friends...Of course, that goes without saying. Which is why, my dear Jamie, you will leave all this for a week and then you will call him early in the morning, after I've spoken to you. Now you're not going anywhere in the immediate future, are you?'

'I was planning...'

'To stay put until we speak again. Such a flexible chap you are.'

'If you say so.'

'You can't do this by remote control from Sicily, you know, Jamie. So don't sulk. Just stay put and I'll contact you very shortly.'

'Annie I don't know how you do this but you have me now completely under your thumb.'

'Try reading some Jane Austen, Jamie, and you'll understand the techniques.'

'And which one should I start with?'

'Persuasion, of course.'

'Oh dear...Ouch and touche'

'Sorry about that, Jamie, but you asked for it. But thank you very much... That was very helpful.'

Annie put the phone down and prowled around her office. She scented a coup in the offing, but it was all a matter of timing. Tom Stone just had to restrain his wilder urges and stay on for just a little bit longer as editor of the Chron. Just time enough for her, in other words, to fire her bolt down the tube which, she now knew, would hit straight into the Moscow nerve centre. There was a flaw in the Russian scheme and she had found it. That was indisputable. Cyclops Old Lady – that was the size of it. And who was it who bored a hole through the Cyclops' eye...?

But Stone was on board and in play. That was the good news. That could not be denied. Now for Leadon, she thought. Using

Leadon, I can give Stone some briefing, which will keep him in play; alert the odd thinking person in the London market that there is really something very odd taking place; and also tip Joe off that it's time he set off on his travels.

She snapped her fingers in delight at the sheer simplicity of her scheme.

'One and one can make five, if you've spent enough time plotting coups...'

Then she cautioned herself.

She knew that one wrong move and one plus one would total zero...

And that would never do...

$$\star \quad \star \quad \star \quad \star \quad \star$$

At different points in the City, at around 10.30 in the morning, various traders, journalists and market men stared at the e-mail which had flashed onto their screens. Boldly entitled Notes from Threadneedle Street and signed by Christopher Leadon, formerly of the Financial Chronicle, the e-mail had an electric effect. Leadon pulled no punches. The crucial part of the market briefing read as follows:

'...*The first leg in any argument concerning the collapsing Euro involves the Financial Chronicle. Any analysis of its functional role in the City's hierarchy must arrive at the conclusion that the Chronicle normally operates as a willing mouthpiece of the Bank of England when it comes to discussion of the broader issues involving the Bank's demesne. This was broadly the position the newly-formed Chronicle occupied in the immediate post-war years when its' attacks on Chancellor Dalton's policies echoed in public what Bank of England Governors were stating in private.*

The Chron's role has not altered substantially in the subsequent fifty years. The Bank of England still runs the markets and the FC still sticks broadly to its own zone of equity coverage, collects the advertising cash and

442

underwrites in its leader columns more or less what the Bank has decided. A measure of the cosiness of the deal is illustrated by the fact that the FC traditionally made no distinction between editorial and promotional journalism; journalists wrote the advertising surveys and were paid for them.

Fast forward... to the moments surrounding the announcement of the Bank's independence consequent on the election of the current Labour administration. It looks as if the Bank, realising that a golden opportunity lay in its path to establish total freedom from political interference, moved strongly to reinforce its traditional relationship with the Chronicle by conducting a form of ethnic cleansing throughout financial journalism. This maybe is the only way to explain the wholesale changes in personnel which have taken place from newspaper to newspaper in Fleet Street. For the most part, the journalists were replaced by individuals known to be reliable by the Bank and who were disinclined to write analytically about markets per se.

The conclusion looks to be inescapable – the Bank is not in the giving vein today or indeed any other day. It has treated the reality of independence as an opportunity to regress to the niche within which it feels most comfortable- that of a private bank, wholly unsupervised by Government to any practical extent and capable of imposing pressure on government at will by orchestrating disapproval or otherwise through a constellation of willing Press satellites, led by the Chronicle.

Fast forward again, this time to the collapsing Euro. This week it fell again – sharply. This is a catastrophe for Europe. But a feature of the coverage of the Euro's gyrations has been the reporting of these events by the Chronicle. Rottweiler journalism as a term covers pretty well the approach of the journalistic team. The venom of the hostility towards the currency has been remarkable, given the gravity of the situation. It suggests that the Chronicle, and hence the Bank, have no interest whatsoever in participating in the Euro either now or at any time in the future, in stark contrast to whatever politicians might suggest at the other end of town.

Each edition of the Chronicle has contained many stories on the Euro all of which have been written from a negative slant. The destabilising impact of such cumulative negative journalism over time is easy to imagine. Eventually the currency will go into freefall – which is what happened to the Euro last week. The Needler warned last week that the currency might gap down in this way and the Needler has been proved correct. But the Needler *did not expect a sustained onslaught by the Chronicle on Europe's fledgling currency, urging it ever lower.*

The point derives even greater weight when the Chronicle's Euro coverage is contrasted with that of sterling's performance against the $. For the record, the pound hit lows on cable below $1.55 or levels last seen in the early Nineties, while both the Australian $ and the New Zealand $ continued to weaken. But it took real sleuthing by the Needler to find these facts in the Chron. The travails of the pound took place unobserved.

This all looks very much like the Bank of England getting up to its old tricks again. This is a very similar approach to the 'rolling boulder' gambit adopted in the late Forties when the Bank was determined to impose a flexible interest rate structure on the UK economy – and was helped in this objective by the sniping from Chronicle House, although the end-result was only achieved after a massive sterling crisis had been provoked.

★ ★ ★ ★ ★

Darling Ursula, I have just read Leadon's latest piece on the markets – it suddenly appeared on my screen – and I'm mortified. How could I have overlooked such a good man? And how could so many odd things be taking place in Fleet Street, under my nose, which I missed? It's uncanny the way that it has all been organised – and all by stealth. I'm surprised now that Q didn't chop me to bits. The whole thing has been done so ruthlessly and with such calculation. And I'm not the only casualty. There's Bill, and Ian to name but two, and then of course there's Roddy who actually dared to write a book about the Bank and then found himself chopped. And what about this man that I met in El Vino's...? Is he part of all this? I tried ringing his number but all I got was the answerphone...I will try again in a few days...

★ ★ ★ ★ ★

Annie was in high spirits. She'd been doing her homework on the Bank of England as well as the Russians. She'd been chatting here and there to the odd person in and around various investment areas who knew about such arcane matters – and she'd made some startling discoveries. Very rapidly she was able to implement her discoveries

Her plan was to increase pressure on the Bank cumulatively so that the sinews of resistance would be stiffened. That meant that the opposition's freedom to manoeuvre was correspondingly reduced because the surround play had reduced the degrees of freedom in the potential response facility. So when the time came for Annie to play her master stroke, its chances of success would be enhanced by the sclerosis she had induced in the opposition, in this case the Bank. Any animal that feels itself threatened reacts accordingly. Threatened on a number of fronts, it organises a complex response, in effect curling itself into a ball. But when the real attack comes, the scope for resistance is severely reduced, provided there is an obvious loophole...

All very plain and groovy, she told herself, as she beavered away at her planning...

She had found out, for example, that the Bank of England under Stobart and Q had abruptly introduced new employment contracts for all staff at the Bank. The move had taken place very stealthily some months previously. It had not been reported by the Chronicle for obvious reasons.

Stobart and Q had wanted to consolidate their grip on the Bank by eliminating any possibility of a disaffected staff response to whatever they might choose to do, ahead of the uncertain outcome to the US Presidential election. Depending on which candidate was elected, Stobart and Q wanted to be able to move quickly to make a rapid response both in terms of the uncertain external factors, like the US dollar behaviour, and also to fit into what Moscow might want them to do.

In other words, any possible dissent within the Bank at complete reversals of previous lines of policy had to be extinguished immediately. Hence the new deal that was placed on offer. The new contracts offered to Bank staff were far weaker in terms of individual security of tenure and tightened the control structure right throughout the Bank from the top. In effect, the Bank became a fief of Stobart and Q. Naturally the Bank was transformed from being an impartial forum, where advice was freely sought and just as freely offered, into a place-seekers' paradise with all commentary from below carefully crafted to agree with the prevailing line.

This was exactly the outcome which Stobart and Q had anticipated.

The Bank could at that point be viewed as a tightly-controlled and classically organised little soviet right in the heart of the City of London.

Annie found herself dumbstruck at the rich harvest of information that she had uncovered. It was like finding a hoard of gold coins buried in a field. She discovered moreover that meetings were scheduled between the Russians and the International Monetary Fund to fix the terms of debt repayment to the Fund some time ahead of the US Election. No big deal in that, as her informants told her. The IMF was disposed to be indulgent towards the Russians and the meetings should pass off without a hitch. The IMF wanted to tee up the real business that was under discussion between Russia and the West, notably how debt that had been created during the Soviet era would be repaid to the Paris Club. The old lenders wanted their money back. All in all so far as the markets were concerned, it was a matter of routine – the Russians were back in the tent.

But Annie knew differently. She realised that Moscow was headed down a completely different track, because it now controlled London. Controlling London meant that Moscow had guaranteed access to credit – after all London was very nearly the biggest capital market in the world – so it could afford to cock a snook at the IMF and tell the Paris Club just exactly where it got off in terms of getting its Soviet-era debt repaid.

Far from Russia being within the tent, it was not only out of the enclosure but well on the way to setting up its own establishment down the road.

But unfortunately for the Russians, Annie had cracked the code. She had prior information. And she knew exactly how to use it. Which she would do soonest. But not yet. For the time being she did nothing.

Timing was all.

She would have one shot at this little box of tricks, she told herself, just one and no more. She walked around her office, stared at the Thames flowing past almost at her feet, and repeated that statement to herself again and again.

Without the precious luxury of a quiverful of arrows to fire off in a bombardment, she would content herself with doing sweet nothing until the wonderful magical moment came when she could poke out the Russian eye with her projectile down the long tube which Moscow itself had fashioned...

After taking her initiatives, Annie sat back and surveyed the scene. Her situation was of course hopeless. She knew that herself...But, as she told herself, it was not quite as hopeless as it might have been nor as it had been...

And that in intelligence circles is about as good as it gets at the midway stage in an offensive...

★ ★ ★ ★ ★

Joe stared at his e-mail on the screen, as the Perfect outside did whatever perfect secretaries do when they plan to jump ship and transfer their allegiances. In her case, as it turned out, very little, but then that was par for the course with the Perfect. Only she could gauge the difference between activity and inertia, in Joe's opinion. The difference now was that she still did very little – but with attitude...The Perfect's eyes glinted at him suspiciously each time he emerged from his office. Joe guessed that the bush telegraph at ABC was even now beating out on its tom-toms that his demise was imminent. Fortunately, Felix was still away on his training course, so the Master of the Revels was fortunately absent for the time being from the lists. One source of irritation, as well as danger, had been removed.

The Ides of March had come but not yet gone…

The bid for Global was very imminent now; young Nicholas, who had behaved bizarrely, had been blooded in a very odd way at the morning meetings; and Joe had a meeting scheduled shortly with Moley for another game of spooked chess. Joe wanted to know exactly how much to pay Nicholas – that had not been discussed with Moley but it required attention…

Joe was looking at the screens, and following the markets as he thought then about Rivers. That proud but misguided young man was about to be sorely tested by events, when the bid for Global emerged and he discovered that he'd been dumped by the City…Not a pleasant experience, as Joe well knew, when all doors were suddenly closed…

As he brooded, Joe watched the Euro, and to a lesser extent the pound, as they plummeted on the exchanges.

'Mayhem out there,' he told himself as the Euro crashed down through all the support levels to some 90 cents against the dollar. He watched the screen, getting the feel of the markets, and wondering also about Stanley and Maisie and Italy…

'He'll be enjoying riding the rails,' Joe thought, reflecting that he had heard nothing from the errant stockbroker since the imbroglio with Maisie had deepened. Then his eyes flickered back onto the screen.

'The Euro really is very weak. It has no support at all. I can see Germany getting back to cigarettes and chocolate at this rate instead of D-marks…'

And then there was the mysterious business of the e-mail. Yes, the e-mail – that called for some explanation. Joe let his mind wrap itself around that phenomenon as well as he prepared to sally out for a tryst with Moley and discussion about that very singular young man whom Moley had sent to address the morning meeting. The more Joe thought about Nicholas the more puzzled he became.

Talk about trying to trash the Euro! He was like a Dervish at the podium, bulling the $. And it just happened to suit Joe's book to have somebody like Nicholas promoting the contrarian view. Anything to persuade the traders to close off their $ bear positions. Moley's Nicholas was a gift from the gods for Joe.

But back to the e-mail…

Unbidden on his screen that morning there had flickered up an investment appraisal by one Christopher Leadon, whom Joe recognised as a former star reporter on the Chronicle.

Firstly, Joe told himself, the e-mail was well written and well informed and showed Leadon off at his finest. It broached a critical line of analysis that was now entirely lacking on the Chron. It was a pleasure to read. But why had he, Joe, been sent the article? Very few people indeed knew his e-mail address just as the fact itself that he worked for ABC in such a senior capacity was more or less unknown. Pa Lee had seen to that with his customary efficiency. So how had Leadon got hold of his address? And known how to mail him like that?

It wasn't a hoax but it was certainly a mystery.

On a conventional level, it didn't make sense. No rhyme nor reason. But the e-mail was there, flickering away in front of his eyes. Therefore it existed. Therefore it must make sense on an unconventional level, of which, in Joe's world, there was only one of any real significance – spookery! Back to the Gents with the stovepipe hats and mufflers at midnight?

Was that it?

Perhaps, Joe told himself but without conviction. Even that explanation failed to make much sense. The Gents knew his call sign as well as he did, they could contact him whenever they wanted and he was to a large extent already operational with the ABC job. So it might be spookery, or it might not, although on balance Joe considered that it was spookery – but with a special message…

Perhaps that's it, it's a message, he speculated, as the Euro bounced a little around 90.25 cents, then sank again towards the crucial limit point of 90 cents. Red wherever Joe looked on the screen as the bears came in again and again to hit the Euro again with big selling orders…

The currency reminded him of a tiny rowing boat caught in mid-Atlantic by a typhoon. It squalled this way and that, buffeted by the winds, tossed hither and thither, quite out of control…

But no matter how much it bounced, it kept heading back towards 90 cents and almost total immersion…

And likewise the $ was soaring.

It's going to go through that 90 cents mark like a knife through butter, Joe thought. As a currency, it looks doomed. Good for my bid since it's taking the pound down with it. But not good for ABC Bank, not by a long chalk.

Joe left his office to go and meet Moley in the Barbican, still mulling the moves against the Euro in the market and how they impacted on the bid. He realised with a start as he passed by the Perfect's desk that she knew absolutely nothing about the Global bid. She would not be happy when she found out either. All the data and the documentation had been done in absolute and total secrecy, using security printers in the USA. She would be shocked rigid when she discovered how she'd been by-passed.

He nodded to her as he left the office and she gave him a glare in reply.

'Twas ever so, he told himself, realising that the Global bid was in actual fact just a few days away now from announcement. Time had flown and he'd lost track as he coped with detail. The offer would be made on a knock-out basis, helped by the terms of the deal which were considerably sweetened by the weakness of the pound against the dollar. Heavily massaged by a tough-talking Lucia, who had played a starring role throughout the long drawn out bid negotiations, the London institutions sounded happier and happier to take the Detroit terms. These were dressed up via notes and convertible bonds and all manner of bells and whistles but they boiled down in effect to a straight cash offer for Global with a currency kicker. This reportedly had delighted every actuary within the Square Mile because the returns were enriched so massively as a result.

Joe did not anticipate a great deal of fuss over the bid now. It should go through…The job was nearly done…Exit Rivers Pugh?

He left the ABC office and strolled towards the Barbican wondering by just how much Moley would have fixed the chess pieces for their impending chess-game. His desire to cheat and rig the game was almost comical, it was so transparent. Recalling the position of the pieces, Joe reckoned he knew what Moley might have done with one of the pawns…He thought it would have been shifted sideways one square. And if that was so, then Joe had a devastating counter to the move in this weird game of four-dimensional chess, a counter which would set Moley thinking way beyond midnight...

More wind among the high City buildings and more bluster. Joe walked quickly towards Moley's flat, still thinking about his e-mail and Rivers and the end game of the bid for Global...

★   ★   ★   ★   ★

Nicholas caught Grace between meetings. She was walking in Green Park and feeling blithe because she'd won her bet and didn't have to sleep with the wretched Simon; Simon for his part was slow to kick in on his side of the wager. He didn't want to make that trip to the building society with her, the two of them holding the account book in their hand. She was still waiting for the £5,000. But that could wait – the important thing was that she had the whip hand now and Simon was on the run. The client that morning was happy with the final short-list of candidates and the sun was also very bright that morning as it beamed its rays through the park. She and Nicholas were finally starting to get it together again. There had been some soothing dinners together in Flood Street; some hand holding watching TV, and most important, some latent, tumescent exuberance in his nether regions which seemed directly related to his improving job prospects...Yes, he seemed to be getting over it all now very well...She was looking forward to exploring that protruberant excitement more closely in the course of the weekend...So out with the frillies...

She was delighted to take the call from Nicholas.

'Darling, it's all working out so very well. I've now done three new morning meetings this week, all at different City houses and it's gone down very well... It's so wonderful to be back in the markets, I could sing about it.'

Grace thought about early morning tumescence with mellow anticipation. It's been a long time, she told herself. Nicholas chattered on.

'It's bit of a bore having to chant the same song from Moley's hymn sheet each time, but then that's something I have to put up with…'

Grace asked him sharply what exactly he meant by that expression 'chant from Moley's hymn sheet'?

'Oh, it's nothing. That was the condition of the deal. Moley gets me in to address these meetings but he scripts me very closely. He gives me the line. I just say that the Euro is about to collapse and then I mention a figure like 75 cents against the dollar which brings a real reaction from the traders. But it doesn't matter, Grace, I tell you. They all hate the Euro anyway and it's falling like a stone so it's preaching to the converted anyway. You ought to see the Chron these days, if you want aggressive commentary about the Euro – I'm mild by comparison. The Chron is absolutely rabid.'

Grace tried another tack. There was something about all this which she mistrusted. Her problem was simple – try as she might, she didn't trust Moley.

'So what happens when the Euro stops falling, Nicholas?'

'Well, for a start, it won't and secondly if and when it does recover, I hope to be so well ensconced that I can start generating my own ideas then. So it looks a reasonable bet to me…At least I'm getting the exposure…And I'm getting the market right.'

Grace attacked across the ridge, trying to turn Nicholas' flank and hoping to hear good news which would allay her apprehensions.

'But Nicholas this long-range stuff is all very well but are you being paid for it? Have you seen any money yet? You know, like cash in your wallet?'

Nicholas was as blithe about the fee as Grace had been just a few moments before about the bet.

'Moley's looking after all that. He's promised me that he'll see me right. And I trust him on that. He has no reason to lie. Otherwise why would he have put me up for all this? So no money as yet but it's on its way. And then we'll celebrate…'

Grace could find no answer to Nicholas' optimism. They parted on good terms with both looking forward to meeting up that evening at Flood Street.

* * * * *

Joe performed his usual antics with his fingers as he pressed in the code to Moley's establishment in the Barbican. Inverted triangle, followed by natural triangle followed by the numerical combo which described a natural...

Amazing, he thought yet again. Can you beat it? After all these years, the combination of numbers that I find will procure me entry to the flat of an erstwhile good friend is almost exactly the arrangement of numbers which led me into such bad company so many years ago. If I'd got the numbers wrong in Berlin then I wouldn't be here now...Sniper's bullets at five o'clock...

He entered the block and escaped from the wind. The entrance door crashed behind him.

And so the whirligig of time really does bring in its revenges and Shakespeare was not wrong when he wrote that line, Joe reflected as he mulled coincidence and waited for the lift. Who would have thought it indeed!

Very nearly exactly that combination!

The lift snapped open its doors. He punched in Moley's floor and as he mounted into the sky, he thought again about his e-mail. He was certain that it contained some very subtle coded meaning. Equally he was determined to reach no firm conclusion until it was absolutely necessary to form a judgement. He thought there might be a very simple conclusion to be drawn from it – nobody sent him mail – but so far he was stumped. He allowed the lift to take over his train of thoughts by clumping up floor by floor in an anguished bumpy process of squealing hydraulics.

The doors of the lift snapped open this time and he exited on Moley's floor. The door of Moley's flat was ajar, as usual, and he could hear Moley machine-gunning some instructions into the phone from the landing. Doing a trade and using old-style dealing techniques, he thought, as he pushed through the open front door. Just give 'em Hell and complain afterwards to the Council when you're taken upstairs…

That was always Moley's style…

The voice continued insistently.

'No, I don't think I'd bother…No, it's down to me, I'll look after him…Just let him get on with it…I tell you that you're quite wrong…He's under control. Trust me.'

And down went the phone with a crash.

Joe went into the living room and saw the chess set laid out as before on the small table between the two chairs. Then Moley appeared quite abruptly, as if from behind an arras, wiping his hands on a cloth and looking petulant. His broker's smile had not yet been switched on.

'Damn brokers. They won't take No for an answer, some of them…They make far too much money as it is…'

Which speech struck Joe as odd, since the discussion had plainly centred on an individual and not on a market trade. Nor could Moley ever object to the amount of commission that brokers generated since he was one himself. Joe reckoned the simple explanation was the true one – Moley was disoriented and had simply gone into speech mode forgetting his audience…

Joe registered the discrepancy but no more than that. It was merely the first step in a complicated dance of deception. As such it was wholly unremarkable. The half-truths of Moley did not disturb Joe. Far from it. He was in his element. He had spent his adult life waltzing through such hazy shades of grey. It was no more than he had expected.

But he was also impatient. He was eager to get to the board and establish quickly just exactly how, or whether, Moley had re-jigged the position of the pieces.

Had he pushed the pawn that Joe had calculated he would manipulate? Had he pushed another pawn? Had he found another way of cheating that Joe had overlooked? Those were the key questions. It was no longer a question of whether Moley still possessed any integrity – that issue had long since been resolved.

Moley was a cheat and a crook and without honour. He was working some kind of swindle using the hapless Nicholas as his go-between, or his proxy. But Joe didn't care, and he felt blithe; his deal was on its' way.

The irony of it all was that whatever swindle Moley was doing seemed to be working in Joe's favour as the currencies crashed around.

But all that was a given and as such irrelevant for the time being. In the chess game now it was a matter of whether Joe could second guess Moley's perfidy and still come out on top – a very different matter.

Very stylish probabilities at play here, thought Joe.

He looked at the board and he was not disappointed. Moley had pushed the pawn whither Joe had calculated it would go, assuming tampering would happen. Once duplicitous, always duplicitous – that was the rule. Moley had not faltered for a second. He had conformed to type. Thus far, so wonderful and so far so good. Now it was just a matter of time before Joe sprang his own trap.

Joe sat down at the table with the special beam of a smile one reserves for very old ex-friends and prepared for the fray – and his chess coup.

'Chablis, Moley?'

Joe thought Moley was just a touch off centre, just mildly distrait given the occasion. The smile was too rigid. Moley was worried. Rancour was getting to him.

'Of course, Joe. The usual?'

Moley bustled off stage and Joe wondered where the slave was located at that moment. Most likely suspended on a rope by his heels out of the window, twenty stories up, with Moley waving a pair of shears at him. Joe stared at the board again and realised that there was indeed an atmosphere of agitation in the Moley establishment. None of the pieces were quite centred within their squares. That slight element of disorder conveyed the flavour of the greater sense of disorientation.

Slave on the loose? Shrieking in Italian for home comforts and succour? Or worse?

Moley reappeared with the bottle and the two glasses and sat down heavily. He was breathing heavily also as if he'd been running. His household was decidedly out of order.

'Tricky situation this one, Moley. I really don't know how to handle it. I'll have to think about it. You're a cool player.'

Joe glanced at the faked chess board as Moley nodded and focussed on pouring out the wine. It slopped without precision into the glasses. Some wine cascaded out of the glass. Moley with some exasperation moved to mop it away. His mind was plainly very much elsewhere. Joe tried another tack.

'Nicholas…?'

'Yes!'

That hit home, thought Joe. The reply was far too abrupt.

'He's very good, Moley. Knows his stuff. He's gone down a complete storm with the traders. They really like his performance on the Euro. We wanted to know more about him. Is he on the market? I think you suggested that he was. We'd like to make him an offer.'

Which statement was only partially true, although it would serve. The morning meeting had been electrified but not wholly convinced by Nicholas' ranting performance at the podium forecasting a fall in the Euro to 75 cents and below. He had offended some of the traders as he expectorated his venom about the currency. They found him a touch too extreme.

'Oh really, I'm very pleased…Yes, he's very good…Interesting that you should talk about hiring him…'

They both stared some more at the chessboard and Joe, giving every appearance of thinking hard, moved his queen into danger territory. That startled Moley. His eyeballs roamed free within their sockets. He gazed at the board and then went through the whole repertoire of his mannerisms – the tugging of the eyebrows, then the scratching of the earlobe followed by the nose blowing and the thirsty, guilty gulp of Chablis. He looked at Joe and Joe returned his gaze, looking as innocent as thirty years of espionage would permit.

Joe did his innocent look quite convincingly, as Felix had never failed to point out.

'That is a very odd move, Joe. I'm not certain I understand it at all.'

'I'm not sure I do either, Moley. I'm sure that technically it's quite unsound.'

More theatricals from Moley whose range of responses to Joe's predicated moves had not included this pre-emptive strike. Then Moley gave some impression of what was on his mind. It was very strange.

'If Nicholas approaches you for a job, you will be sure to check with me first won't you? It's just that...Well, he's got a poor record in some areas and I'm shepherding him back into the City slowly. He has been known to make mistakes and he has put up some blacks. I don't want him falling into the wrong hands, if you understand what I mean...'

'Of course Moley. I wouldn't dream of taking an initiative without consulting you...'

'Good. That's very good.'

Moley looked relieved at Joe's comment. Too relieved.

'Come on Joe, it's your move now. What are you going to do about that?'

Moley had moved his bishop to counter the threat from Joe's queen. Joe paused to ponder. Moley was a lot happier now.

'You see, I had some people on the phone just now who were interested in hiring young Nicholas. They were very impressed. I don't know if you overheard...'

'I heard nothing Moley...The door slammed...'

'Good...No, that's fine... Well, I had to put them off too. Nicholas is not really on the market yet...'

Joe was still staring at the board. He knew what he was going to do. The move begged to be made. It was inevitable, like the end of a beautiful friendship. But it would take a few more moments before he struck. He held a small future reality in his head and his fingers ahead of the defining moment of its appearance.

The question he asked was like his chess move – defining and well nigh terminal.

'Tell me, Moley, who pays Nicholas? Do we pay him or do you?'

'Oh, I take care of all of that side of things. No, don't you worry at all about that. I'll take care of his money. We have an arrangement you see...'

Like Hell you do, you're going to screw him. I've seen your handwriting, don't forget, and it's a shocker, thought Joe. Moley, you are born to betray – it's in the calligraphy.

Joe reached for the chess piece.

Defining moment, then. So let's do it.

Picking up his piece with careful deliberation, he sacrificed his queen. There and then, without a tremor.

Moley goggled at the queen sacrifice. This was not what he had expected. Again the performance of the eyebrows, the earlobe, the nose blowing and this time the eyes out on stalks, a fresh addition to the repertoire.

'That was not what I expected, Joe. That is very unorthodox. I'll have to think about it. Long and hard.'

Which meant in Moley speak that the seance was over until he'd had a chance to run that particular set of combinations through his computer and then through various friends and then shift a few more pieces hither and thither on the board, in the quiet dark and still of the conspiratorial night. Moley was born to win by hook or by crook. For him, friendship was now just another moment of temporary arrival.

Or always had been.

Providentially Moley's phone rang at that moment. With a sudden smile bursting to his lips, Moley sprang to field the call, nodding the while at Joe. The game was indeed over for the time being. Moley made elaborate hand gestures, intimating that there would be a fresh encounter shortly. Joe beamed assent back. It cost him nothing. The situation was now meaningless as Moley moved back sharply into money-making mode. Joe moved to see himself out of the flat. The conventions were well set.

No sign that afternoon of the slave.

Joe wondered about his morale. Resentful at best, and at worst...? The mind boggled.

And why am I so surprised, thought Joe as he descended via the lift towards the ground floor from Moley's palace in the skies. Moley has moved on and so have I. We are both very different now from what we were. These encounters with the past never work. So why was I ever so foolish as to imagine that our friendship might have survived the years unscathed? Moley was clearly something else apart from what he claimed to be all those years ago, most likely some form of nark for the Bank of England or something similar...

And as for me, well that process of evolution via espionage would be hard to explain to anyone let alone an old friend...Half spy half trader and half vagabond and that's not even the half of it... And too many halves don't make a whole...

The lift hit the ground floor and Joe stepped out into the wind, still thinking about Moley.

...I don't think I ever mentioned the Fat Man to Moley, did I? Now that would have been an encounter and a half...They would both have bought and sold each other within half an hour...Each to his own advantage...

In the absence of Joe's driver, whose behaviour and attendance were now highly erratic as Joe's reputation within ABC started to nosedive, Joe took a cab in the direction of Waterloo Station His mind rolled back to the e-mail and its possible significance as the taxi swung along past St Paul's and down towards Fleet Street and the Strand.

What did the e-mail sing – danger ahead? No danger ahead? Keep calm? Who knew – it had to mean something, but he failed yet again to establish its precise significance. He gave up on the e-mail for the time being.

He brooded about Felix and just exactly how he should deal with that particular irritant, now that the mission looked to be just about completed. Lucia was in place and she could handle the Global details well. The bid should go through. It had been a tough struggle but it might just be entering the final lap or the home straight or whatever other cliche he might care to use... Talking advantage of Felix's absence, it might just be time for him to disappear for the final time, collecting his fat winnings from ABC via the severance cheque or something similar... Perhaps that was what the e-mail signified through the negative inference. Because there was no hidden message qua agent, therefore he had nothing to think about qua agent, while he obviously still had a considerable amount to mull over qua investment banker...

★   ★   ★   ★   ★

Rivers was having a small dinner party that evening for old friends, like Buffet and the rest of them. That was not exactly life-threatening on the face of it, but it did contain elements of vast potential frisson. Buffet had a girlfriend called Pascal, recently divorced from a spouse who lived on the Hampshire coast. Pascal was very beautiful, very striking and with huge presence. So much was obvious from the first minute of any encounter with Pascal. What Rivers and Buffet did not know in any great detail was that Pascal had in the past also been Joe's squeeze. Fortunes of war, thought Joe as he tried to discount the danger from that quarter. She'd been to Pugh Park before, after Joe's relationship with Perdita became more public, and she had breathed nothing about her prior dealings with Joe. She had been discreet. If provoked, she might turn nasty – Joe knew her of old to be a smouldering fireball of a woman. But in the absence of provocation, she hopefully would remain as tight-lipped as before. Joe reckoned she had too much to lose with Buffet to be able to indulge in any fits of temperament. That was his guess and his best estimate. But he couldn't be wholly certain.

So it might all come unstuck. And then, there would be ructions. Anything that she revealed about Joe's less than savoury past would surely create damage.

★   ★   ★   ★   ★

Joe was in the garden of Pugh Park talking to Lucia about the bid. Lucia thought he was in the King's Road. Joe glimpsed Mrs Gulliver waving towards him from afar by way of a late dinner call.

'Let me ask you, Lucia, are you still on-line with the Pru this evening?'

'This is why I've been calling you. They are biting very hard now and they want to talk some more about the sterling angle. If you can firm that up, then they'll bite very heavily for sure. I can go back at any time. They want to commit.'

'Ask them the obvious question. How do they feel about $1.40 or thereabouts for the pound? Maybe even lower. It's $1.50 now. But it's tumbling. Just make the forex call sound like a shot across the bows…'

'They'll be sceptical. But if they thought that was what they'd be offered in dollars, they'll kill to do the deal.'

'Of course they would, but we can talk about all that at tomorrow's meeting. Ask the Pru as well how they'll feel if the attack on the Euro gets worse…Starting almost immediately…If they see that coming over the horizon, then they'll be more inclined to sell out.'

'I'll call you back when I've spoken to the Pru. Don't you dare be off-line for me.'

'I'm just going into dinner now. Don't be surprised if I take some time to come back to you. But I will speak to you soonest.'

'OK, but I want to register a small moan here. It's all A-OK for you going in for dinner. But what about me? So what about my summer holidays, Joe? What about them?'

'Don't get human with me, Lucia. Your holidays will come back. Like everything else. You get your reward before Heaven. Now go for it. Hit those suits as only you know how. And in the meantime, congratulations on signing up the Norwich Union. That is a big break-through.'

Joe saw Mrs Gulliver had advanced within ten feet of him and was looking anxious.

'I must go now, Lucia, I am being summoned. But we will speak later on…'

He snapped the mobile shut and saw that Mrs Gulliver seemed very distressed. She groped at his arm.

'Joe, I think you'd better come quickly. I think that Perdita is not at all well. I can't get her to come down for dinner.'

It was a moment of truce between them, as genuine apprehension for Perdita overwhelmed Mrs G's natural repugnance for Joe. Joe hurried into the house, and past the dining room, where he could see Buffet and Rivers at play together and shrieking with laughter. Then he hustled up the stairs. He caught Perdita emerging from their bedroom. She looked strained and tired and wayward. Joe took her by the hand and led her back into the bedroom. She suffered herself to be escorted back there.

The moon seemed very close to them both outside the window. Perdita sat down on the bed and hunched forward. She was the picture of abject despair.

'I'll go through with it this evening, Joe, and I think I'll be OK over dinner but I can't make any promises. It's not Mrs G's fault at all. She can't help it if she's not Mummy. But you know what happens to me, it's always the same. Just as I'm getting into my stride, I look for Mummy to come round the corner and make her funny, sarcastic comments about me… And…and…Well, she doesn't, does she? So she wasn't there tonight, was she? And she'll never be there again will she…? So my Mummy has gone for ever, hasn't she…? Oh God, oh God, oh God…I loved her so much, so very, very much… I find all of this very hard to bear. It's so hard.'

Her eyes were very full of tears and she heaved her breathing into her mouth. Joe sat beside her and placed his arm around her and drew her very close to him without a sound, trying to let the animal body warmth seep out from him and into her so that she took some succour from him. She was like a wounded stricken bird. Soundlessly she sobbed into her handkerchief, as her blond hair splayed everywhere in disarray.

Then she turned to him with red desperate eyes and her floppy mouth reached out and felt for his lips.

'Joe you're very good to me and I don't deserve it. I give you so much trouble. I always give you grief. You're not going to leave me are you? Promise me, promise me. Go on, Joe, promise.'

Joe nodded his head without a sound as she clung to him with nails dug tightly into his shirt and he held the dead weight of her body mass against his chest. He felt the hot wet salt of her tears as they cascaded down her cheeks. He rocked her to and fro very gently against him and listened to her breathing to detect any improvement. It was thready and she was breathing very deeply and irregularly. He held her very close and said nothing.

Little by little the attack on her from remorse ebbed a little. It was a miracle for Joe to feel the health returning to her. The breathing became more regular and the sobbing began to abate. The flow of tears started to dry up. She sniffed into her handkerchief. Like an animal relieved of its pain, she moved a little and stirred her body a fraction away from Joe, still clad in his sombre City suit.

'Oh, look Joe,' she said with sudden merriment, 'look what I've done to your suit. You look as if you've been snogging some tart.'

Her lipstick had smeared its way down Joe's lapel in a crimson gash and he laughed at the mess on the material. He wagged an admonitory finger at her.

'No tarts, Perdita, no tarts…'

That was reassuring for her. She smiled at him. She was beginning to recover quite quickly now. She grimaced through the tears and began to brush them away from her cheeks.

'Me Perdita, you…?'

'Jesus Christ…'

'That's funny, you normally say John the Baptist.'

'I was going to say that, but I suddenly remembered that he lost his head on account of Salome. I was superstitious. I need to keep my head just for the time being…'

'You really are the clever one, aren't you. I'd like to know one of these days what actually goes on in that noddle of yours, clever clogs…'

She was stirring, like an animal emerging from its covert. She was walking round the room now, looking fit again and ready to riposte at him. The remorse had left her for the time being, although it might return that evening. She was more alert again. Her confidence was returning.

'Can I go downstairs for dinner looking like this, Joe? My eyes are terribly swollen. I look as if I've been beaten up.'

'Go as a private detective.'

'You mean wearing some shades. Looking sinister.'

'I don't see why not. Buffet knows nothing about your little attacks so you can say that you bumped into something. Rivers won't even notice, I imagine, because he's completely tied up in one of his deals, and he'll be talking to the tribe of Pugh, his acolytes. Mrs G won't say a thing. You can always take them off half way through dinner when you're feeling better.'

Gamely, Perdita grinned at the idea. Then she rummaged in the drawers of her dressing table impatiently as the moon outside seemed to draw ever closer to the window, bringing back fond memories of Lady Pugh clumping about the house in exasperation as she organised the menage. Perdita turned around with black shades over her eyes, looking terribly Marlene Dietrich and very fake.

Joe laughed at her.

'You look like the Blue Angel, something out of Berlin in the twenties.'

With relief at finding a solution to her grief, however temporary, Perdita cavorted a little around the room wearing the shades.

'All right, Joe, I'll leave you to get changed out of your tarty suit. I'll be downstairs arresting everybody. You come down when you're ready. But don't be long. Mrs G. will have the food on the table in a few seconds... But of course, I was forgetting, you know everything there is to be known about Berlin, don't you, oh silent one who does not talk about his past life.'

Perdita knew a little about Joe's clandestine life. Not a lot but a little.

'Nobody was as beautiful as you in Berlin, Perdita...Nor as dangerous...'

'And you mean that...?'

'Most sincerely. Yes, most sincerely, sweetheart.'

She kissed him again on the lips. She liked that exchange of banter. It always gave her pleasure. He saw her to the door, and she was still wearing her shades. She seemed a little happier as she left…

As Joe took off his suit, he saw that his mobile had taken another call. It was another call from Lucia. He returned the call quickly. She picked up the phone instantly.

'Joe you really do know how to turn these people on. I've got both the Pru and Standard Life jumping down my throat here at the prospect of seeing $1.40 on the dollar value of the bid. But they want to know more, much, much more. Can you oblige?'

'Not a lot this evening. But ask them to come into ABC tomorrow and we'll run through the rationale. Early, say around 8.30. Tell them it involves Argentina, I think, and the Bank of England's crazy exposed forex position, again as I think. That's what I surmise, but I can't be certain at this juncture this evening. But I can firm a lot of it up tomorrow early…It's an idea that's been knocking around in my head for a day or so. What has happened today has helped to clarify and crystallise everything. In the meantime, just check out $/Euro for me will you and leave a message for me on the mobile. I'll call you when I'm free, say in an hour or so. The shooting may be starting on that one any minute and that will help us enormously over Global. We could be just getting into our starting blocks tonight on the whole deal, if the Euro is as weak in New York as I think it will be. And I have a good feeling about it all now. So well done Lucia and thanks for keeping me posted…'

'A pleasure, Joe. I must say, you sound very confident. Is it your dinner party that's going so well for you?'

'At the moment, my dear Lucia, I am standing at the top of the stairs in somebody else's house after answering a call of nature.'

'And where's this dinner-party you're at?'

'Just off the King's Road. If we didn't have a full table, I'd invite you. That plus the fact that I'm a guest, not the host.'

'Give my regards to the good life.'

'Of course. With pleasure. It's just as good as you remember. Now get me that Euro/$ quote, will you, in an hour or so…?'

'Gladly.'

And for once it sounded as if Lucia meant it. She had not been born over-endowed with a facility for compliments. Nor girlish optimism. She was always more Maitland than female. And she, fully endowed with all her family's legendary feel for markets, could see that the shadow dancing ahead of the bid was drawing to an end. Joe for his part thanked God for mobile phones, which left his precise whereabouts unknowable and untraceable.

He showered swiftly, pulled on his jeans and a shirt and went down for dinner, hoping to chat some more with Perdita.

Rivers knew well how to freeze someone out of a conversation – the laughter at the Pugh dinner table more or less died as Joe entered the room but he was indifferent to the disapproval. Joe was used to a frosty reception chez Pugh. On this occasion, it was attributable as much to the ambivalence of Joe's social position as to the presence of Rivers' crew. The crowd at the dinner table was not quite sure where Joe fitted in. It had never been pointed out wholly clearly by either Joe or Rivers to the likes of Buffet that Joe had inherited Pugh Park on Lady Pugh's death. Buffet assumed that it had all gone through as per natural and per programme to Rivers – or would do shortly – and behaved accordingly. No one wished to disturb the tranquillity of Buffet's assumptions, or anyone else's for that matter. By hugely tacit agreement, therefore, on occasions such as these when his cronies were present, Rivers sat at the head of the table as master of Pugh Park and Joe sat in the well, along with Mrs Gulliver and her husband, Captain Pluperfect and the rest of them. It cost Joe nothing to defer to Rivers in this way and it helped to keep the peace. In some respects the seating plans suited him. As a spy he could hide in the crowds, as he was used to doing. Sometimes at Pugh Park the need for concealment was very strong in Joe and he craved his camouflage. By the same token, the volatile and saturnine Rivers needed all the appeasement which Joe could offer given his long standing disapproval of Joe's presence in any way among the Pugh's and his people. So Joe opted for the easy line and played it long, thinking quietly that before too long, the shooting would start and that Rivers, now seated comfortably at the head of the table, would be on the run.

And how!

As for the Pugh Park ambiance, the shades of Sloane School hung heavily across the table. Office furniture on conspicuous display, along with loudly ticking clocks. As well as his old school friend Buffet, Rivers had invited along a couple of young tyros from Global with their girl friends. They sat there stiff and attentive, with the girls looking gawky and strictly on their very best behaviour. All of them, boys and girls together, were very careful not to put a foot wrong or say a word out of place, so that career opportunities did not go a-begging. The atmosphere was unnaturally subservient. No spontaneous huzzahs of disapproval or loud coarse raspberries blown from that quarter.

Eyes kept moving constantly in the direction of Rivers, watching his every move, gauging his mood and seeking approval or disapproval for continued existence. It was purely feudal. Joe guessed they were all ex-alumni of Sloane School, judging by the way they had been smiling in a ferocious yet indulgent way at Buffet's court jester antics with the walking stick.

Nothing had changed at that end of the table since time immemorial, Joe guessed as he wandered into dinner. Rivers was still smiling at his court jester's antics as he had smiled at the same performance at Sloane School many years before. Nothing to learn from that quarter. He looked around for Pascal, the danger hand in this situation. To his relief, he saw that she was absent. Her place, directly opposite to him was empty. Delayed? Cancelled? Better offer? Who knew? Certainly not Joe, uninterested in questioning the rationale for her absence. For him, it was just another sliver of good fortune in the midst of his social morass.

That evening he was afraid of Pascal, of what she might create.

Perdita sat the other end of the table facing Rivers and wearing her shades. She looked vampy and tantalising, but somewhat restored. The outrageous nature of her appearance had been very largely ignored. The flows of attention were all in the direction of Rivers who graciously dispensed attention from his end of the table to Buffet and the acolytes. She gazed down the table at her brother, an approving smile curving her lips as he spoke.

Buffet was not yet on the table gagging with the stick but he wasn't far away from doing his leaping-around act amid the cutlery. Joe knew the signs; he was familiar with the Buff's antics. Buffet was stirring. The stick in his hands was jiggling up and down and he looked bent on mischief.

More or less unacknowledged, Joe sat down at his place at table and greeted Captain Pluperfect, Mrs Gulliver's husband, seated opposite and sideways, with a quip. Mrs G was fixing the food in the kitchen which duly appeared, borne in by the evening's two helpers. It was osso bucco, done River Cafe cookbook style, and cooked very skilfully indeed.

Joe was offered a starter but he waved it away. Time to get on with the grub

The plates were filled tastefully, the sauce to the osso bucco had just the right bitter tang to it, and Joe for one moment felt like a homecoming had been arranged. Between the kitchen and the dining room, Mrs G was in full control, behaving like a true Hampshire beadle.

The Gulliver buttocks flounced in and out of the kitchen, looking well satisfied with the product of the kitchen. They had a ' job well done' slither to them. Joe avoided Perdita's eye after he stared at her retreating posterior and then began gorging down the food.

After some mouthfuls and feeling the pangs of hunger abate a fraction, he addressed Captain Pluperfect across the table.

'Cross gartered again, I see, Pluperfect. It suits you. Very chic. Wish I had the nerve to wear those socks.'

Joe's jeering reference to Malvolio was lost on the Captain who glanced at Joe suspiciously and then continued eating, head well down. As a matter of course, Pluperfect wore yellow socks every day. That was his moniker. Pluperfect then grunted a perfunctory comment in Joe's direction. His reticence was understandable. Socially he hunted with his wife. He viewed Joe as an unexplained aberration, hardly worth an acknowledgement. Not known, not categorisable and therefore socially negligible.

Pluperfect slurped down some more food, head still well down.

Then turning away abruptly, Pluperfect turned to Rivers at the head of the table and asked him again about his dinner at No. 10 with Tony Blair, the Prime Minister.

Rivers was pleased to share his experiences with the dinner table.

'Hardly worth the trouble. Blair knows nothing about business, his wife is even worse, and so far as I could gather it was a fund-raising exercise. The number of Indian business men around the table would have confirmed that point, I think. No, a complete waste of time, apart from the really quite valuable contact I may have made with one of the Indians. I sniffed a deal there. He wants to sell, and I thought I might quite like to buy....Expensive, but then these deals always are...'

The acolytes perked up dutifully at all this talk of deals and prepared to applaud. In-house at Global, Rivers was clearly viewed as someone who could walk on water. But Pluperfect was not to be fobbed off with such trifling titbits. He wanted more details.

'And Cherie?'

The question pleased Rivers. He weighed in with the county's customary, loud-mouthed abuse.

Pluperfect nodded, perfectly satisfied with Rivers' account and the material he had picked up for on-passing to cronies elsewhere in the county. One of the Global acolytes then dared to ask his boss a question, but only after he had carefully emptied his mouth of food. He paused carefully before speaking. His girl friend, dressed like a squaw and apparently poised on tiptoe although seated, looked on approvingly as her flunkey boyfriend smoothed his fingertips.

'How long before the new deal is finalised, Rivers? We're getting impatient down in M&A to see it through.'

He looked meaningfully at Joe along the table, in silent question about raising such points before an outsider. Rivers nodded as if to intimate that Joe's presence was of no consequence.

Flunkey then added a daring coda to his comment.

'We can't wait to really get our hands on that Czech business. It's just crying out to be ripped apart.'

Rivers nodded his head like a predator.

'Not long now, not long at all, and then we pass onto the big one...'

That was enough for the Global tribe. It guffawed in unison and then subsided back into eating mode, well pleased with the tactical fawning. Mrs Gulliver asked Joe how he was enjoying the osso bucco and Joe answered softly that it was slipping down very well. He had been musing idly about Moley and the loss of 25 years' friendship consequent upon Moley's betrayal.

It trashed the past so unexpectedly, he was discovering. Such a betrayal liquidates the past because it besmirches it, he thought recalling the good hours that he and Moley had spent up and down the City wine bars.

Mrs G persisted in puncturing his musings.

'You would have eaten quite a lot of it when you were in Italy, I imagine.'

Joe nodded in agreement. How typical of Mrs G to get her countries wrong! She knew that he had spent time abroad but precisely where he had been located was a total mystery to her. But it might just as well have been Italy for all she knew. Grateful for the food, Joe improvised to be helpful.

'Masses of it, Mrs G. That and ravioli, were my favourites. Your cooking brings it all back. You certainly know my Achilles heel, Mrs G.'

Joe was conscious that Perdita was glinting at him down the table and he wondered if his crack was the signal for veiled and highly camouflaged warfare to break out between them.

Mrs G was in chatty mode.

'I'm surprised that Rivers even ventured to go so far as to have dinner in No. 10. I know he's forced to do these things for his business but it was asking a lot of him. I do feel that a Labour Government in power is always something odd and unnatural, don't you, Joe?'

It was a coercive rhetorical question, plainly inviting the answer 'Yes'. Joe hardly read Mrs G as a socialist. She was plainly trying to teach Joe the correct social way for Hampshire and to school his replies so that he demonstrated the correct attitude.

Joe was poised to reply in a way that would refrain from offending when at that moment he was forced to field a question from Perdita.

The shades leered cock-eyed at him from the end of the table.

'Joe, what have you done with Dr Foster?'

Perdita's question, dead on cue! So she wasn't out for the count after all. So there was life in the Pugh withers! Joe was briefly stumped for a reply to the tag line but then inspiration came to him on the late evening breezes.

'I said the hounds of spring were following on winter's traces.'

Pause for dramatic effect as the table ignored Joe and got its head firmly in the trough.

'But let it pass, let it pass. And incidentally, what do four ones beat?'

That was two for the price of one. That should take care of Perdita the Minx for the time being. But Mrs G misunderstood the whole thrust of the Q&A session. Glancing briefly at Rivers for approval, she chipped in:

'Oh so you're using Dr Foster, are you? We, that is Ken and myself, we're still using Dr Upcerne. We find that he's so reliable, especially for Ken's...'

Captain Pluperfect broke in quickly. He had no desire to overhear his wife describing his recent anatomical experiences beneath the surgeon's knife. Captain Pluperfect was keen to cut an exciting social dash in and around Hampshire. Haemorrhoids, a natural health hazard of late middle age, hardly helped the blazer-clad, post retirement, boulevardier image.

But misunderstanding the literary allusions, the Captain nevertheless picked up the ball and ran with it, refocussing the conversation at Perdita's end of the table quite naturally on himself.

'You know, Perdita, I've never been able to work out what four ones beat in any game. But do you know my bridge is going from strength to strength now that I've retired. I've very nearly got back to where I used to be twenty years ago...'

The shades nodded with interest. Perdita knew how to play this particular game too. She paused. Then she replied with calculated, wicked intent. Perdita was a naughty girl.

'You should ask Joe to play with you some time. He used to make a living out of it, some years ago. Didn't you, Joe? He's red hot. Aren't you, darling?"

The shades leered some more at him from down the table as Perdita enjoyed herself. Joe nodded vaguely, thinking just what a vicious knowing little bitch she could be on occasion. The way she had put the Captain on the spot was nothing short of masterly.

The Captain squirmed, using his shoulders, and grinning his frank, entirely duplicitous smile, as he tacked away from the idea of being seen in public with Joe. The Captain was most definitely not keen to be seen playing with social inferiors. He talked very quickly.

'Different styles, Joe, and different aims, I would have thought, wouldn't you. We'd play different games all the time. You're a young man and you'll be up to all the tricks. All that new-fangled stuff isn't for me... Which is not to say that I wouldn't welcome a game with you some time when we can get around to fixing it up.'

Joe thought with dreary premonition of what the evasive Captain was going to add. Was his diary perchance a little full for the time being?

The Captain did not fail to disappoint.

'My diary is a little over-booked right now, I'm sorry, but that's no reason why we shouldn't meet some time and play. If you like to give me a ring sometime in the week, we can try to forge an alliance.'

The Captain gave his socially correct explanation and Mrs G beamed approval as the timing of the meeting was left unresolved. Joe needed far more kicking into shape before a date with her Captain could be arranged in Hampshire.

Joe nodded with an apparent semblance of gratitude, wearying abruptly of the poor sport of the whole Pugh Park charade and thinking about Lucia and her check on the Euro/$ quote. He returned to adult mode, as he glanced around him at the table, taking in the fawning over Rivers at one end of the table; the comic idiocy of Captain Pluperfect and Mrs G; Buffet the Mad Clown; and even, sad to say, Perdita herself who at that moment was gazing in admiration from behind the shades at her brother, whom she adored.

Ownership is not possession, he told himself yet again. Meanwhile the memory of Moley's perfidy was not far distant from his mind at that moment...

One of those cold defining moments stole upon him at the Pugh Park dinner table, as carefully etched in his mind as the moment when he pulled the trigger on the Fat Man and blew out his brains in Fleet Street; or when an aghast Spongo shot himself in the Martins dealing room; or when Lady Pugh tumbled from her station wagon close to death after her wild drive from the Rachmaninov concert; or when he observed with deep welling tears her long sad funeral in the graveyard close by the sea.

Or his realisation that Moley would now do him wrong...Without hesitation...

Defining; irreversible; sad; chill; and stark. The buzz at the tables continued all around him but ceased for Joe, leaving him alone with his thoughts, even as he gazed at Perdita, now lording it, shades and all, as she embarked on a deep discussion with the Captain.

Should I be here, he wondered? Am I not wholly out of place, out of time and out of character? Is even my idolatrous love for Perdita not enough to conceal that fact? And is this how it all ends up, with me jumping through the Hampshire hoops and getting snubbed by frauds like the Captain and his ilk? Is there anything more for me now on offer and better than the slow and gradual grinding down by the country social round? Or do I finish up like all the rest of them, walking in line...?

This cannot be either true or for real. It seems too sad a return on all that expensive investment in time and experience...It is unthinkable...I'd prefer the dangers of Berlin to all this...

His patterns of thinking and the wide range of his possible responses seemed to alter as he was struck amidships by sad clear perceptions. Involvement in the hubbub of the table slipped away from him quietly, leaving him standing starkly isolated and alone in the mental landscape, like a solitary, blasted oak, branches cleaving sightlessly to the unforgiving sky.

Alone and detached and remote...

Nothing to be seen for miles around...Unvisited...Moorland, just moorland all around...

Mechanically, he slipped his mobile out of his shirt pocket and holding it beneath the table, checked the calls. Three so far, all from Lucia! My God, what was happening in the markets...? Three calls was a telephone directory on the actual movement of markets for Lucia; normally she didn't like to get too much involved in the minute by minute ebb and flow of securities' prices...

Joe wanted very much at that moment to know his prices. That way he could restore some semblance of control and location to his universe by gauging expectations in the currency markets.

And hence his deal. It would mean a lot, everything in fact, to the deal if the currency angle started coming in very strong.

A sense of inevitable separation from the partying in full swing around the table began to invade him like the slow movement of tides at midnight. He saw Perdita at one end of the table, looking jollier as she doffed the shades from time to time, and then the solemn focussed Rivers at the other end, occasionally smiling as tribute was offered to him. Joe felt wholly de trop, not least because he was poised to break the sacred ties of hospitality in one way or another by orchestrating the brutal takeover of Rivers' company. Joe sensed that he ought in truth to stand up and make his farewells there and then...

Perdita was on the boat with the bunting and the bands playing, as the vessel slipped yet another few feet away from the jetty, so that the gap between craft and land, formerly invisible, had now widened to about twelve feet...Still not a large gap, but too wide now to span with a flying leap... As the distance grew between them all...

His feelings were grey and sad.

What am I doing here, he thought to himself? These people have grown up with each other, they bonded years ago deeply and for ever. They are like vegetation. They are part and parcel of each other's skin and bone. They grow together like trees in the fields or flowers in the meadow. But I'm not like that; my role is separate. There seems to be no place here for me – I'm a townie hobo on the roads, not a fixture in the fields...

Joe thought about his deal. He had forgotten briefly that the head of the company against which he was poised to move without compassion was seated no more than five feet away from him, gossiping with cronies in the full plenitude of his power as CEO of Global. Joe was rejecting the Mansfield Park aspect of it all, where Sir Thomas Bertram, a.k.a. Rivers Pugh, was the necessary and sufficient head of the household, setting the standards without question. Joe was sharply indifferent to any of the rural traditions of control and deference. They meant nothing to him and they never would. Gumboots were just gumboots – they did not sing to him.

But the markets did…! Joe was pretty certain from Lucia's frantic calls that a currency crisis was about to overwhelm the markets. Had the Euro collapsed? Was it holding? Or even recovering? No way of telling. But the deal hinged on all of this – where the Euro went, the pound was following faithfully. He felt certain about that. He wanted to call Lucia to check prices against his expectations and get the feel of the market matrix of greed and fear in full operational mode.

But he was powerless. Until a gap or an interval in the dinner party presented itself he was nailed to the floor, forced to remain at the table, making his polite and meaningless conversation.

It was torture for Joe…

He looked at his mobile again. Four calls now from Lucia…Christ, this is unbearable, worse than playing bridge in Hell with 51 cards.

Eventually Buffet bailed him out. Buffet could wait no longer. The dinner party was too lively. He had to be himself. In the absence of Pascal and egged on by the tribe of Global courtiers, he grasped his stick and was up there on the table in time honoured tradition, gnawing at the handle, shaking his head and making the growling noises, in time honoured celebration of some epic long forgotten cosmic event of his and Rivers' childhood. The table applauded – the dinner party was too staid and needed livening up with some bad behaviour. They were all agreed on that. Like a Capetian monarch, Rivers smiled at the performance – this was more like Buffet and about time too…

The Global boys and girls chortled with careful merriment. The Captain smiled too, squaring his shoulders, after a worried glance at Rivers first to double-check permitted reactions. Mrs G was in the kitchen.

Buffet danced away on the table as Joe worried about his deal.

Then with a clatter of plates, Perdita clambered onto the table to join the party, like a trainee lap dancer. Abruptly, with a smile on her face, she too was up there, shades still hooding her eyes and skirt flying up and down as she tap danced up and down between the diners. Joe looked at her slim ankles highlighted by her light black slingbacks flying past his nose and the long young untested legs that went on and on as they danced past him. He thought about Lady Pugh and Berlin hookers he had known in the past – they too had always done exactly what they wanted when they wanted. An overwhelming sadness at his failure to reach out to Perdita and winch her away from off her fast-disappearing boat began to envelop him as he watched her dance up and down on the table, doing her thing as she had always done it...

Dancing for Rivers and his approval. As she had always done.

Chaos began to reign. Buffet, her old suitor, welcomed her to the dance and they rocked back and forth on the top of the table, occasionally sending a plate here and a wine glass there flying to the floor. Perdita's heels hammered in frenzy on the table oak.

Mrs G took one look at the carnage and fled back to the kitchen, buttocks waving and flapping a distress signal. The Captain remained motionless chained to his chair by the spectacle of the dancing Perdita's slim thighs. She cavorted about with Buffet in high spirits, abandoning herself to the occasion. Buffet was growling and Perdita was shrieking. Joe felt old and detached.

Then Perdita danced alone, rocking her arms back and forth so that her boobs waggled in time to the clapping from the audience, as she danced up and then back from Rivers, like a stripper. It occurred to Joe that he was beginning to understand just exactly why Lady Pugh had willed Pugh Park to him, as Perdita first knelt on one knee before Rivers and kissed him on the forehead in mock-submission, before danced away down the table, roaring at the top of her voice. Then she came dancing back in order to repeat the gesture, this time kneeling on the other leg as she slid the free leg out and along the partial length of the table. Her skirt rode up again over her little bottom as she kissed Rivers again on the forehead...

Truly the gorgeous Salome of the county, thought Joe, observing the performance and feeling his heart chill at her mad rejection of him for the reels on the table...

One of us should be a Boswell taking all this down, he thought.

More clapping from the acolytes and from Buffet, still standing up there beside her...

Then Perdita seemed to falter standing by herself in the middle of the table. She looked dazed as if wondering how she came to find herself up there on the table, on display, wagging her lace knickers and her pussy at the gloating watchers seated all around her...

It's about the moment for Pascal to turn up, Joe thought, recalling an anguished scene of years ago at the Reform Club when Gregory, Emma's poet lover, had fallen off his chair just as Pascal had arrived for dinner.

This is just about the moment when she makes her entrance...

On cue, a voice hit the scene in the Pugh dining room with a crack like a whiplash.

'What on earth is going on here? This is like a bear garden. Buffet, just why are you making such a fool of yourself like this again? Can you tell me quickly please? What are you doing on the table?'

Joe had been right; it was a correct call. Behold Pascal – and then some! It was herself framed in the doorway. Foppishly, Rivers smiled at her like an old Roman at a banquet, waiting for more.

Nobody had heard the front doorbell ring. An angry Pascal, tall and dead white with rage stood there like a Fury. She spoke like an experienced dominatrix, accustomed to using a husky rasp in her voice to gain obedience. Buffet would be taking, not giving, the lashing later that night.

'Get down from there immediately, you fool.'

Buffet cringed, looking like the abandoned little boy that he was at heart and obeyed Pascal's instructions. His walking stick tumbled from his hand and bounced along the table with a terrible clatter. Perdita still turned around herself slowly, aloft and adrift and confused among the crockery. Joe thought she might have lost her wits temporarily. Too much Prozac on the quiet...? To help simmer her down...?

'Rivers, I'm sorry I'm late for dinner, but it doesn't look as if I've missed much...'

Rivers waved a nonchalant arm towards her as Pascal stalked into the room, still white with rage. Joe reckoned this was a good moment to slip away. The market and Lucia were calling him. He just had a few seconds to make his call. Sadly, he was forced to leave Perdita to make her own way down from the table. There was just no time to accomplish both tasks...

It was like a farewell...

He walked through the kitchen and into the fresh air outside, tapping out the telephone number as he went. Lucia was still at her post, but sounded weary.

'What kept you, Joe?'

'High jinks, and rather too much of them. A little local difficulty but it's over now. What are they?'

'Who's a very clever stockmarket operator then?'

Joe laughed and let her give him the news.

'The Euro is collapsing. New York has smashed it apart. It's recovered from the worst but it was down about five cents at one point. It was awesome. And it took the £ with it. They really gave the £ a tonking, after they'd made a meal of the Euro. So forecast made and forecast fulfilled – clever old Joe. Those institutions I mentioned want to meet with you without fail tomorrow morning. They are impressed. We have spoken again. For the time being, they think you walk on water.'

'Which I do, of course, but only on Fridays. Not a pretty sight at the best of times. Ask my dry-cleaner....And the Euro?'

'I'm calling it 86 cents...But it looks very rocky. It could even be easier than that, as we speak.'

'That is a fall and a half. One hell of a drop. And cable?'

'Slipping...Very weak too. $1.49 or so, off about two cents on the session...And slipping, like the Euro. It'll be very weak tomorrow in London.'

' I think it goes a lot further down…Short term, I see it $1.45 or even lower.'

'You're bound to be right, Joe. Downing Street has opined on the problem, this evening not 15 minutes ago. The No 10 Press Office suggested the UK was indifferent to whatever level the £ traded. It was on the wire. That really ripped the guts out of it.'

'Christ, they've totally lost it.'

'Agreed, Joe.'

'I think we'll have this deal wrapped up soonest now, Lucia.'

'It feels good…They'll be eating out of your hand tomorrow, Joe. They smell those dollars –and their forex turn.'

'That's natural and understandable. But you sound tired Lucia. True or false? Or have I got that one wrong…?'

'Trick or treat…Oh not a lot Joe. Not to the marrow. What makes you think I'm fatigued? I've only been here for about fourteen hours so far today…'

'You'll recover, you'll see. But you've done good work today, Lucia, and thank you very much. I think we may have timed it just about right on this deal. The Maitland touch as ever is unerring…'

'It was nothing, Joe. Just hard work, talking to those fucking smug institutions. I'm not really very tired. But I'm just thinking about your party…How is it? Plenty of broken glass flying about? Lots of bad behaviour? It's so long since I was out on the town. I feel quite envious of you…'

'Actually, Lucia, you've missed nothing. It's very dull and all that's been talked about is bridge hands…Everyone here is too old. It's like being in the country.'

Joe wondered whether at that moment Pascal was not actually lashing Buffet into submission, with Perdita slumped either in her chair or across the table. But he refrained from elaboration on the tasteful scene at Pugh Park that night.

Lucia rang off after stressing how important it was for Joe to be punctual the following morning. It could be a full house. She reckoned the word was now circulating fast that something like a mega-deal was afoot with ABC right in the middle of it. There might be more than just two institutions present to hear Joe's presentation. It could be standing room only at his talk in the morning.

'So, don't be late, Joe'

Joe bade her a cheery goodnight and walked back through the kitchen where Mrs G, without comment, was beavering away with the rest of the hired help over the washing up. He went into the dining room. It was empty. Starkly so. The guests had fled and the dinner party was dead. Causality was disjointed. A wind blowing through the room suggested that the front door was open. The guests had departed. It was over for the evening. Buffet had gone and so had Pascal. Rivers and his acolytes were nowhere to be seen.

And likewise Perdita...

Likewise Perdita...

Feeling the same kind of blind red rage rising in him that years ago had made Joe snatch the Fat Man's pistol from him, pull the trigger and blow his brains all across the street, Joe went to the open front door and sat just outside the house, looking at the wind. He breathed quite heavily and he bit at his knuckles in his concentration. He felt angry, he felt a fool, he felt like he was on the road again, and he felt that his deal was going to come up smiling...

He was experiencing a complex set of reactions to the evening's entertainment.

At that moment, he wanted Perdita very much to be with him and beside him, so that his simmering rage might abate. But she wasn't there. In his murderous heart of hearts, Joe felt now she might never be there. He had made his play and he had lost. An alternative reality, more attractive and familiar to her, had abruptly descended from the flies, neatly bisecting their territory together so that she was in one segment – Buffet, pals, larking in the hay wain, high spirits and frivolity – and he was trapped somewhere else in another tranche.

A tranche that was far, far harsher.

And the connect between the two segments was non-existent. That was obvious enough. The connect was that there was no connect.

He looked some more at the dark wind of the night blowing through the house and across the park and failed to glimpse any sight of Perdita. She could be anywhere, he decided. He looked at his watch – midnight. It would be foolish to organise a search party. She could be with Rivers. Or talking to Buffet. Or even exchanging some vicious confidences with Pascal. Then Joe gave up on assumptions. He did not care to pursue Perdita like some uxorious jealous swain. That would be fatal. Closing the door he went upstairs to bed alone, feeling devastated.

She went where she wanted.

He threw off his clothes, discovered that he was dog-tired as the fatigue and the tension hit him, and then fell into bed with his eyes closing as his head hit the pillow...He went out like a light....He felt his mind closing down as his spirit tobogganed down the misty pathways of sleep, down 20,000 fathoms at least as the waters closed above his head... Up again at 6, for the 8.30 meeting, he told himself. Must get some sleep. It won't do to talk to those institutions with bags under my eyes and Lucia glinting at me with rage and jealousy, fearing the deal might be slipping away...

And then he was awake abruptly, as sound struck his ears. What on earth was that, he asked himself, feeling the dead weight of his body as he struggled up onto his elbow, then looking at his clock which read 2 in the morning. The dream was dispatched.

The cry came again, out there deep in the night...It sounded primal, lonely, anguished and painful, some soul in torment... Joe turned to wake Perdita and discovered that his bed was empty apart from himself.

So where was Perdita...?

Oh God, he thought to himself, could that be her out there in the park in the night, screaming away? Finally driven mad by her own sense of contradiction? Must see, must see...He pulled his jeans back on and padded to the door of the bedroom. Then cautiously in the darkness he descended the stairs, heading for the kitchen.

In the kitchen, he found Rivers fixing himself a glass of water. Rivers stared at him and carried on pouring out the water. Rivers and Joe spoke rarely. During the dinner party they had not exchanged a single word. Joe felt more rage bubble up strongly from his spleen.

One of these days, Rivers...And it's coming up fast, Rivers...

'What was that? Did you hear it? Where is Perdita?'

Primly Rivers took a sip of water and replied evenly.

'I don't know, I'm going back to bed. That's your business.'

Joe heard a sound from the dining room which ran the length of the south side of the house, parallel with the lake outside. He crept to the door of the kitchen and opened it a fraction. Nothing but moonlight playing through the windows...Nothing there at all, and nothing to get scared about...But then he saw it all very clearly in the moonlight...

'Oh my God. This is horrible. Oh Christ...'

Quickly, Rivers was behind him at the door.

'What's that...Oh...'

It was Perdita. Stark naked, walking up and down the length of the room, plashed in the moonlight, and arms waving. She was holding an imaginary conversation with her mother, the dead Lady Pugh.

Sleepwalking or plain mad, it was impossible to tell. But her voice was high and rising. She gesticulated as she talked.

'Yes, mother, you see, it's quite simple. Only you don't understand...And of course you'll never understand will you...That's why you're my mother, isn't it...And didn't you like my hopscotch...And wasn't Rivers so very, very clever? Beautiful Rivers, mother dear.'

Then Perdita made her great wheezing porcine sound – the one which had so infuriated her mother – and carried on her dialogue with the dead, this time pointing through the window and across the lake outside. She moved in and out of shade as she moved. The moonbeams played with pleasure on her naked breasts and her long slender body and legs...

'And yes, I'd like my tea now, if you don't mind, and then we can look after the lake...And Rivers, of course. Come on Mummy, you know that I can't make tea to save my life...Mummy, mummy, make the tea.'

Joe heard Rivers draw in his breath behind him and turn around as Perdita continued to march up and down, mad in the moonlight, shouting out now at the top of her voice old scraps of remembered discussion with her beloved mother. She was deafening.

'Come on mother, just make the tea, make the tea, make the tea...'

Something was beginning to snap inside Joe. He knew the symptoms. He wanted to get his hands around Rivers' throat – and fast. He really wanted to see it – those eyes popping out of their sockets like squash balls and Rivers' face turning purple and his heels hammering on the floor as the breath faded within his body.

Joe well knew how to do it. Training helps. It wouldn't take long at all. First, the lunge taking Rivers by surprise. Then two fingers placed round his jugular deep in the pit of his throat... His heels would be hammering out their tattoo of doom after only about four seconds.

He spoke with difficulty to Rivers as the red mist of total murderous rage roiled up and over his brain.

'This is your fault Rivers. You have brought this about.'

Rivers looked at him with level gaze.

'Don't be so stupid.'

Rivers sounded cool. Doctors knew about these things – that's what they were paid to do. It wasn't his affair. Rivers was opting out.

'Rivers, I know what I'm talking about. You do too – that is your sister next door raving away. And I have the leverage on you here, no matter what you think. Don't forget that it was you who brought me into this family when I saved your life. Yes, have you forgotten it all? I saved your life and you owe me......You owe me large.'

Rivers still stared at him without comment. Joe continued to talk. He knew that if he ceased to speak he would murder Rivers Pugh there and then on the spot. Important to parley...

'Forgotten it all have we? How convenient for you! Named in the report? Ring any bells with you? The beating up I saved you from? Battersea Bridge? Walking across together and you poised and ready to jump? My holding your hand? Like so...'

Deliberately, Joe reached across to take Rivers hand. Rivers shifted backwards denying the flesh contact, his eyes still fixed on Joe.

'That's how we held hands, Rivers. Like so. Have you forgotten all that so quickly? Have you? And I like a fool refused to allow you to jump…Like a fool…Well, let me tell you the truth Rivers, I wish that I'd let you jump. Yes, I relive that scene endlessly. Every time I run it again, it changes so that you jump – with a little scream – and then you're frothing about in the Thames and just about to go under again…And I watch you from the bridge. I wish that you were dead, Rivers. Yes, just rotting slime now. I wish that I hadn't flickered for a moment when you wanted to do it. Because what has it led to? It has led to this…'

Tears of rage and pity running down his cheeks, Joe showed him Perdita still marching hopelessly up and down up and down, screaming loudly.

'Your sister's mad, your mother's dead, the house is in my name and all in the name of your wretched little tin pot job selling arms across the world. That and your ego…Get real, Rivers get real…'

Rivers stared at him white with shock as Joe's bitter words ripped into him. It was rare for Rivers to be on the end of a tongue-lashing. It didn't happen at Global.

'I tell you this Rivers, I've been straight with you. I've made no problems for you staying here. It used to be your estate, it belongs to me now but I've drawn no distinction between us. You live here just as you always did. But I've been wrong because you've abused my trust. So I tell you this – that has to change now. This is a crisis, and we have to work together on it. Yes, together. Whether you like it or not. Your sister is not well. She is out of her mind with sadness. She is dying of grief. Even you can see that for yourself…Even a purblind fool could see that…And I'll tell you something else, Rivers Pugh,…'

Joe paused. Even in his rage, he could see the folly of threatening Rivers too far. He refrained from mentioning his murder of the Fat Man in Fleet Street.

'By God, do I want to repair some of the damage that I caused on Battersea Bridge when I helped you across…'

Rivers made to speak but changed his mind. He remained silent. But he looked shocked – and younger all of a sudden. Joe noticed that.

'Where's Mrs G, Rivers?'

'I don't know.'

'Was she staying tonight?'

'I think so.'

'Go and get her. If she's not here, go and fetch her…Now…Do it now… Do as I say.'

A stout figure waddled into the kitchen. Mrs G had finally been woken by the noise. Joe was pleased to see her.

'What's going on? I couldn't…Oh no, the poor lamb…'

Mrs G had glimpsed Perdita in her fit of madness. Perdita was now seated on the sofa, crooning to herself as she stroked the hair of an imaginary Rivers seated beside her, just as she had done the first time that Joe had visited Pugh Park, back in the good old days when Lady Pugh was still alive.

The moonbeams were caressing her like shadowy hands.

'Mrs G, get something on her, will you. She'll die of cold, if nothing else at this rate. She's not well, as you can see. Rivers, you look after your sister. I'm taking your car…No, on second thoughts I won't take your car…I have to be in London early tomorrow. What are the times of the early trains from the station? What time is it now?'

Rivers reached for the timetable.

'It's nearly two thirty. There's a train, I think, around 4.'

'I'll walk to the station. Look after your sister. Good night and thank you Mrs G for being around. You have been very helpful.'

Joe left the room and went upstairs again, full of disgust. He threw himself on the bed and stared at the ceiling for some minutes as dreams faded in his head, dreams that had sustained him through many tough encounters in recent years. It was over. Yes, it was definitely and conclusively terminated.

He felt doors slam in his mind, definition and judgement reassert themselves and the bleak perspectives of common or garden reality heave into view.

The whole Pugh thing…

It was over...The cloud-capped towers of Pugh Park were dashed to the ground as the revels ended...He felt that very strongly. His romance with Perdita the Beautiful, yes that was inevitably now concluded...It had to be so...She came with Rivers and they were inseparable, like twin peas in a pod...Perdita was beautiful, like a dancer, but too, too attached to her surroundings and her memories to change for him...And he was under pressure. He needed her, but she would not be there for him. For her brother certainly; for Buffet even, perhaps. But not automatically for Joe. That seemed to be clear to him. And there was no way that he could take one without the other, Perdita but not Rivers. The truth of it was obvious – that he couldn't support the burden of both of them, not with the oddities of his make-up and background and experiences and his deals...Lady Pugh, that cunning old fox of an aristocrat, had realised all of that from the beginning. He saw it all with great clarity now, including the great risks she had taken. But then she was a risk-taker and a romantic at heart...That was why she had bequeathed the house and the estate to him, knowing his infatuation for Perdita, knowing that Pugh Park would be safe in his hands and gambling thereby that Perdita might then have a chance of escape from her saturnine brother...The slim prospect of a normal life...But it had all failed, because Perdita could not support the burden of ordinary life, had faltered before its challenge and because Rivers had then reasserted his sway...As the dancing that evening had demonstrated. She cleaved to Rivers, as she always had done...The Pughs led different lives with different people, including that oaf Buffet...Joe thought that he had found a way into the enchanted garden but he had been wrong. It was a pardonable mistake but it was still nevertheless a lapse of judgement...He acknowledged that. The result? He, Joe, must quit Pugh Park in some way or other, acknowledging that something had failed, had come to an end and had altered...He had no place there, whereas Rivers and Perdita belonged there like the trees in the Pugh fields. Yes, it was all over for him now. He had a deal in the City to see through, or at least launch, and he had a life to lead or recreate, if such a thing were possible...

There is a world elsewhere, he told himself without huge conviction. And whatever it was, he perforce must find out about it...Alone.

Joe stared at the ceiling of his bedroom in Pugh Park, scene of many carnal joys between him and Perdita, and concluded that he ought to hit the road. He felt grief-stricken at the realisation.

With great difficulty, he hauled himself to his feet, went into the bathroom and shaved himself. He did this with care. Then he took a brief shower and returned to the bedroom. He looked out some fresh clothes from the wardrobe, a blue shirt, a tie, and a favourite suit. He dressed. He refused to think about anything else than the very immediate present as he went through these motions. He cleared Perdita from his mind, something he could just about manage to do. Then he put on his most comfortable shoes. Pugh Park was a few miles from the station. It would be quite a walk. It would take some time. But he would be in London in good time for his meeting. He focused on his agenda. He ensured that he carried his mobile with him.

He glided onto the landing. From where he stood, hanging over the banister, he could just hear the bustling and clucking sounds of Mrs G as she fussed over Perdita, with the occasional interjection from the deeper-voiced Rivers interrupting her flow. He thought they might have carried her into the kitchen. No sound of Perdita's voice. But they would look after her, as they always had done. Safe as houses now to make a discreet exit, he thought. Joe slid down the stairs to the cloakroom. Slipping on an overcoat, he moved towards the front door, at the opposite end of the house to Perdita, Rivers and Mrs G. He paused for a second, before opening the front door which gave onto the drive and the dawn of a new morning. He stood there listening. No sound now. Was she in bed, tended by Mrs G? It wasn't for Joe to know. He raised fingers to his lips as he stood at the door and blew a kiss on the morning air to Perdita elsewhere in the house, somewhere else in her mind and in the world...

His footsteps crunched quietly on the gravel as he walked down the long drive towards the main road. No one followed him. Attention was elsewhere. It took less time than he had imagined to clear the estate; he was unobserved and unhailed. He was on a side road now, which route led directly to the station, provided he took a left turn when it came up. He felt his feet clumping solidly on the ground as he marched along.

The suit fitted well to his body. He felt at ease. Shed of burden. And also limber. Ready for action. He had chosen. Joe felt pleased with his decision.

He turned back to look back at Pugh Park, now glimmering in the morning air as the day dawned crisp and bright with the sun close to an early spritely rising. The birds were shrieking their approval of the coming of the day. Hampshire was bursting into light.

'...And being awaked, I do despise my dream,' he thought, brooding for a second on the wiles of Lady Pugh, the collapse of the hapless Perdita, and the impotent rage of Rivers as Joe had thundered at him about an hour previously.

'Was I wrong to do all that,' he wondered. 'Should I be leaving? Is this really a wrong, hasty decision?'

He found a snap response although in his heart of hearts he was not convinced. All best left to the other guys, he concluded. Mrs G and Rivers know how to handle these things. But he wasn't entirely sure about his call. He knew the phrase was glib, and Joe hated cliches. The fleeting image of the Fat Man came to him. He reflected wryly that that there was little to choose between the oppressive dominance of the Fat Man and the manipulative wiles of Lady Pugh. Both had been professionals, he thought to himself. Both had been tops at their jobs.

But rightly or wrongly, Joe felt his spirits rising with the coming of the sun and the day. The instinctual animal in him had survived the rigours of the night. The profile of the house behind the trees was coming into sharper focus as the light improved. Joe stared for a few seconds more at the house and then waved farewell at the scene as he turned on his heel. He continued to tramp between the hedgerows, now brimming with noisy life and excitement.

'I may be there again at Pugh Park in body but I am leaving it in spirit,' he told himself. 'This is not for me. I am bound for the world's highways, not for the village round – and that's the truth

488

of the matter. Another day, another dollar. It sounds trite but it's true. Give me the deal any day of the week...'

More hammering of the shoes on the road as he strode along. The heels banged out a satisfying noise. He closed his mind to Perdita's desperate pleas of the previous night not to leave him.

And her warm lips and tear-stained eyes? And her collapse?

He still felt confident enough about his decision.

'If Perdita wants to come with me, then that's fine. If not, well then this is a convenient way out. And I am pleased that I did not strike Rivers. That would have been too much for my conscience to bear. Besides, it would have been madness. That young man gets his comeuppance very shortly and it all starts in about four hours time when I give my briefing on the dollar to the assembled suits at 8.30. We'll see how he sings when he learns that the City institutions have turned against him and that they're backing the Detroit bid for Global. He won't be the first CEO to learn about the fickleness of the Square Mile and he won't be the last. It'll come as quite a shock for him to learn that he's yesterday's story... As a bombshell, in fact...'

Joe continued his soliloquy in the fresh early morning air.

'I am not a young man anymore but nor am I an old man either. There is still time and nothing is fixed...Everything in this lane as I walk along sings to me of hope, of optimism, of the freshness of things. I must take my comfort from all of that. It merges with me and my experiences. It is a simple truth. Briefly I feel at peace. I feel at one with the universe. This is no time to lose heart. Even the birds are with me.'

What he said to himself was rubbish on one level and yet wonderfully appropriate on another. Joe knew that, within the vast irrelevance of the cosmos' mighty being... But he refrained from too close a scrutiny of his feelings. He went with the flow of it all. The anger of his encounter with Rivers had given way to a more elegiac mood. He crunched along some more yards and took the left turn as it came up. The walking was sweet, like the rhythm of his movement. He felt the breath come in and out of him fluently. He swung along at speed as his pace began to quicken.

The sweet early morning danced all around him in its ecstasy of naive beginning.

'This is a precious moment of release as burdens slip from me. I am alone to confront not the past but the future. I can still build and I can still fashion. For lo, the winter is over and the time of the singing of the birds is come. That is what all this means. But I must be careful. I must position carefully. My fixed point in the universe has suddenly gone – in a flash. Useless to think that Perdita will be there for me. No way. She has gone and the door has slammed shut and great changes have happened in the twinkling of an eye. She is no longer there for me.'

A great lurch hit him deep in the stomach as he thought about Perdita again.

Then Joe rounded the bend and saw the station directly in front of him. The day was up now, singing and fighting in all its glory and the air was very fresh. Joe saw that he had longer to wait for the train than he had imagined and he sat down on a bench beside the track to pass the time. He hunched into the overcoat as he sat on the bench. Suddenly there was an early-morning breeze. It ruffled his hair.

'Just an ordinary Joe waiting for the train,' he told himself as the minutes ticked by and other early risers gradually turned up on the platform.

'Just an ordinary Joe, early in the morning. Forget the Dick Whittington bit and the David Copperfield touch. I'm just a guy waiting for an early train who's had a long-delayed bust-up with all and sundry – and that's the long and short of it...These things happen and they pass...'

More early morning travellers trickled onto the platform.

'I will breakfast at Leo's in the Fulham Road and talk to the guys on the street,' he told himself. 'It's been a long time since I was back on the street...In London, on the street, getting the buzz...I wonder how Silva is ...'

But would that be enough after Perdita, he asked himself deep down. Yes, after Perdita...It was strange for him to think of her in the past tense when everything about them together had been so much concerned with the present.

Eventually the train arrived, as trains do, even in early morning Hampshire. He boarded it, along with the others, part of the sleepy throng, and found a seat and fell asleep until Clapham Junction. From there he proceeded towards the City but via Leo's in the Fulham Road. Leo gave him a good welcome and served him his usual tea and toast charging him at the old prices because he was such a faithful customer...Good old Leo! Leo was chipper and brisk. It looked as if he was doing well with his cafe. Many of the old faces were still there. Said's back was very bad, but he was still making his usual – and vain – effort to do his crossword in less than one morning.

Normality reigned, Leo style.

The 8.30 meeting with the suits, all very young, went well, not least because the market could see a currency crisis in the offing. Donnelly was also there and looking attentive. Joe was pleased to see that he still had some support at ABC. The chat about the currencies was intense. The Euro was very weak so any discussion about currencies was welcome. Joe outlined his broad idea, that the pound would continue to fall with the Euro and tossed in the idea of the Argentinean connection for good measure – the UK had long standing trading connections with Argentina; Argentina had a fixed 1 for 1 parity with the dollar and the peso looked dear, as the dollar soared; so therefore, the pound must drift down with the Euro in order to prop up the peso. Savvy, boys?

Although it was by and large rubbish, the suits were impressed. Anyone who can proffer a view during a currency crisis is briefly welcome, as the world turns upside down. Joe's attention was straining towards the bid now and its announcement.

He reiterated his forecast of $1.40 or lower for the pound and as luck would have it, sterling was weakening as he talked. That added some lustre to his comments as the screens flickered deepening shades of red in the meeting room. The suits were quiet to open-mouthed and respectful. Not many questions, and all for the most part, friendly – the suits could smell a deal in the offing. A weary Lucia was most impressed by Joe's delivery and gave him her personal congratulations after Joe had finished speaking. Donnelly was beaming. Lucia meanwhile was doing her sums. According to her calculations, the ABC team, acting on behalf of Detroit, might have far more than just the odd stray percentage pledged in its favour. Looking quizzical and sensible but still hedging a little, Lucia opined that they might be going into battle with something like 15-20% of the institutions' votes firmly and irrevocably committed in Detroit's favour. That augured very well for them all.

In the course of the day, Joe took a call from one Nicholas and sanctioned him addressing the morning meeting again very shortly. He talked to Moley and passed on the news. They arranged to play some more of their chess game and Joe assented to the suggestion with what he thought was unseemly alacrity. He also fielded a call from Treadwell and arranged to play a little bridge with him and he picked up a message from Emma's housekeeper. Yes, the tapes had arrived and thank you very much, and yes, they had been forwarded to Emma in Italy. Joe told the housekeeper that he would be tied up, or out of town, for a brief time and after that he would be in Berlin. Emma was very welcome to visit him there at ABC. Glancing absently at his diary but still working on his deal and watching the forex screens, Joe gave the housekeeper precise instructions what day and time he thought would be convenient for Emma to call. Logging the date of Emma's visit in his mind, he told the housekeeper where his office was located in Berlin.

That business concluded satisfactorily, he then left the ABC office and went to the Reform Club. There he took a bedroom and slept undisturbed for seventeen hours.

No message from Perdita on his mobile when he awoke. That would come later, he guessed, if it came at all. Ownership is not possession, he told himself yet again. Not even halfway. He was getting bored with that particular mantra. He wanted another one.

Then it was time to go into ABC again and shepherd his deal through some more via Lucia.

It won't be long now before the deal is announced and the shooting starts, he told himself. And afterwards…? When I leave ABC…? Who knows…? Anything could happen. I will then genuinely be a free man. I will have quit. The whole scene. And for ever.

Emboldened, cheered but also cautioned by that prospect, he got on with his work. Around 11.30, he called Pugh Park but raised the answer phone. No Mrs G there and most likely nobody at all. Perhaps Perdita was in hospital, or perhaps worse.

Joe did not leave a message to say he had called.

*   *   *   *   *

Leadon is on top form and I feel so stupid, thought Tom Stone as he read Leadon's latest offering and watched the Euro collapse under the weight of the selling. It was on a toboggan ride to nowhere now. The hunter-killer packs of the market were out in full force, tracking the currency down every road as it sank inexorably. Every newspaper now had the Euro in its sights. It was a joke currency. It was ready to implode, taking France Germany and the rest of Europe with it. But Tom was slightly comforted. He had a small item for his journal. He was still writing it up diligently.

*   *   *   *   *

Later in the day and touched by some vague form of recollection, Joe leaned forward in the cab and told the driver to forget the Reform Club as a destination and head towards Chelsea and SW3. The Reform Club felt like a sanctuary which perhaps he no longer needed. Was it the moment to explore fresh horizons? After all, he had the time, the money and perhaps even the inclination…

Obediently, the cab swung left out of the Strand and sped down the Mall, turning left again at the Palace as it approached Victoria. Sloane Square, land of fable, vicious intrigue and ladies

493

who lunched in fours or worse, lay directly ahead. It was some time since Joe had sauntered around SW3. He had been away.

'Long time since I was in these parts,' he thought, 'and I have time to kill...Much time to kill...I wonder how the dames are faring now that Liz Playfair has departed from the scene...I wonder how their bridge has improved. Or not, as the case might be...Do they still refuse to lead up to weakness? I wonder where they are now... And Lady C and Ateh? I wonder just how those two got along together. Too bad I wasn't around for any of that. It might have been fun, watching a suddenly widowed woman come to terms with an illegitimate daughter landing on her doorstep.'

A small wave of nostalgia swept over him as he thought of the locust months he had spent in Chelsea, bivouacking penniless at the World's End in his cheap flat with the crack in the wall and then playing grudge bridge on demand at the Liz Playfair bridge club in Lower Sloane Street, the while trading the market desperately to keep afloat.

Matters arising, he thought, as he redirected the cab again, this time away from the King's Road and towards old Chelsea. This was a very traditional haunt for Joe. This was where Pascal had lived in the old days of their relationship. Close by was where Emma Bales had purchased her first London house of note, the Emma Bales who now had land and beefs in Pelham Crescent; the Caribbean; and most likely a myriad of other spots around the globe. The Emma Bales, finally, who by now ought to have taken delivery of the German tapes which he had sent her and to which she was welcome. They came with blood on the tracks, courtesy of the scheming Fat Man who had lent them to Joe on his first espionage mission to Berlin, many, many years ago of spooking by Joe.

'She should be fluent in German by now,' thought Joe ironically as he instructed the cab driver to stop the taxi in Cheyne Walk. He got out and paid the driver off and stood there alone, close to the river, taking the wind off the Thames and wondering if indeed this was the moment to let it all start to slide.

'I could buy a small place here this afternoon if I felt so inclined,' he ruminated, suddenly conscious that opportunities were opening up for him now that the Global bid was on the launching pad, with the countdown starting.

'At this moment, I could do almost anything in the world that I wanted. I could take out my chequebook and just buy a small flat here on the spot and move in just as soon as it was ready. What a wonderful possibility…'

He had forgotten briefly about Pugh Park and his involvement therein. But Perdita was not far from his mind, like Lady Pugh.

He walked along the street, shielded from the traffic by the discreet curve of an embankment garden, and passed by the understated welcome of the King's Head and Eight Bells, formerly an old pub in which he and Pascal had drunk occasionally many years previously. His mind was suddenly alert with possibilities as the potential in the situation began to grip him. He walked with a tighter step.

Ahead of him as he strolled along, there stood a block of flats of imposing size and baroque elegance. Joe paused to stare at the front door of one of the blocks, conscious that he was more or less just a signature away from possession, if anything there took his fancy. It was a heady moment for Joe.

'It's a sunny day,' he told himself. 'Just the time for making a spot purchase… These things don't take long. And I could always invite Perdita here to stay with me. Lure her up here on a visit…We could start again, but this time without Rivers.'

He continued to walk along the quiet street past the blocks of flats.

Just then a head popped out of the front door of the next block and scanned about it, in quest. It was an elegant well coiffed head. The face looked familiar. Joe drew nearer.

'Hullo, Joe,' said the face. 'What are you doing here? In that suit, and for once, you look like a man who works for a living. You should be in your office. Why aren't you?'

'Hullo, Betty. Fancy seeing you here.'

It was Betty, Betty the Cool, Betty the Fixer, Betty of Long-Time-No-See, whose errant son, Marcello, Joe had run to earth, again many years ago, in deepest Chelsea. The first time Joe had met Betty, she had saved him many millions by turning up punctually in the City; the second time was in the South of France in his villa; and the third time was in a smart clothes store in Notting Hill. They got around, those two. They went way back.

'My suit is a long story, Betty. How's Marcello?'

'Marcello's fine, as ever, thanks to you. Settling very easily into married life, I must say.'

Betty paused, hesitated and then asked Joe a question, backing up the request with a no nonsense grin of responsible mischief-making.

'Joe, you may be just the man I need. The answer to a maiden's prayer. Could I borrow you for twenty minutes and then we could have a chat?'

'Of course, Betty, but for what?'

'It won't take long, Joe, and it won't hurt you, I promise. My youngest, Monica, is musical and she's about to give her first public recital at the Wigmore Hall. We're having a little dress rehearsal this afternoon here in the flat for a few friends and we're one short. So there's an empty chair…Which can be very off-putting for a young pianist, as you can imagine. Bells should be here but she just rang – she's stuck in the middle of traffic in Hyde Park, so she's going to be late. But she's on her way. So I popped out to see if I could spot anyone to fill a gap until she gets here. No point in my standing in for Bells. Monica won't have me within a million miles while she's playing – she says I'm intimidating. So Joe…'

'I'd be delighted to stand in, Betty.'

'We can talk afterwards, Joe. The first piece is very short, mercifully.'

'Of course. What is she playing?'

'Something utterly dreary by Ravel, followed by something equally awful by Poulenc…When you think of all the wonderful Schubert she could have chosen, it's simply a crime. It makes me want to scream. But anyway, it's her choice and she has to live with it…So, OK, Joe?'

'OK, Betty.'

'You're a sweetheart, Joe. One of the best. And you really look the part. I couldn't have found a better stand-in. Now follow me…Just twenty minutes, Joe, and that's a promise.'

Joe followed her through the front door and into the ground floor flat to the left as he entered the block.

The room was sparse but quietly full of presence. Very, very uncluttered. Many spaces between the objects. At one end, against the window, Joe saw a baby grand piano at which was seated a young girl, in jeans, with a serious expression, and a cascade of dark brown hair. Joe recognised her. But now she was much more grown up than when he had glimpsed her, in Ateh's shop in Notting Hill Gate, on the occasion of the great reconciliation with Marcello. Almost grown up now, he thought.

In front of the piano, eight chairs were arranged in two rows, on which there were sitting very patiently seven, very obvious, friends of Betty's family, soberly indeed stiffly dressed, all come to lend moral support on a trying and testing occasion for Betty's musical daughter.

An empty chair might have been most off-putting, given the expectations of imminent arrival. Betty made an exuberant introduction and Joe waved a polite hand.

'Look, everybody, what luck! I ran into Joe who has agreed at very short notice to stand in briefly for Bells...'

'Mainly because otherwise I'd be minus most of my fingers...'

That raised a brief giggle of laughter and Monica smiled. She was happier now to play and she composed herself at the piano as Betty exited from the room closing the door behind her. Joe took his seat, the audience settled and the hands of Monica fluttered over the keys before descending in a quiet welter of chords into Ravel's musical vision.

As the music swelled about him, Joe thought of the various layers of his existence which seemed to have centred here in the secluded and studious room in Chelsea with Betty and her family – Moley and the City which were briefly far away from him; Berlin and the Fat Man which seemed even more remote; and then the dames with their excited intrigues; hatreds; and passionate reconciliations here in the heart of old Chelsea.

Was this the moment to stop running and start afresh, he wondered. A reverie of possibilities enveloped him like the music as Monica's subtle fingers twinkled across the keyboard...

Then she paused; the fingers were raised from the keyboard; the music died away; and the applause sounded, very gently and deeply en famille as the audience smiled at Monica for her playing; and as Monica smiled at the old friends for listening sympathetically to her efforts.

A brief pause as Monica adjusted her music for the second piece. Betty stood in front of Joe, flanked by another woman who smiled at him.

'Bells, here's your stand-in. Joe, this is Bells. I must say Joe you are a cool customer. You know, Bells he didn't bat an eyelid when I borrowed him…Maybe he's used to it, like a little library all on his own. Anyway, come on Joe…Let me give you a drink.'

Betty and Joe stole away out of the room, as Bells sat down in her spot. Monica composed herself and the audience settled once more. Then the music started again, as Betty closed the door and led Joe into the kitchen.

Joe sat down at the kitchen table, and Betty rummaged in the fridge for a bottle.

'Joe you don't mind if I offer you some champagne do you? It's all I've got here at the moment…It's for the party after the recital…'

'No, I'll take some champagne. That would suit me very well.'

Betty sat down opposite him with a smile after handing him a glass of Bollinger.

'Celebrating are we, Joe? Do tell…'

'It feels like the end of a long trail, Betty, and I may just be reaching the frontier. I feel tired but I may have made it. Here's hoping…'

They clinked and he drank. Joe looked at the bubbles appreciatively.

'Good for you, Betty, and good for your fridge. They don't serve stuff like this on the wrong side of the border.'

'Living hell was it?'

Joe nodded.

'Middling vicious, Betty.'

'Passport in order?'

'I think so.'

'Anything else to declare?'

'Not only my genius…'

'I agree, Oscar's always a great help on these occasions. So you're walking up to the checkpoint and the guards look relaxed, they're not fingering their guns, and you can see freedom on the other side of the barrier…'

'Something like that, Betty. You're a mother, I keep remembering, and you know about these things.'

'Not exactly in your dimension but I can see what you mean…So how long have you been on this trail, Joe?'

'Too long, Betty, far too long. I think it may be time to quit. Something swept over me just now, or a little earlier in the day in fact, and so I took a cab and arrived here. I was thinking of buying a place here…Probably foolish…The impulse swept over me…I wanted to sign something…'

'Hmmmmn.'

Betty looked at Joe closely. Joe smashed down some more champagne. He grinned at her. She smiled back. Two chance acquaintances who had rediscovered friendship unexpectedly.

'You've been through the mill recently, Joe, haven't you? You're good at hiding it, but I can see through you. You're exhausted.'

'Maybe…It didn't feel so at the time but it does now…I can still handle it but only for so long now. I feel quite empty all of a heap.'

'I need hardly ask, Joe, whether you have acquired a wife on your travels. You do not give me that impression, I have to tell you. So is this the impulse buy that of the genuine buccaneer hoping to hang up his boots? Don't forget Joe that we have come to know each other quite well. We've had many chats in many odd places now. So it does sound as if life is starting to change for you.'

'It could be, Betty, it could be.'

'Joe I don't see any virtue in your buying a flat here in Chelsea immediately. You can always use this place. I'll give you a key and you can give it back to me when you've decided what to do. Nobody uses this flat much now. We bought it for the family after Marcello returned but now that he's flown the nest once and for all it doesn't get a lot of occupation. So if you like it, you can always think in terms of buying it. If you want to, that is…See how you like it…'

'This is very sudden, Betty. But I'm very grateful to you. This might solve a few problems for me.'

He was grateful to Betty for her presence, as he tried to balance in his mind the great weights of obligation and responsibility that he had juggled up and down for so long.

'It might work, Betty, you never know…'

'Why not come out to Hertfordshire and stay with the family? Now that Marcello and his father are reconciled, it's a very peaceful spot. You might enjoy it. Not a lot to do there but what there is of activity is substantial. I don't think I ever asked you before, Joe, but do you play bridge? I rather think you do, but I can't quite remember for sure.'

Lights flashed from the conning tower as Joe approached the frontier. This is no time for sentiment, he told himself.

'In the past…'

'Oh that's good. So you have the rudiments…'

'Just about.'

'You see, we've set up a little bridge saloon in the area for the ladies of the county and it's going very well…'

Joe had a sudden premonition of what was coming. I don't believe this, he told himself. This world is too small even for me. Do not say, Betty, what I think you are going to say.

Undeterred by Joe's psychic waves, Betty chattered on.

'We placed an ad in one of the bridge magazines and we got hundreds of replies, of course. The world and his wife want to teach bridge judging by our post-bag. But one of the entries stood out a mile, it was from a woman by the name of Liz Playfair…'

Joe nodded.

I knew it, he told himself.

'She used to run a bridge club somewhere in London but it wasn't too successful, apparently. There was some argy-bargy of some description and she closed it down. Anyway, to cut a long story short, she eventually came to us and it's all been a huge success. Everybody flocks there but only the women come. There aren't enough men there so you'd be very welcome.'

Joe measured his ground very cautiously as the light from the frontier searchlights caught him in its glare, just about sixty paces from the wire, suitcase in hand and looking vulnerable. Hug dead ground, he told himself, just as the Fat Man said.

'Yes, Liz Playfair, you said. Yes that name rings a bell…Yes, I'd love to come and play with you all. Mind you, I'm a bit rusty…'

'Oh, she'd soon sort you out. She's about six foot tall, very blond, and works out all the time, so if you put up just the slightest show of resistance…'

'I can well believe it. It sounds fascinating.'

Joe was drinking some more champagne and thinking that Hertfordshire might be about the last place in the world that he might wish to visit, granted the presence there of Liz Playfair. Then the memory bank suddenly clicked like a cash machine, to disgorge a small but dramatic fact.

'Tell me, Betty, just exactly what time is it?'

'There's a clock there behind you. I can't see without my glasses. But why the rush? It's only mid-afternoon, I guess.'

'I've suddenly just remembered I have to see a man about…'

'A dog?'

'Yes, something like that, Betty.'

'Who is it that you have to see, Joe?'

'An old friend. Name of Treadwell. I'd quite forgotten. We have some business to discuss.'

'Where?'

'Close to Earl's Court, Betty. I don't have to rush but I have to be departing shortly. He's a doctor.'

Joe absorbed some more champagne as one does on these occasions. It seemed somehow appropriate to hang a little loose, even though Betty looked at him a tad grimly as he hammered the contents of her Bollinger bottle.

They both listened out for the music which could be faintly heard from the front room down the hallway from the kitchen. Betty began to tell Joe about the musical progress of Monica and he listened with half an ear glad of the opportunity to elude her vigilance regarding his rate of champagne consumption.

He did not mention that his date and business dealings with Treadwell would involve gambling for high stakes at the Jack of

Hearts bridge club. Somehow Hertfordshire and the Jack of Hearts seemed not quite on a par with each other, especially given the leaven of Liz Playfair's nostalgic presence.

After a few minutes more of desultory discussion, Joe stood up to go. Betty was complimentary on his appearance.

'You do look well in your suit, Joe. It becomes you very well. Yes, we'll definitely get you out to Hertfordshire. I can just see you breaking a few hearts out there with your innocent withdrawn look. And some of them deserve to have their hearts smashed, I can tell you. Women are pure vixen, I've concluded'.

'I can't wait, Betty. But I must dust down a bridge textbook just to mug up on the bidding...'

'Oh we'll all teach you that.'

Betty made her point with emphasis; rummaged around for a spare key to the flat which she found and gave to Joe; made a point of taking his mobile number so that she could call him; and generally fussed over him to the door, completing the process of farewell by planting a couple of ripe smackers of kisses on his cheeks.

The music still drifted towards them on the doorstep from the room where Monica was still playing.

Joe was thinking about emigration to Patagonia by the time he climbed into a fresh cab and set forth for the Jack of Hearts bridge club. None of what had happened was remotely what he had intended, but he felt in some senses resigned to the process of integration.

Treadwell was pacing back and forth quite slowly in the entrance to the club as Joe arrived. It was some time since they had played together. Joe was struck by the changes. Treadwell was still tall and thin with black hair curling over his hair and severe spectacles perched on his nose but otherwise he had altered considerably. The lips were now set in a thin line, making him look peevish. The restless energy had slowed as he had taken on some extra weight so that he now seemed choleric rather than dynamic. Joe was confronted by a Treadwell lapsing into premature middle age, if not worse.

'You're early, Joe.'

That was another change thought Joe. In the past Treadwell would have screamed at him for being a few minutes late, so that precious minutes of gambling times would have been wasted before he could get into the operating theatre. Now he didn't seem quite so frisky.

'Why are you wearing that suit, Joe? It looks quite new.'

'Interview, Treadwell. I borrowed the suit from a friend.'

Joe had been poor when he first met Treadwell. Now he was rich. But no point in telling the truth now and ruining the image.

'Get the job?'

'Of course not. No one would hire me in their right mind. But it was a good interview. They liked the suit too. They'd have hired that if they could have done.'

'Very funny, Joe. Now what tables are we playing on?'

'$75 per hundred?'

'Are you sure?'

That was another change. In the past, Treadwell had been fearless. He had been very greedy about making money on the tables. Now he sounded uncertain. He also sounded as if he had a wife in tow. There was something plaintive in his tone of voice.

'Maybe you're right,' said Joe diplomatically.

Treadwell took charge of the afternoon to his evident relief. Joe let him get on with it.

'Let's start off at the £25 tables then. After all, you're not exactly rolling in it yourself, are you, Joe, these days?'

'True, Treadwell, very true. The readies are very backward in coming forward. But how's the saw boning these days?'

Treadwell tossed his head.

'There's been a change there which I'll tell you about later. I've moved on from the surgery. But just tell me, Joe, before I start, what exactly is it that you do when you're working?'

That was another change in Treadwell. That was the first time in all the time they had gambled together that Treadwell had asked Joe a word about what he might do for a living.

'Not a lot. I write the odd freelance piece for a magazine about bridge hands for one of the professionals who's too busy to write it himself. That was what the interview was all about. I was trying to get on the permanent staff. But apart from that...'

For some reason, Treadwell looked relieved again as they sat down to play at the cheaper end of the market in the bridge club. Same face opposite Joe; same green on the tables; same smoke-filled atmosphere. Otherwise everything had changed. Like their fortunes as a partnership, which flattered to deceive. At first, they prospered at the £25 tables. Their old partnership understanding still seemed to be intact despite the long gap when they had not played together.

After a little time they had made a few hundreds. Emboldened, they moved up a gear to the £50 tables. Treadwell had looked more like the Treadwell of old – lean, hungry and ruthless.

The cigarette was stuck jauntily out at the corner of his mouth, as of old.

Treadwell had looked super-confident. But perhaps that was his undoing. He took it too fast. There were cracks in his game and there were flaws in the partnership understanding. Treadwell tried for a slam – which he shouldn't have done – and then failed to make the slam, which in the past would have been cold. Whipsawed, in other words. He grew angry with himself and barked at Joe. Things went from bad to worse at that point.

Then they were losing money, principally to a couple of quiet sallow-skinned Italians who said nothing but played together like waltz kings.

After an hour or so, Joe and Treadwell were both standing on the pavement outside the Jack of Hearts, feeling disconsolate and minus about two thousand pounds between them. Joe thought it was regrettable but for Treadwell it seemed like the end of the world.

He spoke quickly and urgently to Joe as they mooched away for a coffee.

'Do you think you could take this one on your book for once, Joe? It's not that I'm short but…'

Joe cursed the suit he had worn to the betting. Had he looked more down at heel, Treadwell would never perhaps have asked him to shoulder the losses.

The confession continued.

'You see Joe I'm not exactly raking it in as I was before. A couple of cock-ups in the operating theatre – nothing serious but the old hand/eye coordination isn't quite what it was and the insurance started to rocket. So I've switched to shrinking...'

'You'd be good at that, Treadwell. You've got a confiding bedside manner, I would have thought.'

About as comforting as a crocodile on heat, thought Joe as he placated a Treadwell ruffled by his losses. Treadwell was disposed to talk about himself to Joe.

'It was rather forced on me by other factors as well. You see, Mrs Treadwell' – Treadwell spoke about his wife as if referring to something monumental and separate like the pyramids – 'yes, Mrs Treadwell came into some money. Quite a lot of money, actually...'

So that's it, thought Joe. It's the dollar sign between them. Mrs T now has more dosh than Mr T – she's sprinting ahead and she also has signing power for the joint account...

'Between ourselves she won some lottery money. Not for repetition of course, but it was a sizeable sum. It was a rollover week and she shared some of it but nevertheless...'

'So you could retire immediately, Treadwell, and live off the wife.'

'Not exactly, Joe, it's not as easy as that. Mrs T and I, of course, discussed it but we reached the conclusion I couldn't quite cope with such a large compression of the differentials. No, it's quite a long story. Quite complex and quite fascinating in a way. You see, Mrs T has always nurtured social ambitions – yes, I think that's the fairest and kindest thing to say – and of course when she won her ...when she won her money...she was able to indulge this little fantasy of hers. So she discovered yachting. Had to, had to. Inevitable. At least, that's what she said to me. Route to the top in this country if you want to socialise. Anyway, it was something she'd always wanted to do. So she's bought her yacht and put together this crew on her yacht and it's – I mean they're – going to sail around the world.'

'And you're going with them?'

'Not exactly. It's an all-female crew. So I'm barred. Of course. That much must be obvious even to you, Joe. But I've been roped in as the official psychiatrist to the expedition. You know, just running the rule over them, that kind of thing. Just checking...

I'm going to do daily counselling by satellite, and the girls have rigged up a special isolation cubicle so that they can talk freely about…'

'How wonderful for you, Treadwell. No need to bother with Tubes then. You can get it from the horse's mouth.'

A far-away look came into Treadwell's eyes. He seemed to be mulling something like an event, remote and yet painfully present. He paused for a second.

'I suppose you could look at it like that, in a way. Yes, I suppose you could…Some of them are very strong-minded, yes, quite surprisingly so…And they do know their own minds as well…As I found out…'

Treadwell snapped to attention.

'Yes, I've had to be quite stern with two of them. It turns out they were at school together, so they've got a lot to catch up on…God knows what the Roaring Forties will be like…'

Pause from Treadwell and more faraway look. Then he resumed.

'…They'll give a whole new meaning to the concept of Cape Horn…I can see that one coming. But of course, that means nothing these days. It was always the men who fainted in the operating theatre, never the women…'

He seemed to drift off into a reverie. Mercilessly, Joe prompted him.

'So what are their psyches like? I mean from a sailor's point of view, of course. Good? Bad? Crazy? I suppose in the end they're just like women, really…'

Treadwell seemed to come to then with a jolt. He glared at Joe, like an outraged apologist.

'No, Joe I don't think you understand. The girls are OK. A little larger than life but then they always were. No, my problems lie elsewhere. I have other clients as well and one of them is causing me a great deal of concern…'

Disappointed at Treadwell's adroit switch of topic, Joe let him ramble on. Any minute now and he'll be telling me about the power to prescribe, the greatest benefit that a medical qualification confers…Far superior to the power to arrest… Treadwell pounced on his opportunity to discuss a business problem with an impartial outsider.

'...Yes a great deal of trouble. I really don't know what to do at all. You see, well, anyway, you judge for yourself. I can discuss it with you because you're so far away from the action.'

He paused for a second.

'I have this client who works in the City. He's a banker in fact. Not a very edifying specimen but then none of them are. Never have been. Been doing his banking for years and slowly climbing the tree. Not quite at the knighthood stage but in the running...'

Joe was suddenly all ears. Very much all ears.

'...He has a tight little team around him, and no big deal in that. It's a very tough outfit and they all have big jobs to do. I'll come back to the team in a minute. For the time being, the banking job appears to be going well. Anyway to cut a long story short, my man starts blacking out every now and then. At home, not in the office, but regularly. His regular doctor can't find anything wrong with him, so he's sent along to me. We start talking and I get nowhere. I've never met anyone who's quite so defensive or quite so buttoned in on himself. Terrified of his colleagues of course, and terrified that he'll miss out on his K, so winkling anything out of him is both a struggle and a terrible disappointment. It takes a lot of very tough medication in the end to force him to loosen his tongue and meanwhile the blackouts are continuing. I have to tell you I was quite severe with him. Eventually I get to the bottom of it all, or so far anyway. This happened today, this morning in fact, which is why I'm so preoccupied. He's part of a racket, is my man. He's in it up to his neck. That's what I've found out. It's organised by someone even higher up in the City than my man – he won't tell me who it is but I can guess – and they're both in this together, along with most of the City, by the sound of it. These two – my man and his God – were at school together, and one of them has got something on the other, something like a murder years ago which looked like an accident. Something which would turn very nasty for someone with ambitions for a K if it ever came out. So my man has to go along with the racket – he's not prepared to tell me yet what that is but I'll worm it out of him eventually; I think it's a currency swindle but I can't be sure. Pretty unsavoury whatever it is. But that's not all…'

Treadwell stared out of the window at the London traffic bustling by on an ordinary afternoon. Joe waited to hear what sounded uncannily familiar. He felt very tense. And very isolated. This was bad.

'My man has two deputies. No names, no pack drill obviously, but you get the picture. One of them is very tough. Apparently he spent most of his life in East Berlin, so he knows a thing or two. Came over the border when the Wall came down and then scaled the European banking hierarchy. The other one, nobody knows anything at all about him, keeps himself very much to himself and he is suspected of being some sort of agent. Useless at his job, of course, but clearly fronting for someone…'

Here it comes, thought Joe. Here it comes…This is just as bad as I thought it would be.

'The boys in the racket are nervous about the agent. If he is an agent, he could be fronting for anyone. So they've decided to knock him off. Yes, kill him. They're taking no chances. My man is going to action it, very shortly…Or at least, he's being told to action it…Whether he does sanction it, who knows. Who knows what goes on in his mind, or indeed in the minds of any of these City moguls. The Communist is going to do it. He's working on the best way to effect the killing, even as we speak. My banker client rather wants me to come up with a solution for him…Tell him what to do, you know, that kind of thing. So what a ghastly situation for me…What do I do?…I can hardly tell him to take compassionate leave can I? So what do I do, Joe? What do you think as the impartial observer…?'

Joe tried to play it very cool. His heart was pounding and he felt the sweat break out on his forehead.

Pure fear gripped him.

He could see the training manual in front of his eyes as clearly as Treadwell sitting opposite. 'If the operative finds that an extreme situation has developed which is potentially life-threatening, then he should take one of the following courses of action…'

Pure bollocks of course. This was real and it was deadly. The training manual fought rather shy of reality. In the limit, it was dainty.

Times; dates; schedules; and programmes tumbled together in his mind, as Treadwell continued to talk. When was Felix back? That was crucial. When was the bid due? When was the killing due? Was any of the bid do-able in the time? Could he finesse it? Was that possible, even remotely. Maybe, but it felt tight, very tight.

Joe could feel the gun jammed up his nose as his thoughts raced ahead.

And the e-mail?

He understood about the e-mail now, not as a truth cast in bronze but as a working hypothesis. It had been sent as a warning, that he was deep in a tough game and that he'd better watch his step.

So tough in fact that the e-mail was the only possible sign of communication which could be sent.

OK, thought Joe, I accept that view now and I'm grateful. But it's ancient history now. What about the Felix schedule? That is key…And the bid schedule? That also is crucial.

Hug dead ground, hug dead ground – the mantra came flashing into his mind like a neon sign in the desert. Yes, I know how to do that, of course I do, it's perfectly easy. I just find a hole, and burrow into it. Easy.

What Joe had spurned as a vicarious option not a couple of hours ago – the key to Betty's flat in Cheyne Walk – had now become a vital part of his survival kit. I can go to ground there, thought Joe. Impossible to track me down there because if they're looking anywhere for me it's bound to be in the Hampshire direction. Felix will bribe my chauffeur to spill the beans. And that's where the spoor will him lead him.

And the bid?

It's due out this time next week. No more waiting. Big headlines, big market reaction, then it'll all be over for me. I have a week to survive, no more. It'll happen on schedule, though. Then I go to Berlin for meetings. Then the following week, after I'm back from Berlin, Felix returns…Provided he doesn't try anything stupid, then perhaps – and this is a big 'if' – I might be able to pull it off and then depart in one piece.

Treadwell broke in on his reverie.

'Another coffee, Joe? You look puzzled.'

'Not at all Treadwell, I was mulling your conundrum…It's a tricky one isn't it…Obviously, if your man decides not to do the deed then it's a different story…'

Treadwell laughed his bitter medical guffaw.

'We can't have that. Then my man gets killed and I lose a patient. We can't have that.'

'Of course not. How foolish of me. But what about the poor blighter that they knock off…?'

'It's a tragedy of course but there again he's not one of my patients…It's his problem. The Oath doesn't cover any of this, thank God.'

'Yes, I suppose that's the case…'

'It's all like something out of Le Carre. Did you ever read any Le Carre, Joe?'

'About half a page. I gave up. I couldn't follow it.'

'As little as that. I'm surprised at you, Joe. I think Le Carre is wonderful. I've read them all.'

'Yes, but I couldn't make head or tail of it.'

Just bridge players' chat. Treadwell looked at Joe across the table.

'No I suppose not. I can see that…'

Then he prepared to shamble off from the Jack of Hearts and back to his thought-fucking of the all-girl crew. Treadwell had carefully refrained from making another bridge date with Joe. Any overtures therefore would come from Joe which in turn would make him liable again for any losses at the table. Such a scoundrel, thought Joe, watching him depart, as he thought about bladders; Shakespeare's boys adventuring too far onto the deep; ambition; and Wolsey.

'Fling away ambition, Cromwell, I charge you. By that sin fell the angels…Or similar rubbish,' thought Joe, as he watched Treadwell climb into a cab after much discussion with the driver.

All of a heap, London felt much like Berlin, as Joe wrapped survival around him like a winter cloak, even in the street.

510

Darling Ursula, This is a very tiny item to add to the journal but it will explain why I have not yet resigned from the Chron despite everything that I said beforehand about jetting off and away from it all. The stranger in my life – male, so don't worry – has approached me with an article which he says I should run in the Chron very shortly. He hasn't written it yet, in fact he won't tell me anything about the contents of the piece, but he is about to put plume to papier. He won't tell me what it concerns. But he stresses that when he gives it to me I must run it immediately. Now I went along with what he said but for my money the line he is suggesting is ridiculous. I have about as much chance of influencing what goes into the paper as Mary Magdalene. I ventured to tell him as much but he would have none of it. So here we go – Last Chance Saloon for one busted editor. That is my crazy position after God knows how many years in Fleet Street. I will do as he suggests. After that, irrespective of the outcome, I will resign and go my way, darling Ursula. I may show you this journal before I go or I may not – I haven't made up my mind. But whatever happens, and even if you're reading this alone in your kitchen on the table with your mad spectacles wired across your nose, you must know and be aware that I love you very much. Wherever I am, I will be thinking about you. I cannot bear to think of you being upset by whatever I do. Or disappointed. So I may just disappear, and leave the hard copy for you to read…I don't know anything any more…

★ ★ ★ ★ ★

Annie had everything more or less under control now ahead of her one golden shot down the tube. She knew the risks but she was prepared to stake everything on her one glorious fusillade.

511

She had nothing to lose. The Russians had the upper hand and she had just one shot left in the locker. Tom Stone had been told to expect an article from Jamie and had promised in his own characteristic way to do what was necessary, without much conviction. His scepticism did not surprise her but no matter... She had got one of her minions to write the piece for Jamie. To add a final flourish to the proceedings, she had conjured up something else even more exotic out of the ether just to help the proceedings along. They were very close now to denouement time, she reckoned. Only a few more cents off the Euro: dollar rate and then they could go for it. She could hardly wait...

$$\star \quad \star \quad \star \quad \star \quad \star$$

Joe sat in Betty's flat, watching the evening go down over the river and thinking about Julius Caesar. Treadwell had told him about the killing to be arranged – his killing – about four days previously. So four days had passed. The bid for Global was due in two days' time. From what Lucia had told him that morning it was a shoe-in. Lucia had tugged at her nose a great deal as she spoke, a sure sign that she was both excited and confident. The pound has fallen against the dollar to around $1.40 and was heading lower. But the dollar value of the bid, cutting through all the guff in the offer document, was at the old parity of $1.60. So there was a free ride of 20 cents or so in the deal. Lucia had sewn the whole thing up beautifully. The stampede of the London institutions to accept the terms would be like a thundering herd – and then some. Snouts well down shortly at the watering hole...

Very shortly indeed after the bid came out, Joe was scheduled to be in Berlin for his big board meeting. This would include the American presence, including Pa Lee and it would be Joe's farewell board meeting. The day after that again, Felix returned to the office. Felix would not be at the board meeting where Joe intended to resign. Joe had managed to winkle those details out of the Perfect. So some time between now and Felix's return to the office would be the killing time – or just afterwards. It would be in that zone, either just before or just after Felix's return. That had to be the schedule. No other slots looked suitable.

Joe could now pin down the timetable reasonably precisely. He thought that Felix would make his move just after he returned from his course. He was more or less sure of that, not 100% but maybe 95%. He was trying to read Felix's mind and he thought that would be the way that Felix would approach the matter, partly because Felix himself would be hoping that some factor which he had overlooked, like the Quiff dropping dead, would present itself and give him an excuse for cancelling Joe's execution. Felix, if he had to make the killing, would want to start again at ABC with a clean slate. Joe knew how Felix would go about it. He knew his man – they'd worked together in the past. Felix was a compassionate man. That would be the way he would have planned it himself. That was how the niche of opportunity tended to slant itself. So likewise with Felix. They had both been trained in the same school; they would both tend to think alike on this matter.

Or so Joe hoped....

And if he gambled wrong...Joe closed his eyes and his mind to that possibility and refused to contemplate the probabilities. He did not want to confront a raging Felix with a loaded pistol, not anywhere at all...

So Joe took the orderly route. He would wait until the Berlin board meeting. He thought he was crazy but he knew that he was going to that meeting. It was important for him to sign off correctly. He had to ring-fence the whole business of Berlin; spying; and the business of his dual existence before he could start on a new life.

There had to be a final determining event.

Joe would like to have fled beforehand but additional factors, all of which surprised him, like protocol, a sense of procedure, gut feeling, and a general reliance on his own sense of savvy, prevented him from quitting. By the time of the Berlin board meeting, Pa Lee would know that the bid for Global was going through. Hopefully he would therefore move a board motion thanking Joe for his sterling contribution and hand over masses of dollars or whatever. Joe wanted to be paid for what he had done.

It seemed only proper.

The mission was at an end. The Global bid was on its way. It was just a matter for Joe of making sure he avoided entanglement with the rudders of the thing as it went down the slipway. Easy, he told himself, easy…Just a matter of avoiding whatever Felix was going to throw at him.

Easy, easy…

But Joe was not so sure that it was all so straightforward. He felt less than confident. His sense of survival told him strongly that events would defy the logical view. That was in the ether. More brutally, he had to survive for around 100 hours or so and then he'd be in the clear.

But it only took about two seconds to kill a man stone-dead.

So Joe's situation was highly leveraged. He knew that. He could do the sums quite easily.

Life, like a will 'o the wisp, beckoned to Joe over the waves of the river as he tried to concentrate on what might be Felix's game plan. No way that he was quitting before the deal was announced and no way that he planned to hang around after it had been announced and he'd done Berlin…

Why was he going to Berlin, Joe asked himself? Was it foolish? Would Felix find him there? Joe doubted it – Felix would think to cross him in London. That was part of Joe's survival kit. He was gambling on double-bluffing Felix. The other part of it all was instinctual. Joe was focussing on Berlin because he was using the odd logic that fugitives adopt as they try to draw a line in the sand.

On the run, with no fixed point of reference, fugitives try desperately to rearrange the jangled space-time coordinates so that somewhere in their existence there features a zero, a central point in the matrix. That allows data to coordinate. Otherwise there is chaos.

So for Joe it would all end, as it had begun, in Berlin. He was adamant on that point. No way that he would flee before Berlin. No way either would he be around afterwards. Like the Nazi High Command remnants in Berlin in 1945, as the Russians closed in on the doomed city, Joe planned to slip away after his big ABC meeting.

Take a train…A plane…Anything to escape Felix. And his gun popping into his hand so fast without any preamble, and the flame spurting from the black deadly barrel…

Joe was not keen on that image.

Which was why in turn the idea of Julius Caesar came popping into his mind.

How had Caesar felt on the day of the Ides of March, the day that he was assassinated in the Roman Senate with 43 stab wounds, himself vainly resisting the attackers with a writing stylus? That was the question for Joe as he thought about Berlin and the end, the very end, of his affair. It preoccupied him. He couldn't work it out, even though he felt himself cornered in much the same way that Caesar had been trapped.

Had Caesar been confident? Apprehensive? Disregarding?

Like Joe, Caesar had clearly been warned. He knew that mischief was afoot that day, before he was due in the Roman Senate. He would have got the message early. He would have thought about it and he clearly could have turned back, after deliberation, just as he had paced about the Rubicon for a whole day before he crossed it and threw Rome into civil war.

But no, the greatest adventurer of the ancient world had disregarded the advice and gone about his business as normal. That had been his view. He had the girl friend, Cleopatra, installed down the Tiber in his villa with his new son, Caesarion. She was part of his plans. Caesar must have reckoned he had it all worked out. Cleopatra, a nice enough girl but prone to an excess of personality, would bring the granaries of Egypt with her in the marriage which he had carefully planned. This in turn would help Caesar buy off the Roman mob with cheap food and thus finesse the old senate. His new son linked the dynasties – he had it made!

He was nearly there! He was closing on the deal!

So that morning of March 15, after he'd been warned, perhaps even by Brutus himself via a slave, Caesar would have sat down in his villa and worked it out as the girl friend slumbered next door, perhaps a touch restlessly, as the sun came up over the Tiber. Caesar would have thought about it hard. He'd been in many tight corners before and he was a careful man, although ailing now in health and vigour. Caesar would have reached his view alone on that day as the sun came up. He would have bet on Brutus, in Joe's view. Caesar would have calculated that Brutus was not up to it. Brutus was the king pin but he would bottle – that would have been the judgement. A weak man, Caesar would have estimated, and one run by his wife – no assassin him! That in turn would have convinced Caesar that he would survive, that factor plus his natural desire to get on with the business and tough it out with the boys, all of whom he had known since his own very early youth. It was a showdown, no doubt about that, especially after the warning.

But Caesar would have gambled that he would escape with a parade of strength without having to do anything at all, lion tamer style.

So he backed his judgement and gambled on the finesse and walked down to the senate – and lost! That was beyond doubt. They rushed him. Brutus had the bottle after all. Forty-plus stab wounds later, just a minute or so after he'd walked into the senate as the most powerful man in the entire world, Caesar's gamble looked less clever.

Caesar died without a word, sinking to his knees beside a pillar and pulling his toga around him as the daggers rained down, holding out his stylus in mute defence.

Joe didn't like the trend in these thoughts one little bit. He disliked the pull in his thoughts towards the melodrama and exhibitionism of Caesar's end. That disturbed him. Was Caesar a chancer, he asked himself, a man prone to overestimate his survival capacity? Had Caesar the hustler grown old and careless? Had Cleopatra the girl friend convinced him he was immortal?

She might even have been in on the assassination deal herself...

Or, more intriguingly, had Caesar planned it all himself, knowing that his powers were failing and knowing that Caesar Augustus, his appointed heir, could after all wing it? Had Caesar arranged his own assassination?

Nobody knew for certain. The jury was out and the decisions even after 2000 years were unclear.

Like the result of Joe's trip to Berlin.

Play it cool, play it long and look for the breaks. Stick to the manual, he counselled himself. Felix will think you'll behave like an idiot because that is the only way he can summon up the nerve to kill such an old colleague. So duck smoothly. You know nearly everything at this stage, apart from one or two details. In particular you know that Felix is poised to kill you, which Felix himself does not know. So you have edge there. Most likely too, Felix will have had you followed one way or the other. Don't be fooled on that one – Felix will have tailed you. So he will know about Pugh Park and perhaps even the Reform Club…

But what he will not know about, cannot know about, will be Betty's little hideaway here in Cheyne Walk because there is no way that he can know about it. It's a circular argument. So there again you have edge…He will be nervous that you have disappeared…Perhaps he too will make a mistake and expose himself in open ground unnecessarily…

Edge, edge, edge, that is all that is needed. Felix will be nervous…Remember that single moment of relaxation when the two of you chatted about the forgeries – he was more human then and he smiled. So he too will be driven by compulsions, like the promise of the top job at ABC if he succeeds in the assassination attempt…So his timing may be poor and he may bungle it…He may concede you a vital second…He will not be certain either of his ground because he knows you of old and he knows that you too have blood on your hands. That will deter him.

Use that edge…Take the bus…Once in the office, stick with people like Donnelly…Mingle…It's hard to knock a man out in an office, so Felix will not even try…Go to the club in the evening and then escape by the garden at the back…You know the exits so use them there…It's cat and mouse but every now and then be the cat…Think of the real training manual…Think about getting through and nothing else but getting through…

Probability of survival, he asked himself at the end of his quiet evening?

No better than 40%, if that even, in all honesty. But at least it was 40%. It could have been even lower without Treadwell's indiscretions.

He was sure of that.

Joe, he told himself in the end as the evening went down over the river and the sky darkened, be careful and be lucky. You simply cannot go down at this stage when it is all very nearly just completely fucking over...

Just be lucky and keep it very, very tight...

Besides, you still have one meeting left with Moley when you will see how he copes with the queen sacrifice. Now that's not a meeting to miss, is it...?

Joe went to bed but slept fitfully. It is hard to relax when you expect to find a shooter shoved up against your face at any moment from close range by a man with attitude. So sleeping was hard. But just before he finally drifted off, a happy thought struck him. He had at least squared his account with Nicholas that morning.

After Nicholas had done his dervish act at the podium, talking the euro down to fresh lows, Joe had taken him to one side and given him a cheque for £10,000.

'Just in case anything goes wrong with the transmission process,' he had reassured the analyst, 'I've earmarked the funds, but do give me a call just before you encash it, so that I know. This is kosher money. Don't worry about a thing.'

The look of gratitude on Nicholas' face would have melted stone, Joe reckoned. It was the look of a man who had been too close to the evil side of the Square Mile and had ceased to believe in salvation. Nicholas' eyes had glistened as he stared at the cheque. Joe reckoned that he had at least made one establishment quite happy that evening.

Moley was obviously a very late payer. Treason, like murder, is only ever a matter of dates.

*   *   *   *   *

'Nicholas?'

518

'Yes, Grace.'

'That was very nice.'

'It was good for me too.'

'It's been a long time.'

'Too long.'

'I really enjoyed it.'

'Me too.'

'You're really still very good at it, you know...I can't believe it...It's like starting over and I feel like a young girl...There's no one else, you know...'

'That's wonderful news.'

'So tell me what happened again this morning...'

'With the greatest of pleasure, darling Grace. I did my usual talk on the podium and it was all A-OK because the Euro just kept on going down. Afterwards, Joe came wandering over to me and he just handed me the cheque and told me that it was kosher money. After I'd picked myself up from the floor, I called you and here we are, back where we belong, between the sheets... Or rather, sprawled on top of your sofa.

'So little time, so much opportunity."

She nibbled his ear some more.

'How long before you start to revive?'

'Not long at all, Grace.'

'Well, then. Let's get into bed and do it more comfortably.'

So obligingly, Nicholas followed her upstairs to bed, keeping his hand clamped hard against her pert little rear. Grace wriggled in excitement at his touch. Once installed in their big bed in Flood Street, London SW 3 he turned over towards her – and got on with it.

Moley called quite early the following morning, after a visibly more relaxed Grace had departed and as the Euro started to tank well and truly towards $80 cents and below. Europe was in pandemonium and the flames of a real financial crisis were now licking around every European capital. There was simply no precedent for what was happening to the Europeans' cherished currency – it was ceasing to exist. But Nicholas missed Moley's call. He'd gone out to buy some breakfast down in Oriel at Sloane

Square, celebrating his windfall of £10,000 – with more to come of course from Moley.

Moley was an honest man and Nicholas trusted him.

So Nicholas wasn't there to take the call. Moley left a quiet message on the answer phone saying that Nicholas' services were no longer required in the City. He promised that he'd be in touch in due course about the money. But Nicholas shouldn't consider calling him for a few days. Moley had lots of business on and would be too busy to talk to him.

★   ★   ★   ★   ★

Annie placed her first card on the table. She was taking the initiative, at last. It was a simple play – but highly deceptive. As the Euro collapsed, she arranged for the President of the European Central Bank, Lim Dowberg, a man of blameless reputation whom the Chron had reviled for weeks in its columns, to give an interview to The Times in London. Meanwhile the Euro was over the edge. Dowberg made a few honest plodding comments which were duly seized upon by the Chron and distorted out of all recognition. The roar of disapproval at Dowberg's remarks by the world's press could be heard in every trading market across the globe. Dowberg's job was on the line. The Euro fell through 80 cents. It looked to be all over for the European dream. But Annie had secretly arranged for buyers to support the currency at these low levels. At 78 cents to the $, they came into the market and bought the Euro very hard, pushing it back up and over the precipice on the right side this time. It was like watching Niagra Falls flow backwards. Unwittingly, therefore, it looked as if Dowberg had found the bottom of the market – all very sweet and easy.

★　★　★　★　★

Leadon took up the theme in his Threadneedle Street commentary, a commentary which here and there was starting to attract attention, raise some unanswered questions and develop a following.

Leadon wrote as follows:

...Markets have become highly politicised as three larger than life characters played starring roles on the world financial stage – Lim Dowberg, President of the European Central Bank; Alan Greenspan, chairman of the US Fed; and, to roars of muted applause from connoisseurs, the Old Lady of Threadneedle Street herself.

Dowberg emerged as the hero of the hour. This is the Needler's view. It, clearly, is not the consensus view of the market for whom currently the ECB President is something slightly worse than unmentionable. But the market is hysterical in its short-term judgements and the evidence in his favour is overwhelming. Consider the position he found himself locked into towards the end of last week. It looked dire. The support facility for the Euro, for example, which he had painfully negotiated with the US was patently unravelling. The slow ebb of US support was taking its toll of confidence in the currency. At the same time, raising European interest rates appeared to have failed in its intent of stabilising the currency. Finally, the ploy of fresh intervention had most likely to be ruled out for fear of leaks. On the first occasion that the G-7 central banks had intervened, these early whispers to the market had done a great deal to nullify the impact of the buying support programme. Fresh intervention coupled with fresh leaks would have completed the demolition of that vital piece of equipment in the central banks armoury, had it gone off at half-cock.

Those roughly summarised were the problems which Dowberg faced to his left.

To his right, he could see the glittering ranks of a deeply hostile world financial press spearheaded in its assaults by the Financial Chronicle. More on the wrecking role of the FC later. But for the moment suffice it to say that Dowberg's every move to placate markets was greeted by a hostile press commentary which in turn had the effect of enforcing a self-justifying and self-feeding downward spiral in the currency through the doleful $0.80's support level – and most likely beyond.

Rather than stand by and witness the gradual decline of the currency to further destabilising lows, Dowberg moved to take the initiative by granting his interview to *The Times*. By speaking provocatively and feeding the market's worst fears, he was trying to achieve two ends – to find the bottom of the market for the Euro and also to establish rapidly a low enough level for the currency against the dollar so that the US authorities of whatever political colour would feel able to intervene in support without fearing that an adverse chain-reaction against the dollar would be set in motion. It was a very brave gambit by a tough- minded and experienced central banker forced by the exigencies of the situation to step out of role.

Whether Dowberg has succeeded in his ploy remains to be seen. Most likely in the short term, granted special factors in abeyance, he might well have been successful. Given the selling momentum that was building up behind the Euro it looks to the Needler as if the Euro might well have sped through the $0.75 support level had Dowberg not made his move. As it is, he may well have bamboozled forex markets.

The Needler now focuses on the third member of the trio who dazzled markets so much last week – the Bank of England. In more ways than one the Bank seemed to succeed in conveying its characteristic two-faced Janus expression all across town. But it did nobody any favours. Increasingly the independent Bank of England looks like an institution without a home in the evolving world of global markets – and certainly a very complex animal in both motivation and agenda.

Consider first the scale of the attacks by the Financial Chronicle on the Euro; the European Central Bank; and Dowberg himself. The battery was constant and the impact on confidence in the Euro most likely very damaging, although not easily quantifiable. This kind of unbalanced journalism is not new. It has characterised the FC's reporting on the Euro for many months. Where it changed last week was in the personalised nature of the venom. Dowberg took a very heavy pounding indeed. At the height of the storm surrounding his words, the FC carried a note which very roughly read as follows:-The only point of optimism in this whole affair is that Dowberg expects to have departed before the end of his full term as ECB President.

This is yellow journalism.

* * * * *

Indeed it is, thought Annie as she blessed Leadon for his aggressive commentary and received reports about the support buying for the currency. The moment to support the currency had been well chosen. The Euro was deeply over-sold. At the first whiff of support buying, the bears trundled off into the woods. It was fairly easy to engineer a small rally in the currency from the frightening lows around 79.50 cents to some 82 cents, although the Chron, typically, was still looking for Armageddon around the corner. The Euro was still very fragile.

Undeterred, Annie prepared to make a fresh play. Now for card number two, she thought, the vital one this time....The Russians will be very puzzled that the currency has not sold off even more, especially after the hysterical attack on the Euro by the Chron. They will smell a tiny rat about the Euro but not enough to alter their plans. Because they do not know what I know. That is their great weakness – I know their structure and I know just how inflexible it is, relative to their game plan. So the failure of the Euro to collapse totally will serve to whet their appetite for more when I play my ace of trumps...They will be more exposed than they might have been. Now is the time and now is the hour. We'll see whether Stone is a man of straw or what very shortly...

Everything has been arranged...

* * * * *

Mid-morning in the City. Joe sat in his office at ABC looking at Bloomberg on his TV screen. The work was done and the bid was out. It had been announced at 8.30 sharp and it had been completely unexpected by the traders. A knock-out blow. After initial surprise, the market had responded most favourably to the terms and the wire services were buzzing with the news. Interviews; commentary; share price movements; much shouting in the Square Mile streets. The cameras were everywhere and likewise the interviews. Everybody liked the currency play.

A grim-faced sector analyst was being interviewed by one of the gorgeously pouting pretty ladies on Bloomberg about the bid. She wide-lipped her questions at him and the analyst took undue encouragement from her attention. Joe had watched her in the past. She framed her questions like chat-up lines and signalled entirely the wrong message. The analyst bored on forever about earnings and synergy and management possibilities, quite oblivious of the main point about the deal – the US was pulling military hardware out of the West and did not want to leave too much behind in its wake, as happened in Vietnam.

Joe felt that an era was coming to an end for him. His mind was still focussed on Felix but he could see a door swinging open…Only a matter of making those last sixty feet or so and then he was away…Only a matter of time…Time for the last sprint…

Suddenly Newsflash came up large and red on the screen; the Bloomberg babe reacted as if someone had boshed her around the head – clearly the ear mike had received a message – and then they were over at Global House interviewing Rivers Pugh on the steps of his head office.

Joe leaned forward to scrutinise Rivers as the camera caught him in close-up.

He was shocked for a second. It was a very different version of Rivers Pugh which the viewers glimpsed. The change in him was remarkable.

'This is one event you just did not foresee in a million years, Rivers, and it shows,' Joe told himself.

The eyes were fluttery behind the lenses; the tongue licked around the dry lips; and the head shook backwards and forwards in amazement. Hunched in his coat, Rivers looked more like a captured drugs dealer than a CEO. He was evasive and very nearly speechless. No sense of power and no projection of authority. He seemed to have crumpled on the news. He looked, in fact, very like his sister on one of her bad days. The idea that the London institutions no longer venerated him in the fawning way they had approached him in the past had hit Rivers Pugh hard.

Peer group betrayal of Pugh – he'd never experienced that before. Or rather, he had been through something similar but that had been some years ago at the Foreign Office. The tyro was taking a second time out, in effect, but this one was more deadly because Rivers would have assumed that he was invulnerable by now.

'This bid is going through and then some. It'll be over in a flash...'

Joe was quite clear in his own mind that everything about the deal was a coup. Rivers looked out for the count. That would have been noticed by the London institutions as they watched the interview. The body language was atrocious. Rivers' poor showing would have encouraged them even more to accept the terms of the Detroit bid, especially given the generous terms of the bid. Our cock won't fight, they would be saying. No sense in staying with a loser...Let's take the money and run – who knows what might happen now. There's lots of money, too. Who knows, anything might happen here. The pound might start to recover...Now that would be a blow...

The stampede to sell Rivers Pugh futures was only just beginning...Not a stock that was tightly held by any means, to everyone's surprise in the market.

Joe was also struck by another aspect of Rivers' demeanour as he mumbled along to the camera, mouthing rather than articulating his replies as his eyes moved sharply sideways away from the camera. He seemed younger, almost buoyant but in an inverse sense, although Rivers Pugh the business hustler was giving way to a fresher, reborn but more innocent Pugh, such as Joe had first encountered in and around Battersea Bridge and the Rivers' suicide attempt. And such as his sister again was becoming as she tried to recover from the shock of her mother's death. Rivers seemed to be shaking off the mantle of commercial hustler even as he spoke...

With an ache, Joe thought about Perdita and Pugh Park, a forbidden topic with him for many days...

The blond tresses swirled about in his imagination. He thrust the image of her from his mind...

'Congratulations, Joe. Well done. A very fine piece of work indeed.'

It was Donnelly. He had stolen into the office as Joe stared at Rivers on the TV. He reached out a hand to grip Joe on the shoulder and Joe smiled at him. It was a good moment for them both.

'Lucia did most of it, you know, Donnelly. She worked night and day on this one. Most of the credit is down to her. I'm hoping she'll step by so that we can both offer our congratulations. She fixed the currency angle by and large...'

Donnelly smiled. Indeed his face was a quilt of pleasure. A big moment for them all as the deal came out into the sunshine and was well received.

Joe's phone rang. It was Nicholas. Joe heard from his tone of voice that something was wrong. The voice was cracked. Trouble and large...

'One second, Nicholas, I'm putting you on hold. Don't go away.'

Joe turned to Donnelly.

'This call may take some time. I'll catch up with you in two or three minutes. If you see Lucia on your travels, send her in and you come too...Come to think of it, tell the Perfect to stir her stumps and get some champagne out for the troops. Let's have a couple of snoots...'

It felt like high days and holidays that morning. The sun was breaking through...Joe returned to Nicholas. He sounded very crestfallen.

'We wondered what had happened to you, Nicholas. We missed your Nuremberg rally performance on the podium. Have you not been well?'

A snatch of breath at the other end as Nicholas attempted to salve his dignity. Joe's fingers played on the key pads on his phone as he waited for Nicholas to speak. Tap, tap, tap, up and down and across in the old familiar hopscotch as Nicholas returned to speaking mode.

'That £10,000...'

Joe saw it all. So it conforms to trend. No surprises here at all. He came to the point straightaway.

'Aha, so Moley has been a naughty boy, has he? Welshed on you, has he?'

'I got a call from him out of the blue, telling me not to turn up any more at any of my morning meetings and that he'd pay me sometime. He's a skunk. I've been used.'

The voice was flat and stony.

'Nicholas, I thought you were exclusive to us. How many meetings were you doing?'

'Four or five a day by the end of last week.'

'All on the same topic? The end of the Euro as we knew it?'

'Exactly, and all scripted by Moley…'

'Aha. So he loaded the bullets and you fired them?'

'Exactly. I feel such a fool.'

'But you did get the market right. That won't be forgotten here at ABC. Our boys have made a small fortune out of shorting the Euro.'

'Thanks. But I can do so much better in the markets than just regurgitating Moley's views.'

That sounded like a job application. Joe's fingers tapped away at the phone. Nicholas continued to talk down the phone at Joe. All of a sudden it came to him. Structure emerged. Joe was hit by an idea of such devastating and cruel simplicity he felt the hairs on the nape of his neck rise in excitement.

That afternoon was the agreed date between himself and Moley for when the queen sacrifice was due to be explored. Now Joe saw another Queen's Gambit very clearly.

'Nicholas, tell me, just what are you doing this afternoon at three thirty precisely?'

'Killing myself, most likely.'

'Premature, I would say. It's a sunny day. And you've still got my cheque to encash.'

'OK, point taken, and so I have. But what did you have in mind?'

'You say Moley owes you money?'

'Masses. But how can I get hold of him? I don't know his address and he won't take calls from me.'

'One second, Nicholas. I have an idea. Just tell me where you're calling from. I don't want you going off-line while I work this one out.'

'I'm not in a callbox, if that's what you wanted to know.'

'Fine, now Nicholas first things first. You pay that ABC cheque in soonest.'

'You're sure?'

'Perfectly sure. You got the market right, it helped us hugely to hear your views, for whatever motivation, so you go right ahead and pay in the cheque. You deserve the money. It's a legitimate expense.'

Large exhalation of breath down the line.

'Joe thank you. That's a great relief. Thank you very much. That makes a difference. I can't tell you just how much of a difference...Domestically...'

Joe tapped away at his phone pad. The idea was hot and strong. Triangle, then inverted triangle then cross to make a perfect...Yes that was it – his call sign of old but with a difference. Moley was the difference...

The number was unforgettable.

'Nicholas, you have a pen there?'

'I do indeed.'

'Moley's address is as follows...'

Joe dictated the Barbican address down the line. Joe could hear the intake of breath as the precious information was conveyed across London and space, making Moley suddenly accessible – and vulnerable...

Joe then made him very vulnerable, very carefully. With intent. That was what old friendships were all about.

'Moley's flat is at the top of the tower. You can tell that from the number of the flat. But no way that Moley will let you in...'

'Agreed.'

'But I happen to know that at 3.30 precisely this afternoon he is expecting a visitor. He will be there in his flat expecting his visitor. And he always leaves his front door open to let the visitor free access to the flat. Something about his hospitality protocol. So here is the code which will give you entrance to his block at the front door of the block. Then you take the lift, march into his flat and put your points to Moley himself in person. Just march through his front door.'

Triangle, inverted triangle, then cross to form a perfect...Joe gave the vital numbers down the line to Nicholas. Nicholas took them down very carefully. He then repeated them back to Joe. Joe confirmed that the numbers were correct as he pronounced in that way a valedictory renvoi to his friendship with Moley.

Pity about the chessboard, he thought. I will never ever know now just how Moley would have rigged the board to recover from that queen sacrifice. Too bad...

'One further point, Nicholas.'

'Yes.'

Nicholas' voice was hard now. That did not bode well for Moley.

'When you go into Moley's flat, you have to shout a word. Does that make sense? Just one word.'

'What kind of word?'

'I'll tell you. The word is Aiuto! It's Italian. Do you know what it means?'

'I haven't a clue.'

'No matter. You'll find out its true significance this afternoon. But you have to really bawl it out. So repeat the word after me – say Aiuto! Very loudly. Now!'

'Aiuto!

Nicholas' shout very nearly smashed Joe's tympanum.

'That's good. Very good. Assume it's a form of greeting. Now write it down so that you don't forget it. You'll be very surprised and very pleased by what happens when you shout Aiuto at Moley.'

'Walls of Jericho?'

'Something like that but more intimate. The reaction will be instantaneous. But make certain that you shout the word out.'

'This is all very irregular.'

'So is your situation, Nicholas.'

'I was forgetting...'

'A cheque for £10,000 does that to a man. Instant amnesia. But I tell you that if you follow my instructions this afternoon, you will recoup everything that Moley owes you...Perhaps more besides…Now don't call me again for some weeks. I'm off now out of town and you just caught me.'

Nicholas sounded peeved that Joe was departing just when he thought he'd made a catch.

'Give me your number, Nicholas, and I'll call you when I'm back in town.'

Nicholas fetched across his number and Joe noted it down. Important, he thought to go through the motions. Then the interview was over. Joe rang off, wondering just how Moley would cope with both Nicholas' sudden manifestation and the Italian slave emerging from the kitchen like a buzz-cock. That'll tax his negotiating skills… Cornered by two very angry young men…And owing both of them, big time. It'll take more than a swift castling to extricate Moley from all this.

Joe turned back to the TV and then looked up to find Lucia standing over him.

'Get out! Just get out!'

Lucia was quivering with fury. She was wound up with rage like a top. Her bulging eyes were out on stalks at Joe.

'What was that, Lucia? Run that past me again, will you?'

More vibrating from Lucia as the TV flickered in the corner and Rivers pretended to answer some more questions.

'I said Get out. You're a cheat and you're fucked.'

'I'll be the judge of that, young lady. But hey, hey, easy, we're supposed to be celebrating, not slagging each other off.'

Joe heard Donnelly return to his office. From the clink of glasses, it sounded as if Donnelly had secured some help from the Perfect over the booze. Donnelly brought a merry sound into Joe's office.

Rivers was still on screen, muffled to his ears in his overcoat. Lucia gestured at him.

'See that, Donnelly! See him, do you? Do you know who that is?'

Donnelly was smart enough.

'That's Rivers Pugh, your vanquished foe.'

'Correct. And do you know where he lives…'

Joe was beginning to see Lucia's drift. And behind that drift he glimpsed the hand of Felix. So Felix had tailed him – and had established where he lived…One up to Felix…! But one up to Joe too, by the most stupendous piece of good fortune – Saint Betty herself!

He thanked God for her blessed manifestation.

'Tell me, Lucia, where Rivers lives…'

Donnelly had his humouring tone on him. Joe thought Lucia might strike him in her rage. Lucia was a stickler for the rules. She did not like bank officers talking down to her. Joe reckoned she was nearly three inches off the ground at that point. Her rage was making her almost levitate as she hopped from foot to foot.

'He lives in a place called Pugh Park.'

'Sounds nice. Where is it? Kent? Surrey? Shall I open the bottle?'

Here it comes thought Joe. But Felix, old boy, I've just missed your knife thrust…By a fraction…And by pure good fortune…Unbelievable…

Joe waited for Lucia to make a fool of herself. She flung herself into the mire.

'And who lives there with him…?'

Donnelly looked fogged. Was this some kind of game show?

'Posh and Becks?'

'Yes, come on now, don't be so dim. Who lives there too?'

Donnelly was starting to get angry as well now. Lucia gestured wildly at Joe. Joe reckoned that Felix had not been able to come up with the full story – as yet. He would not have been able to establish that Joe owned Pugh Park. So Joe could lie his way out of the encounter…

Lucia was almost frothing with rage.

'He lives there too. Yes, him, standing there in front of us. None other than Joe himself. So where does that leave us? Yes, where? We're guilty of insider trading? He actually lives in the same house as the man who runs the company we're bidding for. And he never told us…Wait until the Panel hears about this. We are completely and utterly fucked. The bid will be declared null and void…Oh Christ…It's not an arms' length deal…You fucker, Joe, you absolute fucker.'

Almost idly she picked up an ashtray, eyebrows semaphoring in a frenzy, and smashed it down against Joe's desk. Fortunately, it did not break. Donnelly looked at Joe for confirmation. Joe could see that all his old doubts were now resurfacing.

Joe paused. The God of Spooks had been riding shot-gun for him. He was in the clear. I'll give this to them both very slowly, he thought.

'I moved out.'

'You did what?'

'I moved out. I live in Cheyne Walk, in the flat of an old friend of mine. It cost me an arm and a leg to do this. It's completely destroyed my domestic life...I did it for the bid so that nobody would be compromised. I'll take you round there and show you, if you like.'

Lucia was nonplussed. Her mouth fell open.

'That's not what I heard...Prove it!'

'As I said, come round immediately and I'll show you my living quarters. It's a nice enough flat but not a home from home. You're very welcome to come and inspect.'

Lucia still looked dazed. This was not what she had expected. Joe saw a gap. He pressed home his advantage.

'But who told you, Lucia? It's your turn now.'

Joe asked the question very gently. She blushed scarlet.

'I...'

Joe took charge. He talked quickly and very quietly to the two of them so that the rest of the room, now filling up as a party beckoned, could not eavesdrop.

'Donnelly, if I told you that I had known Lucia too in another life, then you'd be surprised by that as well, wouldn't you?'

Donnelly looked amazed while Lucia was panic-stricken. She waved a taut hand in denial. Her anger was abating giving way to deep apprehension. She had an inkling of what Joe might say now. This was an encounter of long ago which they never, ever, mentioned between them. It had never happened. That was the unspoken pact.

'If I said to Lucia – and I want you to bear witness to this Donnelly – remember a certain restaurant in Sloane Square and a certain conversation, then you'd be surprised because my discretion has been total...But look at Lucia, Donnelly...So no betrayals of confidence...Likewise over Global, you can take my word for it...But look at Lucia again. You can see from her expression that she does recall the lunch and the chat, and that she does not want that mentioned one little bit...'

It was true. Lucia was now a deep scarlet. Hardly surprising. At the lunch, years ago, Lucia had asked Joe to fuck her, quickly and expeditiously, as a matter of course. But she had been young then, knowing no better. And being young, she had been more in love with grunge sex than mergers and acquisitions.

That had been then. Oh, foolish youth.

Lucia was waving her hand and tugging furiously at her nose again, eclipsed by the situation. She was retreating from the blame game very fast. Joe breathed again. His dancing ankles had carried him just clear again of Felix. By about 2 centimetres, no more. Joe could blackmail Lucia into silence. She would be no trouble. But it was a damn' close run thing.

Felix had very nearly torpedoed the whole bid by his indiscreet revelations.

Donnelly came into his own. Like any bank official he moved to restore order. He saw the problem and acted accordingly. He hustled and bustled around the room pouring out the champagne, asking questions loudly, and crafting equilibrium where there had been chaos. Joe warmed to him in the moment of crisis.

Lucia was quieter now.

Joe walked up to her, put his arm around her and kissed her on the forehead. The room roared with approval. Little hot tears burned their way down her cheeks.

Meanwhile on the screen the share price of Global was booming. The market liked the bid. Just as well Donnelly was working the room. This was no time to go wobbly, not with so much money and prestige at stake and in play.

Joe suggested that point to Lucia and Donnelly made it too. Taken off guard by Joe's unexpected revelations and suffering also from nervous exhaustion, Lucia allowed herself to be humoured into taking some champagne and joining in the general sense of celebration. The champagne gradually went to her head.

That reassured Joe. He mooched around his room, distributing the champagne to more and more of Lucia's team who were now flocking in spontaneously, full of buoyant optimism. The judgements flowed back and forth in quick patter. The boys too had seen Rivers being interviewed on TV. They had formed the quick impression that he was a busted flush; a pretty boy but no more than that; a City rent-boy like the rest of them.

So on with the drinkie-poo's…

Ties were loosened; gestures grew larger in the exuberant mid-morning; and each movement of the Global share price was greeted by 'Oooh's and 'Aaah's as fists smote the air and the champagne flowed around and about.

Time to relax. It had been a hard slog getting the bid to the starting line – they were all agreed on that. But the spirit of the team was with them. Joe saw Tommy, another brief casualty of the run-up to the deal, smite the air with the crowd before pulling out the mobile to call the wife with the good news.

Meanwhile Joe could see Donnelly going to work discreetly on a faltering Lucia, just behind the TV screen. He saw the words 'Italy' and 'holidays' framed in his mouth. The logic of Donnelly's position flowed from those suggestions. By taking a short break on holiday, he was urging that Lucia could take stock. No sense in hanging around in the short term. There was nothing much to be done in the next few days. The event had taken place – the bid was out. That was all that mattered. A short intermezzo would now follow as a matter of course, as the institutions took stock.

Joe admired the way that Donnelly poured oil on troubled waters. He admired still more the gracious way that Donnelly allowed himself to be persuaded into taking over the administration of the deal in the very short term…In Joe's view he showed real tact with no apparent trace of ambition… Joe acknowledged that Donnelly would do a wonderful blocking job in the short term as the bid for Global evolved into something quite unexpected. Donnelly could get a deal. This was just as well since Joe was poised to jump ship, or he was casting off – one of the two. Either way, he was going. He had very nearly reached the end of the line.

He could glimpse the opportunity coming up fast to slip away from both the company and the job… Take a train and just fade away, alighting at a random spot somewhere God knew where, on some strange platform in an unknown country. Then quickly, walking with determination, it would be into the forest, down the hidden pathways, into the half light, far from Felix, far from the obligations of the market, far from almost anything apart from the memory of Perdita, haunting him at every turn of the path, like a nymph...

Fade far away, dissolve and quite forget...

Oh Perdita...

* * * * *

'Nicholas, what has happened to your jacket?'

'I bought a new one.'

'But you liked your jacket, you always said it was a part of you. You've had it almost as long as I've known you.'

'I bought a new one. See – don't you like it?'

'It's alright – ish...But I liked the old one, where have you put it? I don't think I'm too keen on that stripe at all. No, that definitely isn't you at all, not in a month of Sundays.'

Grace turned Nicholas round so that she could view the jacket from the rear, smoothing down the flap as she did so. She tut-tutted in disapproval at the cut.

'I left it with the shop. They promised to get rid of it for me.'

'Such a pity. But whatever possessed you to make such an impulse purchase?'

'Moley paid up.'

'He didn't. You're telling me the truth, that Moley paid up...?'

Nicholas nodded, a little shakily, in Grace's closely-observed view.

'He most certainly did.'

'I take it all back then. How much?'

'I'll tell you in a second.'

Nicholas was playing for time and testing out his version of events. Grace distrusted anything to do with Moley.

.

'So, Grace, I felt rich. I went into the nearest shop I could find and I celebrated by buying a new jacket.'

'What happened?'

'I rang him.'

'Even though he told you not to ring...'

'I got lucky. I must have caught him on a good day...'

Nicholas faltered slightly but he managed to keep his eyes fixed on Grace's face as he spoke. The memory of Moley's startled face as he burst through his front door in the Barbican, full of real balls – aching rage, was still with Nicholas. Moley had been white with fear. But Nicholas thought also of the quite appalling, unexpected manifestation of another body in the flat who burst suddenly from the kitchen as soon as Nicholas had shouted, as Joe had instructed, the magic word, 'Aiuto'.

If anything the stranger had been even more angry than Nicholas... Everything had rapidly reached terror-pitch...Had Joe known about any of this...? Nicholas embarked some more on his carefully-constructed tale of events.

'So Moley said he would pay. We met at his club...'

'Oh which one was that?'

'The Army and Navy.'

'Very posh, I am impressed. What was the dress code?'

'Negative, so far as I was concerned.'

Nicholas' mind returned to Moley's flat as he lied to Grace...

Seeing that he was backed by reinforcements, the strange young man had immediately pulled Moley's phone from the wall, hence severing all communications with the outside world. Moley had come hurtling across the room to Nicholas and asked him to help protect him from the madman, now spitting rage. Moley had been pursued...The young man was insane with anger, like an animal suddenly scenting freedom. There had been a chessboard carefully positioned between two low chairs, Nicholas recalled, but the young man had kicked it to one side, scattering the pieces all across the room, as he pursued Moley.

'Adequate for my purposes. Yes, he gave me all the money in cash, which was nice of him...'

It turned out that Moley kept a sizeable amount of money in the flat with him. He had offered all of it to Nicholas if he would help keep off the madman who Nicholas now assumed was Italian from what he was saying. The scenes of wreckage in the flat were indescribable as Moley had cowered behind Nicholas. The Italian had gradually gone berserk.

But so far, at that point, nothing major had happened. Only property had been destroyed. Moley handed over the money to Nicholas, which he had pulled out of a drawer in his desk, thrusting it into his hand...

Then the Italian had gone a stage further. He had opened the window...

The wind had rushed in from outside blowing papers, and what have you, everywhere in a storm of bits and pieces...Nicholas had his money, so he had no further interest in the situation. He relinquished protection of Moley, surrendering him to the Italian. Moley had screamed in pure terror as the Italian grabbed hold of him and began to drag him towards the open window, many, many floors up in the middle of London's skies...

Moley had grasped Nicholas' jacket, tearing a massive rent in the sleeve, and would not let go. There was pandemonium in the flat. Nicholas had started to shake with fear.

The situation was by now completely out of hand and getting worse. Nicolas had realised that he was potentially compromised. He was holding a large, unspecified, amount of money in the flat of a rich and prominent City stockbroker as some Italian maniac tried to throw him out of the top floor of a Barbican tower block...

'Did he give you lunch, Nicholas?'

'No, he was too busy to do that. I just took the money and more or less scarpered...I'm afraid I was a little ungracious.'

Grace nodded and Nicholas told some more lies about his encounter with Moley.

Nicholas found he could not forget the wolfish, starved look that had come over the Italian's face as Moley clung to the jacket. His eyes had seemed to light up in his skull as a mad idea had presented itself to him. For a second he released Moley on his side, as the wind howled into the flat from the sky. Moley had flown into Nicholas' arms and the maniac had vanished. Moley had sagged like a dead weight against Nicholas.

Then the maniac had returned with a scream and grabbed hold of Moley once more. As Moley had stretched out a hand to the table to hang onto something else, Nicholas had seen a great knife describe a wheeling arc against the ceiling before plunging into Moley's unprotected upturned hand with a thud, nailing it to the table. Blood had spumed out from Moley's hand and the maniac had cackled his pleasure at the bloodletting and his handiwork.

Pinned to the table, Moley screamed again...

More blood, this time cascading across the table...

Nicholas had fled at that point, clutching the money, slamming the door behind him and leaving Moley to his fate...

He had clanked down from the skies in the lift, clutching the thick wad of money in his trouser pocket and desperately trying to manipulate the jacket so that the rent could not be seen. He got to the ground floor, stepped out of the lift and glimpsed his face in the mirror opposite...

To his horror, he saw that it was smeared with blood, a great slash of red running from his ear to his neck...He checked the jacket and found more blood soaking the sleeve...He was shaking with fear and excitement after the encounter. But he still clutched his money...

'I'm not surprised that you went out and celebrated. But tell me Nicholas, how much money did Moley give you?'

'Oh, it was another windfall...He gave me £5,000...'

'Like manna falling from heaven. So now on account of your little jaunts up to the City you've got £15,000 in cash. Amazing. You're not exactly rich, Nicholas, but at least you can make a contribution to the household...'

'That's right, I'd love to...'

Nicholas had come away with substantially more than £5,000 from Moley's flat but he was saying nothing about the excess. He was terrified now. Every single sterling banknote had been worth £50. But there had also been a tightly rolled wad of dollar bills, at least fifty of them. All in all, Nicholas had come up away with something like £15,000. He had buried all the dollar bills in a box in Grace's tiny little garden...

Right at the end of the garden.

He had been panic stricken and shaking with fear and shock, as he had shovelled away at the earth. A neighbour might pop a head over the wall at any moment and ask him why he was suddenly taking up gardening, he who had never been known to stir a step in the garden apart from doing some ineffectual weeding. But the neighbours had been too busy playing bridge or whatever to disturb him. The box had gone deep into the earth, which he had just as hastily shovelled back into the small hole. He was still shuddering from the memory of his wild-eyed and dishevelled walk through the Barbican, jacket over his arm, which he had done immediately after exiting from Moley's lift.

His arms at the small trowel had been weak and shaky.

As he had paced along the windy walkways of the Barbican, at any moment he had expected to hear the polite but firm policeman's cough behind him – 'Excuse me, sir, but could I ask you to step this way... A murder has been committed... You look to me, sir, as if you might be able to help us with our enquiries, bearing in mind that your jacket is ripped and soaked with blood. You look as if you've seen a ghost, sir...And there's blood all over your face, sir.'

But no cough had come. He had made his way into the Barbican theatre and there mingled with the crowd amongst whom he had been indistinguishable with his fervid look. He had blended with the throng.

Grace meanwhile was still probing. She was inexorable.

'Show me the money.'

'I can't do that, I've paid it into the building society...But you can look at the passbook...'

'No, forget it silly...But I would like to see an entry like that, when you're disposed to show me. It's been a long time since you've handled money like that, Nicholas my love...'

Nicholas noted with surprise that Grace was both more perky and also more deferential to him than normal...But he wanted to go to sleep and forget about the horrors of his day...He excused himself, went up stairs and fell asleep almost immediately.

When Grace came to bed later, his feet were sticking out from the end of the bed. She noted first with surprise and then with horror that his left ankle had a long streak of what appeared to be paint but which turned out to be blood, running up and over his Achilles tendon. She looked at his feet, heard the slight snoring, and digested the implications of what she had seen.

Grace was no fool. She realised she had much food for thought.

She'd come a long way in the headhunting game by using her own head. She was not going to make a sacrifice of anything now for anybody. Her business had legs, even though Simon's were slightly wobbly.

And even though his bank account was now minus £5000.

So she looked at the blood for a long time before deciding what to do. She was mulling the implications. Nicolas' story had not fooled her. She smelled a rat.

Nicholas for his part lay inert on the bed and slept heavily. No job but clearly some money. She still had her investigations to make. She looked around the room and finally ran his building society passbook to earth in one of the drawers, beneath his shirts. She opened it silently, watching him carefully as she turned the pages. She found the relevant entry which confirmed that Nicholas had paid in £15000 to his account that day, £10,000 by cheque and £5000 in cash.

So he had not at that stage, so far as she could establish, lied to her…That decided it. He was still partly honest although he had fallen among thieves, it had to be added. He had that smell and that look of dishonesty about him. Grace went to the bathroom, took a flannel, washed it in warm water and very carefully, so as not to disturb Nicholas, cleaned the blood from his ankle. Just to be on the safe side she rinsed the flannel in warm water, then wrapped it in some cling film and walked downstairs to stow it with the rest of the kitchen rubbish for collection the following morning. She stowed the flannel right at the bottom of the can.

Only then did she dare go to bed. For most of the night she lay there with eyes wide open. She slept fitfully because she was preoccupied by many thoughts. In particular she reflected on the irony of Nicholas' building society account being now full to overflowing with cash, whereas her account with Simon had just been closed, because the relevant deposit now graced her personal account. Another £5000 flowing into the coffers!

But Nicholas was dead to the world and slept through the whole night.

The following day was dustbin day, just off the King's Road, as if that had ever concerned Nicholas. She filled the dustbins and thought that on balance living and sleeping with Nicholas was better than sleeping with Simon. But only by a small margin…

That wasn't much in it. They were both cretins.

★ ★ ★ ★ ★

Darling Ursula, I think this is my Waterloo. This is the day when I have to do the deed and it is also the day when I imagine that my whole career in journalism comes to an end. Sad times…I am full of remorse…

It is about 10.15 in the morning now, and I'm sitting in my office at the Chron as Editor-in-Name of the paper. It may well be my last day here as Editor. On balance, yes, I think I'll resign today…

To begin at the beginning, the stranger and I met yesterday evening and he gave me his article. It is a very straightforward piece. It is long and it is an editorial, not a feature, and this surprised me. It is also very strong. It amounts to a warning to the Russians to pay their debts when they come due, as they will do shortly when I think the Paris Club meets to discuss the borrowings the Russians ran up during the Soviet era. All the world knows that the Russians want to monkey around with everyone over these debts. Predictably the Chron has been supportive of the Russians at best and at worst simply silent on the whole issue. But the editorial, which I have strict instructions to run today for tomorrow's newspaper, takes a very stern line on the Russian position. Now assuming that the editorial gets run, which I very much doubt, then the Russians will of course be shocked.

They're used to an easy ride from London and the Chron and they'll wonder at the change in tone. That's all I know about anything.

So now I'm sitting in my office, waiting for conference, and the boys to show. I'm supposed to put my foot down here but there's a fat chance of that happening when the whole of the meeting and the day's agenda for the paper will be dominated by the likes of...As if I stood a snowball's chance in hell of getting anything I wanted into the paper, still less an editorial...I will go through with the idea but I have no faith at all that by the end of the day we will be any more advanced...I'll close now briefly but I'll be back shortly to chat some more with my little electronic confidant...

★ ★ ★ ★ ★

Annie sat at her desk, looking at the waves outside and thinking cool thoughts. It's now or never and so it might as well be now, was the dominant idea that ran through her head as she stared out across the Thames. Come on, Tom, she thought, do your stuff. It's all laid on for you. All you need do is just walk into conference. It can't be made any easier than that, now can it?

Her idea was simplicity itself. The Russians had built a salient right into London via the Bank of England and the Chron, which were to all intents fused in the operation. It was like a bridge extending across continents. But the Russians did not know that London was fully aware too of the existence of the salient. Very well, Annie had surmised, that gives me an edge. Or rather just one shot at trying for edge. If I suddenly make it very clear that we in London have the operation under full surveillance – because we know all about it – and if I make this obvious at a very crucial moment, a very, very crucial moment, just when the Russians are poised to play hardball over their debts, then there will be consternation at the other end in Moscow. The message will go right through to the end of the line, right down the tube in fact to Moscow and into the eye of the observer at the other end of the tunnel. But such is the fused nature of the Chron and Bank tie-up with the old Soviets that the Russians will have no means of withdrawing from their position. What they have gained in outreach they will have lost in manoeuvrability.

Tom Stone's role in all of this is to run the editorial which he will no doubt at this very moment be fingering in his hot little hand...

Our billet doux sent to Russia with love, thought Annie.

Now as soon as the Chron appears, carrying its changed message, what will the Russians do? Very difficult for them because they risk being stranded over the credit negotiations, on the assumption that their access to London credit has been rumbled. Effectively, they will be caught between a rock and a hard place. They won't want to miss out on the credit access...Annie calculated that a first class row would break out in Moscow between the liberal wing, which believed in the West, and the old Soviet cadre, both of which were jostling for power. That was Gamble No 1. Gamble No 2 was even better if it came off. In the ensuing melee between the various competing Russian power blocs, the consensus would emerge that the London end had been penetrated and must therefore be abandoned. So the Russians would be tempted to pull out both on the Bank and on the Chron, closing off their salient of their own volition and leaving Stobart and Q and the rest of them to their fate...

Playback time and then some...

So that was the plan...

Annie now proceeded to dwell on the specifics...The Chron would be a different paper, just for the day, as Stone's Last Charge began.

★   ★   ★   ★   ★

Darling Ursula, I have to report more shocks and surprises. Conference was very nearly empty and all the old wrecking crew have been detained at home or elsewhere for a variety of reasons. Hurricanes...! I talked and everybody listened to me for a change. So I have my slot back again and I can be Editor for a day...It's a great pity that I have to spend my precious moments of liberty running somebody else's article but then I suppose that I must do it, even though I have a wonderful idea for an editorial on space travel...Hey ho but it does me good to be back in charge...The pacing of the corridors, the chatting with the subs, and the general feeling that the whole place hums and throbs through my veins and mine alone...

*   *   *   *   *

Annie had left nothing to chance. Arranging for Tom Stone to have a free run at the paper had taken the kind of planning and organisation that went into getting people over the Wall in the old days. But she had gone further. She had arranged for one of the Chron's remaining 'independent' columnists to write a piece that approximated closely to the line taken by the Chron editorial. Obligingly, he had written as suggested. Even more helpfully, he had written the piece early so that Annie had sight of it well before publication. She had been able to trim Jamie's editorial so that it came into line with the column piece. The message that came across from the paper was overwhelming... And very hostile to the Russians...The Russians were bound to take the bait, in Annie's view. They could do nothing else. That was the overwhelming virtue of her playback gambit. The old Soviet wing had no experience of anything approaching a free press, so the simultaneous publication of two pieces both on the same topic with identical points of view would amount, to the Russians, to one thing and one thing only – penetration of the Bank/Chronicle cell. Lacking alternative intellectual apparatus, they could take no other view.... That was part of the beauty of the scheme... And Jamie was lunching that day with Stone, just to make even more certain that everything would run just as it should...

★ ★ ★ ★ ★

Darling Ursula, I've done it. I've resigned. It's 7 o'clock in the evening now and I'm just putting the paper to bed. Everything is in order, just as it should be, and the editorial has gone in just as planned with not a word altered. My last edition as Editor and perhaps in the context my best issue. My compliments to the Russians and all who sail in her. The wreckers will be back tomorrow but tonight I'm on a high... This seems like the time to do the deed and so that's what I've done. I'll go out on a good note. I wrote my chitty to Graham Dune-Jones – what a waste of space he turned out to be – just a few moments ago and I've sent it via the internal mail in such a way that he'll get it first thing tomorrow. After that who knows...! So later on this evening, darling Ursula, you're going to get some shocks. I've put all this on floppy, and I'm going to sit you down in front of the screen, watch you put on your mad-granny specs, and then I'm going to leave you to read it all just so that you know why I've done all of this...It hasn't hit me yet, but here's a career that just now has come to a screeching halt. I think I'm leaving everything now, Ursula, and I feel so unhappy about everything for you but I do feel a burden starting to lift from me. Can we talk about it, do you think, as we did in Hampstead so many years ago, when I first tried to break stories in London? It seems such a very long time between then and now, almost another age. Can we sit down and talk it through? I will understand if you don't want to discuss anything. But I would so like to retain some contact and access after I set off on my travels...I know I'm going to miss you hugely...So I'm closing this diary as of now. I know you won't be happy with what I've done and I know you won't be coming with me but nevertheless...Anyway I'm on my way home now to see you and give you the good and bad news...Click, click, as they say.

★ ★ ★ ★ ★

Annie got the good news about the Chron very early. Then she decided to talk it all through with Pa Lee. She thought it was time he knew what she had been doing...Pa Lee was on his way to Berlin but he had time for the two of them to meet for an early dinner. She left the office feeling pleased with her business.

★ ★ ★ ★ ★

Darling Ursula, it's nearly one in the morning but I have to record what happened earlier this evening. I know I said that I'd closed the diary but what happened was so bizarre that I must just get it down on something like paper. None of this incidentally has anything to do with the Chron...

So I got home, entered the domain, kissed you – or should I say kissed Ursula, since this diary is not addressed now to Ursula but is a record of what she did -so kissed Ursula and then had some food. I then fed the dish washer which occasioned some surprise but no matter. I put her in front of the p.c. machine, which I must add she does not prefer to my old typewriter, to my surprise; I turned on the p.c.; fed it with a floppy; got hold of her spectacles; put them on her nose; and told her to read. I then departed for the Barley Mow.

Where I stayed for the next two hours drinking slowly before venturing back home...

In through the door I crept, only to find Ursula in the hall, pacing about, with a savage expression on her face...Of course at that point, I feared the worst but no, she then smiled at me, and invited me to come into the kitchen.

'You're a lucky man, Tom Stone. That's all I can say, you're a lucky man...'

She was still pacing about. This was not at all what I expected to hear.

'You've read the diary?'

'Of course I have. I read it in a flash. You're a fool, Tom Stone.'

I bridled.

'So what do you mean by that?'

She did not answer me at all. She stared at me. But she then came right up close to me, took my face, and kissed me full on the lips...And then burst into tears...By this stage I was perplexed and I stood there like a fool, wondering if I was in a some form of lunatic asylum. But then she spoke. She said the nicest sentence that I have ever heard in my life or indeed ever hope to hear.

'I'm coming with you.'

'What?'

More tears and sobbing and clenched fists and more heaving of the Ursula bosom. I was crying too by this stage. I liked the look of the Ursula bosom though.

'Could you doubt it? I'm staying with you. It's taken half a lifetime for us to get to this point and I'm not losing you now. I just couldn't bear all the hassle of going through the search process again. So I'm coming too and stuff the job. I don't care if you're the editor or the tea boy – I'm not losing you. Damn you.'

'Ursula, you darling...'

'You heard what I said. I'm coming with you.'

So, to take everything, dear diary, in logical sequence, first Ursula was mightily relieved to read the diary because she had assumed that I was having some form of affair, judging by my furtive manner. So that point was cleared up. Next, I don't think in the end she cared tuppence about the job provided she had her Tom – which came as a big surprise to me.

That's the basic message from the command module and I do not know whether or not to caper about in hysterics because I've hung onto my girl.

★   ★   ★   ★   ★

Joe was still alive. He knew that because he knew that he wasn't dead. Felix hadn't got to him yet...No bullet holes...At least, he wasn't conscious of any...And he didn't feel like a ghost...

He knew that Felix hadn't reached him yet because he was on his way to the airport, en route for the board meeting in Berlin later that day. He was seated in a cab, streaking clear of the early morning traffic and headed towards Heathrow. So if he was still a sentient being, then it stood to reason that so far he had escaped Felix's clutches.

Easy...

The late summer dawn came up over the motorway traffic in exuberant splendour and Joe took its hale welcome to the day as a hopeful augur. Streaks of gold already among the blue of the morning as the fist of God spread out across the heavens...

So Felix definitely hadn't got to him yet...

But he was still on the run and under the cosh. Nevertheless, Joe judged that it was all still moving in his favour, although extrapolating from trend, in the guff of the market jargon, he still had to achieve value in the context of an event horizon. In other words, it was all A-OK, data wise, until Felix poked a shooter up his hooter and pulled the trigger- that altered the risk profile considerably.

But so far, so good...

He'd fixed the bid – the market was very optimistic about the outcome and falling over itself to take the Detroit money. Lucia? Safely packed off to Italy, so far as he knew, where she could rest up after her amazing labours and take in some holiday and simmer down, after Joe's half-truths.

Felix remained an unknown quantity. Idly, Joe wondered just how much money Felix had syphoned off from the ABC Bank by now. Millions most likely. Felix was a clever boy and an accomplished operator and he would think that it was all working in his direction now. He had the ear of the Quiff; he had an undetectable and simple scam working; and he had a quarry to eliminate who just happened to be the chief impediment against Felix's continued and substantial personal enrichment at the expense of both ABC and most likely the Quiff himself. All the more reason therefore why he should come a-hunting in Joe's direction. But somehow it didn't feel quite like that for Joe. Future shock of a terminal nature seemed to be absent from his scenario. That was what his spook sixth sense was telling him. Joe felt in his bones that somewhere out there in the ether, at some date and time still to be confirmed, something not entirely disagreeable would happen between himself and Felix. It was hard to define this feeling but it was definitely there, like the premonition of a sunny day or the glimpse of a beautiful girl strolling in the sun. He had a sense of secret, pending joy.

That morning, his esp felt almost benign. That cued Joe in beautifully. He was still alert, still on tip-toe relative to danger and looking out for the sniper on the roof. But he could grant himself a brief respite from worry, seated there in his cab as he reflected on his calm and tranquil night's sleep alone in Betty's flat beside the fast-flowing river Thames.

And he could finger the envelope in his jacket inside pocket...And wonder what it contained...And tried to decide when and where he would open it.

That was where the real danger to life and continued existence lay, he told himself. He had picked the letter up from the Reform the previous evening, after he called in there on the off chance of receiving mail just before his departure. Sure enough, there had been post for him.

More esp?

Perhaps – Joe had had no certainty that events lay quite so exactly pat for him as to receive a letter. But then on the other hand he had not been exactly bowled over with surprise to find the slim manila nestling in his pigeon hole. His heart had leaped as he realised that it was a letter from Perdita – and hand delivered at that. So she had been in town, then…And why hadn't she contacted him…? Well, that was obvious, was it not…? She didn't know where he was…

Joe had recognised the handwriting and now he tried to imagine what the message of the letter might be. Impossible – he and Perdita had never communicated by letter. So fuck off, Joe? Or come home, Joe? Joe hardly dared think about it, even in the sunny dawn of the day; he felt too fraught to contemplate a return to home comforts. They had lived together for some time now and they had never been apart since they had met. So there had been no cause for epistles back and forth…They had bedded down in the countryside together, like creatures in the hedgerows. He had no knowledge of how well, or how badly, she might compose a letter.

This was the first letter she had ever sent to him.

Still less did he know what she might have written to him after his Great Desertion. That was how he termed his raging walk-out from Pugh Park early in the morning as the sun came up, after Perdita had performed her Ophelia act up and down the living room in the moonlight. He now knew why he had departed. Beneath the blind rage, there had been a sensible motive. It had been a matter of survival. Under pressure on all fronts and needing to keep his vigilance in all directions as Felix stalked him, he had simply had no choice. The spy in him had been uppermost, and likewise the desire to live and complete the assignment. Nothing else had counted at that moment. The struggle to survive had prevailed over everything else, any known form of morality, including any version of the social laws.

So he had departed…

And most likely would not return for some time, such had been the strength of his rejection…

But now, as the final, final mission of his espionage career dragged itself haltingly and erratically towards a conclusion, and as the augurs looked good in terms of future survival – and Felix was nowhere to be seen – Joe found himself looking back with an extraordinary sense of regret at the brutal way that he had slammed the door on Perdita, Pugh Park and that whole halcyon way of mannered county life. Even Mrs Gulliver seemed less of an ogre and figure of fun as he surveyed her from a distance in his cab heading towards Heathrow…Had he miscalculated? Misprision in the highest degree?

And Rivers…?

The thought of Rivers squashed his mellow mood quite flat. Now that was another question, Joe thought, as the cab swung left off the motor way and into the airport complex. The vision of Rivers which Joe had glimpsed on the TV screen suggested that one version of Rivers Pugh – furtive, brutal, arrogant, fast moving and ambitious – might now have died the death, as his City peer group traded him in for a newer and more attractive model. So cue the alternative Rivers, that person who could weep his heart out? Had Rivers renounced it all?

The cab drew to a halt at Joe's terminal. He got out of the cab, paid off the driver and walked into the terminal to join the jostling travellers, still deep in thought.

He stood in line waiting to board his plane.

He decided to open the letter in mid-flight, half way between one existence and another, albeit briefly, departing from one set of possibilities and returning to embrace the past in Berlin while still remotely hopeful about the future. That seemed appropriate.

But he was still a pale face at the window, travelling swiftly through unknown territory in a strange direction. He knew that for a certainty.

★   ★   ★   ★   ★

Grace had an early-morning meeting with a client, so she took the bus to Sloane Square and prepared to take the Underground. She glanced at the unshaven hoarse-voiced newsvendor and his wares beside the station as she pushed through the crowd and into the station. She caught a glimpse of the headlines as she jostled past. All the newspapers carried the same lead story. The treatment varied but the message was the same – Millionaire City Financier Found Slain in Penthouse Flat.

Grace felt sick. She decided not to buy a newspaper that morning. She hurried onto the Sloane Square platform, drawing comfort from the masses of normal business people milling around and waiting for the next train to come curving round the bend and into the station.

The train arrived and she pushed and scrambled aboard, taking more comfort from the proximity of so many straight forward people all around her. She found herself jammed up against someone who looked like a banker who was reading his Times avidly. Glancing unavoidably over his shoulder, she found the news story, which she had avoided reading just a few minutes previously, now jammed right up against her.

The story was horrifying. It was obviously Moley. Everything which she knew about him fitted the description. He had been found late the previous evening by a window cleaner who had looked into the flat from his vantage point on the outside of the block. Moley had been dead for some time...The flat was soaked in blood...Moley himself had been mutilated; his fingers had been torn from his hands....Moley was unmarried, so the inference drawn by the newspaper was obvious...There was also a suggestion that he had been sexually assaulted, perhaps even after he had died...

There was an ambiguous reference to chess pieces...

Grace got off the train at Victoria and sat down very quietly on a bench on the platform. She needed time to think about this...

She didn't like it one little bit of it...Perhaps Nicholas had to go, after all...Or perhaps she ought to wait upon events. Would that be more sensible?

★   ★   ★   ★   ★

Pa Lee called Annie. He was jubilant in his quiet way.

'Seen this morning's press, Annie? Concerning our Moley?'

'Indeed I have.'

'That kind of evens things up a little, I guess'

'Exactly what I thought. It's a big plus for us. And a big setback for the Soviets. It means we're back in the game and maybe bigger than we thought. Maybe, maybe, time will tell. They didn't like those Chron pieces one little bit, I can tell you. The Moley story is icing on the cake.'

'Well done. That's what I thought. It'll come as an even greater shock to them because they won't know for certain whether Moley's was just a random killing. Taken along with the Chron pieces, they'll suspect a coup.'

'More mayhem in Moscow.'

'Exactly.'

*   *   *   *   *

Joe took his seat on the plane and ignored the newspapers which the smiling hostess thrust at him. He sat quietly in his seat, waiting until the plane took off before he reached inside his jacket and opened the letter.

It was a long letter, written on Reform Club notepaper, of course, and it read as follows:-

Joe darling,

Where are you? I'm missing you and I just don't know what to do when you're not around like this. Where are you? What have I done? Have I sinned so grievously? I only danced on the table, which doesn't seem a terribly naughty thing to do but does that mean that I have to suffer this kind of persecution by your absence? Why aren't you in my bed – that's what I want to know? It seems a pity to have bought the new one together and then to find that I have to spend the rest of life sleeping alone...I reach for you in the morning and I just find nothing there and everything else is just flat and dull. Waking up is horrible and getting up is worse. I didn't think that it was possible to feel so vacant in the absence of another human being but it's true – another of life's discoveries for Perdita the Stupid. So why aren't you here? It's starting to become intolerable and I don't like it. That's why I journeyed up to town and to the Reform Club in the hope of finding you there. I had a feeling that you'd be there. But of course you weren't…That's what second sight does for you.

And Joe the autumn is on its way. All the trees are so beautiful as they start to shed their leaves. I want to go on another of our slow walks but not quite as we did before. I am feeling so much better. Really, truly, Joe, so much better, my darling…

All the news from Pugh Park of course is about Rivers who's had a terrible pounding from everybody because his company is about to be taken over. He's gone very quiet indeed, almost religious, and he just mopes about when he's here, looking like a ghost and sitting silently in one room after another. But I'm secretly pleased because when he's not miserable he's almost his old self again instead of the wicked monster that he turned himself into when he became the boss of that awful Global What's-it company…I'm having to do some mothering of him, in Mummy's absence, but I find that I'm starting to cope quite well with all of that. I enjoy the challenge of it all. When he starts looking miserable I just shout at him and tell him to do some gardening – and lo and behold off he trots quite happily to do his weeding or whatever… Such a surprise… He's quite an obedient little boy really beneath all that tough exterior. Unlike you, of course, Joe…Apart from the obvious things, I think it's your eyes that I miss most – always flashing here and there and taking it all in quite soundlessly. I miss those little orbs of yours…

In strictest confidence – and I mean that – Rivers is going to get a lot of money when his company goes to the Americans. I mean quite a few millions. He was talking to me about buying Pugh Park from you, making an offer and that kind of thing, but I told him not be so silly – I said to him why couldn't we all just sit down and try to work it out together like adult human beings especially since I don't think you will want to sell. He <u>seemed</u> to agree but I couldn't be sure of that…When he's in old man Rivers mode, he's quite reasonable but when he slips back into being businessman Rivers Pugh – you know just what I mean – then he becomes devious. To tell you the truth when we spoke I don't know which mode he was in. Then he talked about becoming a priest and I told him not to be so ridiculous. I said he wasn't pompous enough to be religious and do you know he suddenly laughed out loud. It was an astonishing sound, like an ass farting or something even worse…I nearly ran out of the room I was so frightened…So Rivers may be on the mend as well, you never know your luck, babe…

Here's looking at you kid and all you have to do is whistle – aren't those lines ridiculous? Fancy whistling in the street – ugh! But I do see myself in a kind of Bogey-Bacall set-up with you, I must admit. It's those sweet little eyes of your'n, honey child…They really truly turn me aaarn…

There's nobody here apart from Mrs Gulliver and all the people on the estate and what have you, so I'm in charge and I have to say, I am quite enjoying myself. I seem to have got over Mummy really quite suddenly, after my night in the moonlight – Mrs Gulliver told me all about it – and all that seems to have acted like a purge for me. Yes, a purge – that's a good word and I like it. Mrs Gulliver told me that these things happen and that I had to be quite philosophical about it all and I think that she's right. Of course I still miss Mummy dreadfully but the sheer gut wrenching pang of it all seems to have subsided, at least for the time being. Now she seems to have floated off into wherever it is people go when they die quite happily, after seeing me capering around in the moonlight, whereas before I just felt that she was desperately unhappy and intent on showing me just how anxious she was…I think she was afraid that that I didn't love her any more whereas now she knows…And you know how close she always was to death, so these comments which are <u>strictly</u> between ourselves will not surprise you. All of which is very healthy, I think.

So, Joe my darling, I'm better and you can come home now. I don't promise not to shout at you – I'm getting quite good at that – but I do promise to give you a very warm welcome. The house is still standing, you'll be pleased to know so there is also somewhere to come home to as well. You can always call me on my mobile if you're afraid of talking to Rivers and just in case oh mighty one you've forgotten the number I'll give it to you again...I'll scrawl it very clearly at the bottom of the page...

Now here's my joke for you, Joe – Have you no code, man? Isn't that a good one? You didn't think I knew that line did you, but I do and the proof that I didn't crib it is that I'm sitting here in your club writing this letter to you without any prompts at all.

So it's au naturel, mon brave and toute cette sorte de chose...

I'm going to close now Joe. There's an old gentleman over there in the corner who is starting to get over anxious about the way that I'm staring into space seeking inspiration. It may be the blouse which is ever so slightly unbuttoned too far but you never know. You never can tell these days, my dear. Anyway, he is threatening to wander over and give me some help...Which I don't want at all...Ah yes, I was nearly forgetting, Mrs Gulliver bless her soul, wants you to come back as well – she had been very complimentary about you recently although why I can't imagine – because she wants to consult you about the gift fair, which as you know is pending...She thinks that we should have some kind of lottery but she wants to talk to you about it.

So darling Joe, come back soon, nothing is forgiven – natch! – but everything is forgotten and you are much missed and I will never forgive you if you don't get in touch with me very, very soon,

Your darling ever-loving and much abused

Perdita (who is thinking about you night and day)

P.S. Here's another one – Have you seen my pistol, honey bun? (I'm off now – the old gent is standing up and looking meaningful...).

*　　*　　*　　*　　*

This is not fuckoffski, thought Joe as he read and re-read Perdita's blissful warblings during the flight. Under pressure, I may have misjudged all of this.

The warblings were balm to his soul. He particularly liked her threatening tone. That was how she had sounded when he first met her. She was getting back to her customary bossiness. That was good news. So now she was on the road to full recovery... And even Rivers sounded faintly manageable...

The plane began its downward descent as Joe's spirits began to lift. Maybe he hadn't lost his girl after all.

'Even I can see that it isn't fuckoffski, which proves a great deal. I have no plans to do a Diana right now and get killed 10 minutes from freedom. I'm going to take it nice and slow. Caesar, eat your heart out. I'm not going your way, Jules, I'm going to take every precaution possible. I'm out of here.'

The plane landed in Berlin and Joe, clearing passport control etc. at speed, headed for the big concert hall which used to stand right beside the Wall. That was where he had gone on his first evening in Berlin so many years ago when he had arrived to do his first tentative piece of espionage. Felix had no idea that Joe had any interest in music. None whatsoever. So that would be the last place he would think of seeking him out, if indeed Felix was in town at all.

Now there was a thought. Berlin and no Felix – yippee!

Joe mused to himself about the past in the cab which carried him back to the centre of Berlin from the airport.

'It was a piano recital given I think by Pollini and he played some very difficult Brahms, I seem to recall. All very proper. Audience very restrained. But then in the encores, he played a Schubert Impromptu and the audience dissolved in tears...Wild stamping and clapping as the old Viennese sounds filled the concert hall. Then afterwards, as we came out, we could see the Wall out there, some forty yards away, floodlit, almost within touching distance, with the guards up above on sentry duty, protecting another brutal world...And so we came to the Fat Man...'

★　★　★　★　★

Emma got to Berlin in good time for her meeting with Joe. Her flight from Antigua was punctual to the minute. She decided to do some sightseeing in the hour or so that remained before her appointment with him. She wanted to go around where the Wall used to be.

In the end, though, she thought better of it and she stayed in the Ku'damm trying to get the feel of the city. She had the tapes with her in her bag, ample justification for her journey. And she had a bone to pick with Joe. She had been very surprised to find that they were blank. That was surprisingly forgetful of Joe and quite unlike him to be so careless. He was normally so punctilious...

Perhaps he had just sent the wrong tapes? But the tapes were not the real reason for her visit. Of course they weren't, although they would provide her with an early talking point. They were an excuse. They would help to break the ice...After that, it was up to her; she was on her own.

Full of hopes about Joe, Emma realised at the same time that she was missing Italy already, even though she had only been away from Lucy-Miranda briefly. She missed the square in Repugia, the slow turning wheel of the day and the sun and the gossip and the hot shadows at sunset, and the sense that the square and the boy waiter would always be there to greet her, inviting her to make herself well at home, notwithstanding any act of any earthquake dimension.

But had it all made such a great impression on her that she couldn't tear herself away from it for such an important visit as her trip to Berlin to parley with Joe...? With a view to...? Emma refused to approach such a thorny question. It was far too early for that, she thought, as the image of Joe danced before her eyes. Far better to see how the day went before she returned to that particular topic. But Emma had made some concessions to Italy even as she journeyed to Berlin via Antigua's Sentry Point. She had made good use of her vacation in one respect – she had worked hard on Italian fashion. Now in Berlin, tanned, relaxed and carefully dressed in superb Italian chic, she could see the returns on that investment accruing very quickly judging by the number of appreciative glances she attracted from the Berliners as she wandered about the city for an hour or so. She was an emissary from an alternative way of life, an ambassador whose letters of accreditation were well received, indeed welcomed by the subject people whom she was visiting.

'Die in a ditch , Joe you dog, if you don't react to all this mannequin parade, launched, planned, and conceived entirely in your honour, you beautiful, loveable swine of a man…'

She could hardly have been more explicit.

★　★　★　★　★

Joe wandered about his office. He had just about an hour to go before the ABC meeting, scheduled for 3.30 in the afternoon. He was nearly there now, he told himself. So no heroics, no grand gestures, no Caesar-like pacing up and down to impress the people. That was not the style. Joe was taking the discretion option. He would stay in his office until the last possible moment then slip into the meeting, accept the thanks of a grateful board as he resigned, plus hopefully the more concrete expression of their gratitude in the shape of a large severance cheque for services rendered.

That was the plan. So far it was working. He had made his Berlin office and he was still in one piece.

No sign of Felix.

Joe stared out of the window, thinking about old times and trying to spot the odd nook or cranny in which he might have crouched, years ago behind the Wall on the wrong side, waiting for the guard to pass. To no avail…The entire landscape had changed in his absence back in London. He gave up on the Proustian moment game and finally just sat on the edge of his desk bracing himself for the meeting and the shock news of his resignation.

His phone rang. It was reception, speaking in perfect, almost idiomatic, English.

'We have a young lady here with an appointment to see you. She apologises for being a little late…'

Young lady? Who on earth could that be? He had made no such appointments…There were no young ladies in his diary…

Or had he made an appointment? Memory tugged at him, just a stride behind events, as he recalled some date he might have made with Emma…

Was it Emma? Was that the date?

'It's Miss Emma Bales, I think. Is that correct?'

'Indeed it is. That is the name. Shall I send her up?'

'Please do…'

Joe felt more comforted than before. He could spend his remaining minutes in her company, ahead of the Great Farewell. That surely would be fun…

The door to Joe's office opened and in walked a vision of tanned Italian loveliness, escorted by his secretary. Joe recognised the hip modern Venus with difficulty as being Emma nee Bales. Or something.

She looked amazing.

Emma smiled at him with confident ease and Joe's mind flew back to good times he had enjoyed with Emma years ago in her Norwich hideaway. He felt more optimistic already.

'Emma, you do look good. Magnificent, in fact. And quite scrumptious. Can I eat you up all at once? Or do I have to pause between courses? I'm starting with the lower left thigh, if you please.'

'I don't know what it is about you, Joe, but you're always about 1 pace ahead of me in the repartee. How do you manage it? I ask merely for information.'

'Early training. Plus I say the first thing that comes into my head and then improvise. But when it's vision of such pulchritude, such as I behold before me right now, then the words somehow frame themselves. You look gorgeous.'

'I think that's the most dishonest thing you've ever said to me...'

'How can you choose? I'm surprised at you. There've been so many...And there's plenty more where that came from.'

Emma was open-mouthed at Joe's brazen impertinence. Her ensemble creaked a touch as she withstood the barrage of Joe's wit.

'There you go again. I can't stand it. You're one pace ahead again which means that I'm one pace...'

'Behind. Should be two paces, not just one. I'm slowing down. Tell you what, I'll give you a start. I won't talk for 1 minute flat...'

They were back immediately to their old pattern of dialogue, such as had carried them from Chelsea through Sloane Square and Earls Court to the West Indies and back. And now via Italy in Berlin, the chatter continued...They were both pleased to find that the cut and thrust was still there. And in full working order.

Joe glanced at the clock. Not too long to go now...Caesar and Diana, eat your hearts out!

'Joe, I have a bone to pick with you. Not a very large bone, but a bone of contention nevertheless. Those tapes you sent me, the German language tapes, they don't work. They're kaput. There's nothing on them.'

Impossible, thought Joe. Those were the Fat Man's tapes. I haven't touched them ever since he gave them to me. She must have wiped them, the silly bitch.

'I don't believe you, Emma. That's impossible.'

'No, truly. Let me show you. Have you got a machine here that I can use?'

Joe's office was a wonderland of German gadgetry. He waved her to the sound system in the corner. She could almost play the tapes and brew up some coffee at the same time on his machinery. Well pleased with the way the encounter was shaping up, the bronzed Emma slinked across the room and shoved the first tape into the machine and turned on the system.

'You know, Emma, you shouldn't walk in front of me like that. I've got a board meeting in about 5 minutes. I may not be in fit shape to attend after watching you walk like that across my office.'

Better and better, though Emma. She grinned at him and curtsied in mock deference. No sound from the tapes. Mere silence instead.

'Looks like you're right Emma about the tapes. How strange…That is truly unaccountable.'

Then Joe recalled just what point of difference against Emma he had nurtured for many months.

'…Which reminds me, the young and beautiful Emma, just what happened to you when we were supposed to meet on the beach front in the Caribbean? You stood me up? What happened? It's a long way to go just to get the elbow…'

Emma looked awkward.

'I…'

A voice interrupted their conversation.

'Not half as far as you're going in a few minutes, Joe.'

The shock of the voice was deadly. Reality iced over both of them as the room temperature dived to zero and below.

Felix advanced into Joe's office, toting a machine pistol which he waved at the two of them meaningfully. Joe eyed the weapon carefully. He knew it of old. It was Felix's favourite. Because Felix knew about these things, it would be well fitted with a silencer.

At that moment Joe knew exactly how Caesar felt as the crowd closed in on him. Joe was cornered. He had gambled wrongly. No easy way out now, or at least none that he could see.

'Easy with that, Felix, easy. It might be loaded.'

Felix made no reply but looked grim. He motioned them both back against the wall.

Emma looked scared but also outraged.

'Is this a joke, Joe?

'No, Emma, I'm afraid it isn't. I'm afraid you've stumbled into something really quite nasty. Everything has now turned quite upside down from what it was five seconds or so ago… Isn't that so, Felix?'

'Exactly right, Joe.'

More to play for time than in the hope of finding a means of escape from the imminent death which stared at him down the blank tunnel of Felix's machine pistol, Joe continued to talk.

'With your permission, Felix, I'll explain to Emma here just why she now risks having her head blown off in the next twenty minutes or so...'

Felix nodded.

'Felix here is going to shoot me – and most likely you – in a few minutes, just before the ABC board meeting at which I was intending to resign. He will choose that moment because it will enable him to walk from here more or less straight into the meeting, so that he has a pretty cast-iron alibi...Yes, Felix?'

'Quite right Joe. You always were very smart. You see things very fast.'

'You see, Emma you're being here is a double slice of luck for Felix. He will shoot me and then you, put the gun into your hands with the appropriate fingerprints, of course, before going into the meeting. Then when it is all discovered the police reaction will be obvious – crime passionel...It couldn't be working out better for Felix here.'

Emma stood there dumbstruck, watching her world collapse and feeling nauseated.

'I'd better explain, Emma. It's not a long story and I won't take forever. Years ago, Felix and I knew each other in another life. We were both spies in Berlin working for the British under a boss whom I shall call, for want of a better name, the Fat Man. The details of all that don't matter much – all you need know is that both Felix and I have been, or were, full time spies for many years; we know the game well. Felix here was on one side of the Wall, and I and the Fat Man were on the other. Now to cut a long story short, it turns out that Felix's father was also working with the Fat Man although employed by Stasi, the East German and all powerful secret police. It also transpires that the Fat Man was working a racket, ferrying politico's and what have you back and forth across the frontier as the Cold War suddenly drew to a close and the Wall came down. Everything was out of control and the Fat Man had a very cool eye for a bargain. A very lucrative business in which of course the Fat Man was the banker. Now at a given moment, the Fat Man suddenly disappears and so does Felix's father who we think was tortured to death by the Stasi after having been betrayed to them by none other than the Fat Man.'

Emma caught her breath in horror at such treachery.

'Now all of that would have been ancient history and you, Emma, would not now be facing almost inevitable extinction in twenty minutes, had not Felix and I happened to find ourselves working for the same bank, the ABC Bank. That is coincidence No 1 which has worked out badly for us. Naturally Felix suspects that I have banked the swag somewhere and he is anxious to recover it, for the perfectly understandable reason that most of it is perhaps due to him. He is wrong, of course, to think that I hold the keys to the loot but there again I have told him that before in the recent past to no convincing avail. If he did believe me, he would not be waving that machine pistol at us. Agreed, Felix, so far?'

Felix nodded again. He seemed to be in no hurry, which might or might not be favourable, Joe calculated.

Joe thought that if he kept talking, something might turn up. The horse might talk. He was trying to work out in his own head as he spoke whether he should divulge how much else he knew about Felix and his role at ABC – the dummy accounts; the syphoning off of the bank's deposits; the connivance with the Quiff; and the broader racket in which they were all involved, Joe and Pa Lee always excepted.

To go nuclear on that kind of data at such a moment seemed to add up to an open invitation to Felix to go terminal instantly. Much better perhaps to parley a little and play dumb and offer some kind of deal...? Even though, according to Treadwell, there was a contract out on him anyway within ABC?

Joe reckoned there was nothing to be lost in trying to offer a bribe.

'I was wondering, Felix...'

Felix interrupted abruptly.

'No deal, Joe. Out of the question. Even if I was tempted...'

That way now looked blocked.

'So why don't you just go ahead and shoot us then, Felix?'

'It's too early. I need to do it in ten minutes' time and not before.'

Emma gazed at him in horror.

'What...'

Joe cut in quickly before she became hysterical.

'Felix, let her go. I told you the Fat Man was dead. Why don't you believe me?'

In full control, Felix shook his head adamantly.

Suddenly, Joe was interrupted in turn by another voice, a voice well known to both Joe and Felix. Its knowing mocking rasp filled the room suddenly in booming tones.

'So, Joe, you will be surprised to hear from me…'

It was the voice of the Fat Man.

Felix's eyes went crazy as he turned white and spun around, clearly rattled. He hadn't bargained on a third party present. Joe was at his elbow in a flash. He took the machine pistol from Felix with gentle force and Felix did not resist. Feeling more hopeful about events, Joe then retreated some three feet from Felix still holding the pistol at him. The balance of power had changed – he had the gun now. Felix disregarded him. He looked shattered. He was listening.

The voice continued. It came from the tapes. Felix had known nothing about the tapes silently winding onwards over in the corner. Nor had anybody else, for that matter.

'This is by way of being my last will and testament, Joe, and it may or may not reach you. That depends on whether you play the tapes I gave you or not…You may throw them away, who knows…'

Joe recalled the last moment of anguish on the Fat Man's face as he shot him dead in Fleet Street one sunny weekend morning.

'I don't suppose you ever will listen to the tapes again, so what I am about to tell you and the legacy I am about to give you will remain for ever locked away…Such a shame…And you worked so hard for it all in Berlin…I am recording this by the way while you lie asleep next door in your room. We have just returned from a sortie across the Wall, a sortie, I must tell you has been very lucrative for me although you will not know anything about that side of things…'

The voice then proceeded to detail exactly the story which Joe had just recited for Emma's benefit. Felix listened with tears running down his face. He looked broken. Eventually Joe put the pistol away in his desk, after emptying the magazine. The moment of assassinations had come and gone...

The voice continued.

'...All of this is very well, I can hear you saying, Joe, in your impatient way, But where's the folding stuff? Where's the loot? I can hear you saying that now. Very well, I will tell you. I devised a plan with no questions asked...I wonder if you can crack my little plot, Joe...? I will pause now for a few seconds as you sleep next door in one time dimension – I can hear you snoring because you were tired out after that little hazardous trip across the Wall – and perhaps ponder my little puzzle in another area of space and time, if you ever get to listen to these recordings. The money is in a bank, it is well protected and it is in a bank which will ask no questions when you call with the special codes which I am now about to give you. That and your left-hand signature, the one I taught you to make. The rate of interest paid on the deposits is guaranteed for about twenty years and since the money has gone onto deposit when interest rates are very high, there should be a very considerable endowment sum awaiting your collection. OK, ready, for the legacy? Time's up...Got it, Joe? Of course not...Right, now listen very carefully. The bank in question is of course the Bank of England which still has a few private customers and which incidentally raised no objections at all when I wanted to open an account with them...Did you get that...? Did you guess it was the Bank of England...? My master stroke, Joe'

Joe walked across to the machine and stopped the tape. Silence in the room.

'I guess this changes things a little, Felix.'

Felix looked at him with reddened eyes. No reply. Joe made a quick decision based partly on his revulsion at the revelations than anything more substantial. But he also had an idea. Berlin Rules.

'50-50, Felix? But no more shooting, OK?

Joe put his idea into play.

'Except on my say-so...'

A cowed Felix nodded.

'You know very well Joe that I might not have been able to pull the trigger...'

'I'm not so sure about that, Felix, I've seen you pull the trigger before, don't forget. And I know more about your activities in ABC bank than you imagine. What about the Fat Man account you've been operating…?'

Felix grinned. He looked younger. Joe whistled very softly the Bobby Shaftoe tune at him, insistently but with smiling eyes. Felix reached out a hand towards him. Joe took the proffered gesture of reconciliation. Felix was back to being Felix.

'Par for the course, Joe, the Fat Man account. If the Quiff is so stupid as to leave me in charge…'

'Your nonchalance appals me…It sounds plain immoral to me. But then Felix, you're an expert in the field, so I'm told…Anyway, to business…Emma here, who is just catching her breath and tapping herself to make sure she is still alive, will, I'm sure, make the call for me to the Bank of England as we listen to the tape in private. You, Felix, will attend the ABC meeting on my behalf when it starts in ten minutes and announce my resignation. Make sure you winkle a damn good settlement out of them…And that will just about wrap it up…Apart from one thing which I will discuss with you now, Felix. So come on Emma, let's get those blasted codes and get on with it….It's not that I don't trust you, Felix, but I grew slightly nervous a while back that you might have forgotten some basic training elements…'

Felix stood in a corner of the room without comment. Emma and Joe played the tape through at the vital point and established the codes which the Fat Man had set up in order for the account to be activated. Without further ado, she then rang the Bank of England in London. It all went through like clockwork. The sum involved was colossal although not so large as Felix might have imagined – £850 million in all. Compounding up over the years had done all the damage. As nest eggs go, it was more than substantial.

At a stroke, instead of receiving a bullet through the back of the head – Felix's preferred method of termination – Joe found himself richer by over £400 million. Felix likewise.

Berlin was that kind of town for Joe.

It was always one way or another, but strictly in spades.

Joe went to talk to Felix over in the corner for a few moments as a deeply concerned yet relieved Emma checked thoroughly the arrangements with the Bank. Then quietly Joe left the room and then the bank leaving Emma to make arrangements.

Joe began to wander about the city...

It hadn't taken long for Joe to reach agreement with Felix. He felt sick, flat but also curiously calm and detached. Everything was now apparently over for him in finance and in espionage. An old world had suddenly reared its head against him and then just as abruptly collapsed. Joe carried on walking......A world and an existence and an identity had come to an end. So the Fat Man had been a shit, but not quite that kind of a shit....The years of angst had returned an enormous dividend...And he was free of it all... He felt like a puff of wind, a feather on the breath of Fortune.

And Felix would stick to his side of the bargain. Joe was sure of that. Berlin Rules still held sway.

Eventually Joe fetched up at the Berlin railway station, where he drank heavily for most of the rest of the day and until late into the evening. It was solid, unemotional drinking, one glass after another, in just a seat at the bar, as Joe set about methodically dosing himself into oblivion. Then while his head was still just about on his shoulders, he repaired to the lavatory. In one of the cubicles, after closing the door, he took off first one shoe and filled it with his cash; then filled the other shoe with his credit cards. He tied his shoe-laces very tight.

Then he went to the public waiting room and fell asleep among the drunks and the down and outs and the stranded. Just as he had one night when he had first arrived in Berlin. It seemed somehow appropriate to him. Back to the streets and away from the smart and the elegant...The following day he would take the first train from Berlin out in which ever direction suited him.

He was a feather now on the breath of Fortune...At some point, he would call Perdita but not yet...Old life was shutting down very fast...

★　★　★　★　★

Emma slept like a dead person. Initially as she climbed into bed she was mortified – Joe had eluded her once again. She was highly chagrined. It was too much...After coming such a mighty distance to find him he had slipped artfully from her grasp like an eel. But not for long. She was confident of that; the details of the Bank of England account would need all sorts of ratification and she as a solicitor would of course have all sorts of business to transact with the Bank and with Joe...Wherever he might be...Communication would be established sooner or later. And there was always the Reform Club. He couldn't escape her now.

Then she passed out, as the strain of coming so close to immediate extinction caught up with her. Blackness invaded her brain.

She had decided to take an early train back to Italy the following day.

★　★　★　★　★

It occurred to Joe as he washed his grimy face the next morning in the station's public washroom that he owed Emma a great debt.

'Had it not been for her turning up with the tapes, Felix would undoubtedly have shot me in the office. That was the plan. I can see it all very clearly. But for her I would now be very definitely something like brown bread. No come backs from that...Just charred toast and nothing more...I owe that girl more than I can say, or estimate.'

After transferring his cash and his credit cards from his shoes back into his pockets he left the washroom.

He made his way to the middle of the station, stood under the indicator board and tried to decide where to go. Paris? Vienna? Moscow? Rome? Istanbul? He could go anywhere...He had no sense whatsoever of decision or of orientation. It was all over for him for the time being. He could barely put one foot in front of another, such was his fatigue and absence of volition. He was literally without any sense of direction whatsoever.

After a long pause, during which trains entered and left the station without ceasing, like so many wasted opportunities, he decided to go to Paris, largely because the train was leaving in 15 minutes. He went to the guichet to buy a ticket.

★   ★   ★   ★   ★

Emma turned up at the railway station feeling more depressed now. He had escaped her and God knew how she would catch up with him. And where was he now…? Drearily she prepared to take her train back to Repugia. Her Italian chic seemed less radiant now. She walked about the main concourse thinking about the Italian sun, the errant Joe and the extraordinary outcome to her Berlin mission…Why did all these ventures always have to end in some form of ritual self-abasement, especially when it was a case of dealing with Joe? You would think a man who had just picked up over £400 million for a day's work would hang about to do some celebrating. But no, not Joe. Not him, sir…He was off like lightning into the shadows, like a small, perfectly formed predator…But there again Felix had spilled the beans on him well and truly. She had never realised just how deeply involved he had been in spookery. It had almost been a vocation with him, like a priest.

Glancing along the line of one of the platforms she then saw, as in a dream and right on cue, what she thought was a well known figure. It was strolling along beside the carriages, walking obviously with a view to finding his seat and taking the train.

She looked more closely – yes, it was unmistakeable!

It was Joe! Joe the Elusive! And now by the looks of things Joe the Runner!

Hold hard, my boy! Not so fast, my friend! Such good fortune! You're nicked, my good friend! Now for it!

She rushed to the barrier, just as it closed ahead of the train's departure. The figure was still walking along beside the carriages, questing the precise location of the seat. She tried to get through the barrier but the guard shook his head quite sympathetically but still firmly. She stood there, fuming, trying to explain her plight in German, in which language she spoke not a word. The guard stared at her looking resolute. 'Nein' was written all over his features. Out there on the platform, the figure had paused for a second and was checking something on his ticket.

The train was about to depart, as trains do, with whistles blowing and flags waving.

Inspiration came to Emma on gilded wings. She recalled an earlier life when convention was non-existent. Yes, and so what! The situation called for desperate measures. She'd done it then and she could do it again, even though the butcher's boy had always done it better than she could.

Carefully, filing back over the years, she put two fingers into her mouth and blew very hard...

An ear-splitting screech like the Last Trump burst from her lips and cut through the bustle and noise of the station like a fusillade. The station ground to a halt. Heads swivelled. Eyebrows shot up. But no reaction from the figure. She whistled again, louder this time and with even greater brio. Then she waved her arms wildly...Heads turned, as she continued to whistle...More waving...The figure put the ticket away and prepared to climb aboard, as one of the train guards approached him; addressed him; and then pointed him in the direction of Emma and the barrier...

* * * * *

Joe turned around and saw the figure waving wildly at the barrier. He felt awkward. He recognised the person as Emma.

'Of all the gin joints in all the world. This is too romantic for words. I have a split-second now to make a decision,' he told himself. 'Either I take the Paris train or I go with Emma. So which is it to be, sunshine, or...And I owe that girl large time...'

He stood there in a paroxysm of indecision, quite drained of volition. The guard asked him if he was taking the train. Joe did nothing. The guard asked him again. Again no reply. The guard shrugged; smiled; rolled a cocksure eye; climbed aboard; and waved the train out from the station. It chugged away. Joe watched it depart seemingly inch by inch but then faster and faster as new perspectives came into view and into play.

Then the track was empty...

There was nothing for it but to walk back along the platform towards an Emma who was by now hopping up and down with excitement. His mind seemed to empty itself of content as he prepared for her warm and tender embrace....

'You put your lips together and you blow,' he thought, still in Bogey mode. It seemed mildly appropriate.

★　★　★　★　★

They sat opposite each other on the train to Italy and Repugia, which raced through the German countryside at top speed. Joe was pleased to be leaving Berlin. He listened to Emma who talked non-stop.

Excitedly, she told Joe parts of her tale about the Italian summer. Joe listened intently. It was all coming back to him, like the sun and the sea and the vacation...Joe had been to Italy before many times. But it seemed churlish to interrupt Emma's description.

Emma talked on and on about the special friend that she'd met by chance; how the relationship had blossomed; the wonders of the square; how her friend was preparing to set up a kind of hostel for women who had stumbled etc. etc.

Joe listened with half an ear, staring out of the window, and thinking about Felix. Felix had been dazed by it all. Even more dazed now, Joe reckoned, as he trousered his share of the booty. That kind of thing can change a man, even if he is ripping off his own bank at 120 miles per second per second.

'Yes, Joe, she is a very go ahead kind of woman…'

'And what is the name of this paragon?'

'Her name is Lucy-Miranda, Joe. It's a very unusual name for a very unusual woman. Now let me tell you about the great celebrations she has arranged….'

Joe stared out of the window even more fixedly than before. He thought about nothing in particular for a few minutes. Then he thought about Caesar, stepping out from his villa and preparing to make the short journey to the Capitol and the assassins. It would have been a sunny day, just like today, he thought. But Joe had passed through his Ides of March, unlike Caesar, only to face something now which seemed far more serious and life-threatening.

But even so, the sun was out and the train was racing through the countryside. And there was the little matter of the overnight increment to his bank account. Joe no longer felt like a wan immigrant face at the window. He looked out of the window some more to take in the sunshine. It was going to be a very hot day. He could feel the heat in the fields.

After some time he interrupted Emma's chatter. He was starting from memory to feel the pull of Italy from the hot soil upwards.

But so soon…?

'Tell me one thing, Emma, will you?'

'What's that, Joe darling? You do look well, you know…I have to say that. I feast my eyes on you…'

'Thank you, sweetheart. Here's looking at you, kid. But you did say Lucy-Miranda didn't you?'

'I did. Wait until you meet her. She's a remarkable woman. Such a friend.'

'I can't wait. But tell me one more thing, Emma. It's a funny thing to ask, I know. But does this train stop before the frontier?'

The BBC TV reporter was highly excited.

He was covering the Lord Mayor's Banquet in the City and it was his first real break at the Beeb, presenting live direct to camera on a big occasion. He'd done his homework and he spoke fluently from the pavement beside the Mansion House, just opposite the Bank of England headquarters and the Royal Exchange – the Governor and his Deputy and the Chancellor would be arriving there in a few seconds, along with the Lord Mayor. The assembled dignitaries would speak on policy in the Mansion House to the assembled City which comprised the usual traders; spivs; racketeers; wowsers and wide boys, all kitted out for the occasion in the regulation soup and fish and masquerading as decent God-fearing people.

The man from the Beeb assured his watching audience that this ceremony, or something like it, dated from the Middle Ages. It represented continuity within change and symbolised the solidity of the financial institutions within the Square Mile. When the Governor spoke, the world listened....Etc. etc...The man from the Beeb was so mesmerised by the sound of his own prose that he started himself to believe what he was saying, such was the splendour of the occasion.

The cameras were well positioned to pick up the Governor and his Deputy when they arrived by car at the side of the Mansion House, after making the short trip through the City's Byzantine roundabout which included Threadneedle Street; Poultry; Cornhill; King William Street; Moorgate; Walbrook and Queen Victoria Street in its rays from the centre.

Camera lights flashed as the Governor and his Deputy emerged from the Bank of England Rolls Royce and prepared to enter the building.

Up above the banqueting hall, well ensconced in his nest concealed in the darkness and among the rafters, sat Felix, also wearing his soup and fish but nursing the stock of his rifle. Reliving on just one occasion an agent's past life in East Berlin,

Felix was preparing to take out via his single bullet either the Governor or his Deputy – he hadn't as yet decided which of the two was booked to take his bullet in the brain that evening.

But one of them was sure to go. And that in the next few minutes…It was preordained.

Felix had never missed from that distance in all his career as an assassin.

Just like in the old days, Felix had rigged up a small stand for the rifle so that it was rock steady in his hands as he hugged the darkness in the rafters. It was just like the old days, he thought as he waited for the enemy to show up and move into his sights. His black polished shoes were beside him.

One shot; the advantage of surprise; and then away swiftly in his stockinged feet – that was the plan. Felix had taken care to secure his exit, away to his left and down the stairs that led to the street behind the Mansion House and so over the wall into the churchyard of St Stephen's at the back of the Mansion House. Felix had been thorough in his reconnaissance – it should take no more than 15 seconds for him to unscramble himself from the scene of the crime after the fatal shot.

And then he would rejoin the hordes spilling out from the Mansion House in their panic after the shooting. And since he had a marked and named place at the ABC table, it would be assumed that he had been present in the banqueting hall at the time of the shooting. So no comebacks. It was a perfect alibi.

'Guest appearance, just for one more time and one more shot,' the sole Deputy Chief Executive of ABC Bank told himself as he surveyed the scene far below of the City men taking their places at table ahead of the Governor's arrival. A patchwork of white and black as the small ant-like figures sought and found their places. Felix even thought he recognised the Quiff from his vantage point. But of course he had no plans to murder his boss.

This occasion was strictly business. Felix sat waiting for the Governor. Outside the man from the Beeb continued his orisons. In the BBC mobile control room, located in the alleyway behind the Mansion House, and directly impeding Felix's planned escape route, they sat and smoked and watched impassively as the man from the Beeb, direct to camera, milked the occasion for all it was worth.

More dates; more background; more panoramic sob stuff.

In the rafters, Felix was fulfilling his contract with Joe, hatched in Berlin immediately after the Fat Man's dramatic monologue had overwhelmed them all. It had been sealed at Joe's insistence at the basic cost of some £400 million. This was Joe's price for splitting the Fat Man's legacy – Felix had to shoot either the Governor or his Deputy.

'With that amount of money in your back pocket, Bobby Shaftoe, you don't have to worry about working any more any time. True or false? Deal or no deal? It's easy money for you Felix, you've done this a thousand times. Deal or no deal?'

Joe had assumed the upper hand, which was not difficult since he was still holding Felix' shooter as he spoke to him. He had also been very persuasive and very insistent, Felix recalled. Brutally, he had rubbed thumb and forefinger together in front of his nose in a reprise of Felix's insult to him way back in the spring. But he had been smiling.

It had been just like those desperate times in the old, Berlin days, before Felix had accessed respectability.

All this dialoguing and bartering of souls had taken place in harsh whispers on one side of the room and wholly unbeknown to Emma. At Joe's prompting she had been making her safety calls to the Bank of England at that moment to check that the Fat Man's legacy was intact and accessible. Fortunately, Joe's bribe to Felix had passed her by.

So now Felix sat waiting for the Governor, who by now had passed through the welcoming throng of bystanders and was processing to his place at the top table in the banqueting hall. The City mob thundered out 'For He's A Jolly Good Fellow' as the Governor approached and clapped his arrival. Some brave souls pounded the tables with their cutlery.

There was a fair old racket taking place below as Felix high above squinted down through the rifle sights, lining up the Governor's head in the cross-wires as the body of dignitaries appeared at the entrance to the hall.

Perfect vision; perfect target. Unmissable.

'I'll shoot him during Grace,' thought Felix. 'The shock will give me just that extra fraction of time to escape. The Deputy maybe...?'

The professional in Felix mused as he pondered which of the two bankers to kill. The dignitaries were by now arranging themselves around the top table; grinning to themselves; and exchanging the odd pleasantry with guest in the well of the room.

Felix prepared to shoot.

As he leaned forward taking aim, he became aware of a cone of light sweeping across the rafters to his right. It was a flashlight, held so far as Felix could determine, by a security guard who was checking the top of the building for heat from the TV cameras. There were two of them. Felix could hear them talking about temperatures.

'They will soon go. No worries,' Felix told himself, working as ever off the probabilities.

They turned to go and Felix began to relax and refocus on his sniping. But one of them, still faintly uneasy for whatever reason, turned as he prepared to descend from the flies and flashed his light again. By ill-fortune, it caught in silhouette, Felix's little stand for his rifle.

'There's something here that shouldn't be here. Let's take a look...' came from over on Felix's right. This time Felix knew the jig was up. He reacted as he would always have done – he created a diversion.

Taking his shoe, he hurled it in the direction of security but at an angle. Then he took flight to his left. In his stockinged feet and invisible in his black coat, he glided from the nest as he heard the guards plunging about in the rafters. In a flash he was down the stairs and heading for the street.

As he neared the ground floor, he realised that his reconnaissance had been faulty. The TV mobile control room barred his way to the churchyard opposite. Thinking ahead very quickly, Felix realised that with the mission aborted – which was now obvious – he had committed no crime; that he was free to go; and that he should resume his normal identity.

Take it easy, babe; they can't hold you.

He stopped running as soon as he emerged from the back of the building and started to stroll towards the entrance, preparing to take his place among the guests.

The man from the Beeb, smiling, barred his way.

'And just what do you think the Governor will have to say to us tonight, sir?' he started by way of preamble.

Felix raised a cool eyebrow at the question.

'Oh, not a lot, steady as she goes, that kind of thing. It will be very reassuring whatever he says. The Governor is careful in his choice of words. He knows he is playing with fire if he says the wrong thing.'

Like a bullet in his brain, which was the plan until five minutes previously, Felix thought.

But as, indeed, it behoved a senior ABC executive to do so on TV, Felix spoke in measured tones before eluding the man from the Beeb and moving on up Walbrook.

In the control room, they scratched their heads.

'I will never, ever, ever fathom this City lark; no wonder we get it wrong,' said one to the other. ' Take that geezer we just interviewed, case in point. I dunno if you noticed this, but he wasn't wearing any shoes. No, 'e 'ad no shoes on. Just play the monitor back and you'll see. So he's going to this top table do in 'is stockinged feet. Now top that, Arnie, can you? Would you Adam and Eve it for a second ?'

FINIS

Printed in the United Kingdom
by Lightning Source UK Ltd.
101218UKS00001B/10-24